WHERE IT ALL BEGAN

THE HEARTBEATS ROMANCE COLLECTION

FIVE NOVELS THAT SHOW GOD'S LOVE

LORANA HOOPES

Copyright © 2018 by Lorana Hoopes

All rights reserved.

❀ Created with Vellum

NOTE FROM THE AUTHOR

Thank you so much for picking up this book. I hope you enjoy the story and the characters as they are dear to my heart. If you do, please leave a review at your retailer. It really does make a difference because it lets people make an informed decision about books. Below are the other books in this series. I would love for you to check them out. I'd also like to offer you a sample of my newest book. Free Sample!

The Heartbeats series:
The Power of Prayer

When Hearts Collide

A Past Forgiven

WHEN IT ALL BEGAN

*M*esquite, Texas 1980

I touched the white paper that had been burning a hole in my pocket all day and took a deep breath. Though I hadn't had the courage to read it earlier, I knew I would have to sooner or later. Pulling it out, I unfolded it and scanned the words. My heart sank. What were we going to do? We couldn't have a baby right now; we were both still working on getting our careers started. I could hear Peter opening and closing drawers in the bedroom. He was such a creature of habit that I could almost see him pulling on his blue plaid pajama bottoms and buttoning up the shirt. Next he would pull back the crisp white sheets, making sure they were exactly half way down the bed; then he would climb in. My heart thudded in my chest, and I bit the inside of my lip. *Should I tell him now?* Folding my fingers around the incriminating paper I had brought home and taking a deep breath, I exited the bathroom.

"Hey babe, is everything all right?" Peter looked up at me as he finished pulling back the comforter on our queen sized bed. Exactly half way, and then he ran his hand over it to crease it.

I shook my head, blinking back tears. Stepping closer to him, I slowly held out my right hand and opened my fingers to reveal the paper.

He tilted his head at me; confusion gleamed in his brown eyes, but he followed my gaze down to my outstretched hand. He picked up the white paper, and his eyes scanned back and forth. "I don't understand; how did this happen?" He plopped down on the bed, turning wide eyes up at me.

I sat down beside him and picked at a thread in the comforter. My throat was dry, and I couldn't meet his eyes. "Peter, you're training to be a doctor. You know how it happens."

He closed his eyes and shook his head, "No, I know that, but we were always careful."

"Not careful enough, I guess." I forced my eyes from the comforter to his face. "I knew something was off; I just felt weird, so I asked them to run a pregnancy test at work today. What are we going to do?"

A sigh escaped his lips as he ran a hand across his forehead. "I don't know. We both work too many hours to raise a baby right now." He trailed off and lowered his eyes to the paper again. "Let's sleep on it and discuss it later." He folded the paper carefully, as if it were contaminated, placed it on the nightstand, and crawled into bed. Right now, for him, the discussion was over.

Though I nodded, his words didn't make me feel any better. Instead of the advice I sought, he had dismissed the discussion. A little part of me had been hoping that he would be excited and propose, but he wasn't. He seemed unenthused, to put it mildly.

As I walked around to my side of the bed, I blinked back tears. Climbing in beside Peter, I stared at the white popcorn ceiling. It didn't hold answers, but it was something to focus on as questions charged through my mind. *Could we raise a baby right now? Will I have to give up my career? Would I be happy if I did? What will my parents say?* Peter let out a soft snore, and I glared at him. Men had it so easy. They never had to worry about pregnancy and how it was going to change their lives.

❀

I entered the hospital the next morning in a daze. My mind had raced through questions and pondered possibilities until past three in the morning, and when the alarm went off at six am, I felt like I had just fallen asleep.

As I shuffled down the hallway, I rubbed my eyes. They burned from lack of sleep. The training room door loomed on my right, but just as I touched the handle, the door swung inward, and Raquel bounded out. She nearly collided with me before stopping short and squinting her green eyes at me. "Whoa, what's up with you? You look like you were hit by a train."

I shook my head, swallowing the lump of emotion that had lodged in my throat. I couldn't talk about it yet, even with my best friend. It was important to decide how I felt about it first.

Raquel took the hint and wrapped an arm around me. "Don't worry. Whatever it is, I'll be by your side." I nodded, thankful for the support, and followed Raquel back into the training room. We took a seat around a back table as Nurse Hatchett – our nickname for her – entered the room.

She was a large German woman. Her tight blond bun demanded compliance, and her harsh brown eyes scoured the crowd, looking for the victim of the day – the student she would focus on and correct relentlessly. "Today, we will be practicing blood draws on the bags in front of you. Your job is not to screw it up, because if you do, that's a life you may not save."

"Nothing like fear to motivate you," Raquel whispered under her breath.

I nodded, but not even Nurse Hatchett could garner all of my attention today. My mind veered back to the possibilities of my more current problem. Maybe I could find time to have a baby and still go through nursing school, or maybe I could take a year off. It wouldn't be that long, and I could always go back.

A fist pounded on the table, and I jumped. "What are you doing?" Nurse Hatchett's eyes bored into my own; her large meaty paws sat on either side of my equipment. My eyes darted around, not sure at first what she meant, and then realized I had poked my bag in the wrong place.

"Sorry," I stammered as heat flamed across my face.

She folded her arms and leaned back. "Your patient just died. Don't be sorry. Do it right."

I nodded, shaking my head to clear the invading thoughts. Focus, I had to focus, or I'd get kicked out of the program, and a baby really wouldn't matter. Raquel squeezed my arm in reassurance as Nurse Hatchett stomped off to terrorize the next student.

The rest of the day passed in a fog; I had no clear memory of anything I'd done. Though I'd managed to focus on work, it hadn't really been conscious. I'd been operating solely on auto pilot.

Relief flooded my body as I pulled into the apartment parking lot and saw Peter's car. Maybe we could finally talk about this pregnancy so I could get my brain back.

The smell of pasta filled the air as I entered the front door. Peter stood in front of the white stove, stirring a pot. He turned at the sound of my footsteps and smiled. "There you are. Just in time, the spaghetti is just perfect."

"Okay." I hung up my purse on the rack just inside the door and shuffled into the kitchen. Peter had already set our small dining table, so I pulled out my chair and sat down. A minute later, he loaded my plate with spaghetti. The smell was enticing, but I had other things on my mind. I looked up at him as he pulled his chair into the table across from me. "So, did you think any more about the baby?"

He wrinkled his brow and frowned. "Let's not discuss that right now. It was a long day; let's just have a nice dinner, okay?"

I bit my lip, but nodded. Why didn't he want to talk about it? How much longer would he wait? As I ate the spaghetti and listened to Peter rattle on about his day, my mind traveled a million miles away. What kind of mother would I be? Would it be a boy who took after Peter or a girl who resembled myself?

"Sandra, Sandra," He was shaking my arm.

"Sorry what?" I shook my head and forced my eyes to focus on him.

"I was asking you which direction you think I should go: Emergency Medicine or surgery?"

"Umm, I'm not sure. Which do you like more?" My fork twirled aimlessly on the plate. *Really? This is what he wants to discuss right now?* We had a much bigger elephant in the room. A tiny spark of aggravation flickered in my heart.

"Well, Emergency Medicine would probably be more exciting; you know never knowing what's coming in, but surgery would pay better. Of course, I'm not in it just for the money, but wouldn't it be great to get a Porsche like Dr. Rhodes?"

The spark ignited. I dropped my fork and glared at him. A Porsche would never be a good family car. "Do you even want this baby?" A tightening sensation squeezed my heart, and the words came out barely more than a whisper.

He sighed and scratched his chin. "I don't know. I mean I want to be a father someday, but I don't know if now is the right time. I'm not saying for sure yet, but maybe you should look into an abortion."

My jaw dropped. "Abortion? But Peter, this is our child. Yours and mine." *I couldn't abort my own flesh and blood, could I?*

He threw his napkin down on the table. "I know. I know. Look, this is why I didn't want to talk about it yet. Just give me some time to think, okay?" He shoved his chair back, causing it to tip and clatter to the floor. I jumped, clasping my hand to my mouth as he stalked out of the room.

The agitation flamed, and my hands clenched. Tears pooled in my eyes. I thought babies were supposed to bring people together, but this one seemed to be tearing us apart. Blinking the tears away, I grabbed the plates and rinsed them in the sink before throwing them in the dishwasher. The sound of the TV reached my ears, and I rolled my eyes. The agitation turned into ire. Here we had a real problem that needed to be discussed, but he was watching football on TV.

I stomped out of the kitchen – past Henry sitting on the couch – to the guest room. A bed, nightstand, and dresser were the only real furniture in the small room, but what I was looking for was in the closet. Opening the sliding door, I pulled out my easel, paints, and a canvas. I wasn't sure when it had actually started, but painting had become a cathartic therapy for me. After setting the easel up, I opened a jar and shoved a brush inside before bringing it to the stark white canvas. Angry red splashes appeared. They matched my mood perfectly.

Two hours later, I had calmed down, and I had an angry piece of artwork covered in reds, browns, and blacks. Sighing, I put the lids back on the paints and took the brushes with me to wash them in the kitchen sink.

The living room was quiet now; Peter must have gone to bed. I washed the brushes, dried them, and then headed to the bedroom myself.

He lay in bed with his eyes were closed, but I could tell from the uneasy cadence of his breathing that he was still awake. After brushing my teeth and changing into pajamas, I crawled in my side of the queen-sized bed. As I pulled the stark white sheet to my face, I could almost feel the tangible chill in the space between us. Once again, I found myself gazing at the ceiling, searching for answers it couldn't provide.

When the alarm went off the next morning, I turned it off and held my breath. Silence met my ears: no shower, no TV, no kitchen noise. I rolled over and sighed in relief that Peter's side of the bed was made up, and he was clearly gone. The previous night had been too tense, and I didn't want that same feeling this morning. My head needed to be in the game today. After dressing, I curled up with a cup of coffee on the leather couch and watched the news before heading to work.

Raquel waved from across the room as I entered the training room. "You look better today," she said when I sat down beside her.

"Really?" I raised an eyebrow in surprise. "I don't feel any better. Look, let's talk at lunch, and I'll tell you what's going on."

The door swung open, and Nurse Hatchet stomped in carrying an armful of bandages. "Today you will be working on wrapping. You'll use this skill often, so be sure and get it right." Her eyes found mine, and I cringed inside. She tossed a few bandages on our table, and we began wrapping. The routine movements were oddly cathartic; I found my mood lifting as I wound them around and around.

"Hey, come on," Raquel tapped my arm, "It's lunchtime."

Putting my bandage down, I followed her out of the room. The hospital cafeteria was two floors up and down the hall. Though there weren't many people in this area of the hallway, Raquel still managed to draw the eyes of every man we passed. With her long black hair and emerald eyes, Raquel defined beauty and turned heads wherever she went. She smiled and waved at the men, and I shook my head.

The lunch rush was beginning, but plenty of open seats remained. We grabbed the silver metal trays and picked up a salad and a drink from the buffet area. "Are you going to tell me now?" Raquel asked as we waited in line to check out.

I glanced around, shaking my head. "Wait till we sit down; there's too many people here." After paying the cashier, we crossed through the sea of conversation to the far side of the room where a few empty tables sat alone.

"Okay, seriously, why the secrecy?" Raquel asked as she put her tray on the grey Formica table.

Setting my own tray down, I pulled out the hard plastic chair. A deep breath and a glance around assured me that no one was listening; I didn't want the gossip. I leaned in to keep my voice from carrying, "I'm pregnant."

Raquel's eyes grew wide. "Is that a good thing?"

"That's the problem," I sighed. "I don't know. I mean I always thought kids would come after marriage, but the more I think about it, the more the idea grows on me. But I'm not sure Peter feels the same way. He won't even talk about the baby, and the one time he has, he said we both work too much."

Raquel bit a chunk of her carrot stick. "That is tough," – she said between bites – "I guess I can see his point. This program does take a lot of time, but I can see yours, too, even though I know I'm not ready to be a mother. So what are you going to do?"

Sighing, I picked at my salad, scooting a tomato around the plate. "I don't know; I really don't know."

Peter's car was in the lot when I got home, and I braced myself for the strain I was sure was still there. Sure enough, Peter glanced up as I entered, but turned his face back to the TV. Clearly, he was not ready to talk tonight either.

Sighing, I crossed to the kitchen. After throwing together some food for dinner, I ate in silence and then retired to the guest room. I took the canvas from the night before and laid it on the beige carpeted floor, leaning it against the dresser. Then I removed another blank canvas from the closet. This time my painting took on hues of blue, and, when finished, it also perfectly mirrored my melancholy mood.

Peter still sat glued to the TV. He spared not even a passing glance as I passed through the living room to clean the brushes. After finishing my nightly ritual, I lay in bed and placed my hands on my abdomen picturing the baby. I could see myself running after the chubby legs or going for long walks pushing a stroller. As a smile pulled at my lips, I realized I might really want this baby.

WHEN PUSH COMES TO SHOVE

*P*eter still wasn't talking to me the next day or the day after, and I was steadily running out of canvases. Though painting was therapeutic, we'd have to discuss this baby soon, or I would have no place to put all the art. As we drifted apart, thoughts of raising the baby on my own invaded my mind. I stared into my cereal bowl, watching the cheerios swim and imagining a toddler munching on them.

"How would you feel about a weekend at the lake?"

The sound of Peter's voice shattered my daydream. I blinked and raised an eyebrow at him. "I think we need to discuss this baby first."

He put his fork down and ran his hands along the table beside his plate. "Yeah I've been thinking about that. I just don't think we have time for a baby right now. I think you should just have an abortion and move on."

Silence descended on the room. My heart dropped. Could he be serious? "I don't know if I can do that. I've been thinking too, and I think I might really want to be a mother."

Peter scowled from across the table. "But I just said I'm not ready for kids."

Anger fueled inside me. "You also haven't been talking about the baby for a week. I have been thinking about it non-stop."

"It's not a baby right now," his face reddened, and he slapped his palms on the table top, causing my bowl to jump. "Stop calling it that. It's just a clump of cells."

My mouth dropped open. "Peter, we both learned about human development. We both know that isn't true."

He shrugged and folded his arms across his chest. "It's mostly true. It's not like it could live by itself right now, and seriously with our schedules the kid would always have to be in daycare, Sandra. What kind of life would that be? We should wait till we have more time and can be good parents."

I closed my eyes and took a calming breath, "I don't want to kill this baby, Peter."

When I opened my eyes, he was staring at me, rage fueling his eyes and distorting his features. "You have two choices," – his voice, cold as ice, cut to my soul – "You can get rid of the pregnancy or raise it alone. I'm not giving up my career." He pushed back from the table, sending his plate and my bowl clattering to the ground. Then he stormed out of the apartment. The slam of the door reverberated down my spine.

His empty chair mocked me as the silence set in, and tears filled my eyes. If those were the choices, then so be it. I grabbed the fallen dishes and threw them in the sink. Returning with a towel, I mopped up the milk that had spilled on the floor and begun spreading out. Then I yanked my purse from the bar and pulled out my checkbook and a notepad. I began writing down the bills, rubbing my temples as the list grew. How would I ever be able to afford a baby on top of all the bills? The numbers swam together as the tears threatened to spill over. Would my parents help? Probably not, they had been disappointed when I had let Peter move in; they would probably be angry about a baby out of wedlock. There was no brother or sister to turn to as I was an only child. All that left was Raquel.

A light went off in my head. Maybe Raquel would let me move in with her. If I split the rent, surely I could afford a baby. I scooped up the checkbook and notepad, throwing them back in my purse, and hurried to the bedroom to get ready for work. Lunch could not come fast enough today.

"So, let me get this straight," – Raquel said over the noise in the cafeteria that afternoon – "You want to try and have this baby even though Peter wants you to have an abortion?"

"I can't bring myself to have an abortion, but I can't pay the bills and cover the baby alone, unless I had a roommate maybe." I stared into Raquel's eyes, hoping she would get the hint.

Her eyes widened, "You don't mean come live with me and bring a baby?"

"Well, it would only be for a little while until I got a better paying job. I could help with rent, and I'm sure the baby would be no trouble." The words tumbled out of my mouth in a rush.

Raquel shook her head. "Look, I like you, Sandra, but I like men too. Having a baby would totally ruin my image. How many men do you think want to stay the night and be woken up by a crying baby? It's why I had my own abortion a few years ago. I don't do kids."

Her words pierced my bubble of hope, and my jaw dropped, "You had an abortion?"

Raquel shrugged. "Yeah, a few years ago; it wasn't a big deal. I had a little too much to drink one night and hooked up with this really cute bartender. I guess we forgot to be careful. Anyway, as soon as I found out, I went and had it taken care of."

Her callous words coursed over me, and my forehead wrinkled. I'd always thought I was pro-choice, and if Raquel had had an abortion, then maybe they couldn't be that bad. A seed of doubt erupted in my chest and began strangling out my desire for the baby. "Did it hurt?" The words came out small and quiet.

"A little, for a day or two, but then I had my life back, so it was worth it. Look, you have to make up your own mind, but maybe Peter is right. Wait until you guys are settled in your careers, and then you can have some kids if you still want them."

Raquel's words collided with Peter's ultimatum, and together they began to make sense in my head. After all, if I couldn't move in with Raquel, I really was out of options, and as Raquel said, we could always try again later. A small voice insisted that this wasn't right, that abortion was murder, but I pushed it aside. The thought of abortion had taken hold, and the knowledge that Raquel had done it caused the thought to grow. Ending the pregnancy would be the easiest option, and no one would ever have to know besides Peter and Raquel, and they would never tell.

As soon as I opened the door that evening, Peter rose from the couch, folding his arms across his chest. The anger still radiated off him. "Well, have you decided what you're going to do?"

Sighing, I set my purse down on the coffee table. Had I decided? Even though the abortion made sense, I still didn't want to do it, but what choice did I have? "I'll do it," I said softly, and an icy cold sensation trickled through my veins.

A smile broke out on his face as his posture softened. He crossed the room and embraced me. "I knew you'd see it my way and make the right decision," he said into my hair.

I nodded against his chest, but a seed of doubt remained. I just wish I knew it was the right decision.

DOWN THE PATH OF NO RETURN

A few days later, I stood in the parking lot of a small nondescript brick building. It didn't look fancy, but surely that didn't matter. My heart galloped in my chest like a wild stallion, and I took a deep breath to calm my nerves. As I walked up the sidewalk to the front door, I fully expected lightning to strike me when I touched the door handle, and when it didn't, I pulled the door open. The air inside was much cooler than the summer heat outside, and a shiver shimmied down my spine as the air conditioning chilled me.

"Can I help you?" To my right, a girl with short blond hair and an ear full of piercings, sat behind a desk.

"Um yeah. I'm Sandra Baker. I have an appointment." As I crossed to the desk, my throat constricted and ice coursed through my veins. I shivered again and swallowed the bout of nausea that clawed up my throat and threatened to choke me.

"Okay, here's your paperwork. Have a seat, and we'll call you back in a minute." The girl handed over a clipboard and some forms, and I took them to a nearby chair and sat down. As I picked up the pen, my hand began to shake. Closing my eyes, I took a deep breath. *It'll be okay. It'll be okay.* The mantra played over and over in my head, though it did nothing to stop the freight train roaring in my heart. Somehow I managed to force the pen down and write information on the form. I had no idea if it was correct or not. A door opened, and my eyes flicked up. A hardened woman with steely grey eyes and a clipboard met my glance.

"Sandra Baker?"

The lump in my airway grew, and I swallowed it down and nodded. My legs shook as I pushed up from the chair and stumbled in her direction. The weight of anchors pulled on them. Were they even part of my body? A screaming erupted in my head, urging me to flee, and I froze. My eyes tore about the room, but there was no one screaming. *What am I doing?*

I turned to flee, but then I remembered Peter's ultimatum, and the fact that I couldn't raise this baby alone. It's for the best. The mantra started again and propelled me to the waiting woman. Up close, she was even more harsh looking. Ice for eyes, no smile, a don't-mess-with-me aura, hair pulled back in a tight brown bun. Executing a nearly perfect three-point turn, the nurse spun as soon as I reached her and marched into the back. Shoulders down, I followed even as a small voice pounded in my head to turn around.

The nurse turned into a tiny room with a bed, a stool, a hard plastic chair, and a tray with instruments. "Undress from the waist down and put this on," the nurse said as she picked up a gown off the tray. She shoved it unceremoniously into my arms and left the room.

The cold sterility of the room tightened the fear on my heart, but somehow I managed to pull off my clothes and fold them on the chair. I slid on the paper thin gown, wrapping it around my body. I shouldn't be here. I thought about bolting, but what good would it do? Instead, I climbed up on the bed; the paper crinkling beneath me. Surely, something in the room would calm my nerves. I glanced around, but there was nothing on the stark white walls, not one picture. No beaches, no calming words. Just a harsh white. Why did the walls present nothing calming? Surely other women felt the same anxiety.

A knock at the door arrested my attention, and I jumped. An older man with bushy white eyebrows and a wrinkled forehead entered along with the hardened nurse. I waited for a comforting word, but none came.

"Lay back," the nurse pointed. I acquiesced and focused on the white tiled ceiling. No comfort there either. "Legs up." I positioned my legs in the cold, metal stirrups and shivered again.

"Am I going to be awake?" I asked as the fear squeezed ever harder.

"Yes, did you think we would put you out?" A sharp stare from the icy eyes.

That was exactly what I had expected. I didn't want to be awake for this. If I got up to leave now, would they let me? A sharp sting caused me to suck in my breath.

"That was a local anesthetic. It will help."

A weight like a stone rolled on my chest, and it grew hard to take a breath. I squeezed my eyes shut, but that only intensified the sound of the clanking metal instruments. I opened them and began counting the holes in the tiles. *One, two, three,* "Ouch!" Tears filled my eyes as the pain intensified. Why had no one warned me about the pain?

"Hold still." A cold hand held my legs apart, and the freezing sensation crawled up my leg. Then the scraping started. I bit back the screams, though moans escaped, and tears flowed freely down my cheeks now. Scrape, tug, scrape, tears, moans, scrape, tug. My hands clutched the side of the bed. The scraping stopped, and I sighed with relief. Surely this was almost over. Then the whirring started, and my heart stopped. More suction, more tears, and still no comfort. The sound stretched to eternity; the pain never ceased. And then it was silent.

"You can get dressed now," the nurse said, and they left the room. The doctor had never spoken; I didn't even know his name. How different from all the doctors I worked with, who always introduced themselves. I tried to sit up, but my body fought me. The feeling of being punched repeatedly in the abdomen kept me prone.

Then the guilt crept in. What had I done? A moan that didn't even sound human reached my ears. *Was that me?* And then a baby's cry echoed throughout the room. My eyes darted about, but I was still alone. The cold returned and hungrily licked up my body. Crossing my arms, I hugged my own shoulders, wishing I had never entered this vile place.

After some time, I managed to force my body into a sitting position. My head pounded like a drum, and my stomach ached as though I'd lost a terrible boxing match. Nausea bubbled in my belly as I stood, and I clasped a hand to my mouth to keep the contents in. My shaky legs could barely hold my weight as I struggled to calm my quivering hands and redress myself. The nurse re-entered just as I finished.

"Come with me." She pivoted and marched out the door. I followed, pulling my shirt close around my neck. The feeling of being naked and exposed lay on my shoulders like a coat. Would everyone know what I had done? Would it flame on my chest like a scarlet letter? I suddenly knew exactly how Hester Prynne must have felt in the novel I was forced to read in High school.

The nurse opened a door on the left. "Take a seat. You have to wait at least an hour before we can release you."

I nodded and entered the room. The door clicked closed. Nothing but hard plastic chairs and three other women filled the room. One woman nonchalantly read a book, but the other two mirrored my feelings. One girl, probably only in her teens, sat rocking with her knees at her chest. Her dark hair covered some of her face, but her vacant brown eyes stared at nothing. The other woman, a young Hispanic who appeared about my age sniffled softly into a tissue. Tears streaked her face. I sat down in the chair one away from her, but the girl did not even glance at me. Her brown eyes also focused on nothing.

As I studied my brown hands clasped together, the questions barraged me again. *Why did I let Peter talk me into this? Will this massive guilt ever go away? Will the child ever forgive me?* The cry of the baby came again, and my head popped up. I glanced from one woman to the next, but they appeared to hear nothing. Was I going crazy then? The cry grew louder, and my body began to shake uncontrollably. *I must be going mad.* I jammed my fingers in my ears to block the sound, but the cry echoed in my head. Nothing seemed to stop the sound. My hands found the side of my head and squeezed. Black dots swam before my eyes, but finally the noise grew silent.

The nurse came in, and the woman with her book exited. How could she be so calm? Had she not had the same procedure? Why had no one told me about this guilt? Was it not normal to feel so much guilt? Or the pain? The pain in my stomach but also in my heart. Pain I had never felt before. Emptiness.

The blond girl went next, but she had to be carried from the room by two nurses. She never once looked at anything. Her wild eyes remained vacant. I wanted to talk to the Hispanic girl, but how do you strike up a conversation after you've done the unthinkable? Then the Hispanic girl left, shuffling as a zombie after the nurse, and I was alone.

Why had Peter not come with me? He said he'd been too busy, but he should have been here. This was his idea. He'd given me the money like a prostitute and sent me to do the dirty deed myself, and I hated him for it. The silence in the room pressed in on me, and I swallowed. The room began to spin and my breath . . . I couldn't get a full breath. Nothing but shallow gasps. I tried again, clawing at my throat. What was happening to me? My eyes grew wide as I struggled, but the darkness won.

When I opened my eyes again, I was no longer in the small room. I blinked a few times, taking in the cream colored walls before realizing I was home in my own bed in a pair of pajamas. How had I gotten home? I pushed back the covers and sat up, but immediately the room spun.

Slamming my hands to the side of my head, I waited for the room to stop turning. When it finally stilled, I pushed myself off the bed. As soon as my feet touched the floor, I nearly crumpled from the pain. A burning sensation blazed through my abdomen, and I wrapped one arm around my stomach. The other grasped the wall, and slowly I limped down the hallway and into the living room. Peter sat on the couch watching TV. He glanced up as I entered.

"Hey, how are you feeling?" he asked, before returning his eyes to the black box.

My eyes narrowed, and I glared at him as hatred fueled in my heart. I bit back the hateful words I wanted to spew and took a breath, "How did I get here?"

"Evidently you passed out, and they called me. We still need to go back and get your car."

"No," – I shook my head as the nausea reared up again – "I never want to see that place again, so find someone else to drive it home, or they can have it towed, and I'll pick it from the tow place."

Peter wrinkled his forehead, "Don't be silly. It's just a few minutes down the road. We'll get it when you feel better."

"If I ever feel better," I whispered as the grief pulled at my heart and the tears tumbled down my cheeks again.

Peter rose from the couch to comfort me, but his touch only ignited the nausea and repulsed me. I shook him off and limped back to the bedroom, shut the door, and crawled back into bed. Pulling the covers up over my head, I closed my eyes, wishing I could redo today and make a different decision.

At some point Peter came in to offer me dinner, but I couldn't eat. I wasn't hungry; I wasn't sure I'd ever be hungry again. He didn't come back that night, and I was glad. The mere sight of him stirred the seed of hatred, and the thought of his body next to mine made me cringe.

The cry of a baby woke me some time later, and I glanced around. A tiny baby in a blue sleep suit lay at the foot of my bed crying softly and flailing little arms. Was it a boy then? I reached for the baby, but my arms continually fell short. The cries grew softer and softer, and my heart squeezed tighter and tighter. And then they stopped, and the baby regarded me with empty dark eyes. A guttural scream reached my ears, and I snapped my eyes shut and clapped my hand over my mouth.

Drenched in sweat and tears, I slowly opened my eyes, but there was no longer any baby. There was no baby. I had killed him. I curled into a ball as racking sobs wrenched my body. When there were no tears left, I touched my stomach and the pure emptiness consumed me again. I had killed my own flesh and blood, for what? Convenience? I couldn't go on like this, and I couldn't get back to sleep. How could I deaden the pain?

The image of the small stash of liquor Peter kept for parties jumped in my mind, and I limped my way into the kitchen. He was snoring softly on the couch as I passed, and the hateful thoughts that jumped in my mind surprised me. I shook my head and continued limping along. A few more steps landed me at the little chest. Opening the door, I took stock of the offerings. I had never been a big drinker, so I had no idea what I was looking at or what each tasted like. Rum, Tequila, Gin, Whiskey, Scotch, I played a quick mental game of "Eenie-Meenie-Miney-Moe" and grabbed a bottle, closing the door softly and shuffling back to the room.

As I sat on the edge of the bed staring at the bottle, I wondered if it would help? Unscrewing the lid, I lifted the clear liquor to my mouth, took a deep breath, and swallowed. Fire burned my throat as the liquid slid down, and my eyes watered.

I coughed and slapped my hand over my mouth. Had I woken Peter? I held my breath and listened, but no sound came back. I swallowed the fire completely and then tilted the bottle up and downed another large gulp. When the bottle was half gone, the glorious numbness set in. I screwed the lid back on and placed the bottle in my nightstand drawer, covering it up with pajama shirts. I crawled back in the bed, closed my eyes, and let the spinning room rock me to sleep.

It was late when I woke up the next day. The apartment was quiet, and though I wasn't really hungry, the alcohol mixed with the lack of food created an unpleasant sensation in my stomach. I pushed myself up, grimacing at the amount of pain still coursing through my body, and repeated the previous night's limping expedition to the kitchen.

Nothing appealed to me, so I settled on a bowl of cereal. It was easy, and hopefully it would soothe the swirling sensation in my stomach. The walk to the living room was even slower, as the hand holding my abdomen now had to hold the bowl of cereal, but finally I made it.

I sank onto the brown leather couch and clicked on the television. Pictures flashed, but I saw none of them. The sound, however, was better than the silence. The silence scared me as the cries of a baby seemed to come in the silence. As today was Saturday, there was no need to go to work. Peter must have gone in, though, which was fine by me; I still didn't want to see him.

When the cereal was gone, the sensation in my stomach waned, but as it did, the pain in my heart returned along with the need for a drink. I limped the bowl to the sink and then back to the bedroom where I rescued the bottle and downed another fourth. It was nearly empty. I had no idea how often Peter checked the stash or if he'd even know if a bottle was missing, but I decided I better replace it and get some more. I shrugged on a cardigan, not bothering to brush my teeth or my hair. I didn't care what anyone thought about me, as long as they didn't know my secret. Clutching the cardigan high around my neck, I grabbed my wallet and limped out of the apartment.

A liquor store sat a few blocks up, and I thought I could make it, but about halfway there, the pain blossomed in my stomach. The sun beat down causing beads of sweat to pop out on my forehead. If anyone peered out their window, they would probably wonder why I was wearing a cardigan in the summer heat, but I didn't care; the layers helped me hide.

By the time I reached the store, sweat was pouring down my face, and I couldn't stand up straight. A small bell announced my entrance, and the clerk, an older man in a short sleeved t-shirt, raised his eyebrows as I entered. Avoiding his gaze, I dropped my head and pulled the sweater closer. Because I had no idea what I was looking for, I just grabbed the first few clear liquors I saw and carried them to the front.

"Are you having a party?" the man asked kindly, scanning the bottles.

I chanced a quick glance at him and then returned my attention to my wallet. "Something like that," I said as I fumbled with the zipper. Forking over the money, I picked up the brown paper bag and tucked it under my arm. The bell jingled again as I exited, and taking a deep breath, I began the trek back toward the apartment.

By now, my stomach was screaming at me, but I kept pressing on until the cry of a baby stopped me short. I closed my eyes briefly before looking around, expecting to see nothing like the last few times the phantom cry had come, but this time there was a young mother playing with a small child in her front yard. Somehow that hurt even worse as the reminder of what I had done to my own child seared my heart again. Gritting my teeth against the pain raging in my abdomen and now my heart, I quickened my pace to escape the "accusing" cry. My vision blurred as tears built up behind my eyes, but I blinked them away until I reached my front door. Then they came back with a vengeance causing me to fumble with my keys at the front door.

"Are you okay? Do you need some help?"

A glance to my right revealed a man with dark tan skin watching me. I sniffed, "No, I'm fine. It's just allergies," and jammed the key in the lock again. This time it clicked into place and opened the lock. "See? But thank you." I shuffled inside as quickly as I could and closed the door, leaning against it as the tears overwhelmed me. I let them come, pouring down one after the other. I couldn't have stopped them anyway; I was like a leaky faucet.

When they finally tapered, I dropped my keys on the entry table and wiped my eyes with the free hand. The aching pain was so bad that all I wanted was a drink and to curl up in bed, but I had to make it there first. I tucked the bag close to my stomach so I could hold the contents and my abdomen, and I limped to the bedroom.

Pushing the door open, my eyes tore around in search of a hiding place. Peter was such a minimalist that the bed, dresser, and nightstands were the only furniture in the room. I could hide one bottle in the nightstand as the one residing there currently was nearly empty, but where to place the others? I quietly cursed my neatness as there were no piles to hide them under or behind and shuffled to my side of the bed. As I pulled open the nightstand drawer, I realized I could probably fit two bottles there, so I plucked one from the bag and placed it next to its friend. Then I sank to the floor and peered under the bed. Only our slippers were there, but maybe if I put the other two close to the wall and my slippers in front, they wouldn't be easily seen. I pulled them out of the paper sack and situated them against the wall.

A key in the front door grabbed my attention, and I shoved the bag next to the bottles. I'd have to retrieve it later. Stripping off my cardigan, I tossed it under as well, and then I crawled into bed, pulling the covers up over my ears. Peter's steps came down the hallway, and I wished I'd had time to sneak another drink. I couldn't talk to him right now. I squeezed my eyes shut, hoping he'd either think I was asleep or I needed more space.

"Sandra?" Hesitation colored his voice, but it didn't ease my hatred of him. "Sandra, I'm really sorry you aren't feeling well. Liam and I went and got your car, so it's back in the parking lot for when you have to go to work on Monday."

I held my breath, surely if I was quiet he would go away.

He sighed, "Okay, I'll leave, but I'm going to make lunch, and I hope you'll join me." His footsteps receded, and I sighed. Would I ever be able to forgive him? More importantly, would I ever be able to forgive myself?

Saturday turned to Sunday, and I stayed holed up in the bedroom as much as possible. When I heard the front door close and knew Peter was gone, I would venture out to get a small bite of food. It still held no taste, but the sensation of being hungry was slowly creeping back in, and my stomach would grumble in complaint.

To Peter's credit, he hadn't bothered me again and was either sleeping on the couch or somewhere else. I didn't care as long as it wasn't with me in the bed. The first bottle of liquor was gone, and only half of the second one remained. I hoped I wouldn't have to make another trip to the corner store, but the liquor seemed to be the only thing getting me out of bed in the morning and asleep at night.

THE SLIPPERY DOWNWARD SLOPE

When the alarm went off Monday morning, I glared at it. Could I make it through work today? Did I even want to? If I didn't go, what would I do for money? The questions continued to parade in my mind while I forced my legs out of bed. Without even thinking, my hand opened the nightstand drawer for another drink. The quenching fire burned down my throat, giving me the courage to get up. I pushed myself off the bed and shuffled to the closet. The pain was less today, almost manageable.

I perused the closet and reached way back on the shelf for a pair of sweats and an oversized shirt. Nothing skin tight, I wanted to hide in the layers and bagginess. Thankfully, I was still in the training program, and we were allowed to dress more casual. I wasn't looking forward to the day I had to wear the rather tight-fitting scrubs. The blue button-down shirt hung from my body, but that was okay, I didn't want anything touching me tightly. I still felt naked and exposed as loose as my clothes were. A glance in the mirror shocked me. My skin was splotchy and pale, and my hair was oily, but I had no time for a shower today; it would wait. After splashing a little water on my face, I patted it with a towel, and decided I didn't care. I hastily pulled my hair up, securing it with a clip, and then I turned out the light and left.

Peter was gone. I had no idea when he had left, and I didn't care. The less I saw him, the better. Grabbing a banana from the bar, I picked up my keys from the table and locked the door behind me.

My car was sitting right where Peter had said it would be, but my feet didn't want to move to it. Images of where I had gone the last time I sat in it flooded my mind, stirring a feeling of nausea. I closed my eyes and began to count. The sound of my heart pounding in my ears almost drowned out the numbers, but as I neared fifty, it began to lessen. My hands stopped shaking, and my feet finally stumbled to the car.

I had loved this car. All through college, I had begged my father for a dark blue mustang, but he had always said no – they were too frivolous – but on my graduation day, it had been waiting for me outside.

My fingers touched the door handle, remembering the first day when I had driven it until it completely ran out of gas. My father had had to come and bring me gas, but he had been smiling when he showed up. Images of Raquel and I with the windows down and the music blaring replaced that one, and then images of Peter and I scrunched in the back seat beneath foggy windows. But the image of the clinic lasted longer. The cold sterility of the place invaded my mind, and my hand flew back as if burnt as the memory invaded. I knew I would have to get rid of this car as soon as I could. I'd have to tell my father I needed something more reliable. He would understand; I hoped.

After several more minutes and a few deep breaths, I was able to open the door and climb inside. As soon as the door shut, the car began to squeeze in on me, and black spots impeded my vision. I dropped my head in my hands and tried to slow my breathing. *Just get me to work. That's all I ask. Just get me to work. I can take care of the car after work.* The dots faded, my breath slowed, and I put the car in drive and headed to the hospital.

As I pulled into the parking lot, the panic hit again. Surely everyone would be able to see what I'd done just by looking at me. Why hadn't I called in sick?

My pager buzzed and Raquel's number popped up. I had to make it inside before she sent a search party looking for me. Taking a deep breath and swallowing the large lump of fear, I exited the car and forced my feet toward the entrance.

Each crack in the sidewalk I passed increased the pounding of my heart in my chest as I crept closer to the door. Beads of sweat broke out on my forehead and tumbled into my eyes, burning. I wiped the sweat away and pulled the door open.

The cool rush of air conditioning engulfed me, causing a shiver, but it didn't cool the fever burning inside of me. No one yelled accusations at me though, and the pounding softened. I kept my head down, weaving my way through the halls to the training room. Sweat had broken out on my palms even in the cool hospital, and I ran them down my pants before opening the door.

Closing my eyes against the onslaught of judgement I knew was coming, I stepped inside. No conversation stopped. No one screamed in horror. Slowly I opened my eyes. No eyes even looked my direction. Relief flooded my body, and I slunk to an open table at the back of the room. Though no one was staring at me, I still felt exposed, and I shrunk down in my chair as much as possible.

Raquel entered the room a few minutes later, and her eyes scanned the tables, widening as we locked glances. She crossed the room quickly, "What happened?"

"What do you mean?" I asked, pulling the collar of the shirt even tighter around my neck.

Raquel raised an eyebrow. "I mean you look like crap. There are dark circles under your eyes, your hair barely looks combed, did you even shower? And you're wearing clothes two sizes too big for you. What's going on?"

My eyes dropped to the table as my finger scratched something on the surface; I wished she'd stop asking. Though I knew it was only because she cared about me, I had no desire to talk about the dirty deed I had done, at least not yet. "Nothing." A glance out of the corner of my eye indicated she wasn't buying it. "I just didn't sleep well."

Raquel pursed her lips and shook her head but said nothing. I swallowed a tiny sigh of relief.

"Look, I know you don't want to talk right now," Raquel said that afternoon when class had ended, "but I'm here if you ever need me." Worry surfaced in her bright green eyes, and tears filled my own in response. The pain, still raw, flared anew.

"I'll tell you soon," I said, hugging her and then hurrying out of the hospital and to my car before the floodgates opened. As I closed the door, the tears won and spilled down my cheeks. Would this ever end?

As soon as the tears ebbed enough for me to see, I backed the car out, heading to the nearest used car dealership. I parked by the front door, and a man with a pot belly and a mustache came out to greet me. The last button on his Hawaiian shirt didn't cover his enormous belly and dark hair poked through. The small name badge on his shirt read Jerry. Swallowing my disgust, I wiped my eyes and exited the car.

"How can I help you?" he asked, scratching his belly and causing his shirt to rise, exposing even more flesh and hair. I forced my eyes to his face.

"I need to trade this car in for something else," I said.

He drew his eyes together, tugging on his mustache with thick fingers, "What's wrong with it?"

"Nothing, I just want something different." I crossed my arms and rubbed my palms up and down my biceps.

"Well, what do you have in mind?"

Turning, I scanned the rows of cars. I didn't honestly care, but a small, silver, four-door caught my attention. "How about that one?"

He followed my finger, and his eyebrows arched up. "You want to trade a Mustang for a Ford Taurus?"

"I just want something reliable that won't cost me more than the trade-in. I don't want monthly payments."

"Are you sure there's nothing wrong with your car?" He scratched the rotund belly again.

"Just memories I no longer want."

"Oh I hear that little lady." He winked at me. "Okay, follow me, and we'll get you set up."

I cringed at his word choice and familiar gesture, but followed him inside. The dealership was small and dark, even with rows of windows as the outer wall. A few other smarmy salesmen glanced up as we entered, but no one bothered us.

Jerry sat down at a cluttered desk, shoving the papers spread out on his desk onto the floor. A fake potted plant sat behind him, and a picture of what I assumed was his family rounded off the rather impersonal area. I stared at the two vinyl chairs across from the desk, afraid of what might be growing on them, but I took a breath and sat down on the very edge, careful to touch as little as possible.

Thirty minutes and a stack of signed papers later, he handed me the keys to the Ford Taurus, and I exited the stifling building. Opening the car door, I slid inside. The grey interior matched the exterior, giving it a bland monochromatic look, but it was comfortable, and it looked and smelled clean enough, so as long as it drove fine, I'd consider it a good trade.

By the time I got back to the apartment, Peter's car was parked outside. After putting the car in park, I turned off the engine. *Do I go in or wait for him to leave?* I chewed on my right thumbnail and tapped the steering wheel with my left. *Who knows how long he'll stay; I might as well go inside.* Sighing, I grabbed my purse, locked the car, and entered the apartment.

The smells of dinner accosted me as I stepped inside, and I paused. My stomach rumbled, but was I hungry enough to see Peter? He stepped out of the kitchen just then and stopped short at the sight of me.

"I made dinner." A feeling of sadness threaded his voice. "I hope you'll join me." His eyes darted back and forth across my face, and his normally strong shoulders seemed slumped in defeat.

A spark of sympathy flickered in my heart, and I nodded.

"Yeah?" A flicker of hope danced in his eyes. I could only nod again; I didn't trust myself to speak.

I followed him into the kitchen and sat down at the table. Peter placed a plate of grilled chicken and vegetables in front of me, and while my fork mechanically brought the food to my mouth, my mind wasn't focused on it. Instead, it was whirring a million miles a minute through future possibilities. *Can we get over this? Will the guilt go away if I just give it enough time?* I could hear the sound of Peter's voice discussing his day, but I couldn't muster much more than a nod or "hmm" in response.

After dinner, I helped with the dishes, but the proximity to Peter began to churn the nausea that had developed in my stomach over dinner, and I quickly retired to the bedroom for the evening. A small drink was enough tonight to quiet the pain, and after returning the bottle to its hiding place, I closed my eyes, letting the darkness overtake me.

The sound of crying snapped my eyes open. I slapped the empty bed beside me and shot up. A tiny baby, wrapped in a blue blanket, lay at the foot of my bed. The little hands waved, and the tiny mouth wailed. I reached for the baby, but again my arms could do nothing but brush the blanket. The baby stopped crying and turned sad brown eyes on me. The grief in the tiny orbs seared my heart, and tears rolled down my cheek. It must have been a boy then. I'd now had two dreams of the baby wearing blue. The baby faded away, but the echo of his cries remained. I pulled the sheet over my head. "Go away. It was my choice; I don't need the guilt." The echo slowly tapered off, but sleep was slow in returning.

I slapped the alarm the next morning, eyes still closed. When the incessant beeping stopped, I rubbed my eyes. My eyelids felt like stone slabs glued to my face. After getting them open a tiny crack, I pulled the nightstand drawer open and felt around for the bottle. Clasping the neck, I unscrewed the lid and brought the bottle to my lips for my morning ritual. When the fire had burned down my throat and created a nice buzzing in my head, I managed to fully open my eyes and roll out of bed. I shuffled to the closet, but everything still looked too form fitting, so I threw on another pair of sweats. I cringed at the puffy eyes and the splotchy face staring back at me from the mirror. It was no wonder Raquel had caught on that something was wrong, I wasn't even sure I recognized myself.

The hospital loomed a giant steel beast as I pulled into the parking lot, and I dreaded entering. There were too many people, too many eyes. I counted the cracks in the sidewalk this time as I approached, fifty-four, and then the lines in the floor on the way to the training room, sixty-two. I was early enough today that a few tables were empty at the back. I slunk to the farthest one and tried my best to disappear.

"Uh oh, was it a bad day?" Raquel slid in the chair beside me, looking immaculate as usual in her dress pants and Guess shirt.

I stopped chewing my rapidly disappearing thumbnail long enough to nod. "I'll tell you at lunch." Nurse Hatchett entered the room and began her lecture on disposing of needles. I tried to focus on her words, but the image of the baby kept appearing in my mind.

"Come on; it's lunch." Raquel nudged my arm, and the baby vanished for the moment. I followed her down the hall, my stomach churning at the thought of telling Raquel what was going on. Raquel had seemed so nonchalant about her abortion; she couldn't have gone through anything like what I was facing.

After standing in line for food, we headed to a far table. "You had the abortion, didn't you?" Raquel asked as we sat down. My eyes widened, and my jaw dropped.

"Is it obvious?" I whispered, glancing around to make sure no one overheard.

Raquel's smile was full of sympathy. "To me it is. You've been acting weird, so I figured you must have decided on abortion. You certainly don't have that pregnancy glow about you, but aren't you glad you have your life back?"

I dropped my eyes to the Formica table top and shook my head. "It's been horrible. The procedure was awful; there was so much pain afterwards; and . . ." – I raised my eyes to her – "I keep hearing a baby cry, but then there's nothing there. But the dreams are the worst."

Raquel raised an eyebrow. "Dreams? What dreams?"

"Dreams of the baby. He just stares at me and cries, and I reach for him, but I can't ever touch him."

"Him?"

I shrugged, pushing my food around on my plate. "I guess it's a him; the baby has been in blue both times I saw him, so I'm assuming my baby would have been a boy. Did you never have dreams?" A vein of fear ignited and began to course through my body. What if there was something really wrong with me?

Raquel shook her head slowly. "No, I never had dreams, and I never heard phantom crying. You probably have just been thinking about it too much. You need to let it go, and realize you have your life back now."

I nodded, but the words fell on loose sand and blew away. Maybe I was overreacting, but Raquel didn't hear the cries; she didn't see the baby. But she was right; I did need to get on with my life. I had made my choice, and even if I regretted it now, I could do nothing about it. The question was, how did I go on about my life when I was being haunted by my child?

Raquel continued to pour affirming words into my head over the next week, and slowly they began to take root. The physical pain was all but gone, and the nights had been blissfully dream free, thanks to the alcohol coma I practically put myself in at night. I hadn't seen Peter much, but I had even started thinking that maybe we could work it out, with time, so I was disappointed when his car wasn't at the apartment when I arrived home that day.

As I was locking the car, a small pink ball rolled up to my feet. I picked it up and looked up to see a little girl with brown braids staring back at me. She held her chubby hands out for the ball and smiled. Breath caught in my throat. I tried to smile back, but the grief gripped me and began its vice grip on my body again.

A woman carrying a baby approached, "I'm so sorry. Karen, I told you to keep the ball in our yard." As she was speaking, the baby cried, and a tiny hand waved. The dream came flooding back, and I fell to my knees. The pebbles in the asphalt bit into my skin, but I couldn't move. The little girl took a step back, reaching for her mother's hand. "Are you alright?" the woman asked and pulled her daughter close to her with her free hand.

"I'm sorry." My voice was quiet, choked with emotion. I rolled the ball to the girl, who scooped it up, and the trio turned quickly, leaving me on my knees in the parking lot. My body shook as the grief took hold once again. The darkness began to cloud my vision until a hand landed firmly on my shoulder. I forced my eyes upward. The same man from a few days before stood beside me, staring down with gentle brown eyes full of concern.

"Can I be of assistance?" He extended his other caramel hand to help me up, and I accepted.

"I'm sorry," I said when I got to my feet. My knees still shook beneath my pants, and cold tendrils gripped my stomach. "Thank you."

"Can I walk you to your door?" Though I didn't know him, his voice soothed my raw nerves like balm on a burn, and I nodded. I took his arm, grateful for the help, and pointed out my apartment.

My hands were still shaking when we reached the door, and the keys tumbled out of my grip to the ground. He picked them up, holding them out to me. I shook my head and pointed to the middle silver key. Understanding my silent request, he inserted the correct key, turned the lock, and opened the door.

"Will you be alright now?" he asked. I nodded, though his raised eyebrows told me he didn't necessarily agree. "Okay, well my name is Henry. I live in 2B. If you ever need anything, you come knock, okay?"

I grasped his hand and squeezed. "Thank you," I whispered. He nodded, and after a final look, he turned away. I entered the apartment, shut the door behind me, and sank to the beige carpeted floor. How was I ever going to get over this? If just seeing a baby sent me into a tailspin; how was I ever going to continue to be a nurse?

As if on cue, the phantom cries started again. I slammed my hands over my ears and rocked back and forth, willing the sound to go away, but instead the sound grew louder. My heart accelerated, and a weight fell on my chest. The air wouldn't come; I clawed at my throat, but the darkness crowded in, pressing down like a vice until it won.

"Sandra? Sandra?" A hand was shaking my shoulder. I snapped my eyes open, but there was no cry. There was only Peter staring at me with wide frightened eyes.

"Are you okay?" Peter asked, "What happened?"

"I'm not," My head shook. "I am definitely not okay."

WHEN SORRY ISN'T ENOUGH

I lay on the brown leather couch, staring at the ceiling. I didn't want to be here, but I had agreed with Peter after the mini-breakdown that I needed to try something. His solution had been to introduce me to one of his doctor-friends, a psychologist named Dr. Munch. At 45, he was nearly twice my age, and not being a woman, I figured he would not understand my issue, but here I was lying on his leather couch anyway.

"So why don't you tell me what's been happening?" he asked as he sat in a chair across from me and pulled out a notepad.

"I lost my baby, and now he's haunting me." I glanced over, but he showed no reaction. His calm brown eyes returned my gaze.

"Go on," he said.

"That's it." I wasn't telling this man I had an abortion. "I hear phantom cries, but there's no baby there, and sometimes I have dreams where I see the baby but can never touch him." His pen began scratching on his paper, unnerving me. I wondered what he was writing. Was he writing that I was crazy?

"It's affecting my work and my relationship, and that's why I'm here." I took a deep breath, expecting some kernels of wisdom to flow out of his mouth and heal my pain, but he simply stared back at me.

Unease set in and filtered through my body, "Don't you have anything to say?"

"That isn't how it works," he said and raised his eyebrows.

"So what am I supposed to do? I can't keep going on like this." I crossed my arms over my chest.

"Well, I don't think you've told me everything, and that would be a start. I think you should also look into a support group, but I'll give you some positive mantra exercises, and I'll see you again when you're ready to be honest." He stood and walked to his desk.

Heat and anger flared within, and I shot up. "That's it? That's all you can do for me?"

"It takes time to heal." He held out a piece of paper. I snatched it and still shaking, stomped out of the door. The slamming door brought a small semblance of satisfaction. Peter jumped, and his eyes widened. He opened his mouth to speak, but quickly closed it. Instead he stood and took a tentative step to me.

"All done?"

I glared at him and shoved the paper in his hand. "That was a waste of time." Pushing past him, I flung the outer door open. Behind me, a sigh, but then footsteps.

The car ride home was quiet, uncomfortable. As soon as Peter parked, I opened the door and hurried into the apartment, making a beeline for the bedroom.

My hands were still shaking as I locked the bedroom door and as I opened the nightstand drawer. The bottle smiled at me from its snug bed, and I jerked the lid off, downing a large swig. A knock on the bedroom door caused me to jump, spilling just a little of the clear liquid. I cursed at the wasting of the liquid courage.

"Sandra? Are you okay in there?"

I rolled my eyes and shook my head. "I'm fine. Just leave me alone for now." Silence descended, and then his footsteps receded. I tilted the bottle again and hugged my knees to my chest. The fire spread from my throat to my toes. After recapping the bottle, I placed it back in the nightstand and curled into a ball. Maybe I could just drink the pain away.

When the alarm went off the next morning, I sighed before

turning off the buzzer. As soon as I was sitting, I opened the drawer to upend the bottle. It was going too quickly. I knew I was probably drinking too much, but I told myself I could give it up when the pain went away, when the dreams stopped. I put the bottle away and threw on some clothes for work.

As I drove home that evening, I hoped Peter wouldn't be there. I was so tired of the tense evenings. I just wanted him to be gone or for things to be the way they had. The decision seemed to change from moment to moment, but the former seemed much more likely than the latter. I sighed as I pulled in next to Peter's car; another tense night loomed ahead of me. Grabbing my purse, I locked the car and stepped to the door. The key had just touched the golden lock when the door swung open, and a beautiful woman I didn't know met my stare.

"Oh, I'm sorry," – she raised a perfectly manicured chocolate brown hand to her smooth throat – "You scared me." Her white dress shone against her darker skin, and her hair was long and smooth, straightened.

The keys clenched in my hands, turning my knuckles white, and I narrowed my eyes. "I'm sorry, but who are you?"

Peter appeared then behind the woman's shoulder. His eyes darted between the woman and me. "This is Sheila. She's an associate at the hospital. We were studying for exams." His words tumbled out in a stream, and I ground my teeth together.

"Nice to meet you, Sheila," I pasted a smile on my face and stuck out a hand, which Sheila cautiously shook back. "Now, if you're done studying, I'd like to spend the evening with my boyfriend."

Sheila's eyes flashed, hardening at the implication. "Of course, I'll see you tomorrow," she said to Peter, laying a hand on his chest. Then she glided past me, sashaying her hips as she left and leaving a floral scent in her wake.

I stepped over the threshold and slammed the door behind me. Ice flooded my body, and my nostrils flared. "Are you cheating on me?"

Peter crossed his arms across his chest and leaned back. "Nice to see you too; no, I am not cheating on you. She really was here to study with me, but could you blame me? You can't even look at me, much less let me touch you."

My jaw dropped as heat flared all over my body. "Are you kidding me? You forced me to kill our child. You have no idea of the guilt that I face every day. The thought of you touching me just brings back the memory, and what if we got pregnant again? Would you encourage me to have another abortion?"

He threw his hands in the air. "That's not fair."

"Fair?" I screamed, my voice rising in pitch. "Was it fair that you made me go to the clinic alone? Was it fair that I had our child cut out of me or that I'm haunted by dreams of him?"

Shock colored his face, and he crumpled to the floor, bringing a shaking hand to his mouth. "It was a boy?"

The rage fizzled at his reaction, but I still couldn't cross to him. Instead, I crossed my arms. "I think so. Every time I see him in my dreams, he's wearing blue."

His hand ran across his face, and when he turned his face up at me again, his eyes were hollow. "We would have had a son?"

My eyes narrowed. "Are you saying it would have been okay if it were our daughter?"

He blinked, caught off guard by the question. "What? No, I guess, I just . . . What did we do?" He dropped his head in his hands, and compassion flowed over me. Maybe he was finally feeling a small portion of what I had been battling.

I crossed and sat down beside him. "We did the unthinkable." I rubbed my arms, but I had no more words. He didn't either. After a moment, he reached for my hand and squeezed it. I leaned into him, hoping that this time it would be different, that this time maybe the nausea wouldn't rear its ugly head, that maybe we could move on, but as soon as his arm went around me, the familiar churning began. I swallowed the sensation as long as I could, but as the turmoil grew, the need to detach myself won out. "I need to change clothes." I stood and rushed into the bedroom.

As soon as I closed the bedroom door, I leaned my head against it and swallowed repeatedly. The sickness began to subside as I breathed evenly. Pushing myself off the door, I crossed to the nightstand and uncapped the bottle. A sip of the fiery nectar sated the nausea. Another cooled it completely. A third created the welcoming fog, and the sensation slowly faded away. I smiled. *That wasn't too bad; I just needed a few sips, and, surely with time, it will get easier.*

After changing into comfy clothes, I rejoined Peter in the living room. He smiled and opened his arm to cuddle on the couch. Forcing a smile in return, I swallowed and sat down beside him. He pulled me close, wrapping his arm around my shoulder. The alcohol helped me relax for a while, but when Peter's hand caressed my shoulder, the nausea ignited, and when he cupped my chin to kiss me, it enflamed. Putting my hands on his chest, I pushed back with tears in my eyes. "I'm sorry," I said and hurried back into the safety of the bedroom. As I crawled under the covers and curled into a ball, the flame sputtered and died out. A solitary tear rolled down my cheek.

Sometime later a knock sounded at the door. "Sandra? Can I come in?" I crawled out of bed and opened the door for him. Shoulders slumped, Peter stood on the other side. He flashed a weak smile. "I can't do this anymore, Sandra." My eyes blurred with tears, but I nodded. I knew he was right. It had been weeks, and I still couldn't forgive him or myself. I stared down at my hands and then up at him.

"Where will you go?" As much as I hated him for pressuring me into the abortion, a part of me still loved him.

"Liam's offered to let me move in with him for a while until I decide." He scratched his fingernail against his pants as if scraping off a crumb. When he met my eyes, tears glistened in his as well, "I wish it could have been different," he whispered.

I bit the inside of my lip to stop the flow of tears. "Me too." He reached out and squeezed my hand, and then he brushed past me and walked to the bedroom. I decided to give him some space and wandered into the hallway and then into the guest room. The canvases I had painted before the procedure silently accused me of never coming back to them. I'd had no desire to paint; I didn't even now, so I packed up the paints, put the canvases and easel back in the closet, and shut the door.

After leaving the guest room, I wandered into the kitchen to busy myself with the dishes. The sound of Peter packing in the bedroom reached my ears, and I sighed as the melancholy filled me. I had been so sure that Peter and I would marry; we had always been so good together. The memory of the first day we met popped into my mind.

We had been waiting for the same drink at a local coffee shop, and when the barista called the order we both reached for the cup. "Sorry," our voices said in unison. He let go, giving me the first drink, which I took to a nearby table. A few minutes later he sat down beside me. "Can I join you?" His smile had caused my heart to stutter, and I had nodded. As we drank our coffees, we discovered we were working at the same hospital. Peter was interning to be a resident, and I was just starting the nursing program. It had been love at first sight for both of us. We exchanged numbers and went out the very next night. We'd been almost inseparable since then, until now.

I guess there are some things you can't get through together. I washed the lipstick off the last glass, and ire flared briefly again. It wasn't my shade, but what did it matter? He was free to date Sheila or whomever he pleased now. After placing the dishes in the blue rack to dry and wiping my hands on the checkered towels, I wandered back to the bedroom to check on Peter.

He stood in the closet doorway, surveying the holdings. At the sound of my footsteps, he turned to face me, the Hockey jersey I had given him last Christmas in his hands. Defeat weighed down his shoulders. He folded the jersey and placed it on top of his other clothes in his large black suitcase. After zipping it up, he turned downhearted eyes on me. "I'm really sorry," he sighed, "If I had known, I would never have pressed for an abortion. Maybe we could have done it, found the time, I mean, to raise a baby."

I knew he was trying to apologize, but his words cut like a knife and only deepened my regret in killing our child. *Why couldn't you have given the thought a chance before I ended our child's life?* A lump formed in my throat, and I clenched my hands at my side. He was waiting for me to say something, but the words wouldn't come. All I could do was nod.

Sighing, he picked up his suitcase and walked past me, out the bedroom door. Rooted to the spot, I listened for the click of the front door; only then did my body release my feet. I sank to the floor and wrapped my arms around my knees. The beige carpet swam like a muddy sea before me. Silence descended, and I let the grief wash over me in waves. Then I spied the remaining bottle, a life raft, under the bed and grabbed it. After unscrewing the cap, I took a long sip and let the fire burn my pain away.

NEW BEGINNINGS

I expected the next few weeks to be hard, but a relief descended in not having to see Peter. He was gone, my car was gone; there was almost nothing to remind me of the "procedure" months ago, and I felt like I was slowly beginning to heal. The phantom crying hadn't returned, and the liquid courage at night kept the dreams mostly at bay or at least kept me from remembering them.

"Let's go get some drinks tonight," Raquel suggested as we finished the day. I grabbed my purse from the locker and shut the door. The sound of liquor excited me, even though the thought of dressing up and hanging around strangers held no appeal.

I agreed only because it had been some time since we had gone out. We went our separate ways to change clothes and freshen up, agreeing to meet up at the bar an hour later.

When I got home, I peeled my clothes off and rummaged in my closet. Though I wasn't looking for romance, I pulled on a simple black dress and applied a little makeup before heading back out to meet Raquel at a nearby bar.

The parking lot was full when I got there, and I had to park farther from the door than I would have liked. A few people lounged in the parking lot, and I scurried past them. Something about the bar crowd at night had always rattled my nerves. Raquel was waiting for me at the front entrance in a sparkly white dress.

"Well, I feel underdressed," I said looking down at my dark dress.

"Nah, you're good. It's nice to see you looking better," Raquel said as we flashed our IDs and entered.

I smiled. "It's nice to be feeling better."

We maneuvered through the smoky crowd up to the bar. Then my heart froze, and my feet melted into the floor. Peter sat at the bar with his arm around Sheila. Her hand lay on his thigh, and their heads were just inches apart. I shouldn't have been surprised; I had seen the way he had gazed at her that day and the glass with the lipstick, but a part of me had hoped it wasn't true.

"Sandra," Raquel tugged on my arm and then stopped. She turned to me, face white as a sheet. "Let's just go somewhere else."

"No, it's fine." I shook my head. "I just wasn't expecting it is all."

Peter looked up at that moment, and his eyes grew wide. His arm slipped off Sheila as a red flush crawled across his face. Noticing his change in demeanor, Sheila turned, and as she saw me, a malicious smile spread across her face.

"Look just order, and I'll go find us a seat," I said to Raquel, forcing my feet to move and heading farther back to an empty booth. I brushed the crumbs off the table and sat down on the wine colored pad. I wasn't really angry at Peter, more confused. How long had he been cheating on me? I shook my head. It didn't matter; we would never have made it. Raquel plopped a large Pina colada down in front of me.

"I'm so sorry. I had no idea he'd be here."

I peered up at her, "Did you know he was with her?"

She bit her lip and dropped her eyes, turning her glass in a slow circle on the table top. "I'd heard some rumors today, but I didn't see how telling you would make you feel any better."

She was right about that. I nodded and picked up the drink. "It doesn't matter. Here's to a girls' night out." I tipped the drink back, downing half of it. Raquel raised her eyebrow at me, but followed suit. One drink turned into two, and a couple of handsome men bought our third and fourth drinks. Raquel's eyes began to glass over. "Come on, let's go home," I said, taking her arm.

"What? No, the fun is just getting started." Her words slurred, and she tipped to the side, righting herself before falling.

"Not for you. You've had too much." I pulled her toward the door, but she shook my hand off her arm.

"No, you're just no fun anymore. Ever since you . . ." I slapped my hand over her mouth to keep the condemning words from escaping. Rage burned inside me.

"Don't say another word," I hissed. "I am trying to keep you from doing something you'll regret."

She pulled my hand from her mouth, her eyes afire. "I didn't regret mine, remember?" Her words were cold like ice, and that was all it took.

"Fine, do what you want." I turned around and stormed out of the bar, my cheeks flaming. As I walked to the car, the cool night air chilled my anger, and I realized she was right. I didn't do anything fun anymore. I went to work, and then I went home. I rarely ever left the house for any other reason. This was the first time I had been out in ages. As I climbed into my car, I decided that I needed to get out more. If Peter was moving on, maybe I could too, as long as it was with someone else.

Back at my apartment, I climbed into bed and closed my eyes, only to open them minutes later to the sound of cries again. A baby boy about six months old was lying next to me in the bed. He reached out a hand and smiled, and I reached for him. My arms had always fallen short before, but this time I was able to hold him. I wanted to hate him for the guilt he brought; I knew I'd done a terrible thing, but maybe he was coming to see me for a reason. Maybe there was relief in acceptance.

Tears flowed down my cheeks as I studied his perfect features. Warm brown eyes peered at me from his chocolate skin, and his toothless smile began to mend my broken heart. The baby cooed, but all the words sounded eerily like mama. My breath caught at the words, and then tears streamed down the baby's cheeks. There was no cry, just the echo of mama as the tears tumbled down. I pressed the baby to my chest to comfort him. Somehow, I would tell him how sorry I was, and then my arms were empty. I stared at my hands, nothing; the bed next to me, empty. Tears fell down my cheeks as well; my baby was gone, Peter was gone, and I had nothing but dreams to look forward to.

I woke up the next morning determined to be different. I was still sick over what I'd done, but being able to hold the baby had somehow allowed me to accept some of the consequences of my decision. I knew I couldn't go back, though I still wished I had made a different decision, but I could enjoy the dreams of him whenever he came. It might hurt my heart, but it would also be the connection to the child I had lost, and somehow I would make sure he knew how sorry I was.

Raquel was waiting for me when I arrived in the locker room at work to clock in. She rushed to me, chagrin written all over her face. "I am so sorry," she gushed. "I'd had way too much to drink. I didn't mean what I said."

"Stop," I held my hand up, and she paused, pursing her lips together. "You were a jerk last night, but you were right. I haven't been any fun lately, and I'm sorry."

"Really?" Raquel squeaked.

"Really," I nodded. "I've decided I need to try and get on with my life."

"How much so? I mean are you willing to try dating?"

I raised my eyebrow at her and crossed to my locker to load my personal items for the day.

"Hear me out. Philip has a single friend who's very nice. Just come on a double date with us and see." Philip was the chiropractor that Raquel had been dating for a few months. I had to give him credit; he'd lasted longer than most of Raquel's flavors of the month.

I closed the locker and turned around. "Okay."

Raquel shook her head and smiled. "I'm not taking no for an answer. Wait, did you say okay?"

I returned the smile and shrugged. "I said okay." She enveloped me in a giant hug, squealing in my ear. "Alright, alright," I said pushing her off. "You're excited, I get it."

"You have no idea," she said. "Tonight, my place, seven pm."

I agreed and headed to the front desk for my assignment. Thankfully I wasn't in pediatrics or labor and delivery today. Those were the hardest rotations for me. The day flew by uneventfully, and before I knew it, I was standing in my closet trying to decide what to wear on a blind date.

I hadn't been on a date in years. Peter and I had been together for three years, and we had met at a coffee shop. I had no idea what this guy even looked like. Sighing, I pulled a simple blue dress off the hanger and shimmied into it. My hair, I piled on my head, and after applying some lip gloss, I decided I looked good enough.

As I pulled into Raquel's apartment parking lot, butterflies began to swarm in my stomach. What if this man nauseated me like Peter had? *Maybe I can return home and pretend I forgot. No, Raquel would never believe that, and she'd never stop nagging me.* Sighing, I parked the car, grabbed my purse, and smoothed my dress before walking up to Raquel's door.

The door swung open just as my hand hit the wood. "You made it," she smiled. "I was afraid you were going to flake on me."

I gazed down at my feet as a blush spread across my face. "I thought about it."

Raquel laughed and pulled me inside. "Well, I'm glad you didn't. Come on in; Philip just called to say he and his friend were on their way. Do you want some wine?"

Relief flooded my body; it wasn't my normal drink anymore, but surely the alcohol would work the same. "Yes, a tall glass; lead the way." I shut the door behind me and followed Raquel into her immaculate designer kitchen.

Raquel's father owned several hospitals in the area, and Raquel had never been wanting for money. The marble countertops had probably been cleaned by a maid just that day. I ran my hand across the tan, speckled surface, wishing I had the money Raquel did. Maybe if I'd had the money, I wouldn't have had the abortion. I shook my head to clear the thought as soon as it emerged; I'd never get through this date if I kept thinking about that.

A wine glass filled with red liquid appeared before me, and I tipped back the glass. The comforting fire didn't accompany this liquid, but it still seemed to infuse me with courage.

"Woah, try not to get drunk before dinner," Raquel said, laughing. "Since when did you get so good at holding your liquor anyway?"

My face flushed as I surveyed the now half-empty glass. "Sorry, I guess I'm just nervous." Inside, my heart sped up. *Would Raquel buy that? I'll have to be more careful.* I picked the glass up again for a dainty sip, and a knock sounded at the door.

"Ooh, they're here," Raquel squealed. "Do I look okay?"

I smiled as Raquel bounced on her toes. Her black dress hugged her figure and set off her pale skin and green eyes even more than normal. "You look radiant." I placed my glass on the countertop and followed Raquel to the door.

As the door swung open, my breath caught in my throat. Standing beside Philip was the man from 2B who had helped me the day of my mini-breakdown. What was his name? All I could remember was that it started with an H. Would he remember the breakdown? My throat constricted at the thought.

"Hey baby," Philip said, embracing Raquel and planting a kiss on her lips before turning to his friend. Philip was just as put-together as Raquel. His dark brown hair was perfectly combed, and his button down shirt and chinos appeared freshly pressed. "This is Henry; Henry, my girlfriend Raquel."

Henry stuck out his hand, but his eyes focused on me. My heart thudded loudly in my chest, and I brought a hand up to cover the noise. "Pleased to meet you ma'am." Raquel tossed a conspiratorial wink at me before smiling and returning the handshake.

"Please come in," she said. "This is my friend Sandra."

Henry crossed the threshold, and my heart froze. Would he tell them he knew me or how we met? His smile widened, and my heart began to melt. Somehow, it comforted me.

He stuck out his hand as if we'd never met. "Pleased to meet you, Sandra." His brown eyes twinkled, putting the ball in my court. I could play along or tell them the truth; he had given me the choice.

I swallowed as my mind went over both options. I didn't enjoy lying to my friend, but she didn't know about my drinking either, so I guess I'd already been lying to her, and telling them about my mental breakdown before dinner wasn't appealing either. Besides, Henry was being very nice to let me save face. I took his hand and returned the smile. "It's nice to meet you, too."

"Okay, small talk over," Philip broke in. "We have reservations, so we better get going."

"Thank you," I whispered to Henry as we followed Raquel and Philip out of the apartment. He smiled and nodded and then held out his arm in a lead-the-way gesture. We all piled into Philip's red BMW to make the trek to the restaurant. Raquel and Philip caught up on their day in the front seat, which gave me the chance to speak quietly to Henry in the back. "Why didn't you say you knew me?"

He smiled. "I'm going to guess that wasn't a good day for you, and probably not a usual one. Why would I call attention to a time that was obviously hard for you?"

Those days were more regular than I would have liked, but I smiled and nodded. There was something about Henry. I observed his open face, trying to figure out what made him seem so different. He was handsome, but not model handsome. In fact, one eye looked a little larger than the other. His teeth weren't perfectly straight, but that didn't affect his warm smile. His suit was nice, but didn't appear overly expensive; it made me wonder how he and Philip were even friends. Of course, I felt the same way about Raquel and myself sometimes, but we had been friends since meeting in college.

As we pulled into the restaurant's parking lot, Henry touched my arm. "Please wait here and let me get your door." I raised an eyebrow at him, but did as he asked.

When the car parked, he got out first and then came around to my side of the car, opened the door, and held out a hand to help me up. I smiled as I took his hand. How long had it been since a man had held a door open for me? It seemed to happen less and less as feminism grew and women demanded equal treatment. While I agreed women should get paid the same if they did the same job, I did miss the chivalrous gestures that men used to do.

We walked into the upscale restaurant and Philip gave his name to the hostess, who sat us immediately. A white cloth covered the table, and a candle centerpiece emitted a romantic glow in the dim restaurant. I reached for my chair, but Henry beat me to it and pulled the chair back for me. I flashed him another smile before sitting down. Then he pushed my chair in before taking his own seat. Raquel raised an eyebrow at me, but I shrugged in response.

The delicate paper menu held only a few choices, and my eyes widened at the prices. I should have thought to ask where we were going before I agreed. I didn't have the money to spend so much on dinner, especially since Peter had moved out and money was much tighter. My heart thudded in my chest as I quickly scanned for the cheapest item on the menu; even the side salad was nearly fifteen dollars. *How do people afford this? Well, the salad comes with bread and a bowl of soup, so at least it should be enough to fill me up.*

The waiter, clad in a white dress shirt and perfectly pressed black pants, appeared just as I laid the menu down. "Have we had enough time?" he asked politely, glancing at each of us before focusing his attention on Philip, who took the lead in ordering.

"Yes, we'll have two glasses of your finest red wine and two plates of the steak and lobster, grilled medium well." He handed his and Raquel's menus to the waiter.

"Very well," the waiter nodded and turned his attention to me.

I swallowed. "Um, I'll have the side salad and the tomato soup."

The waiter cocked his head. "Will that be all miss?"

My face flushed, and just as I was about to answer, Henry jumped in. "Yes, and the same for me please." He handed our menus to the waiter.

The waiter nodded. "Yes, sir, and anything further to drink?"

Henry glanced at me; I shook my head. "No, water will be adequate for now, thank you."

As the waiter turned away, I regarded Henry. Who was this man, and why was he being so nice to me? He caught me staring and shot me a small wink as he picked up a piece of bread.

"So, Henry, what do you do?" Raquel asked as she nibbled her own piece of bread.

"I'm in sales," he said. "Not glamorous and I don't save lives like you all, but I do get to meet some interesting people."

"Was that how you met Philip?" I grabbed a piece of bread for myself.

Philip laughed, "No, we actually met at the gym. It turns out, we both like racquetball."

"Well, I need to freshen up," Raquel said, pushing back her chair. Immediately Henry pushed back his chair and stood. Raquel and I both gawked at him. "Um, Sandra, will you come with me?" she stammered. I nodded, but before I could push back my chair, Henry was pulling it out for me. I flashed him a small smile and followed Raquel to the bathroom.

As soon as the door closed behind us, Raquel whirled to face me. "He seems nice, right? I mean a little odd with the standing thing just now, but nice, don't you think?"

"Actually, yeah he does, and the standing thing just now was him being chivalrous. At military balls, all the men at the table stand anytime a woman gets up from the table. It's a sign of respect."

Her eyebrows knitted together. "Really? How do you know that?"

"My dad was in the military, remember? He always told me growing up how a man should treat a lady and being chivalrous was one of his big points. I've never actually met a man who does it outside the military though, but it kind of makes me feel special." Warmth flooded my body at that realization.

Raquel turned to the mirror and pulled out her lipstick. "I wish Philip would do that for me, or even open my car door like Henry did for you. Maybe not every time, but once in a while would be nice."

I nodded absently. This new feeling of appreciation and lack of nausea had me distracted. Could I be developing feelings for this man or was I just reacting to the kindness he had shown tonight? I sat down on the plush red couch and peered around as the realization that there was a couch in the bathroom sunk in. Above me, an elegant chandelier hung from the ceiling. The counter was a white marble, and the walls were painted gold. White tile gleamed on the floor, and even the stall doors were white with gold trim. This restaurant bathroom was nicer than any I had ever seen.

Raquel finished touching up her makeup, and we returned to the table. Henry stood as we approached and again helped me with my chair. Our soup and salads arrived a moment later, and everyone reached for a fork, except Henry. Out of the corner of my eye, I noticed his hands folded on the table, his eyes closed, and his head bowed. Realizing he was praying, I put my own hands down and waited for him to finish. It seemed the respectful thing to do and a small way to say thank you for his kindness to me. Only when he picked up his fork did I follow suit.

As we finished the appetizer, Philip and Raquel's meals arrived, and I tried hard not to stare at the beautiful plate. The tantalizing smells of meat tickled my nose, and though I was no longer hungry, my stomach complained it wasn't getting the delicious food accompanying the aroma. Henry and I each took another slice of bread and smiled at each other. Had he ordered the same to be nice or was he short on cash like I was? The talk turned to Philip's practice and the crazy stories from the hospital while Raquel and Philip finished their dinner. Henry and I listened in a companionable silence.

Then the waiter returned. "How was everything?"

"It was very good," Philip spoke up before the rest of us could say a word.

"Wonderful, now there is no rush, but how would you like to handle the bill sir?" His eyes jumped from one person to the next. I blanched and swallowed.

"I'll take ours," Philip said, pointing to himself and Raquel.

"And I'll take ours," Henry jumped in. I shot him a relieved smile. A few minutes later the men paid the tab, and we headed back to Philip's car. Though it was still fall, a chill had descended while we were in the restaurant, and I shivered as it breeched my skin.

"I have a coat in the car," Henry whispered.

"I'm fine, really," I smiled up at him even as I hugged my arms tighter around myself. Little goose bumps popped out on my arms.

When we reached the car, he opened my door before climbing in his own side. He passed his brown leather jacket to me, and I accepted, pulling the jacket up to my neck. The smell of leather and sandalwood tickled my nose as I took a deep breath. I missed the masculinity. The ride back was quiet, but I couldn't help stealing glances at Henry. He seemed so nice; could he be genuine? And even if he was, could I handle male companionship again? Before I could completely sort that thought out, we arrived back at Raquel's apartment.

"I'd love to stay babe, but I have an early day tomorrow," Philip said, giving Raquel a quick kiss. She sighed up at him, but relented and crawled out of the car. Henry followed suit and then opened my door.

"It was a pleasure to meet you." Henry executed a little bow at Raquel and then at me. "I sure hope we can meet again." His eyes stared directly into mine.

Heat crawled across my face. "I'd like that." Henry climbed into the passenger side of Philip's car. As the men drove off, I realized I still had his jacket in my arms. A little smile tugged at my lips at the thought that I'd have to see him again to return his jacket.

"So do you think you'll see him again," Raquel teased.

"Maybe," I smiled, "I think I'd kind of like to."

I hugged her goodnight and returned to my own car. My heart fluttered as I replayed the night in my mind on the drive back.

As I entered the apartment, I hung Henry's jacket on the coat rack by the front door and changed for bed. It wasn't until I was in bed with my eyes closed that I realized I hadn't taken a comfort sip from my stash.

UNDERSTANDING A LOVING GOD

The sunlight filtering in the window woke me the next morning. As I yawned and stretched, I realized I had actually had a decent night's sleep. No dreams, no crying baby, just silence. Blessed silence. Better still, I didn't feel the need for a drink this morning.

Smiling, I rolled out bed, dressed, and shuffled into the kitchen to make a cup of coffee. On my way, I passed the brown leather jacket, and my heart warmed. There was definitely something about Henry that was affecting me, and I couldn't wait to find out about what it was.

As I was putting the grounds in the coffee maker, a knock sounded at the door. I glanced at my watch. *Who could that be? It's only 9 am.*

After pushing the button on the coffee maker, I crossed to the front door. No one was visible through the peephole, so I turned the lock and opened the door cautiously. There was no one on the stoop, but a bouquet of beautiful flowers lay there. I poked my head out as I retrieved the flowers, looking quickly left and right, but no one was to be seen. Whoever had dropped them had disappeared without a trace. I brought the flowers inside and shut the door.

In the kitchen, I pulled down a vase from the top brown cupboard.

After filling it with water, I unwrapped the flowers and placed them inside. A small white envelope poked out from the top of the pink carnations and white daisies. Plucking the envelope, I opened it up. A handwritten note stared back at me:

Thank you for a wonderful dinner last night. I hope to see more of you. —Henry

Would his charm never cease? I tried to remember the last time Peter had brought me flowers. Maybe our first Valentine's Day together over three years ago? Yes, there had been a bouquet of roses that day. Once we had started dating seriously though, his practicality had kicked in; flowers no longer made any sense because they just died, so he had bought books or clothes. One Christmas he had even bought a vacuum cleaner. That had not gone over well. I kind of missed the flowers.

The coffee finished brewing, and I poured myself a mug, bringing it and the vase to my small kitchen table. As I admired the flowers, I thought about the previous night. There must be something wrong with Henry; he was too nice, too charming to still be single. Though I was interested, I'd have to keep an eye out for whatever his fault was. I finished my coffee, a smile still on my face, before dressing for work.

I arrived at work just a few minutes before shift; Raquel was already there dressed in her scrubs and putting her purse in her locker.

"Well, you look happy," she said, closing the door.

"I do?" I tilted my head and smiled. "Well it might have to do with the fact that I received flowers on my doorstep this morning."

Raquel's eyes lit up, and she clapped her hands together. "Ooh do tell."

I laughed at her childlike display. "Not much to tell yet. I was making coffee, and I heard a knock at my door. By the time I got there, no one was there, but a bouquet of pink carnations and white daisies was on my doorstep. There was a card from Henry saying he had a nice time and he hopes we can get together again soon."

"He likes you," Raquel teased, "I knew he did. You could tell just from the way he looked at you."

A blush colored my face. "It's still early; I think he was just being nice."

Raquel raised an eyebrow. "Uh huh, sure, nice. I don't think Philip has even bought me flowers yet."

"What? That's terrible."

"Well, he's handsome and rich, so flowers aren't that big of a deal." Raquel flicked her hand in dismissal. "Oh, we better get going," she said, glancing at her watch.

I finished shoving my purse inside and closed my locker door. As I followed Raquel out, I couldn't help wondering if money was really more important to her than simple gestures?

When I returned to the apartment that evening, Henry's brown leather jacket greeted me at the door. As much as I enjoyed having it in my apartment, he probably wanted it back. My watch showed 7 pm, surely it would be okay to bring it back to him now. After approving my reflection in the mirror, I grabbed the jacket, locked the door, and headed the few doors down to 2B.

As I stood outside his door, my stomach knotted. *Will he consider me too bold coming over here? No, he had sent me flowers after all.* I wiped my sweaty palm on my pants, took a deep breath, and brought my knuckles down on his door. Waiting, I held my breath until the click of the lock sounded. The door swung inward, and Henry smiled from the other side. His blue shirt complemented his skin tone and hugged his muscular arms.

I swallowed, forcing my eyes to his face. "Here," – I pushed the jacket out to him – "I didn't mean to keep this last night."

His eyes danced back and forth as he reached for the jacket. "Thank you; I know you didn't. Would you like to come in for some tea?"

I bit my lip. I did want to come in; I wanted to know more about him, but should I go in? Even while the mental battle raged, I found my head nodding and my feet stepping forward.

His apartment was similar in layout to my own; we entered the living room first, which was decorated much more masculine in browns and blues. A kitchen was off to the right, and a hallway led out of the living room to the bathrooms and bedrooms. He was obviously neat as everything was in a place, but he was no minimalist. Three bookcases sat about the room, each teeming with books. A brown coffee table sat in the middle of the room and held a thick black book, a notebook, and a pen.

"Have a seat," he said, pointing to his tan couch. "I'll get the water going." As he crossed to the kitchen, I sat on the couch, taking the room in. There were a few nature paintings hung along the walls, but the most prominent art was a small wooden cross hanging over one of the bookcases. I don't know why it commanded my attention in the room; it wasn't even ornate, but I found my eyes drawn to it.

The sound of running water finally pulled my attention away from the wooden figure, and I glanced down to the coffee table. I picked up the thick black book: The Holy Bible. I sighed; I should have known from him praying at dinner. Maybe this was why he was still single; he was one of those crazy religious nuts. Quickly glancing over my shoulder, I opened the book. I'd never really examined a Bible before, and the thinness of the pages surprised me, but not as much as the markings in the book. Yellow highlighter sprinkled across many verses and handwriting covered the blank spaces. I touched the thin paper; I'd never written in a book, and he had filled nearly every blank space.

"Do you read the Bible?"

I jumped at his voice and slammed the book shut. "I'm sorry," I mumbled up at him, "I should have asked first. I was just curious."

He smiled, "I have nothing to hide in that book. You are welcome to look through it any time." The tea kettle whistled, and he turned back to the kitchen. A cupboard opened and dishes clanked.

I opened the book again. I didn't know much about the Bible, but like the wooden cross, I felt an odd pull to the pages. My finger ran down the words and tingled. I wasn't even reading them, just skimming, but something felt different than other books.

"I was studying John," he said, sitting beside me and placing a tea cup on the coffee table for me. Steam curled above the brown mug. "Have you read it?"

I peered up at him. "I don't think I have. I mean I've never had a Bible, so unless I read part of it somewhere else, I guess I haven't."

"Ah, well the Bible is comprised of lots of books written by men inspired by God. John is one of the books that talks about Jesus coming down to earth to die for the sins of the world. Have you heard of Jesus?"

"A little, I think." I grasped the mug and let the warmth travel up my arms. "Wasn't he a nice person who did good deeds a long time ago?"

Henry nodded. "He was that, but also much more. He was perfect and sinless, and he performed miracles when he was on earth before he was killed. But there was something different about him. He rose from the dead after being crucified and ascended back into heaven three days later."

My head dropped forward, and I stared at him not sure I'd heard correctly. Alarm bells sounded in my head as my eyebrow shot up. "You think he came back from the dead?"

"No," – Henry shook his head and smiled – "I know he did. You see the Bible is God's word to us. It is a map of what happened, and a map of what will happen. It tells me that Jesus died and rose from the dead three days later."

"Why did he have to die?" I took a sip of my tea and peeked at him while trying to decide if he was delusional. The story seemed crazy, but also a little interesting.

"Well, God used to allow sacrificial lambs to cover the sins of his people, but he knew humans aren't perfect, and he wanted to give a sacrifice that would last forever. He sent his son, Jesus, to be a sacrifice for all of us so that when we get to heaven, we will be able to stand clean in God's presence."

"So, everyone goes to heaven?"

Henry shook his head and studied his cup. "No, I'm afraid not. God gives everyone free will. He wants us all to go to heaven, but he also wants us to choose him, and, sadly, not everyone will."

"Why would people not choose God?" I didn't know much about God, but it seemed if choosing him was the way to heaven, then it was an easy choice. Cocking my head to the side, I waited for his answer.

"Well, some people don't want to give up control of their lives. They want to be able to do what they want when they want. You see when you believe in God, then you also believe Jesus died for your sins, so you first have to believe you sin; many people don't. Then, Jesus told his disciples he was leaving them with the Holy Spirit when he returned to heaven.

"The Holy Spirit dwells within each believer, and therefore we should not want to do anything that would grieve the Holy Spirit. A lot of people don't like that part because they might have to give up something they love, like premarital sex or cursing or a multitude of other sins. Of course, God knows we aren't perfect and allows us to ask for forgiveness but Jesus said, 'Go and sin no more,' so we have to try and stop the sinning.

"What these people don't understand is they may have to give up some things on earth, but this life is fleeting, and the eternity spent with God will be so much better than anything here. It makes the sacrifices worth it."

Henry's words had stirred my excitement, until he mentioned premarital sex. A weight descended on my shoulders, and I dropped my eyes to the mug cooling in my hands. I not only had practiced that, but had been living with my boyfriend and had eliminated a baby conceived in it. If premarital sex grieved God, how much more would killing my baby? He certainly would never allow someone like me into heaven.

"Sandra? Are you okay?"

Henry was staring at me. Biting my lip, I tried to come up with something to tell him. I certainly couldn't tell him about my past; he'd never like me if I did. My eyes darted to the large wooden cross and quickly away as I conjured up an excuse. "Yes, sorry, I just remembered that I have something important to do." I placed the cup back on the table and stood.

His face pulled at my heart strings; I didn't want him to think I didn't like him, but the sobering thought had stirred the desire for a drink. Plus, I needed clarity to decide what to do about the new knowledge of Henry's character. "I'd love to chat together again though," I offered in hopes of soothing the situation.

That seemed to soothe his ego as his eyes brightened, and he led the way to the door. "I'd really like that, too."

As I walked back to my apartment, I wondered if my terrible deed and Henry's religious outlook could ever co-mingle. I didn't know much about God, but Henry had made him sound wonderful. With so many huge mistakes though, would God ever accept me? And would Henry if he knew how damaged I really was? Henry had said God sent Jesus to die for our sins, but would he forgive my biggest sin? I didn't even know if God was what made Henry so different, but if it was, I wanted a taste of what he seemed to have.

After locking the door behind me, I headed straight for the bedroom like a missile. I needed the clarity and peace only the bottle could supply. A satisfying swig soothed the ruffled nerves, but the questions continued to swirl about in my head.

THE LIES WE TELL

*W*ork consumed my next few days, not leaving much time to think about Henry or God's acceptance. I had just shrugged off my coat when a knock sounded at the door behind me. Glancing at my watch, I wondered who could be knocking on my door at seven at night. As I opened the door, Henry smiled, looking boyish and nervous.

"I was wondering if you might feel up to a walk?" His hands were jammed in the pockets of his tan pants, and he rocked back and forth on his heels.

A warm sensation trickled over me. "I'd like that, but I just got home, and I haven't eaten. I'm starving."

"There's a little cafe about three blocks from here," he suggested, "We could get our walk and dinner." He raised an eyebrow, and hope danced in his eyes.

I smiled, opening the door wider. "That sounds great. Come on in; I just want to change into something more comfortable."

As he entered the apartment, his eyes surveyed the room. "You can have a seat there if you'd like." I pointed at the couch. "I'll be right back."

I dashed into the bedroom and ripped off my scrubs. Donning a pair of jeans and a peach shirt, I checked my makeup and breath and then slipped on some tennis shoes before heading back to the living room.

Henry rose from the couch as I entered. "You look nice in that color," he said. "Are you ready?"

"Yes, and thank you." I followed him out the front door, locking it behind me.

As we walked, he talked about his family back in Louisiana and his short stint in the Air Force, which was how he ended up in Texas. "I wanted to be a pilot, but after they found out I was color blind, they said it was a no go. I tried doing the different jobs involving planes, but my passion was flying, so after I served my four years, I got out."

"What made you stay here?" I asked.

"Well, I liked San Antonia, where I had trained, so I figured when I got out, I'd see what else Texas had to offer, and I found a job in Dallas, so I stayed."

"Do you miss your family?"

His eyes clouded over, and he turned his head away. "I do, but I try to see them once a year or so."

Something about his demeanor led me to believe there was a bigger story there, but I didn't press the issue. "I'm an only child. My parents live in Houston, but I couldn't handle the heat, so when I had a chance to go to nursing school in Dallas, I jumped at it."

"Do you like nursing?" he asked.

"Yeah, I think so, for now anyway." As the words tumbled out of my mouth, I realized I didn't enjoy nursing as much as I had before the "procedure." I didn't deal with babies much or pregnant women for that matter, but the hospital itself held some kind of memory, and it just hadn't been the same. Plus, there was always the chance of running into Peter and Sheila.

We arrived at the quaint cafe then, and a waitress led us to a table. The cafe had an eclectic feel with brightly colored walls and healthy sandwiches. Large potted plants sat in the corners, and music played softly through the restaurant. The menus were single sheets inside plastic casings, and after ordering, we engaged in more small talk.

The food came, and once again Henry prayed over it before he ate. I took the opportunity to really focus on him while his eyes were closed. He was a handsome man, but even more than that was his demeanor. I wondered again if this God of his had something to do with that.

After dinner, we sauntered back to the apartments. On the walk there, Henry grasped my hand, and I smiled at the touch and the fact that no nausea accompanied it. I laced my fingers in his and enjoyed the warmth that traveled up my arm, enflaming my body. As we walked, I wondered if he would try and kiss me goodnight and found I wanted him to.

When we reached my door, I paused, giving him the opportunity. Henry's brow furrowed as if he wanted to say something, but wasn't sure what. His mouth opened and closed. He took a deep breath and squeezed my hand. "I know this might sound kind of strange, but I really feel like God is telling me to invite you to church on Sunday, so will you go with me?"

I had my head tilted up and my eyes closed when his words sank in. My eyes popped open. "I'm sorry, but what did you say?" Surely, I had heard him wrong. He couldn't want me to go to church with him, but then again he didn't know my secret.

He cleared his throat and brought his other hand up so that he was holding my hand in both of his. "I'm asking you to go to church with me on Sunday. The service starts at 9:30, so I could pick you up at 9 am. It isn't far from here, and I'd really like you to see why God is so important to me. Will you come?"

His eyes pleaded with me, and my mind drew a blank on excuses. The only one I had, I couldn't tell him about. I nodded, unable to actually form the word yes on my lips. His eyes lit up as he squeezed my hand again.

"That's great," he said. "Thank you again for accompanying me to dinner, and I'll see you soon." He dropped my hand and walked to his apartment; I stared after him, missing the warmth of his touch, but still a little in shock.

Unlocking my own door, I stumbled inside and locked it before ambling numbly to my bedroom. *Why did I say yes? What if God strikes me down at the church door? Does he do things like that? Would everyone in church be able to see I didn't belong and my past sin?* The questions circled over and over like a gerbil on a wheel as I changed into pajamas and brushed my teeth. Even after I climbed into bed, they plagued my mind, keeping sleep at bay.

At lunch the next day, I picked at my salad contemplating what I could say to Henry to get out of church on Sunday but not scare him off. A metal dray dropped beside me, causing me to jump. Raquel's bright green eyes met my gaze when I peered up.

"Guess what?" she squealed as she pulled out a chair and plunked down. "I'm getting married. Philip proposed last night." She held out her left hand where a large diamond ring adorned her fourth finger.

"Wow, isn't that kind of fast?" The words escaped before I could stop them, and I felt bad when Raquel's face dropped. "I'm sorry; I mean that's great."

Raquel tilted her nose up and away. Her feathers were definitely ruffled. "It may be fast, but when you know, you just know."

"You're right," I agreed, hoping to appease my friend. "Let me see it."

Raquel held her hand closer, and I oohed over the ostentatious ornament.

"Now, tell me how are things with Henry?" Raquel's voice lilted in a sing song manner, and she raised her eyebrows in a teasing gesture.

I sighed, *back to the question of the day*. "It was going great, and then he invited me to church."

Raquel shrugged and plucked a grape off her tray, popping it in her mouth, "So what? Go to church with him. It's probably not a serious thing. I know a lot of people who go to church on Sundays just to atone for their Saturdays if you get my drift." She nudged me with her elbow and winked.

"I don't know." I shook my head, ignoring her insinuation. "God seems really important to him, but what if he hates me?"

"Who? Henry?"

"No, God."

Raquel leaned forward, her eyebrows arched. "Why would God hate you? You're amazing."

I bit my lip and whispered, "Because of the 'procedure.'" I

glanced around quickly to make sure no one had heard.

She sat back and picked up another grape. "Look, *if* there's a God, I'm sure he understands that you just did what was best for you. Isn't that what people always say, God wants the best for you?"

"I don't know if that's what they mean." I was no expert on God, but that didn't sound like the same one Henry described.

"Well, I've been in a church since mine, and I am fine. I'm sure lots of other women have, too. Besides, Henry is worth it. He's a catch." She smiled and winked at me.

Raquel's words sunk in and churned around in my stomach, sprouting a seed of confidence. Maybe I could go to church. Maybe it wouldn't be so bad.

When Sunday rolled around, I woke before the alarm clock. Doubt gnawed on my insides. After showering, I stood in the closet, surveying the contents. What did people even wear to church? I'd only ever seen TV shows about it, and they always appeared dressy. I pulled on a simple peach dress and checked the mirror. Dressy but not overly, pretty but not too sexy.

I swallowed the seed of fear that was steadily growing and entered the kitchen to start the coffee. When it finished, I sat down on the couch with a steaming mug, trying to calm the nerves roiling in my stomach. At 9 am on the dot, a knock sounded at the door. Henry stood on the other side looking dapper in a charcoal suit and blue shirt.

"You look very nice," he said and held out his hand.

I stared at his outstretched hand and ran my hands down the peach dress, smoothing out imaginary wrinkles. Swallowing the lump in my throat, I took his hand and shut the door, locking it behind me. He dropped my hand as we began walking. I eyeballed him, expecting an explanation, but he gave none, nor any indication that what he had done was out of the ordinary.

"We're not driving?" I asked as we exited the parking lot on foot.

He smiled. "Not when God made it so beautiful outside. It's not a long walk anyway." We continued in silence down the cracked sidewalk. Redbud trees lined the sides, and the sun warmed my skin, but inside my nerves were balling together. I had hoped he would take my hand again; it was a calming presence, but he didn't, and I was too confused by his action to try taking his.

We turned the corner a few blocks down, and a white clapboard church came into view. A few trees dotted its yard, and a solitary cross sat atop its steeple. Groups of people milled outside chatting, and as we approached, a few waved at Henry. He returned the wave, but he didn't stop to chat. Relief flooded my body like a gently lapping wave. I didn't know these people from Adam, and I didn't want to try and have small talk as nervous as I was.

He led me into the small sanctuary. Rows of pews with red velvet seats lined the left and right but the center aisle was open. As I followed him to a pew on the right, in about the middle of the church, I gazed up at the beautiful stained glass windows that adorned the church. Each one depicted a different scene, but they made no sense to me. I'd have to remember to ask Henry about them later. As we sat, I noticed the brown shelf holding books on the back of the pew in front of me.

"What are these?" Picking one up, I began turning the pages. It was similar to the Bible, though not as big and with thicker pages.

He smiled. "Have you never been to a church before?"

I shook my head as I focused on the pages. Music bars stared back at me.

"That's a hymnal, so you can read the words if you aren't familiar with the songs, and that other book is the Bible in case you don't have your own."

I nodded and continued turning the pages as the church filled around us.

A few people came over and shook Henry's hand. He made introductions when that occurred, and I would smile, but I wished people would stop coming over; I just wanted to listen to the service. Finally, a choir clad in black robes took the stage. One man stepped up to the mic.

"If you'll open your hymnal to page 584, you'll be able to follow along as we sing 'At the Old Rugged Cross.'"

I flipped the pages until I found the correct number. People began to stand all around me, including Henry, so I rose to my feet as well. I didn't know the song, but not wanting people to know that, I mouthed the words and enjoyed the deep sound of Henry's voice beside me.

The song was slow, but the words had a power to them. Different emotions played across people's faces: mostly joy, some sadness, and a few of indifference. I couldn't understand those people. I didn't even know what I was doing here, but I certainly felt a power. A slower song followed and then a faster song. I gasped as people began raising their hands and dancing in the aisles.

"Do they always do that?" I whispered to Henry.

He smiled. "Only on the fast ones."

When the song ended, a black man in a light suit took the stage and began to preach. I tried to listen to the words, though the "amens" from those around me were often distracting. I found myself turning to see who had shouted the word every time. I'd had no idea church was so lively. Church had always been something I thought was formal and stiff. As the preacher closed, the choir stood up and sang one last song before the service was over. When the music stopped, Henry stood, and I followed him out of the aisle and out the front entrance of the church. Again people waved, and Henry returned the waves and smiled, but he didn't stay to chat.

"What did you think?" Henry asked as we made our way back to the apartment complex.

I tilted my head and pursed my lips. "I think I liked it. I definitely enjoyed the music, and the sermon was nice, too."

His smile stretched across his face. "I'm glad. Would you like to come again?"

As much as I had enjoyed the service, a small seed of doubt still remained. I squished the seed and returned the smile as a warmth enveloped me. "Yes, I think I would. Also, I think I'd like a Bible to read. Do you know where I could get one?"

"Any bookstore would have one for sale, but I bet the library at our apartment complex has one you could check out."

I sucked in my breath, hope building inside. "Really? Will you go with me to check?"

The rather small apartment library consisted of two bookshelves in the corner of the main lobby. They held mostly trashy romance novels with a few classics sprinkled in, but at the very bottom of the first bookshelf, I struck gold. A black leather book with "The Holy Bible" embossed in gold down the spine called out to me.

"You were right," I said, handing the book to him. He smiled as he ran his hand over the cover. I signed the book checkout log sheet, and we walked back to my apartment, the Bible tucked to my chest like a Christmas gift.

"I'd really like to take you to a movie," Henry said outside my apartment door. "Are you free Friday night?"

"I'll have to check my schedule, but I think I can make that happen." He said goodbye, and I entered my apartment, Bible cradled against my chest. I sat down on the couch and opened the book to the first chapter. Genesis 1:1 "In the beginning God created the heavens and the earth." Hmm, that wasn't what I'd learned in school, but I always did have a problem buying the whole evolving from a monkey thing because monkeys were still around. I continued reading.

"How was church?" Raquel asked as we ate lunch the following day.

I smiled. "It was actually pretty fun. There was lots of music, and the message was good too."

Raquel wrinkled her nose. "I can't imagine church being fun. I've gone a few times, and you're right the music was good, but the sermon . . . ugh. Philip and I spent the morning in bed, much more fun I think."

I chewed a bite of salad as I thought. "I don't know; the people I saw yesterday all seemed pretty happy. I started reading the Bible as well. Some of it is hard to understand, but it was fascinating."

Raquel's head dropped as her eyes widened. "You aren't going to go all religious on me, are you?"

A small laugh escaped my lips. I certainly didn't know enough to be considered religious, besides – the realization sunk in again – God probably wouldn't accept me anyway. "No, I guess not," I sighed.

"You say that like it's a bad thing." Raquel picked up her tray. "I think you're being smart. Get to know his interests, but don't get sucked into the crazy."

I nodded as I followed her out of the cafeteria, but it didn't seem all that crazy. In fact, it seemed rather nice.

When Friday evening rolled around, I sat in my apartment drumming my fingers on the couch arm, waiting for the knock on the door. I was really looking forward to spending the evening with Henry.

Seeking the peace he seemed to have, I had been perusing the Bible nightly, but couldn't find the answers I sought. Perhaps tonight I would be brave enough to ask him about it.

At 6:45 on the nose, the knock sounded. I jumped up from the couch and smoothed my pale yellow dress. As I opened the door, I smiled at Henry on the other side dressed in khaki slacks and a light blue button down shirt, holding a red rose.

He bowed and held the flower out to me. "For you, pretty lady."

My heart skipped a beat, and a blush heated my face. "Thank you." Pulling the apartment door shut behind us, I followed him to his car.

"How was your week?" he asked after shutting my door and getting in on the driver's side.

"It was okay. Oh hey, did you hear Philip and Raquel are getting married?" His eyebrows furrowed as he started the car and pulled out. "What?" I pressed, "I thought you liked Philip."

He sighed. "I do, it's just he doesn't seem like the marrying type."

Concern bubbled up for my friend, "What do you mean?"

He shook his head. "Nothing, it's just Raquel is the fifth girl he's dated since I've known him, just over a year, but maybe she's the one."

I bit my lip and my own retort. As much as I loved Raquel, she was quite the player herself. I would just have to be extra vigilant to make sure she didn't get hurt. The conversation stalled, and I mentally kicked myself, wishing I'd chosen a lighter topic so maybe I could bring up my questions.

When we arrived at the theater, Henry paid for the tickets and held the door open for me as we stepped inside. We waited in line to get popcorn and drinks and then filed into the theater. I wanted to ask him about his peace, but the right words wouldn't form.

He picked seats in the middle of the theater, and we munched on the popcorn as we waited for the movie to start. Warmth spread up my arm every time our fingertips touched. The lights dimmed.

When the popcorn was finished, Henry set the bucket down and grasped my hand. The tingling warmth ran up my arm and spilled over onto the rest of my body. Though I tried not to react when the characters in the movie kissed, I couldn't help wondering what kissing Henry would be like, and I was glad the theater was dark because I knew every time the thought popped in my head a red blush covered my face.

After the movie ended, we exited the theater still hand-in-hand. The outside warmth had gone away with the sun, and I shivered when the cool air hit my exposed skin. Henry wrapped his arm around me, pulling me close, and I smiled into his chest.

As we reached the car, his posture stiffened. Looking up to see the cause, I followed his gaze to a red BMW with fogged windows. "Isn't that Philip's car?" I asked. I knew nothing about cars, but his license plate 1CHIRO had stuck in my mind. Henry nodded, his lips pinched. "Should we go say hi?" I pressed, wondering at his silence.

He shook his head. "No, he looks busy." I couldn't figure out why was he so upset by the sight. Had he never steamed up car windows? Henry opened my car door, but he was quiet on the drive back. When we returned to the apartment complex, he still seemed distracted.

"Is everything okay?" I asked.

He shook his head and smiled, but it didn't quite reach his eyes, "Yes, I'm sorry. I had a great time tonight."

"Me too." I placed my hands on his chest and tilted my head up to him. He took a deep breath and squeezed my arms.

"So, I'll see you Sunday for church?"

I blinked; I had been expecting a kiss. "Um, yes, I'd like that."

"Great, I'll see you then." He squeezed my arms again and walked away.

"Okay." I watched him walk back to his apartment unsure of what had just happened. Shaking my head, I entered my own apartment and changed for bed. As I lay in bed staring at the white ceiling, I realized I still hadn't asked him about his peace.

The ringing of the phone jolted me awake the next morning.

Blinking my eyes, I glanced at the clock before grabbing my phone. 10 am? I rarely slept that late. "Hello?"

"Sandra? Were you still sleeping?" Raquel asked on the other end.

I rubbed my eyes and yawned. "Yeah, I guess I was tired from last night. I'm surprised you're awake; you were out later than I was."

"What are you talking about?" Raquel asked, "I stayed home last night and caught up on soaps."

Ice flooded my veins, and I was instantly awake. I pushed myself into a sitting position. "You weren't with Philip last night?"

"No, Philip's sister was in town, so he took her out," Raquel said. "Wait, why did you think I was out late last night?"

I swallowed and bit my lip. I'd really stepped in it this time; should I till Raquel the truth? I traced the seam on my bedspread, "Um, no reason. I just thought I saw Philip's car when we were leaving the theater, but I must have been mistaken."

There was a long pause and when Raquel's voice came across the phone again, it dripped deadly icicles. "What did you see?"

I cringed, glad this exchange was happening over the phone and not in person. "Um, we saw his car at the theater with the windows all fogged up. We thought it was you, or I did. Maybe that explains why Henry was acting so weird after," I trailed off, realizing the last part was more for my benefit than for Raquel's.

"I'm going to kill him," Raquel screamed into the phone. "I'll call you later." The phone went dead in my hand before I could even respond. Grimacing, I replaced the phone on the cradle and kicked off the covers. I would not want to be Philip today. Actually, Henry had some explaining to do as well.

After showering and dressing, I squared my shoulders and marched over to Henry's door. I rapped three times and leaned back, crossing my arms.

"Well, hello," he said with a smile as he opened the door.

"You knew, didn't you?" I poked my finger in his face.

He blinked and took a step back. "Knew what?"

"About Philip, last night, you knew he wasn't with Raquel, and that's why you acted so weird."

His face fell, and his shoulders slumped. "I wasn't sure. I thought I saw blond hair before the windows fogged up, and I was hoping I was wrong. I wasn't though, was I?"

The sadness in his voice calmed my ire, and I unfolded my arms. "No, Raquel just called me and said she was at home last night because Philip was taking his sister out. I don't have a brother, but I doubt I'd be steaming up a car with him if I did."

"I'm so sorry." Henry gathered me into his arms. "I was hoping I was wrong about him, and that maybe Raquel was the one he would finally settle down with."

Tears filled my eyes as I raised them to meet his, "What can I say to Raquel? I feel so bad for her."

He brushed a tear from my cheek. "We can pray for her and for wisdom to know what to say," he said. His finger continued down my cheek to my lips and traced them. My breath caught in my throat, and my lips parted. *Please kiss me.* His eyes stared deep into mine, and as he lowered his head, I closed my eyes, savoring the soft velvet feel of his lips as they met mine. It lasted only a moment, but it left me breathless. "Come on," his voice was husky with emotion, "Let's go pray for Raquel."

I followed him inside and to the couch. He held my hands in his as we sat down. Then he closed his eyes and opened his mouth. "Lord, we bring our friend Raquel to you. We know she is hurting at this time, and we pray for peace for her. Though it's hard now, we pray for her to see the benefit in finding out before she married Philip. We also pray for the words to say to her. Help us be examples of you and show her your love as she grieves. Lord, I also want to thank you for bringing Sandra into my life. Please bless this relationship, and help us grow it in a way that would be pleasing to you. Amen. I hope that last part was okay," he said. "It kind of just slipped out."

"It was perfect," I said.

Henry squeezed my hands and then leaned in to kiss me again. My heart skipped double time in my chest, and I wrapped my arms around his neck, pulling him closer. The familiar tingling ran down my spine, and my breath grew labored. Then he pulled back.

"What's the matter?" I asked, snapping my eyes open.

He ran a hand over his face and took a deep breath. "I just needed to take a break before we did something we might regret."

I regarded him, trying to decide if I was flattered or insulted, but he appeared genuine. Then I remembered what he had said about the Holy Spirit, and it made sense. "Oh right," I agreed. "Better to take it slow."

His face lit up, and then he sighed. "I'm so glad you understand. I have to get to work anyway, but you'll still come to church tomorrow right?"

"Of course," I agreed, "I want to do some reading today anyway." Though my mind understood Henry's reluctance to go further, my body was still upset. A fire raged within. As I curled in my couch and opened the Bible, the fire slowly simmered and died out. The words themselves had a calming effect, and I found myself relaxing into the story.

*R*aquel looked terrible when I entered work Monday morning. Her eyes were puffy and red, and her usually spotless face was splotchy. Even her lustrous hair was piled lazily in a disheveled ponytail. "I guess it wasn't good," I whispered to her as we filled out charts at the front desk.

"No, he denied it at first, but when I told him you guys saw his car, he fessed up. I guess he had been seeing his assistant, Tiffany, the whole time we were together. I really thought he was different." Her voice dripped with disdain as she said the other woman's name. She sniffed and discreetly ran a hand across her eyes.

I touched her arm. "You know I saw a lot of single men at Henry's church yesterday. Not that you would go there for that reason, but maybe they would treat you better. Henry seems to, at least."

She stiffened slightly and drew her shoulders back. "No offense, but I don't think that's my cup of tea."

I smiled. "I didn't either, but it's kind of growing on me."

"Heads up ladies," – Nurse Hatchet roared behind us – "We've got a trauma coming in."

We dropped our charts and turned to the incoming door.

❦

I sighed as I collapsed into bed that night. While I loved working in the ER, excessive traumas always wore me out. Today had been no different. A ten car pile-up on the Interstate had sent thirty or so people into the ER. I hadn't had time for a lunch or even a break, and I had scarfed down dinner when I finally got home before soaking in the tub.

Spying the Bible on the nightstand, I picked it up and began reading where I had left off. I still didn't think God would accept me, and I hadn't asked him to, but I found there was peace in reading the Bible and discussing it with Henry. The dreams had lessened, though I wasn't entirely sure if that was a good thing or a bad thing. Sometimes I missed seeing and holding the boy, even if he wasn't real.

Most evenings I spent with Henry, having dinner and discussing our respective days. I continued to go to church with him and even made some new friends, but I still didn't feel "good enough" for God. Raquel had started seeing another rich doctor, and was already sharing her apartment with him on weekends.

When the year anniversary of my "procedure" rolled around, my heart grew heavy again. The dreams came back with a vengeance, and though I thought I had accepted them, they began to take a toll on my concentration. I found myself turning to the bottle to sleep at night again, and every baby seemed to pull on my heartstrings.

"What's the matter?" Henry asked as we sat at dinner in a crowded restaurant.

My head popped up. "What do you mean? Why would something be the matter?"

He grasped my hand and stared into my eyes, "You've flinched at every cry from that baby over there, and you physically turned away when a toddler walked past you. Now, if you hate babies, we might need to have a talk because I really care for you, but I want children in my future."

My jaw dropped along with my heart. "Hate babies? I don't hate babies." *I just killed my own a year ago, but I can't tell you that.* What could I tell him though? I had to give him some reason; maybe a half truth? "It's just that," – I bit the inside of my lip as the words formed in my head – "It's just that I lost a baby a year ago." It wasn't the complete truth, but it was close.

His brow furrowed, and he sat back. "I don't understand. I didn't know you were married."

"I wasn't, but I was living with my boyfriend . . ." I trailed off as his face fell. Maybe this hadn't been a good idea; I suddenly remembered him saying premarital sex was a sin. Was that why he hadn't made a move beyond kissing? "I'm sorry, is that a deal breaker for you?"

He took a deep breath and tapped his finger to his lips. My heart beat like a jackhammer. *Please don't say yes* repeated over and over in my mind. He opened his mouth but said nothing. *Ba-bam, Ba-bam,* the sound was deafening in my head. *Just say something.*

Finally, he leaned forward again. "It's not a deal breaker for me, but I'm a little disappointed. I always hoped that was something I could share for the first time with my wife on our wedding night."

My mind raced as I blinked repeatedly at him. *Does he mean to say he's a virgin?*

"You also have to know that I don't condone living with someone or being intimate outside of marriage, and I won't do that, but I do believe Jesus forgives, and it's not my place to judge your past. I am sorry about your baby, though."

I barely heard the words that fell out of his mouth. "I'm sorry; do you mean to tell me you've never been intimate with a previous girlfriend?"

Henry smiled. "No, I haven't. I'm saving myself for marriage because that's what Jesus would want me to do. You see God made marriage between one man and one woman as a way to procreate. He never meant for us to be intimate with everyone we date. That's why the Bible says the man will leave his family and become one with his wife. God only meant for us to become one with one person."

I couldn't wrap my mind around a man who didn't crave sex. "But don't you want to? I mean haven't you in the past?" My face heated up at the scenario I was implying.

"Yes, my flesh has often wanted the intimacy both with you and with past relationships, but I have chosen not to give in to the flesh. You see when I accepted Jesus as my savior, and the Holy Spirit indwelled in me, I didn't want to do anything that would grieve him. I'm not perfect by any means, but I try my best to avoid temptation that would lead to sin. It keeps me from having to make hard choices I might regret later."

My breath caught at those words. Had he decoded my lie or was he just speaking in generalizations? Then the words sank in; I could have avoided that terrible choice if I had chosen the path that Henry had. Why hadn't I ever heard about saving myself? The TV shows always showed people being intimate, sometimes even on the first date, and, even in school, we had discussed how sex was normal – if not expected – and we'd been handed birth control and condoms. We'd even spent a class period learning how to put them on bananas. But no one had ever said you didn't have to have sex. No one had said there was power and respect in waiting. Would I have listened if they had? Probably not, once the imprint of "do it, it feels good" was there, it would have been hard to listen to anything else, but I was listening now. "I wish I had waited. What you're saying makes a lot of sense, and it would have saved me a lot of grief."

Henry squeezed my hand. "Whatever grief you are experiencing, God can help you overcome it, if you put your trust in Him."

"I want to," I began, "but I don't think he'd want someone like me." Tears welled up in my eyes and threatened to spill over. I blinked and wiped them away.

"Hey, God meets you where you are and changes you from there. You don't have to be perfect to meet Him."

Though I nodded, I didn't really believe him. I wanted to, but it was such a terrible thing to have done. I just couldn't give it all away.

That night as I lay in bed, Henry's words ran through my mind again. Could God forgive even the sin of killing my own child? I wanted it to be true, but how could he? I had thrown away the gift he sent me.

I woke to the feeling of something on my face. Startled, I snapped my eyes open to see a toddler. His tiny hand touched my face again, and he smiled.

"Mama," he said and flashed a grin with only four teeth. He stood on the floor beside my bed, holding onto the side and bouncing up and down. "Mama," he said again and clapped his hands.

I tried to smile, even though a part of me knew he wasn't real. I had taken his life a year ago. He was so beautiful, though. "Hi baby," – I whispered as a tear rolled down my cheek – "Mama is so sorry. I'm so sorry I never gave you the chance to live."

The boy's smile faded, and his small hand touched my wet cheek. I grabbed his little hand and kissed it. If only I could go back. If only. I closed my eyes as I thought of how to make it up to him, but when I opened them again, he was gone.

"Even if God could forgive me, I don't think I'll ever forgive myself." Sleep did not return that night.

"Whoa, what happened to you?" Raquel said as I clocked in the next morning.

I glared at her. The dream and the lack of sleep had left me grouchy this morning. "You don't remember?"

Raquel cocked her head, "No, should I?"

"It's been a year." I slammed the locker door and sank onto the bench in front of the lockers. "I thought it was getting better, but I had another dream last night."

"Oh, the procedure," Raquel said, sitting beside me.

I dropped my head in my hands. "And I lied to Henry about it. I was acting weird at dinner and he wanted to know why, so I told him I lost a baby."

Raquel shrugged, "That's mostly true."

I whipped my head up, daggers in my eyes. "It's not true at all. I killed my baby. I thought it would be easy and I'd forget, and some days I seem to, but then he comes to me in my dreams and breaks my heart again. And things are going great with Henry, but I don't think he'd support my decision, and now I've lied. How do I build a relationship on a lie?"

Raquel touched my arm, "Okay, first you need to calm down.

While I agree lying isn't the best thing to do in a relationship, it happened before you knew Henry, and you only stretched the truth a little. You seem really happy with him, so I'd try to come up with a way to forget..." I narrowed my eyes at her. "Or at least accept your stretching of the truth," Raquel continued. "Maybe it was a mistake, but you can't take it back, so perhaps if you accept it, it will get easier."

I sighed, but she was right. If I told Henry, I might lose him forever, and that thought scared me to death. I realized I was falling in love with him and didn't want to be without him. "I guess you're right. There is nothing I can do now, so I'll just try to make better choices from here on out."

"That's the ticket," Raquel smiled. "Now come on, let's go save some lives."

I decided the best way to convince myself I could move on from the past was to be the best person I could be from then on, so I joined Henry's church and the choir. We joined a Bible study that met weekly, and I even began memorizing verses. On the outside, I tried to live as righteously as I could, hoping eventually it would change the inside to match.

As Christmas rolled around, my joy grew, and I whistled as I decorated the apartment. This would be my second Christmas with Henry, though we hadn't exchanged gifts the first year as we had only been dating a few months. I had bought him the perfect gift; it was now sitting under the tree, begging to be opened, and he was due any minute. Raquel and her latest fling, Greg, were also coming. I hung up the stockings and had just finished lighting a candle when a knock sounded at the door.

Henry stood on the other side dressed in a green shirt and khakis. Warmth flooded my body as he held up a piece of mistletoe and kissed me. When we parted, I grabbed his hand, pulling him into the apartment.

"I come bearing gifts," he smiled and held up a small square box wrapped in red paper.

"Ooh, I can't wait to see what it is," I squealed as I took the box. "Can I shake it?"

He laughed, "Go ahead; it's not breakable."

I held the box to my ear and shook it back and forth, but no sound came forth; it tightly held its secret.

"Knock knock," Raquel said as she pushed open the door that had been left ajar. "Merry Christmas."

I rushed to my friend, enveloping her in a hug. "Merry Christmas to you, too. Here let me take your coats." After I hung up Greg and Raquel's coat, I led them to the tree to deposit their packages. "Who wants egg nog?"

"I'll help," Raquel offered, following me into the kitchen.

I pulled four festively colored mugs down from the cabinet and filled them each with the creamy liquid. Handing two to Raquel, I picked up the other two, and we returned to the living room where we chatted idly as Christmas music played in the background.

When I could contain my joy and curiosity no longer, I clapped my hands and surveyed my friends. "Okay, who's ready for gifts?"

They smiled, laughing at my exuberance, and I handed out a gift for each person. The little red box from Henry I picked for myself, holding it like a cherished toy. "Open yours first," I nudged him.

He smiled and unwrapped the gift I had gotten for him. As he pulled out the book he had wanted, his smile deepened. "You remembered."

"Of course I remembered." I swatted him playfully on the arm. "You didn't already buy it for yourself, did you?"

"No, I was hoping my very attentive girlfriend would cover that base." He laughed and kissed my nose. "Okay, now you." He stared at me as I began to unwrap the little box.

Beneath the red paper was a small black jewelry box. A lump formed in my throat, and I raised silent eyes on him.

"Go ahead," he teased. "Open it."

I took a deep breath and eased the lid open, anticipating the sparkle of a diamond ring, but there was nothing there. I blinked in confusion. "It's empty."

Henry rose from the couch and knelt on one knee before me. He clasped my hand with his left as he reached for his pocket with his right. "Sandra, I know it's been just over a year, but I can't imagine my life without you in it. Will you do me the honor of becoming my wife?" His right hand pulled out a simple gold band with a small diamond. It wasn't much, but it filled my heart with joy.

Unable to contain my excitement any longer, I threw my arms around his neck. "Of course I'll marry you," I whispered and met his lips with my own.

"Hey get a room," Raquel teased from the love seat across from us.

I blushed as we pulled apart. Henry slid the ring on my finger and swung me around. We finished opening the gifts, but I couldn't help staring at the simple flash on my left hand. As the evening came to a close, Raquel pulled me aside. "I'm so happy for you."

A feeling of astonishment raced through me. "I kind of can't believe it."

"You deserve it," Raquel said.

Though the words were meant to console me, they hit my weak spot instead. I didn't deserve Henry; I had lied to him. A rock settled in my stomach, and I tried to swallow the guilt away. Flashing a hesitant smile, I walked my friend to the door and bade her and Greg good-bye. As the door closed, Henry enveloped me in his arms.

"What's wrong?" He asked into my hair, "You seem a little off."

I turned my head up to kiss him. "No, I'm fine," I lied, "I'm just so happy."

"Well, it's late, and I should retire and let you get some sleep." Henry cupped my face, "Can I come see you tomorrow?"

"Of course," I smiled. He placed his lips on mine one final time before leaving.

After the door closed behind him, I retired to my bedroom. I sat on the edge of the bed and examined the ring. I wanted to marry him more than anything, but would he want to marry me if he knew my past? Would it be right not to tell him? My stomach churned at the thought of starting our marriage out in a lie, but I had worked so hard to be different. I couldn't lose him. I just couldn't. I pushed the thought aside. It wouldn't be important. What was important was us starting new. That was all that mattered.

TOO GOOD TO BE TRUE?

The days wore on in much the same fashion: work, evenings with Henry, planning the wedding with Bride magazine in my room late at night, and church on Sundays.

It was around Valentine's Day that Raquel announced her engagement as well, with a ring three times the size of mine. Though I tried not to be jealous, it was awfully hard to ignore the sparkle on Raquel's hand. That being said, there's nothing like sharing ideas for your wedding with your best friend, and I was elated to share the experience with her and gather her advice.

"We should go look at dresses," Raquel said one afternoon as we were clocking out.

I shrugged. "Sure, I'm not seeing Henry tonight. He had to work late. Do you think any stores are still open?"

"One way to find out." Raquel slung her purse over her shoulder and led the way to the parking lot. Deciding to just take one car to conserve gasoline, we climbed into her BMW.

A few minutes later we arrived at a shopping center. A bridal store sat prominently in the center, but it oozed the definition of expensive. Its sign alone was bigger than the other stores' signs put together. I bit my lip as I exited the car. Though I wouldn't be able to afford anything in here, it couldn't hurt to look. I just had to remind myself not to get excited.

As we entered the store, a woman in a spotless blue suit with her hair pulled back in a bun greeted us. She clasped her hands in front of her chest and tilted her nose upward. "Welcome to Bonita, who's getting married?" Her eyes darted from Raquel to myself, but they returned and fixed on Raquel.

"Actually we both are," Raquel smiled, "but I think her wedding will be first." She pointed to me, and a blush burned across my face as the woman turned her attention to me.

"Yes, I'm getting married in six months," I stammered.

"Well, that should give us time." She unclasped her hands and pursed her lips. "What are you looking for?"

"Oh, something simple, white, maybe some lace," I said as I ground my toe into the ground.

The woman cocked her head, and her eyes traveled from my feet up to my head. "You're an eight or a ten?"

"Umm, a ten usually."

"Right; follow me, and we'll see what we have."

"Oh, this is going to be so much fun," Raquel squealed.

I smiled half-heartedly and followed the woman, but I didn't really see the fun in trying on dresses I could never afford. As we traversed the sea of dresses, I glimpsed a tag and nearly laughed out loud. $4000? I'd never be able to afford even half that much.

The woman led us to the changing rooms at the back of the store. To the left was a raised platform, carpeted in pink and surrounded by three full length mirrors.

"Take the middle one," the lady pointed, "and I'll bring you some dresses."

I obliged and waited until the first dress appeared over the top of the changing door. It was a beautiful white satin dress with a long train covered in lace and beads. Finding the tag near the zipper, I turned it over and sighed. $6000. I almost didn't want to try it on in case I loved it, but I knew Raquel would never let me go without trying something. It fit perfectly. As I opened the door, Raquel gasped and clapped. I blushed but continued to the raised platform. The dress was a dream come true, if not a little showy, but I forced myself to focus on the negative so that I wouldn't get excited, knowing I'd never be able to afford it.

"What do you think?" the sales lady asked.

"It's beautiful," I said, "but a little out of my price range. Even if I could clock a lot of overtime, I'd never afford this."

The woman's lips flattened and her nose rose in the air. "I see. Well, I'll check to see what we have on the sales rack." She spun around and marched off.

"I don't think she liked that," Raquel whispered smiling.

"I don't either, but I can't afford six thousand dollars."

Raquel whistled. "Yeah that is a pretty penny, even for me. It is beautiful, though."

The woman returned a few minutes later with another few dresses. I took one and returned to the dressing room. After carefully removing the first dress so as not to harm any piece of it, I then slipped the new dress on. It was much simpler: no beads, but still plenty of lace. The price was better – only $3000 – but still way out of my league. I rolled my eyes, but opened the door to show it off.

"Oh, that's nice too," Raquel said as I stepped on the platform for the second time.

"How's the price on that one?" the woman asked with disdain.

I blushed. "Um, better, but still more than I can afford."

The woman flipped through the tags of the other dresses she had brought over. She pulled out a dress near the bottom and held it up. "$1000 is the cheapest one I have." The contempt in her voice was nearly palpable.

"Well, it's very nice; they all are, but I'm afraid I can't afford it either." The woman scowled – probably feeling that we had wasted her time – so I quickly added, "Maybe Raquel should try some on now since she can afford more than I can."

The woman's face brightened at that prospect. "Yes, let's do that. What are you, a six?"

Raquel nodded, and I returned to the dressing room to change back into my clothes. If $1000 was the cheapest dress, I'd either have to find a way to earn the money or find a store that sold cheaper dresses. After putting my street clothes back on and hanging up the dress, I returned to the platform area to watch Raquel try on dresses.

Raquel's personality was much flashier than I, and her dresses matched her taste. All of them had plunging necklines and long trains, and it seemed each one had more beads than the last. The final dress she tried on was off the shoulder, had a bodice bedecked in beads, and a six-foot long train. "This is perfect," Raquel sighed.

"It's one of my favorites," the woman agreed smiling. "Shall I put it on hold for you?"

"Oh, I'd love that," Raquel smiled back, "but do you have a temporary hold? I'd like my mother to see it before I decide to buy it."

"Of course; we can hold it for seven days, but then we'll have to put it back on the floor."

"That's fine." Raquel winked at me and returned to the dressing room to change. Afterwards, we followed the woman to the front where Raquel filled out some paperwork.

"Are you really going to buy that dress?" I whispered as we pushed open the door of the shop and walked into the parking lot.

"Doubtful," Raquel said, knitting her eyebrows together, "That dress was $10000. That's even out of my league."

My jaw dropped. "But you asked her to hold it."

She waved her hand in the air. "Of course I did; the sales people are always nicer if they think you'll come back. I didn't give accurate information though."

Shaking my head, I climbed into Raquel's car. I didn't think I'd ever understand rich people.

Raquel slid into her seat and tapped her fingers on the steering wheel. Her brow furrowed and she twitched her lips to one side. Then she snapped her fingers, her eyes sparkling. "Aha, I've got it. Do you feel up to going to one more place?"

I shrugged. "As long as it has dresses under a thousand dollars please."

"Yeah, I think this place will be perfect. I can't believe I didn't think of it first." She pointed the car north, and fifteen minutes later, we pulled into another shopping center. This one was smaller and much older.

I scanned the store names but nothing appeared very bride-like. "Where is it?"

"There." Raquel pointed to a small shop at the very end of the strip mall. The sign was so tiny that I couldn't even read it from where we were. Raquel parked the car, and we walked up to the door. LE BRIDE was stenciled in white lettering across the glass door. Raising an eyebrow, I swallowed my apprehension and followed Raquel into the shop.

A short plump woman greeted us as a tiny bell tinkled our arrival. She wasn't dressed in a suit, but an old blue and white dress. However, she exuded an air of friendliness. "Welcome to Le Bride. How can I help the two of you today?"

The knot of apprehension fizzled as the woman spoke. The woman looked like an older version of Mrs. Butterworth, though with gray hair and the name of Helen on her name badge. "I'm getting married in six months," I said. "I need something white and affordable."

Helen smiled. "I have just the thing. Come with me."

She moseyed toward the back, and we followed her. Helen flicked through a few racks, clicking her tongue and grabbing a few dresses as she went.

"Here we are dearie; try these on." She folded the bundle over my arm, and I stepped into the small dressing room and hung the dresses up on the supplied hook. I inspected the first dress, but with its overzealous beading pattern, it didn't fit my style. Moving it to the side, I gasped as my eyes landed on the second dress. It was simple, but elegant. Lace covered the bodice and part of the back. The satin rippled like a sea of milk. I slid the dress on before even looking for a tag and sighed. My hands ran down the sides; it was a perfect fit. The white offset my darker skin, making me appear to glow. I twirled in front of the full length mirror in the room enjoying the vision from all sides.

I opened the door and smiled as Raquel gasped. "Right?" I asked. "I think it's perfect."

"I agree. You look like an angel."

The woman appeared and pulled a pencil from somewhere in her gray hair. "Ah, yes, I knew this would be lovely. It is absolutely perfect on you, my dear."

I bit my lip hoping it was affordable. "Can I ask how much?" Butterflies fluttered in my stomach as I waited for the woman's answer.

"It's on sale this week for $300."

My heart fluttered. It was expensive, but not unaffordable. "I'll take it." I turned back to the mirror and beamed at my reflection. This was really happening.

After paying the bill, I carried the new dress, wrapped in a beautiful gold lame box with a white bow, out to Raquel's car. "Now, I just have to make sure Henry doesn't find it, and I don't gain a ton of weight."

"I'll make sure of the latter, but the former is up to you," Raquel smiled.

✺

A few weeks later, Henry and I met up to taste cakes for the wedding.

"Are you sure about this place?" I asked, raising my eyebrows at the small brick building that seemed out of place amidst the taller, newer buildings filling the rest of the block.

He smiled. "Don't worry, she's a client of mine. I know it doesn't look like much, but she's the best baker around." He opened the front door, and we stepped inside the little shop.

Just three small silver tables with two chairs each sat in the small room. A glass cabinet housed a variety of tasty-looking treats. I had to admit the shop inside did look much better than the outside. A bell above the door announced our entrance, and a petite blond woman emerged from a door at the back, wiping her hands on her flour covered apron. A stray smudge covered her right cheek.

"Henry," – she smiled, and her eyes lit up – "It's not Thursday; what brings you here today?"

"Hi Cassie. This is my fiancée Sandra. I told her you were the best baker around, and I'm hoping you have some cakes we can taste today. I'd love to have you do the cake for our wedding."

She clapped her hands together and swayed back and forth on her feet. "I'd love to do that. I'm so happy for you." She turned her attention to me. "You've got a good man here. He's one of the best."

I gazed at Henry and smiled back. "I think so too."

"Okay, have a seat, and I'll bring you some cakes to taste." She turned and disappeared into the back again, and we chose the table nearest the small storefront window.

"She seems to know you well." I tried not to sound as jealous as I felt, but images of Peter and Sheila flashed in my mind.

Henry's eyes twinkled. "Don't be jealous. I helped her write a great insurance policy when everyone else was trying to get her to close shop so they could take over her lot. That's why she likes me. Plus, I come nearly every Thursday for her fruit tarts. They are amazing."

"I wasn't jealous." I wrinkled my brow at him, surprised that he could read me so well. "Just curious."

Cassie appeared a moment later with four small white plates. Each held a different slice of cake. "We have classic white cake with a lemon filling, classic chocolate cake with a strawberry filling, a German Chocolate cake, and a marble cake with raspberry filling." She handed each of us a fork. "I'll let you taste, and I'll be back in a moment."

I picked up the dainty silver fork and eyed the tasty desserts. "Which one shall we start with?"

"Whichever one you like; I'll let you decide because I'll probably love them all."

"Hmm, I think the white cake first." I pushed the fork through the soft cake and brought the bite to my mouth. The tart lemon flavor lit up my taste buds. "Mm, that's good."

Henry took a bite and smiled back. "Pretty good, and I'm not even much of a lemon fan."

After a drink of water to clear the taste, I decided on the marble cake next, which was even more delicious. Then the chocolate cake, simply to-die-for. Finally, I took a bite of the German chocolate cake.

Though delicious, it didn't scream wedding cake fare to me. "Okay, so which do you like?" *Please say chocolate.*

He twisted his lips and narrowed his eyes in thought. "I think . . . I think I like the German chocolate cake the best."

I wrinkled my nose and blinked. "Are you sure? I mean it is delicious, but don't you think it's kind of odd for a wedding cake?"

"I like being different," he said. "Why? Which one is your favorite?"

"The chocolate one, but really they were all good." I thought for a moment. "I'll tell you what, you can have the German chocolate cake, but you have to give me something in return."

He tilted his head back, one eyebrow raising on his forehead. "Like what?"

I tapped a finger to my lips. What might be something he would fight me on? An idea popped in my mind, and I smiled. "I get to choose the wedding colors."

Henry cocked his head. I could almost see wheels turning in his head as if trying to decide if this was a good choice or not. "Okay, deal."

"Shake on it," I demanded, thrusting out my hand.

He grasped it and pumped twice. "Cassie? We've decided."

Cassie entered the small room carrying a notepad and pen. "Okay, what's it going to be?"

"We're going to do the German chocolate cake," Henry said as he stood up and crossed to the counter.

Her eyes widened slightly, "Really?" She turned her eyes to me, "You agree?"

I joined Henry at the counter. "I traded. Cake for wedding colors."

Cassie nodded knowingly. "Ah, smart girl."

"Why do I get the feeling I just got played?" Henry glanced from Cassie to me and back again.

"Oh, I'm sure it will be fine." Cassie threw a conspiratorial wink at me. "Now, do you know how many people you need to feed?"

Henry's brow furrowed. "We haven't really discussed that yet. Maybe fifty?"

I scratched my head as I ran a brief mental tally of my friends and family. "Um, I'd have to sit down and make an actual list, but I probably have close to fifty myself."

Henry's head snapped back in surprise. "Really? Okay, well then I guess we better make it one hundred servings."

Cassie's pencil scribbled on the notepad. "And do we have a date picked out yet?"

"Yes, September 14th at 2 pm," I said.

"Okay, I'll log this in, and if I have any more questions, I'll contact you. Will that work?"

"That's perfect, Cassie, and thank you," Henry said.

"No, thank you for the business," she replied.

We exited the little shop and returned to his car. "Thanks for bringing me here; she's amazing," I said, buckling my seatbelt. "We'll have to come back to try her other desserts."

"I already have." He laughed as he started the car. "Okay, where to next?" Henry put the car in drive and headed out of the parking lot.

"Let's go look at a tux for you."

"Uh oh, what is that mischievous look about?"

I smiled but said nothing.

A few minutes later we pulled into a tuxedo rental shop, The Penguin Shoppe. Henry opened my car door, as usual, and took my hand as we walked in.

A shorter man with a mustache that covered most of his face greeted us. "What can I do for you today?"

"We need to look at a tux for him," I said, squeezing Henry's hand.

"Okay, come with me." The man turned and waddled like a penguin towards the back where three mirrors were set up for viewing. I wasn't sure if he just suited the shop, or if the shop had rubbed off on him.

A small desk sat to the right of the mirrors. The man whipped out a measuring tape – seemingly from thin air – and began taking Henry's measurements. "Mmhmm, okay, yes, that's perfect," he mumbled as he wrote numbers down on a little white pad.

Henry raised his eyebrows at me, and I smiled in return.

"Wait here, and I'll be right back." The man disappeared into a side room and returned with a sharp black tux. "Let's make sure this fits." He slipped the jacket on; it was a perfect fit.

"It's perfect." I sighed, and my pulse quickened at the sight of Henry in the suit jacket. There was something about a man in a suit.

"So, what else do you need? Vest, tie, cummerbund?"

"No cummerbund," I said, "but definitely vest and tie. Do you have a color chart?"

The man nodded and produced a white board with color swatches lined four across and four down. The colors ranged from deep purples and blues to bright reds and oranges. I touched the color swatches and pursed my lips. Sneaking a glance at Henry, I smiled. "I like this color for the groomsmen," – I pointed at a dark blue – "and this one for Henry."

Henry leaned over my shoulder. "Purple?" he asked.

"Magenta," I smiled.

"Um, why can't I wear the blue?"

"Because you got German chocolate cake," I teased, "and I got to pick the colors. Besides the magenta will look great on you." I held the board up to his face. "Wouldn't you agree?" The salesman nodded.

Henry pleaded with his eyes, but I remained resolute. Finally, a smile tugged at the corner of his mouth. "Okay, you win."

*A*s the planning continued, invitations were ordered, the caterer and photographer were hired, and, of course, the pastor of our church was asked to officiate. Summer burned through Mesquite and the school year ended. Children of all ages ran around the apartment complex and splashed in the pool. Though the sight and sounds of children still rubbed the wound, it was less. Planning the wedding kept my mind off of the past, and I convinced myself that I was healing, that once I got married the dreams would end and the guilt would go away. That if I could just make it to September the past could be forgotten.

The scorching heat faded into the beginning of muggy fall. The leaves on the few trees turned brown and began their descent from the limbs. Children returned to school, and quiet resumed during the day at the apartment complex. I sat at my small kitchen table addressing invitations and enjoying the blissful silence on a day off. A stack of white envelopes lay on one side of the table and a stack of invitations on the other. I stuffed the invitation in the envelope and licked it, but as I pressed the seal down, a sound reached my ears and froze my heart.

I paused, hoping it would go away. Sucking in a breath, I closed my eyes and listened. "Mama? Mama, why?" The voice was faint, but it was there. I squeezed my eyes tighter, willing the sound to disappear.

I hadn't been visited by the baby recently, and I had hoped it would stay that way. I had almost convinced myself that I had miscarried instead of what I had actually done.

"Mama?" The voice was closer this time, and the soft pitter patter of tiny feet hitting the floor joined the voice. *Oh please*, I clenched my hands at my side, *please go away*. "Mama, why didn't you want me?"

The words broke my heart, and my shoulders heaved. The lies and the walls I had built so carefully began to crumble, and I began to shake. Then a tug came at my pant leg, and I couldn't keep my eyes closed. My eyes snapped open; a toddler, clad in blue overalls and a red shirt, stood beside me. His chubby hand tugged again on my pants, and his wide brown eyes spoke sadness.

"Why did you let them take me, mama?" His mouth turned down as a solitary tear spilled out of his eye and rolled slowly down his cheek. I longed to touch his soft brown curls and breathe his scent, but I glued my hands to my thighs. If I could just get through this, maybe they would stop. I had thought once that maybe I could live with the visions, but the child seemed to grow every time. I was getting to see what my son would have been, and it was breaking my heart every time.

"You're not real," I whispered, but it didn't ease the ache in my heart. "I'm so sorry. I wish I could take it back. I'm trying to do it right this time."

"But what about me?" he asked.

"I didn't know." My vision blurred with tears. Unchecked, they tumbled down my cheeks, one after the other. "I didn't know. I thought I couldn't handle it. I was selfish. I'm so sorry." Through my blurry vision, I saw the boy hang his head, and his shoulders slump. The vice on my heart squeezed ever tighter. Closing my eyes and wrapping my arms around my chest, I let the sobs take control. I don't know how long I cried, but when I opened my eyes, the boy was gone.

Isaac. The name blazed in my head. *Is that what I would have called him, or is that what God named him when he got to Heaven?* I hoped he was in Heaven. I'd never had the courage to ask Henry or anyone else because I was too afraid of the answer, but in my reading I had convinced myself that all babies went to Heaven because Jesus found them so precious, and it had helped. But these visions made me ever more unsure about lying to Henry. I got up from the table and wandered into the bedroom. I hadn't had a drink in a long time, but my nerves were on edge. I needed the calming sensation.

The nightstand was empty; I had never replaced the bottle. Dropping to my knees, I peered under the bed. One lone bottle remained. When I had retrieved it, I held it up to the light. There was only a little bit of liquid in the bottom. Hoping it would be enough, I screwed off the lid and downed the fire.

❦

*a*s I sat in the last pre-marital counseling session with Henry later that evening, I wanted to tell him what I had done, but fear convinced me to keep my mouth shut. My finger ran up and down the seam of the leather couch as the events of the afternoon paraded through my mind again. The drink had helped a little, enough that I had returned to the kitchen and finished the envelopes, but not without turning on music first and situating my chair so that my back was to the wall.

"What do you think Sandra?"

I whipped my head up at the sound of my name. "I'm sorry, what?"

"I was asking you about joint accounts. Do you plan on combining your accounts when you get married?" the pastor repeated.

"Um, sure, I guess, I mean why wouldn't we?" I stammered.

Henry shot me a concerned look, and I plastered a smile on to reassure him.

"Okay, good," the pastor said, "I think it's a good idea. If you are truly going to join together, then it ought to be with everything. Well," – He glanced from one to the other – "unless there's something else, that's all I have."

Out of the corner of my eye. I saw Henry shift in his chair and cough into his hand. "No, I think we're good. Right, Sandra?"

My head nodded. "Yep, feeling good. Ready to be married."

The pastor narrowed his eyes at the forced statements, but said nothing. He rose from his chair and held out his hand. "Alright, I'll see you in two weeks for the ceremony then."

We both shook the proffered, outstretched hand and then left the office. As soon as the door clicked behind us, Henry whirled on me. "What's going on? You seemed really out of it in there."

I sighed. "It was just a long day is all. I'm sorry. I am excited to be marrying you."

He stared at me as if deciding if that was all and then nodded and continued walking. I couldn't help but think that he was hiding his own secret.

WHEN OPPOSITES COLLIDE

Though the wedding planning kept my mind busy and the dreams mostly away, a new worry replaced the dreams. My parents were flying in today to help finish the final details and, of course, attend the rehearsal dinner. I was pretty sure my mother would like Henry; she was a traditionalist – though with a flair for fashion – but I wasn't sure about my father. He was ex-military and very strict. His distaste for Peter had been obvious, but whether that was because of Peter or because we were living together, I wasn't entirely sure.

Even more nerve wracking was the fact that Henry's family was flying in soon after. He rarely spoke of them, so I had no idea what to expect. What if they hated me? What if I hated them? They did live back in Louisiana, so it wasn't like we'd see them all the time, but still it unnerved me. I wish I knew more about them.

As I pulled into the Dallas-Love Field airport and found a parking spot, I grimaced. I hated coming into the city, but hopefully I wouldn't be here long. After locking the car door, I trekked into the airport, trying to calm my nerves. Would they like Henry? What would I do if they didn't?

I scanned the big TV screens to find their flight and then made my way to their gate. Suddenly my mother's flashy garb caught my eye; she always did dress larger than life. Today she sported a bright red and gold dress. My straight-laced father in his black button up suit stood next to her.

"Sandra." My mother bobbed up and down, pumping her hand. I blushed at the shout, but stepped in that direction. A moment later, I was enveloped in a giant hug.

"Hi mom," I said into her shoulder.

"My baby," she cried, "I can't believe my baby's getting married."

"Mom, I'm twenty-seven. I'm not a baby anymore," I sighed.

My mother waved her hand in dismissal. "You'll always be my baby."

Rolling my eyes, I turned to my father, the antithesis of my mother. He stuck out his hand in lieu of a hug, and I shook it. Though I had always hoped he would show more affection, it seemed some things never changed. I led them through the busy airport to the baggage claim.

"So, when do we get to meet the man?" My mother asked as we waited for the baggage carousel to cycle around.

"Um, well we can probably meet up for dinner," I replied, keeping my eyes on the carousel, hoping it would start up and give me a reprieve, "but his family isn't here yet."

"When are they coming?"

"Tomorrow, I think." The conveyor belt revved to life, and we moved forward to watch for luggage.

"There." My father pointed as a hard grey suitcase came into view. I elbowed my way closer and grabbed it off the belt.

"Are there more?"

"No, just that one."

He took the handle, and I led the way back to the car.

"Where is your Mustang?" my father asked when I stopped at the Taurus. I bit my lip. I had gotten so used to this car that I had forgotten all about the Mustang.

"Um, it was economics really. This car gets much better gas mileage, and when Peter moved out, I needed to cut finances somewhere." I hoped this would satisfy his practicality.

"Well, I hope you at least got a good deal," he said.

I convinced him I had as we loaded in. My mother spent most of the ride complaining about the lack of humidity, but my father remained quiet, true to his nature.

When we arrived at my apartment, I took the suitcase to my spare room. My mother followed, still prattling on.

"Ugh, you need to do something with this place. It's so . . . bland." Her nose wrinkled as she waved her hand at the white room.

I rolled my eyes at the familiar criticism. Though I loved my mom, she always pointed out the negatives first. "Mom, it's a guest room. It's not supposed to be exciting."

"I'm just suggesting a dab of color. Everything is so white."

"Mary, it's fine," my father spoke up. "We're only here for a week."

I shot my father a thankful glance and hefted the suitcase onto the queen bed. "I'll go make some tea and let you guys unpack."

"Do you have chamomile?" my mother's voice reached my ears as I shut the door behind me.

Sighing, I squared my shoulders and sauntered into the kitchen. It was going to be a long week.

Henry showed up that evening at 6 pm. As I opened the door, I smiled; he looked handsome as always in his casual attire.

"Thank goodness you're here." I hugged him and then stood on my tiptoes so my mouth would be right beside his ear. "My parents are too."

He nodded against me as he returned the hug. "Don't worry, I'm good with parents," he whispered back with a wink, following me into the apartment.

"Mom, Dad, this is Henry. Henry this is my mom, Mary, and my father, Bruce."

My parents rose from the couch where they had been sitting. Extending his hand, my father nodded curtly, "Henry."

"It's nice to meet you, sir," Henry replied, shaking the outstretched hand.

I watched the exchange intently, biting my thumbnail. My father was measuring Henry with this handshake. An initial opinion would be formed based on this one simple greeting. He nodded again, and I smiled inwardly that he seemed pleased with the strength of Henry's grip.

Henry turned to my mother, prepared to shake her hand as well, but she engulfed him in a hug instead. His eyes widened in surprise though he recovered nicely and returned the hug.

"You'll have to forgive my mother," I said, pulling her back. "She forgets not everyone is as into hugs as she is."

"It's no problem," Henry replied as he smoothed his shirt.

"Well, aren't you just a tall drink of lemonade," Mary smiled, and her eyes roved up and down Henry in appreciation.

"Mom," – I hissed as Henry's face colored – "Why don't you come help me in the kitchen?"

She threw a wink at Henry, but acquiesced and followed. As soon as we rounded the corner and were out of sight of the men, I whirled on my mother, hands akimbo.

"What?" my mother asked holding out her hands defensively. "I was just saying he's handsome."

"You don't have to say it so loud or with those words. You're embarrassing me."

"Oh, I'm sure a man like that is used to hearing it."

She waved her hand in dismissal again, and sighing, I turned to the cupboard and pulled several plates down. "Here make yourself useful," I placed the plates in her hands and pointed to the table.

My mother rolled her eyes, but took the stack and began setting the table as I finished the last minute preparations. When everything was ready, I called the men in, and we sat down around the small table.

Dinner was polite though reserved. My father grilled Henry on his job, his plans for the future, and his past. Henry, to his credit, answered each question as it arose, and his answers seemed to satisfy the ex-army man, though both my mother and father seemed surprised about Henry's religious views.

After dinner, the men retired back to the living room while my mother and I cleared the table and put the dishes in the sink. Leaving them to be washed later, we then joined the men. I was surprised to hear my father discussing religion with Henry as I had no idea he had an interest. The conversation progressed for a while, but when my mother began stifling her yawns, I suggested we call it a night.

Henry rose, and I followed him out, promising to be right back. The air was still warm, even though it was dusk, and it lay like a light shawl on my skin.

"Thank you for being so amazing." I touched his arm. "I know my parents are rather quirky."

Henry smiled and took my hand. "I thought they were sweet. Besides," – his eyes clouded over – "my family has some quirks too."

"Do you want to talk about it?" I asked hesitantly.

He stiffened, displaying his answer before he voiced it. "No, we'll talk about it later."

I nodded, curious, but deciding to let it go for now. "Are they arriving tomorrow?"

"They are. Shall we meet for dinner again?"

"We might as well," I agreed, "they have to meet sometime."

We kissed goodnight, and I re-entered my apartment.

My mother stood waiting to pounce on me. "He seems lovely."

"He is," I agreed. I curled up on the couch with my mother beside me and began to tell her of how Henry and I met, minus the breakdown and the abortion of course. I had decided I was never going to tell anyone about it besides Peter and Raquel, both of whom I was sure would keep my secret.

It was nice having my mom around to talk to. We hadn't really spoken much since college, though I couldn't really remember why. After getting her up to date, we decided to call it a night.

The next day, I took my parents around the town. There wasn't a lot to see in Mesquite, but we found some antique shops my mother loved, and some trails that kept my dad's interest for a time. We stopped for barbeque as a late lunch before heading back to the apartment.

Once inside, my parents each got out a book to read, while I went to take a shower to freshen up. As I pulled on a soft yellow dress, my throat grew dry at the prospect of meeting Henry's family. Because he rarely spoke of them, all sorts of images played in my imagination.

Promptly at six pm, the doorbell rang. I gave myself one last glance and shuffled to the door. Henry stood looking uncharacteristically stiff in a blue button down shirt. Behind him was an older man who was clearly his father as the resemblance ran deep. He was also dressed smartly in a blue dress shirt and slacks. Henry's brother, a younger version of himself, stood to the left of his father, but it was the woman who stood out to me. With her short hair, suit, and severe expression she seemed such a contrast to Henry.

"Come in," I smiled, opening the door wide to allow passage. The group shuffled in, and I wiped my sweaty palms down my dress as I shut the door behind them. Introductions were made around the room, and then a tense silence descended. Sylvia, Henry's mother, checked her watch, while David, his father, and Anthony, his brother, dug their shoes into the carpet. My eyes darted to Henry for some clue as to what to do.

"Well, I'm hungry," Henry said, breaking the tension. "Who's hungry and wants to join me?"

"I'm famished," my mother spoke up, and the tension fizzled for now.

"I'd offer to make something, but my kitchen table barely seats four, and I don't have extra chairs, so . . . out?" I suggested.

Everyone agreed, and since neither of us had a car large enough to hold seven people, we decided to take two cars to the restaurant. Henry and his family piled in his car, while my mother and father came with me.

We drove in silence, until we pulled into the parking lot of a fairly upscale restaurant. I wrinkled my forehead hoping Henry knew what he was doing because I didn't have the money to afford dinner here.

Henry spoke to the hostess, and after a short wait, we were shown to a table. Henry held out my chair as normal, but before I could sit down, his mother spoke up.

"Stop doing that. Is she broken? She can get her own chair."

All conversation stopped as a silence fell on the group. Henry's father stared down at his feet. I glanced up at Henry in surprise, but he mirrored his father's embarrassment. My own father stiffened, the strain of holding his tongue evident on his face. My mother put a hand on his arm, and he relaxed, but his eyes remained on me to see what I would do.

"It's fine, ma'am. I actually like it," I smiled.

Henry's mother scowled. "It's women like you who will set us back years."

"I'm sorry?" My eyebrows raised at the tone. How dare this woman who didn't even know me, attack me?

"Equal rights. You know women get paid less than men. We have to prove we are equal and not pulling out your own chair shows weakness." Sylvia pulled her own chair out and sat down, not even glancing at her husband.

My face flamed, and a fire licked up my belly. I splayed my palms on the table to control their shaking. "I happen to think that it was just a nice gesture. I don't think Henry was trying to say I was weaker. I thought," I said pointedly, "that he learned such manners from you."

Sylvia scoffed. "Not from me, my dear. I never let him do such things for me. I tried my best to instill in my children that men and women are equal and deserve the same rights."

"Yeah, and look what that got us," Anthony spoke up softly.

Henry shot him a look, and Anthony dropped his eyes to the table. I considered one brother then the next; what did that mean?

Another tense silence descended. Whatever implication was in Anthony's words had at least quieted Sylvia. She surveyed her menu, silently, as did Henry's father. Henry sat down next to me, and I turned questioning eyes on him, but he shook his head slightly to indicate that now was not the time.

"Well, I think I'll be having the steak," my mother spoke up, trying to change the mood.

"Yes, me too," my father added, and while the topic lightened to food and drink, the damage was done. Sylvia and I shared a terse silence the rest of the evening. When I wasn't deciding if I wanted this woman to like me, I was trying to decipher what secret the brothers were sharing and if it would impact our wedding and our future.

When dinner ended, the waiter brought the check. "Will one check be fine or would you like me to split it up?" he asked, looking at each of the men.

"Actually, I'll take that," Sylvia said, snatching the bill. While I was grateful — as I didn't have the money to cover it — I wasn't sure if Sylvia was doing it to show off her money or her "equality." Regardless, I was relieved I wouldn't have to return in the same car with her. After hugging Henry goodnight and promising to meet up later, I climbed in the car with my parents.

"Well, they seem lovely," my mother said with a fake brightness. My father and I both whirled to face her.

"Sylvia seems horrible," I sighed. "What am I marrying into?"

"Perhaps you should have found out more about them before accepting the proposal," my father suggested softly.

I opened my mouth to reply, but before I could, my mother interrupted. "The thing to remember is that you are marrying Henry and not his mother."

"But she's bound to be a part of our life." I backed the car up and began the short drive home.

"I'm curious how Henry turned out so chivalrous," my father murmured, "Did he serve in the military?"

"Yes, a short stint in the Air Force," I replied, "but I think a lot of his behavior has to do with God. I've been attending church with him, and most men there are very respectful of women, just like Henry."

"Tell us more," my father said, and I found myself kind of excited as I rattled on about the church and all that I had learned. I still didn't believe God would forgive me, but maybe if I enlightened my parents, they could be saved. Telling them about Jesus gave me a sense of peace as well, and by the time we reached the apartment, I had almost forgotten the tense evening.

THE JOINING OF TWO LIVES

The next few days were filled with so much last minute preparation that I never did get to ask Henry about the secret with his brother. Surely it couldn't be that important or Henry would have told me, so I let it go a little longer.

Though the rehearsal dinner had been a little stressful, there had been so much going on that Sylvia didn't have time to be overly assertive, and before I knew it, the morning of my wedding day dawned.

I woke with butterflies zooming around my stomach. After showering and dressing, I wandered into the kitchen for a cup of coffee.

"Are you ready?" my mother asked, turning from the coffee pot and holding a mug out to me.

I took a deep breath. "I'm more nervous than I thought I'd be."

"Don't worry, I was too." She sat down at the table, and I took a seat across from her and listened as she replayed her wedding day. Though I had heard some of the story before, I had never listened as intently as I did now. I just wanted some consolation that I wasn't crazy; that butterflies were okay; and that I wasn't making a mistake.

My father came in a few minutes later, but after pouring his cup and staring at me briefly, he left the room.

"What's up with him?" I asked my mother.

"He thinks he's losing a daughter," she smiled and took a sip of her drink, "and it's hit him kind of hard." I sat back in the chair and crossed my arms. My father had never shown much emotion, so I certainly hadn't expected my impending nuptials to affect him. "You're his baby," she continued. "Though he hasn't always shown it, he really loves you."

"Huh, I never would have thought." My mother tossed me a wink, and we finished our coffee in silence.

A few hours later, we parked in the church parking lot, and my mother helped me pull the dresses and supplies out of the trunk. My father grabbed his suit and pulled me in for a fierce hug. As I drew back, my eyebrow raised at him. I couldn't remember the last time my father had hugged me.

"I'll see you soon," he said, emotion coloring his voice. He sniffed loudly, drew his shoulders back, and walked off to join the other men getting ready on the other side of the church.

I shook my head as my mother and I entered the church through a side door. A white door on the left sported a handwritten sign: "Bride's Room" and we entered. The room held a few chairs, a small table, a full length mirror, and a clothing rack. I hung the wedding dress on the rack and set my shoes down in a chair near the mirror. Raquel flew in a few minutes later.

"Sorry I'm late," she said as she threw her purse in the corner. "Greg decided he had to do some last minute rounds. He does this all the time; I don't know if we're going to make it. He's always working so long." She began unzipping her garment bag, seemingly unaware of my mother and I staring at her. "What?" she asked when she finally noticed the silence in the room. Suddenly her face shifted, and she clasped her hand to her mouth, "Oh, I'm so sorry. I didn't mean to jinx you. You guys will be wonderful together."

I sunk down on the chair and dropped my head in my hands. "What if I'm wrong? What if I shouldn't be marrying him?"

Raquel came over and touched my shoulder, "Hey, from the time you guys met, you have seemed perfect together. He treats you like a princess. I can't imagine you finding anything better."

I stared up at my friend who evenly returned the gaze. Something in her serious expression calmed my nerves. "Okay, you're right," I said, pushing myself up. "Let's get ready for a wedding."

Raquel smiled and hugged me and then turned to slip her dress on. I pulled out the white satin dress and took a deep breath. This was really happening.

After removing my street clothes, I slipped on the milky satin and then sat to put on my makeup. Raquel, in her dark blue dress, came over and helped pull my hair up and attach the veil. My mother also had on a dark blue dress with a maroon flower pinned on.

When the makeup was completed and the hair was in place, I stood to admire the final look in the mirror. Though the dress was simple, the white stood out against my caramel skin. The butterflies begun another loop around my stomach, and my heart pounded a double step in my chest.

"Are you ready?" my mother asked, lightly touching my shoulder.

I nodded. "Ready as I'll ever be, I guess." I picked up the bouquets I had brought in and handed Raquel's to her. While there weren't very many blue flowers, we had added what we could and then filled the bouquets with the deepest red roses and whitest baby's breath we could find. We exited the door and turned right towards the small sanctuary.

The doors were closed, but my father stood outside them, picking lint from his tux and shifting his weight from side to side. He pulled me in for another hug and sniffled in my ear. I patted him awkwardly on the back, not sure what else to do for a man who had never shown much emotion. The doors opened slightly, and Greg and Anthony slipped out.

"Are you ready ma'am?" Greg asked, holding his arm out to my mother. She nodded and squeezed my hand before placing it on Greg's arm. My father and I stepped to the side, out of sight, and he opened the door and walked my mother down the aisle. The music coming from the sanctuary hit home again how real this was, and my throat dried up. A minute later, Anthony took Raquel's arm, and they disappeared inside as well. The music changed, and I signaled to my father that it was our turn.

"You look beautiful," my father said in a shaky voice, "and I'm sorry I didn't tell you that enough."

His words brought tears to my eyes which I quickly brushed away. "Thank you, daddy. Are you ready?"

He nodded, and I hooked my right arm in his. As we stepped onto the maroon carpet, my eyes sought Henry who stood at the front with Anthony and the pastor. I barely registered the friends sitting on either side of the aisle as my heart sped up in my chest. The room grew quiet, but the sound of the beating of my heart thundered in my ears.

"You look like a princess," Henry whispered, taking my hand as I stopped next to him at the end of the aisle in the small Baptist church.

I fidgeted, touching the simple white dress, "It's not much, but I didn't want to start our marriage in debt."

"Better than this maroon tie," he said as he winked and leaned his head in close to mine.

"It looks handsome on you, and besides it was the compromise for German chocolate cake, remember?"

The pastor cleared his throat to get our attention. Heat flamed up my neck and ears. Henry's face colored as well. We turned to face the pastor.

"Dearly beloved," he began, "We are gathered here today to celebrate the union of Henry Dobbs and Sandra Baker. They have made a commitment to each other and stand before us today to publicly declare that commitment. Henry James Dobbs, do you take Sandra Elaine Baker as your wife, to love and to cherish, to have and to hold, through sickness and in health, till death do you part?"

"I do," he said and squeezed my hand.

"Sandra Elaine Baker, do you take Henry James Dobbs as your husband, to love and to cherish, to have and to hold, through sickness and in health, till death do you part?"

"I do," I breathed softly.

"Do you have the rings?"

Anthony pulled the rings from his tuxedo pocket and handed them to Henry.

"Repeat after me, Henry. With this ring, I thee wed."

Henry repeated the words and slid the ring on my finger. Then he handed the other ring to me. I too repeated the words and slid the ring on his finger.

"I now pronounce you husband and wife. You may kiss the bride."

Henry leaned in and touched my lips with his own. It felt different this time, more real, more serious, and my arms wound around his neck. I had completely forgotten about the people in the room until applause and cheering erupted. My face flamed as I pulled back. Henry must have felt the same pull of desire I did because the need was visible in his eyes. I smiled softly and took a calming breath. We turned to face the crowd, and then hand-in-hand, we rushed down the aisle and out of the sanctuary.

I pulled him towards the room I had changed in. As the door shut behind us, Henry pushed me against the wall. Passion enflamed his kisses, and his hands roved up the sides of my waist. My breath grew ragged as desire flooded my body. Heat radiated through me, and then a coldness descended. I opened my eyes to see Henry pulled back, panting.

"We should wait until after the reception," he said in a halting cadence.

My body screamed "no" but the thought of all our guests waiting for us flooded my mind. Even if we were quick, we would be longer than normal, and everyone would know what we had been doing. The dampening effect was immediate. Though the desire remained, the intense need lessened, and I nodded.

"Besides," he added, "I don't want my first time rushed and in a church."

A blush crawled across my face at the thought. "You're right." I smoothed my dress as Henry readjusted his tux, and we exited the room. Holding hands, we walked down the hall to the kitchen area where the reception had been set up.

A small kitchen attached to a large open room, where tables had been set up and covered with maroon and blue table cloths. As we entered the room, a cheer erupted. Friends gathered around us to issue congratulations. After a plethora of hugs and handshakes, we made our way to the center table. A buffet had been set up with sandwiches and fruit, and though I was hungry, I could barely eat.

As I sat at the table, nibbling on a sandwich, I examined the room. Beautiful flower arrangements in reds, blues, and whites sat atop the tables, and white Christmas lights hung from the ceiling, creating a soft, romantic glow. I couldn't believe the transformation. A glance at Henry sent another blush heating across my face. The thought of what was coming after the reception kept jumping to my mind.

When most of the guests had finished eating, the music began. Henry took my hand and led me to the floor. As I gazed into his eyes, the rest of the room faded from sight, and for a moment, it was just the two of us. When that song ended, my father stepped up and took my hand. His eyes were still red and watery, and I wished I knew the words to say to him. He smiled down at me as we swayed to the music. Across the floor, Henry danced with his mother, who, for the moment at least, appeared happy. When the song ended, I headed back to the table, but Anthony met me before I got there and asked for a turn. Agreeing, I returned to the floor with him.

"You've really made Henry happy," he said. "I haven't seen him this happy since Camilla died."

I turned my head up at him, my brow wrinkled. "Who's Camilla?"

"Our sister. Didn't Henry tell you?"

I shook my head and sneaked a glance at Henry. "What happened?"

He sucked in his breath, and his eyes darted around. "I'm not sure I should say if Henry didn't tell you, but she died five years ago. Henry took it hard. That's when he moved away and found religion. I guess it helped him heal."

"So the rest of your family aren't believers?" I asked.

Anthony shook his head. "I doubt mom ever would; she considers it a weakness, but I've thought about it, and I think dad has. It sure seems to give Henry something, a peace or something, you know?"

I nodded; I knew exactly about that peace as I had seen it in him myself. Unsure of what to say next, I pondered how Henry could have failed to tell me about his sister. Was that why his demeanor changed whenever he discussed his family? The music ended, and, after thanking Anthony, I returned to Henry, more questions than ever coursing through my mind. Time seemed to crawl from that point on, but finally the end of the reception neared.

"It's time for the bouquet toss," the DJ announced into the microphone. Blushing, I grabbed the bouquet and headed to the middle of the floor where a chair was set up. Stepping onto the chair, I surveyed the small crowd of single women. Then I turned the opposite direction and tossed the bouquet into the air.

"I got it," Raquel's voice called, and I smiled. I figured she would be marrying soon whether she caught the bouquet or not, but I had hoped it would land in her hand. Slowly the guests began filtering out. Henry and I stood at the door, hugging and shaking hands as they left.

After the majority of the guests had departed, I handed my parents my spare keys. "Please enjoy the apartment. You can leave the keys on the table when you leave, but don't forget to lock the door."

"It was so good to see you baby. Don't forget to come visit," my mother cried, hugging me as tears streamed down her face.

"Mom, why are you crying?" I asked, shaking my head.

"Because my baby is married." She sniffled into a tissue.

"Good grief, mom. I'm not going anywhere. You're just gaining a son."

My mother nodded and embraced Henry. "Take care of my baby."

Henry nodded, promising he would. Then he turned and shook my father's hand. Sylvia and David came next and hugged Henry. David hugged me as well, but Sylvia could only muster a tepid handshake. I wondered if I would ever have a relationship with my mother-in-law. Raquel and Greg wandered over and offered to help load the mountain of gifts into Henry's car. We handed them the keys while we said goodbye to the final few stragglers. When they had finished loading the car, they returned the keys and bade goodbye as well.

"Well, shall we?" Henry opened the door and stood looking at me.

Suddenly the ball of nerves began to tangle in my stomach. I bit my lip, but nodded. The weight of Henry never having been intimate settled on my shoulders. What if it wasn't good and he hated it or felt cheated? What if he wished he'd never married me?

"What's wrong?" Henry asked touching my arm and causing me to jump.

"Oh, nothing," I blushed, but decided to be honest anyway, "I just don't want you to be disappointed."

"Hey," – he folded me in an embrace and kissed my forehead – "I followed Jesus' commandments. He will bless our union, so I am not worried."

I nodded again, but the ball of nerves continued to tangle.

The drive to the hotel was quiet, and the ball wound tighter. The check in was awkward, tighter still. The walk down the hall, silent. Henry inserted the key and turned the lock. The door swung open, and he flicked the light on.

A king size bed filled my view, and the nerves began to fray. This would be my first intimate encounter since "the procedure," and I had no idea if I'd be able to do it. The nausea had never surfaced with Henry, but what if it did in the middle of the act? I had never been able to be intimate with Peter again, but was that because it was Peter or because I was ruined for life?

Fear glued my feet to the floor, and Henry turned to see why I hadn't entered. His eyes roamed my face, and he smiled and stretched out his hand. My arm wouldn't move at first, even though my heart wanted to go inside. I closed my eyes and took a deep breath. My hand ventured up. The touch of his hand jolted my feet, and I crossed the threshold. The door clicked shut behind me.

On autopilot, I followed Henry to the bed, flanked on either side by a small brown dresser. The flowered pattern of the bedspread filled my vision as I let Henry lay me back. His lips moved down my neck, and as desire welled up inside me, I held my breath, hoping the nausea would not flare up.

An hour later, I lay smiling in his arms. As I traced a pattern on his chest with my finger, I felt a little lighter, as if one brick of the wall I had built over the last couple of years was finally crumbling. Sighing, I listened to the sound of his even breathing. I couldn't remember the last time I had felt such peace, and then I stiffened as another thought filled my head. What if I had a dream of the baby tonight? How would I ever explain them? The thought dimmed my good mood. I'd been so used to sleeping alone that I hadn't thought about sharing the night with Henry. Suddenly the urge for a drink blanketed me, and I licked my lips. I hadn't noticed a mini-bar in the room, and I didn't want to chance waking Henry by leaving the room, so I sent up a prayer for peace. I wasn't really expecting an answer, but the desire ebbed, and my eyes grew heavy.

The next morning, Henry and I drove to the airport. I knew Henry didn't have much money to spend either, so I was surprised when the ticket he handed me said Hawaii. I peered up at him, questions in my eyes.

He smiled. "My mother has made quite a fortune," he said, "she bought us these tickets before she knew you weren't her kind of feminist, but she decided to let us use them anyway."

I laughed, and we headed to the terminal. After passing through security, we hurried to the gate and onto the plane. I had never been out of the continental United States, so excitement and nervousness battled within me at the same time.

The flight was long, but it was worth it. When we exited the plane, a woman handed us a lei in the airport. After grabbing our luggage, we took a shuttle to the hotel Henry's mother had booked. All I could do was stare out the window at the beautiful view. The hotel sat right on the beach, and after dropping our bags in our room, we decided to take a walk down the sandy beach. As we walked, I realized how happy I was, and I began to think that maybe, just maybe, life was going to be okay now.

THE CALM BEFORE THE STORM

*A*s we pulled into the parking lot from our week in Hawaii, I laughed out loud.

"What is it?" Henry asked.

"Well, I guess we better decide whose apartment we are going to live in. It makes no sense to keep both."

He smiled. "Actually, I thought we'd look at a house."

"Really?" An image of a wrap-around front porch and a white picket fence jumped into my mind.

"Of course, apartments aren't great for kids. I want to have a big yard, so the kids will have lots of room to run. And maybe a pool." His eyes lit up as he was speaking, and I smiled back, hoping it would come true. Somewhere in the back of my mind though, I worried that I had ruined my chance of having kids. I knew, from attending church, that God did not condone abortion. What if my punishment was to never get pregnant again?

"That sounds lovely. I can't wait."

"For now, let's stay in yours. I have fewer clothes I would have to move," he laughed.

We each grabbed a stack of presents and carried them inside. After setting them on the table, Henry went back out for the rest of the gifts and our suitcases, and I took the moment to glance around the apartment. I didn't have any bottles still lying out, did I? I was pretty sure I had thrown away the last bottle when I had finished it.

Henry returned, and we stared at the mountain of gifts flowing off the table.

"I guess we better get started," I said, grabbing a notepad to keep a list of what was given by whom so I could send thank you notes later. We sat on the couch and took turns opening the gifts. Most of them were things we could use like towels and matching plates, but a few oddball gifts made their way into the stack.

"Does anybody actually use these?" I asked, holding up an ugly gravy boat with a weird blue symbol on the side.

"No one ever did in my house," he agreed, smiling, "but then we didn't eat a lot of gravy."

After finishing the gifts, we retired for the night. The jet lag was kicking in, and we both had work in the morning.

As I curled into Henry's arms in bed that night, I thought again about how perfect everything seemed.

❀

*R*ising for work, after being off for a week, proved no easy task, and Raquel cornered me as soon as I got in to let me know she had set a date. I plastered a smile on my face and congratulated her, but I wondered if Greg would end up like Philip and so many other guys she had dated.

I invited her to church with us again, but like always, she declined. I wasn't sure how much I should push her, especially since I wasn't sure on my own "status" with God, so I let the topic go and just enjoyed her company for the rest of the day, but I was really looking forward to going back home to Henry's arms.

I had always loved intimacy, until the "procedure" anyway, but there was something much more special about being intimate with a spouse. No fear existed of him seeing someone else another night. No worry loomed about picking up some unknown disease or getting pregnant out of wedlock. In fact, I wrestled with the desire of wanting a baby now. On one hand, I really wanted children with Henry. I wanted them to fill the yard we didn't have yet and hear them laughing, but then I would remember how I threw my first child's life away, and I would wonder if I really deserved more children. How could I love them when I couldn't love that first baby enough to fight for him?

When I got home that evening, Henry stood waiting just inside the door, keys in hand.

"Are you ready?" he asked.

My forehead wrinkled, and I tilted my head. "Ready for what exactly?"

His eyes gleamed as a steady smile spread across his face. "Ready to see a house? I talked with an agent today, and it sounds like everything we want. It just came on the market, and he can meet us in fifteen minutes. Want to go?"

I had never seen him so excited; he was nearly bouncing up and down.

"Let me just change clothes," I said and hurried to the bedroom to pull on some jeans.

"So where is this house?" I asked as we drove.

"You'll see." Henry tapped his fingers on the steering wheel and hummed. A contagious smile stretched across his face from ear-to-ear. I found myself smiling and singing along with the music too.

The drive wasn't far, just twenty minutes or so to the edge of Mesquite. As he pulled into a driveway, I sucked in my breath. It was like he had read my mind. A white picket fence surrounded the property, and a huge wrap-around porch circled the house. The house itself was a light blue with white trim.

He parked next to what I assumed was the agent's car, and we got out. The gate squeaked just a little as he pushed it open, so we could walk up the gravel path to the front porch. The door opened as we stepped up to it, and a man I vaguely recognized from church stood on the other side.

"Henry, Sandra, you made it. Welcome."

"Thank you James for letting me know about this." Henry stuck out his hand, and the men shook hands.

"You bet. Come on in. So, this house is 2100 square feet. Four bedrooms and three bathrooms."

Immediately dollar signs filled my head, and I flashed back to the first wedding dress shopping fiasco. Was I going to fall in love with the house only to find out we couldn't afford it? "That's way more house than we need," I said, imagining the payment and trying not to get my hopes up.

"Not if we plan to fill it with children," Henry teased and squeezed my hand. My face flushed hot, and James laughed.

"Well, this is the living room," James continued. The beige carpet in the spacious room was in decent shape, but the floral patterned wallpaper would definitely have to go. "And here's the kitchen." James led us into a charming beige and blue kitchen with white appliances.

"Plenty of room for a large dining table," Henry said, holding his hands in a square as if picturing it.

"And back here is a guest room or an office."

"Or a playroom for all the kids."

"And a bathroom," James continued. The bathroom was small – just a toilet and sink – but it was painted a soft rose which helped offset the size. "And upstairs we have the bedrooms, if you'll follow me." The staircase had an ornate brown rail, and as my hand trailed up it, I could almost see children sliding down it in the future.

The landing opened up to another beige carpeted hallway. The three bedrooms were all about the same size and shared the guest bathroom on one end. The master bedroom was situated at the other end, and as James opened the door, my jaw fell. The huge room gaped with space; plenty of room for a king-sized bed, a dresser, and even a desk and chair if we wanted. To the left, another door opened into a large walk-in closet and a large bathroom with both a shower and a soaking tub.

"Here's the best part." James brought us back into the room and led us to the large window. When he pulled back the curtain, a small balcony that oversaw the backyard appeared. A small swing set and slide were set up, and there was plenty of open grass for kids to run around in.

"It's perfect," I sighed, "but it has to be more than we can afford. It's so much house."

"Why don't we go back downstairs, and we can talk price," James suggested.

We followed him back to the kitchen, and he laid out some papers on the bar. "Okay, now, generally speaking this house would go for $120,000, but the owner is a friend of mine, and she specifically said if I found the right family for this house that she would take $100,000. I know you don't have children yet, but Henry told me about your dream house and his dream of a house full of kids, and I think you guys are that family."

"I can't do that math in my head; what does that come out to each month?" I held my breath, hoping the answer would be low enough for us to afford.

"It's about $500 a month, depending on taxes and your credit, of course."

My heart stopped; he couldn't be serious. A smile broke out across Henry's face.

"We can do that," he whispered. "We can do that."

I nodded and squeezed his hand. "What do you think?"

He gazed into my eyes, and together we turned to face James. "We'll take it."

❦

It took a few weeks for all the paperwork to go through, but soon we were moving into our new house. I convinced Henry to take down the hideous wall paper in the living room, and, though he grumbled, he agreed the final result was worth it. We did a few other minor touchups, but the house had been pretty move-in ready.

Raquel, Greg, and a few other friends from church showed up to help us move. The men did most of the heavy lifting, while Raquel and I began unpacking. She rattled on about her upcoming wedding as I put away clothes in the dresser.

"Did you hear me?" she asked.

"I'm sorry, what?" I turned to face her.

"I said, I think I'm pregnant."

My heart froze. I knew Raquel well enough to know she probably still wasn't ready to be a mom, but I couldn't believe she would have another abortion and tell me about it, knowing how terrible my experience was. "What are you going to do?" My voice came out barely more than a whisper, and I realized I had twisted the shirt I was holding into a knot.

"I don't know," she sighed, "I'm not sure I'm ready to be a mom yet, and besides I would never fit in my dress." My jaw dropped at her. Was that all she could care about? "But," – she continued, seeing my face – "though I didn't have the bad experience you did, I'm not sure I want to have another abortion either. It certainly wasn't the best thing I ever went through, and it can't be good on your body. I don't even know why I'm telling you; I guess I just needed to say it out loud. I haven't told Greg yet."

I pursed my lips, trying to think of the right words. Raquel was my friend, and I loved her, but I could no longer condone an abortion, and I wasn't sure if I would be able to be around her if she had another one.

"I'm sorry. I shouldn't have said anything," she said. "Maybe I'm wrong anyway. It's only been a few days."

"If you're not wrong," I said, "please don't have an abortion. Give the baby up for adoption if you guys can't raise him or her, but please don't kill the baby. Henry would probably even want to raise the baby, if you can't."

Her eyes grew wide at the serious tone in my voice. "Okay, I'll think about it." A tense silence fell on us as we went back to our tasks.

I could think of nothing else the rest of the evening, and as I lay in bed with Henry that night struggling to focus on our devotional, he touched my arm.

"Hey, what's the matter? You've been acting weird all day."

I sighed. "I'm not sure if I should say anything; it isn't about me, really."

He picked up my hand and caressed the top. "I'm your husband. You can tell me anything, and I promise to keep your secret."

His brown eyes seemed so sincere that I decided I could trust him, at least with part of it. "Raquel thinks she might be pregnant, and she isn't sure she's ready."

His finger stopped its circling pattern on my hand. "I see. Are you jealous because she might beat us, or is there something else?" His voice sounded slightly off, and I glanced up at him. A hardness burned back in his eyes.

I had never seen this side of him. "Are you okay?"

He stared at the ceiling and took a deep breath. "Do you remember the night you met my parents?"

"How could I forget?" I scoffed.

"Do you remember what my brother said?"

I thought back to the night a few months ago, and the image replayed in my head. Suddenly, I remembered I had wanted to ask him what that was about, but I'd gotten so busy that I'd forgotten. Then my mind jumped to the wedding and Anthony telling me about their sister. I had no idea if I was right, but suddenly I was sure the conversation had had something to do with her.

"What happened to Camilla?" I asked. Henry's head snapped my direction. His eyes widened and filled with questions. "Anthony mentioned her at the wedding. He didn't know I didn't know."

He sighed and rubbed his forehead. "I should have told you a long time ago, but I guess I was ashamed."

"Of your sister dying?" I asked.

He shook his head. "Of the way she died." He took a deep breath. "Five years ago, my sister – who was a lot like my mom if you get my meaning – had too much to drink at a college party and ended up getting pregnant. I don't know if she wanted an abortion, but my mom convinced her to have one. For a while everything seemed okay, but then one night I went to surprise her with a pizza and . . ." his voice faltered as tears fell from his face. I squeezed his hand and waited.

He wiped the tears and continued, "I got to her room and found her in bed. An empty bottle of pills lay on her nightstand. I called the ambulance, and they rushed her to the hospital, but it was too late." He ran a hand over his face, "When I went back to the dorm room to help pack up her stuff, I found the note she had written under her bed. She took the pills because she was so depressed from the abortion. We never even knew."

My heart fell as I thought about my own past. I could never tell Henry the full truth now. He would hate me forever.

"My mother refused to believe she was depressed over the abortion; she even accused me of forging it, and that's when I knew I had to get out of there. I moved out the very next day. In fact, I hadn't seen my mother face to face until she showed up for the wedding."

"Oh Henry, I'm so sorry. And I don't want Raquel to make the same mistake, but what can we do?"

"We can pray," he said, and he grabbed both of my hands. Together we prayed for Raquel, for God's will and his wisdom, for the life of the unborn child that might be growing in her belly at the very moment, and for healing for Henry. Though our subject was heavy, both of us felt lighter after giving the worry over to God. "Now, what do you say we work on making our own baby," he said, and I curled into him.

THE SECRET THAT WON'T GO AWAY

"So, any word yet?" Henry asked, looking up from his plate as we ate dinner one night.

I pushed the green beans around on my plate. "It was negative again."

He touched my hand. "Hey, it's okay. It's only been six months. I'm sure we'll get pregnant soon."

I nodded, but the old doubt resurfaced. Peter and I had gotten pregnant the first time we didn't use protection, so why wasn't I getting pregnant with Henry? Now, when I was finally ready for a baby. Even worse, I couldn't understand why Raquel was pregnant and I wasn't. She had had an abortion too and thought about a second, but thankfully Greg had convinced her to choose life. They had married, but it had been a rushed wedding before she began putting on weight. Henry and I had done it the right way, and I was remorseful of my procedure. So why was she pregnant and not me?

Henry switched the subject then, and began discussing his day. I nodded in all the right places, but my mind was a million miles away.

As I lay in bed that night, I tried reading a book, but the words blurred together as my vision filled with tears. Henry was being so supportive, but what if he wanted a divorce since we couldn't have kids? Here we had bought this huge house for kids, and we couldn't have any to fill it. I folded the book on my lap and closed my eyes.

"Lord," I whispered, "I know you probably don't listen to prayers from people like me, but please help us to have kids, for Henry's sake. I promise this time I won't squander the life you give."

I had prayed the same prayer nightly for the last few months, but every month the answer had been the same: a negative pregnancy test. As more tears fell down my cheek, I put the book away. There was no way I'd be able to read tonight. I clicked off the light on the bedside, thankful that Henry was still watching news in the other room, and darkness descended.

The creak of the bed woke me some time later. I rolled over, expecting it to be Henry coming to bed, but a toddler in blue train pajamas bounced on Henry's side of the bed.

"Mama!" Pure joy lit up his face, and he toddled across the bed to me. My throat swelled as I blinked back the tears threatening to flow again.

"Baby," I reached out to him. The baby jumped into my arms, and I squeezed the boy tightly. The fresh clean scent of soap radiated from him. He put both of his chubby little hands on my face and peered into my eyes.

"Mama, I miss you."

The tears broke the dam, spilling down my cheeks. "Oh, baby, I miss you too."

He laid his little head on my chest, but it was the three words that broke my heart the most. I squeezed him even tighter and cried into his dark hair.

"I'm so sorry," I said over and over.

"Sandra, wake up." I opened my eyes to see Henry above me, hand on my shoulder. "What's wrong, Sandra?" He wiped a tear from my cheek, and I bit my lip, deciding how much to tell him.

Pushing myself into a sitting position, I asked hesitantly, "Do you remember when I told you I lost a baby?"

He nodded.

"Well, I have dreams of the baby sometimes. This time the baby was almost four, and he told me he missed me. I'm sorry if I woke you." *And I'm sorry I can't tell you the whole truth.*

"It's okay. I have dreams like that about my sister sometimes."

I nodded, "I can understand that. I'm sorry I didn't tell you about my dreams. They haven't come recently, and I thought they were over, but I guess not."

"Losing a child is hard."

I bit my lip. He had no idea. I lay back down and curled into Henry, but sleep didn't return for a long time.

❧

Three months later, I was at the hospital holding Raquel's beautiful baby girl, Alyssa. Dark brown hair covered her head just like her mother's. She was perfect. My heart ached as I held her. I so wanted a child of my own.

"You were right," Raquel said when it was just her and I in the room.

I glanced up from Alyssa's face, "Right about what?"

"How wrong we were. The moment I saw the first ultrasound I knew. She was a living being even then, and then I felt her move," she broke down in tears. "I've felt so guilty for months."

Unsure of what to do, I rose from the chair and, cradling Alyssa in one hand, I placed another on Raquel's arm.

"How did I not know? Why didn't we have ultrasounds then? Maybe it would have stopped me."

I sighed, "I don't know, I didn't get the feeling that they cared about me when I was there. Maybe it's just about the money to them. If it were really about choice, I would think they would want to give us all the options."

"How do I go on?" she cried. "How do I forgive myself?"

I squeezed her arm, "I don't have all those answers, but I know that you have to try. You have a beautiful daughter now, and she needs you. You can't just leave her."

Raquel sniffled. "I know. I would never do anything to hurt her, but I can't stop thinking about the other baby now."

"I understand. That's how it's been for me from the beginning, but hopefully you can move on now. We can't even get pregnant, and I'm starting to think something's wrong." It was the first time I had voiced my suspicion aloud, and ice trickled through my veins at the thought.

Raquel gasped, and her eyes widened, "Oh, Sandra, I'm so sorry, and here I was going on. Do you know for sure?"

I shook my head. "No, I've been too scared to check. I'm going to give it a little longer. I keep hoping it's just stress or something else, but I'm so afraid." Tears spilled down my cheeks.

Raquel squeezed my arm back, and together we cried over our past mistakes.

❀

Six months after that, I sat on the floor of my living room playing with Alyssa. Raquel sat nearby reading my Bible. After our discussion in the hospital, she had started coming to church with us, and like myself, she had found comfort in the words of God. Unlike myself, she seemed to have been able to forgive herself and move on, not that she still didn't have bad days where she cried for the baby she had lost, but she seemed more like Henry, more complete. I wondered if I couldn't get there because I couldn't get pregnant. Would I be able to forgive myself more if I had a new life to look after?

Alyssa cooed, and I smiled down at her. Raquel had asked me to be her godmother, and I had gladly accepted, but even all the time I spent with her couldn't take away the desire to have my own child.

"You know what's odd?" Raquel spoke up from the couch. "I can't actually find anything about abortion in the Bible. Why do you think God didn't put a specific commandment in there? Do you think he didn't know how far we would fall?"

"I don't know about that. I've heard people at the church say that God knows everything we will ever do, so I guess he would have had to see this coming. And there is a commandment about killing: Thou Shall Not Kill, but I think more importantly, and what people forget, is that God believes life begins at conception. There are many verses that talk about women being "with child" and God breathing life into their wombs.

"I've heard a lot of times that Jesus spoke in parables to make sure those who read them really wanted to know, and I think some of the other big questions are like that too. God didn't want someone to just be able to open the Bible and pick out a specific verse; he wanted us to gain knowledge from reading and letting the Holy Spirit talk to us."

Raquel regarded me with wide eyes.

"What?" I asked, shrugging. "I listen when they speak. Just because I have a hard time believing God could forgive me doesn't mean I wasn't paying attention."

"You know he will forgive you if you ask," Raquel said quietly. "He forgave me, and you are no guiltier."

"What if I ask, and I still can't get pregnant?" I asked. "What will I do then?"

Raquel sighed and shrugged her shoulders. Here we were, two people who didn't really understand God or his word completely, trying to help each other and failing miserably.

Alyssa took that moment to move forward just an inch on the carpet, and the discussion was forgotten. "You did it," I scooped her up, planting a kiss on her delicate porcelain cheek. She smiled in return and babbled at me. As I hugged her close, I relished the smell of baby lotion and milk. She slapped her hands on my face, and my mind wandered back to the last dream of the boy touching my face in the same way. The dreams had been surprisingly absent, and I wasn't sure whether that was a good thing or a bad thing.

The front door opened, and Henry entered laden with bags. I handed Alyssa to Raquel and hurried to see if he needed help.

"What is all this?" I smiled as he set down the bags.

"Well, I thought maybe we could use some positive vibes, so I bought paint, and I'm going to paint the nursery. Maybe if we get it ready, the baby will come."

Hope glistened in his eyes, and a stone fell in my stomach, but I pasted on a smile for his benefit. "That is awesome. Do you want some help?"

"No, I've got it. Hi, Raquel." He planted a kiss on my cheek and then took a bag in each hand up the stairs.

"You have to get checked," Raquel whispered as I sat beside her on the couch.

I dropped my head in my hands, "I know, but I'm so scared."

⁂

I sat in the doctor's office biting my nail. After nearly two years of trying, Raquel had finally convinced me to at least get checked out. When the exam ended, the doctor had showed me to her office while she went to view the tests and gather the paperwork. As terrible as the thought was, I hoped it was a problem on Henry's side. It would be awful having to tell him, but we could look at other options, but if it was my fault . . . what would I tell him?

The door opened, and Dr. Warren entered with paperwork in her hand. Her blond hair was pulled back in a ponytail and her horn-rimmed glasses sat on her nose, but it was the expression on her face that enlarged the lump of fear in my stomach. Normally a pleasant serene woman, the serious expression appeared out of place on her face. Dr. Warren sat at her mahogany desk across from me and pushed her small grey glasses up her nose. She cleared her throat and clasped her hands. Her eyes still focused on the papers on her desk.

She shuffled some of them around before looking up at me. "Um, I have to ask you, Sandra. You said in your history that you lost a child; was that a natural loss?"

My blood ran cold, and my throat tightened. I dropped my eyes to my lap. "What . . . what do you mean?"

When I peeked up, steely gray eyes met my gaze. "I mean that you have scarring in your uterus as if you had a pregnancy terminated. Did you have a pregnancy terminated?"

The lump clawed its way up my stomach and lodged in my throat. "I did," I whispered. "Five years ago. Is it bad?"

The gray eyes softened, and Dr. Warren sighed, "I'm sorry, Sandra, the scarring is so bad that you'll never be able to have children again."

The world grew silent around me, and my hands clenched into balls in my lap. "No, there must be something we can do," I shook my head, willing her to be wrong.

"There isn't. The damage is too extensive. I'm sorry."

"But . . . but they told me it was safe. It was supposed to be easy." I tried to grapple with the knowledge, but my brain refused to accept the words coming out of the doctor's mouth.

"I'm afraid there is a risk with any surgery." She leaned forward in her chair. "Are you saying they never went over any risks with you?"

I shook my head. "I don't remember any."

"Well, that is unfortunate. They should have at least informed you of all the risks. You might be able to take some legal action if you can prove it. Take as long as you need, and again I'm really sorry, Sandra." Dr. Warren stood and picked up the papers. She paused for a minute, as if unsure if she should say more, but finally she exited the room.

I stared at my hands. What was I going to tell Henry? He'd be devastated. He had made no secret of the fact that he wanted a big family. He had even painted two of the rooms, one pink and one blue, so we'd be prepared either way. Worse yet, I'd have to tell him about the abortion.

Embarrassment compounded on the grief, and my long forgotten loathing of Peter and myself bubbled back to the surface. Why had I ever let him convince me to have an abortion? It had not only ruined our relationship, but now my chance to have children, and he was probably married to Sheila by now with kids of his own. The anger boiled inside of me, and I grabbed my purse and stalked out of the office.

As I drove home, the anger turned to despair as I practiced ways to tell Henry the bad news. Nothing sounded right. The white picket fence came into view, and sweat broke out on my palms. What was I going to do? I pulled into the driveway and took a deep calming breath. I'd just wait until the time was right. That would be the best way. Thankfully Henry was still at work, and I hadn't told him about the appointment, so I wouldn't have to tell him right away.

I set my purse down and wandered into the living room. The

wedding picture of us called to me from the coffee table. I picked it up and touched Henry's face. Happiness shone on both of our faces. Could we continue that happiness now that we couldn't have kids? Would Henry forgive me and look at adoption? Or would he want to leave me as he'd wanted to leave his mother when she convinced his sister to have one?

At five-thirty, Henry's key sounded in the lock. "Sandra," he hollered.

I put the picture frame down and met him in the front entrance. "What is it?" I asked, hoping my face wouldn't give me away.

"I just wrote a huge policy. We should go celebrate. Let's go out to dinner." He picked me up and twirled me around.

His enthusiasm was contagious, and I found myself smiling in spite of my news. "Okay, let me go change."

"Yes, something special. Let's go somewhere nice."

I headed into the bedroom and picked out a nice black dress. Henry entered behind me and changed his shirt, adding a tie. Within thirty minutes, we were both ready and locking the door behind us.

Henry drove to an upscale steak restaurant, and after a short wait, we were seated at a table near the back. The dimmed lights created a romantic glow. I nibbled on a slice of bread as Henry regaled his day. If only I had good news to share with him as well; instead I had the ball of lies roiling around in my stomach. I took a drink of water, but it did nothing to douse the acidic flame churning inside.

The waiter came, took our order, and left. Henry continued to share the details of his policy, and I tried to listen and nod in all the right places. Dinner came, and I forced the food into my mouth, even though my appetite had disappeared as the churning grew. Henry chatted on between his bites, and thankfully, he didn't seem to notice my lack of conversation. He even ordered dessert, and we shared a warm chocolate brownie topped with ice cream. Then the check came, Henry paid, and we arose from the table.

Fall was approaching, and the air held just a bit of chill as we exited the restaurant. Henry wrapped his arm around my shoulders as we walked to the car, and the guilt grew. As he opened my door, I thought for just a second that maybe we could just go on like this or adopt. Maybe everything would be okay. Maybe I could just never tell him. Henry started the car and turned on the heater. The warm air conflicted with the icy turmoil inside me, and beads of sweat broke out on my forehead

"This policy will pay for college for the kids, I think," he said pulling onto the street. "And maybe we can look into in vitro fertilization. I know it's expensive and still relatively new, but there must be some reason we aren't getting pregnant, and maybe that can help. If I can just write a few more policies like the one today, then we could probably afford it..."

My guilt grew as he continued talking.

". . . Maybe they'll let us do a payment plan. Then we could really look into it."

And finally it bubbled over, and I burst out, "I can't have kids."

He turned to look at me, "What do you mean you can't have kids? I thought you said you lost a child five years ago. You got pregnant then; why couldn't you get pregnant now?"

I took a deep breath. Now was as good as time as any. "About that, I haven't been completely honest with you." His face had turned back to the road, but his eyes glanced over at me. I twisted my hands in my lap. "I told you I lost a child about five years ago, but the truth is I had an abortion." He sucked in his breath and his knuckles, gripping the steering wheel, turned white. I hurried to spit the rest out before I lost my nerve.

"Evidently they botched the procedure, and it scarred my uterus. The doctor told me today I would never be able to get pregnant again." His head whipped to stare at me, and I shrank back from the anger in his eyes. I had never seen him angry. "I'm sorry," I repeated and clutched my hands together. His mouth opened, but no sound came out, and then a horn blared.

I turned as lights filled my vision. "Henry," I yelled. He yanked the steering wheel to the right, narrowly avoiding the oncoming car, but the car over-corrected and hit the gravel on the side of the road, spinning out of control. "Lookout!" Henry tried to turn the steering wheel, and the squeal of tires braking hit my ears, but it didn't keep us from slamming into the big oak tree. My head slammed forward hitting the glove compartment and everything went dark.

❦

*T*he sound of scraping metal woke me. The air was metallic and cold. I tried to turn my head, but it was too stiff, and the pain was too great. Out of the corner of my left eye I could see Henry, blood pouring down his forehead. "Henry," I called, "Henry, talk to me."

"This one's alive." A male voice reached my ears and the scraping of metal grew louder. I wanted to plug my ears, but my hands wouldn't move either. The scraping stopped, and the man spoke again. "We're working to get you out ma'am. Just hang on. What's your name?"

"Sandra," I replied, "How's my husband, Henry?"

"I'm not sure, but we're working on getting you both out. Try to hold still now."

The scraping grew louder again, and then cooler air hit my skin. How long had we been in the car?

"My name is Brad. We're going to get you out. Does anything hurt?"

I closed my eyes to focus. "My head, and I can't move my arms or legs."

"Okay, just hold on." Hands reached in and cut the seatbelt off. Then more hands pulled me from the car, and I found myself leaning back on something hard. The stars were out.

"What time is it?" I asked.

"It's two am." Kind brown eyes filled my vision. "Do you know what time you crashed?"

"Um," – I closed my eyes trying to remember – "we left dinner at eight-thirty so between then and nine, I guess."

"Okay, that's good." Blocks appeared and were placed on either side of my head. Straps closed across my middle and my forehead. The bright flashing lights of the ambulance blinded me. I blinked and tried to look around for Henry. "Hold still."

"My husband, Henry. Where is he?"

The gurney was hoisted up, and the ceiling of the ambulance came into view. The light was bright, but I had to know. The kind brown eyes glanced at the other EMT in the back of the ambulance as the doors slammed, and it started moving. "I think they're still working on him. We'll know more when we get to the hospital. Try to relax."

I closed my eyes and sent up a small prayer for safety for Henry and for myself. The ride to the hospital felt long and bumpy. The EMT set up an IV, but I barely felt the poke in my arm. The loud siren squealing in my ears deepened the pounding in my head, and the lights were too bright, even behind my closed eyelids.

Then the ambulance stopped, and the door opened. The gurney was pulled out, and the cool night air chilled me again. I heard the whoosh of the hospital doors, and a bevy of doctors appeared on all sides. The EMT rattled off medical jargon that should have made sense to me – if my head hadn't been so fuzzy – and then the doctors took over. Hands unstrapped my head, my torso, my feet. *My feet had been strapped?* One doctor held my head as the others rolled me slightly to remove the wooden board. Then I was on my back again.

A Hispanic woman with dark curly hair came into view. "I'm Dr. Torrez. We're going to take you for an x-ray to see what we need to do, okay?"

"Okay," I whispered as I still couldn't move my head to nod. The tiles of the ceiling flashed by as I was wheeled down the hall. How different the view was this way! Though I had walked this hospital a million times, it appeared so odd being wheeled down the familiar hallways. We turned left into a darker room with a large x-ray machine. A team of nurses hefted the gurney onto the x-ray machine.

"Ma'am?" Dr. Torrez's face appeared in my vision again. "We're about to do the x-ray. Is there any chance you're pregnant?"

Tears welled up in my eyes again. "No, no chance at all."

The woman squeezed my hand and departed. The whir of the machine was the only sound in the room. When it was finished, the team came back in and hefted me back on the rolling gurney. Then I was wheeled back down the hallway and into a room in the emergency room.

"I'll be back as soon as I have the x-rays," Dr. Torrez said.

"Wait, can you tell me about my husband, Henry?" I asked before the doctor left the room.

"I'll check for you."

The woman left, and I was alone in silence. Pity crept in and blanketed me. This "easy" procedure five years ago had already taken a relationship, my chance to have children, and now caused an accident. What else was it going to rob from me? I bit my lip as worry for Henry crept in as well. No one seemed to know what had happened to him, but he there had been so much blood on him in the car.

I could hear the bustle of doctors and nurses outside and a hum of some kind of equipment in the room. Finally, Dr. Torrez re-entered the room.

"How are you doing, Sandra?" the doctor asked.

"I'm nervous. I still can't feel my feet, and no one has told me about Henry. Do you have some news?"

Dr. Torrez's eyes shifted quickly to the right, and she took a deep breath. "I have some news about you, but I still haven't heard anything about Henry."

Her mannerisms informed me the news was not good. "What is it?" I asked as a sinking sensation swam down my throat.

"I'm afraid you've injured your T4 and T5 vertebrae."

"What does that mean?" Even though I had studied anatomy, the words were not forming a conclusion in my brain. The room began to close in on me.

"I'm afraid it means that you are paralyzed from the waist down."

I heard the words, but they refused to register any meaning. "So, I'll never walk again?"

"No, but you have full use of your arms, and you should be able to drive a modified car if you need to."

"Are you sure? Maybe if I exercise enough? Or Therapy? Surely, there's some surgery . . ."

Dr. Torrez shook her head. "I'm sorry, Sandra; your injury was extensive. I don't see walking in your future."

As the words began to sink in, tears pooled in my eyes again. "I see. Can you check on Henry for me?"

"I can. Do you want me to call anyone for you?"

I bit my lip thinking. I didn't want to tell my parents yet. Was there anyone else? "Yes, can you call my friend Raquel Miller? She works here."

"Sure," Dr. Torrez nodded. "I'll have the nurses come make you more comfortable. We'll want to keep you a while for observation and some therapy." She turned and left the room, leaving me in silence once again.

I tried vainly to wiggle my toes, but I could feel nothing. Still, I wasn't entirely sure I trusted the doctor's opinion. Perhaps a second opinion would yield different results.

A few minutes later, two nurses entered the room. One was tall and muscular with short brown hair, and the other was shorter and blond.

"Hi, I'm Jennifer, and this is Alex. We'll be your nurses tonight till six am. We're going to unstrap you and get you off this uncomfortable gurney, and then we'll get you in something more comfortable, okay?"

I nodded at the taller one speaking. I didn't trust my voice to say much.

The taller woman, Jennifer, pulled out a hospital gown and a pair of scissors. She cut my dress, which was already ripped in several areas, and the two of them helped me sit up. Then Alex helped me slip my arms in the faded purple flowered gown, and they tied it in back and laid me back down, pulling the black dress out from underneath me. Jennifer pulled the sheet up over my legs. "I'm going to go get you some water, but is there anything else we can do for you right now?"

I shook my head.

"Okay, well here's the remote if you want to watch some TV." She handed me a white remote. "We'll be in to check on you every hour or so. There's a call button here if you need us before then." Jennifer pointed to a button in the rail of the bed.

"Thank you," I managed, and the two women left the room. I glanced at the ceiling as tears slid down my cheeks. "Is this my punishment, God?" I whispered. "It took this long, but finally I'm being punished. I'm so sorry. Please forgive me."

Though I had been attending church with Henry for years, I had never truly asked for forgiveness because I had thought God would not forgive me and because I could not forgive myself, but now as I lay on the bed, certain I would never walk again, I realized I had nothing to hold on to but hope. So for the first time in five years, I truly gave it over to God, hoping that he would help Henry and myself. A tiny sliver of peace formed in my heart.

A knock sounded at the door and Dr. Torrez poked her head in. "Hey, Sandra, how are you doing?"

"I guess as good as I can be. Do you have news about Henry?"

Dr. Torrez shuffled in, shutting the door behind her. "I do. It took them a little longer to get him out. He fractured his skull and suffered a concussion. He's in critical condition, but they're hopeful that he will recover."

My heart froze. "What . . . what does that mean?"

Dr. Torrez stepped closer and took my hand. "It means there's hope. He's got a brain bleed in both the front and the back of his skull, so they're going to be closely monitoring him for a few days. We need his brain to stop bleeding, but as long as it doesn't get any worse, he should recover."

Relief coursed through my veins. A skull fracture was bad, but he was alive, and that was what mattered. "Can I see him?"

She shook her head. "Unfortunately, you are on bedrest of for the foreseeable future, but I'll have someone give you updates."

Tears pricked the back of my eyes, but I nodded. More than anything, I wanted to see him just to assure myself that he was okay.

"Can I get someone to come and talk with you until your friend arrives?" Dr. Torrez asked.

"Um," I searched my mind. The only one I wanted was Henry, but I did have questions, and I knew of someone at the hospital who could answer them. "Is there a pastor or chaplain on site?"

Dr. Torrez blinked. "Uh yeah, I think so. Shall I call him for you?"

"Please."

Dr. Torrez nodded and squeezed my hand. "I'll have him check in soon with you."

"Have you called Henry's family? His parents and his brother?"

"Yes, I believe they've called them. Would you like me to tell them to come see you when they get here?"

"Yes, I need to talk with them."

"Do you want me to call your family?"

I thought about my mother, how excited she had been the last time we had seen her and told her we were trying to have kids. I pictured my father, who once again had hugged me tight when we left their place, and I didn't have the heart to tell them right away. Still they would be mad if they found out the news from someone else. "Yes, please call my parents. They'll have to take a flight in."

The doctor nodded and left the room again. The peace I had felt just moments earlier was ebbing away, and I desperately wanted it back. "Lord? Are you there, Lord? I don't know how to go on without Henry. Please Jesus, help heal him and show me what to do. Help me. Please help me." The little kernel of peace began to grow again, shrouded as it was in sadness.

Sometime later, a knock sounded again. A short balding man with gray hair stepped in the room. "Sandra? I'm pastor Clive. The doctor said you wanted to see me?"

"I did. I need help." I poured out my story from sordid beginning to sad present. Pastor Clive sat by the bedside holding my hand.

"My dear, I am so sorry for your loss. Have you talked to your family?" he asked.

I shook my head. "They aren't here yet. Neither are Henry's, but I don't know what to say to them. I knew he hated abortion after what happened to his sister; I don't know why I told him in the car."

"Some things are not for us to know. Now, let me ask you daughter, you said your husband is religious. Do you know God as your father and savior?"

"I don't know. I've been attending church and reading the Bible, but I never thought God could accept me because of the abortion, you know?"

He patted my hand. "That is a grave sin, you are right, but God can forgive even that if your heart is in the right place, and you confess that it was a sin."

"It was the worst thing I've ever done, but I want to move on. I want to know God the way my husband does; how do I do that?"

He led me in a prayer of confession, and amid my despair, a peace like I'd never felt before trickled down my spine. However, it didn't erase the sadness and confusion raging through my body.

"Did God take my ability to walk because I didn't ask for forgiveness a long time ago?"

"That isn't how God works. Unfortunately, this world is imperfect and sinful, and bad things happen. You need to ask God to give you peace and ask him how to use you now. It won't be easy, but God will be there for you."

Pastor Clive shared some verses from the Bible with me, and we prayed again before he left.

Raquel arrived shortly after the pastor left, dressed to the nines in a form-fitting black dress. "Oh honey, I'm so sorry. They told me what happened at the front desk." She hugged me, and the tears I thought were gone started anew.

"What am I going to do, Raquel?"

"I don't know, but we'll find a way to work through this together. We'll pray, and we'll figure something out."

She pulled up the stool beside me and grabbed my hand.

"Where's Alyssa?" I asked.

"She's still with the babysitter. Greg and I were having a nightcap out. He went home to be with her, and I canceled my shift for tomorrow, so I have a little time with you."

"Did they let you see Henry?"

Her eyes shifted from my face. "I did. Only for a minute. It's probably good that you can't see him right now. Both of his eyes are swelled shut from hitting the steering wheel, and he's pretty out of it." A tear streamed down her cheek, and she brushed it away.

I nodded and filled Raquel in on the rest of the story, the part they hospital wouldn't have known about. Together we cried until there was nothing left. Then we sat in silence until my lids grew heavy.

Sylvia, David, and Anthony arrived the next day. I had just finished lunch when the knock sounded on my door. As the door opened, I hit the button to raise the bed, so I could sit up to talk to them.

They entered slowly, and I swallowed. Sending up a quick prayer for the words to say to them, I started with, "I'm so sorry."

David and Anthony crossed to either side of the bed, but Sylvia held back.

"Can you tell us what happened?" David asked quietly. His face was more haggard than I remembered, as if he'd aged ten years in the last two.

I bit my lip and glanced from one man to the other. "Well, Henry and I were trying to have children. After nearly two years with no positive results, I went to the doctor." I took a deep breath. "Five years ago, I was with another man, and we got pregnant. He wasn't ready to be a father, and he convinced me to have an abortion." They all noticeably stiffened, but I continued. "The procedure caused scarring and left me unable to have children. I didn't mean to tell Henry in the car, but he kept talking about our future kids, and it just spilled out. He took his eyes off the road, and we veered into traffic. Then he overcorrected, and we hit a tree. I'm so sorry." I had thought I had no more tears left, but after telling the story again, they made their way down my cheeks like soldiers in formation.

"It's my fault," Sylvia moaned behind us as she sank to the floor. "It's all my fault. If I had never pushed Camilla to have an abortion, she wouldn't have died, and Henry wouldn't have left and had the reaction he did. I didn't want the shame of a pregnant daughter who was not married, and I told Camilla the abortion was empowering as a woman, but I was wrong. It's horrible." David went to his wife and put an arm around her.

"Have you seen Henry yet? How is he?"

"He's still in the ICU," Anthony said. "The brain bleed is pretty bad, and he's had some disorientation. They're taking him in for another CT."

I nodded, wishing the news were better, but knowing I had to share what was on my heart before I lost my courage. "I don't know if you know God like Henry does, but I just truly found him yesterday. Can I pray for all of us?"

The family nodded, and I led a prayer, feeling closer to his family than I had in the last two years. They stayed a little longer to chat and then left to check back on Henry. The doctors had said one of them should stay in the room at all times to watch for signs of seizure.

My parents arrived later that afternoon. My mother entered the room, frazzled, an unusual look for her. She rushed to my side and enveloped me in a hug. My father hung back at the door. Thankfully Raquel had filled them in on the story when she picked them up at the airport, so I didn't have to go over it again. I returned my mother's hug and then motioned for my father to come closer. As he stepped to the bed, I realized he was struggling to contain his emotions. His red and puffy eyes betrayed the fact that he had recently been crying.

"It's okay dad. I don't know how, but I know God is going to take care of us."

He nodded and clasped my other hand, but he didn't seem convinced.

"We're going to stay until you get out. Maybe a little longer. Your dad's going to work on adapting the house for you," my mother's words tumbled out in a rush.

"You don't have to do that," I said.

"Yes we do," my father added, "and we aren't taking no for an answer. Neither of you will be able to drive for a while, so consider us your personal chauffeurs."

I nodded, and my eyes filled with moisture. I guessed some help would be necessary to get reacquainted with our new life.

❀

*H*enry was released later that week. They wheeled him in to see me, and I was shocked by the transformation. The bruising around his eyes was a deep purple, and he looked like he had lost ten pounds. His speech was slower, and he would pause every now and then as if trying to remember a word.

"I'm so sorry you can't come home yet," he said, holding my hand. "But I'll come visit whenever I can. They told me I can't drive for at least a month, but your father has offered to drive me until I can again."

"I'm so sorry," I said. "I never meant for this to happen."

His eyes clouded a moment, and I wondered if he was still angry.

"We'll talk about that later. Just concentrate on getting well for now."

That was easy to say, but much harder to do. The therapy was intensive and often painful, but the worst parts came at nights when I was alone with my thoughts. It was those lonely nights when pity crept in, and I began to hate myself again.

THE LIGHT AT THE END OF THE TUNNEL

 *A*fter three months of extensive therapy, the hospital finally released me. Henry had healed slowly over the time, but I couldn't help the jealousy running through me that he could walk while I was lifted out of bed and placed in a wheelchair. He still leaned on a cane as his strength had been the slowest in returning, but it was a step up from the walker he had been sporting just a week ago.

Raquel and my parents were there as well, all smiling as if this were the best day, and it should have been. I was ready to get out of the grey, sterile hospital, but I had little to look forward at home. There was now so much that I couldn't do for myself.

"Wait until you see the van Raquel helped set us up with," Henry said. Raquel had set up a fund to cover some costs that insurance wouldn't cover and had used the money, along with a lot of her own, to purchase a modified van that would allow me to drive when I felt up to it. Forcing a smile on my face, I tried to cover the depression I was feeling.

As we pulled up to the house, and Henry helped me out of the car, the sadness set in again. Though the house appeared the same on the outside, except for the ramp my father had erected over the stairs, I knew the empty inside loomed. There would never be children sliding down the banister, and the swings would remain motionless in the backyard. Before I could stop it, a giant sob escaped, and I began crying uncontrollably.

Henry rushed to my side, "Are you okay? Are you hurt?"

"It's gone," I said, "It's all gone."

"Oh, Sandra, it will be okay," Raquel said, joining him. "We're all here for you. I'll bring Alyssa to come play, and it will be okay."

I nodded, but that seed of jealousy flared inside me again, and all I really wanted was her gone. Why had I been unable to have kids while she had Alyssa? Why had my ability to walk been taken while she walked on two perfect legs?

Henry pushed my chair up the ramp and opened the door. "I want to show you what we did," he said, leaning over my shoulder. He pushed me down the hall toward the guest room.

My father ran ahead, sporting the biggest grin I had ever seen on his face. He pushed the door open, and I gasped. They had completely redone the guest room, adding on a larger closet and a walk in bathroom with modified features, so I would be able to use the necessities myself.

"We converted this into the master bedroom, so you don't have to worry with the stairs. Everything is right where you need it."

My smile was genuine this time. The gesture had been really thoughtful.

"We've also modified the kitchen for you. Would you like to see?"

I nodded, and Henry wheeled me down the hall and to the kitchen. My father had lowered several of the counters, making them accessible to me and brought several of the most used accessories forward. I would be able to reach the toaster, the microwave, and the coffee pot.

"We'll work on fixing the stove for you later, but for now you'll just have to suffer through my cooking," my mother said.

I turned questioning eyes on her.

"I hope you don't mind," Henry said, "but I asked them to stay a little longer. I still tire easily, and I want to make sure you are taken care of until you are fully recovered."

"Thank you," I said.

※

ith my parents around, there was little I couldn't do, but it didn't stop the depression from sinking in. The hospital, though sorry, had fired me, and I had nothing to fill my long days. I had taken to driving aimlessly around town, with the excuse that I needed some time alone. In reality, I had begun drinking again, and those times out were often spent buying alcohol and drinking it in my van. I usually drove to a church parking lot as they left me alone and would sometimes let me use the bathroom if I needed to go while there.

Mesquite View church was one of my favorite places. The green manicured yard reminded me of spring and the tall, old trees gave shade to my van. Plus, the staff always let me in to use the bathroom.

I lifted the freshly bought bottle to my lips, enjoying the fiery burn that slid down my throat. When the lack of feeling started to sink in, I set the bottle down and closed my eyes for a minute. I had a bottle of pills with me that I was contemplating taking, but I hadn't found the energy yet.

A rapping at the window startled me. A young man and woman with dark hair stood outside the window, motioning for me to roll the window down. Fear formed as a lump in my throat. Surely the worst they could do was call the cops. Grasping the handle, I turned it clockwise just enough to be able to hear them. They seemed nice, but what if they were trying to mug me?

"Hi, what's your name?" the man asked.

"Sandra," I said cautiously.

"Hi, Sandra. I'm Tony, and this is my wife Margaret. We've seen you parked here a few times and wondered if there was anything we could do for you?"

I bit back the rude reply that immediately came to mind, but what did spill out wasn't much nicer. "No, I'm fine. I'm just enjoying the view and a little drink."

They glanced down at the half empty bottle beside me before meeting my eyes again. "Well, Sandra, I'm the associate pastor of this church, and Margaret is our counselor. God told us we needed to come and talk to you, so would you let us do that? Just talk with you?"

These two were complete strangers, but something in me said yes. Maybe it was the fact that I had missed going to church the last few months, and though the chaplain had come by often, his visits hadn't filled the need in my heart for some purpose, some reason that God had left me the way he had. Maybe it was because of the bottle hidden in the glove compartment. Whatever the reason, I nodded and maneuvered out of the van.

They led the way into the church, much bigger than the one Henry and I had attended before the accident. Tan carpeting covered the floors and ahead I could see a large sanctuary with a raised platform stage. Tony, however, turned left down a hallway labeled offices.

At the third door, he stopped and pushed it open. Inside was a small conference table, a desk, and a bookshelf laden with books. I wheeled inside and Tony and Margaret followed, each grabbing a chair from the conference table.

"So, Sandra," Tony said, folding his hands in his lap. "Why don't you start at the beginning and tell us how we can help you?"

I gazed into their sincere eyes and dropped my head. "I don't know why God would want to help me. I've blamed him for everything, and I certainly haven't been a good Christian. Even when I had a chance, I was only strong for like two weeks, and then I drifted away."

"Because God loves you no matter what you've done," Tony said. "He understands when we are angry with him when things happen that we don't understand, but he still loves us. He waits patiently for us to come back to him, and when we do, he welcomes us with open arms. You may see brokenness, but God sees you mended and loved."

A glimmer of hope sparked in my chest. "Do you really believe that?"

"I know it to be true," he said. "Not only because I've read it in his word, but because I lived it once. You see, just after I finished seminary school my father got cancer. I couldn't understand it because cancer didn't run in our family, but my dad was a fighter. I prayed every day for God to heal my father, and being a new pastor, I was kind of cocky and just believed he would.

"After a year-long battle, my father passed away. I was angry at God. My father had been a wonderful father and a good Christian; I couldn't understand why God would take him and not the other people who seemed much worse in my eyes. I even gave up preaching for a time, but then my wife reminded me that not only was my father in Heaven and no longer in pain, but that God answers prayers in many ways.

"While I thought God wasn't answering my prayers, maybe his answer had been that extra year. Maybe he was supposed to die earlier, but God gave me more time. Also, she reminded me that God said we should all long to be there where it's perfect. I missed my dad, but I knew he was no longer hurting and that I would get to see him again one day. Slowly, I turned back to God and to ministry and God began to bless my ministry."

"I wish my story were that easy," I sighed.

"It wasn't always easy," Margaret said, "but it was always worth it. God is an amazing and loving God, and he only wants what's best for us."

Margaret's face held lines that showed her ability to laugh, and her eyes sparkled. Though these two were perfect strangers, there was something in their open faces that gave me peace, and I opened my mouth.

"I . . . um, I'm not sure where to start. Five years ago, I had an abortion. It was the worst thing I could ever have done. When I met my husband Henry a year later, he brought me to church and introduced me to God, but I didn't totally accept him, and I never told Henry about the abortion." I looked down at my hands, waiting for the courage to rise again.

"A few years into our marriage, I found out I could no longer have kids, and when I told Henry, he lost control of the car and we crashed into a tree. It paralyzed me and Henry suffered a head fracture. I think I really found God after that, but now I'm wondering why I'm still here. I can't have children; I've lost my job; and I just don't know what purpose God has for me."

Tony let out a low whistle. "Wow, that is a lot. Now I see why God wanted us to meet. Your story reminds me of Job, are you familiar?"

I hadn't read Job since my life had fallen apart, but I remembered most of the story, so I nodded for him to continue.

"I think one of the biggest things I've taken from Job is that suffering isn't always deserved. I have so many people ask me what they did to deserve what they're going through, and if you look at Job, he did nothing. God allowed Satan to try and tempt Job to show his righteousness," Tony said.

"Why does he do that?" I asked.

"Well, sometimes it's to show his glory. Remember God made the world and us. We are no one to question him, but remember that he also blessed Job tremendously at the end. It's not always easy, but it's always worth keeping our faith in God."

"I know I always have trouble with God allowing Satan to tempt us," Margaret spoke up. "Sometimes it hard to reconcile that a loving God would allow us to be tempted, but again I think it speaks to what Tony was saying that God is blessed at the end if we are strong enough."

"I guess I just don't understand how God can be blessed from my story."

"Have you ever thought" – Margaret began quietly – "about telling the women who go to the center your story?"

I regarded her with raised eyebrows. "You mean sit outside and talk to the women coming in?" My heart sped up at the very thought and I dropped my eyes to my lap. I never wanted to see that place again.

Margaret touched my arm, "I know it would be hard," she said, "but imagine how many women are going in like you did, not really wanting an abortion but feeling pressured to. What if telling your story to them could help them make the choice to save their baby?"

A wave of emotion rolled over me. The very thought of going back there made me sick to my stomach, but I didn't want any other women to end up where I had. What if I could make a difference? What if I could save a baby from the same fate mine had met and a woman from the awful guilt I felt? What if someone like me had been there that fateful day when I had gone? "I want to, but I don't know if I could."

"I know it's a big step, and maybe it's not something you can do right away, but I'll be happy to go with you if you ever do decide it's something you want to do."

"Why don't you try something in the meantime?" Tony suggested. I raised an eyebrow, waiting for him to continue. "Why don't you let us help you get a job, and" – he rose from his chair and walked over to the desk. A drawer opened and closed, and then he was back. – "become a prayer warrior." He handed me a brown leather journal.

I held it in my hands. The leather still smelled new. As I opened the cover, it creaked, and I peeked at him with questions in my eyes.

"It's to write down prayer requests. That way you can pray for people by name or by physical description if you don't know their name. You can put checks beside them when you've prayed for them, so you know who you've done each day. Sometimes praying for others is the best thing we can do for ourselves."

"Thank you," I said running my finger over the cover again. "I'd like that." As I held the book, peace like I hadn't felt in a long time covered my shoulders, and I knew the first thing I had to do.

I called Raquel on my way out of the church and asked her to meet me at the house. It would be easier to share if everyone were there at the same time.

Raquel arrived as I was rolling up the ramp.

"What's going on, Sandra? Are you alright?"

The first tug of a smile I had felt in a long time pulled at my face. "I think I will be."

She followed me into the living room where Henry and my parents were already sitting, quizzical expressions on their faces.

"I know I haven't been myself lately, and I've been worrying some of you." I glanced at my mother as the pill bottle popped into my mind. How close I had come to ending everything! "But I met some people today who, for some reason, gave me the words I needed to hear. I'm going to go back to school and look into being a counselor."

"Honey, that's wonderful," my mother said.

I held up my hand as she began to stand up. "I'm also going to try sitting at the center where I had my abortion. I'd like to tell women my story in hopes of saving other lives."

I turned my focus to Raquel. "I know you work a lot during the days, but I was wondering if on your next day off you might come with me."

She looked down at the floor, and I waited. Though she had told Henry and my parents about her abortion, I knew it was still a hard subject for her. I wanted to know what she was thinking, but I didn't want to pressure her. When she peered back up, tears glistened in her eyes. "I don't know if I'm strong enough," she whispered.

I rolled to her and squeezed her arm. "I know I'm not, but I'm counting on God to give me the words, and if we can save any of them from going through what we did, isn't it worth it?"

Slowly, she nodded. "I still wonder; you know? Would Alyssa have a brother or a sister? I don't even know. Some days it gets really bad, and I think I don't deserve to live, and then I look down at Alyssa and realize I have to. I'm sorry I wasn't there for you more; it must be even harder for you." She squeezed my hand and tears rolled down both of our faces. "I'll be strong for you."

"I'll pray that God gives us both strength," I said, squeezing her hand back.

Henry and my parents gathered around us, and Henry led us all in prayer.

That night, before I fell asleep, I pulled out the prayer journal Tony had given me and opened it up to the first page. The smell of leather reached my nose, and I smiled. *Strength for Raquel and I*, I wrote and paused. It needed more. *Give me the words to say to reach women.* Filling the first line in the journal filled my heart with joy for the first time in a long time. I felt almost complete.

A NEW BEGINNING WITH A NEW PURPOSE

*M*argaret, Tony, and I prayed together the next morning before Margaret and I headed out to the center. I let her drive as my nerves were still balled up, and my hands were shaking. I hadn't been back to the center since the horrible day, and fear consumed me. What if I couldn't handle it? What if they yelled at us? What if I passed out like I had the day I was there last? I sent up a prayer for peace and slowly the questions dissipated from my mind.

Margaret pulled into a nearby business, and we made our way to the center. My heart began to speed up in my chest, and my breath didn't want to work. A hand touched my shoulder, and Margaret smiled down at me. I took a deep breath and nodded.

There was a small bench out front of the center, and we parked there- Margaret on the bench and me in my wheelchair next to it. For a moment it was silent. There were no cars, no birds, no talking. It was just us and God. I could feel his presence there with us, like a comforting blanket. Minutes later, a young woman, probably in her late twenties, came walking up the concrete path. Her hair was pulled back in a tight bun, and her blue suit looked very expensive. My mind told me she would not be receptive to my words, but God told my heart to speak anyway.

"Please don't kill your baby," I said softly as she approached us.

She looked up, fear in her eyes. Although she appeared completely put-together in all other ways, her eyes told the real story.

"Please don't kill your baby," I repeated. "Can I tell you my story?"

"Leave me alone. It's my choice." And she hurried past us into the clinic.

I sighed, "I don't think that went well."

Margaret squeezed my arm. "We won't win them all, but when we can't reach them with our words, we pray for them." She closed her eyes and bowed her head, and I followed suit. "Lord, we don't know the woman who just entered this center, but we saw the fear in her eyes. Please Lord, work on her heart and help her to see the error in her decision. Lord, protect the unborn child growing within her as only you can. Help us to have the right words to say to reach the women coming and going from this place. Amen."

We waited in silence. Soon another girl came walking up the pathway. Her blond hair covered her face as her head was down, focused on the ground. Her hands clenched and unclenched at her side.

"You don't have to do this," I said to the girl. My voice was louder this time.

Her head lifted to reveal a pale face with wild eyes, "I'm not doing anything." She had to be young, seventeen or eighteen.

"You're planning to have an abortion," I said, "and you don't have to. In fact, I don't think you even want to. You know it's a baby, and that God has a plan for that baby's life." The girl's eyes widened. I had no idea where the words had come from; they had just flowed out, but I could see that they affected this girl.

"I . . . I've messed it all up," the girl said, her eyes shimmering.

"No, you haven't. Not yet."

"You don't understand. My father's a pastor, and I slept with my boyfriend on prom night, and now I'm pregnant. This would ruin my father's reputation."

Margaret spoke up then. "Let me ask you this. Would your father be angrier that you had sex or that you killed your baby?"

The girl's eyes darted to the left, to the right, to the ground. She clasped her hands together. "I don't know."

"Well, I'm a pastor's wife and while I don't have children yet, I can tell you that while I hope my daughter won't get pregnant out of marriage, I would never want her to have an abortion. People make mistakes, but God forgives, and our reputation is not worth a child's life."

A spark of hope flickered in the young girl's blue eyes. "Do you really think so?"

"I know so," Margaret said, "and if you'd like help talking to your parents, I'd be happy to be there with you."

The young girl sank to her knees on the sidewalk and put her hands on Margaret's lap. "Thank you. I've been praying for a sign not to do this, and you were my answer. I'm so glad you were here. Will you go with me now before I lose my nerve again?"

Margaret glanced over at me, and I nodded.

"Of course," Margaret said. "Let's go talk to them now."

The two headed off, leaving me alone in the chair. I sent a prayer of thanks up to God, and also a prayer requesting clarity. It seemed like having someone talk to these girls and tell them there was hope was good, but actually telling their families with them might be needed as well. Was that what I should be doing? My prayer was interrupted by a shout.

"Hey, you, you can't harass patients here."

I opened my eyes, and my heart froze. The same woman who had been my nurse six years ago stood before me now. She appeared even more hardened than before, but it was her.

"I'm not harassing anyone. I'm simply telling them what you won't." My hand shook on my lap, and I tucked it under my leg to conceal it.

"What are you talking about? We give full disclosure here. We are strictly by the book."

I tilted my head and gazed evenly at her. "You don't remember me, do you?"

"No, why would I?" The woman flapped her arms in exasperation before crossing them across her chest.

"Because six years ago, I had an abortion here, and you were my nurse."

"You had an abortion and now you're trying to take the choice away from other women?"

"This center never told me of the risks. My abortion caused scarring on my uterus that prevented me from having a child when I was ready."

"There are always risks to surgery. It was on the form you filled out when you came in."

She could have been right about that. I remembered filling the form out, but had no memory of what was on it. "I was young, and I was scared. The risks should have been told to me, so I truly had a choice. What you do here isn't choice. It's an assembly line butcher shop. I lost my ability to have children, and I may not reach them all, but I will sit here and talk to as many women as I can to try and save them from what happened to me. You can't stop me from talking. I'm not blocking them from entering your building."

"I'm calling the police," she said, whirling around back to the building.

"Go ahead," I called, "the law is on my side." As the door closed behind her, I shook my head at the boldness that had come out of me. It had to be God, because inside I was shaking like a leaf. I took a deep breath to calm my racing heart, and the door opened again.

The woman in the blue suit was exiting. It had been too fast; she couldn't have had the procedure that quickly. Maybe I was being given a second chance. When she saw me, she dropped her eyes and walked a little faster.

"I regret my abortion," I said, "Please don't make my mistake."

She stopped and slowly raised her face to look at me. "You had an abortion?" Her voice was barely a whisper.

I nodded, "It was the worst mistake of my life. I had it here, and they botched the procedure and scarred my uterus. I'll never be able to have kids. When I told my husband, we ended up in an accident, and that's how I ended up in this chair. I'd do anything to take mine back. Please don't make the same choice."

The woman sat down on the bench beside me. "I'm not ready for children though. I just started my career, and my husband just started at his firm. He's working long hours, and we can't afford a baby right now."

"What's your name?" I asked her.

"Melanie."

"Melanie, people always say they can't afford a baby, but God provides. He has given you a precious gift. I know it seems impossible right now, but if you ask him, God will show you how you can make it through a difficult time. Have you told your husband?"

Melanie shook her head.

"Well, I think he deserves to know. Maybe he'll surprise you and tell you he is ready for a child. Even if he doesn't, if there's even a chance that you could end up like me, are you really willing to take it?"

"I don't know," Melanie wrung her hands. "I don't know God; so why would he help me?"

"Because he loves you, and he loves that child growing inside of you right now. This is not what he wants for you. If you need help, there are churches and agencies who will help you throughout your pregnancy. I'd love to introduce you to my church if you want. Please, at least take a few days and think about it."

Melanie nodded slowly. "Okay, I will. Thank you."

As the woman walked away, I sent up another prayer for her.

We stayed the whole day until the clinic closed. We didn't reach everyone, but the fact that we saved even one baby had us excited on our way home.

"The parents were so understanding," Margaret said. "They were disappointed, naturally, but they told her that they still loved her and that they would love the baby whether she decided to keep the baby or put him/her up for adoption. I wish more kids knew their parents would be supportive."

"Maybe we can start a class at church, a communication class. We can teach parents how to communicate with their teens and teach teens that their parents will listen. Do you think people would come?" I asked.

She smiled at me. "I think that would be amazing, and yes I think people would come. There are so many issues that I think parents miss today. Opening communication between parents and their teens would be huge."

That night after the devotional with Tony and Margaret, I lay in bed looking over the prayer journal. I had written down the name or description of every woman who had come into the clinic that day. As I ran my finger down the list, I prayed for them all again. Though it had been hard to be there again and even harder to know we didn't save all the babies, just knowing that we had saved one gave me a new purpose for life.

"I'm glad to see you smiling," Henry said next to me.

I closed the journal and set it on the table beside me. "I'm glad to be smiling," I answered.

He set down his own book and took me in his arms.

❀

The next day Margaret and I spent the morning at the center and the afternoon at church talking to Tony and the other pastors about our idea for a communications class. Though most of the men, besides Tony, were all older, they agreed that there was definitely a need for a class.

"I also wanted to ask if we had or could set up an outreach program of sorts?" I spoke up. "There were a lot of women who seemed to want help telling their spouses or parents and others who needed help knowing how they would get through the nine months. Do we have something like that?"

The men exchanged glances and then returned their gaze at me. "We don't," Pastor Dan, the head pastor, said, "but how would you feel about starting one?"

My heart thudded. I didn't know the first thing about starting one, but if they believed I could, I would do it. "I don't know how, but I'd be honored to."

"In fact," Dan continued, "Tony's been telling us a lot about you, and we'd like to interview you as our ministry outreach person. It doesn't pay a whole lot, but it would be enough to supplement your income."

My head dropped forward, and my eyes widened, "You want me?"

"You have a gift for talking to these women, and you've already discovered ways to help them. We think you'd be a natural. We'd even like you to continue your ministry at the clinic, so the position would be in the afternoons here so you could meet with women or hold classes, and in the morning you'd be out at the clinic."

"I'd like to pray about it," I said trying to control the smile bursting on my face. Though I had no idea what it would entail, this sounded like a dream job for me.

"We wouldn't have it any other way," he agreed, "and of course we need to do a formal interview."

Margaret squeezed my arm, and after shaking all the pastor's hands, she and I left. "Oh, Sandra, that's wonderful," she said when we were in the hall.

Emotion overwhelmed me, and I stared at her through watery eyes. "It's amazing, and it never would have happened without you and your husband. I can never thank you enough."

Henry and my parents were equally excited when I told them the news that evening. Together, we all prayed for guidance and wisdom in this new chapter of my life. Peace descended on me, and I had no doubts whatsoever that this was what God was calling me to do. I couldn't wait to tell Raquel the next morning when I saw her.

When I pulled into the parking lot, the fear fell on me again. While I knew what I was doing was right, it didn't stop the fear and disgust I felt for this place. I wondered if it would ever get easier.

The sun was shining today, and it seemed odd. Here was this black, soulless place in the middle of the warm sunshine. I shivered and brushed the thought away. A few minutes later, Raquel came walking up. She shivered too and wrapped her arms around herself.

"Ugh," she said as she sat on the bench beside me, "it's like this place steals the heat away."

My eyes widened at her, "You feel it too? I thought it was just me because this was where I killed Isaac."

She shook her head, "No, it's not just you. I didn't have my procedure here, but it feels dark. I don't remember feeling like that when I went to the clinic for the procedure, do you think we feel it now because we know how wrong it is?"

"Maybe," A glance around revealed no ominous shadows lurking.

"So, what do we do now?" she asked changing the subject.

"First, we pray," I said and led us in a prayer for strength, wisdom, and the ability to reach the women who were undoubtedly coming. Then I filled her in on my interview later that day.

"Sandra, that's wonderful, and what a great idea. I'll ask at the hospital if there's anything we can do to help. Do you think we would like your church?"

"I thought you guys were happy at the old church?"

She smiled, "We are, but now that it appears I've got my friend back, I'd like to go to church with her, especially since I don't see her at work anymore."

A warmth flooded over me, and I returned her smile. "I'd love that."

At that moment, a dark haired woman came up the sidewalk. "Please don't kill your baby," I said to her.

She whipped around to glare at us. "It's my choice," she said, "I can do what I want, and it's none of your business."

"I thought it was my choice too, but it took my ability to ever have kids," I called to her, but she had hurried ahead, and my words bounced off her back.

"Are they always like that?" Raquel asked as I pulled out my journal to write down the woman's description.

"No, sometimes they're worse, and sometimes they're better."

"What are you doing?" she asked.

"This is my prayer journal, and I write down every woman who comes by so I can pray for her."

"What if they have the procedure though? Not much to pray for then."

I tilted my head at her, "Do you think you and I don't need prayer?" Her face scrunched in confusion and then she brought her hand to her mouth, and I knew she understood.

The morning was slow, which gave Raquel and I time to talk and catch up. Only five women came in while we were there, and while we didn't save the first one's baby, we saved one for sure and left the other three thinking. Raquel hugged me goodbye and wished me luck on the interview, promising to come to church on Sunday.

I should have been nervous on the drive to church, but God had granted me peace today. I knew this was where he wanted me right now, and I knew that unless I made some giant mistake that the job was mine.

The interview room was small and windowless. The two men and two women took turns asking me questions and writing down my responses. The words flowed out of me without much thought. At the end, the four smiled and the pastor in the middle offered me the job on the spot. I accepted, and one of the women showed me to what would be my office.

It wasn't much, a small room with a desk, two chairs, a bookshelf, and a window, but as I rolled behind the desk, I knew it was where I belonged.

A NEW OUTLOOK ON LIFE

a year later, the phone rang on my desk. Somehow, I knew this was the call I had been waiting for.

With my life on track, my parents had finally moved out of our house, though they had decided to move to Mesquite to be closer to us in case we needed anything. They now lived a few doors down, but I welcomed the proximity. Henry's parents too had become more of a feature in our lives, coming to visit during the summer for a few weeks.

My job had taken off, and I felt fulfilled with the help I was providing women and their families, both through the church and the sidewalk ministry. I had decided to delay going back to school because the job allowed me to do everything I wanted, but the biggest change had been our decision about children.

After several long discussions and lots of time spent in prayer, Henry and I had decided to become foster parents. We had attended the informational meeting and gone through the thirty-five hours of pre-service training. The case worker had conducted the home study and approved our application. The last few months we had been waiting, waiting for the phone to ring with the news that a child was coming into our lives.

My hand was shaking as I reached for the phone. "This is Sandra. How may I help you?"

"Sandra? It's Claire. I have a child if you and Henry are ready. A boy, about seven years old."

My heart froze in my chest. Isaac would have been seven if he had lived. I hadn't thought that we might get a child that would be Isaac's age, though we had agreed to foster any age.

"Sandra, are you there?"

"Yes, I'm sorry," I said, recovering my voice. "We would love to foster him."

"Great, his name is James. He was being raised by his mother, but she was just arrested for drug use again. Unless she gets time off for good behavior, I suspect you'll have him for at least a year. I'll bring him by this evening. Will that give you enough time to get whatever supplies you need?"

"Of course." I was already making a list in my head. We had made one room ready for an older child with a bed, a dresser, and some toys, and the other room ready for a younger child with a crib. There was also the original master bedroom that we had converted into two more rooms, but we hadn't decorated them yet. I figured we would need to get some clothes for the boy and maybe a few older toys. After getting his size from Claire, I hung up with her and then called Henry to tell him the good news.

Later that evening, after the shopping was all finished, Henry and I sat in front of the front door waiting for Claire and James. His hand was on my shoulder, and I could feel his nerves flowing through his touch. My stomach was also a bundle of nerves.

At seven pm, the doorbell rang, and Henry and I looked at each other. A mixture of love and fear passed in that glance.

He opened the door. Claire stood on the doorstep next to a caramel-skinned boy, whose hands were jammed in his pockets. His eyes were focused on the ground, and his thin shoulders held the weight of the world. A small blue bear was tucked under one arm, and a backpack slung over his shoulders held all his other possessions.

"James, I want you to meet Henry and Sandra. They're going to take care of you until your mother can again, okay?"

James nodded and hugged his bear tighter. Sandra's heart hurt for him. No child should have to go through what he was going through.

"Okay, I'll be back to check on you in a few days, James." She shrugged at us over his shoulder and pushed him forward. His little feet shuffled over the threshold and into the house.

Henry thanked Claire and shut the door behind her.

"Hi, James. Welcome to our home," I said. "Would you like to see your room?"

James shrugged again, but I took that as a sign he might. Wheeling over to the banister, I climbed out of my wheelchair and into the sliding contraption that Henry and my father had installed.

The whirring of the motor began, and James looked up.

"What is that?"

"I lost my ability to walk in a car accident, so this helps me go up and down the stairs."

"You mean you can't walk?" His voice was incredulous.

"Nope, but I can still do almost anything." The seat hit the end, and I climbed into the wheelchair we kept at the top of the stairs. "It's very important this chair is always at the top of the stairs for me, okay?"

James nodded, his eyes still wide.

Henry had caught up to us and led the way to the blue room we had readied for James. I wasn't sure what he might be into, so I had picked up some pictures of airplanes and sport paraphernalia that Henry had hung on the wall. A simple blue bedspread covered the bed and matched the curtains hanging from the window.

"James we have some new clothes for you in the dresser and the closet," I said.

James blinked. "Is this all for me?"

"Why of course it is," Henry said. "Why wouldn't it be?"

"In my last foster house, I had to share a room with three other boys."

Henry and I shared a glance.

"James, are you hungry?" I asked.

He gave a small nod.

"Would you like to put your stuff down, and we'll go back downstairs? I have spaghetti cooking?"

James dropped his bag, but the tattered blue bear remained in his grasp.

I couldn't blame him. It sounded like he had been bounced around a lot in his young life, and the bear was his only hint of stability.

After dinner, Henry took James outside to see if he knew any baseball, and I cleaned up the kitchen.

When the boys returned, I was reading my Bible in the living room.

"Did you have fun?" I asked James.

His answer was once again a nod, but he made eye contact this time, which I considered a plus.

That night as Henry and I lay in bed, I thought about what James had said about his last foster home.

"Henry?" I asked. "Do you think we should try to get more foster children? We have the room, and if they are jammed into other houses, at least we could give a few more space with us."

He shut his book and flashed a warm smile. "Sandra Dobbs, I love you. I was thinking the exact same thing. Let's give James a week or two to adjust to us, though. Plus, it will give me time to finish the other rooms."

Scooting over, I turned my face up to kiss his lips. "I can't believe we didn't see this before, but I think this might be exactly where God wants us to be."

The next morning, I decided to take the day off and spend the whole day with James. I called his school, so they wouldn't worry, and then I made him a breakfast of blueberry pancakes.

His bear was still clutched to his chest as he came into the kitchen.

"Good morning," I said, placing some pancakes on a plate for him. "Did you sleep well?"

My answer was yet another shrug. He was going to be a tough one to crack.

"I hope you like pancakes."

I placed the plate in front of him and saw his eyes light up, but again no words. However, I was pleased to see him pick up his fork and begin eating.

"I took the day off work and excused you from school, so we could spend the day together," I said, putting a few pancakes on a plate for myself and wheeling over to join him at the table. "Is there anything you would like to do?"

He kept his eyes focused on his plate.

"Come on, anything at all."

"Could we go to the library?" he asked, his voice just louder than a whisper.

"The library? Of course we can go to the library." I had expected him to say a movie or a video game store maybe, but not a library. What kind of life had this kid led that he didn't get to go to libraries?

"How will we get there?" he asked.

I smiled, knowing he referred to my wheelchair. "I'll drive us, of course. I have a special van that allows me to drive."

"You'll see."

With breakfast finished, I put the plates in the sink, and we headed out the door to the modified van. I unlocked his door so he could climb in, and then rolled around to the driver's side and hit the button to lower the ramp.

The driver's seat had been removed, and the van had been modified so my entire wheelchair could lock in behind the steering wheel. Two buttons had been installed on the wheel, so I could hit the gas and the brake with my hands.

James watched the whole loading process in wonder.

"I told you I could do almost anything," I said, winking at him.

A few minutes later, we pulled into the library parking lot, and he walked in beside me. He beelined for a section without a second glance, and I realized he had been at this library before. Perhaps library books were the only kind of books he could get, or perhaps he just loved to read.

As I got closer, I realized he was in the non-fiction section. He already had three books out and open on the floor.

"Look, Sandra," he said, holding one up to me. "This is Saturn. I learned about it in school. It's my favorite planet because it has rings."

His enthusiasm brought a smile to my face, and I hoped I would get to see more of this side of him.

We spent almost an hour in the library with him showing me all sorts of different books on planets, and we walked out with a stack of books for him to look into later.

"Would you like to get some planet posters for your room?" I asked as we loaded into the van again.

"Why?" he asked. "I probably won't be there long."

His words tore at my heartstrings. "Well, that room is yours as long as you are with us. We might as well make it something you like."

He stared at me as if my head were on fire, but I just laughed and turned the car towards the local Walmart.

Once inside, he picked out three planet prints, a solar system bedspread, and a book he could keep with planetary facts in it.

"Why are you being so nice to me?" he asked as we headed back to the car after checking out. "None of my other foster houses were ever this nice."

"I'm sorry they weren't," I said. "They all should be, but we're this nice because we want you to enjoy your time with us. We can't have kids of our own, so you're helping us out too."

"Is it because of your accident?" he asked.

He was too young to hear about my sordid past. "Something like that," I said.

When we arrived back at the house, I grabbed some pushpins from a kitchen drawer, and we headed upstairs to decorate his room.

"I'm afraid I can only put this them high," I said, holding one up. "If you want them higher, you may have to wait for Henry."

"No, it's fine," he said. "I don't mind them low."

I smiled to myself as I hung up the posters and then helped him change the bedspread.

"What do you think?"

He placed his hands akimbo on his little hips and turned in a circle, surveying the room. "I think it is satisfactory," he said.

I stifled the laugh that rose in my throat as I had no idea if was he serious or being silly. "Wonderful, well here at the Dobbs house, we aim to please."

He walked over to my chair and held out his hand for a shake. "Thank you, Miss Sandra."

"You're very welcome, Mr. James." I said, returning his shake.

The rest of the afternoon was spent poring over his books, and when Henry arrived home, he started over with him while I prepared dinner.

As we sat down at the dinner table, we reached for James's hands.

"What are you doing?" he asked, folding them in his laps.

"We're going to pray," Henry said. "In this house, we pray before meals and before bed. Plus, anytime you feel the need to pray."

"I don't pray," he said, shaking his head. "God doesn't love me."

"That's not true, James," I said after a moment's shock. "God loves you very much. I know it's hard to see that sometimes when life deals us crappy hands, but it's true. I was angry at God for a while too when I lost my ability to walk, but if I hadn't ended up in this chair, I would probably still be working long hours as a nurse, and we might not have become foster parents and met you."

"If God loves me, why doesn't he fix my mom?"

I looked to Henry, hoping he had a good answer for James.

"James, God gave us this thing called free will, so that we had the choice to follow him or not. He wants all of humanity to want to be with him, but some people use their free will to deny God, and some use their free will to make poor choices that hurt others, but we'll pray that your mother stays straight this time."

James still didn't offer his hands, and we didn't force him, but we did still pray over dinner, and we prayed when we tucked him into bed that night.

"It hurts my heart that he has suffered so much," I said as Henry and I got ready for bed that evening.

"Mine as well, but we'll keep praying for him."

The next day, I had to take James to school, even though I would have preferred to continue bonding with him. I was thankful that he was able to stay in his familiar school. At least that gave him some stability in this trying time.

Slowly, he began opening up to us and sharing more of his likes and dislikes with us. I found out that he loved hamburgers, but hated tacos and that he was scared of moths.

A month later, I invited Raquel and Alyssa over. We hadn't had much time to chat as she was busy with work, and I was busy with James, so it was nice to catch up.

James was playing on the floor with Alyssa, and I could hardly believe he was the same boy who had come to us so shy. His eyes sparkled as he regaled Alyssa with his vast knowledge of the solar system. At three years old, she had no idea what he was talking about, but she would nod and repeat after him.

"They seem to be getting along well," Raquel said. She and I were crocheting blankets to take down to the pregnancy pantry I had started at our church. In it we stocked diapers, wipes, blankets, clothing, and other items to help women get started. We had also begun partnering with the local food bank to help low income women get food assistance so they could feel secure they could provide for their babies.

"Are you guys going to have any more?"

"I don't know," Raquel said. "We want more, and it's not like we aren't trying, but we can't seem to get pregnant again."

My heart went out to her; I knew exactly what that felt like. James wasn't blood, but he was filling the empty hole that had been in my heart for years.

"Do you still see him?" she asked, placing a hand on my arm.

I didn't have to ask her who; it was almost like she had been reading my mind.

"Sometimes, but never as clear. I can't seem to see his face anymore, it's more like a shadow or a feeling of him. He would have been a little older than James, can you imagine?"

Raquel nodded. "My first would have been twelve, almost a teenager." We sat in silence for a time, remembering the children we'd never had.

※

*W*hen I received the call from Claire that she had another child, I asked her for a few hours to discuss it with James first. He had adjusted so well, that I didn't want to do anything that might disrupt his progress.

I picked him up from school and drove to the Dairy Queen where we ordered two small ice cream cones.

"James, Henry and I have three other rooms in our house, and we were thinking about asking to foster some additional children. Would that be okay with you?"

His big brown eyes regarded me, a maturity beyond his seven years showing through. "Will I have to share my room?"

I smiled at the sincere question. "No, though we would love to help as many children as we can, we think that it's important you each have your own room."

"In that case, I'm okay with it. It would be nice to have other kids to play with."

He shrugged and returned to eating his ice cream, and I marveled at his resiliency. When we got home, I called Claire to share the good news.

That night, Stephanie, a four-year old blond pixie who had been abused by her parents entered our home. James took her under his wing immediately, giving her the grand tour of the house.

As he tugged her little hand and pulled her upstairs, I looked up at Henry. Tears shone in his eyes, mirroring my feelings.

"I always thought I needed my own children to feel fulfilled," he said, "but there is something special about being able to help these kids."

I couldn't have agreed more.

AS TIME GOES ON

*a*fter Stephanie, two more children came to our house. The house was soon full of children's laughter and fighting, but I wouldn't have traded the sound for the world. So when Claire showed up on the doorstep, I wasn't prepared.

"Hi, I wanted to tell you in person, but James's mother is getting released next week, and James will be returning home." Her stoic face told me that this was often her least favorite part of the job.

My heart broke. Losing James was almost like losing Isaac all over again, but I had known when we started this process that it might happen. "Can I tell him?" I asked.

"I'll be back for him next Wednesday. You have until then." Claire turned and walked back down the porch.

With the door shut, I rolled back to the backyard where James and the other children were playing. "Lord, give me strength," I said. I watched them play until it was time to call them in for lunch.

When Henry came home that afternoon, I met him on the front porch.

"Uh oh, what's wrong?" he asked upon seeing my face.

"Claire came by today. James's mother is being released next week."

Henry sighed and ran a hand over his forehead. "I knew it wasn't forever, but I guess I had hoped it would be longer," he said.

"I know it's selfish, but I had hoped it would be forever. I feel like we've all become a family, and I don't want to lose him."

Henry grabbed my hands and together we prayed for strength and for the will of God to be done regarding James.

"Let's not tell him until tonight," I said. "I think he should know before we tell the others."

Henry agreed, and though the words ate at my heart the rest of the day, I pasted a smile on, so the other children wouldn't suspect anything.

As we sat at the dinner table, I focused on James, wondering how different our lives would be without him in it. Though he wasn't the oldest, he had been with us the longest and was therefore kind of the leader of the group. As I looked from Matthew to Jessie, I wondered if one of them would step up and be the new leader.

Then my eyes wandered to little Stephanie, and I wondered how she would take it. She and James had bonded, almost like real siblings, and as she was so young, I worried that it would hit her hard.

When it was time for bed, Henry and I helped get everyone to bed, and then we returned to James's room together.

He looked up in surprise as we entered as we had already prayed with him and said goodnight. We prayed with each of the children before putting them down for the night. Because we had no idea what they might return to, we wanted to be sure they at least had some knowledge of Jesus to help them through.

"James, we need to tell you something," Henry said as we approached his bed.

"What is it?" James asked, his chocolate brown eyes jumping from Henry to me.

"It's your mother," I said. "She's being released next week, and you're going to get to go home."

I don't know what reaction I expected, but it wasn't the expressionless face that stared back at me.

"I suppose I don't have a choice," he said.

"You don't want to go back?" I asked.

The eyes he turned on me were so much older than his seven years. "I love my mom, but she'll just go back to drugs, and I'll wind up in care again. Do you think I'll be able to come back here?"

I glanced at Henry, who was fighting the same struggle with emotion that I was. Grabbing James's hand, I looked into his eyes. "You will always have a place with us."

We told the other three children the next day, and Stephanie burst into tears and clasped onto James's leg with a death grip.

"You can't go," she said. "I'll miss you too much."

"I'll miss you too, Stephanie, but I'll leave you my planet comforter to remember me by, okay?"

Tears stung my eyes as I watched the exchange. I wondered if it was this hard every time, or if someday we'd get so used to it that it wouldn't phase us.

Stephanie spent every moment she could with James over the next few days, and Tuesday night, Henry and I helped pack his little suitcase.

I shoved in as many clothes as I could since I didn't know what he was going back to. Then Henry and I each penned a heartfelt letter to him in his planet book, so he'd have a memory of us whenever he looked in the book.

"I'm scared," he said as we finished praying.

"There's nothing to be scared of," I said. "You're going home, and God will protect you, you hear?"

Though James nodded, the fear didn't leave his eyes, and as soon as we were back downstairs in our room, I burst into tears.

"It will be okay," Henry said, pulling me into his arms. "We have to trust that God knows what's best."

❦

A somber mood filled the house the next morning, and we sat like statues in the living room waiting for the dreaded sound of the bell. When it came, it sliced through my heart.

Henry opened the door for her and then hugged James. He whispered something in his ear, but I was too far away to hear it.

James nodded and hugged Matthew, Jessie, and Stephanie before turning to me

"Don't ever forget that you can do anything," I said as I pulled him tight.

He brushed away a tear. "I won't, Miss Sandra."

As the door closed behind them, the mood in the house fell. We had all been living in a happy glass bubble, but the reality hit that each of these kids had another family and would probably be returning sooner or later.

I offered ice cream in an effort to lighten the mood, but no one felt up to it. The two older children went out back, and Stephanie crawled up in my lap, content to be held most of the day.

"I didn't know it would be so hard," I told Henry that night in bed. We had spent the last hour praying for peace, but I still wasn't finding any.

He wrapped his arm around me, pulling me to his chest. "I didn't either. Do you want to stop?"

I shook my head. "No, anytime with them is better than no time at all. I just wonder how many times my heart will break."

⁂

With such a full house, I had taken to working mainly from home. Matthew and Jessie were both in school, so it was just Stephanie and I in the mornings.

She would usually color and play with her dolls while I did an hour of work, and then we would take a break together and practice her reading.

We rarely had visitors, so I was surprised when the doorbell rang a month later. I was even more surprised to find Claire and James standing on the stoop.

He rushed to hug me, and when we parted, I sent him inside to play with Stephanie. The look on Claire's face told me he didn't need to be around for whatever she had to tell me.

Needing no convincing, he raced into the kitchen and the sound of happy squeals carried to my ears.

"I figured it was okay to just bring him by since we hadn't given you another child yet," Claire said.

"Of course it's okay," I said, "but Claire, what happened?"

"His mother went right back to using when she got out. I suspected it on my first home visit, but I couldn't find any evidence. Evidently, the man she was seeing was a dealer, and they shorted a customer. The retaliation was a hit. James's mother and the dealer were involved in a suspicious auto accident yesterday."

My hand flew to my mouth. "Does James know?"

She nodded. "He does. I had to tell him when I picked him up from school yesterday. He's holding it together quite well, but you may need to have him see a counselor."

"Absolutely, we'll do whatever needs to be done."

"There's more," she said. "He no longer has any family, so he's available for adoption if you and Henry are interested."

I barely registered the rest of her words after she said adoption. "Yes, we would love to adopt him."

"Good, I was hoping you would say that," she said, relief evident in her voice. "There's just one more piece of news, but it's not about James. Stephanie's parents have signed away their rights. She's also available for adoption if you are open. If not, I'll need to get her placed in a home that is right away."

I stared at Claire, unsure I had heard her correctly. Not only were we getting James back, but we were going to get to keep him and Stephanie. In a daze, I nodded. "We would love to adopt them both."

She smiled. "I kind of thought you would, but I have to officially ask. Okay, I'll start getting the paperwork underway. It's still a long process, but when we finish, they'll be legally yours."

Claire turned and walked back to her car, and I watched her go, still floored by the change of events. I needed to tell Henry. Wheeling back inside, I grabbed my phone and dialed his number.

"Henry, can you get off early? I have some great news."

He walked in the door twenty minutes later while I was making lunch in the kitchen.

"What is it?" he asked. "Is everything okay?"

My gaze shifted to the back window where James and Stephanie were playing in the backyard.

His eyes followed mine. "Is that James?"

My smile stretched across my face. "It is. There was an accident, but long story short, James is available for adoption."

"He's...?

I nodded, knowing exactly how he felt. "But there's more. Stephanie's parents signed away their parental rights, and she's available for adoption too."

"Both of them?"

"Both of them." I smiled as the happiness flowed over me.

He grabbed my hands and squeezed. "Do they know?"

I shook my head. "I was waiting for you, so we could tell them together."

he End

If you enjoyed this book, please leave a review at your retailer. It really does help and only takes a minute. http://amzn.to/2BoOFnx

RESOURCES

*F*ree prenatal care if you put your baby up for adoption: http://www.adoptionstar.com/birth-parents/yourpregnancy/prenatal-care/

The loss of fertility after abortion: http://www.lifenews.com/2012/11/30/abortion-is-a-war-on-women-death-infertilityemotional-damage/

Dreams after abortion: http://www.afterabortion.com/dreams.html

Pray to end abortion app: https://www.humancoalition.org/

Abortion stories: http://www.abort73.com/testimony/

Adoption: http://www.pregnantpause.org/adopt/wanted.html

*P*lease reach out to someone if you find yourself pregnant unexpectedly. There are resources and loving couples who would love to raise your baby.

DISCUSSION QUESTIONS

1. What do you think the theme of this book is? What's the message the author is trying to get across?

2. As an English teacher, Lorana Hoopes loves literary devices. What was your favorite literary device she used and how do you think it enhanced the story?

3. Who was your favorite character in the book and why?

4. What are some ways we can encourage women who are in Sandra's position?

5. How can we ensure our daughters don't go through the same struggles Sandra did?

. . .

6 . What did you learn about God from reading this book?

7 . How can you use that knowledge in your life from now on?

8 . Is there something you could do at your church to help inform or love on women in this position?

9 . Sandra struggled with masking her pain with alcohol. How do you mask your pain?

1 0. What would be a more productive way to deal with your pain?

WOULD YOU LEAVE A REVIEW?

As an author, I highly appreciate the feedback I get from my readers. It helps others make an informed decision before buying my book. If you enjoyed this book, please review at your retailer.

Do you like free books? I'm offering a free sample of my next book Free Sample!

THE POWER OF PRAYER

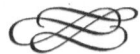

DEDICATION

Dedication Page:

The Power of Prayer is dedicated first and foremost to my grandmother who chose life when she was pregnant with my mother even though she was informed she might not survive delivery. My grandmother lived until I was four.

To my mom and dad: thank you for editing and adding your two cents. Most importantly, thank you for raising me in a Christian home and encouraging me to write.

To my husband and my children: thank you for allowing me to spend time working on this in the evenings.

To Ryann Woods: thank you for your tough questions about God. You were my inspiration for Lexi, and I'll keep praying for you.

To Kathryn and Beth: thank you for your support and feedback.

CHAPTER 1

checked the diamond studded watch on my left wrist for the fourth time and sighed in annoyance. Only two minutes had passed since the last time, but I couldn't keep my eyes from returning to the classic timepiece. I had been planning this day for the last year, and Shaina's delay was disintegrating my perfectly laid plans.

"Where is she?" The agitation spilled into my voice, and my mother's brow furrowed in the mirror behind me. My mother had never understood my need for lists and order; she preferred going with the flow, which had never been my strong suit.

"I'm sure she'll be back any minute." Her voice was calm and soothing, but she couldn't hide the flicker of doubt that crossed her eyes or the furtive glance she shot at the door. Something was definitely not right. "I'll go check."

As if on cue, a knock sounded at the door, and Shaina, my best friend and maid of honor, poked her blond head in the changing room.

Shaina and I had met in college and become friends our Junior year because Shaina had been just as driven as I was. She had been fierce competition for the top spot in class, but I had welcomed the challenge and only gloated a little when I had won, if only by a tenth of a point.

Relief flooded my body. Surely Shaina had taken care of whatever the problem was. "Is everything ready?"

"Well, sort of." Shaina's brow furrowed and her whitened teeth bit her perfectly pink bottom lip. She shuffled into the room past my mother, who took the chance to exit, closing the door behind her.

"What do you mean sort of?" A knot appeared in my stomach as I whirled to face Shaina. This could not be happening. "Did that photographer flake out on us? I knew we shouldn't have hired him. I thought he seemed flighty. I mean what kind of photographer has his studio in a garage for goodness sake? Or is it the food? I told Daniel the shop we ordered it from seemed a little dirty but he insisted on them because he *loves* their food . . ."

Shaina held up her left hand; her right stayed conspicuously behind her back. "No, the photographer is here, and the food is fine." Her eyes darted around the room, focusing on anything except my face. That was not a good sign. Shaina was terrible at hiding information and even worse at sugar coating. It was a characteristic I normally loved about her. "It's uh . . . it's Daniel; he's . . . uh . . . he's not coming."

The knot intensified, threatening to choke off my breath. My hand flew to my chest as the first signs of a panic attack coming on began. I hadn't had one in ages, but my fiancé not showing up to his own wedding would certainly be cause for one. "What do you mean he's not coming? Has he been in an accident? Is he in the hospital?"

"No, Callie." Shaina lowered her eyes and brought her hidden hand forward. She turned her palm up and offered up the cell phone it held.

I snatched the phone and swiped the screen to turn it on. Daniel's message still glowed on the screen.

-Tell Callie I'm sorry, but I can't marry her-

What does he mean he can't marry me? This had to be some kind of joke. My shoulders slumped forward, and my knuckles holding the phone turned white. "That's it? That's all? What does this mean?

What am I supposed to tell everyone out there?" There were nearly two hundred people waiting in the sanctuary.

Shaina lowered her head, unable to meet my eyes and bit her lip again.

My eyes narrowed to slits as I crossed the room and grabbed Shaina's arm, eliciting a yelp of either surprise or pain. I didn't know which, and at that moment, I didn't care. "What aren't you telling me?" Her eyes narrowed to slits. "There's someone else, isn't there? Who is it? If you know Shaina, then you have to tell me."

When Shaina lifted her head, tears glistened in her eyes. "I'm so sorry, Callie."

I dropped my arm and stared at Shaina. *She's sorry? What does she have to be sorry for? It's not like her fiancé just left her. It's not like*—Anger flared up in me as the realization set in. The world flashed red, and my nostrils flared. A vice grip squeezed my heart as the loathing flooded my body. *I'll kill her. I'll strangle her with my bare hands.* My hands curled into fists and my lip quivered even as my words came out more a snarl than a statement. "You? How could you?"

Shaina shrunk under my glaring eyes and took a step backwards. Her shoulders curled inward, and her head dropped. "I didn't mean to, honest." Her words tumbled together, spilling out of her mouth as her hands wrung together. "We spent so much time together planning the wedding while you were working. It was one time, and I had no idea he had feelings for me until this morning when he called. I even tried to talk him out of leaving you."

"You?? And Daniel??" Flashes of black dotted my vision. "Were you ever going to tell me?" *You little --* My knees began to tremble from the rage boiling inside, and I fought for control of them as my carefully laid plans crumbled around me.

Shaina turned away, her voice higher than normal. "Um, no? I was pretty sure he thought it had been a mistake, so I was going to try and forget him for your sake."

My nails dug holes into my palms, and the vein in my throat pulsed. I could almost see my heart beating. "For my sake?" The words were soft, deadly. "Shouldn't you have thought about my feelings before you slept with my fiancé?"

Shaina flinched as my words pierced like an icy dagger. "I never meant for it to happen. If you hadn't been so busy --"

My body tensed, shaking. "Don't you dare make this my fault," I seethed through clenched teeth. "I trusted you. I trusted him, and yet while trying to move up in my career you both threw that trust away."

Shaina's shoulders dropped, and she stared at her feet, her voice losing its power. "That's part of the problem, Callie; your career always came first. You couldn't even plan your own wedding. How do you think that made Daniel feel when you could never be there?"

"Get out; get out now!" Unable to contain the rage any longer, I grabbed a nearby glass of water from a small table and hurled it at Shaina. Shaina ducked and the glass missed cutting her face, but the resulting explosion of shards as the glass shattered against the wall mirrored my feelings and brought a smidgen of satisfaction. "Go be with MY fiancé and have a great life, but don't ever contact me again. I never want to see you, either of you, again."

Shaina cowered in the doorway, hands covering her face, tears spilling down her cheeks. "I am sorry Callie, and I hope someday you forgive me."

As the door closed behind Shaina, my knees finally gave out, and I collapsed on the floor. How could this happen to me? This was supposed to be my perfect day, the day I had dreamed of since I was eight years old.

An ugly, wretched sound escaped my mouth, and before I could stop them, more sobs poured out. My shoulders rose and fell as if pulled on strings by some sadistic puppet master. Darkness began to claw into the sides of my vision, and my throat closed up. My hands pulled at my throat, desperate for a little more air.

The door opened and closed. I vaguely registered my mother as she entered the room, scooped me up, and rocked me like she had when I was young. As she caressed my hair, she whispered a prayer, and for once I didn't stop her. "Please God, please heal her pain."

CHAPTER 2

*A*s the beeping intensified, I threw the alarm across the room to shut it up and pulled the pillow over my head. I had no desire to go to work today. It had been much nicer sitting in the dark yesterday feeling sorry for myself.

Though I could tell myself no one would know, I had little doubt that everyone at work would know by now that I had been stood up. They'd probably be happy. For once, I wanted to curse my braggadocios attitude and constant need to appear superior. If I hadn't made such a big deal about the wedding and invited nearly everyone in the office to it, then I might have been able to pretend the jilting never happened and go on about life. It wasn't like I had close friends at the office anyway, more like associates that I only spoke to between the hours of nine and five. But no, I'd had to brag about how amazing it was going to be and now everyone would know of my humiliation.

Sighing, I slammed my palms down on the bed. *No, I can't let him win. I have to at least act like it didn't bother me. Besides, they're announcing Junior Partner this week and if I don't show up, I'll never get the promotion.* Lowering the pillow from my face, I blinked at the intruding sunlight, and threw back the covers.

With the last reserve of energy, I rolled off the bed and stalked into my closet. A myriad of designer clothing crammed the closet, but I saw none of it. Instead, I yanked on the first black skirt and white top my hands touched. I should have wanted to make a good impression, to prove that I was doing fine, but I couldn't muster the energy.

The image staring back at me from the mirror was cringeworthy. Dark patches circled my normally bright green eyes, and they looked dead and void of life. I looked like I'd gotten punched in the face. *Better do something about those.* It was one thing not to care about my outfit, but I couldn't go in looking shabby and beat up. Grabbing some concealer, I placed a few dots under my eyes and rubbed it in. The look wasn't much better, but it would have to do. I ran a quick brush through my long dark hair that normally flowed in gentle waves, but as I hadn't showered in two days, it now hung limp and lifeless. Sighing, I pulled it into a lackluster bun, and decided "good enough" would do, for today at least.

I grabbed a quick cup of coffee and a banana and headed to work. The closer I got to work, the more the unease bubbling in my stomach grew.

By the time I parked the car and stood outside the building that served as my second home, I had to fight the urge not to turn around, go home, and crawl under my sheets again. Would everyone be talking about me? Would I have to fake my way through looks of pity all day? The very thought sounded worse than a root canal at the dentist, but somewhere deep inside a spark of courage flickered, and I grabbed ahold of it. Squaring my shoulders, I gripped the door handle to Schuster and Tuck, my firm's office, took a deep breath, and pulled it open.

Linda, the receptionist, lifted her hand in a wave and then returned her focus to her phone call. Everyone else seemed engrossed in their tasks as well. Not one eye stared at me. That could mean no one knew or that no one cared enough to make a big deal of it. The knot in my stomach untangled slightly, and my shoulders relaxed a smidgen. Maybe this wouldn't be so bad after all.

With my head held high and with deliberate braver-than-I-felt steps, I covered the distance of the lobby. I was feeling good until I turned down the hallway that led to my desk, and then I sighed. I had spoken too soon. Tina stood at her desk, staring at me with sympathetic doe-brown eyes. Ignoring them, I pulled my shoulders even farther back and marched to desk.

Tina had been my assistant since I started at the firm a few years ago, and while she was professional, I often found her overly sensitive about things.

"Are you sure you're okay?" Tina's voice oozed concern, accentuating her southern drawl. Her voice had often irritated me, and I had worked hard to break my own accent. "We're all so sorry about what happened."

Stiffening, I rolled my eyes. *Of course I'm not okay. What kind of a question is that? My fiancé left me on our wedding day for Pete's sake.* "Good news sure travels fast," I said instead, forcing a tight-lipped smile. "At least I have more time for work now, right?"

Tina's return smile would have appeared condescending coming from anyone else, but I had known her long enough to know that even with all her faults, one things she prided herself on was honesty. She held out my messages. "Sure; maybe it will even influence the partner position." Her eyes broke contact with those words, and I knew she didn't believe them, but she was saying them in hopes of making me feel better.

I flipped through the messages, my foot tapping against the floor – one of my nervous gestures. "I don't understand it, though. How could I have missed the signs?"

Tina's lips pinched together, and she looked down at her lap.

"What?" I leaned back, folding my arms across my chest. My lips drew into a tight single line as I waited for her to say the dreaded "I knew" words.

"Well, I never thought it was my place, but Daniel always seemed . . . what's the word I want? He always seemed too focused."

"Too focused? How is that a bad thing?" I thought about my recent past. Sure, I had skipped a few family occasions, but ever since my mother and father had split, they weren't as much fun anyway. My father was always off with his new wife and kids. He had tried, for a time, to see me on weekends when I was young, but once he married his girlfriend, I had gotten lost in his priorities and rarely seen him after that. My mom had been my best friend growing up, at least until she started going back to church. Now, all she ever talked about was what the church was doing and how God was working in her life. I had no time for someone I couldn't see or hear, so our relationship had grown distant.

Tina's toe ground into the floor as she mumbled the words, "Well, it seemed like he cared more about his own work than what really matters sometimes."

His work? Heat flooded my body, and my hands clenched, crumpling the messages. "It seems he cared even more about my best friend than his work." I paused, mentally forcing myself to calm down and relax my hands. A deep breath completed the outward transformation. "Anyway, it's done, and now I have more time to focus on my career. Who needs a man anyway?"

Tina nodded, timid as a mouse, and returned to her work.

I stepped into my office and sat down at the familiar, mahogany desk. A mountain of manila folders stared back at me. I drummed my fingers on the desk, hoping the monotony of the familiar would take control, but all I could do was stare at the pile.

Thoughts of Shaina and Daniel flooded my mind, constricting my throat and making it difficult to swallow. What were they doing right now? Was she cuddling with him as I used to? Was he nuzzling her neck finding that sweet spot in between her collar bones and the curve of her throat? The beep of the office phone intercom interrupted my nightmare, and I jumped.

"Yes, Tina?" I said, punching the intercom button.

"There's a Lexi on the phone for you."

Lexi? She was more of an acquaintance than a friend. I had met Lexi in college, but she had always been into partying, which had never fit in my perfect plan. Right now though, letting loose sounded like a nice diversion from the torturous thoughts of Daniel and Shaina. "Put her through."

"Callie, I'm so sorry about what happened," Lexi began. I ran my hand across my forehead. Maybe this had been a bad idea. Her overly sympathetic tone made her sound like a valley girl, which only increased my irritation, "but I know how to cheer you up. My brother's band is playing downtown tonight. Come with me to hear them. I guarantee you will have a good time."

This wasn't the first time Lexi had invited me out. In fact, I was surprised Lexi was still trying as I never bothered to come up with a good excuse when I turned her down. How many times had I told Lexi I was working late or getting a massage when I was really going home and curling up with a good book or with Daniel? Daniel, ugh. I needed a distraction from Daniel.

"Sure, that sounds like fun," I said, pushing the thought of Daniel out of her mind. It actually sounded about as much fun as watching golf on TV, but at least I wouldn't be alone, and it would get Lexi off my back.

"Really? I mean that's great," Lexi stammered in surprise. "Okay, let's meet at the Blue Banjo at eight."

"I'll be there." I hung up the phone and rubbed my temples. Would this day ever end? No answer came, and as the mountain of paperwork continued to mock me, I picked up the top folder to begin the tedious research. "Junior Partner cannot come fast enough."

When five o'clock rolled around, there were still a few folders on the desk. A week ago, I would have stayed until they were all done, but I had promised to meet Lexi tonight and surely one more day couldn't hurt. Clicking off the computer and then the light, I enjoyed the blessed darkness for a moment before heading home.

Though I normally had no trouble throwing outfits together, I stood in a pile of discarded clothes liking nothing. Nothing seemed to say 'my fiancé just left me for my best friend so leave me alone.'

Deciding I needed something to draw the attention away from my vacant eyes, I grabbed my green cowl-necked shirt. As I tugged it on over my head, I wondered if I would ever feel normal again.

A hand swipe down my jeans sent a piece of lint flying into the air.

I watched it fall, realizing my life now felt a little like that, blown off course and subject to whatever force came near it.

Out of habit, I glanced over my shoulder for Daniel, who was always ready before me. He usually stood by the door, phone in hand as he made business deals while waiting. He wasn't there, but his jacket was, hanging on the hook, taunting me. He must have left it the last time he was here, stupid jacket. I wondered what else of his might be lying around and realized tomorrow I would have to do a thorough sanitizing of the place to get rid of all his things.

Grabbing her keys, I stalked out the door, determined to have a good time and forget about Daniel.

"*A*nother round," I hollered at the blond waitress who ambled past us on the dance floor. The lights flashed, and music flooded my body, relaxing the tense nerves that had taken root. The noise filled my brain, allowing me to forget about Daniel, for the time being.

Lexi's slender body moved to the beat, her blond hair flowing against her bare shoulders. "Wow, no offense, Callie, but I can't remember the last time you were this fun to be with."

"Me either." I lifted my hair to relieve the sweat trickling down my neck, and a pair of hands, not my own, landed on my hips. They were tan, strong hands, and no ring marred them.

Twisting my body to see who the hands belonged to, I hoped for someone handsome. If I was lucky, maybe it would be someone who could make me forget Daniel for a night.

The face that met mine did not disappoint. Bright blue eyes above an impish grin stared back at me. Taut muscular arms extended from what was likely an equally chiseled chest. Yes, he could do. Desire flooded my veins, and my eyes roamed over the rest of him. The hint of a tattoo peeking out of his shirt sleeve gave him the air of a typical "bad boy," and tonight I wanted to be a "bad girl." I locked my arms around his neck, pulling him closer so the rhythm of his hips could match mine. He flashed a sexy grin and tightened his grip on me.

He leaned his head down, lips brushing my ear as he whispered, "My name is Brent, and I think you're hot."

Inwardly, I cringed at the pedantic come-on, but tilted my head back and smiled anyway. *Handsome, though not eloquent; I guess I could do a lot worse.* I ran my fingers through his short blond hair and let my mind go blank. One dance turned to into two, then three, and the rounds of Tequila kept coming.

"It must be late." My words slurred, and I realized too late that I had had too much to drink. Though we sat at a table on the side of the dance floor, the room still spun. I put my hands to my temple in hopes of stopping the roller coaster I seemed to be on, but it was no use

"I think you're right," Lexi stammered, equally inebriated, "and I have to work tomorrow, so I'm heading out." She stood and then grabbed the tabletop to keep from toppling.

"Are you okay to drive?" Brent offered his hand to steady her, and I wondered briefly how he seemed so sober. Hadn't he had as many drinks as we had? I tried to think back in my mind, but the exertion increased the pounding, and so I stopped.

"No, but my brother is." She pointed an unsteady finger to the stage where the musicians were packing up their instruments. "He can drive me."

I tried to focus on Lexi, but I wasn't sure whether the left or the right Lexi was the real one. I had always thought people were full of it when they said they were seeing double, but now I realized I had just never been drunk enough. "Thanks for getting me to come out. We should do it again soon."

Lexi flicked a sloppy salute and stumbled off.

Brent turned his attention back to me and brushed a curl from my face. "How about I drive you home?"

His fingertips felt nice on my face, soothing. I nodded, my eyes already trying to close for the night. The image of my warm apartment and soft bed called to me, but then the jacket flashed in my mind. I couldn't go home and face the jacket. My eyes flew open, and my lips parted. Leaning into Brent, I placed a hand on his solid chest, "How about you take me back to your place instead?"

Brent licked his lips, and his eyes roved my body, "I thought you'd never ask." He placed a hand on either side of my face and brought his lips down on mine. It was a rough kiss and his stubble scratched my chin, but I didn't care. Wrapping my arms around his neck, I surrendered to the feeling, or lack thereof, and leaned farther into him.

When we parted, I thrust my car keys into one of his hands and grabbed the other, stumbling after him to my red mustang parked around the corner.

The cool, night air woke me enough to acknowledge the tiny seed of doubt sprouting in my head. This wasn't like me. I was no prude, but I didn't go home with men I didn't know. I wasn't even intimate until we had both said, 'I love you.'

Shivering, I pressed my lips together, fighting the urge to call it all off. I wanted to be bad tonight. I needed to feel attractive again. Before any words could form, we were in the car; the warmth enveloped me; and I stopped caring. My eyes closed as I leaned against the leather seat.

"Come on." His voice cut through my sleepy fog. He had parked, but I had no idea where we were or even how far we had driven from the club. Tiny alarm bells sounded in my head, but I couldn't focus on them. He stood outside the car door, a hand held out to me.

I placed my hand in his, struggled to stand, and fell against him. His chest was indeed chiseled, masculine. He spun me around and pulled me to his side, wrapping his arm around me to help me walk. We crossed the parking lot and then he deposited me against a wall while he rummaged for his keys.

The sound of silence crept in on me, stirring a little more awareness into my head. "Why is it so quiet?"

He cocked his head at me, "It's two in the morning. Everyone else is asleep."

"Right," I nodded, pointing a manicured finger at him, "sleep."

He pushed his door open and grabbed my hand, pulling me across the threshold into his apartment. The door shut behind me, and the click of the lock on the door registered something in my mind, but a thick fog obscured it.

Brent took my other hand as well and began walking backward, pulling me down the hall. I vaguely registered the clutter of clothes strewn about before we entered his bedroom. He spun me around and backed me to the bed until the back of my legs hit the frame, and I fell back, letting desire and fatigue take over.

"*G*o away," I moaned, throwing my hand over my face to block the bright light, but the sun filtered through the gaps of my fingers. "Ugh." My head felt like it weighed a thousand pounds as I tried to lift it. Giving up the fight, I lowered it back to the pillow and opened my eyes slowly to adjust to the light. White walls covered in Green Bay Packer paraphernalia filled my vision. Where was I? I didn't even like football.

I glanced down at the sheets – white. My sheets were purple Egyptian cotton ones. A feeling of unease ignited in my stomach, and I clutched the sheets tighter in my hands. How did I get here? A shuffling noise grabbed my attention, and I turned, recoiling at the sight of the muscular man lying next to me. What had I done?

My audible intake of breath woke the sleeping giant, and he rolled over and smiled. "Good morning, sunshine."

I swallowed, racking my brain for his name "Um, hi--"

His blue eyes danced at my obvious discomfort. "Brent; we met at the Blue Banjo Club last night."

The events of the previous night flashed in my mind, and a soft pink blush crawled up my cheeks. "Right, and I guess we --"

"Oh, come on," he said, reaching out a finger to caress my face, "I thought you would at least remember that."

Trying not to flinch at his touch, I pulled the sheet to my neck and glanced around for a clock. "Um, what time is it?"

He rolled away a moment – there must be a clock on his side - "Ten."

I jumped. "Ten? Oh no, I am late, very, very late." I rolled off the bed, pausing for a moment as the world swam around me. When it stopped, I wrapped the blanket tighter around me, and tried to ignore the flame burning my ears.

"Call in sick," Brent patted the empty bed next to him. "We can order in and have breakfast together, right here."

"No, I can't do that," I said, agitated. "I am a candidate for Junior Partner. I can't take a day off." I rummaged in the clothes on the floor, tossing them in the air until I located my jeans and shirt, wrinkled from their time on the floor. Another few minutes of searching yielded the rest of my clothes.

"Suit yourself." He laced his hands behind his head and stretched out, as if he didn't have a care in the world.

I shot him a dirty look as I pulled on my clothes. Cringing at the thought of wearing jeans to work, I tried vainly to smooth out the worst of the wrinkles and then grabbed for where I normally kept my keys, but came up empty-handed. Of course, this wasn't my apartment.

Planting my hands on my hips, I turned to face Brent. "Where are my keys?"

"By the front door; on the table, I think." He pointed out the bedroom door.

I swallowed the knot growing in my stomach and hurried out of the bedroom and into the living room, scooping my keys off the hall table on the way. Slamming his front door behind me, I glanced around for my car, spotting it halfway across the parking lot. Hurrying across the asphalt already radiating heat, I climbed into it and turned the ignition on.

Easing out to the street, I glanced around for a point of reference, but nothing seemed familiar. *Oh, great.* I eased up to the intersection to see the cross streets. Baker and Yates? Where was I?

My jaw clenched as I whipped out my cell phone and turned on the GPS app. The low battery icon flashed eliciting a groan. *Please just last until I get to work.* I kept an extra cord in my desk drawer as my phone often needed a charge during the day, but I needed to get there first. I punched in the office address, and my heart sank another few feet; *thirty minutes? I am so dead.*

"*W*here have you been?" Tina asked in a harsh whisper as she hurried toward me. Her brows furrowed, creating a pattern of wrinkles across her forehead and making her appear older than she really was.

I shook my head, "It's a long story." The sordid events of the previous night lay on my shoulders like a heavy blanket. What had I been thinking? Now I knew why I never had one-night stands. I felt dirty and cheap.

"Well, Mr. Reid said he wanted to see you in his office, as soon as you arrived. I've been trying to stall for you."

Her words hit like a punch in the stomach. "This can't be good; the partner position wasn't supposed to be announced until next week, and I can't see Mr. Reid looking like this."

"I have a skirt if you want to borrow it," Tina offered. "I know we aren't exactly the same size, but it might look better than jeans."

I raised an eyebrow at her. I'd known she was different, but why would anyone keep outfits at work? "Why do you keep a skirt at the office?"

"Oh, gosh, I am such a klutz that I keep a whole outfit here in case I spill on myself. I've already had to replace my replacement outfit twice."

I weighed the options. Tina was probably a size smaller than I was, but borrowing a skirt from her would be better than showing up in jeans, if it fit. "Okay, thanks."

Tina opened her right bottom drawer and handed over a simple black skirt. Tucking it in my arm, I headed to the nearest bathroom and peeled off my jeans. The skirt reluctantly shimmied up over my slim hips, but I couldn't tug the zipper up all the way. I pulled my blouse out over the skirt and turned to the mirror. The effect was still a little unkempt, but it was better than before. I rolled up my jeans and dropped them at my office before continuing down the long hall to Henry Reid's office.

. . .

*B*eads of sweat broke out on the back of my neck and trailed down my back as I pushed open his door.

His assistant looked up from her desk and wrinkled her nose. With her blond hair pulled back in an immaculate bun and her pressed black suit, she appeared impeccable – the way I normally dressed myself. My unease grew, but I squared my shoulders, portraying a confidence I didn't feel, and approached the desk.

"I'm here to see Mr. Reid. I'm Callie Green."

"Yes," her eyes traveled up and down my form. "He's expecting you." Disdain dripped from her words.

Ignoring her scorn, I crossed to the inner office door and smoothed my blouse one more time for good measure before stepping into the dark and masculine office.

His mahogany desk color was captured in the dark wall coloring and complemented by the dark mauve carpet. Various plaques and commendations hung from the walls and garnered my attention as I made my way to the dark brown chair across from his desk. Smoothing my skirt, I sat down and folded my hands in my lap.

Henry Reid met my gaze across the desk. He was the oldest of the partners. White hair circled his head, but the middle of his pate had lost its battle long ago. "Hello Callie, how are you doing?"

The truth was that I was a wreck, but I couldn't say that. "Not too bad sir, considering. I am throwing myself into my work." I forced a stiff laugh and then forced my hands, which had begun to curl into fists, to lay flat on my lap. My traitorous right index finger, however, continued to tap a pattern to the steady staccato of my accelerated heartbeat, displaying my nervousness.

"Yes, that is what I need to talk to you about." He leaned forward, "Do you remember the Mead case?"

I tilted my head and closed my eyes, reviewing the cases I had pored over yesterday. "I'm sorry sir. It isn't ringing a bell, but I still have a few files on my desk."

He cleared his throat. "That's the problem, Callie. It still WAS on your desk, and an injunction was supposed to be filed yesterday."

My heart dropped to the floor, and my shoulders curled inward under the heavy weight of the mistake. "I am so sorry sir."

"Normally, this would be an offense we fire for," Mr. Reid began. "We can't afford such costly mistakes."

I dropped my head into my hands and shook it back and forth. This couldn't be happening.

"But considering your history of success here and your recent personal event, I have convinced the board not to fire you."

I lifted my face to look at him through splayed fingers. "Thank you, sir."

"They have agreed to a one month suspension, without pay. I suggest you take a vacation, regain your footing, and come back ready to work. And Callie," he emphasized, "they won't be this lenient IF there is a next time."

"Yes sir." I gave a curt nod and then stood. The Junior Partnership flashed in my mind, and I cleared my throat, unsure of how to ask the question on my mind. "I don't suppose---" I broke off mid-sentence, unable to form the rest of the question, but he read my mind.

"I'm sorry, Callie. I couldn't recommend you this time."

My head fell. "I understand, sir."

"But there will be another junior partnership next year. If you come back refreshed and re-focused, I could recommend you then."

Another whole year? The weight of the prospect of another year of doing grunt work bore down on me, threatening to release the tears now crowding my throat. As my heart shrunk in my chest, I fought to compose myself.

"Thank you, sir." I forced a tight smile and shook his hand. Drawing myself as straight as I could manage under the heaviness descending my body, I shuffled out of the office and past the perfectly put-together, snarky assistant to the hallway.

As the door closed behind me, I pressed a hand over my mouth to hold back a sob. My eyes darted around for the bathroom sign, and I hurried to the women's room. Locking the stall behind me, I sank down on the toilet. Tears obscured my vision and tumbled down my cheeks. *What is happening to me? Why is everything going wrong? How am I going to get back on track now?*

When the tears were spent, I splashed water on my still puffy face and scuffled back to my office. My head was down, all of my bravado gone.

"Oh, no, what happened?" Tina asked. The concern in her voice nearly broke the dam holding back another flood of tears.

I swallowed and bit my lip. "I missed filing an injunction yesterday."

"Are you . . .?" Tina averted her eyes and wrung her hands together.

My head shook back and forth, "No, I've been given a one month suspension." The words tasted dirty in my mouth. Suspension? I would have never thought the words would be applied to me, the girl at the top of her class who had her whole life planned out. I swallowed the vile words to dislodge them from my throat.

"Well, that's not so bad," Tina said, touching my arm.

"It could be worse," I agreed, "but what am I going to do for a month?" The thought of sitting around my empty apartment that long chilled me to the bone. I had never been one to sit at home. In fact, in the time I had been at the firm, I had taken only one sick day.

Tina's eyes lit up, and she snapped her fingers. "Do you still have your honeymoon tickets?"

"Yes, I think the information is on my computer. Why?"

"Send it to me. I have a friend who's a travel agent. I bet he can work something out and send you to a nice place for most of that time."

A spark flickered in my dark heart. "Really? That would be great." I pulled Tina into a hug, turning her in a circle before realizing what I had done. I never hugged people and especially not people at work. Dropping my arms, I mumbled an apology.

Tina laughed, ignoring my apology. Her eyes sparkled. "I'll call him right away. Go home and rest, but be sure to have your phone on."

I didn't know how to thank Tina. Even after all the years we had worked together, I barely knew anything about her, but that was going to change. An escape to a tropical island sounded like just the thing to help me forget Daniel and focus on rebuilding my self-esteem, and I couldn't believe Tina was willing to help me. As I gathered up my things, I promised myself that I would be different when I came back and that I would pay more attention to others around me, especially Tina.

As I entered my apartment, the silence seemed almost palpable. Rubbing my neck, I looked around for some way to pass the time. A book on the coffee table garnered my attention, and I scooped it up and reclined on the brown, leather couch.

I couldn't remember the last time I had read this book, and as I had no idea what was happening in it any longer, I flipped back to the beginning. I read the first page, then read it again, and again. Sighing, I closed the book and glanced at the clock. I'd managed to kill a whopping five minutes.

Setting the book back on the small coffee table, I grabbed the remote. Maybe some mindless TV would help pass the time. A click of the power button brought the screen to life and the news filled the screen. Election coverage, ugh, I was so over the presidential race this year. Politics had never held my attention anyway. I clicked the channel up button: soap opera, talk shows, game shows. There was nothing worth watching on TV in the middle of the day. A rerun of Friends was the only thing that seemed remotely interesting, and I soon got lost in the friendly banter of the characters.

The shrill ring of the phone broke my trance, and I snatched it up before the end of the first ring. "Hello?"

Tina laughed on the other end. "Hello? Callie? Wow, it didn't even ring on my end."

"Sorry, I seem to have no life right now," I replied, sitting forward on the couch and fingering the gold chain around my neck. It held no special appeal or sentimental value, but touching the chain often brought comfort when I was nervous.

"Well, you will soon. Can you catch a plane tomorrow?"

"Of course I can." I listened in rapt attention as Tina rattled off the details of the vacation. Twenty-one days in the Caribbean, a hotel on the beach, and all-inclusive; it sounded like heaven. I'd have to come up with a special way to thank her.

After hanging up the phone, I danced a little jig to the hall closet and opened the door, pulling out my red suitcase. It was nice to be feeling something other than dread and despair.

I threw the suitcase on the bed and began rummaging through my drawers for swimwear, tank tops, and skirts. With the bag packed, I phoned my mother for a ride to the airport the next morning and then turned to the task I was not looking forward to – gathering all of Daniel's things.

I wandered around the apartment picking up books, ties, socks – anything that was Daniel's or reminded me of Daniel – and shoving it in a box. The coat was the last item. I snatched it off the coat rack and flung it on the top of the pile to take out in the morning.

*T*he next morning, I glanced around the apartment for anything I had missed as I waited for my mother to arrive. The list on the coffee table had been checked off – the clothes were packed, the major appliances unplugged, the mail was taken care of. My eyes landed on the box of Daniel's things, and a new surge of anger flooded my body. Snatching the box up, I flung open the front door and stomped around the corner to the communal trash dumpster. I threw the whole thing in, box and all, and then wiped my hands together, feeling a smug sense of satisfaction.

The deed done, I retraced my steps and found my mother standing at my front door.

"Dare I ask?" she said, one eyebrow raised.

"Just taking out the trash," I said sweetly and stepped past her into the apartment.

"Okay," she said slowly, drawing the two syllables out in an exaggerated effect. She followed me into the apartment and tried another tactic to get me to open up. "Do you want to tell me why you're running away then? It's not as if that is going to soothe your grief."

I pulled the handle out of the rolling suitcase and rolled my eyes as I answered her. "I'm on suspension, mom; I was told to go on vacation."

"You were told to take a break and clear your head—which isn't the same thing. You know, honey, I've started praying again and that has helped clear my head."

My muscles tensed at the mention of God. I'd had no use for him before, but I certainly didn't want to hear how loving he was now, after being left at the altar. "That's great mom. I'm glad it works for you, but I am not praying to anybody, especially to a God who cared so little about me that he let my life get so far off track. After all, if he really cared about me he could have stopped Daniel from leaving me on my wedding day or from sleeping with Shaina in the first place."

My mother's lips pursed as she shook her head. "Well, at least let me pray for you and your safety."

I checked my watch and sighed. "Fine, mom, as long as it's quick."

A look of reproach crossed her features, and she opened her mouth as if to scold me, but deciding against it, she sighed and closed her eyes. Her prayer was short, a prayer of safety, but I couldn't resist tapping my foot against the carpet. I couldn't wait to get out of Texas and go somewhere where no one knew my shameful secret, either of them.

CHAPTER 3

Sighing, I collapsed on the king size bed in the hotel room and flung my arms out. What a long flight! It had been just my luck lately to be seated next to an elderly man who wouldn't stop talking and didn't seem to know how to read body language. I had thought if I stuck my nose in a book or plugged in my headphones that he might get the message I wasn't interested in a conversation, but he had kept prattling away until he had finally talked himself to sleep.

Rolling over, I enjoyed the feel of the soft comforter on my skin. It wasn't a tacky flower comforter like most hotels. Instead it was some soft material in a light blue color.

The salty, fresh air wafting in the slightly open window relaxed my muscles, and the stress began to peel off my shoulders in layers. This was exactly what I had needed. I glanced up at the peach colored walls and stifled a laugh at the picture of the ocean hanging on the wall I was facing. Though it was pretty, I could hear the real thing seeping in the window.

Sitting up, I grabbed the suitcase and hefted it onto the bed, unzipping it. My current clothes lay sticky and molded to my skin from the long plane ride, and a sniff revealed they needed a wash. A pink maxi dress and matching sandals seemed appropriate for the beach, and I slipped them on after removing my other clothes.

My hair was also flatter than I would have liked, but a few shakes gave it some body. I touched up my makeup and pulled the sliding glass door open.

The warm night air caressed my face much like Daniel's fingertips used to, and I breathed in a deep breath. This was perfect; I'd have to buy Tina lunch when I got back to Texas. Maybe Tina wasn't so bad after all.

I slid the door shut behind me and stepped onto the cream-colored sand that appeared almost white at the base of the various palm trees dotting the landscape. The palm leaves stirred slightly with the gentle breeze which also lifted my hair, swirling strands about my face. Blue water licked the sand and called to me like an old friend. *I'll have to go swimming tomorrow.* As I stepped closer to the water, I could see the colorful fish swimming back and forth in the clear, calm glass.

The soft sound of music to my right caught my attention, and I turned to see a small bar surrounded by tiki torches. A handful of people sat in the few barstools and tables and several more stood around sipping their drinks. The glow of the light pulled at me, daring me to come and join it, and since the beach area to the left was empty except for a few occupied lounge chairs, I accepted the invitation and set off to check out the scene at the bar.

Probably twenty people, who seemed close to my age, professionals at least, hovered around the bar. An iPod speaker system sat on the bar's counter playing soft reggae music that my head began to bob to.

"What'll you have?"

The voice was deep and masculine, and as I turned to find the man who owned it, a small gasp escaped my lips. Broad shoulders that had been tanned in the sun stood out against his cream tank top, and dark brown hair fell in waves to about his chin. He was probably the most handsome man I had ever seen, but it was his piercing green eyes that I couldn't seem to look away from. He stared at me expectantly, an empty glass in his hand as he waited for my order.

"Uh, tequila sunrise," I stammered as the blush climbed my

cheeks. Had he heard my gasp? I tried to look away, but his gaze was a magnet drawing my eyes back to him.

"Tequila, huh?" His lips pulled into a smile revealing perfectly white teeth, and my heart fluttered in my chest.

"It's my weakness." My lips parted, and my tongue darted across her bottom lip. I wondered how his lips would feel against mine. Apparently, he was a weakness for me as well.

"In that case, how about a double shot?" The wink he flashed solidified the notion that he was flirting with me, but I couldn't tell whether that was because he liked me or because it was part of the job description.

"Sure." My heartbeat magnified in my ears, and despite his magnetic pull, I forced my attention away from the bartender and back to the crowd, hoping to hide the red on my face. Though the bartender was easily the most handsome man there, several other nice looking gentlemen filled the area. Most appeared to be chatting with women already, but one man sat alone, tapping at his laptop and nursing a beer.

"Here you go." The bartender slid a colorful glass her way.

I grabbed the drink, smiling at the tiny blue umbrella attached to the side, and reached for my bag. I froze as I realized I didn't have my bag or any cash on my person. My dress didn't even have pockets. "Um . . . any way I can charge this to my room? I forgot my purse."

"No need. It's all inclusive here." He tossed another wink at me and flashed a lopsided grin.

"Oh right. Thank you." I raised the glass in a mock salute and headed to an empty table. Smoothing my dress, I sat in the wicker beach chair and glanced around. *Why didn't I think to at least bring a book?*

The answer to my question appeared a moment later as a tall man approached the table and motioned to the empty chair across from me. "Mind if I sit down?"

I nodded once in agreement, checking him out as he folded his frame into the chair. He appeared about thirty with blond hair and blue eyes.

"So," he took a sip of his beer and raised his eyebrows suggestively at me, "What do you do?"

I fought to keep my eyes from rolling. He came across like a frat boy who hadn't quite realized he was no longer in college, but I was determined not to be judgmental and to have a good time, so I pasted a smile and answered, "I'm a lawyer, here on vacation, clearing my head."

"Lawyer, huh? That must be interesting." He leaned across the table bringing a whiff of alcohol with him. He had clearly had more than one beer already.

Forcing another smile, I leaned back, away from his breath. "Hah, that's rarely the case. TV makes it look exciting, but I do a lot of paperwork and research right now."

"Well, then I'd say you definitely deserve a break, huh?"

"You have no idea," I agreed, taking a long drink of the tequila. I was not usually much of a drinker, but the alcohol felt good as it burned down my throat.

"My name is Owen." He stuck out a large hand which I shook after only a moment's hesitation. His hand was smooth and . . . manicured? He obviously did not do physical labor for his job.

"I'm Callie. Nice to meet you."

Owen's eyes roamed my face before beginning to slide south. Why was it that men couldn't keep their eyes focused on women's faces? "So . . . are you here with your boyfriend?"

Images of Daniel flashed into my mind, and I squeezed my eyes shut, shaking my head to clear the treacherous face. The last thing I wanted to do on this vacation was think about Daniel. "I most definitely am not."

"I'm single too," he hinted, tracing a circle around the top of his glass with his index finger. "Would you like to have dinner with me tomorrow? We could meet at the hotel restaurant here."

I opened my mouth to decline and then closed it. While he wasn't my normal type, it was just dinner. Besides, my normal type had ended up sleeping with my best friend. The fact that he seemed drunk already bothered me – I didn't need any more drunken trysts, but maybe it was his first night, and he was just relaxing. I wasn't here to psychoanalyze people, and I'd probably be enjoying more of these drinks while I was here. Besides, if dinner turned out to be a disaster, I wouldn't have to see him again.

"Sure, that sounds nice." With the words out of my mouth and unable to be recalled, I tilted back the last of my drink. Though not drunk, the jet lag, combined with the alcohol, created a soft buzzing in my head, and I excused myself before I ended up passing out on the table.

Waves of fatigue bombarded me as I opened the sliding glass door and closed it behind me. Kicking off my sandals, I crawled into the inviting bed, not bothering to change. My teeth felt fuzzy, and I knew I should get up and brush them, but the bed had wrapped its comfort around me, and I couldn't lift my head, much less my body. *I'll brush them tomorrow* was the last thought in my head before the darkness won.

The sunlight peeking in my window woke me the next morning. Yawning, I stretched out my stiff muscles and did a double take at my watch. *Nearly noon? I guess jet lag does mess you up.* This trip was my first out of the continental United States, and I'd had no idea how tired the flight over would make me. I never slept past eight am unless I was sick or drunk. I cringed as the night with Brent blazed in my memory again.

Pushing it away, I plodded out of bed and into the bathroom. After turning on the water in the tub, I slipped off my dress and stepped into the bathtub, letting the warm water energize me. When I felt thoroughly refreshed and washed, I toweled off and, wrapping the white fluffy towel like a sarong around my chest, traipsed back into the main room to pick today's outfit.

I wanted something comfortable but also eye catching, so I grabbed a green tank that brought out my eyes and a pair of shorts. After slipping them on, I ran a quick brush through my dark hair and grabbed my sunglasses. It was time to check out the rest of what the island had to offer.

The hotel itself was gorgeous, but very much like other hotels I had been to: a spa, a gift shop, and a few small restaurants sat on the premises but not much else, so I headed out of the hotel to the village outside.

The sun beat down, sending small beads of sweat trickling down my back as I traversed the walkway. I needed a hat or a fan, something to keep the blazing sun off my head.

As small shops straddled the quaint street, I approached one that was laden with clothing and begin to search through the wares. Dresses, skirts, and tops filled the tiny shop, and a dark-skinned woman sat on a stool, eyeing me and fanning herself.

My hand landed on a beautiful green, blue, and red maxi skirt that called my name, and I handed it to the lady to wrap up for me. I added a straw hat before leaving and was just about to place the hat on my head when I saw a man braiding hair a few feet ahead. I'd often pictured a braid in my hair whenever I thought of myself lounging on a beach, so I tucked the hat in the bag for now and sidled up to his stand.

He was just finishing a braid on the current customer, his skilled hands deftly weaving the hair back and forth. "How much to do one small braid in the front of my hair?" I asked, pointing to the front right side.

The dark man smiled at me as he wrapped a small rubber band around the bottom of the woman's braid. "For you, pretty lady, I take ten dollar."

The lady thanked him and smiled at me as she vacated the chair, and I handed over the ten-dollar bill I had just fished from my purse. I couldn't believe I was actually letting a stranger run his fingers through my hair, but I had to admit the feeling was rather nice.

"Blending in, are you?"

I glanced out of the corner of my eye to see the handsome bartender from the previous night. My heart fluttered in my chest. He looked just as handsome today in cargo shorts and a green t-shirt. "Uh yeah, I figured I should try some of the local culture." Why did I lose the ability to speak coherently around this man?

"Well, Sammy here is the best braider around, so you are in good hands." He clapped a hand on the shoulder of the man and flashed another charming smile.

My pulse drummed in my ears. What was it about this guy? Why did he have such an effect on me? "Are you not working at the bar today?" I hoped the question sounded nonchalant, though I feared my attraction to him was showing through.

His head tilted as he regarded me, his eyes twinkling. "I don't work here; I was covering a shift last night, for a friend."

Something in the way he answered led me to believe there was more to that story, but as he didn't seem inclined to share, I decided not to push. "What do you do then?" I asked, finally recovering the ability to string intelligible words together.

"I manage a few companies back in the states."

"Are you vacationing then?"

"I guess you could say that." That twinkle in his eye was so distracting as was his uncanny ability to give vague answers to my questions. "Listen, do you want to get some lunch after Sammy finishes your hair? I'd like to show you a fantastic, local eatery."

Yes. My heart flip-flopped, and my pulse revved, accelerating in her chest, but I took a deep breath to regain control. "I don't even know your name." I glanced up at him, and Sammy smirked.

"It's JD, and people around here can vouch for me."

"I'm Callie, but I don't know people around here so them vouching for you doesn't mean much."

"He's a good guy," Sammy interjected.

"See? I'm a good guy." JD smiled. "Come on." His bottom lip protruded in just the hint of a pout, and desire flickered in my veins again. I wanted to gently nibble on that protruding lip and then . . . I squeezed my eyes shut, stopping the tempting thoughts. What was wrong with me?

"Okay, fine, but just lunch." Of course, if it turned into something more, I wasn't sure I would be upset.

Sammy finished the braid and tied it off, and JD stretched out a hand to me. It was large and masculine, as Owen's had been, but there were also callouses. He had probably never had a manicure in his life.

I placed my hand in his, enjoying the roughness that rubbed against my smooth skin. Tingles raced up my arm at his touch, sending another flush crawling up my neck. I lowered my eyes, afraid of what he might see in them, but as soon as I was standing, he dropped my hand. My eyes shot to his face, but he was already walking on. Ignoring the empty sensation pulsing through my hand, I hurried to catch up to him.

"You aren't a vegetarian, are you?" JD asked as we strolled past various shops.

"No, I like to eat—I need the protein," I laughed, "because I work out a lot."

"What do you do?" He turned into an eatery on the left side of the street.

"I kick box."

His eyes widened, and a laugh escaped my lips. I was used to that reaction. Though athletic, my 5'7" frame did not scream 'heavy hitter.'

"I'm sorry," he said, holding up his hands in apology, "I don't know many women who kick box."

"I don't either," I agreed, though more women were joining my gym every day, "but it's the only workout that I have continued for any length of time; I've been training for ten years. I guess I get bored easily, but it's never the same workout, so it stays fresh." A furtive glance at his well-toned body sent another flame of heat across my face, forcing me to look away. "What about you? Do you work out?"

"Mainly running and lifting, but I've been known to hit a bag now and then."

Images of JD shirtless flooded my mind. I pictured the two of us in one of the small changing rooms in my gym icing each other's wounds in between stolen kisses or crawling into an Epson Salt bath together after a hard workout. My ears burned with heat, and I shook my head to clear it. What was wrong with me? I didn't even know him, and I had just warmed the bed of another man I didn't know.

Daniel. He was the reason. His leaving me at the altar had damaged my psyche and these lustful thoughts must be my way of regaining it.

The waitress approached, and I followed her, thankful that JD appeared not to have noticed my face or crimson ears. She led us to an empty table with a bright blue and orange umbrella attached to offer shade. Several similar tables sat throughout the restaurant, each with a different colored umbrella.

JD pulled out my chair, and I cocked her eyebrow at him as I sat down, unsure whether to be flattered or offended. I could pull out my own chair, but the gesture had been nice.

I picked up the paper menu and wrinkled my forehead. Everything was in Spanish. *I have no idea what any of this is, how am I supposed to pick something to eat? Okay, pollo is chicken, I remember that; thank you Ms. Alvarez. So maybe I'll order something with chicken.*

JD scanned the menu before laying it down. "Do you trust me to order for you?"

Narrowing my eyes at him, I considered his offer. Was he offering because he could sense I had no idea what to order or was he being chauvinistic and assuming I couldn't order for myself? "I thought you were here on vacation. How do you know so much about the cuisine?"

He shrugged, "I come here every year."

My eyebrow inched up my forehead. He must make a lot of money to afford a trip like this every year. While I wasn't poor, most of the money I had spent the last few years had been Daniel's. Even Junior Partners didn't make as much money as people thought. The realization that I was going to have to cut back on my spending habits when I returned home slapped me in the face. "Sure, order whatever you think will be good."

I placed the menu back on the table and removed the hat that I had donned after leaving Sammy. I placed it on the empty chair next to me as JD called the waitress over and ordered. Lifting my hair off the back of my sweaty neck, I twisted it up into a roll, so the cool breeze could the spot. With the other hand, I pushed a stray tendril behind my ear until I realized that JD was staring at me. My face flushed, and I released my hair.

JD dropped his eyes and cleared his throat. It was the first time he had appeared flustered. "So, are you seeing that guy from last night again?"

His question caught me off guard, and I leaned back in the chair and crossed my arms. It appeared I hadn't imagined his interest last night. "Were you spying on me?"

"No, just observing. I see guys like him come and go while I'm here every year. I didn't want you to get hurt."

"You don't even know me." Defensive walls shot up at his insinuation, and my arms pulled tighter to my chest. "What do you know about how I might get hurt?"

JD softened his voice, "I could see the sadness in your eyes last night. I sense that you are dealing with some pain, but guys like that won't make it go away."

"Guys like what?" I didn't know why I was arguing with him, I hadn't been that attracted to Owen, but my eyes narrowed to slits anyway as I dared him to continue.

"You know the kind I mean." He leaned back, folding his arms across his muscular chest. "Here for a week, hoping for a fling, never going to call again after that."

"Well, how do you know that isn't what I'm looking for?" It was a challenge, and I didn't even know why I was throwing it.

He considered me for a long moment, his eyes never wavered from mine.

What is he looking at? Frustrated, I broke his gaze and glanced away.

He leaned forward, propping his head on folded hands, still never shifting his eyes. "I don't think that's really what you're looking for."

I stared down at my wrists as I thought of the night with Brent again. *Maybe he's right; I can't say I'm proud of that night, but who could blame me? Still, who I see is none of his business.*

His words spurred my need to always be right and have the last word, and I raised my head, returning his stare and almost daring him to contradict me. "Well, as a matter of fact, I am seeing Owen again tonight for dinner."

Though he couldn't hide the flicker of surprise that flashed across his eyes, he managed to keep his voice even. "Ah, well, I am sure you can handle yourself, but do remember my advice."

Before I could retort, the food arrived. A colorful mix of red, brown, green and orange tantalized my eyes as the savory smell delighted my nose. My mouth watered, and I grabbed my fork, scooping up a mouthful, but JD's hand stopped my arm before it reached my mouth.

"Wait, can we pray over it first?"

"Are you serious?" I raised an eyebrow and stared at him, "You pray before you eat?"

"Of course, don't you?"

Lifting my chin, I pointed my nose in the air, "I don't pray at all; I don't believe in praying to a God who allows someone to experience intense pain."

"But you do believe in God?"

"I---" I stopped, unsure of how to answer his question. My forehead furrowed as I thought. Did I believe in God? "I don't know," I shrugged. "My mom does, and when I was young we went to church." A vague memory of entering a church, holding hands with my mother and father before they divorced flashed across my mind. "Maybe I used to."

"Well, I do believe in God, and I believe everything happens for a reason. I don't know what happened to you, but I do believe that God had a reason for whatever it was."

My body tensed as I clenched my fork, "Yeah? A reason to be stood up at the altar?"

JD cast his eyes down. "I'm sorry. That had to be painful, but yes, even in a situation like that; I think God has a plan for you."

"Well, let's agree to disagree on this point." I shook his hand off my arm and brought the fork back to my mouth. Across from me, JD closed his eyes and bowed his head but remained silent. I opened my mouth to take a bite; then sighed, put my fork down, and closed my eyes as well.

"Dear Lord," JD prayed, "Thank you for all the blessings you have bestowed upon us. Thank you for this food we are about to eat and for the hands that have prepared it. Thank you for new friendships, and Lord, please allow us to understand your reasoning regarding events that are beyond our control. Amen."

"Interesting prayer," I said, cocking my eyebrow at him when he opened his eyes. "Are you hoping that something will be revealed to me that will change my mind about who God is?"

The twinkle flared again in his eyes, and his lips formed a teasing smile, "I think it will in time."

"How could you possibly know that? You don't even know me." Why was I even continuing this conversation? I'd heard enough religious mumbo jumbo from my mother; I didn't need it from a stranger too. Yet, I couldn't muster the desire to leave. Not only was I physically attracted to him, but there was something else about him that intrigued me as well.

"Not yet, but I know God and even though I don't always know the way He works, I have seen people receive various truths from Him, and I know he works in mysterious ways that we don't always understand at first."

My gaze lingered on him a moment longer as I tried to decide if he were serious or playing me. Deciding it didn't matter for now, I returned my attention to the food and took a bite of the delicious dish, savoring the flavors that exploded in my mouth. I sneaked a glance at JD curious if he just had good taste or if somehow he knew exactly what I liked?

The rest of the meal was finished in a comfortable silence; and after lunch JD paid for the meal and escorted me back to her hotel.

"Thank you for having lunch with me," he said as they reached the front door. "I wish you well on your dinner tonight and the rest of your visit here."

He bowed slightly and before I could respond, he turned and walked back the way we had come, leaving me battling confusion over his baffling behavior.

I lay around the pool the rest of the afternoon pondering the time with JD. What was it about him? True, he was handsome with his toned body and tanned skin – I could picture myself enjoying being wrapped in his arms – but he was also obsessed with God, which I had no stomach for. So, why couldn't I get him off my mind? I'd probably never even see him again after leaving the Caribbean, but I couldn't shake the image of his face from my mind.

At four o'clock, I headed back to the room to shower and prepare for dinner with Owen, which I was no longer remotely excited about. For whatever faults he had, JD was right that I didn't need another man like Owen, but U had promised to go, and I didn't like reneging on my word.

I chose the new colorful maxi, which ended up hugging my hips, and a matching blue tank top I had brought with me for dinner. As I regarded the image in the mirror, I thought about changing because I didn't want to look too good and lead him on, but a check of my watch showed 6:02. Perfect. I hated being the first one when meeting people, but if I were any later, it would be rude. Exiting the room, I headed to the hotel bar to meet Owen.

The music spilled out of the restaurant before I even reached the entrance. *Well this isn't going to be the best place to have a conversation.* I scrunched my nose, coughing at the smell of cigarette smoke that permeated the air as I made my way toward the bar. Owen sat perched on a barstool, drinking a beer and surveying the crowd. His eyes lit up, and he lifted his hand in a wave when our eyes met. I took a deep breath, exhaled, and headed that direction. *It's just dinner, remember?*

"Well, hello gorgeous." He grabbed my hand and his eyes traveled my body up and down. It was a gaze that left me feeling dirty more than desirable.

The hair on the back of my neck bristled with his gaze. "Hello yourself." I flashed a tight smile and extricated my hand as politely as I could.

"Do you want a drink?"

"Sure; I'll have a Tequila Sunrise." I was going to need quite a few drinks to get through this evening.

After the drinks were ordered and poured, we made our way to a secluded booth in the back. The low lighting set a romantic air and since the booth was surrounded on three sides, only the general buzz and not specific words of the conversations around them reached my ears.

"So, why did you decide to become a lawyer?" Owen's eyes focused briefly on mine before trailing down to stare at my lips.

I placed a finger to my lips. Why had I become a lawyer? It seemed so long ago I wasn't even sure. "Well, I always loved arguing when I was younger, and TV made it look glamorous."

"Yes, it does. I bet you would be fantastic on TV." He placed his fingers on my arm and traced an imaginary pattern.

My skin crawled, and I grabbed my drink, dislodging his hand. "What about you? How did you get into . . . what do you do again?" I took a sip, but as soon as I set the drink down, his hand resumed its position.

"I sell insurance. My dad owned the company, and I joined him." He traced his fingers up my arm.

Stifling a shiver, I tried my best to ignore his hand. "You don't want to sell insurance?"

He scooted closer and laughed, "No, not at all, but the money is good, so why change?"

Something in that answer sounded so wrong, but I wasn't sure what. I loved money, too; it was one reason I had gone into law in the first place, though I wasn't at the point where I was making good money yet. Still, money equaled power which equaled happiness, right?

"So, how long are you here for?" Owen changed the subject.

I focused back on Owen and the current conversation. "Um, I'm here for about 20 more days."

He pouted his lip, "Well, I leave in five days, but I hope we can spend a lot more time together." As he inched closer, he winked and licked his lips. Unlike the wink that JD had thrown last night in the bar, Owen's wink was leering and creepy.

"Mmmhmm," I nodded, pursing my lips together and glancing around. How long had I been here? More importantly, how much longer did I have to stay before I could leave without appearing rude? As Owen continued rattling on about his work and his hobbies, I snuck a quick peek at my watch. 6:30, *ugh I am going to need more tequila if I have any hope of staying here much longer.* I caught the waitress's eye, and motioned for another drink.

Tuning back into the conversation long enough to hear "Nascar is like the best sport," I rolled my eyes and tuned out again. *Oh Lord, does he have nothing intelligent to talk about?* I stirred the straw in my drink and thought back to the afternoon with JD. He had been so easy to talk to and had intelligent things to say. True, he was a bit of a "Bible thumper," but so was my mother and perhaps I could loosen JD up.

I jumped as Owen's hand relocated from my arm to my knee. *I don't think so mister.* Picking his hand up, I smiled and placed it back on the table. Owen never missed a beat, just kept rattling on. My second drink arrived, and I downed it, sighing as the alcohol relaxed my muscles. *Maybe Owen isn't that bad, after all. At least he's cute and I could probably shut him up easily.* The third drink arrived, and my lids grew heavy. I shook my head and took a deep breath, opening my eyes wide, but the spinning room stirred nausea in my stomach, and I blinked them closed again.

"Another round?" Owen leaned forward.

"I shouldn't," I replied, pushing my glass away.

"Oh, one more won't hurt," Owen pressured, signaling the bartender.

"No really---"

"It's no problem."

"The lady said she's had enough."

The commanding voice sliced through my fog, and I raised my head to see JD standing at the end of the table. Though the rest of the world spun, my eyes locked on his, relief coursing through my body.

"Excuse me, but we're on a date here." Owen stood, squaring his shoulders and throwing his chest out.

JD didn't take Owen's bait. Instead, he crossed his arms and returned Owen's stare. "And it just ended." His words were cool but confident. He unfolded his arms and stretched out a hand, "Callie?"

I looked from one man to the next, mumbled an apology toward Owen, and took JD's hand.

"Whatever," Owen said and stomped away.

My world tilted as I stood up, and my knees buckled. JD wrapped an arm around me, and I leaned into him, placing one hand on his chest. I closed my eyes and took a deep breath. He smelled clean and salty like the ocean. Sighing, I laid my head on his shoulder as he led me out of the bar. There was a safeness and security in his arms. I couldn't remember the last time I had felt so protected.

"What's your room number?" JD asked, shaking my shoulder.

"103," I whispered, and my eyes closed again.

"Whoa, whoa, no falling asleep yet." JD shook a little harder this time.

It was a struggle, but I managed to keep my eyes open until we got to my door.

"Key?" he prodded.

"Somewhere in there," I mumbled and held out my bag.

He rummaged in the small purse until he found the key card, inserted it, and opened the door. Taking my hand, he pulled me into the room. The light clicked on and illuminated the room.

"Thank you." I turned to face JD and fell into him, placing both hands on his chest. His muscles quivered, and I bit my bottom lip, turning my face up to his as desire coursed through me.

JD stared down at me, closed his eyes, and took a deep breath. Then he grasped my upper arms and tried to turn me around. "You need sleep."

I doubled my effort, shaking off his hands. "I know what I need." My hands moved up his chest, enjoying the feel of his taut muscles beneath them, and wrapped around his neck. "Don't you find me attractive?"

JD sighed and removed my arms from his neck. He held both hands and stared into her eyes. "That isn't the issue, Callie. You aren't yourself right now; you've had too much to drink."

A seed of anger flared inside, and I yanked my hands from his. "I'm fine." The feeling of rejection was sinking in yet again, "You can leave now."

"Callie – "

"No, really," I crossed my arms, "You can go."

JD shrugged and sighed. "I'll be around if you need me."

"I won't need you." With the little sobriety I had mustered, I slammed the door behind him and threw myself down on the bed. "Why? Why is this happening to me?" I thrashed back and forth and pounded my fists on the bed. "I want my perfect life back and my Daniel back," I shouted to the room. I don't know who I expected to answer me; I just needed to get the words out. Grabbing a pillow, I covered my face and screamed into it. Slowly, the screams subsided to moans, and I removed the pillow, cradling it to my chest. "I don't even care about the affair. Just send Daniel back to me please. I want my old life back." I curled into a ball as the ocean of tears poured down my cheeks until I fell into a fitful sleep.

JD leaned against the hallway outside Callie's room and rubbed his temples. The urge to knock on her door and talk things through coursed through his body. He hated leaving angry words as the last words. He'd promised himself after Alexa that he'd never do that again.

The more important question was why did he care so much about her? He barely knew her, but there was something in her eyes that affected him. He wanted to ease her pain and make sure she never felt any again, but what if he never saw her after this? What if he had ruined his chance with her? He couldn't remember the last time he had been so affected by a woman. His hands shook as he ran his fingers through his hair. There was nothing more he could do tonight, so he pushed himself off the wall and forced his body down the hall to his room.

When his own hotel room door closed behind him, JD crossed to the nightstand where his Bible lay. He turned to the book of John in the New Testament, where he had been reading yesterday, but the words kept swimming together. His heart still drummed too fast in his chest, so he closed the Bible and got down on his knees. Placing his elbows on the bed, he folded his hands together and leaned his forehead against them.

Blackness filled his vision but words formed in his mind and flowed out from his lips: "Lord, I don't know Callie or what her pain is about, but I sense that her heart is hurting. I want to be a good example for you before her. Please help me find the words I need to say and help me be the witness you would have me be." He remained silent, listening for the still, small voice and hoping that tomorrow he'd get a chance to see Callie again.

CHAPTER 4

The ringing of my cell phone jolted me from sleep the next morning. Eyes still closed, I patted the bed until I found my purse and pawed through it until my fingers touched the phone. Pulling it out, I swiped the screen without looking at the caller ID. "Hello?" My voice still held the heaviness of sleep.

"Callie?" My eyes snapped open at the familiar voice on the other end, and I scrambled into a sitting position, instantly awake. "Callie? Don't hang up," Daniel's voice pleaded.

My heart thudded in my chest and my pulse quickened. Why was he calling? Had he broken it off with Shaina? My nostrils flared, and my grip tightened on the phone. "Why shouldn't I?"

"I . . . okay, you have a right to, but Callie, I think I made a mistake."

"You think?" My shrill voice echoed in the hotel room, and my hands began to shake. Heat flared inside me as my eyes narrowed to slits. "You bet you did."

"I know. I know," Daniel stammered. "I just...I guess I got cold feet, but Callie, I miss you. I can't concentrate or eat."

A small segment of satisfaction flooded me at his admission. I was glad he was suffering, now he knew how I felt. "What about

Shaina?" The poison in my voice matched the ice flowing through my veins.

He sighed, "That was a one-time thing, Callie. I never meant for it to happen, but you were always so busy."

"I was trying... to get a promotion... to junior partner... to make a better life for us," I spat, biting off the string of obscenities I wanted to scream at him.

"I know and I should have been more understanding," he paused, "Hey, did you get the partnership?"

"No," I snapped. "I couldn't concentrate either, and I made some stupid mistakes. I'm lucky my boss didn't fire me."

"I'm sorry. I should have handled the situation better."

"You think?" A pregnant pause ensued, and I held the phone out, my finger hovering over the "end call" button, I should just hang up on his sorry butt, but the memory of my late-night plea made me pause. Maybe he was sorry. He did sound remorseful, but could I trust him? Would I ever be able to trust him again? I returned the phone to my ear and plucked at some lint on the comforter, waiting to hear if he had more to say.

"Can I come see you?" he blurted out.

I sucked in my breath? Did I want him here? Yes, I missed him, and I had asked for his return, but did I really want it or had that been the alcohol and JD's rejection talking? "I...I'm not home. My boss told me to take some time off, so I changed our honeymoon tickets for a trip to the Caribbean."

More silence. "Then I'll come there."

"What?" My head shot up.

"I could use some time away too, and it's not like I can't afford it. Besides I think the time together would help us reconnect."

I chewed on my thumbnail as I thought about it. The biggest question was whether I could forgive Daniel or not. Maybe it had been a one- time thing; I had been working a lot of hours, but that didn't make what he did right. Plus, we had been together for three years; that was a long time to throw away, but could I take him back? And what would my friends and family say? I sighed; I knew exactly what they would say. They would tell me to kick the creep to the curb, but they weren't the ones in love with him. If she were going to give this a try, this would be the perfect place to take the first step, away from prying eyes and accusing or pity-filled stares of those who knew. "Okay, but you'll have to get your own room."

Daniel chuckled on the other end. "Okay, it's a deal; I'll be there in a few days."

As I hung up the phone, I wondered if I had just made a horrible mistake. I wasn't the type to give cheaters a second chance, but what if there was a God who had listened and heard my plea last night, drunk though it was? *What am I saying?* Rolling my eyes, I tossed the phone down. I didn't believe in God any more than I believed in the Lochness Monster or Big Foot. *I need to clear my head. I must be suffering from extreme hunger.*

I headed down to one of the hotel restaurants on the ground floor and chose a table near a window that faced the ocean. The waiter took my order of oatmeal and fruit and then left me with my view of the enormous ocean and the waves that ebbed forward and backward – endlessly lapping the sand and then returning. The water appeared peaceful today, like a shimmering sea of blue glass. I wished my mood matched the serene picture, but churning inside me was a ball of turmoil, partly from Daniel's phone call and partly from the previous night with JD. I had no idea why, but I didn't want that to be the last impression he had of me. *Maybe I'll take a walk outside; the fresh air would do me good.* When breakfast was finished, I placed a small tip on the table and wandered out the side door to the beach.

The warmth hit me first, and my face turned up to grant the sun's kisses. The hotel had been cooler, and the warm air pressing down on my body sent a shiver down my spine. I inhaled a deep breath of the still, salty air, invigorating my senses as I strolled to the water's edge. Slipping off my shoes, I dug my toes in the sand, enjoying the feel of the tepid water licking my ankles and tickling my toes. If only I could stay here where life seemed easier and clearer.

As I turned to the right, my heart sped up at the sight of the familiar figure. The strong shoulders and longer hair gave away JD's identity before he even turned around. I opened my mouth to call to him and then shut it again. Would he want to talk to me? I had been so awful last night, but at least this would give me a chance to apologize to him. I scooped up my shoes and jogged toward him.

"JD," I hollered when I was within ear shot. He turned, and his face brightened. Relief flooded through me; he didn't seem angry.

"Hello Callie." He smiled as I stopped in front of him, "Are you feeling better this morning?"

My gaze dropped to the ground, and I dug a toe in the sand. "I am so sorry about last night. That wasn't me."

He placed a finger under my chin, lifting it until my eyes met his. Up close, his emerald green gaze was even more arresting. I felt like he was staring deep into my soul. "I know it was the alcohol talking, but Callie, maybe you should stop drinking."

My chin tingled at his touch, and I licked my lips. The tingle was crawling down the rest of my body, which wanted to press against his. "Says the bartender who gave me a double my first night here." I had meant it as a joke, to lighten the desire I was feeling and to keep my arms from wrapping themselves around his neck, but his gaze remained serious. I cleared my throat. "The funny thing is that I rarely drink at all. This has just been a horrible week for me." His eyes never wavered from mine. How different he was from Owen who couldn't seem to keep his eyes focused on mine. The urge to lean forward and taste his lips blared in my brain, but I pushed it back.

"I was doing my job," he said finally, dropping his hand, "but your day must be getting better. You're smiling."

"Well, it might be." I tucked a dark strand of hair behind my ear and lowered my eyes. "My fiancé is coming to spend some time with me." I glanced up to see his reaction, unsure exactly why I cared.

JD's eyes widened, and his mouth parted. "Your fiancé? You mean the one who left you at the altar?"

"Well, yes," I stumbled, my toe twisting in the sand again, "but he called this morning and apologized, and maybe we can work things out." *What am I doing? He doesn't even know me and he's not convinced. Why did I say yes to Daniel?*

JD tipped his head to the side as he stared at me. "For your sake, I hope so, but I also hope you know what you are doing. Remember, Callie, sometimes things happen for a reason."

"Are you trying to tell me God planned for him to leave me?" I replied, taking a step back and lowering my brow. "Maybe Daniel's call was an indication that God wants us back together. I mean, I did pray for it."

"You prayed?" His eyebrows shot up, and his eyes gleamed.

I bit her lip. It hadn't exactly been a prayer. "Well, sort of. I asked out loud for certain things to happen."

JD's shoulders fell. "That sort of request isn't what God wants to hear from any of humanity. He wants to hear our plea for help and that we need Him to guide our lives. Besides, God isn't the only being who listens to the verbal requests and prayers we make."

"What do you mean?"

"I mean Satan also listens to what people say out loud, and he intends to interfere with God's plan for individuals – especially believers. That is the whole point of the book of Job in the Old Testament. If you haven't read it, you should."

My eyes narrowed, and I crossed my arms. Who did this guy think he was? Why couldn't he be happy for me, and why did I care so much what he thought? "Are you suggesting that my fiancé is only returning to me because Satan wants to hurt me?"

He held his palms out like a peace offering, "That's not what I said; I'm saying that Daniel's coming back to you might be Satan's doing to distract you from God's purpose for your life."

Uncrossing my arms, I moved them to my hips in a show of defiance. "Well, then why doesn't God stop it?"

JD cocked his head and gazed evenly at me. "You haven't asked him to, Callie. If you want God to influence your life, then you have to let him into your life. Jesus said that he will give us rest and carry our burdens, but we have to ask him to. We have to confess that he is Lord and that God raised him from the dead in order to be saved. Salvation is the starting point in having a working relationship with God."

I had no idea what to say to that. *Why does he have to bring God into everything?* The silence stretched out.

"Look, I head back to the states in a few days, Callie, but I'd like to show you more of what the island has to offer while I'm here, if you're up for it."

I paused for a moment. I was a little miffed that he couldn't just be happy for me, and I certainly didn't buy into his religious nonsense, but I did have some time to kill, and he had saved me last night. Plus, as much as I wanted to, I couldn't deny that I wanted to see him again. "Sure, I'd like that."

He smiled, "Great, I want to show you Dunn's River Falls. Why don't you change into an outfit you can hike in and meet me back at the hotel entrance in half an hour?"

We walked back to the hotel, parting at the front desk to go to our separate rooms. I changed into a pair of shorts and a crop top and then made my way back to the atrium to meet JD, who stood by the front door, looking quite handsome in tan cargo shorts and a green tropical shirt.

I pointed to the bag at his feet, "Did I need to bring a bag?"

"No, I packed us a lunch, some water, and my camera. Follow me." He led the way out the front door where a grey shuttle van was waiting. As he opened the door, I noticed five other people already squished inside, and my heart sped up. Only two spots remained in the far back, just enough room for JD and myself. The space was tight, and as he scrunched in, his skin pressed against mine from the top of my shoulder down to my foot. A tingling shot down my skin, and I breathed in his clean, masculine scent.

As the van pulled out of the parking lot, I sneaked a glance at him from the corner of my eye, but his gaze focused out the window at the scenery. I took the opportunity to study his features. While his face wasn't as chiseled as Daniel's, his strong jaw commanded attention, and his soft lips eluded gentleness. What would it be like to kiss them? Would they be soft and gentle or hard and passionate? *What are you doing? You can't fall for this guy; you agreed to give Daniel a second chance.* I forced my eyes from his face and stared down at my hands. What was happening to me? My whole life, I had always been so sure of what I wanted, and now I seemed to have no clue.

A few minutes later, the van parked and everyone tumbled out.

Though not extremely loud, I could hear the roar of the falls. *We must be close.* A sign near the parking indicated the direction to follow, and I fell in step beside JD as we climbed the path. "Have you been here before?"

"Yes, it's one of my favorite places, though it's much more fun to come with someone who hasn't seen it before."

His smile warmed my heart and caused another flush to spread across my face. The way he looked at me was so different from the way any other man ever had. I couldn't quite place the difference, but it made me feel special.

Trees and other green fauna surrounded us on either side as we continued up the gradual incline of the trail. My breath grew more ragged as the ascent grew steeper. I had thought I was in shape – I made it to the gym on average four times a week and walked the other days, but the incline was testing my endurance. Sweat broke out on my forehead and trickled into my eye. As I raised a hand to wipe it away, I bumped into JD's unmoving back.

"Why'd you stop?"

JD stepped to the side, and I gasped. The falls lay ahead. Clear blue water rushed over the edge, and white rocks peeked out from under the overflowing waves. The green of the jungle around complemented the blue and white foam making the view pristine and untouched. Breathless, I whispered, "Wow, it's beautiful."

He smiled and pointed to a large tree stump, "Come on, we can sit there and eat."

At the stump, he dropped his bag, and I sat down, enjoying the opportunity to catch my breath. He pulled out two turkey sandwiches, some fruit, and some extra bread from the backpack and laid them in the middle.

I grabbed a sandwich, unwrapping the saran wrap surrounding it. "Mmm, I am so hungry." I had the fresh bread in my mouth ready to bite down when I realized JD had his face lowered and his eyes closed. *Oh, good grief.* A sigh escaped my lips, but I lowered the sandwich and closed my eyes. "Okay, fine. Go ahead and pray."

"Lord, thank you for the beauty all around us. Thank you for making yourself known in the amazing things you have created. Help us to always keep our focus on you, Amen."

My eyes snapped open at the ending word, and I took a bite of the sandwich. *This is nice. I can't remember the last time Daniel and I did anything outside.* I cocked my head, thinking back over the last few years for a time we had gone hiking or camping or even on a picnic, but came up empty. Daniel and I both worked too hard to sit down and admire nature, and when we did go out, it was almost always to fancy restaurants or less-than-memorable parties, never outside enjoying nature.

My eyes turned to JD, who was chewing his own sandwich. Suddenly I was curious about him, the rest of him that I hadn't seen yet. Did he eat like this back in the states? Did he take his dates on picnics or romantic carriage rides?

"Where do you live?" The words escaped my mouth before I could stop them, and while he raised his eyebrow at the suddenness of the question, he didn't seem put off by it.

"New York."

"Do you like it there?" I couldn't reconcile my image of busy New York with this laid back man. Did he wear a suit to work every day or jeans and a button-down shirt? Did he take the subway or walk?

"Some days," he smiled, "Sometimes it's too busy for me, and I wish I lived somewhere a little slower and less intense, but right now that's where my business is, so that's where I am. Come on," he offered a hand to help me up and then pulled a camera out of his bag. "Stand over there." He pointed to a spot where the falls would be visible to my right and a crop of beautiful rocks would fill the background.

I followed his direction, feeling self-conscious as he raised the camera, pointed it at me, and clicked the button a few times. However, the more the camera clicked, the more relaxed I became.

"My turn," I said, reaching for the camera when he paused.

"I've got a better idea." He glanced around for a minute; then he placed the camera on a tall rock. He checked the view, hit a few buttons, and ran to my side. Leaning his face in close, he whispered, "Smile."

I would have smiled anyway. There was something about him that kept a smile on my face almost constantly, but I heeded his instruction, fighting the urge to turn and look at him. The camera's audible click reached our ears, and JD collected it.

I was hoping he would take another, so I would have a reason to be close enough to breathe him in, but he packed the camera and the leftover food and threw the pack over his shoulder. We spent the rest of the afternoon hiking around the falls, taking pictures, and admiring the view. As the sun set, we made our way back to the van.

Disappointment filled me as I opened the van door. I had been looking forward to another ride with JD pressed up against me, but some of the other people must have taken an earlier shuttle because only two people filled the backseat. Sighing, I climbed into the front bench seat. JD climbed in beside me, but without another person in the seat, plenty of room still separated us.

As the van pulled up to the hotel, I dared a glance at JD. His brown hair was tousled from the hike and the wind, and my fingers itched to touch it. Would it be as soft as it looked? What would it feel like between my fingers? I wondered if he found me as attractive as I found him.

He climbed out the van first when it parked and offered a hand to help me down. My pulse skipped as heat from his hand radiated up my arm, but as soon as my feet touched the pavement he let go. Why wouldn't he hold my hand? Was it because of Daniel? Why had I told him about Daniel?

I rubbed my arm and stared into his eyes. "Thank you; today was fun and so beautiful."

His gaze locked on mine and electricity crackled between us. Could he feel it too? "You're welcome. I have to cover a shift tomorrow evening at the bar, but would you like to do lunch?"

"I'd love that." My lips parted, and I raised my chin – my sign that I wanted him to kiss me. *Come on, kiss me.* I willed the words at him and his eyes dropped to my lips. My eyes closed waiting for the feel of his lips on mine, but nothing came.

JD cleared his throat, and my eyes snapped open. "Okay, well I think I'll call it a day." He brought his hand up in an awkward wave and lumbered off to his room.

I sighed and ran my hand over my face as I watched him walk

away. When I was sure he wouldn't change his mind and come sweep me up in a kiss, I returned to my own room. As I changed into pajamas, brushed my teeth, and climbed in bed, I couldn't help replaying the day in my head, though in my imagination, it always ended with a kiss.

The sunlight woke me again the next morning, and as I yawned and stretched, I realized I could get used to this not waking up to an alarm clock life. I folded my arms behind my head and stared at the exposed wood ceiling wondering what JD would have in store for today. A flurry of excitement fluttered in my stomach at the mere mention of his name and I stretched out my left arm out to glance at my watch. 9:05; plenty of time to eat breakfast and soak up some sun before meeting JD.

I pulled on my swimsuit and a cover up, grabbed an apple and a bagel from the breakfast bar, and continued to the crystal blue pool. A few other people lay in chairs, either reading or listening to music. *Why didn't I think to bring a book? It would have been a perfect time to read.* Choosing a chair near a table, I peeled off my cover-up and donned my sunglasses. I had just closed my eyes when a shadow blocked the sun from my face.

"Hey beautiful," Owen leered down at me. I rolled my eyes and bit my lip to keep myself from telling him to get lost.

"I wanted to apologize about the other night and see if you wanted to get some lunch today."

Fat chance, buddy. "I already have plans for lunch, sorry." *Now please go away.*

"Dinner, then?" He was clearly not taking the hint.

"I don't think so, but thanks for asking." I closed my eyes, signaling the end of the conversation, and his shadow moved away. I let out a deep breath and continued soaking up the sun's gentle touch.

A splash in the pool and the quiet buzz of conversation told me more people had arrived, but I didn't open my eyes to see how many. I hoped no one else would bother me, but a shadow appeared above me again, and I sighed. "Owen, I said no." My eyelids flicked open and I gasped. JD, and not Owen, towered above me.

"Good thing I'm not Owen then, huh?" JD's smile was mischievous. "Are you hungry yet? I have a great place I want to show you."

I lowered my glasses and cocked an eyebrow. "I'm not dressed for a restaurant," I said, pointing to my swimwear.

"You're dressed fine for where we're going," he said.

I sat up, pulled my coverup back on, and followed him. *Where on earth could we be going that a swimsuit is appropriate attire?*

He led us out of the pool and down a quiet street into a residential neighborhood. Small peach-colored houses lined both sides of the street. An old man on his front porch lifted his hand in a wave.

I returned the wave with a lopsided, self-conscious smile. "Where are we going?"

He held up a hand, "Wait." Just past the last house on the left side, a little shop sat nestled between the houses. Three tables filled the outside area, and a barbecue pit off to one side smoldered. Tree trunks cut in half circled the tables and served as other places to sit. "This is the best barbecue in town," JD led the way to one of the tables and pulled out a chair.

"Then where is everyone?" The other two tables hosted no one, and the slight rustling of the tree leaves was the only sound.

"We're early for a reason. Wait and see."

A dark-skinned woman with long dreads and a bright green dress approached the table. "Welcome JD, you having the usual today?"

"Yes, make it two please."

The woman nodded and turned back to the small store front. She hollered something in her language, unintelligible to me, and a male voice hollered back. Soon tantalizing smells began wafting to my nose, and people began to arrive. Within minutes, the other two tables filled, and more people arrived with chairs, seemingly out of nowhere. A dozen people now dotted the little yard, and conversation hummed around us.

The woman returned with two steaming plates of barbecue, rice, and beans. This time, my fork remained untouched as I waited patiently while JD prayed before taking a bite of the delicious food. At the first bite, flavors exploded in my mouth. Typical barbecue flavors, but something else as well. Closing my eyes, I rolled the food back and forth on my tongue, trying to figure out the mysterious taste causing my taste buds to dance, but it remained elusive. When I opened my eyes again, JD was starting at me. A blush colored my cheeks, and my eyes dropped to the plate.

"How do you know of all these places?" I glanced up at JD through lowered lids.

He smiled. "I told you I come here every year, and I try something new every time I do. The good stuff I come back to every year."

"I could get used to coming here every year." A small sigh escaped my lips as I picture JD and myself having every lunch and dinner together in this tropical paradise before retiring to bed. I imagined that he would be the type of guy who wanted my head on his chest, so he could wrap his around me while I slept. Desire coursed through me again, and I felt the first fingers of heat clawing up my face. A small beeping interrupted my daydream.

JD frowned as he touched his watch. "Drat, I have to get back and get ready for work tonight."

I smiled and bit back a laugh. *Did he say "drat?" Who says "drat" anymore?*

"I'll bring some travel books over tomorrow, and we can pick another place to go," JD finished.

"That sounds great," I replied and, after paying for lunch, we traipsed back to the hotel.

As JD headed one way, I meandered to the pool to finish sunning. My previous chair was still open, so I slipped off my coverup and reclined again, thinking back to lunch. I stifled another laugh at JD's anachronistic word and lack of cursing. When was the last time Daniel had chosen a different word when he was upset? For that matter, when was the last time I had? JD might be a religious nut, but he was also positive and optimistic, which I found refreshing. Perhaps that was what made him so enjoyable to be around.

*H*umming, I finished dressing and stood in front of the mirror applying makeup. My twinkling green eyes glistened back at me. I couldn't believe they were twinkling again. Just a few days with JD and the vacant stare was gone. I finished the lipstick and practiced a pout. Perhaps today would be the day he would kiss me.

A knock at her door sped my heart into overdrive, and my toes curled in excitement. *Right on time.* I skipped to the door, throwing it open, and beamed from ear to ear. "Come..." My heart stopped, and I stumbled back, covering my mouth with my hand. Instead of JD's long hair and muscular frame, Daniel's lean frame with close-cropped dark hair and blue eyes leaned in the doorway.

"Hey baby." His eyes traveled the length of my body as his arms reached for me.

I took another step back and gulped, "Daniel, hi, I, uh, wasn't expecting you so soon."

His smile faltered a little. "Well, that's not quite the greeting I was expecting. I took a red eye the night we hung up so I could get here right away. I couldn't wait to reconnect."

I blinked and tried to recover. "I'm sorry; I thought you were going to call first, but come on in." Grabbing his hand, I pulled him inside and then poked my head out and glanced down the hallway. No sign of JD yet. Sighing with relief, I closed the door and turned to Daniel. *What's he doing here so soon? He's going to ruin everything.*

He wrapped his hands around my waist and pulled me close. "How about a proper greeting?" His lips nuzzled my ear and began trailing down my neck. Pushing against his chest, I tried to extricate myself enough to keep from being in an awkward position when JD arrived. Daniel, not taking the hint, propelled me towards the bed. I stumbled, falling closer to him and breathing in his familiar scent. My resolve started to crumble and my arms found their familiar space around his neck, but a second knock jolted my head back.

"Oh," I gasped, pushing away in surprise. "That's my friend."

A flash of irritation distorted his features momentarily, but then his game face was back in place. He couldn't keep the annoyance out of his voice though. "Well, let's meet her."

I bet my lip and looked away. "Um, him," I mumbled. *Oh no, what am I going to say to JD, now?*

My heart caught in my throat as I opened the door. JD stood smiling on the other side. "Good morning friend; I brought the books." He held up a bag loaded with books.

I swallowed the lump forming in my throat. "Hi JD, come in. There's someone here I'd like you to meet."

Questions surfaced in JDs eyes, but he stepped inside; His smile froze at the sight of Daniel, and his eyes darted to me. Before I could stay anything, he painted a polite smile on his face and stepped forward with an outstretched hand. "Hello, you must be Daniel."

Daniel's eyes hardened to narrowed slits. His voice held the veiled threat of retaliation if JD didn't answer just right. "I am; and you are?"

"This is my friend JD," I said, jumping in. "He's been showing me around the island."

"Oh, well, thanks for taking care of my girl until I got here." Daniel stopped the handshake and put a possessive arm around my shoulders, pulling me close to him in a clear show of ownership. I glared up at him.

"It was my pleasure," JD replied, shifting his weight from one food to the other. "Well, um... I'm heading out, but I wanted to say good-bye and bring you these." I'd never seen JD look so uncomfortable, and I wished I had words to make it less tense.

JD put down the bag he was carrying and rifled through it a bit. He paused, seeming to consider something, and then came up with a few books and brochures. "I also found some books on the island's history you might like and some maps and brochures of the best spots to consider for exploring." He held the books out to me.

"Thank you." I ducked out of Daniel's grasp, grabbed the stack, and placed them on the dresser. The silence grew deafening as I glanced from one man to the other. *Someone say something.* JD and Daniel continued to stare at each other, like a pair of lions about to fight for the title of king. The palpable tension pressed in on me.

JD broke eye contact first. "Well, you guys have fun with what's left of your trip. It was great to meet you." His green eyes caught my gaze; unsaid words glistening in them. "Both of you." And then JD picked up his bag and left.

The door shut, and Daniel grabbed my arm, pulling me back to him. "Well, that was awkward," he leaned in to kiss my neck again, "Now, where were we?"

I pried his hand off her arm, "Hold on a minute, Daniel." Opening the door, I ran into the hallway after JD. "I'm sorry. I . . . I didn't know he was coming today."

JD paused and then turned around. His flat voice pierced my heart. "It's okay, Callie; I have to get back to the states soon anyway." He turned to leave.

"Wait." He turned back around, silent, as if waiting for an explanation. "I... I didn't want to leave it like this," I stammered, my heart pounding in my chest.

"Callie, you have a fiancé waiting for you," his shoulders dropped, "You should get back to him." Then JD turned and walked out of my life.

I stood rooted in the hallway, watching him leave. A tightness in in stomach emerged, doubling me over. What had I done? Would I ever see him again? Why did I care so much? Leaning my head back, I took a few deep breaths, before standing and trudging back to the room.

Daniel's rigid posture and folded arms greeted me when I crossed the threshold. "What was that about? Were you seeing him?"

I tensed at the biting tone in his voice. "It wasn't like that." Suddenly, a spark of anger flared inside me, and I took a bold step, jabbing my finger at him. "Besides who are you to question me? I'm still not sure I have forgiven you. You did sleep with my best friend and leave me, through a text of all things, on our wedding day."

He raised his left hand to ward off my angry advance. "Alright, you're right, but geeze Callie, it was one time, and I said I was sorry."

"I know you're sorry, but it isn't easy to forget an experience like that." My throat closed up, and I swallowed back tears.

Daniel's body relaxed as he took a step forward, "I understand, but I promise I will spend my life making it up to you."

I stared at him a moment longer; questions raging in my mind. Could he really change, or was this all an act? Could I care for him again? Daniel's blue eyes pleaded with me, and the wall of resolve chipped away. I took a step and let him wrap his arms around me, but I couldn't stop the thought that I was staying with the wrong man.

CHAPTER 5

Though not in the same way as JD, Daniel had been very attentive and enjoyable the final two weeks spent in the Caribbean. That no one knew who we were or what our past entailed had calmed my nerves, and I was almost able to imagine the time together was like a honeymoon.

However, as we headed back to my apartment in Mesquite, my unease grew. What would my friends say? What would my mother say? JD's reaction had been utter shock, and he had barely known me; how much worse would the reaction be of those who did?

Daniel squeezed my knee, "You're quiet."

"Hmm?" I removed the thumbnail I had been chewing from my mouth. "I'm sorry; I was thinking about what to tell people regarding what happened between us."

"Who cares what they say?" A note of agitation crept in his voice.

I scrunched down in my seat at his forceful tone. "That's easy for you to say, but you weren't the one cheated on and left alone at the altar."

His hands tightened on the steering wheel, and his jaw clenched. The vein in the side of his neck pulsed out. "How long am I going to have to keep apologizing?"

"I don't know," I said, my own anger building, "but try to see it from my side. If I had cheated, left you, and then come back, what would your friends say?"

Daniel relaxed his hands and flashed his charming smile. "They'd say I was lucky because you are so beautiful."

He knew I was a sucker for his smile, but I wasn't buying what he was selling today. *Quit trying to change the subject.* "I'm serious."

"Okay, okay, you're right. If you think it will help, I will apologize to any of your friends and family personally, okay?"

I nodded, but the pit of uneasiness extended its tendrils up to my heart cutting right through Daniel's flippant words.

As my apartment came into view, my heart lightened. It had been nice having some time away, but I was looking forward to the familiar. I carried my bag into the bedroom and began to unpack. Under all the clothes, at the bottom of the bag, the books from JD lay. I picked the top one up, opening the cover, but before I could read anything, Daniel entered the room and wrapped his arms around me. The book fell from my hand as he pulled me backward onto the deep purple bedspread.

"Ah, I've missed being in this bed with you. What do you say we refresh my memory of how much I enjoyed this?" He pulled me close, meeting my lips. Familiarity took over, and my body melted into his as his lips roamed down my neck.

A few hours later, I awoke with a start. Something wasn't right. I lay still for a minute, listening; then I jumped up and raced into the bathroom, reaching the toilet as my stomach heaved its contents out. *Whoa, what was that about?* I washed my mouth out and splashed water on my face, noting the paler-than-normal complexion as I looked in the mirror. After drying my face, I headed back to bed.

"Everything okay?" Daniel words were mumbled from the bed without even opening his eyes.

Irritation flared inside me as I crawled back in beside him. "I don't know; it might have been something I ate." I spent the rest of the day in bed, in and out of consciousness.

. . .

$\mathcal{T}$he feeling wasn't gone the next morning, but it seemed less intense as I lay in bed breathing. Deciding I was okay, I swung my legs off the bed and plodded to the closet.

Daniel came up behind me and pushed my hair to one side so his lips could have easy access to my neck. "Are you really going into work today? We just got in last night."

"I have to. I need to prove I'm still partner material, even though I'm going to have to wait a whole year to get it." I pulled my favorite black skirt off the hanger and ducked out of his reach so I could pull it on. It slipped on easily enough, but the zipper wouldn't go all the way up. "Ugh." I shimmied out of it, tossing it on the floor and reached for another skirt. It didn't fit either and neither did the third. Frustration surged through me. What was going on? Finally, an older skirt with an elastic waist slipped on.

"Eat a little too well while you were gone, did you?" Daniel asked, noticing my choice of skirts.

I wasn't sure if he were teasing or hinting that I needed to go on a diet, so I glared at him for good measure as I yanked a long blue shirt off the hanger that would cover the hideous elastic waist. It was not my usual put-together look, but it worked. "I'll be back later," I said, pushing past Daniel. "Don't make a mess while I'm gone."

Without kissing him goodbye, I left the apartment. I was miffed at his ribbing and contemplating if I already regretted letting him back in my life. JD would never have said something so insensitive. JD? Where had that thought come from? I hadn't seen him in two weeks. He was probably back in New York doing whatever he did there. Shaking my head to clear his smiling face, I focused on paying attention to traffic as I drove to her office.

Tina stood, smiling, as I neared the office. "Welcome back. How was your trip?"

"It was good.... and interesting." I thought about telling Tina I was back with Daniel, but the memory of her earlier reaction and opinion of Daniel flooded my mind. *No reason to face the disappointment in case it doesn't work out. I'll tell her in a few weeks if he's still in the picture.*

Tina raised an eyebrow, but didn't press the issue. "Okay, well the work is on your desk, in piles, and here are your messages."

As I reached for the messages, my stomach turned again. Clapping a hand over my mouth, I bolted down the hall to the bathroom, making it to the stall just in time.

When my stomach was empty and still, I gargled some water to lessen the lingering taste in my mouth and splashed some water on my face. The color of my face was not right, and there were splotches that had never been there before. *What is wrong with me?* I gave it a few more minutes to make sure there wouldn't be a repeat performance, and then I headed back to the office.

Tina's eyes were wide. "Are you alright?"

"Yeah, it's food poisoning, I think. It started yesterday when we got back. I feel fine otherwise though. In fact, I seem to have gained weight even with my frequent deposits to the porcelain god." I meant it to sound light – joking was a habit when I got uncomfortable – but the words sounded flat even to me.

Tina wasn't buying it either. "Food poisoning doesn't usually last that long," her voice oozed concern. "Promise me you'll go to the doctor if this keeps up."

"I promise." I flicked my hand, dismissing the conversation, and headed into the office to tackle the mountain of work. It hit me as I closed the office door that I had said "we" instead of "I." Thankfully, Tina hadn't noticed, but I would have to be more careful in the future.

My food stayed down the rest of the day, and I got so engrossed in work that I forgot my promise to Tina. I climbed in my car, planning to head to the gym, but Tina's words reared their ugly head and bounced around in my head, and instead my car pulled into a local emergency clinic.

I entered the small grey clinic, and a petite brunette with glasses looked up from the desk. "Can I help you?"

"I hope so," I said, signing the check in form on the counter, "I've been vomiting several times for the last twelve hours.

I figured it was food poisoning, but my friend thought I should see a doctor."

"That's probably a good idea," the receptionist agreed. "Have a seat, and we'll call you back shortly."

I sat down in one of the many empty chairs and picked up a magazine from the table next to me. On the cover, a couple on a beach lounged in chairs. It looked so much like the ocean in the Caribbean that my thoughts wandered back to that time. *I wonder what JD is doing now?* There they were again, thoughts of JD crowding into my head.

"Callie Green?" A short, stocky nurse with dark hair stood at the open door, clipboard in hand. Her eyes scanned the waiting room.

I set the magazine down and followed her into another small grey room. A computer terminal with a stool in front of it and one other grey plastic chair were the only furniture in the room. As I assumed the stool was for the nurse, I took a seat in the chair.

"Any fever?" the nurse asked as she began taking my vitals.

I shook my head. "I don't think so; I haven't felt hot anyway."

The nurse ran the thermometer across my forehead. "98.6, that's normal. Any other aches or pains?"

"No, but I just got back from the Caribbean. Could I have picked up something there that's made me sick?"

"It's possible." The nurse sat on the stool and began typing on the computer, filling in the electronic chart. "We will look at all the possibilities. Have you had intimate relations in the last month?"

I blinked, taken aback by the prying question. "What does that have to do with anything?"

The nurse paused her typing and turned her hazel eyes on me. "It could be significant if you've also been tired lately, have you?"

I shrugged. "Maybe a little more than usual, but as I said I just got back from vacation. I think it's probably jet lag, you know?"

The nurse looked at me again, raised an eyebrow, and then turned back to the computer screen. "Okay, well the doctor will be in soon." She exited, leaving me alone in the small room.

As I glanced around the bland room, I pondered the nurse's questions. Could she be insinuating an STD? I thought back to

High School health class. Was vomiting a symptom of any STD? Not like it mattered, Daniel and I always used protection anyway. He always claimed he wasn't ready for a family yet. I couldn't remember the last time we . . . and then the night with Brent flashed in my head. I sucked in a large gulp of air. What had that been, three or four weeks ago? Pulling out my phone, I furiously tapped the calendar app. *One , two, three...Oh no, I haven't had a period in six weeks.* My fingers touched my parted lips as a coldness erupted in my core.

The doctor, an older woman with greying hair but kind eyes, entered at that moment. She registered the shock on my face. "Are you alright?"

"Could I? I mean, is it possible . . . Am I pregnant?" The cold clamored through my insides sending a shiver down my spine.

A warm smile spread across the woman's face. "I was about to ask you the same question."

"We are always careful, but there was this one night...." I dropped my head as the guilt of what I had done roiled around in my stomach. It weighed on me like the heavy anchor of a large ship that had been thrown overboard.

"It only takes once," the doctor laughed. She picked up a small cylindrical container off the counter tray and handed it to me, "Here, provide me a urine sample, and we can know in ten minutes." After pointing out the bathroom down the hall, the doctor left. and I fought for air.

I brought my knees to my chest and wrapped my arms around them. *Oh no, not again. I can't be pregnant; I can't.* I was trying to make it work with Daniel; I was trying to become partner; and I was pretty sure the baby would belong to a man I had met once. Once! This wasn't me, and this definitely did not fit in my perfect plan. After a few calming breaths, I grabbed the plastic container and headed down the hall to the bathroom.

My hands were shaking as I unscrewed the lid and filled the jar. When finished, I set the cup in the cupboard that opened to a lab on the other side and washed my hands. Back to the small grey room to wait. The hallway seemed longer, like I was walking to a death sentence. My feet felt heavy and clunky, the way they feel when you try to run through mud.

I sat back down in the chair and stared at my watch, watching the second-hand turn, my mind blank. A knock at the door jolted me back to reality, and I raised my head.

"I have your results back," the doctor held a small white piece of paper in her hand. "Would you like to read them, or shall I give them to you orally?"

"Um, I'll read them, I guess." I swallowed hard and reached for the folded white paper.

"Here you go. Take your time, and I'll be back in a few minutes to answer any questions you might have."

I stared at the paper burning into my hand. The words on this paper could change my life. Icy fear returned, clawing up my neck. I took a deep breath and unfolded the paper. My eyes scanned it but no words registered until the all caps "PREGNANT." It mocked me with its capital letters. What was I going to do?

The doctor reappeared a few minutes later. "Have you had time to look over the paper?"

Inodded, unable to form words.

"I can tell this is a bit of a shock for you, but I don't think there's anything else wrong with you. Do you want information on options?"

"Options?" I asked in a haze, the words fuzzy in my mouth.

"You know, what to do about your pregnancy. My dear, you can keep it, put it up for adoption, or have an abortion. I can give you great names to consider for all three choices, if you want them," the doctor gathered some pamphlets from the clear plastic holder on the wall as she spoke.

Grey fog surrounded me, making my voice sound distant, "Okay, I guess I should take all three."

"It's still early in your pregnancy, so you have time to think about what to do, but if you choose abortion, you shouldn't wait too much longer." The doctor pulled a business card from her pocket and wrote names and numbers down on the back of it. "The first one is for a counselor if you decide to keep the baby and need help while carrying it. The second one is of a local adoption agency, and the third is an abortion clinic that is down on State Street. And here are some pamphlets to read about pregnancy."

I took the paperwork and stared at the white card, my mind still foggy. In a daze, I gathered up my things and left the room, moving on autopilot. I stopped only once, at the receptionist's desk to pay for the services, before leaving the building.

When I got to the parking lot, I opened my driver's side door, sat down, and shut the door. I put the key in the ignition but didn't turn it on. My hands shook on the steering wheel, and I stared out the windshield at nothing. What was I going to do?

Daniel had always stated he didn't want a family right away and I had agreed, because kids before age thirty had not been in my perfect plan, but was I sure Daniel and I would last? If we didn't, could I raise a child alone? I supposed I could put the baby up for adoption, but that would mean going through all the pain of pregnancy and gaining all that weight to give the baby to someone else in the end. I didn't know if I could do that. That left abortion. Though I'd always been "pro-choice" in general, I had never thought I'd have to make the choice myself. It couldn't hurt to at least look into it. I stared down at the card and found my fingers punching the number in my phone.

"State Street Clinic," the lady on the other end of the phone said after the second ring.

I jumped at the voice, though I didn't know why. Had I been expecting a machine? "Uh hi, I was hoping to get your address, so I could swing by and ask some questions."

"1400 State Street, and we are open till 7 P.M."

Fifteen minutes later, I pulled into the parking lot and stared at the small brick building. Was this really what I wanted to do? I exited the car and glanced around for a sign, but none hung on the building. I started up the small cement path, dotted only by a few trees and finally saw a small stenciling on the door that told me I was in the right place.

Just before the entrance, an older black woman sat in a wheelchair next to a green bench. She held a sign in her hands that read: Abortion stops a beating heart. I stared at her, and the woman returned the gaze. Then, she bowed her head. *Oh, no, not more prayers.* I hurried past the woman and opened the door.

The room was small, but comfortable looking with a few chairs and a TV on the wall. Two young girls looked up as I entered, fear evident in their eyes. A petite brunette with glasses and a messy bun sat at the desk answering the phones and typing on a keyboard. She finished the current call and glanced up at me.

"Can I help you?"

I rubbed the business card in my hand. "Maybe; I was given this number by a doctor to talk to someone about having an abortion."

"Have you decided to schedule one?" The lady tapped the mouse a few times to open a date book.

"Um, not yet. I don't really know much about them and was hoping you had some information I could read, to better understand the process."

"Sure, there are pamphlets over there you can take," she pointed to her left and returned to her computer, dismissing me at the same time.

I crossed to the wooden rack hanging on the wall, picked up a pamphlet, and sat down to read it. The pamphlet explained how the "lump of cells" would be suctioned out. I bit my lip and cocked my head to the side. *Lump of cells, is that all it is right now? And if so when does it become a baby?*

Returning to the desk, I tapped the counter to get the woman's attention, "Um, excuse me."

"Yes?" The woman didn't look up, just kept clicking on her computer keys.

"Does it hurt?"

"You might be sore for a few days, but it's not that bad."

I shook my head. "No, I meant does it hurt the baby? I mean will the baby feel pain?"

The woman stopped typing and turned a blank face to me. "It's not a baby. It's a lump of cells."

"So, when does it become a baby?"

The woman took a deep breath and then sighed. "When it's born; do you want to schedule?"

I didn't feel like I was asking dumb questions, but the abrupt response of the woman made me uncertain. "Um, I don't know yet. How soon do I have to decide?"

The woman pushed her glasses up her nose. "It's best to have it done before 12 weeks, but you can do it as late as 24 weeks, although if you wait that long the process costs a little more."

"Why?"

"Why what?" Irritation laced the woman's voice. She obviously did not enjoy all of my questions, which I found confusing. Weren't these people supposed to help me decide?

"Why does it cost more?" I repeated.

The woman dropped her head and picked at something unseen on her pants. "There's more to remove because the cells are bigger then."

I raised an eyebrow at her. What wasn't she saying? "Okay, thank you." The woman turned back to her computer and resumed her tapping.

I tucked the brochure in my purse to read it more thoroughly later. My analytical mind had begun to whir, and it wouldn't allow accept such hollow answers without research. I was glad Daniel had texted that he was working tonight because I didn't think I would be able to hide this secret from him for long and I wasn't quite ready to tell him about it yet.

"God has a purpose for your baby." The words pulled at my heart, and I stopped.

"Excuse me?" I asked, whirling to face the woman.

"I can see the pain in your face, but death is not the answer. This baby was made by God, and He has a plan for it."

Anger sparked within me. "Yeah, well it's my body, so I can do what I want with it," I snapped back and continued to my car. *Sheesh, why can't people keep their opinions to themselves?*

*O*nce home, I sat on the couch and pulled out the brochure again. The brochure portrayed the procedure as quick and easy, but questions swirled in my head. *If it isn't a baby yet, it wouldn't really be murder, would it? I mean I barely knew the father, and I doubt Daniel* *would stick around to support me and a baby by another man. This would be easier. I can pretend it never happened and get on with my life, and I'll never make that mistake again.* An odd sensation stirred in my stomach, but I put the brochure away, dismissed the thought, and headed to bed.

As I pulled back the blanket, a colored corner of something on the floor caught my attention. Bending down, I picked up a travel book. It was one of the books that JD had given me the day he left; it must have fallen from my bag when I was unpacking. Giving no further thought to it, I tossed it on the bed and plodded into the bathroom for my nightly routine.

As I brushed my teeth, I turned sideways and eyed my belly in the mirror. Was it really only a lump of cells? What would it look like? Was it a boy or a girl? I shook my head to clear it. No use thinking like that if I wasn't going to keep it. I finished brushing and flossing and then climbed into bed. The travel book caught my eye again and I opened it. A picture fluttered out, and as I picked it up, I gasped. The picture of JD and I atop Dunn's Falls stared back at me.

I traced his face and then looked at my own happy smile. Turning it over, I found a note scrawled in pen:

*D*ear Callie,
    I enjoyed our time together. I hope everything works out for you and your fiancé, but if it doesn't, please remember that you are loved by the God of Heaven. He loves you and is always looking out for you. If you let Him, He will bless you in abundant ways. I'm not leaving my number as it wouldn't be appropriate right now, but know that I will be thinking of you, will pray for you, and if it is in God's plan, then we will meet again. –JD

I read the note again and again as I thought back to the time spent with JD. He had been so different and so refreshing, but I wondered how he would react if he knew my latest news. He hadn't been like other men and he never seemed to want anything from me, but would he still find me attractive if he knew I was pregnant? Then reality crashed in again. Why was I even thinking about JD? Other than New York, I had no idea where he lived. I didn't even know his last name. The chances that I would ever see him again were abysmal. Sighing, I set the picture on my nightstand and turned off the light, falling into a fitful sleep.

*J*D sighed as he finished his dinner for one, yet again. It wasn't that he wanted to be alone, but after his last relationship he'd become pretty picky. The good news was that he was becoming a half decent cook. He had tried microwave dinners for a time after Alexa, but those had grown old quickly. Then he'd taken to dropping in to see his parents, right around dinner time, in the hopes of a home-cooked meal, but now they were in Florida and he was in New York, a little far to go for dinner. So, he'd taken up watching cooking shows in the evening after work and he'd learned how to make a few decent meals.

He placed his plate and utensils in the dishwasher and wiped up the counter. Walking into his living room, he sat down in his favorite blue recliner, turned on the TV, flipped through a few channels, and turned it off again. Nothing on TV appealed to him anymore. He picked up the book he had been reading from his coffee table, and his eyes landed on a piece of paper. It was his prayer list. *No time like the present.*

Scanning the list, JD sent up prayers for each name. When he finished, he placed the paper back down, but an unease in his stomach called him back. He perused it again; he had prayed for everyone on the list, but the feeling did not abate. *Did I forget someone?* He closed his eyes, trying to remember if he had forgotten to write one down, but nothing came to mind. Shrugging, he placed the list down again and froze. Images of Callie flooded his mind. He hadn't thought of her in weeks, but tonight the feeling was strong. He fell to his knees, and whispered a prayer for her.

CHAPTER 6

"Mommy?"

I woke up and glanced around trying to find the owner of the voice. A small girl, about the age of three, with long blond hair and blue eyes stood by my bed, little hands hanging on the edge.

"Mommy? Why didn't you want me?" Tears glistened in the girl's big blue eyes, and her lips formed into a pout.

"What do you mean?"

"Why didn't you want me? You had me in your tummy, and you let them cut me and suck me out?"

The anguish on the cherub face tugged at my heart, and my breath caught in my throat. "They cut you up? But, they told me it was a bunch of cells, not a baby yet."

"Mommy, I had a heartbeat and a brain. I felt everything they did to me. Didn't you feel me try to move away from that thing? Aren't mommies supposed to protect their children?"

"I..." I stammered, but no answer came. My forehead wrinkled; mommies were supposed to protect their children, weren't they?

The little girl's eyes dropped to look at her hands. "Was I not pretty enough? Did I make you mad?"

"Oh, honey, I wasn't mad. You are beautiful. I... I wasn't ready to have a baby, I guess, and it was my choice."

"What about my choice, mommy?"

Again my mouth opened, but no sound came out. I had never considered that question. I believed that what I did with my body was my choice alone, but here was this tiny life showing me that she too had a body and a desire to live. "I'm so sorry." The little girl was so beautiful and angelic. The child began to fade. "Where are you going?" I stretched out a hand to touch her, but the girl was too far away.

"I have to go, but mommy, I would have loved you; I really would have."

The girl faded, and I woke with tears running down my face. My eyes searched around the dark room, but there was no girl; it had all been a dream. I placed a hand on my stomach, but nothing moved yet. Could it be true?

I clamored from bed and retrieved my laptop from the desk. Taking it back to bed, I propped up some pillows and turned it on. Where to begin? I typed in "abortion procedures" and pages after pages filled the screen. The "procedure" was much more graphic than the brochure from the clinic had claimed. In fact, it seemed almost barbaric, but there was a non-medical procedure, a pill I could take if I was early enough. That seemed less awful until I read that the women were usually just sent home to have the miscarriage themselves. The thought of what I might see as I miscarried made that an unappealing option as well.

As I kept scouring, I ran across a page discussing side effects of abortions. *There are side effects?* I clicked the link and stories of women who regretted their abortions littered the page. There were stories of women having miscarriages or ectopic pregnancies after abortions and stories of women having hysterectomies in their mid-twenties because of previous abortions. Fear coiled in me like a spring. I didn't want a baby right now, but I did want one in the future. If I aborted this baby, would I have pregnancy issues later like these women? I tried to convince myself that there couldn't be that many instances of these complications because I'd never heard of any. The media certainly had never mentioned them.

I scrolled back to the top of the page and searched for abortion side effects. Again, links filled the screen. I clicked the first one, and my eyes devoured the page. Thirty percent? The spring coiled tighter. Thirty percent of women who had abortions went on to have reproductive issues including miscarriages, premature babies, and infertility? More than half of all women later suffered from mental health issues including depression and suicide. The coiled spring turned cold, and my mouth dropped open. How had the media never discussed these statistics? Wasn't it their job to give all the information? I bit the inside of my lip. Thirty percent wasn't the biggest number, but what if I wanted to have a baby in the future and couldn't?

The alarm blared beside me, causing me to jump and shut the laptop in surprise. Could it be time to get up for work already? My stomach still churned like I'd just gotten off a roller coaster, and the fear gripped ever tighter. *I'll have to tell Daniel about this and get his opinion. After all, it could affect him too.*

I wiped my palms on my skirt as I exited the car. Pulling my shoulders back to portray a confidence I didn't feel, I entered the coffee shop. Daniel stood at the counter ordering; I took a deep breath and marched up to him. As I touched his arm, he whirled to glare at me, but his eyes softened when he realized it was not some stranger.

"You're late, so I ordered for you already." Agitation colored his voice, and I cringed. This wasn't going to be easy.

I cleared my throat and swallowed a few times, "How was your morning?"

"It was awful." He grabbed a pastry and our coffees and led the way to the last empty table. A few other couples were in the small cafe, but singles with laptops comprised most of the crowd. "I had meeting after meeting that accomplished nothing. It was ridiculous . . ."

As he droned on about his frustration, I ran my finger along the coffee cup lid. I wished he didn't sound so angry, but maybe the coffee and pastry would relax him. A few nearby patrons glared at Daniel's loud voice before returning to their work. I continued listening, waiting for a softer side to emerge, but Daniel's posture never loosened. He checked his watch and rolled his eyes which I assumed meant he had to get back to work. It wasn't the perfect time, but if I didn't ask now, I might not get the chance.

"Daniel," I said, putting my hand on his arm to keep him from standing, "how would you feel about having a baby?"

He turned his mouth down and stiffened. "A baby?" The nearby heads popped up again, agitation in their eyes. His voice had not been quiet. "Did you not hear me talking about how stressful work was? A baby would make it worse. You aren't pregnant, are you?"

I bit my lip. This wasn't going as planned.

His nostrils flared and he lowered his voice to a harsh whisper, "Callie, how could you be so irresponsible?"

My teeth clenched together, "In case you forgot, it takes two people to make a baby."

He leaned back in his chair and stared at me. "I know that, but I thought you were on the pill. You were supposed to take care of that."

His words stung, and I drew a deep breath, sending back my own biting words, "Well, I guess in the whole leaving me at the altar thing, I might have forgotten to take them for a while."

"Oh, here we go again," he threw his hands in the air. "Is that always going to be your excuse? I left you at the altar?"

My eyes narrowed, "Well, you did, and it had repercussions."

"Look," he took a deep breath and ran a hand through his dark hair, "that event is behind us; it's water under the bridge, but surely you can see that a baby would not be good right now. We have to take care of us first. Get an abortion and be done with it. Then we can move on with our lives."

I looked down at my hands. Had he always sounded so callous and selfish? "I've been doing some research on the matter though, Daniel, and I found that thirty percent of women who have abortions either have trouble conceiving later or have pregnancy complications because of it. What if I can't have a child later, when we might want one?"

Daniel waved his hand and scoffed, "Thirty percent is nothing. Think about the seventy percent that aren't affected. That is a much bigger number." The wall of defense that I had built earlier began to crumble under Daniel's harsh words.

I leaned forward, splaying my hands on the table and playing my last card. "Yes, but don't you think it's a baby? Isn't it murder then?"

"Come on, do you think the Supreme Court would honor the procedure if it were murder?" he smirked. "It's a bunch of cells right now, so think of having an abortion like removing a scab from a sore."

My face wrinkled in disgust at the thought. "Still the procedure seemed pretty gruesome, Daniel; they cut the baby up and then suck it from the womb. I saw pictures of cut up little arms and legs online."

He flicked his hand, dismissing my concerns. "First off, those pictures are doctored; you can't believe everything you read online. Besides, you have to think about us, about yourself. Do you think you could make partner while trying to raise a baby? Then, there's the problem of our schedules – we both work long hours and would have no time for a baby. Wouldn't it be worse to raise a baby we didn't have time for?"

His words began to make sense in my mind. I didn't have time for a baby, and surely the mass in my belly was only cells right now; it was still early in the pregnancy. A small voice inside insisted again that it was wrong, but Daniel's words were louder and the fear of the unknown drowned it out. "Okay, I'll think about it again," I agreed.

He frowned, but let the subject drop.

*T*hat night I eyed the bed warily as I undressed. Though I still wasn't comfortable with the decision, I had decided the abortion did make more sense. All of Daniel's arguments were true, but the dream from the previous night continued to haunt me. I didn't want to see the girl again, my daughter? I didn't want to feel the guilt. Climbing into bed, I turned on the TV, hoping for some mindless entertainment. Though I fought sleep as long as I could, eventually my lids fell closed.

*M*y eyes opened to a clear blue sky and a field of white daisies. A small child's hand was encased in her own. I looked down to the top of a blond head. The girl appeared younger this time, maybe eighteen months, walking but not super steady on her feet. Her blue eyes locked on mine and then filled with tears, which streamed down her face.

"What's wrong, baby girl?" I picked up the girl and brushed her hair back.

"Why you not want me? Why you let them take me from you?" The baby's face scrunched and loud sobs escaped her mouth. I searched for words of comfort, but none came. This defenseless baby girl was crying because of my selfish choice, and I could say nothing to soften the pain.

I awoke covered in sweat this time. Was it going to be like this every night? What would happen when I had the abortion? Would the girl go away then? Or would I become like the eighty percent who had emotional repercussions? Questions paraded through my mind, one after the other. I turned the TV back on and watched infomercials till morning, trying to erase the beautiful face of the baby from my dreams.

*A*s I poured my third cup of coffee that day, I fought the emotional turmoil in my stomach. I had to schedule the appointment once and for all. I couldn't keep losing sleep like I had the last two nights or I would get fired. Picking up the phone, I dialed the abortion clinic and set an appointment for later that afternoon. I had expected a feeling of peace now that the decision was made, but a feeling of dread blanketed me instead.

I pulled into the parking lot of the clinic that afternoon after work and sighed. The same older black lady, who had been there before, sat by the front door. *Oh great, just what I don't need.* Locking the car, I ducked my head and strode past the woman. *Please don't talk to me. Please don't talk to me.*

"Please don't kill your baby." The woman's pleading voice reached me just as my fingers touched the door handle.

I stopped, heat searing up my spine. I turned and faced the woman, lashing out at her. "I'm sorry, but what business is it of yours?"

The woman cocked her head and stared at me. Her dark eyes contained a deep sadness. "Can I tell you my story?" She folded her hands in her lap, "And then I'll never bother you again."

I shifted from one foot to another and bit my lip. I didn't know this woman or care to hear her story, but my stomach was curdling again and something told me to give the woman a few minutes. "Fine, go ahead."

The woman paused, closed her eyes for a second, and took a deep breath. "My name is Sandra Dobbs. When I was twenty-five, I thought I had my whole life ahead of me. I was planning to be a nurse, but I made the mistake of being intimate with my boyfriend, Peter, and found myself pregnant. I wanted that baby, but we were young; he was a med student and he didn't have time right then for fatherhood. We fought for a few weeks, but in the end, he won, and pressured me into having an abortion."

My head fell forward, and my eyes widened. It was like this lady's story was my own. My hands curled into fists as the emotions battled inside of me. One part wanted to stay and hear the story, the other wanted to flea and pretend it had never happened.

"I knew I shouldn't have been intimate outside of marriage, and though I wanted a baby, I too agreed it wasn't the right time to have one, so I went through the 'procedure.' On one hand, I was relieved, but on the other, guilt plagued me afterwards. I became withdrawn and started drinking, and Peter and I split up. My drinking grew worse, but then I met a wonderful man, Henry, and he started bringing me to church. I stopped drinking for a time and told him I thought I had accepted God, but I don't think I really had. I hoped if I acted like everyone else that He would forgive me, even though I couldn't forgive myself. My life seemed fine; Henry proposed to me;

and we got married. For several months, I think I was happy, and then things changed. We couldn't get pregnant. After two years of trying, I went to a doctor to see what the issue might be. It turns out the 'procedure' had damaged my ability to ever have a baby."

I clapped my hand to my mouth. *Is she reading my mind? How could she know this is my biggest fear?* As my knees buckled, I grabbed the wall of the building to steady myself. The brick scratched against my palms, but I barely felt the pain.

"Well, my husband didn't know I'd had an abortion before we were married. In fact, I'd never told anyone but my closest friend, but I made the mistake of telling him about it on the way home from dinner that night. He was so upset in finding out that he lost control of the car and swerved into oncoming traffic, over-corrected, and sent us careening into a tree. The crash paralyzed me from my waist down and Henry suffered from a concussion and a pretty bad skull fracture. In one night, that "easy" decision I had made five years earlier produced a drastic result. It destroyed my baby and the life I wanted to have. For years now, I have wished thousands of times that I had just kept Isaac.

"You know your baby was a boy?" I shivered as ice slipped through my veins.

"I didn't at first, but then the dreams came."

My knees buckled again. "He visits you in your dreams?"

"Nearly every night." Tears shone in the woman's dark brown eyes. "At first, I hated those dreams because having an abortion was 'my choice,' and I didn't like the guilt that greeted me every morning when I woke up. Eventually though, I realized that those dreams were the only link I would ever have to the biological child I could have had. He would have been 35 this year, and sometimes in the dreams I get the sense he would have married and had two or three kids himself. Not a day goes by that I don't regret that decision I made so long ago. Now, I know what happened to me won't happen to everyone, but do you want to take the chance of experiencing that risk?"

I stumbled to the nearby bench and hung my head. My hands shook with the intense emotion flooding my body. "I don't want that to happen to me, but how do I keep this baby when my fiancé doesn't want it?"

"Do you know the Lord?" Sandra placed a warm brown hand on my shoulder.

I shook my head and sighed. "My mom does, I think, but how is that going to help me?"

"Ah child, God loves you and wouldn't want you to do anything against his will, so if your fiancé loves you, and if he is a Christian, then he shouldn't want you to do anything against God's will either. As for me, I have no doubt that abortion is against God's will. He has made us all in his image and if we destroy that image, then we are telling God He isn't important. Look... um... I'm sorry, what can I call you, dear?"

"Callie. Callie Green."

The woman blinked, and her mouth fell open. "Callie Green? Is your mother Melanie Green?"

I lifted my head to see the beginning of a smile stretching across Sandra's face. "Yes, she is; how did you know that?"

Her grin grew even bigger, her dark brown eyes sparkling. "Your mother goes to my church. She called me a few weeks ago and asked me to pray for you because your fiancé had left you. I've been praying ever since." Her face grew serious, "Is your fiancé back in the picture then?"

Heat flooded my face, and I stared down at my feet. "I'm not sure. He apologized and I thought he meant it, but now I'm seeing a side of him I never saw before, and I'm not sure I like it. Have you really been praying for me for weeks?"

"Yes; and so have the rest of the prayer warriors I'm affiliated with. There's about fifty of us; so you see, God must have a plan for this baby, because we didn't even know you were pregnant. In fact, God led me to pray double for you as I've prayed for you since the first time I saw you here, not knowing you were already on my prayer list."I stared at Sandra, eyes wide. "Why would you pray for a complete stranger?"

Sandra sat back, but her eyes still shone. "Well, because that is what Jesus commissioned us to do. As Christians, we are to pray unceasingly, and believers in Christ are to tell as many people about him as we can." Her eyes dulled and she stared down at her hands for a minute. When she raised her head, tears sat on her lids. "But I also prayed for you due to my own past. Because of my poor choice and its consequences, this," she pointed to the clinic, "is where I pray for the girls and women who come to make the same terrible decision I did. I see this effort as ministry before my Lord."

I tilted my head and raised an eyebrow. "How do you still seem so peaceful and happy after everything you have gone through?"

Sandra smiled, but it appeared smaller than before, and her eyes clouded over. "Life isn't always easy, dear. I still have many tough days, but Jesus is my peace. I pray to Him whenever I feel sad, and He eases my pain."

I thought of JD and how very much like him Sandra sounded. "I don't think I've ever known anyone so strong with so much pain in their past."

Sandra dropped her head. "I wasn't always strong. After the accident, I hit rock bottom. I reverted back to drinking, so I could dull the pain. I almost lost my marriage to Henry, but God sent Pastor Tony to us." She smiled, and her eyes glazed as she continued, "Henry forced me to go to counseling with him, and Pastor Tony showed me how my life could still have purpose. He and his wife, Margaret, showed me real love. I mean, the love of Jesus shone through that man and his wife, and he showed me how to pray. He even gave me a leather prayer journal, and this time I really did come to know God. They arranged an interview for a job so I could get back on my feet, and they connected us with an adoption agency. If God hadn't sent those two, I don't know where I'd be, but you see with Jesus, you can do anything. And remember, if your fiancé tries to pressure you again or gives you an ultimatum, and if you lose him because you don't do what he wants, Jesus will be there for you."

"Is that true, even if I'm not a believer in Him?"

Sandra's eyes crinkled as a small laugh escaped her lips. "Yes, even then, because He died for you. Have you ever heard of John 3:16?"

I shook my head. I couldn't remember the last time I had read anything in a Bible, though I was almost certain I had one somewhere at home, a present from my mother one Christmas. I hadn't bothered to read it, and I had always tuned out my mother when she began talking about the Bible, so even if I had heard the verse, I wouldn't remember it.

"Well, John 3:16-17 says: 'For God so loved the world that He gave his only begotten Son, that whoever believes in Him shall not perish, but have eternal life... God did not send the Son into the world to judge the world, but that the world might be saved through Him' He wants you to choose Him, Callie, he wants all of us to choose him, but it is your choice to reject or submit to Him while He waits at the door of your heart."

"I think I like what you're saying," I said slowly, surprised to find that it was true, "but I'm not sure I'm ready to make that decision."

Sandra folded her hands in her lap. "That's okay, dear; Jesus will be there when you are ready to decide. He never gives up on us. I'll keep praying for you, and so will the prayer warriors at my church."

I left the abortion clinic relieved and uneasy at the same time. The tightly coiled spring of fear in my stomach had abated with the decision to save my baby, even if I ended putting him/her up for adoption, but a new trickling of nervousness emerged every time I thought of telling Daniel my decision. Would he stay with me or would he leave again? And did I even care if he left? Lately I had seen a different side of him than before. Or had he always been so terse and demanding? Had I been so focused on myself that I hadn't seen the real him?

Sandra's words still rattled around in my head as I entered my apartment. I turned on the lights and headed straight to the bedroom. *I think my old Bible is somewhere in here.* Crossing to the bookshelf, I scanned the titles. No Bible. I tapped my cheek, furrowing my brow. *Now where did I put it?*

As I turned to the bed, the picture of JD and I called to me from the top of the nightstand. A tingle tiptoed down my back, and I crossed to the nightstand. There on the bottom shelf was the Bible, covered in a light coat of dust. I picked it up, wiping the dust off. As I held the book, the tingling flooded into my hands.

I sat down on the bed and stared at the Bible. Having no idea where to begin, I simply let it fall open. My eyes scanned the black and white page and focused on Proverbs 3 verse 5: 'Trust in the Lord with all your heart, and do not lean on your own understanding. In all your ways acknowledge him, and he will make straight your paths.' I stared at the words and read them again. If I trusted God, would he clear the difficult path ahead of me and if he did, what would that mean?

The sound of a key in the door pulled my attention from the page. Daniel. I snapped the Bible closed and placed it on the nightstand. After a deep, steadying breath, I headed to the living room to greet him.

"What a day," Daniel stormed in and threw his coat down on the couch.

My stomach clenched, and my hands shook slightly at my side. "Oh, was it not a good day?"

He rolled his eyes. "When is it?"

I stared at him wondering if he had always been so negative or if I had been wearing blinders and was just now seeing his true colors? I tried to think back to the last time I remembered him being positive, apart from our time in the Caribbean, and drew a blank. Instead, images of quiet dinners when we were both absorbed in our work appeared. Instances when I wanted to talk to him, but his focus had been on the sports game he was watching and his body language had portrayed that now was not a good time followed. *Was I ever really in love with him or was I just in love with the thought of him?* I took a deep breath. It appeared there would be no perfect time and now was as good a time as any, "Well, I had an interesting day."

"Do you have dinner ready?" Daniel interrupted me, glancing toward the kitchen.

"What? No, I... I must have forgotten about the time, Daniel; I'm trying to tell you something that's important to me. I went to the abortion clinic today."

He sat down and grabbed the remote, not bothering to look at me. "Oh, good, did you get rid of the problem?"

I winced at the harsh words falling from his mouth. Had I sounded like that? The image of me snapping at Sandra the first day flashed in my mind, and I cringed. I didn't want to sound like that anymore. "No, I didn't. I couldn't. Daniel, I believe it is a baby."

He glared up at me, coldness in his eyes. "I thought we'd been through this already."

Rage bubbled in my core, and I bit back the words I wanted to shout at him, taking a deep breath instead. "You had, but I hadn't. I've been having dreams – dreams of this beautiful little girl who is so sad. I think she's my daughter. Then, I met one today."

"One what?" he said.

"Remember when I told you that thirty percent of women who have abortions have reproductive problems later? Well, I met one of them today. She had one abortion, and then years later when she wanted to have a baby, she couldn't."

Daniel stood, his eyes fire, and I took a step back in fear. "That doesn't mean it's going to happen to you," Daniel advanced on me, and I took another step back unsure if he was going to hit me. He never had before, but I'd never seen him this mad either. "I thought I made this clear. I don't want a baby right now, and I'm not sure I ever will."

The words stung as if they'd physically slapped me. "What?" I had always thought two children were in our perfect plan together.

He took a deep breath, and his posture relaxed. "Look, Callie, I love you, but I don't want to be a parent right now. I want to be able to do as I please, go where I want when I want, and I don't want to be held back by a child's needs."

"Do what you want? Like have more women like Shaina on the side?" I spat. "I thought she was the problem, but now I see she was just one effect of your bigger problem." My hands balled into fists at my side, and my nostrils flared. How could he be so selfish? And why hadn't she seen this side of him sooner? "I'll tell you what, I won't hold you back any longer either."

"Come on, Callie, be reasonable. You don't need a baby if you have me." He flashed his familiar charming smile and held out his hands, but I wasn't fooled this time. For the first time in a long time, I was thinking clearly.

Flexing my hands, I took another deep breath. The steadiness of my voice surprised me. "I don't need you, Daniel; I thought I did, but I'm beginning to think I need Jesus instead."

"Wait, what?" His mouth dropped open and his eyebrows drew together. "Are you becoming a Christian too?" Disdain distorted his voice.

"I'm not sure yet," I replied, crossing my arms, "but this lady I met today was a much better example to me than you have ever been."

"Well, when you come to your senses, you know where to find me," Daniel picked up his coat and jammed his arms in the sleeves, "but not while you still have a baby."

He slammed the front door behind him, and I sank down on the couch dropping my head in my hands. Questions flooded my mind. Had I done the right thing? How would I deal with this pregnancy alone? My head popped up. My mom, of course; she was always there when I needed her. I pulled out my phone, but then paused, biting my lip. I hadn't even told my mom I was pregnant yet, but surely she would still support me. I tapped the numbers and listened as it rang. "Mom, can you come over? I need to talk with you."

CHAPTER 7

*J*jumped up from the couch when the knock sounded and flew across the room to open the door. "Oh, mom, I need your help." I stepped into my mother's bewildered embrace and squeezed her tightly.

"I know something has been bothering you," my mother said as we pulled back. "Why don't you tell me what it is?"

After shutting the door, I motioned her to follow me to the couch. "I've made such a mess of things." I took a deep breath and began the sordid story. "I was feeling sorry for myself after Daniel left, and I went drinking with Lexi. Daniel's coat was hanging by my door and it was mocking me, so I didn't want to go home."

My mother shook her head in confusion, and I tried again to make the words in my head make sense as they spewed out of my mouth. "I met a guy; he seemed nice; and he made me feel pretty." I glanced up under lowered lids, "I know I shouldn't have, but I ended up staying the night at his place."

My mother sucked in her breath, "Oh, Callie."

I held up a hand. "It gets worse, mom. Daniel contacted me while I was on vacation, and I agreed to give him another shot."

I hadn't thought my mother's eyes could get any wider, but they did. Still, she said nothing, letting me continue the story.

"Anyway, after we got back, I started getting sick. I thought it was food poisoning or something, but, mom, I went to a doctor, and I'm pregnant."

My mother's face froze, and her posture stiffened. I couldn't tell what was going on in her head. I waited for a minute, but she remained silent, so I continued, "Daniel wanted me to get an abortion."

She gasped and brought her hand to her mouth. "Tell me you didn't, Callie. Even though I wouldn't encourage a pregnancy out of wedlock, I would never want you to terminate it."

My chin trembled, "I was going to, but then I started researching the procedure and having dreams of this beautiful little girl, and I almost changed my mind. Then Daniel seemed to make so much sense about timing, and I went to the clinic, but I still wasn't sure; the final straw that changed my mind was Sandra."

"Sandra? What does she have to do with this?"

"She sits outside the abortion clinic, mom. She told me her story, and I couldn't go through with it. Then she said you asked her to pray for me after Daniel left. She's been praying for me for weeks"

"Thank heavens she was," my mother sighed. "So, is Daniel gone for good this time?"

I nodded and dropped my eyes, still battling the embarrassment of being conned. "I started to see his true personality, and I didn't like it. He was so callous, and he told me I had to choose between him and the baby, so I chose the baby."

"I'm glad, Callie." She squeezed my hands. "You may have made some mistakes, but that decision was very smart. Now, you need to find the father and tell him. He deserves to know, too."

I blinked in surprise. The thought of telling Brent had never occurred to me. It was too embarrassing to think about, but I supposed my mother was right. He did deserve to know. "I drove from his apartment the next morning, so his cross streets are still in my GPS, and I think I would remember his apartment. I'll go tomorrow."

"Don't go alone, and let's pray for God's hand to guide this situation from now on," my mother suggested.

I nodded, suddenly deciding that what I wanted more than anything was God in control of my life. "I think I'm ready now, mom; can you tell me how to pray to accept Jesus as my savior?"

"It would be my pleasure," she said, hugging me.

*A*fter my mother had gone, I plodded into the bedroom. *I wonder if she'll visit again tonight.* A smile tugged at my lips at the thought. If she came tonight, surely the dream would mirror the peace and happiness that I was feeling. As I brushed my teeth, I stared at my reflection in the bathroom mirror. Did I look a little different? I sure felt different. Now I understood why JD and Sandra had seemed so content. They must feel this same peace that was flowing through my veins. Why had I waited so long to accept God?

After I finished in the bathroom, I changed into pajamas and climbed into bed. I picked up the Bible, no longer covered in dust and spied the picture of JD. Turning it over, I read the message again. JD had been praying for me, too. *It can't be a coincidence, all those people praying for me at the same time.* I touched his face, feeling a tiny pang of regret. If only I hadn't let Daniel back in, maybe something would have happened with JD. I wondered if I would ever get another chance with him. With a small sigh, I replaced the picture and turned back to the Bible.

I turned the thin pages, realizing I still wasn't sure how to read the Bible with purpose. The word 'womb' caught my eye, and I stopped. "Before I formed you in the womb I knew you, before you were born I set you apart; I appointed you as a prophet to the nations." Jeremiah 1:5. What did that mean? I didn't feel like a prophet. What would I prophesy about? I filed the question in the back of my mind to ask my mother or Sandra about later and replaced Bible on the nightstand. Turning out the light, I placed my hands on my belly and pictured the life that was inside. Was it a girl as I had dreamed before? "Lord, whatever gender, please let this baby be healthy and help me to be a good mother."

. . .

I woke and glanced around; the field of daisies surrounded me again. I held a hand up to my eyes to shield the bright sunlight, and warmth flowed from my heart. The little blond angel frolicked through the flowers. She turned and smiled at me, then ran toward me. I scooped her up in my arms and breathed in her fresh scent as I whirled her around. She was older again this time.

The little girl placed two tiny hands on my face causing sheer joy to plummet through my body. "Thank you, mommy, thank you for choosing life for me."

I hugged the girl closer and caressed her soft hair. "I'm sorry I ever thought of ending your life before it began; I hope you can forgive me."

"Of course, mommy," the girl giggled. "Now, let's go get daddy." She wiggled out of my arms as I looked around.

"Who's daddy?" I asked.

"You'll see," the little girl called and ran towards a wide tree that I hadn't noticed before. As the girl neared it, an arm shot out and grabbed her hand. The tinkle of laughter carried on the wind and I held my breath, waiting for the face to appear from behind the tree.

Before the face became visible, an incessant beeping filled the air. As I turned to find the noise, the dream world shattered and my eyes opened to my bedroom. I pounded the bed in frustration. If only I'd had a few more minutes.

I found Brent's apartment without too much trouble and stood outside his door, paper in hand. I ran my empty palm down my jeans and stared at the door. Would he even remember me?

"You have to knock," Lexi said, nudging my elbow.

I smiled at Lexi, who had agreed to come after I told her the whole situation. I was pretty sure it was because Lexi felt guilty, but I was still thankful for the moral support in case the situation took an undesirable turn. I took a deep breath, calming the acid churning in my stomach, "I know." Bringing my hand up to the door, I knocked and waited, hoping that he wouldn't be home, but a lock clicked and the door swung open.

Brent stood in the doorway, clad in a pair of cut-off shorts and a white tank top, commonly referred to as a wife-beater, though I had never liked the name.

He looked from me to Lexi and smiled. "Well hey there, pretty ladies." Leaning against the doorframe, he tucked his hands in his cargo shorts' pockets. "Long time, no see."

I chewed the inside of my lip, swallowing the disgust building in my mouth. "Hi Brent; you're probably wondering what we're doing here."

"You back for seconds?" he winked at me.

I cringed and closed my eyes. *What did I ever see in this guy?* "Um, no. I'm here because I'm pregnant, and I thought you should know. I'm pretty sure you're the father due to the timing."

His swagger sobered up; he stood straighter and took a step back. "What?"

"Don't worry, I'm not asking for anything. You don't even have to be in the child's life, but I thought the proper thing to do was to tell you."

His face mottled with color as his nostrils flared. "I don't want anything to do with a baby."

"I'm not asking for anything from you," I sighed and rolled my eyes, "I just thought you might want to know."

He held out his hands as if warding off evil. "You do what you want, but don't come asking me for any child support."

My temper flared, and I sucked in my lips to keep it in check. "I won't, but I was hoping you could sign this." I thrust out the paper I had been holding in my hand.

"What is this?" he narrowed his eyes as he scanned it.

"It's the termination of your parental rights. It keeps you from having to pay child support, but also says you can't come back later and try to take the baby."

"Fine, whatever." He signed the paper in the appropriate spot, shoved it back at me, and slammed the door in our faces.

"Well that went well," Lexi smirked.

I grimaced, shaking my head, "Come on; let's get out of here."

CHAPTER 8

*J*D adjusted his dark blue tie in the bathroom mirror. He smoothed his hair back and patted his suit coat one more time. This ten o'clock meeting could open up an entirely new chapter in his life; one he had been thinking about and working on for a few years now. He took a deep breath and exited the bathroom.

The board room doors were closed when he arrived, which gave time for the kernel of unease in his stomach to grow. He knew most of the board members, but that didn't mean they would go for his idea. "Lord, send me the words and help them to see," JD whispered as he pulled the door open.

A large dark wooden table and thirteen black leather chairs were the only pieces of furniture in the almost entirely beige room. The members of the board occupied twelve of the chairs, and JD took a breath as twenty-four eyes regarded him. He sat in the remaining empty chair at the near end of the table and cleared his throat, "Welcome members of the board; I know this is a special session, but it's been weighing on my heart, and I feel like now is the time to move forward."

The members nodded telling JD to continue. "As you know, when my father built this company, one of his stipulations for success was that we always try to help those who are in need. As I watch the news each night, I feel like our country is in greater need now than ever before in a lot of areas, but the one that has been on my heart lately is crisis pregnancies. I'm not sure if my father ever told you my story, but I was adopted, and I've been feeling a need to set up a crisis pregnancy center that will specialize in adoption along with helping pregnant women find resources they need."

A few eyebrows went up at this news, but the other faces remained stoic. They were waiting for the details.

"My biological mother was too young when she became pregnant with me, and without my father's help, I don't think I'd be here today. He shared God's love with her and helped her find the resources she needed to carry me to term and put me up for adoption."

One of the women sniffed and dabbed her eyes.

"I sense that God is calling me to be that same voice for other women, and that is why I am asking for the board to help me fund a pregnancy counseling center in Texas, which I hope will be the first of many to come."

Fred, the longest standing member, leaned forward. With his white hair and bushy beard, he had often reminded JD of Santa Claus. "Why Texas?"

JD folded his hands on the table top. "Well, as you know, our culture is pretty divided on this issue, and not all places would be welcoming of a center like ours. Texas tends to be one of the more conservative states in that regard, and I'm hopeful that the community there will be more receptive. I am thinking we could set up our first center in Mesquite, which is outside of the Dallas Metroplex. I believe that location will attract many women, but it's still far enough outside the city limits that I hope the more liberal communities of the metroplex will leave it alone."

"I assume you have some specific property in mind?" Terry, another long-term board member, asked as he stroked his dark brown beard.

JD nodded, "Yes, I have checked out a few possibilities online and narrowed it down to three, but I'd like to fly out and inspect them in person. I have contacted a local realtor there, and he's offered to line up showings."

"And who will be managing this clinic?" Paul, the youngest board member, inquired. Paul was only a few years older than JD and head of the finance committee so JD knew that he was thinking about the dollar signs.

JD drew his shoulders back and let out a deep breath knowing this could be the make or break point. If they didn't feel the company could run without him, they might say no, but he had to chance it as he really felt God calling him to set up the center personally. "I will, at least to begin with. God's plan on that part isn't as clear yet, though I have no doubt he will reveal it in time. You all can manage the company while I'm away. You've done a great job so far. So... what do you think?"

"Why don't you step outside and give us a minute?" Fred asked.

JD's throat dried up. He had known the decision would require a decision, but he had thought he would be there for it. Nodding, he turned and stepped into the hall. The door swung shut behind him and he leaned his head back against the wall. "I've done my part, Lord. The rest is up to you," he whispered. A feeling of peace covered his head and slowly trickled down the rest of his body.

A moment later, the door opened and Fred motioned him back inside the room. All eyes were trained on him once again as Fred clapped a hand on his shoulder, much like his father used to when he was growing up.

"Well, I think I speak for everyone," Fred began, "when I say that your father would be very proud of you, and that we are happy to extend the money you will need for this project." Fred was the first to extend a hand for JD to shake, but the rest of the board members stood and joined the line, voicing their congratulations as well. The final kernel of unease fizzled out, and JD sent a silent prayer of thanks heavenward.

When he returned to his apartment that afternoon, the realization of the decision finally hit him. He looked around at everything he was going to have to pack. He had no idea how long it would take to get a center up and running, so he was planning on putting most of his items in storage and moving to Texas at least temporarily. Of course he had a few things he had to wrap up here first, including finishing out his current lease, which bought him a couple of months.

He hated the thought of losing his rent-controlled apartment, but he was no longer sure New York was where he was supposed to be. Even before he had met Callie, he had been feeling restless, like he was being called elsewhere, but after meeting her, the feeling had intensified. When she had mentioned she lived in Texas, the place where he had often thought of opening his first center, he had thought maybe it was a sign that they were meant for each other, but then her fiancé had re-entered the picture and shattered that dream.

He picked up the picture of the two of them he had placed on his bookshelf and perused her face again. Though he knew it was a long shot, he had realized long ago never to assume something was too big for God, and as she kept popping into his mind he had to assume that their paths would meet again.

CHAPTER 9

a s I dressed for work the following Monday, I was still smiling and felt lighter than I had in a long time. The meeting with Brent had gone about as good as could be expected, but I had the paper signed now, so he couldn't come back and try to take the child. That in itself gave me a measure of peace, but I'd also gotten the chance to share my story with Lexi over lunch. While Lexi hadn't been convinced she needed Jesus, she had agreed to try church with me the next day.

At church, I'd been able to thank Sandra for playing such a pivotal role in my life, and I'd been able to introduce Lexi to her. I didn't know why, but I had this feeling that people who met Sandra eventually accepted Jesus. She just had this air about her. Sandra, ever the enigmatic one, had smiled and given the credit to God, but I knew my decision had given her heart some joy.

My life was not turning out the way I had planned, but I was pretty content with where it was going so far. The only regret I had was JD. I couldn't change the past, but I now believed that prayer could change lives and so every morning and every evening I prayed for God to send JD back into my life.

I spared a look in the hall mirror on my way out the door and smiled at the change I saw even in myself.

"Well, what happened to you?" Tina asked as I approached the desk.

My smile deepened at the thought that my transformation was so evident. "Follow me into my office, and I'll tell you." Tina's brow rose, her curiosity piqued.

With the door shut, I spilled the story of my trip, my breakup, and my pregnancy, ending with my acceptance of Jesus into my heart.

"Oh Callie, I'm so excited for you. I've been praying for you since I started working here," Tina wiped tears from her eyes.

My eyes widened. "You have?"

"Of course," Tina nodded, "I want you to be in Heaven with me when I get there. I had an all-night prayer vigil with the Lord the night I suspected your pregnancy. I was concerned you were so focused on your career that you would choose an abortion."

I blinked as Tina's words sank in, "I can't believe how close I came to doing just that, and I can't believe how many people were praying for me when I didn't even know what was happening. I hope I too can become a prayer warrior like you and the others who have been praying for me."

"I think God has big things in store for you, Callie," Tina smiled. "Now tell me more about this handsome man you met there."

I sighed. "I wish I could, but I never even got his last name. I messed that up so badly."

"Don't worry about it. I thought I had messed things up when I first met Gary, my husband. I told him I wasn't interested and tried to date his best friend. He ended up moving across the country, but eventually he came back and God brought us back together. I think if you are patient, you'll find that God can do anything. Just remember to pray about it and be open to God's prompting."

I nodded and hugged the assistant that was quickly becoming a friend. Next on my list was Lexi. Though she had gone to church, I could tell she still wasn't ready. I'd call her today and see if she wanted to do lunch again. With that settled, I sat down and faced the pile of work on my desk.

CHAPTER 10

Three Months Later

*T*he taxi dropped JD off in front of the bed and breakfast he had researched online. The pictures had not done justice to the quaint Victorian house. The steps creaked a little under his footsteps, but the porch was clean and homey. Two wooden rocking chairs sat in front of the large window.

He pushed open the cream-colored door and stepped into the homey front entrance. A small brown desk filled the area just to the left of the carpeted stairs. The older woman manning the desk looked up as the door closed behind him. Her dark hair had some strands of grey, but she was still a beautiful woman.

"Welcome to the Parson House," she said. "Do you have a reservation?"

"Yes, under the name of Peterson."

She tapped a few keys in her computer and then flashed a smile at him. His breath caught in his throat. Her smile reminded him of Callie's the day they had taken pictures at the falls. Of course lately nearly every woman he saw reminded him of Callie in some way or another.

"Yes, room 202. I hope you'll enjoy your stay. Do you need help taking anything to your room?"

He shook his head, both in answer and in an effort to clear the image of Callie from it. She smiled again and handed him a key.

"Up the stairs and first room on your right. The bathroom is just across the hall."

Thanking her, he grabbed his bag and stepped up the stairway. The room was decorated in browns and golds, giving it a masculine feel. A single queen-sized bed filled most of the room, but a small dresser hugged one wall, and a squat nightstand sat next to the bed. It wasn't much, but it only had to be home for a few days until he found an apartment.

He unzipped his bag and pulled out his Bible. The realtor was showing him three buildings tomorrow and he wanted to be sure his mind was clear and focused on his purpose.

CHAPTER 11

"Mom, are you ready? I'm hungry." I patted the belly that was just starting to protrude past my pants. Luckily, I was still able to work out, though modified, so I hadn't gained too much weight.

"Why don't we just eat here?" my mother said, gesturing to the small dining room to the left.

I rolled my eyes. "Mom, you eat here nearly every night. Let's go out somewhere tonight."

She shot a glance upstairs before sighing and gathering her purse. "Okay, I was just hoping the handsome new check-in might be at dinner. I think you'd like him."

"Mom, I don't have time for a man right now and really, who's going to want a pregnant one? He'd have to put up with all my cravings and mood swings and get nothing in return." That wasn't entirely true. I did want a man, but only one specific man that I had no idea how to find.

"A good Christian man would understand," my mother insisted.

"And I'll find one, but right now I'm a little swamped with work and preparing for a kid."

Though my words were confident, as we stepped into the

evening air, I did wonder when God would provide the perfect man. I had been praying for months, and while I wasn't getting discouraged exactly, I was beginning to wonder how much longer I would have to wait. I knew it was a long shot that I'd ever see JD again, but surely there had to be more men like him that God could send.

*J*D had scoped out three buildings and settled on a small office building in the middle of town. It seemed to have everything doctors would need; it was centrally located; and it was affordable.

JD surveyed the rooms one more time and nodded. "I'd like to pray about it, but I'm pretty sure this is the one I'm going to want. Can you draw up an offer for me Scott?"

"Of course, but do you think God cares about which property you buy?"

"God cares about everything I do, and if I decide this without him, the business may not succeed."

Scott smirked and scoffed, "Wow, you must take this God thing seriously."

JD turned serious eyes on Scott. "I do. God has had a hand in my life – from day one, and when I follow Him, things always go better for me."

Scott tilted his head, "Can I ask what you mean?" There was no condescension in the words, just an honest question.

JD smiled and laughed. "Where do I begin?" He pointed to a nearby table with chairs, and the two men sat. "Well, I guess at the beginning. My mom was 15 when she became pregnant with me. When that happened, everyone told her to have an abortion because she was so young and having a baby would ruin her life. One day, she met my father at the coffee shop where she worked. As he had opportunity, he spoke to her about God. Then he told her how he and my mother wanted a baby more than anything but couldn't get pregnant. One day, after several conversations, he invited her to church and explained to her who Jesus was and what He did for her.

She accepted Christ as her Savior and decided to let my father and mother adopt me.

"That was the first time God intervened in my life. Later on, when I was twelve, I was hit by a car. The accident should have killed me, but after a policeman helped me up, I barely had a scratch on me. I gave my life to God that very day and committed to follow him from then on. However, years later, when I got to college, I met a girl. I knew she wasn't a Christian and that God didn't want me involved with her, but I ignored Him. Soon thereafter, my life fell apart when I got involved in drugs, drinking, and partying. Then I flunked out of college and of course the girl I fell in love with, well, she ended up breaking my heart. At that point, I was at the end of my rope; realizing I could not effectively govern my life; I went back to God and then joined my father's company. As I began to pray for its success, it grew in size. Next, I began to pray for something bigger to be involved in and God put a calling on my heart to establish pregnancy counseling centers. Therefore, given my level of success in prayer so far, I'm going to pray about this location and ask God to bless it."

Scott sat back in his chair and raised his left eyebrow. "So, because you had one bad relationship you think God was punishing you?"

JD smiled and shook his head. "No, He wasn't punishing me. God has a plan for all believers and when we don't follow his plan, we won't receive the blessings He wants to give us. I decided that I'd rather be blessed than suffer from fighting against Him. Besides, I want to honor Him in all that I do."

"So, are you saying that if you follow God, he will make you rich?" Scott placed his hands on his knees and leaned forward.

JD laughed. "No, I said blessed, not rich. Being blessed isn't about money; blessings can come in many ways - for the rich and poor alike. The company I represent is one blessing; the feeling of peace I have when I wake up every morning is another. God can and does bless His children in so many glorious ways one cannot begin to count them all. We need to look for them to see what they are."

"Well, being blessed does sound good to me," Scott leaned back in his chair. "But how do you know when God is calling you? I've been to church a few times, but God never spoke to me."

"God works in many different ways to call people to salvation. He works through preaching, through print, radio and TV media, and through a one on one witness from a believer. Unbelievers come to Christ when they are convicted of their sin through one of these means and realize they need Him to be their Savior because they cannot save themselves.

"Once a person becomes a Christian, the Holy Spirit, who fills the hearts of believers in Christ, often uses a still, small voice when He speaks, so a Christian has to read the word of God, pray for guidance and be quiet long enough to sense His leading. That's the hard part. Sometimes God even moves in your life by reminding you of something you need to do. It might be something your mind keeps coming back to, like starting counseling centers has been for me. I've been thinking about this goal and looking into it for a few years now and even though I couldn't do anything about it previously, the thought has always been there."

Scott nodded and rubbed his chin with his right hand. "I think I'd like to know more about what it's like to be a Christian. Can we get together in a day or two for coffee?"

Warmth flooded JD, and he smiled. "Of course, I'll be staying in town until the project is done. Would you like to meet on Thursday, say at 10 am, at that coffee shop right over there?" He pointed at the Cup O'Joe across the street.

Scott opened his satchel and grabbed his schedule book. He flipped a few pages and nodded "Sure, it looks free, so I'll see you then."

Sighing, I pushed open the door to my apartment. It had been another long day, and though I didn't stand all day, my feet still managed to ache by the time I got home and tonight they were throbbing fiercely. Dropping my purse by the couch, I shuffled into the kitchen to boil some water for tea.

When the tea kettle whistled, I turned the stove off and poured the water into my cup of tea. Enjoying the warmth, I carried the cup to the living room and lounged on the brown suede couch to rest my weary feet and read. I set the tea cup down on the end table and picked up my Bible. The crinkling sound of the thin pages brought a smile to my face.

As the pages separated, my eyes landed on Ecclesiastes 3. "To everything there is a season, and a time to every purpose under the heaven: 2 A time to be born, and a time to die; a time to plant, and a time to pluck up that which is planted; 3 A time to kill, and a time to heal; a time to break down, and a time to build up; 4 A time to weep, and a time to laugh; a time to mourn, and a time to dance; 5 A time to cast away stones, and a time to gather stones together; a time to embrace, and a time to refrain from embracing; 6 A time to get, and a time to lose; a time to keep, and a time to cast away; 7 A time to rend, and a time to sew; a time to keep silence, and a time to speak; 8 A time to love, and a time to hate; a time of war, and a time of peace."

The words reminded me of a time months ago when JD had told me that everything happens for a reason. I hadn't believed him then, but I knew now that I probably wouldn't have given my life to God if I hadn't gotten pregnant. He had taken that mistake she made and turned it into something wonderful. As I rubbed my belly, I thought back to the time I had spent with JD. *I wonder what he's doing now and if I'll ever see him again.* I sent up a short prayer for JD wherever he was and then resumed my reading.

CHAPTER 12

$\mathcal{I}$ entered the doctor's office at 9am. Butterflies tumbled in my stomach; today was the day I would find out for sure the gender of the baby.

"Morning Callie," the perky brunette receptionist greeted me.

"Good morning," I smiled back, signing in on the sheet.

"Are you ready for the ultrasound?" the receptionist asked.

I touched my stomach, smiling as the baby moved against my hand. He or she had started moving a few weeks ago, and I still couldn't get over the sensation. "I sure am." *Though I'm pretty sure I already know the gender of this one.* I sat down in a brown chair and waited to be called back in the room.

"Are we waiting on anyone?" the technician asked when I was called back.

"No," I raised my shirt and lay back on the cold hospital bed. "It's just me."

"Okay," the blond technician pushed her glasses up her freckled nose. She grabbed the tube of gel from the tray by the bed. "Sorry, this will be a little cold." I flinched as the cold gel hit my stomach. The technician grabbed the wand and began spreading the gel around.

"So first, I'm going to take pictures, and then maybe we can determine gender if you want, and if this little one cooperates."

Grainy black and white images began to appear on the screen and I drew in a quiet breath. While I wasn't sure what each picture was, I could easily pick out the baby's head.

I glanced at the technician and weighed whether the woman would be offended by the question I wanted to pose, "Can I ask you a question?"

"You want to know what everything is?" the technician laughed. "Everyone does."

"Well, yes, but that wasn't my question. It's kind of personal I guess, but I wanted to know how anyone can look at an ultrasound that clearly shows a baby like this and then choose an abortion."

The technician stopped for a minute, lowered her voice, and leaned in. "It's not my area, but I honestly don't know either. You see this here?" She pointed to a grayish part at the top of the picture, "That's your baby's brain, fully formed and full of pain receptors like ours. And here?" she moved the wand, "baby's feet. Ten perfect toes by the way. I know some people say fetus, but I've done so many of these; they are all babies to me."

I smiled at the young blond. "Don't worry, I won't tell your secret," she winked.

"Would you like to know gender now?" the technician smiled back.

My heart sped up as I nodded eagerly. "Well, I'm 99% sure it's a girl, but I wouldn't mind the verification."

The wand circled some more and I held my breath. "Well, it's always a little harder to determine with girls, but I'd say your inclination is correct."

"Does everything look okay? I mean is she okay?"

The technician patted my arm, "She looks great, and I'll print out some pictures you can take with you."

As she stepped out the room, I wiped the rest of the gel off my stomach and returned my shirt to its proper position. Relief flooded me with the knowledge that the baby was okay. My hand touched my stomach again. *A girl. I knew it would be a girl.* The technician re-entered with several black and white photos of the little life that was inside me. As I held them, a warm sensation spread from my head all the way to my toes. I studied each one carefully, marveling at how much I could see. Hands, feet, heart, brain, profile. There was no doubt in my mind now; this was a baby. My baby. My Hope.

*A*bout the time I was beginning my ultrasound, JD was meeting with Scott at a nearby coffee shop.

"So what did the big man upstairs say?" Scott joked as he poured his tall frame into an empty chair. The shop was relatively slow, so they had their choice of seats.

JD smiled and sat across from him. "Well, I prayed, I listened, and I'm 98% certain this is the right building for us." He lifted his cup and took a sip of his coffee.

"Only 98%? Why not 100?" Scott cocked an eyebrow.

"I would never confess to know 100% of God's plan. There is still a lot of my old ways in my head that try to mislead me, so even though I try hard to make sure I'm hearing what He is saying, I can never be completely sure I'm not at the same time influencing myself a little."

Scott raised his eyebrow and leaned forward. "You really are into this God thing, aren't you?"

JD smiled and took a sip of his coffee. He could tell that Scott thought he was a little nuts, but he was used to that. "God has been there every time I needed him. And besides, it's nice to know where I'm going when I die."

Scott blinked and took a sip of his coffee, "What do you mean?"

JD set his cup down and leaned back in his chair a little. "Well Scott, there's only one of two places any of us can go to after death. Those who have a relationship with Jesus will get to fellowship with him in Heaven - forever. Those who don't . . . well, the Bible says that when they stand before God He will say: 'Depart from Me, I never knew you' and that statement will earn a non-believer a one-way ticket to a place that is nowhere near heaven. It's a place where men and women will forever be separated from Him."

Scott's mouth fell open before he could catch himself. "Do you really believe in a Heaven and Hell, JD?"

"I do, and believe me, the Bible's description of Hell is a place no one would want to go and that's why we believers work so hard to tell people about Jesus."

Scott narrowed his eyes and glanced around the coffee shop. JD followed his gaze, but the coffee shop was just getting busy and no one seemed to be listening. "So, you're saying, if I don't choose Jesus, I condemn myself to Hell and you are trying to help me prevent that by telling me about him?"

JD nodded and picked up his drink again. "I think everyone deep down inside knows that God exists, Scott. I mean, how else did we get here? Scientists don't even buy the whole amoeba theory anymore because they can't recreate it. No one can because God made us in His image, according to the book of Genesis. So, whether anyone talks to you about Jesus or not, you choose to reject Him by default, because you do not follow your suspicion and try to find out about Him for yourself. You did not pursue the truth to see if He exists. You simply choose to ignore Him and continue to follow the world's thinking on the matter and thereby, you turn your back on God and you must live with the consequence of that decision."

Scott leaned back, sipping his coffee. JD could tell that his words were having an effect, but he wasn't sure what effect. He wished, not for the first time, that he could read minds. "So, are you telling me that almost everyone today is wrong?" Scott finally said.

JD held up his hands, palms out. "Look, I'm not to judge; only God can do that. I've done a lot of things in my past that I'm not proud of, but what's going on in our country today is not what God wants for America. As a nation, we removed Him from schools and kids started killing each other. We allowed sex education to be taught in schools, and now we hand out condoms instead of teaching kids to wait until after marriage to have sex. Scott, this country was founded as 'one nation under God, indivisible,' but we have become divided because we as Christians haven't been standing up against the atrocities that have been occurring over the last several decades of time. We let them continue and hoped that somebody else would do something about it, but no one has. God destroyed earlier cities for practicing things we praise today, and I don't know how much longer He'll keep watching all of the evil we are not confronting before He feels the need to cleanse the Earth again."

Scott gripped his cup tighter. His eyes darted around again. JD's words were obviously making him uncomfortable "You don't really believe he will wipe the Earth out, do you?"

"Actually, I believe He can and someday will. You see, God had the Bible written to tell us about Him; about what has happened, and will yet happen. While He hasn't told us when the end will come, He has told us to be ready for what will precede it- the rapture of God's children – the removal of believers from the earth will occur first. Then the world will be thrown into seven years of horrible tribulation. After that, there will be one thousand years of peace on earth because Jesus – the Son of God will for that time period reign over everything. God did reveal some signs in the Bible that let us know when the end time is getting close and some of those signs are happening now. There's a lot of debate about the signs and what they mean, but one or two that are very clear are that the world will have the power to destroy itself, which we do now with all our nuclear weapons, and there will be worldwide communication because, at one point, two prophets of God will be killed and will lie in the streets for three and a half days for the whole world to see them.

"Now the world hasn't been introduced to these prophets yet, but we're technologically advanced enough that when they die, they will be seen by everyone in the world at once. Plus, Christians will be persecuted, and that also is happening now. Finally, Jesus said that once these signs begin, the generation of that day will not pass away before He returns to govern the whole earth. Now, of course, we aren't sure how long a generation is in God's eyes, but it seems that if these prophecies can now be fulfilled - they soon will be."

The color drained from Scott's face, and his shoulders dropped as leaned forward. "So what happens to the rest of the population when the believers are taken from the world?"

"Well, no one knows for sure, but did you ever read the Left Behind books?"

"I'm not much of a reader," Scott admitted, "more of a football fan."

JD could tell Scott was trying to make light of the situation. "Hey, I like football as much as the next person, but this is about eternity. I'll tell you about the books someday or loan you mine; I tend to think something along those lines is what will happen. First, many will die in crashes because driving believers will disappear. Airplanes will spin out of control or crash for the same reason. Second, those who live will see other signs. They will see a man claiming to be God and doing miraculous things, and they will have to decide whether to take his mark on their body or chose to follow God instead."

Scott scratched his chin. "So, people could still get saved during that time?"

"I believe so, but Scott, please don't wait. What if you are left behind and you die because believers who were responsible for you have disappeared? That's a lot to hedge a bet on."

Scott nodded and sipped his coffee. His eyes stayed focused on the beige cup in his hands and JD couldn't gauge his reaction. He held his tongue as the seconds ticked by, giving the man time to think.

"You're right." Scott raised his eyes. The humor was gone from them, replaced with a serious expression. "You've definitely given me a lot to think about."

Relief flooded JD. This was always the hardest part of being a believer – sharing with non-believers. He didn't like telling people they might be wrong, but he didn't want their souls on his conscience either. It had taken him years, but he was finally feeling more comfortable sharing the word. "Look, let's sign the papers, and then why don't you find a church nearby and we'll go together this Sunday?"

"Deal," Scott agreed.

I tapped the steering wheel, impatient at the long line. Rotating my wrist, I glanced at the face of my watch. Ten minutes left. I was going to be late, and I hated being late. If I wasn't sandwiched between two cars, I would have just backed up and foregone the drink, but a car had pulled in right behind me, and now I had no place to go. My thumbnail returned to my teeth. I had to kick this nervous gesture before I chewed my nails completely off. Maybe if I texted Tina, she could stall until I returned.

As I reached for the phone in my purse beside me, two men exited the coffee shop. The broad shoulders and chin length hair grabbed my attention and my breath caught in my throat. It couldn't be.

Forgetting the phone, I craned my head to follow the man as he walked to the cars in the parking lot. He had the same gait, the same grace, but what on earth would he be doing in my town?

A horn blared behind me, returning my attention to the line I was in. The car ahead had moved, and I inched mine up to fill the empty space. I glanced back for the man, but he had disappeared into a car, and I had no idea which one.

Frustration roared again, and I pounded the steering wheel with open palms. I couldn't lose him again.

The line moved again, and I forked over my money, no longer caring about the steaming chai tea I placed in the cup holder before exiting the drive-thru and returning to work.

"You're late," Tina hissed as I approached the desk.

I slapped my forehead. I had forgotten to text Tina and ask her to cover. "I know; have they started?"

A smile broke out on Tina's face. "No, I told them your appoint ran late, but they're waiting for you."

"Thank you," I mouthed and turned to the hallways that led to the conference room.

"Wait, don't take your drink."

I had forgotten the tea was even in my hand. "Here, it's a chai tea. Enjoy."

Tina blinked in surprise, but took the outstretched cup, and I continued to the board room.

The other members of the small team were already inside. Issuing a quick apology, I pulled out the open chair and sat down. The stiff back made it impossible to get comfortable. Discreetly, I tried to adjust and switch positions.

Jeff, the man heading the team, began speaking, but his words flew by my ears. My thoughts were still on the man at the coffee shop.

There was a chance that it hadn't been JD. After all, the country was huge and last I knew he was in New York, but if it had been him. . . If it had, I had to find a way to run across him again, but how?

"Does that work for you, Callie?"

The sound of my name cut through my interior monologue, and my face heated as I realized I had not been listening. "I'm so sorry; I was distracted. Can you repeat?"

Jeff sighed. He had never been a fan of mine, probably because I had once beaten him at a case and then rubbed it in his face – I should apologize for that. He had fought to keep me off this case, but hadn't won. "I asked if you could handle researching previous precedent."

"Yes," I nodded, determined to keep my mind on the discussion for the rest of the meeting. "I can handle the research."

"Perfect." Jeff turned his attention from me and continued detailing his plan. To keep my mind focused, I retrieved a pen and a small notepad from my bag and took notes on the rest of the meeting.

"Thank you for covering," I whispered to Tina at the end of the day. Tina was busy putting the work in neat little stacks for the next day, which was one reason I loved having her as an assistant.

I'm not sure Tina had always been so organized, but when she had first started working for me, I had insisted that everything always be in neat piles. It was the only way I could work, and Tina had promptly conformed without complaint.

"You're welcome." Tina placed the last paper and then neatened the pile before looking up. "Thanks for the tea. What happened by the way?"

"I think I ran into my past."

Tina's face clouded over and she crossed her arms. If this was the face she used on her children, I could see why they behaved so well the few times they had been in the office. "Don't tell me it was Daniel."

"No." I stole a furtive glance to the left and right to make sure no office gossip lingered nearby. "I think I saw JD."

Tina squealed and then clapped a hand to her mouth as I shushed her. "Sorry," she said softly. "Are you sure?"

"I'm not. I just saw him for a moment while I was waiting in line at the drive-thru – what a dumb idea that was – but that build was hard to forget." My face warmed at the thought of JD's muscular frame and the solidness of his chest. "Now, I just have to find a way to find him again."

"Do you know what he does? Maybe we could check out some of the similar companies and see if he is doing work for them here."

I mentally kicked myself for my previous self-absorbed attitude. "I don't," I sighed. "All I ever knew was that he owned a business." Why hadn't I asked him more questions about himself?

Tina's eyes held the same question, but she was nice enough not to voice it out loud. "Let's pray then that God finds a way for you to meet. After all, if it is JD, the Lord brought him here."

Tina had the knack for always finding the positive. Though I was growing daily, I was still floundering in some areas and seeing the silver lining was one of them, but Tina and my mother seemed to have it down. I hoped one day it would become second nature for me as well.

After another secretive glance – praying at work wasn't forbidden, but it could cause problems – we whispered a prayer and then walked out of the building together. I waved goodbye as we separated at the parking lot. Tonight was my mother's night off from the inn, so she was making dinner at home. Though not a bad cook myself, I still loved her mother's cooking. It reminded me of a simpler time in life.

My mother's old Ford Taurus was in the driveway of the small yellow house when I pulled up. An old tattered rope swing still hung lopsided from a branch of the sole tree in the front yard. I remembered always begging my mother to go outside and swing on that swing. I hadn't known it then, but I realized now it had been my coping mechanism after my parents split. On the swing, I could pretend to fly to another world where daddies never left and mommies never cried.

I parked the car and stepped out. The grass covering the rest of the yard was a faded yellow and crunchy under my feet as I walked up to the front door. I'd have to remind my mother to water the yard or see if I could afford to hire someone to do it all the time.

Twisting the front handle of the faded white front door, I stepped inside. The smell of Mexican seasonings flew through the air, mingling with the sound of meat browning in a skillet. That meant burritos or tacos, my favorites.

I closed the door behind me and crossed through the living room to the bright airy kitchen. Mother had decorated it a few years ago in a country type flavor with blue gingham prints and pale yellow cupboards. I was more a fan of contemporary style with dark cabinets and lighter countertops, but my mother had been insistent.

"Hey honey, how was work?" My mother turned from the stove at the sound of my footsteps. The house was so old that many of the floorboards creaked. It was impossible to sneak up on someone. I had found that out the one time I had tried to sneak out to a party in High school. My mother had been up before I even hit the front door, and I had been grounded for two weeks after. I hated the floor back then, but now it brought comfort.

"It was okay. I have a new research project on my plate that is going to mean some late nights of work." I situated myself in one of the barstools, leaning back as far as I could to stretch my ever-increasing belly. People did not think about pregnant women when the made straight-backed chairs.

A line of worry etched across her face. "Are you sure you want to keep doing this job? Those long hours can be hard when you're pregnant, and they'll be impossible once she comes."

"I know mom, but I'm not sure what else to do yet. I might as well stay as long as I can because the money's good and will sure help out when Hope comes." My mother's worry had been the same one running circles through my mind. The late nights were taking a toll on my health, and I knew I couldn't continue them much longer, but not many companies were looking to hire a woman five months pregnant. Still, I kept my ears open and perused the ads daily on my break. I'd definitely have to find another job once Hope arrived, though I would definitely miss Tina.

The worry didn't fade completely from my mother's face, but she nodded and turned back to stir the meat.

I traced my finger across the ecru bar counter. "Mom, do you believe in coincidences?"

"What do you mean, honey?" With the meat at the temperature she wanted, my mother lowered the flame and turned to the bar where a cutting board held a few tomatoes and some lettuce. She picked up the knife and began slicing the ripe red fruit.

"This afternoon I could have sworn a man I met while I was in the Caribbean was at the coffee shop." I smiled, remembering the waterfall and the van ride that had allowed me to jostle against him, and a tingle ran down her spine.

"I take it you liked him."

I sighed. "I did, but I didn't realize it back then. Then Daniel called, and I was so confused that I took him back. JD, that was his name, left, and I thought I'd never see him again. But a few months ago, I found a travel book he had given me the day he left and inside was a picture of us and a note; then the other night when I was reading, I ran across a verse that reminded me of him. And today, I could have sworn he was at Cup O' Joe."

"Did you talk to him?" Mother chopped the tomato slices into squares, scraped them into a bowl, and grabbed the head of lettuce.

"No, I was in the drive thru lane, and he was getting in his car. There wasn't time." I dropped my head into my hands, all my confidence from my earlier talk with Tina fading.

"Well, I don't believe in coincidence," my mother smiled. "See, God knew us before we were born and had a plan for us, so I tend to think that God has a hand in everything that happens in our life, including things we might see as coincidences."

"That's basically what Tina said – that God brought him here, so maybe we are destined to meet again."

She smiled back at me. "What do you think Callie?"

"I think I'm going to continue to pray about it and ask God's wisdom." A wistful smile crossed my face, "but I have to say, I don't think I'd mind if JD were in my life."

As my mother chopped the lettuce, I regaled her with stories of the few days I had spent with JD. With every detail I remembered, I felt more and more sure that my mother was right – I had met JD for a reason.

*S*unday morning, I woke up with butterflies zooming around in my stomach. Last month, I had decided to get involved at church, and this morning I was going to be singing on stage with the choir. A part of me was excited because I had always loved singing, but another part of me was still worried about what people might say. No one had said anything out loud to me, but a few people hadn't been able to keep their eyes from wandering to my left hand in search of a ring as my belly began to show. Mother and I had agreed to tell people as they asked instead of making a blanket announcement. As this would be my first time on the stage, I hoped to be a blessing and not a distraction.

The baby turned, sending a fluttering sensation through me. Lately, Hope seemed to read my moods and react to them. Placing a hand on my belly, I rubbed in a slow circle to soothe her. "I know girl, but I think it will be okay." Turning my face heavenward, I whispered a soft prayer. Peace flowed over me and the fluttering in my stomach calmed as well.

❦

*A*cross town, JD was meeting Scott at Cup O'Joe.

"Did you pick a place you'd like to try out?" JD picked up one coffee and handed it to Scott before grabbing the next one.

Scott shrugged, "Yeah, I mean I don't know much about it, but according to all the events its website listed, Mesquite View sounds interesting enough to visit and it's right down the road."

JD nodded and took a sip of his coffee. The hot liquid was perfect, one sugar and just a hint of cream. "Well, let's give it a shot. I've often found that a church either feels right or not quite your style."

The coffee shop was mostly empty, so they had their choice of table. Scott picked one by the door and JD followed him. The unease radiated off Scott in the way he never set his drink down and took a sip every few seconds. JD wanted to allay his fears, but he knew that sometimes it was best just to be quiet and let God work.

However, when Scott finished his drink first and began turning the cup in slow circles on the table, JD decided his energy would be better spent in moving.

"Is the church close enough to walk?" JD downed another sip, but he still had half a cup of coffee remaining. Sine he couldn't stomach the thought of throwing away perfectly good coffee and he was pretty sure the church would have a trash, if not some other place along the way, he decided to take the rest of his drink with him.

"I think so." Scott pulled out his phone and swiped the screen. He tapped a few times and pulled up a map. "Yes, it looks like it's right around the corner."

"Wonderful," JD said, holding the door open for Scott as he threw his empty cup away. "Let's walk."

The wind whipped leaves around them as soon as they stepped out of the wind block the restaurant had offered, and JD pulled his coat tighter around himself.

How different Texas was from New York. Fewer people crowded the streets and the sun appeared closer and warmer, even in the dead of winter. Small mesquite trees lined the sidewalk, but there weren't tall buildings obscuring his view as they strolled. JD took a breath and realized even the air smelled different.

As they turned the corner, a large brick building came into view. The church along with its front and back parking lot covered a quarter of a block. Three large crosses sat atop the middle roof. "It's a pretty big place," JD said as they crossed the crowded parking lot. A few people milled around the front entrance conversing with each other and greeting people that approached.

An older gentleman with a bald pate but a white fluffy beard and mustache trundled their direction. He was dressed in a black suitcoat, pants, and a blue tie. JD hoped they wouldn't be too underdressed in their dress slacks and button down shirts. "Welcome," he said and handed them a program.

Another man opened the door for them, younger and with a full head of hair. JD was relieved to see he wasn't wearing a suitcoat, though he did still have on a tie. "The sanctuary is ahead, and the bathrooms are around that corner. Have a great morning."

JD nodded back, and he and Scott filed into the large sanctuary. A stage with a piano, guitars, and a drum set adorning it stretched across the front of the room and a large cross stood on the left side. White screens behind the stage and on either side flashed announcements. Instead of pews, rows of padded chairs filled the room, separated into three sections. JD led the way to an empty row on the right side and sat down. Scott followed, though his gaze was flicking from one item to the next in the large room.

JD opened the pamphlet and began reading the offerings. "Look, Scott, this place has Bible studies and a great men's group. That's one thing you want to look for in a church, because you need to find a place to get connected. They also have a worship team if you sing or play an instrument and a prayer team if you want to join."

As if on cue, people began filing onto the stage. JD hadn't noticed the rows of risers in the back, but they drew his attention as the people filed onto them. It was a large choir as the top row soon filled, then the middle row, then the bottom row began filling. At the very end of the line of people currently taking the stage was a woman with long dark hair that rippled like moonlight on the ocean.

JD's heart stopped and his breath caught. He remembered that hair, how it had smelled of flowers and vanilla and how he had longed to run his fingers through it. He blinked his eyes. Surely, it wasn't her though as the Callie he had met didn't seem like the type to be singing in the choir on Sundays. As she stepped on the riser and began to turn, he leaned forward in his seat.

"What's wrong?" Scott asked beside him.

His change in posture must have caught the man's attention. JD held his finger up. He just needed another minute. The woman turned and JD's heart shattered. He fell back against the chair back feeling as if he'd just gotten punched in the gut.

"Are you okay?"

Scott needed an explanation, but JD didn't have the words yet. He couldn't even make his mind grasp the image he was seeing; how could he explain it? He had been so sure.

The worship team had taken the stage some time in his shock, and the music began. Though it was like looking at a car crash, JD couldn't keep his eyes from returning to the woman on the bottom row.

He couldn't see the color of her eyes from here, but he knew they were green, deep like an emerald but with flecks of gold in them. They were emblazoned in his memory both from their short time together and from the countless times he had stared at the picture. She smiled and the dimple on each side of her mouth became visible. The sight both elated JD and broke his heart even further, if that was possible. He wanted to know what had happened to her, where this change had come from. He couldn't imagine that the man he had met on the last day he had seen her had inspired this change in her. The look of apprehension had been visible in her eyes even then when that arrogant man had pulled her close, staking his claim, but clearly something had happened.

Though he was no expert, the hang of her maxi dress on her otherwise thin frame displayed a protruding baby bump. Had she known back then that she was pregnant? He thought back to the double tequila he had served her the first night and the drinks she must have consumed the second night to have been so bold. She must not have. She had her faults, but she was so logical that he couldn't imagine her playing Russian Roulette with her baby's fate.

Did it happen after then? He didn't want to imagine her sharing a bed with the man who had broken her heart and upended her life, but he knew she must have. He wished he could gauge how far along she was until he realized it didn't matter. Whether she was one week or thirty-eight, she was clearly now attached to another man and therefore off the market.

Scott was still staring at him, waiting for some explanation.

"I'll tell you after the service," JD whispered, surprised that his voice wasn't shaking when the rest of him seemed to be. "Let's just enjoy the message."

JD forced his eyes to the screen farthest from Callie's face and tried to join in the singing. He felt terrible that he was ruining the experience for Scott and even worse that he felt angry at God. He had been so sure when she kept appearing in his thoughts and entering his mind that God would re-unite them; he hadn't expected it to end this way.

The music ended and the choir filed off the stage. JD's eyes followed Callie, unable to look away and curious to see who she sat with. She crossed in front of their section and turned down the aisle. JD shifted in his seat to follow her path. A right turn brought her into a row and she took the seat next to . . . *Is that the woman from the inn?*

There was no man beside her, which set off another round of questions. Was he at work or maybe a non-believer who was at home watching football instead? Was there a small chance that maybe there was no man? JD hadn't pegged the fiancé as the type of man ready to settle down and he could certainly imagine the fool fleeing the responsibility of a child.

Though that situation would be worse for Callie, JD couldn't help holding onto the tiny shred of hope that had taken root. However, he was now also tasked with the need to find a new living arrangement soon. He had been so busy the last few days that he hadn't begun looking at apartments yet, but he didn't want to take the chance of running into Callie at the inn either since it appeared the owner was her mother or some other close relative or friend.

Forcing his focus back to the message, JD adjusted his position so that his back was to Callie. He'd have to make an obvious shift to see her now, and that thought kept his eyes on the stage and the thin man with graying hair that was speaking.

*W*hen the service ended, JD glanced back at where Callie had been sitting as he gathered his coat and Bible, but the seats were empty.

Scott turned to follow his gaze. "Are you going to tell me what's going on?"

JD nodded. "Let's grab some lunch and I'll fill you in. Hopefully you can help me with another problem too."

. . .

*M*y hand rubbed my belly as I smiled and waved goodbye to a family with one small rambunctious toddler. Though the little girl was beautiful, I couldn't help but hope that my own daughter would be a little calmer. My mother, no longer much of a singer, had gotten involved in church by joining the greeting committee instead, so each week she either greeted the people coming in or stood at one of the exits to bid those leaving farewell.

I wasn't sure how I had gotten roped into helping today, but I pasted a smile on my face and did my best to ignore the throbbing in my feet. Standing on the stage for the twenty minutes of singing had taken its toll, and I couldn't wait to get home and put my feet up. If only I had someone who would massage them gently as well.

As I scanned the thinning hallway for anyone else headed our direction, two men exiting the front entrance caught my eye. Could it be?

"I'll be right back mom," I called over my shoulder already heading down the carpeted hallway.

The man I could see clearest I didn't recognize. He was tall with short brown hair, but I could have sworn that I'd seen a flash of that chin length brown hair that haunted my dreams. The taller man moved, unhampering my view of the slightly shorter man beside him and my feet stalled. There was no mistaking that face, even though it was only in profile.

Though the hallway traffic had thinned, there were still too many people for me to maneuver through and reach them on time, and besides my feet no longer seemed to want to cooperate. I could yell, but that would be rude in church. Plus, it would attract more attention than I wanted, and on the slim chance that I was wrong, it would be extremely embarrassing. So, for the second time in less than a week, I watched JD walk out of my life again.

With his passage out the door and out of sight, my feet regained their ability to move, and, shoulders sagging, I returned to my mother.

"What was that about?"

"It was him again. I saw JD but I couldn't reach him in time. I have to find him, mother. I just have to."

"So, let me get this straight," Scott said after JD had laid out the whole story, "The girl you thought you loved is pregnant with another man's baby here in this town, and her mother is the owner of the place you're staying?"

"Okay, so I'm not positive it's her mother, but that's the gist of it," JD said. "Why are you smiling?"

"I'm sorry," Scott laughed, "It's just that your story sounds a little like a bad Lifetime movie. My ex-girlfriend used to watch them all the time. I think that might be one reason we broke up."

A small smile tugged at the corners of JD's mouth. It did sound like a bad lifetime movie. He just wished it weren't reality and that it wasn't his current situation. "So, can you help me or not?"

Scott nodded as he finished chewing the bite of burger he had in his mouth. "I can. I have a friend who deals with the residential. I'm sure she can get you a great place quickly."

JD should have felt relieved, but that nagging seed of hope reared its head and reminded him that he didn't know for sure. There had been no man next to her during church, and he hadn't seen a ring, though she had been too far away to see her hand clearly. What if there was a chance she was single and he was leaving the best connection to her? Of course, on the other hand, he couldn't stay there forever anyway. He would need to get an apartment for the rest of his stay regardless of Callie.

"Cindy said she can meet you tomorrow at ten to show you a few places. Are you free then?"

JD glanced up. He had been so absorbed in his own thoughts that he hadn't even seen Scott texting on the phone he held in his hand.

"Yes, I can do that." The image of Callie's raven hair faded from his mind as he forced his mind to focus on Scott. He could deal with the torturous thoughts of her later.

CHAPTER 13

*A*fter a long night with little sleep, JD packed his bags and headed downstairs to let the owner know that today would be his last day.

The woman looked up from the counter as he descended the last step, and JD realized she really did resemble an older version of Callie. She had to be her mother, with the same dark hair and eye shape. Her eyes were more of a hazel color than the emerald green of Callie's but the shape was the same.

"Hello," he said as he approached. "I wanted to let you know that I'll be checking out today."

Her smile faltered as her brow knitted together. "Oh, I'm sorry to hear that. Is there anything we can do to make you want to stay?"

He thought about asking about Callie right then. The words 'Can you set me up with your daughter' jumped into his brain, beating against his throat to come out, but he swallowed them away. The woman would probably think he was a stalker if he uttered them. "No, thank you. It was wonderful, but I'll be staying longer and thought an apartment might be a little more convenient."

The smile returned to her face at the realization that he wasn't dissatisfied with her inn or her service. "I can certainly understand that, though I'm still sorry to see you go." She clicked a few buttons on the computer to her right and a small printer whirred to life, spitting out a single sheet of paper. Picking up the sheet, she glanced over it before sliding it across the countertop to him. "I just need you to fill this out."

JD perused the charges. Nothing seemed out of the ordinary, so he initialed on the lines and signed at the bottom.

"Thank you, Mr. Peterson," she said, picking up the paper. She glanced at the lines and then her eyes widened. "I'm sorry, does this say JD Peterson?" A quiver of excitement laced her voice, and her eyes held the look of a kid at Christmas.

"Yes. I'm JD Peterson."

A smile broke out on her face before she could contain it, but just for a second. A blink of his eyes later and she had composed herself, and only the sparkle in her eyes remained, making him wonder if he had imagined the whole thing.

"And what time will you be leaving tonight? So I can have the cleaning crew do your room," she added hastily.

"I should be ready to vacate by six."

"Six," she repeated, "Wonderful."

JD wondered at her odd behavior, but he had only an hour before he had to meet Cindy and the rumbling in his stomach reminded him that he hadn't eaten, so putting the incident out of his mind, he turned into the quaint dining room to grab some breakfast.

Four small circular tables covered in white tablecloths filled the room. This morning they were all empty. Everyone else must have already eaten.

Dropping his coat over the back of one of the chairs, he grabbed a plate from the buffet table and filled it with food. He was going to miss this aspect. The woman was an amazing cook, presenting an array of delicious delicacies. This morning there was a green and gold quiche that smelled heavenly, some sort of breakfast casserole that reminded him of campfire meals, and a plate of homemade cinnamon rolls. Since it was his last day, he piled one of each on his plate. Might as well eat his fill.

. . .

*M*y phone buzzed again on my desk. Someone was sure insistent; the phone had buzzed at least four times since I had started reading this document, but I knew if I picked it up, I would be distracted and lose my place. When I finished the document, I picked up the phone. Four text messages from my mother filled the screen. Was there an emergency? My mother never texted; she always said she hated the impersonal aspect of it. As I scrolled to the top to read the first message, my hand flew to my mouth.

JD was at the inn? The last message stated that he was checking out and leaving at six. I glanced at my watch. It was almost noon. If I worked through lunch and finished this research, I could leave at four, which would give me a little time to clean up.

The intercom buzzed as I hit the button. "Tina? I need you to order me in some lunch. I'm working straight through today."

"*I*t doesn't look like much, but it comes furnished. All it really needs is a woman's touch." Cindy leaned against the small bar in the kitchen and flashed a seductive smile.

Instead of answering, JD turned away pretending to consider the place again. All morning she had been dropping suggestive hints, blocking doorways so he had to touch her to walk by, dropping her hand flirtatiously on his arm as she pointed features out in the apartments, and now striking a seductive pose. It wasn't that she wasn't pretty. With her short dark hair and small build, she was nice to look at, but she wasn't Callie.

"I'll take it," he said, partly because it fit the bill he was looking for and partly because he didn't want to see another place with Cindy.

While she drew up the papers, he perused the small apartment one more time. It wasn't anything grand, but it would do for as long as he was here.

The front door opened to a spacious living room with plush beige carpet. A brown recliner and loveseat filled the room facing a medium sized television. The kitchen had a direct view to the living room and was decorated in beiges and tans. The lone hallway led from the living room down to the bathroom and the one bedroom, both large enough for his needs.

Cindy was right that it needed a woman's touch, and he couldn't help picturing Callie hanging pictures or helping him pick out throw pillows.

"All done," she said in her sing-song voice. "Shall we celebrate?"

He did want to celebrate, but not with Cindy. "I can't. I need to get my things from the bed and breakfast I was staying at."

Her full lips formed a perfect pout. He wondered if she practiced the look in the mirror and how many men stumbled over themselves when she flashed it. "Well, another time then," she purred. "You have my number now, and I know where you live."

He tried for a polite smile and shook her hand, hoping she'd pick up on the hint that he wasn't interested. With a final longing look at him, she handed over the keys, gathered her paperwork, and left.

After locking the door to make sure she didn't return, JD collapsed on the loveseat with a sigh. He needed to pick up some food from a grocery store to stock the fridge, but he could afford to rest for a moment. Avoiding Cindy's advances had been quite exhausting.

I sat in the car staring at the front of the inn. My heart was thudding in my chest and my throat felt like the Sahara Desert. In a moment, I would be face to face with JD for the first time in months. Would he still be interested in me now that I was pregnant? Only one way to find out. With a final deep breath, I stepped out of the car.

The wind caught my hair, whipping it about my face. So much for the thirty minutes I had spent making sure every lock was in place.

I shoved my hands deeper in my coat pockets as the chill in the air bit through my layers. Though it was a short walk up the steps, I found myself shivering as I reached for the door handle.

"Callie?"

The timbre of the voice behind me sent a tingle down my spine. I had missed that, the way he said my name.

I turned around slowly. JD stood at the end of the sidewalk

wearing a pair of jeans and a brown leather jacket. The wind tousled his hair as I longed to.

"Hi, JD." I wanted to say more, to sound eloquent, but words failed me yet again.

He took a step toward me, his eyes never leaving my face. "What are you doing here?"

"I could ask you the same thing." Pulling my coat tighter across my belly − I'd explain that to him later − I stepped down to the sidewalk.

"I'm here for work." Another step, only three steps separated them now.

"My mother told me you were here, and I needed to see you before I lost you again." Only two steps remained.

"Why?" One step. "What about Daniel?"

"There is no more Daniel." A small smile tugged at my lips, and I covered the final distance, feeling the heat radiate off his body even as the wind blew against us. "There hasn't been since a few weeks after I returned from the Caribbean." I could reach out and touch him now if I wanted, if I wasn't afraid he might bolt. The emotion in his eyes was unclear, but I hoped he was happy to see me.

His eyes roamed my face, but he said nothing. I couldn't handle the silence. "I found your travel books and the picture when I got home. It sits on my nightstand. I've looked at it every night, wishing I had done things differently there. I should never have taken Daniel back. You were right, and I'm sorry."

As conflicting emotions battled across his face, I wondered why. Was he seeing someone now?

"What about the baby?" he asked.

My eyes widened. "How did you know?" I had picked this coat particularly because it hid my baby bump.

He stared at me; he clearly wasn't answering my question until I answered his.

"I'll tell you all about it, but the father isn't in the picture." The wind found a hole in our electric current and nipped at me; I shivered, wishing he would take me in his arms.

"So, there's no one?"

The small smile broadened as I shook my head. "No one, but you, I hope."

The words were barely out of my mouth before his right hand was in my hair, his left on the small of my back, and his lips on mine. They were everything I had imagined, soft and firm and intense, like he couldn't get enough. The electricity traveled down my body, warming me against the chilly wind.

He pulled back, his eyes wild. "I'm sorry. I didn't mean – "

"Don't be sorry," I said, placing a finger on his lips. "I've wanted you to do that since the day at the falls."

He brought my hand to his chest as he pulled me closer and met my lips again. The kiss was softer this time, slower, but no less full of emotion.

When he pulled back, I could see that he was struggling to catch his breath just as I was. A tingling was still racing through my body, and my heart was beating so fast it was like a drum in my ear.

A slow smile spread across his face. "I've wanted to do that from the moment I saw you."

We stood there at the end of the sidewalk with the wind whipping around us. He held both of my hands in his, and though the temperature was chilly, neither of us felt the cold.

"I have so much to tell you," I finally said, breaking the magic spell for the moment, "but first I have to tell my mother I found you."

"I get the feeling I owe your mother a thank you," he said entwining his fingers with mine.

"I think we both do."

Hand in hand, we walked into the bed and breakfast. My mother stood at the counter but her eyes were trained on the doorway. As we entered, her eyes lit up, and she hurried out from behind the counter.

Her eyes landed on our clasped hands and her smile magnified. "I take it this is the right JD then."

I smiled up at the man I had only dreamed about, still unable to believe he was here next to me. "It is."

"I assume I have you to thank for Callie showing up here," JD said.

She shrugged, "A mother has to do what she can."

"Well, I truly thank you, but if you don't mind, I'm going to steal your daughter to dinner. I'm starving."

With that, he whisked me back outside and into his car. Minutes later, we had parked at a quiet Italian restaurant.

After opening my door, JD took my hand again and led the way inside. The building was small from the outside, but opened impressively inside. Ten tables and a few booths filled the dimly lit room. Candles glowed on every table, and soft light from the ceiling completed the ambiance.

A young woman in a black skirt and starched white shirt greeted us and led us to the farthest booth. There weren't many other patrons in the restaurant, but the booth blocked out most of what little noise there was. It was almost like being in our own private world.

JD reached for my hand again as soon as we sat down, but I didn't mind. My hands felt empty now if they weren't touching his.

"I have so much I want to ask you," JD said. "Tell me what happened since you left the Caribbean."

I took a deep breath. "That's quite a story, but I'll try. When Daniel and I returned from the trip, I started to see parts of his personality I didn't like." My face clouded as I remembered the ultimatum he had issued. "When he found out I was pregnant, he said he didn't want the responsibility of being a parent. He wanted to be free to do what he wanted, so he forced me to choose between him and the baby. I chose the baby."

"He didn't want to raise his own child?"

A heat seared across my face, and I dropped my eyes. I hadn't wanted to tell him so soon, but it was the perfect opportunity "It's not his, but he didn't even know that, and he didn't want to raise the child. I knew I couldn't stay with someone like that." I bit my lip, hoping that my admission of my philandering behavior wouldn't scare him away. IO looked up through lowered lids, but JD's face was passive. His hand still caressed mine though.

"The baby's not Daniel's?"

Though I had known he would ask the question, the actual words coming out of his mouth speared my heart. "I had a bad night shortly after Daniel left me. I drank too much with a friend and ended up in the apartment of a guy I met that night. I've never done anything like that before, and I promise it will never happen again." The words spilled out in a rush; I was so afraid that he would get angry and leave before I had a chance to explain.

"Callie, I'm not here to judge you. I've done some things I'm not proud of in my life too."

I wondered what he had done, but he didn't elaborate.

"What matters to me is the father. Does he want the baby? Will he come back in our lives?"

I shook my head slowly. He wasn't angry? I should have known; he was so different. *Wait, did he say 'our' lives?* "I don't think so. I told him about the baby as soon as I knew, and he was not pleased. He signed away his parental rights, so even if he tries to come back, he has no standing."

He nodded, and just like that the discussion was over. I stared at him, my affection deepening.

The waitress appeared with a tray of freshly baked bread and I snatched one before it even had time to cool. I had been so nervous about meeting JD that I hadn't eaten much all day, and my stomach was definitely protesting now.

Across the table, JD's lips pulled into a bemused smile. "Are you going to save some room for dinner?"

A tingling swept up the back of my neck and across my face. I swallowed the bite in my mouth and put the rest of the bread down. "I'm sorry. I didn't eat well today, and I'm eating for two now."

"Don't be sorry. I find it endearing." His voice was soft; his eyes steady on my face.

Though I knew he was sincere, I wasn't used to someone looking at me the way JD was now. My eyes dropped to the table top and the remainder of the bread I hadn't shoved in my mouth.

"I've told you my story. Now tell me more about you. We never talked about what you did while we were in the Caribbean."

JD took a sip of his water glass, "I manage my dad's companies because my dad had a heart attack a few years ago, and he decided to retire to Florida with my mom. We run a few Christian publishing companies. In fact, you should write about your story. I bet it would make a great book."

The thought of sharing my story with complete strangers mortified me. I was still embarrassed by my choices and often felt people were looking at me wondering where my ring was, but the verse about being a prophet pushed to the front of my mind. Could that have been the verse's cryptic meaning? Using my own mistakes to help others from making the same ones? "I'll think about it." I smiled. "So what were you doing in the Caribbean? You said you go there every year."

The waitress interrupted the conversation to take our order, and then JD continued. "I do. I take brochures and books about Jesus that we've printed that year and distribute them down there. My dad used to do that every year when I was a kid and so I sort of grew up there. Remember Sammy who braided your hair?"

I nodded. What I remembered more than Sammy was the tingle I had felt at JD's touch and the beginning sparks of attraction.

"Well, he also owns the bar I was working in the night we met, and he helps run a local church there that distributes our materials. I guess it's kind of like missionary work, except I only stay there for a couple of weeks. I give him the books and he gives them out to the people."

"Wow, that's nice of your company. So are you opening a publishing branch here?"

He chuckled. It was a deep, lovely sound, coupled with an even lovelier smile. "No, I'm starting a pregnancy crisis center here."

My eyebrows drew together, creating a stream of wrinkles across my forehead and nose. "What does that have to do with publishing?"

"Nothing," JD laughed, "but the need for one's been weighing on my heart, and my father always taught me to listen to my heart's desire because it's from God when it's also based on principles from His word. So, here I am looking into a place to open up a clinic to help pregnant women make the same decision you did."

My eyes widened and I leaned forward, "Sandra will be so excited. She's been praying for a local clinic, and I want to help your clinic.

Whatever you need. Well, whatever you need that I can do with a baby on the way," she laughed.

"I think you look even more beautiful with a baby on the way. The glow suits you. While you were stunning then, you don't even look like the same woman I met in the Caribbean."

"I'm not." My gaze dropped to our entwined hands and then back up at him through lowered lids. "You were right. Having a relationship with God changes you."

Before JD could reply, the waitress returned with our plates, setting down a delectable chicken alfredo in front of me and a large plate of lasagna in front of JD. My mouth watered as the aroma wafted up to my nose.

This time, I joined JD when he prayed over dinner. When the prayer ended, I filled my fork with pasta. The creamy alfredo sauce flowed like honey down my throat and before I knew it, my plate was empty. As JD still had half of his lasagna, I reached my fork onto his plate and scooped up a bite.

"Hey, what do you think you're doing?" he asked.

"Helping you out." I smiled and brought the forkful to my mouth. Though I wasn't the biggest lasagna fan, it too was delicious.

JD shook his head, a smile playing at his lips. As I watched him finish eating, I pictured my life with him. An image of the two of us in the kitchen cooking while a small child played at our feet filled my mind. He turned to kiss me before I leaned down to scoop up the child.

"What are you thinking?" JD asked.

His voice shattered my daydream, and a blush spread across my cheeks. I didn't want to tell him about the daydream, not yet at least, not until I knew for sure how he felt. "Nothing," I said. "I just can't remember when I had a nicer dinner."

"Me either."

"What does the JD stand for?" Though I hadn't been curious when we met, I had often wondered over the last few months when I thought about him. This time the question jumped out before I could stop it.

He smiled at the odd request, "Jonathon Daniel."

I blinked at him, sure that I had heard him wrong.

"What is it?" he asked.

"Do you remember the day back in the Caribbean when I told you I prayed?" He nodded, and I continued, "Well, I prayed for God to send Daniel back to me. It appears he answered my prayer, only with a different Daniel than I thought."

"I told you he works in mysterious ways," JD said. His broad smile perfectly matched the feeling coursing through my body."

He finished his plate, and when the bill came, JD picked up the tab. I tried to protest, but he reminded me that I would be taking a pay cut, at least for a while when I went on maternity leave.

The cold hit again as soon as we stepped outside, and I shivered. The sun had set while we ate and the temperature had cooled even more. JD wrapped his arm around my shoulder, pulling me closer to him. I basked in the warmth and security he offered.

He allowed the car to idle a minute, letting the heater warm up. "Shall I take you back to the inn?"

I wanted to say no. I wanted him to come home with me so I could stay wrapped in his arms. An unnatural fear that this was all a dream and I would lose him again had settled on my shoulders, and I longed for his reassurance. "I suppose that would be best," I said instead. I knew he wouldn't have come even if I asked. "I do have work tomorrow, but will you come over after I get off?"

"I'd love to," he said, and the fear abated. I nestled down in the seat, letting my mind wander again, as we drove off.

The inn was close, and too soon, we had arrived. Before my hand touched the handle, he was out of his side of the car and opening my door. I had never felt more like a princess. His warm hand enveloped mine, pulling me up from the car and to his chest.

His arms wound around my waist, and as if on instinct, my arms encircled his neck.

JD's eyes were bright, full of emotion and unsaid words. My lips parted, and my face turned up to his. An invisible current seemed to run between us, pushing his face closer to mine until our lips met. As the kiss deepened, my hands tightened around his neck, and his arms pressed me tighter against him. I felt molded to his body, a perfect fit.

Though desire was running rampant through my body and it would have been easy to get back in the car and head to my place, I forced myself to sever the kiss. This time was going to be different, but I couldn't help feeling pleased that he was just as breathless as I was.

"Good idea," he said, shaking his head. "I could lose myself with you." He placed a final soft kiss on my lips and then headed to his own car.

I took those words to bed that night. We both had agreed to wait on an intimate relationship, but I couldn't keep my mind from wandering. Clad in my favorite oversized t-shirt, I curled up in bed, imagining JD beside me. I had never felt sexier or more desired. My hand absently rubbed my belly, and Hope moved against it.

"I don't want to jinx it, little one, but I think he could be 'the one.'"

CHAPTER 14

*J*D woke before the alarm the next morning, a smile still on his face. He had slept better last night than he had in ages, and he had Callie to thank for that.

He was whistling as he met Scott for coffee that morning. After their lunch on Sunday, they had agreed to meet once a week for coffee. Scott hadn't said he was ready to accept Jesus, but JD was pleased that he seemed willing to meet and discuss it.

"Well, someone looks like the cat who ate the canary," Scott said as JD slid in the chair across from him.

JD tried to contain the grin on his face, but it was impossible. "You would be too if you'd had the night I did."

Scott's eyes widened under raised eyebrows. "I didn't think that fit in your philosophy."

"No, not that," JD laughed, shaking his head, "though it was the first time in a long time that it was hard to control that urge. No, I ran into Callie."

"The pregnant woman from church?" Scott's face twisted with confusion. "I guess I'm not seeing why that's a good thing."

"Because," JD said, wiggling his eyebrows, "she's not with the guy anymore."

"Ah, now I see. Good for you, man, that's great." Though Scott's words were positive, there was a wistfulness in his tone.

"Spill it," JD said. He didn't know Scott well, but he could tell something was troubling him.

Scott shrugged. "It's the anniversary of my divorce. I guess it always gets me down a bit. I thought we'd be together forever, you know?"

JD did know. Too many marriages ended in divorce these days, and no one ever came out unscathed. When he married, he hoped his wife would be as committed as he was to making the marriage work, no matter what came their way. An image of Callie walking down the aisle toward him filled his vision, and though he wanted to see it, he pushed it away to focus on Scott.

"Anyway, just ignore me. I'll be fine tomorrow."

JD doubted that, but he hoped that the more Scott came to church with him, the more God would fill the hole in his heart until the woman God had in mind for him came along. He made a promise to keep up his coffee meetings with Scott no matter how busy he got.

*J*D spent the rest of his day buying office furniture, painting, and getting the electricity and plumbing turned on and switched over to his name. It was tedious work, and he couldn't wait to get a staff hired that could help him.

All of that could wait though, because he had a movie date planned with Callie. He stopped at a local florist for a bouquet of flowers on the way to her house. Bypassing the traditional roses, he asked the woman to make up something special. What she handed him was a veritable feast for the eyes. Roses of several different colors, some blue flower he didn't recognize, a few carnations, and sprigs of baby's breath filled the purple tissue paper. It was perfect, original and special just like Callie.

I bustled around the apartment as quickly as I could given my size; no one had told me how much harder everyday tasks would be when my stomach grew. JD would be here any minute and while I normally kept the place neat, I had been too tired lately to clean when I got off work. Because of that, there were a few papers lying about and several dishes in the sink.

As I put the last dish in the dishwasher, the doorbell rang. Perfect timing. A glance in the hallway mirror as I passed it reassured me, and I threw the door open with a smile.

JD stood on the other side with the most beautiful bouquet of flowers I had ever seen.

"For the prettiest woman I know," he said, holding them out.

"Oh, JD, they're beautiful. Come in." Taking the flowers, I ushered him inside. "Let me just put them in some water."

He followed me into the kitchen and leaned against the counter as I pulled out a vase and filled it with water. Though I tried to keep my focus on the task, my treacherous eyes kept darting to the left to admire the way JD's jeans hugged his form and how the hunter green of his shirt made his eyes a darker shade of green, like a forest at dusk. I didn't think I would ever tire of looking in those eyes.

"There all done." I pushed the flowers into the middle of the bar, a kind of buffer to quell the tension stirring inside me.

"Good, let's watch a movie. Did you pick one out?"

"I wasn't sure what you liked to watch, so I picked a few. I have a few romantic comedies and an action movie." I led him back to the living room and motioned to the movies spread out on the coffee table.

"You have The Princess Bride? I love this movie." The smile on his face brought out his boyish charm and I laughed.

"Me too. I used to watch it all the time in High School. And then I found the book." The book had become a favorite of mine, and I was a die-hard fan of the movie and could quote nearly every line, but he didn't need to know that.

After inserting the movie, I joined him on the couch. He opened up his arm, and I accepted the invitation, nestling myself in the crook. His hand began to trace slow circles on my shoulder, sending tingles all the way down to my toes. Snuggling closer, I laid my hand against his chest. The urge to unbutton his shirt and feel his chiseled chest first hand flitted through my body, but I pushed it aside. No matter how hard it was, I was going to do this relationship God's way. Besides, there was a comfort in just being held and inhaling the masculine scent that JD exuded. It had been months since I'd had that.

I turned my face to look up at him. His skin was still the same bronze color I remembered, but a light stubble dotted his face this time that hadn't been there before. He caught me looking at him and lifted my chin before lowering his lips to mine. Heat flooded through me, and my heart thudded in my chest. This time he was the one to pull back, and though I didn't want the kiss to end, I was grateful he had done it. All of my plans to go slow seemed to fly from my mind when he kissed me.

He smiled and brushed a strand of hair from my face. I could get used to his touch and the way he looked at me, like I was the most valuable item in the world. Daniel had never looked at me like that. He had desired me sure, but not with the same respect that JD did. I understood now what Sandra had meant when she said a Godfearing man wouldn't want to do anything to cause you to sin. I could tell that JD desired me in the same way Daniel had, but he was going to do it right, as God had intended. I just hoped I would be able to remain as strong.

CHAPTER 15

*J*D's fingers touched the black velvet box in his pocket. He had picked it up on his way to meeting Scott for coffee, and he'd been unable to keep his fingers from touching it.

"Okay, what's going on, man?" Scott snapped his fingers in front of JD's face. "You haven't heard one word I said."

JD blinked, bringing his focus back to the present. He wanted to tell Scott his news; heck he wanted to shout it from the rooftops, but he also knew Scott was battling a feeling of loneliness, and he didn't want to rub it in.

"Spill it." Scott leaned back and crossed his arms.

JD withdrew his hand from his pocket and held out the black box. "Before you say anything, I know it's fast, but I've known I loved Callie for months, and I don't want to take the chance of losing her again."

Scott opened the box and let out a low whistle. "It's exquisite, so what's the problem?"

A sigh escaped JD's lips as he thought back over the last week. Callie had been home late every night, and while she usually called to let him know, he still wasn't enjoying eating dinner alone. He'd had enough of that to last a lifetime. "It's her job. She's been working long hours, and while I want to propose, I don't want to marry someone who will be gone most evenings, you know?"

Scott closed the box and handed it back. "As you know, I'm no expert, but I'd say talk to her. If she knew how you felt, maybe she'd decide to make a change."

JD nodded. Scott was right. He'd talk to her tonight, and if all went well, then he could propose. He didn't want to think about what he'd do if all didn't go well.

I groaned as I glanced at my watch. I was going to be late again. This latest case had me working nearly twelve hour days, and I'd had to cancel on JD twice already this week. He'd said he had something important to talk about, so I could only hope that he'd forgive me.

Grabbing my purse as soon as the car was parked, I hurried up to his door and knocked.

It opened a moment later, but JD's face was not smiling. "Come on in."

He held the door open, and I bit my lip as I stepped inside. He wasn't going to break up with me, was he? I knew this week had been hard on him, but I'd thought he was the type to stick it out.

"Sit down." He pointed to the couch, and a feeling of dread blanketed me. "Callie, I love you. I'm pretty sure I've loved you from the moment I saw you, but I'm not loving your job right now."

I nodded. "I know. It is busy this week, but when this case is over, it will get better."

"What about when the next case comes along?"

"I . . . what do you want me to do, quit my job?" Anger stirred in my stomach.

"I was wondering if you would come work for me. The hours will be better, and I need someone to help with hiring the staff and putting the final touches on the office."

I considered his proposal. Once, I had thought of nothing other than being a lawyer, but the hours were taking their toll on me, and I knew it would be worse once Hope arrived.

"I could offer you a generous benefit package with maternity leave. Plus, it would be amazing to work with my wife every day."

My head popped up. *Did he say wife?*

JD pulled a black box from his pocket and opened the lid.

My breath caught in my throat, and tears of joy pricked my eyes. I looked from him down to the quarter carat diamond ring sparkling in his hands, and nodded.

He slipped the ring out of the box and onto my finger. The light caught the stone, sending arcs of color on the wall. It was the most stunning ring I had ever seen. "Yes," I said, "to both your questions."

"I know it's getting closer to your due date," he said, "but I wanted us to at least be engaged before Hope comes. Then we can have the wedding after, when you are up for it."

I shook my head. "No, I want to do it before. We can do a small service at the church. I'm sure Pastor Tony would marry us."

"Callie, are you sure? We've got the opening of the center coming soon, and we still need to get your apartment ready for Hope –

"I'm sure," I said, cutting him off. "I want Hope to be officially yours before she's born."

He smiled. "Okay, we'll ask Pastor Tony tomorrow."

I looked around the office I had called my second home for the last few years. Though I had often thought I would be leaving this place, I had always assumed it would be for a bigger office, not a completely different career.

I wasn't sad though. The long hours had taken their toll on my pregnant body, and I was looking forward to getting off earlier. Plus, my priorities had shifted. I no longer longed to be partner; now I just wanted to have time to spend with my daughter and my fiancé. Fiancé. I still hadn't totally wrapped my head around that, but the ring on my finger served as a constant reminder.

Hopefully, there would be no hitches in the wedding planning. Getting married eight months pregnant hadn't been in my dream wedding, but I knew I loved JD, and I wanted both of our names to be on the birth certificate when Hope arrived. That was now more important than a fancy wedding or even wearing the perfect dress. I just hoped we could get it all planned in three weeks' time.

"I'm going to miss you," Tina said, sniffling back tears as I approached her desk. In my hands was a small box with my few personal items packed.

"I'll miss you too, but I'll still be in the city. We'll get together. Plus, I'll see you at the wedding." Of all the things I would miss about my job, Tina was at the top of the list. I gave her a final hug, waved goodbye to everyone else, and walked out of the building.

A mixture of fear and relief washed over me as I climbed in the car. I was excited to be helping JD out at the center, but a worry persisted that I would miss being a lawyer. The last thing I wanted to do was resent leaving. "Lord, please send me your peace." A calmness covered my shoulders and warmed my body, and I eased the car into drive to meet JD at the center.

When I arrived, he ushered me in, planting a quick kiss on my lips and leaving me wanting more. The smell of new carpet and wet paint permeated the air.

"I'm so glad you're here. I set up interviews for today, and I'd really like your input."

I glanced around the nearly finished office space, surprised at how close he was to being able to open. Not only were the new carpets laid and the walls repainted, but the receptionist's desk was installed and the waiting chairs were stacked in one corner of the room.

"So, the doctors have already been hired, but we need to hire three nurses, a book keeper, and a receptionist," JD said, rifling through a stack of papers.

I had hoped the afternoon would be a little more relaxing, but wanting to help JD out in any way I could, I followed him into one of the offices that had also been finished. He had set up a table and a few chairs.

"Make yourself comfortable here, and I'll get you some tea. You won't have to move an inch. I'll bring the interviewees back to you."

I smiled up at him. As my due date got closer, he grew more and more attentive and doting. He had even left his own apartment and driven to the store at midnight the other night to buy me nachos and pickles, which he had dropped off with a quick kiss before returning to his own place.

Minutes later, he returned with a steaming mug of green tea for me, and the parade of interviewees began.

When the last one was gone, we discussed the merits of each, agreeing nearly completely on our favorites.

"How much longer do you think the center needs before it opens?" I asked as he gathered up the resumes.

"Honestly? I think we can open in two weeks just before the wedding. I think Rebekah will be able to handle a few days without me at the very beginning."

An elaborate honeymoon was out of the question for us as I was now too pregnant even to fly safely, but I didn't mind. To me, the honeymoon would just get to be spending the night curled up in JD's arms. I was growing tired of having to say goodbye to him every night and climb into my bed alone.

"What are you thinking about?" JD asked, wrapping his arms around me. Due to my ever-increasing belly, they no longer completely encircled me but landed on the back of my hips.

My lips pulled into a seductive smile as I wound my arms around his neck. "I was thinking that the perfect honeymoon will just be the day I don't have to say goodnight to you and I can wake up with you beside me the next morning."

His lips parted as his eyes filled with desire. "I can't wait for that day either."

My nerve endings tingled as his mouth closed on mine. A heat flared inside as his tongue explored my mouth. His lips then traveled down my neck, landing on the soft flesh between my collar bone and my neck. My breath caught in my throat, and my hands twisted in his hair. If he could affect me this deeply with all our clothes on, I could only imagine the havoc he could wreak with no barrier between us.

*W*ith the wedding quickly approaching, the last thing on my to-do list had been the nursery. I had been pushing it off, due to work, but now that I had some time, it had jumped to number one on the list. The last thing I wanted was for this baby to arrive and have no nursery.

JD had agreed to take the afternoon off and shop with me, and both Scott and Lexi had agreed to help us finish that evening. Lexi's acceptance had surprised me as she had distanced herself after the few times she had come to church with me, but evidently Lexi had a soft spot for babies.

"*L*avender? Are you sure?" JD raised his eyebrows as we stood in the paint aisle debating on colors to paint Hope's room.

"She's a girl, silly." I laughed and swatted him playfully. "She is going to love pinks and purples."

"I guess I'm going to have to get used to all this girly stuff." He smiled as he picked up three cans of paint and put them in the cart.

"If you plan on sticking around you are."

We grabbed some paint brushes and tape and then headed to the baby aisle of the store where I picked out a white crib and changing table, a cream-colored rocker, and a small white dresser. JD muscled them all in the cart and followed me as I turned to the clothing aisle.

My final paycheck hadn't been extraordinary, but the office had pooled together money to present as a wedding/baby gift, and it had been enough to cover most of what I needed to purchase.

Scott's car was in the parking lot when we returned to the apartment, and he hurried over to help JD unload the paint and the heavier nursery furniture we had purchased. Lexi showed up as I was returning for a second time to get all the bags of clothes out of the car.

"These are so cute." Lexi said a she held up a tiny pair of purple jammies dotted with white butterflies.

JD and Scott had taken over Hope's room to paint and assemble furniture, so Lexi and I were sorting clothes in the living room. I was relieved as the couch was much more comfortable to sit in lately.

I smiled and folded a pink onesie. "Makes you think about having one of your own one day, doesn't it?"

"Not until I find a good man like JD."

Pulling a blanket out of the bag, I snipped the tag off. "Well, if you'd come back to church with us, I'm sure God would help you find one."

Lexi bit her lip and pulled out another outfit. "I know; maybe this week."

I changed the subject so as not to make Lexi uncomfortable, but I continued to pray for her as we worked. When we were done sorting, I ordered a pizza and then we turned on the TV to pass time until the men were finished.

Half an hour later, Scott and JD emerged, sporting a few purple spots and a bit more sweat.

"Perfect timing." I pushed myself off the couch and wrapped my arms around JD, placing a quick kiss on his lips. "The pizza just got here."

JD led us all in prayer as we gathered around the table. "Lord, thank you for this food and for the amazing friends you have brought us. Bless them and bless this house and help us to remember the great sacrifice you gave for us and to never waste a day doing what does not honor you. Amen"

"Amen." As soon as the prayer was finished, I snatched a piece of pizza. For some reason tonight, I was craving cheese. I almost had the slice to my mouth when Scott cleared his throat and began to speak. I stared longingly at the slice, but put it down to give him my full attention.

"I want to say something." Scott adjusted his shoulders. "You two have been such an amazing example for me. I've been thinking about it for a while, but tonight after painting Hope's room and hearing your prayer, I've decided it's time. I'd like to have a personal relationship with Jesus."

"That's wonderful," JD and I shouted simultaneously. A burst of adrenaline shot through me, masking the hunger for the moment.

"I'm not sure exactly what to do though." Scott swallowed and tapped his hands on the table.

JD touched his arm. "I don't think there's a perfect way, but I can tell you the one we use on our pamphlets. As long as you mean these words, God will accept you: Lord, I know that I'm a sinner and I now believe that you sent your son Jesus to die for me. I believe in and want to trust Him as my Lord and Savior. Please Jesus, come into my heart and lead me. Amen"

Scott repeated the words and tears filled his eyes. "Thank you," he said, wiping his eyes as he finished. "I can't believe I waited so long. I feel like a huge weight has been lifted.

"You're welcome, Brother." JD clapped his arm. "I'm so happy to have you in the family."

I smiled at JD and sneaked a peek at Lexi, who appeared to be lost in thought. *I hope she's thinking about accepting Jesus, too.*

After dinner, Scott and Lexi said their goodbyes and as soon as they had left, JD grabbed my hand. "Okay, now come see the room."

"I'm coming, I'm coming." His excitement was contagious, and I smiled as he led the way down the hall.

Outside Hope's door, he stopped and turned to me. "Eyes closed."

I closed my eyes, and JD's hands covered them. He stood behind me and walked me into the room before dropping his hands. I gasped. The furniture wasn't against the walls yet, as they were still drying, but the white crib had been set up and decorated with the purple and white heart sheets we had bought. The rocker sat a little to the side, and the dresser and changing table finished the look.

"It's beautiful." I couldn't have imagined a more perfect room if I had tried.

JD smiled and wrapped his arms around me. "You're beautiful."

That night, after JD had left to go back to his place, I sat in the rocking chair, rubbing my belly. "This is your room, Hope. I hope you love purple as much as I do." Hope kicked against my hand, bringing another smile to my face. "I may not have done in it the right order, but in just a few days, JD and I will get married. I think he will make an amazing father." Another kick told me that Hope agreed.

❦

*T*wo days before the wedding, the center's grand opening arrived.

JD and I stood inside the center looking around at the finished product. "It's so amazing." I squeezed JD's hand. The main office was warm and inviting with a soft mauve color on the walls and carpet. Comfy chairs and even a few rockers filled the waiting room, and on the end table were packets from nearby adoption agencies and churches. The exam rooms had each been painted a different color and decorated in childlike themes to entertain any children that might come with mothers. We had hired a wonderful staff of Christian men and women, and I couldn't have been prouder of JD.

"Come on, we better get outside before they come looking for us." I followed him to the back exit where we pushed open the rear door and snuck around to join the crowd in the front of the building.

Thankfully, the weather had smiled upon us today. Though still chilly, it wasn't raining, and the crowd looked warm enough in their coats and scarves. Scott waved as we rounded the corner and jogged to meet us. "There you are." He handed JD a pair of scissors. "The people are getting restless, my friend."

JD took the scissors and stepped onto a nearby bench to be seen as he addressed the crowd. "Welcome everyone; we're so pleased to open Faith Pregnancy Center and be able to give women quality care and alternative choices to abortion." Applause erupted from the crowd. "Please feel free to take a tour and take a business card to share it with a friend." He cut the giant red ribbon that stretched across the front door, and the crowd cheered.

As the people began to file inside, a pain flared in my side and I sucked in a breath.

"Are you alright?" There was a thread of fear in his voice that sent tremors through my body.

"I think so." I rubbed my side, trying to convince myself that the pain hadn't been that bad. "Maybe just Braxton Hicks contractions." I wasn't due for another month, so I doubted it was real labor. I wasn't sure if Braxton-Hicks started that early, but it was the most plausible explanation I could come up with.

The tendons in his neck strained against the skin as his eyes traveled my body.

"I'm sure it's just stress from being so worn out." I hoped I sounded reassuring; I didn't want to ruin his big day. "I'll probably be fine if I just go lie down."

"Are you sure?"

"I'm sure. I feel better already. I bet I'll be right as rain tomorrow."

I hugged him goodbye, trying not to grimace as another pain laced my side, and then waddled to my car. Though I hoped it was nothing, a harbinger of dread fluttered at the back of my mind.

CHAPTER 16

*I*gnoring the pain licking up my side, I stepped into my wedding dress. Though the pain had gotten better after I had rested, it hadn't gone away completely, and I had felt the pangs several times the following day as well.

It had taken all my energy to keep my face from showing the pain, but I had kept the information to myself because I didn't want anything to ruin the wedding.

My mother zipped up the dress and smiled at me in the mirror over my shoulder. "I know this isn't the wedding you dreamed of, but I think it will be the marriage you desired."

She was right. As a little girl, I had always dreamed of the perfect dress – some big designer name – and a big wedding, but I'd almost had that with Daniel, and it hadn't turned out well. As I gazed at my reflection, I realized my dreams had also changed.

Even if I hadn't been nearly nine months pregnant, I would have opted for a simple dress similar to the one that hugged my frame and a small, intimate gathering like the crowd waiting in the sanctuary. In fact, other than the pangs in my side, it was nearly the perfect day.

"I think you're right, mom. I can't imagine a man better than JD."

As the words left my mouth, tiny black flecks dotted my vision, and I shook my head to clear them.

Worry etched itself on my mother's face. "Are you alright?"

"Yeah, I think I just need to sit down for a minute."

She led me to one of the chairs in the room and helped me sit down. I forced a smile, hoping to ease the lines on my mother's face. "Can you get me some water, mom?"

Her eyes bore into mine, as if trying to decide if she could leave me alone. With a lingering glance, she nodded and exited the room.

Exhaling, I dropped my head back. The pain was getting worse, and now with the black dots, I knew something was wrong. If I could make it through the ceremony, I'd have JD drive me straight to the hospital afterwards, but I had to make it through the ceremony first. *Lord, please help me get through the ceremony.*

A few calming breaths, while my hands rubbed rhythmic circles across my belly, helped ease the pain, and when my mother returned with the water, I felt better.

Lexi and Tina filed in behind my mother, looking beautiful in their rose-pink dresses. JD had picked Scott as his best man, and because he wasn't close to anyone else here yet, he had asked Tina's husband to be the second groomsman.

"It's almost time; are you ready?" Lexi bounced from one foot to the other, barely able to contain her excitement. Her blond hair was pulled up on her head with just a few tendrils hanging down.

"More importantly, are you feeling better?" my mother asked.

"Better? What's wrong?" Tina stepped forward, assuming her own mothering role.

"Nothing, I just felt a little dizzy is all."

Tina's stare now mirrored my mother's. Only Lexi, who had never been pregnant, seemed oblivious to the mood in the room.

"I'm fine, really." I pushed myself up, determined not to grimace or pass out. The little spots still swam in my vision, but I blinked them away.

"Callie, maybe you should get checked out first – "

"No." I interrupted Tina more forcefully than I meant to. "I mean, I will, but after the ceremony, please?"

My pleading eyes must have convinced them because Tina and my mother sighed but agreed. Lexi handed Callie me my bouquet, and we headed down the hallway.

As my father was no longer in the picture, I had asked my mother to walk me down the aisle. Scott and Gary, Tina's husband, met us outside the sanctuary doors, looking dapper in their dress jackets and soft pink ties.

"You look beautiful, Callie," Scott said, and Gary nodded his agreement, though his eyes were focused on his wife.

The music began and we all took a collective breath.

Gary held out his arm, and Tina slipped hers inside, flashing one more worried smile at me before opening the door and beginning her walk down the aisle.

Scott held out his arm to Lexi, who smiled and flashed me a wink.

As the doors closed behind them, I turned to my mother. "Thank you, mom, for always sticking with me and for continuing to pray for me even when I didn't want it."

My mother sniffed and wiped away the tear that had escaped from her eye. "Of course, dear, that's is what mothers do. I'm sure you will do the same for Hope."

Hope fluttered at the mention of her name, and I placed a hand on my stomach to calm her. Another wave of dizziness washed over me, and I closed my eyes briefly, hoping my mother wouldn't notice.

The music started, and my mother held the door open. I searched for JD and his calming presence. If I could just make it down to the end of the aisle.

Glad for my mother's arm that lent extra strength, I focused on putting one foot in front of the other. The black dots were returning, making it difficult to keep my eyes locked on JD, but my feet kept moving, and I made it to JD's side. He took my arm, and I sensed the concern in his eyes.

Forcing a tight smile though the pain was now licking at my lower back almost constantly, I took the last few steps to stand before Pastor Tony with him.

"Dearly beloved," Pastor Tony started, "We are gathered here today to celebrate this man and this woman and their union with and before God. The marriage of one man to one woman is sacred to God. He designed us not to be alone, but to share our life with someone. JD and Callie found each other and have decided to share the rest of their life together. They have written vows they would now like to share with you. JD?"

JD took my hand and stared into my eyes. "Callie, I've loved you from the moment I first met you. Even after we lost touch the first time, I never stopped thinking about you, and I prayed that we would meet again. I thought when you came into my life again it was the happiest day of my life, but I was wrong. This is the happiest day of my life, being here with you and all our friends, and I promise to love you and only you, for as long as we both shall live." He reached behind him and picked up the ring Scott held out, placing it back on my hand – its rightful place.

Gazing at JD, I smiled, and summoning all the strength I could to make my voice even and clear, I repeated the words I had memorized a few days ago. "JD, I met you at one of my lowest points in life, and you saw me at my worst and still cared about me. You taught me about God's love, even though I didn't believe you at first, but you never gave up on me. I knew when we crossed paths again that I loved you, and I promise to love only you and never give up on you as long as we both live." Scott brought the pillow to me, and I slid the ring I had picked for JD onto his finger.

"Jonathon Daniel Peterson," Pastor Tony began again, "do you take Callie Marie Green as your wife to have and to hold, to love and to cherish, forsaking all others till death do you part?"

"I do."

JD's hands holding mine sent strength down my arms.

"Callie Marie Green, do you take Jonathon Daniel Peterson as your husband to have to hold, to love and to cherish, forsaking all others till death do you part?"

"I do." The word came out barely more than a whisper as another stream of pain coursed up my back and exploded in my head.

"Then by the honor vested in me by the great state of Texas and the Lord above, I now pronounce you husband and wife. You may kiss the bride."

JD wrapped his arms around me and placed his lips to mine. I could hear the crowd clapping, but the pounding in my head overshadowed it, and I sagged against his strong arms.

"Callie, what's wrong?" JD's voice, full of fear, cut through the noise in my head just briefly.

"I think . . . I need . . ." I gasped and then slipped out of his grasp and fell to the floor. The pain that was happening now couldn't be Braxton Hicks. It licked up my left side, and the spots returned with a vengeance, dancing intricate maneuvers in my vision. A pounding in my head stirred nausea causing me to grab my stomach.

A collective gasp rippled through the audience followed by a hushed murmur. The people on stage all dropped to my side.

"Someone call 911."

JD brushed my hair back and cradled my head. I concentrated on breathing and whispering a prayer that Hope was okay. I hadn't fallen directly on my side, but I knew any fall while pregnant could be bad.

Moments later, two EMTs rushed in, carrying a stretcher.

"Can you tell us your name, ma'am?"

"Callie Green, no sorry, Peterson." I smiled up at JD as the paramedic took my blood pressure and shined something in my eye.

"So, Callie, what happened here?"

The paramedic's blond face appeared again. She appeared close to my age.

"I've been having some pain and spots in my vision."

"Spots? You didn't mention spots," my mother said. Her voice was a mixture of fear and admonishment.

"Sorry, they come and go, but after the headache, they got pretty bad, and I think that's when I collapsed."

"There's a headache now too?" Tina's concerned voice joined in.

"Well, I think you should have come in earlier," the paramedic said, "but you've earned yourself a trip to the hospital."

"At least we're married now, right, Pastor Tony?"

"Don't worry, Callie, it's official. I have the paper right here."

"Oh good, I made it through the ceremony."

The EMT's rolled me onto the stiff board and strapped my arms, legs, and head down. I tried not to focus on all the terrified faces above me. I hadn't meant to scare everyone.

"I'm coming with her," JD said to the paramedics as they began to haul her down the aisle.

"Just one in the ambulance," the blond said. "The others will have to drive themselves."

"We can take the church van. I'll drive."

The inside of the ambulance was bright and silver. A too bright light above my face kept my eyes blinking. JD's face came into view for a moment as he climbed in and then disappeared as he sat down, but I could feel his hand holding mine.

The other EMT, also a woman, but with dark hair pulled back in a severe ponytail, hovered over my face attaching and buckling things I couldn't see. She didn't talk much, and I wished the blond were back here instead. She seemed calmer.

My eyes closed as the ambulance roared to life and the siren began to wail. The sound was too loud, but I had no way to cover my ears with my arms strapped to my side. Instead, I focused on sending words to heaven. Words of supplication in hopes of healing and relief.

When the ambulance stopped, the back doors flew open and the gurney was pulled down. I was now on a bed with wheels, and the world began to whiz by as the hospital doors opened.

The EMTs rattled off my name and age and then some medical jargon I did not comprehend.

A doctor with kind blue eyes appeared, older looking, but maybe that was from the stress of the job. His dark hair was streaked with grey. "Hi, Callie. I'm Dr. Rhodes. We're going to take good care of you."

I smiled and then the pain flared again, and the world went dark.

When my eyes opened again, I was no longer on the hard gurney, but a softer hospital bed instead. My wedding dress had been replaced with a faded blue hospital gown. I hoped they hadn't had to cut it off. An IV tube ran from my left arm to a silver rod holding a clear liquid bag. Some sort of monitoring device was attached to my pointer finger, and there was some weird belt around my belly. A steady beeping and the sound of something scratching on paper filled the room.

There was a small couch and a few chairs in the room, but they were empty. Where had everyone gone?

A moment later, the door opened and JD entered carrying a tray of food. "Oh, thank goodness you're awake," he said, rushing to my side. He set the tray on a side table and leaned over to kiss me.

"How long have I been out?"

"A few hours. The doctors ran some tests, and we're waiting on the results, but they think you passed out from the pain. How is the pain now?"

I took a deep breath and closed my eyes, searching for the pain, but couldn't feel any. "I don't feel any now."

"They gave you some pain killer," he said. "It must be helping."

"Where is everyone else?"

"In the lobby. They're only allowing me until they figure out what's wrong with you."

The door opened again, and Dr. Rhodes entered, carrying a clipboard. "Ah, good, you're awake. How are you feeling?"

"Good for now. Did you find out what's wrong with me?"

His smile straightened, and his face grew serious. "Yes, we did. You have a bad case of preeclampsia. The pain in both your side and your head as well as the vision spots are tell-tale signs, plus your blood pressure is extremely high."

A knife of fear inserted itself and began to twist. "What does that mean?"

"Well, in some cases it would mean that we keep you here and monitor you, but in your case, I fear a seizure. I want to deliver the baby right away."

"But, but she's not forty weeks yet."

He nodded. "I know, she's only thirty-five weeks, but Callie, if we wait and you have a seizure, it could cause you lasting damage."

"Will she be okay at thirty-five weeks? Is she fully developed?"

"Her lungs may still be weak. We'll give you some steroids to help develop her lungs, and I'll schedule a C-section for two days from now. That will give her lungs time to develop. We'll also start you on some anti-seizure medication, but I have to warn you that while it's generally effective, seizures can still happen. The sooner we deliver, the better your chances."

I nodded, trying to abate the fear running rampant through me now, not only for myself but for my daughter. There was one more thing I needed to know though. "Did I . . . did I make it worse by not coming in at the first sign?"

Dr. Rhodes shook his head. "It's hard to say. Your blood pressure might have been a little lower then and we might have been able to get you on medication sooner, but you still probably would have been confined to hospital bed rest so we could monitor you. If you had had a seizure during that time, then yes it would have been worse, but since you didn't, my guess is that the two days didn't make much difference."

Relief flooded my veins and weakened the dam that had been holding back the tears threatening to spill down my cheeks.

"But," he continued, "the next time you have symptoms like that, don't wait, okay?"

Emotion constricted my throat, choking off words, so I nodded. As the doctor left the room, the dam exploded, and a sob escaped. My shoulders began to shake as more sobs wracked my body, and the tears flowed freely.

"Hey, it's okay," JD said, his hand caressing my hair. He leaned down and kissed my forehead, sending waves of comfort over me.

"I'm so sorry. I felt like something bad was going to happen, and I wanted to make sure that you were Hope's legal guardian if anything happened to me."

His green eyes clouded with emotion. "Callie, we could have figured something else out. Please don't keep me in the dark like that again."

"I promise."

*A*s he watched her eyes close, his thoughts returned to a time years before with Alexa. She too hadn't told him when she had first gotten sick, and by the time she did, he could nothing but hold her hand and watch her die. He couldn't bear to do that again. When he was sure Callie was asleep again, he stood and stretched. He needed to update everyone in the hall.

He opened the door as quietly as he could and found Dr. Rhodes waiting for him on the other side. "I'm glad I caught you. I need a word."

His words were solemn and heavy like a lead balloon. Fear gripped JD, its icy talons shooting down his shoulders. His knees buckled and he stumbled back, sagging against the wall. "How bad is it?" The words felt like fire in his mouth.

"Worse than I let on," Dr. Rhodes said, "but I needed to calm her down. Stress will only make it worse. She needs to deliver, but in her condition, the risks are much higher."

"What can we do?"

"Unfortunately, not much. We have to let the steroids take effect or we risk losing the baby, but the longer we wait, the more we risk losing Callie. If you're a religious man, I'd say pray."

JD felt like he'd been sucker punched in the gut. He couldn't lose Callie, not after finally finding her and making her his wife. He thanked the doctor, took another moment to compose himself, and then continued to the waiting room. A voice inside told him not to tell everyone the news the doctor had just shared. He needed them to be positive for Callie. For now, only Scott and Pastor Tony would be informed. Perhaps they could help him figure out what to do next.

Every head looked up when JD entered. He hadn't expected so many, but nearly everyone from the wedding was there, along with several members of the church.

"Callie's sleeping right now, but when she wakes, we can take turns visiting her. She has preeclampsia so they want her to stay positive and avoid stress. They are giving her steroids to help develop Hope's lungs, and then they'll perform a C-section. It would be amazing if you all could be praying for peace and for her safety.

As the group began to pair up and bow their heads, JD approached Melanie whose skin had paled. Her hand covered her mouth, and he could tell she was holding back tears. "Will you go sit with her? I need to talk to Tony, and I'd like someone there with her in case she wakes up."

Melanie's eyes bore into his own. "What aren't you telling me?"

"I promise I'll tell you later, but for now, will you trust me?"

It took another long look, but finally she stood and walked toward Callie's room. JD moved on to Scott and motioned for Tony to join them. The three stepped to the far corner, out of hearing range of the others in the room.

"It's not good," JD said. "I'm not sure what else to do, but the doctor said to pray."

"Of course; I'll get Sandra right on calling our members." Tony said. "I'll also call the other pastors I know and spread the word to their prayer teams."

"What can I do?" Scott asked.

"I'll be in the room most of the time," JD said. "Can you relay information to people here or wherever they're gathered?"

Scott nodded in agreement, and Pastor Tony led the three of them in prayer for Callie and Hope.

Callie was still sleeping when JD returned to the room. Melanie rose and crossed to him. The questions still brimmed in her eyes, but JD couldn't tell her yet.

"Melanie, can you go to Callie's apartment and get some things?" He thought for a moment of all they might need. "The diaper bag, for one. It's packed and in Hope's room. Maybe some clothes for Callie for if, I mean when," he corrected himself, "she comes home. Toothbrush, toothpaste, oh and her Bible, I know she'll want that."

"Okay." Melanie agreed, and though he could tell she wanted more details, she didn't ask and JD was grateful.

He sat in the chair Melanie had scooted close to the bed and grasped Callie's hand. His eyes closed against the emotions battering to be released and he sent up another stream of prayers. He hated feeling helpless, but he knew that the only thing he could do was to pray for Callie, unceasingly.

CHAPTER 17

The two days that followed were the longest of my life. Though the doctor kept making assurances that the time I had waited hadn't made much of a difference, I still battled a massive guilt every time I thought about it, and I worried about Hope constantly.

On top of that, the monitor on my belly to track Hope's heartbeat wasn't very comfortable, and if I moved too far in either direction, the sensors would lose track of Hope's heartbeat and nurses would rush in to check on me, so I couldn't get decent rest. I had to lie almost completely on my back, and it had gone numb sometime yesterday. And as they would only let me out of bed to go to the bathroom, I couldn't stretch or take a shower, which left me feeling sore and grimy.

To top it all off, the doctors didn't want me overstimulated or stressed out, so they capped the visitors to two at a time. Because there were so many people wanting to visit, this meant an almost constant flow of people coming in and out, at least until I got too tired and had to take a nap.

Still, I would gladly relive the past two days over again if it could mean foregoing the C-section today. Though I knew the hospital staff did them every day, one hadn't been in my plan, and as much as I was trying to give everything to God, there were some things I just couldn't let go.

As the nurses came into the room, my breath stopped. The fear I had been pushing away filled my body, and my veins ran ice cold. Unable to speak, I squeezed JD's hand and shot him a look.

JD turned to the nurses. "Can you give us a minute?"

The team left and JD, my mother, and I joined hands. "Lord, I don't know what your purpose is with this event in Callie's life, and we want your will to be done, but we ask that you keep Hope and Callie safe and bring them both back to us after this is over. Give us peace with whatever happens and courage to keep doing your will. Amen." His eyes perused my face, and he squeezed my hand and swallowed several times before he could continue speaking. "I love you Callie, and whatever happens, I will be right here with you."

I could see the sheen in his eyes, and I nodded, trying to contain my own emotion to keep my tears from flowing again. "I love you too," I whispered, hoping it wouldn't be the last time I said it.

My mother leaned down and placed a kiss on my forehead. She was unable to stop the tears flowing down her face. "I love you precious girl, and whatever happens, I am so proud of you."

The door opened and one of the nurses poked her head back in. "I'm sorry, but we really need to go now; the room is ready and the anesthesiologist is waiting." She entered as well as three other nurses. JD and my mother stepped back as the nurses unlocked the bed and wheeled me and my IV out into the hallway.

Usually, JD would have been able to accompany me into a C-section delivery, but the doctors were sure that my case was so advanced that I might need immediate medical attention, so he was not admitted. This information did nothing to calm the ball of nerves in my stomach.

As the bed was wheeled down the hall, I took deep breaths to calm my nerves. Lights flashed overhead, and I closed my eyes to avoid the nausea. I pictured the field of daisies from my dream so long ago and the little blond angel who had visited. It didn't stop my heartbeat from reverberating in my ears.

Suddenly, I shivered. The temperature had dropped, and I lost my hold on the daisies. A cold silver, sterile operating room surrounded me as my eyes opened. A bright light hung from the ceiling, and I blinked. Several doctors were already busy prepping in the room. One was sitting on a stool near the bed.

"Hi, I'm Michael," he said, taking my hand. "I have some music. Would you like music during the procedure?"

I didn't know him; I could barely even tell what he looked like with the mask covering the lower part of his face and his hair hidden under a blue cap that matched his scrubs, but his hand sent a wave of comfort nonetheless.

"Do you have any Toby Mac?" My voice sounded small and distorted.

He smiled and squeezed my hand. "You bet. Now, my job is to make sure you aren't feeling any pain so once we numb you, you're going to focus on me and let me know if you feel anything okay?"

I nodded. Michael and a few other doctors helped me onto the operating bed, and then Michael picked up a long needle and injected my back. I grimaced at the pain. It took a few minutes, but as they laid me back, my legs grew numb.

"Okay, can you feel this?" Michael touched a spot on my leg.

I shook my head. I could see him poking my leg, but I could feel nothing.

"How about this?" He touched a different spot.

Again, I shook my head.

"Okay, then I believe we're ready. Let me turn your music on."

I tried to focus on the music instead of the pounding of my heart. Two doctors strapped my arms down straight out each side, and I couldn't help thinking of a crucifixion. They told me it was so I wouldn't grab at them while they were operating, but I couldn't imagine doing that in the first place. Then they raised a blue sheet and blocked my view of what was happening, which increased my fear even more. The pounding in my head grew to a cacophonous beating.

Michael came back and took my hand once more as another doctor began the incision. I couldn't feel the knife, but I could feel the tugging sensation, like someone was yanking my insides. Glancing up,

I realized I could see a reflection of the doctor cutting my abdomen in the light above me. I closed my eyes and shivered. Ice seemed to be running through me like a liquid maze.

"We've got a bleed somewhere," one of the doctors said and then the pain exploded in my head. *Was this normal?* I tried to open my eyes, wanting desperately to hear Hope's cry, but the pain became too intense and the world went dark.

"*W*e're losing her." The voice was soft, far away, but I thought it was Michael's. Who were they losing? Me or Hope?

Another voice spoke, even softer, almost like a whisper through a door. "Let's get the baby first, and then we can see what's happening."

There was silence in the darkness, and then the sound of a baby's cry. A peace settled on me, and then the darkness took over.

*J*D and Melanie were still praying when a nurse stepped in the room. "I have some news."

They both glanced up, and JD held his breath. Fear and excitement battled for the dominant emotion in his head.

"You have a daughter, and she looks great. We're going to keep her in the NICU for a few days, but so far we don't see any long term problems. She's 5lbs 5 ounces and 17 inches long."

JD squeezed Melanie's hand and flashed her a tight smile. He waited for the nurse to give an update on Callie and when she didn't, his heart tightened, and he focused again on the woman, whose hands were tightly clasped in front of her.

JD swallowed the lump crowding his throat, "And how is Callie?"

The nurse paused, and her eye twitched as she looked at him. "I'm afraid there was a complication. The doctors are still working on her now."

JD fell back into the chair.

"You can come see the baby whenever you're ready," the nurse offered gently.

"Thank you." Melanie gave her a nod before turning to JD. "God is watching out for your wife now; let's go meet your daughter," she said, touching his shoulder.

JD stared at the change in her. The last two days, Melanie had seemed older, frailer, but suddenly it was like they had switched places, and she was the rock giving him needed strength and support. He accepted the change as he had nothing left at the moment to protest with. Surrendering to the mothering spirit she was offering, he stood and followed her down the hall, but inside he was still numb.

Hope Elizabeth Peterson was perfect. She appeared tiny, but the nurses assured them she was healthy. She had no real hair, but the slightest hint of blond fuzz covered her head, and her eyes were a bright blue.

JD feared holding her at first as the emotions were still battling inside him. One part of him longed to hold her, but another part insisted that it was her fault that Callie was in the situation she was in. That voice began to whisper that this baby wasn't really his and that he'd never be able to love her if something happened to Callie.

JD fought the voice, knowing it was Satan trying to turn him from God's plan. He held out his arms, and the nurse placed the tiny bundle in them. As JD held her, she seemed to look right at him, and then she wrapped her tiny hand around his finger. JD's breath caught in his throat. He wondered again how people could throw these tiny human beings away. Even though she wasn't his by blood, JD knew she was his daughter in every other sense of the word. He reluctantly handed her to Melanie after a few minutes and watched them bond as well.

His fear and anxiety flared anew without Hope in his arms. He needed another way to calm his nerves. "I'm going to go see if there's any news on Callie."

He left the room and headed down the hall to the nurse's station. Callie's doctor stood at the counter conversing with the nurses. As JD neared, he turned, a grim look on his face.

JD's heart dropped. "Is she...?"

The doctor held up his hand. "There was a complication, but we managed to stop her bleeding. Unfortunately, she lapsed into a coma.

We don't know why or when she might come out of it, but she is alive."

JD nodded and sank to the floor against the wall. It wasn't the news he had hoped for, but at least she was alive. He stared at his phone knowing he should text Scott to share the news, but how did you write that the love of your life was in a coma?

A nurse touched his shoulder. "She's back in her room now. Would you like to go see her?"

JD wiped his hand across his eyes and pushed himself up, following the nurse on legs that didn't feel his own.

Callie looked frail and pale under the sheet. JD sat beside Callie and stroked her hand, pushing away the thought of Alexa's death that kept crowding into his mind. "She's beautiful," his voice caught in his throat. "Hope is really beautiful. You did a good thing Callie. Please stay with us. You need to see this beautiful life God used you to create, and she needs to know you. I know that may be selfish, but please God, let her see her daughter." JD put his head down on the side of Callie's bed and wept openly.

CHAPTER 18

*W*hen I opened my eyes, I was in my living room. Though everything looked right, something felt wrong. My hands flew to my stomach, but it was no longer large and bulging. It was flat and soft, as if it had never held a baby.

"Hope?" I raced into the guest bedroom that JD and I had turned into a nursery, but it wasn't a nursery; it was still a guest bedroom. The walls were still white, not the lavender JD had painted them for Hope. The roll top desk I had inherited from my grandfather was where the dresser should be, and the black futon couch was in the place of the crib. Clapping my hand over my mouth, my eyes darted around. "What's going on?" Fear massaged my shoulders, and I backed out the room.

Nothing appeared out of place in the hallway, but in the kitchen no sonograms hung on the fridge. I bolted to the bedroom. There was no picture of JD and I on the nightstand, nor was my Bible in its prominent place. The front door lock clicked, and I raced back to the living room. Rooted to the spot, I watched the lock turn and the door open, and then I gasped. It was Daniel and not JD.

"What are you doing here?"

He glared at me as he threw his coat on the couch and his wallet on the hall table. "Cut the crap, Callie, I live here, remember? Have you been drinking again?"

"Drinking? What are you talking about? I haven't had a drink since I found out I was pregnant."

"Pregnant? Are you pregnant again?" His face flamed red, and he took a menacing step toward me.

"No, when I found out I was pregnant with Hope. You know nine months ago?"

"Who's Hope, Callie?"

"The baby, you know the one you didn't want? The one you said I should abort?"

"You did have an abortion, Callie." He rolled his eyes and plunked down on the couch, as if this was a conversation we had had many times.

"What? No, I wouldn't have. I couldn't have. I mean, I remember going, but then I talked to Sandra, and I decided not to. I remember getting bigger and feeling her move. I saw her ultrasound."

He sighed. "I know; you babble about it nearly every night when you toss and turn in bed. But you did have the abortion and then you changed."

"What do you mean?"

"Look at yourself." He pointed a finger at me, and I looked down. I was standing in a bathrobe. "You quit your job. You stay home and drink all day, and now I honestly think you're going crazy."

"It happened." I sucked in my breath and collapsed in a nearby chair.

"What?"

"I became one of the 80%."

"What are you talking about?" He wasn't listening though; he had picked up the remote and was surfing through channels on the TV.

"You know the 80% that suffer mental health problems after an abortion," I said. "Remember, I told you about these abortion statistics when I didn't want to give up the baby, and you said it wouldn't happen to me. But it did."

"Well whatever the reason, you need help Callie. I won't stick around forever trying to clean up this mess. In fact, maybe I'll go see Shaina." He leaned back on the couch with his hands behind his head and shot me a challenging look.

It should have made me angry, but instead it calmed every nerve in my body. "You probably already have been. I get the feeling you aren't ready to be tied down to just one woman."

"Finally, you understand." Smiling, he planted his feet on the coffee table. "I was so tired of coming up with lies. It really is exhausting, you know? And men aren't meant to stay with just one woman. We need flavors." He resumed clicking the remote. "Now maybe we can work out a plan. Like I spend weekdays here with you and weekends with her or maybe a three-four split? Maybe we can even spend a few nights together with all three of us?"

Swallowing the disgust that rose in my throat, I bit my lip to keep the unclean words I had for him from leaving my mouth. "I've got a better idea." I flashed a tight smile at him. "Why don't you take your stuff and spend every day with her?"

"Be realistic, Callie." He didn't even glance up at me. "You're a mess. I can't leave you here alone."

My eyes narrowed, and I placed my hands on my hips. "I'm going to give you ten minutes, and then I'm going to call the cops."

The chill in my voice grabbed his attention, and he glanced up. "Look, I'll go tonight, but I'm serious, Callie, you can't be alone, so I'll be back tomorrow and we'll get you some help."

I picked up his coat and wallet and held them out to him. "Leave." The word came out as two syllables, both accented forcefully and with as much hate as I could muster.

"Whatever," he said, pushing himself off the couch. "You're too much work anyway." He grabbed his things and stormed out of the apartment.

As the door slammed shut, I sank down on the couch and covered my face with my hands. I knew this wasn't the path I had chosen, but how did I leave this reality? The silence in the apartment began to close in on me, and I reached for my Bible, only it wasn't on the table.

A quick glance revealed it was nowhere in the living room. My eyes darted back and forth as I tried to remember where it might be. Then I remembered where I had found it the first time. Racing back into the bedroom, I bent down and looked on the nightstand. There it was, coated in dust, just as before. As I picked it up, peace flowed through me, but I still had no idea how to get back to the reality I knew. I pulled my cell phone from my pocket and called my mother.

"How long has it been mom?" I asked as soon as she answered.

"Well hi, Callie, how long has it been since what?"

I sat on the bed and picked at the robe. "Since I had the abortion, mom, how long?"

"Nine months, Callie. Your baby would have been born any day now. Are you still having dreams? Is that why you're calling?" My mother sighed on the other end.

"No, or I don't think so anyway. Mom, I'm not supposed to be here or at least not this here. See, I didn't abort Hope. I kept her, but I developed preeclampsia. Something went wrong during the C-section, and I ended up here, but I'm not supposed to be here." The words tumbled out in a rush.

"Callie, I think you are suffering from grief over your choice. Now I love you, but I did not love that decision. I would have loved a grandchild and you robbed me of that, but I'm praying to God to forgive you and you should pray for forgiveness, too. I also think it's time you got some professional help."

My forehead wrinkled, but I stayed silent at my mother's accusation. I had no words to convince her, and I was beginning to be unsure myself. "Okay Mom, I will. Thanks." I hung up the phone and stared at it for a minute. *What can I do?* JD's handsome face popped into my head. He would be able to help me. I punched in the cell number I had long ago memorized and tapped my leg as it rang.

"Hello?" a female voice answered.

My mouth opened and closed, unable to form a word. I hung up the phone and dropped it as if it were a hot coal. Of course JD was with someone. In this reality, the last time he saw me was in the Caribbean with Daniel.

Picking up the Bible, I hugged it to my chest. Now that I had tasted it, a world without JD and without Hope held no meaning. "Is this how it would have been, God? Would my life have been so empty?" I lay back, closed my eyes, and prayed for this nightmare to be over.

CHAPTER 19

$\mathcal{J}$D pulled into the church parking lot on his way to his apartment. He hadn't wanted to leave Callie's side, but Melanie had insisted that a) he take a shower and get some fresh clothing at least and b) that he go and see the prayer vigil that Scott had started at the church.

He was amazed by the sheer number of cars filling the parking lot in the middle of a weekday. Locking his car, he stumbled into the building.

Nearly every chair in the sanctuary was filled. He hadn't even known so many people attended their church. Where had they all come from?

"Isn't it amazing?"

He blinked at the sound of Scott's voice and turned to see his friend at the door, Lexi next to him.

"We've gotten so big, we have to be on a rotation basis. We've got local businesses bringing in food as well as a lot of families helping with that."

"Do all these people attend here?"

Scott smiled and shook his head. "No, Sandra organized a lot of this, but when Tony called his pastor friends, several drove over to come pray here. It's amazing. I've never seen a revival quite like this."

"I've never seen anything like this," Lexi said, placing her hand on Scott's arm. A soft pink spread across his face.

"Guess I've missed a lot," JD said, raising his brow at his friend.

Scott put his hand on Lexi's. "Yeah, Lexi accepted Jesus as her savior a few days ago, and we've started seeing each other."

JD wished he were more excited for his friend. Scott definitely deserved it, but a powerful jealousy swept through him. Why should Scott have someone when the love of his life was laying in the hospital, unable to even see her daughter. "That's wonderful," he said, though the words pained him. "I'm going to run home and shower and get back to Callie. I'll keep you posted on any change."

He hurried out of the building before the jealousy made him say something he would regret.

At his apartment, he threw clothes into a bag, then stripped out of his three-day old jeans and t-shirt and stepped into the shower. He turned the water as hot as he could stand it and enjoyed the burning sensation it brought to his skin.

His mind wandered back to Alexa. He had hoped her death would have been the last time he would have to say goodbye to someone in a hospital. She had become addicted to drugs after being diagnosed with cancer. It was how he had started using, partly because she had asked him to do so and partly because he couldn't stand to see her wasting away. The drugs had eased that pain, but only temporarily. When she was gone, even the drugs couldn't quiet the aching in his heart. They had never gotten to have the family he had always wanted, but now he had another chance for that.

JD stepped out of the shower and sighed. This should be the happiest time of his life, and he was happy about Hope. She was like a tiny ball of sunshine. It didn't matter who held her; she always seemed to have a way to touch their heart. But he missed Callie; he wanted her to be able to share in his joy. She had done so much for so many people, himself included, that he couldn't really imagine life without her or life with her comatose. She had to wake up and meet her ray of light. He fell to his knees on the floor, not caring that he was clad only in a towel, and requested God once again heal Callie. This prayer was beginning to feel like a broken record, but he would keep repeating it until Callie woke. After praying, he dressed, grabbed his bag, and then headed back to the hospital.

*T*his time when my eyes opened, I she was in the familiar field of daisies where a sea of white stretched before me and in all directions. Peace blanketed me as I gazed around. The sun warmed my shoulders, and a light breeze tousled my hair. To the right, a blond baby crawled through a patch of grass, and I knew without a doubt that it was Hope. I called out to her, but the baby didn't seem to hear. I tried to run to her, but I couldn't seem to close the distance.

"She can't hear you," a voice boomed behind me. Turning, I saw a man glowing with an intensity I had never seen before. His eyes were like sapphires, and his blond hair waved gently in the breeze. His white robe was so bright that I had to shield my eyes.

"Am I dead?"

"Not yet."

"Then why am I here?" I motioned to the field around us.

The angel smiled. "Because we wanted to show you something. Something you can take back with you." He waved his hand and thousands of people appeared in the field. There were more people than I could even begin to count.

Furrowing my brow, I shook my head, not getting the connection. "Who are they?"

"They are all those who were saved because of your work and your testimony," the angel replied. "Every one of them would never have been born if it hadn't been for yours and JD's center and even more importantly, your message. You touched the lives of the parents of these people, and they chose life for their babies."

My mouth dropped as I stared in wonder. "But there's so many. I haven't talked to that many people."

"You are not done yet," the angel smiled, "You are only beginning, but there is also a ripple effect. You see this man." He pointed to a man near the front, "This is the son of a high school couple you met and set up with counseling services. She and her boyfriend gave up their sinful ways like you suggested, and because of your message she never went to the abortion clinic, but gave him up for adoption instead.

"And this boy, because he knows he was saved from an abortion, has a passion for saving others — he grows up to be the lawyer who becomes instrumental in finally getting Roe V Wade over turned. That change alone saved millions of lives.

"This one," he pointed to a tall brunette, "is here because of a woman hearing about your story right now. She became a believer because of you, and her daughter will become a neonatal surgeon and save thousands of babies a year.

"And this one," this time he singled out a pretty blond with striking blue eyes, "she grows up to be a medical researcher and discovers the cure for cancer. So do you see now how your words, no matter how small they seemed to you, have a ripple effect you could never have imagined?"

I nodded in awe, still focused on the blond woman who seemed vaguely familiar.

The angel continued, "These people, and others you talked to and will talk to in turn, shared your words and their words touched other people." His hand waved and even more people appeared. "Your world is changing, because of voices like yours. Because Christians are no longer silent, people are starting to turn back to God. You must continue to be a part of that voice. Tell anyone who will listen about the awesome power of the Lord Almighty and stand up against the world for the morals you know are true to God's heart."

I nodded, still trying to take it all in. "I will; I will not be silent. Did you show me the other vision too, the one where my world was different?"

He nodded. "In order to really understand what you had, we wanted you to see where you could have been had your choices been different. Callie, you've had the wonderful opportunity to experience what your life would have been like if you had made the wrong decision at such an important time. If you had chosen the selfish, easy path, your life would not be the same. You would have lost your job, you would have sunk into a deep depression, and you would have died of alcohol poisoning at age 35. Had you chosen poorly, all of them would be gone too."

He waved his hand and the people disappeared, "Your decision to choose Christ and a life for Hope made it possible for their parents to choose life for them as well. Now it's time for you to return to your husband and child – and your mission." He leaned closer and whispered, "Inspire people to righteousness when you go back. Tell them that saving even one life can in turn save millions. Don't let the unborn remain silent."

I stood silent, still overcome by the stark differences he had shown me.

"Now it's time for you to return," he whispered.

"Wait, can I ask for one favor?"

The angel nodded, and I thought of Sandra, who had never gotten to see her baby. I twisted my hands and then peeked up at the angel, "Can I see Isaac? Sandra's Isaac, so I can tell her that he's okay."

The angel cocked his head and closed his eyes. He smiled, nodded, and opened his eyes. With a wave of his hand again, a young man with caramel colored skin appeared before her. He had warm brown eyes and a dimple in his left cheek. He was tall with broad shoulders and kept his hair cropped close.

"Isaac would have been a writer, and he too would have touched many lives, but you can let Sandra know that God has fully forgiven her. She has followed His word and His will since that horrible night, and there's a place for her here when it's time for her to come home. Then, she will get to meet this boy she gave up so long ago."

I tried to memorize every feature of Isaac's face. I was no artist so I couldn't draw him, but I hoped to describe him to Sandra. "Thank you."

He nodded and disappeared and so did the field. I stood alone in darkness unsure of what to do next. Closing my eyes, I hoped to wake up in the hospital bed and hold my darling daughter.

As I opened them, I could see my mother sitting by her bed and

Sandra a few feet away, gently rocking the baby. I glanced around but didn't see JD. My voice was barely audible as I began to speak. "Hope." I tried again and got a little more volume this time, although it was still barely more than a whisper. "Hope." It was enough for my mother to hear.

"Callie? Oh praise God. She's awake." She leaned over the bed and embraced me. Sandra wheeled closer and brought a sleeping Hope.

My mother helped raise the bed and then handed the sleeping infant to me.

Her face was angelic, and my heart ached with love. "She's beautiful." Tears of joy fell down my face as my entire body tingled in light.

"Yes, she is." My mother touched Hope's cheek. "I know I've told you before, but I'm so glad you chose life for this baby."

"Me too." I picked up Hope's tiny hand and touched her delicate fingers.

The door opened and JD entered the room, stopping short at the sight of me sitting up. "Callie?"

I waved my hand, unsure what to say, and he ran to me, planting kisses across my face. "Praise God." He pulled back and stared at me; then he kissed me again.

"How long have I been out?"

"Three days, honey -- three long days," JD brushed my hair back.

"I missed nearly an entire week of her life?" My heart ached as I caressed Hope's head.

"You did, but think of how many more you'll get to spend with her," my mother said.

Suddenly I thought of Sandra and the pain she must be feeling. "I'm so sorry Sandra, I wasn't thinking."

Sandra smiled, but it didn't quite reach her eyes. "It's okay. I understand how you feel. I'd give anything to see my baby now."

"Oh, I almost forgot. Sandra, I saw him."

"What?" The word came from Sandra, but my mother and JD registered the question on their faces as well.

I smiled, the excitement lighting up my face. "I had an unusual experience while I was unconscious. Mainly I remember darkness, but then I woke up and I was in my apartment, and Hope was gone and Daniel was still there. I was drinking and depressed, and you were with some other woman." I pointed to JD.

"And then I was in a field of daisies, and I saw Hope and an angel appeared. He showed me all the people who were saved through our message, and there were so many. I don't know how we've affected so many. Well, I think some we haven't affected yet, but he said many are affected because of the center, JD." I tried to slow down, but my words tumbled out in a rush.

"Anyway, the angel told me I had to come back to finish the work I was called to do, but I asked him if I could see Isaac first. He agreed, and, Sandra, he was so handsome. He has warm brown eyes and caramel skin and a dimple in his left cheek."

Tears welled up in Sandra's eyes.

"He was so handsome, and I could tell he was very kind. And the angel said to tell you that God forgives you, and when you get to Heaven, you'll get to see him in person." With the words finally out, I took a deep breath and looked from one person to the other.

"Thank you, Callie," Sandra said softly. "That means the world to me."

My mother squeezed my hand. "We should probably let everyone know you're awake now."

"Let's do that in the hall," Sandra suggested. "These two need a few minutes to get reacquainted, and mother and daughter need that too."

The women exited and JD smiled down me again. "I'm so glad you came back to us and that we will get to be a real family now." He caressed my hair and gazed down at Hope.

"Me too." I touched Hope's tiny hand, marveling at her perfect fingers. "She really is beautiful."

"Callie, I have to tell you something," JD fidgeted with the bed sheet. "I was going to do it before we got married, but then everything happened so quickly and I forgot."

My heart thudded, and a knot of fear developed in my stomach. "What is it? You aren't leaving me, are you?"

"No, not at all." He caressed my arm. "I need to tell you about my past, too."

I could tell that he was troubled by whatever was on his mind. "I'll listen if you need to tell me, but JD, if it isn't who you are today, then it doesn't matter to me. You once told me God would forgive my past when I accepted His son and that lingering on one's past mistakes isn't the thing to do."

"That's true, but I need to tell you in case it ever comes up again in the future."

I nodded, and he continued.

"When I was in college, I met the woman I thought I was going to marry. She was amazing and vibrant and full of life, and she won my heart. What I didn't know was that it was all an act. She had terminal cancer, and she was using some pretty strong drugs in order to appear so happy. We started dating and slowly she introduced me to her drugs. I wanted to support her and so when she offered them to me, I tried them. I must have an addictive personality because I was hooked almost instantly. My life fell apart for a time and it wasn't until she passed away that I realized how far I had fallen. I've been clean for years and have no intention of doing drugs again, but I needed to let you know so you can help me avoid any such temptation in the future."

"Thank you for telling me. I'm sorry you lost someone you loved. The fear of losing me must have been hard for you when I was comatose."

"Yeah, I can't say I'm a big fan of hospitals. Speaking of which, when can we leave here?"

Laughing, I kissed him again. I couldn't wait to get home either.

CHAPTER 20

*A*fter amazing the medical staff with my quick recovery, we left the hospital a few days later - as a family, and headed home.

JD carried Hope's car seat into my apartment. "I guess I can start moving some of my things in here now, huh?"

"Oh my, we didn't even think about that." I laughed as I realized all the changes I would need to make. "I'm going to need to make some room in my closet."

"It's okay. I didn't bring that much with me, but we're going to need to discuss whether we plan on staying here or moving to New York."

His words gave me pause. I hadn't even thought about that when I had accepted his proposal. I had been so excited, but Texas was my home, and I couldn't imagine Hope growing up in New York. My gaze traveled to the floor, and I bit my lip. How could I tell him I didn't want to leave?

"Don't worry," he said, touched my arm, "We'll pray about it."

I nodded and picked Hope up from the car seat, settling her against my chest. As I carried her around the apartment, I pointed everything out to her.

"And here's your room." Pink and purple flowers and butterflies adorned the lavender walls, along with the wooden letters H O P E. Hope smiled and yawned, so I laid her down in the crib and left the room.

JD's arms enfolded me as I stepped into the living room. It was a tight, secure feeling that I had missed. When he released me, he moved his hands to my face. "Are you okay for a bit if I go and grab a few things from my place?"

As much as I wanted him to stay, I was tired myself and looking forward to sleeping in my actual bed.

JD rubbed his thumb over my lip and then followed it with a soft kiss. "I'll be back as soon as I can."

As he left, I crawled into bed and closed my eyes. I didn't regret having Hope for a minute, but I hadn't realized how tiring being a new mother would be.

JD climbed in his rental car. Now that Hope was here, and Callie was awake, there were a lot of things they had to figure out. Even if they stayed in Mesquite, they would need a bigger place soon and a bigger car. JD didn't really miss New York, but he did wonder what would happen to his father's business if he left the running of it up to others. Could he manage it long distance? He did have the board members, and they had been running everything anyway. JD sighed. He had always thought getting married would make things easier, but it came with its own challenges. He prayed for clarity for all the decisions he would have to make as he drove to his apartment to pick up a few things.

He'd already packed a few pieces of clothing when he had stopped by earlier, but he took his time this time grabbing his shaving equipment, toothbrush, hairbrush, and essentials. He added a few dress shirts and pants that he could wear to work at the center and then loaded up his car.

. . .

*J*D was making dinner when I woke later. He stood in the kitchen, cradling Hope in one arm while he stirred a pot of soup.

Yawning, I issued an apology. "I'm sorry, I didn't even hear her cry."

"No worries. She's been great. She helped me pick out all the vegetables." He smiled as he tickled her under her chin.

"Is there anything I can do to help?"

"Not me, but you might want to check your messages." JD pointed a spoon to the machine. "I didn't feel like it was my place yet, and I'm pretty sure they're all for you anyway."

I wrapped my arms around him and kissed his cheek. "For future reference, my messages are your messages, but thank you."

As I pushed the button on the machine, I was surprised by the number of messages from friends who had been praying and then calling to congratulate my recovery.

Tears formed in my throat. "Wow, it never ceases to amaze me how many people were praying for me."

"You've been quite an inspiration to many people." He set a bowl down in front of me. "And I hope you don't mind, but a few of them wanted to throw you a baby shower. I told them this weekend would be fine."

"That's sounds great." The vegetable soup he set down looked warm and inviting.

"I've been praying, too." JD set his bowl down and then sat across from me, still cradling Hope. "You've got roots here, and I've started to put them down as well. I want to continue to see the center grow. The Board has been running my company the last few years anyway, so I'm starting to feel like God is moving me here."

Joy filled my heart. I hadn't even wanted to think about moving to New York, though I knew I wanted to stay with JD wherever he was led.

"I'd like to pray about it some more, but would you be opposed to staying here?"

I shook my head, my grin reaching from one ear to the other. "I would have gone where ever God led us, but I can't tell you how happy I am that we are getting to stay here. I can't think of a better place to raise Hope."

I smiled at the gathering of people in our living room the following weekend. Mine was not the typical baby shower, but I wouldn't change it for the world.

My mother had arrived with a man, and she seemed happier than I could remember her looking in years. I'd have to ask her about that new relationship when I could. It was true I had been busy the last few months, but it was unlike my mother to keep something that big from me.

Lexi and Scott had shown up together. JD had informed me that not only had Lexi had accepted Christ, but that the two were now dating. I smiled at that answered prayer.

Sandra, of course was there, chatting with some of the girls from the center. Evidently, she had stepped in to help at the center while JD and I were at the hospital those five days. Though we had an office manager, I knew that Sandra had a place at our clinic as well, and I couldn't wait to discuss the idea with JD. The group was rounded out with Tina and a few other friends from church.

"Well," Melanie began, "thank you all for coming. Obviously, the baby is already here." Everybody smiled at Hope who was fast asleep in my arms, "but we thought this would also be a great time to get together and celebrate Callie's return to us."

A round of clapping ensued. "Of course, we did bring some things for Hope." Melanie picked up a present.

I stood and crossed to Sandra. "Will you hold her for a minute while I open them?" Hope already had a special place in Sandra's heart.

Tears dotted Sandra's eyes. "Of course," she held out her arms.

I returned to my chair and began opening the gifts and displaying them to everyone.

After all the gifts were open and the food was eaten, everyone packed up and left except for my mother, who was helping clean up,

Tom, who was chatting with JD since my mother was his ride, and Sandra. Sandra wheeled over to the rocker I was sitting in, rocking Hope.

"I wanted to say thank you." Sandra touched my arm.

"For what?"

She grabbed the bag off the back of her wheelchair and pulled out a rolled piece of paper. As she unrolled it, a gasp escaped my lips; the face of Isaac looked back at me.

"Did you see him?"

A soft smile tugged at her lips. "Is it him then?"

"It's perfect." My fingertips grazed the portrait.

"I used to draw a long time ago, and when you told me about Isaac, I knew I had to try to draw his portrait. I used your description and an old picture of Peter, his father, and myself. I was hoping I'd get it close to the real thing."

"You got it spot on." I squeezed Sandra's arm.

"Thank you for asking to see him and for giving me the description. I'll be ready to meet him when Jesus is ready for me, but until then I now have something to look at. I can never thank you enough, Callie."

"I'm so happy I could help you, and I'd also like to ask you to be Hope's godmother. She is going to need strong female role models, and I can think of no one else I'd rather have."

Sandra's eyes filled with tears, and she nodded her agreement. She said goodnight, took her picture with her, and headed home. Melanie and Tom left soon after, and I laid Hope down for a nap.

"Callie, I know we're officially married," JD said, hugging me, "but I feel like we missed out on having a real ceremony at our church. When I get back from New York in a few days, would you like to try again to have a real ceremony?"

I smiled up at him. "I'd love that, though I'm starting to wonder if I have bad luck with weddings." We both chuckled, and then I leaned against JD's chest, enjoying the security he exuded.

. . .

*J*D landed in New York the next afternoon and took a taxi to his office. He had already finished the lease on his apartment months ago before he left, but he needed to hire a moving company for all the things he had placed in storage. Then he needed to tell the board members he was planning to stay in Texas. "Lord, give me the strength and the energy for this."

He climbed the stairs to his office, opened the door, and crossed to his computer to find a moving company. That needed to be his first job so that the movers could be packing up his storage unit while he did everything else. Once he had that lined up, he went looking for the board members.

When the majority of them were assembled, JD cleared his throat and wiped his palms on his pants. "So, I thought I'd give you an update on the center in Texas. Faith Pregnancy Center is up and running. We're starting rather small, but the word is getting out there and people are coming in. Of course, that's not why I asked you to meet me here today. I wanted to tell you that I'm not coming back to New York. I'll be checking in with you all every other week through video conferences, but I'm going to be staying in Texas to run the center and be with my family.

"We sort of expected as much." Fred nodded and pointed to JD's left hand, "Especially when we noticed that ring on your finger."

Relief flooded JD, and he told them all about Callie and Hope.

*O*ne month later, I stood in front of the mirror and stared at my reflection. My brown hair was pulled up, and a few curly tendrils hung down barely touching my cream-colored dress. I thought back to the last time I had stood in front of a mirror like this and shook my head at the difference. Life hadn't turned out the way I had planned.

I was still losing the baby weight from Hope, so I wasn't at my ideal weight yet, but I didn't care. Junior Partner was never going to happen, but I felt more fulfilled helping JD at the center and sharing my story with the women who came in. As I usually had Hope with me, the little girl had also begun her own career in affecting others, even though she didn't even know it. I had, however, married a handsome, rich man, (though not for those reasons) and today I was going to get to have the ceremony I had dreamed of. My only hope was that it went off without a hitch, unlike last time.

A knock at the door interrupted my thoughts, and I turned as Lexi, my mother, and Tina entered the room.

"Are you almost ready, honey?" My mother asked.

I smiled and nodded. "Is everything else ready?"

Lexi nodded. "Yep, JD is standing at the front waiting for you, along with Scott. Sandra has Hope in the front row, and the food all got delivered on time and it looks delicious."

"The cake?"

"Yes, it's here and looks great," Tina said.

"Okay, well then I guess I'm ready."

I smoothed my dress one more time and then followed Lexi, Tina, and my mother out to the hallway. Lexi and Tina had both agreed to reprise their roles as bridesmaids and, to cut down on cash, they were wearing the same gowns they had worn last time. The bouquets were each new though, beautiful bouquets of lilies and carnations. My own bouquet was made up of fire and ice roses and pink carnations. Tina and Lexi opened the doors to the sanctuary and paused before beginning their march down the aisle.

As the doors closed again, my mother turned to me, pulling me in for a hug. "I'm so proud of you; you've grown into a better woman than I even could have hoped."

"Thanks Mom." I squeezed her back, "I'm thankful you never gave up on me."

"Moms don't give up on their children, ever." She wiped the tears in her eyes, and then turned to open the doors.

The music began, and all eyes turned toward me. I glanced to the front of the church where JD stood, smiling at me and handsome as ever in his tuxedo and pink tie. Taking my mother's arm, I marched towards him, glad to be feeling no pain this time.

At the end of the aisle, my mother hugged me one more time and then went to sit next to Sandra, who was cradling a sleeping Hope.

Pastor Tony smiled and addressed the small crowd. "Thank you to everyone for joining us once again. Hopefully, we have no unexpected interruptions this time."

Hope took that moment to let out a large wail, and a laughter scattered through the sanctuary.

Tony continued the vow renewal ceremony, finally pronouncing us husband and wife again.

The crowd cheered as JD leaned in and placed his lips on mine.

When the kiss ended, we walked hand in hand down the aisle, past our many friends and family. Yes, this wasn't the perfect day I had once pictured for myself — it was even better.

HE END

If you enjoyed this book, please leave a review at your retailer. It really does help and only takes a minute. http://amzn.to/2BpOEQr

DISCUSSION QUESTIONS

1. What do you think the theme of this book is? What's the message the author is trying to get across?

2. What was it about JD that finally made Callie start seeing the issues in her life?

3. Who was your favorite character in the book and why?

4. Why do you think Callie gave Daniel a second chance after his betrayal?

5. What Sandra does every day take a lot of courage. What could you do that would be courageous for God?

. . .

6. What did you learn about God from reading this book?

7. How can you use that knowledge in your life from now on?

8. Is there something you could do at your church to help inform or love on women in this position?

9. What are you looking forward to about Heaven?

10. Who are the three main victims of abortion?

WOULD YOU LEAVE A REVIEW?

As an author, I highly appreciate the feedback I get from my readers. It helps others make an informed decision before buying my book. If you enjoyed this book, please review at your retailer.

Do you like free books? I'm offering a free sample of my next book Free Sample!

WHEN HEARTS COLLIDE

DEDICATION

Dedication Page:
 To my family who allows me to sacrifice time with them to write these stories.
 To my friends who inspire me even when you don't know it.
 To women everywhere who have been attacked or forced to do things against their will, your Heavenly Father loves you.

CHAPTER 1

Fear covered Jared like a blanket. The music that had been uplifting now pounded a drum of dread in his heart. Why did it have to be so loud? He pulled desperately on the arm of a nearby boy, spilling some of his beer. "Where's Amanda?" The boy rolled his eyes, cursing a little at his spilled beer, and shrugged Jared off.

Jared turned to another, who gave the same response. His heart pounded like a freight train as his eyes tore wildly around the room. He had known this was a bad idea. Frat parties were often dangerous, this one even more so.

The crowd of bodies pressed against Jared, surging to the beats of the pulsing music. Sweat from those around him joined his own, trickling down his back. He pushed against the crowd, fighting his way to the other end of the house where the bathroom and bedrooms lay. He had to have taken her to one of them. A hand grabbed Jared's wrist, and he whirled on a blond surfer type with long hair.

"Sorry, bro," the surfer dude said, holding his hands up in apology.

Jared continued toward the back. A tipsy blond fell into him, and he shoved her to the side. The bathroom door loomed just ahead.

"Amanda?" Jared pounded on the white wooden door. "Amanda, open up if you're in there." The pounding of his heart was now reverberating in his head, creating a headache that made his eyes hurt.

The lock clicked, and the door opened. A thin brunette in a miniskirt and crop top stumbled out. "There's no Amanda here." Her words were a slur, and her brown eyes barely focused on him.

Jared grabbed the girl's thin shoulders and shook her. "Have you seen her? Red hair? She would have been with Caleb West."

The girl shook her head and fell into the wall as soon as Jared released her. Rolling his eyes, he pushed past the girl and opened the first bedroom door. A couple was entwined on the bed, but the girl had blond hair and the face of the man didn't belong to Caleb.

"Sorry," He pulled the door shut and moved on the next one. Another couple was heavily involved on this bed too, but again no Amanda.

The next door was locked. This had to be the one. Jared rattled the handle, but to no avail. "Amanda?" He pounded on the door, but he heard no noise from inside. Jared grabbed the arm of a nearby male and pointed at the door. "Hey, can you open this? Do you have the key?"

"Sorry, I don't live here." The man shrugged and walked away.

"Aargh!" Jared turned back to the door and rammed his frame into it. The door didn't budge. Perhaps a kick would work. He took a step back and planted a perfect front kick. He felt the reverberation up his leg, but not even a tremor from the door. Cursing under his breath, Jared looked around for anything to wedge in the door. Would they have a crowbar in the house? Would anyone have one in their car?

"Jared!" At the sound of his name, Jared whirled around. Emily was fighting her way to him through the crowd. Thank goodness, she had seen the text. A glance at his watch revealed ten minutes had passed since he had texted her when he'd first lost sight of Amanda.

"Have you seen her?" Emily asked when she reached him.

Jared shook his head, the fear constricting his vocal chords. "Not since I texted you. I saw them at the punch table and then a friend came up to me and started talking. When I turned around again, she was gone. It's my fault."

"It's not," she said, running a hand through her long blond hair. "You warned her, and that was all you could do."

Jared wasn't sure about that. He should have pushed harder. He should have told her the whole story and not just part of it, but none of that made a difference right now. Right now, he needed to find her. "I've already checked those two rooms," he said pointing to the previous doors, "but this one's locked."

Emily glanced around, but like Jared, her search came up empty. "I'm assuming you already tried hitting the door," Emily said, "but what if we tried together?"

"It's worth a shot," he said. "On the count of three, okay?"

Emily nodded, and on the count of three, they both rammed the door as hard as they could. This time the wood did tremble, but the door remained locked.

"Again," Jared said through clenched teeth, and together they rammed the door once more. This time a wonderful terrible splintering sound of wood echoed, and the door opened. Jared rushed into the room.

Amanda lay sprawled on the bed. Her shirt was open and her pants were undone, but still on.

"Check on her," Jared yelled to Emily as he scoured the room for any sign of Caleb. The closet was empty, but a chill crept in from the open window. Jared stuck his head out, but the area was dark and devoid of movement. If Caleb had gone out this way, he had gotten enough of a start to be out of sight. Without knowing which direction he had gone, trying to follow him would be pointless.

With an agitated sigh, Jared turned back to the bed. Emily had wrapped the comforter around Amanda, whose eyes were wide open and filled with fear.

"Can you move?" Emily asked. No head shake, but Amanda's eyes moved left and then right. "Okay, it's going to be okay. We'll get you out of here. Any sign?"

"No, the window is open, but he's gone." A tear slid out of Amanda's eyes. "Don't worry, we'll find him. He won't get away with this." Jared patted her hair tenderly and wiped the tear from her cheek. Then he scooped her up and headed back out the door. "Let's get her to the hospital."

"An ambulance is on its way," Emily replied, pocketing her cell phone.

Jared nodded as he pushed his way through the crowd. A few people turned to gawk at them as they made their way to the front door, but most were oblivious and kept dancing to the loud beats or tipping back their drinks. Jared shook his head as disgust boiled inside him. What was wrong with these people? Did they not even care that someone had been attacked?

The night air slapped him as they exited the stifling house, and the change in temperature sent a shiver down his spine as the cool air licked up the wet sweat dripping down his neck.

The ambulance roared up moments later. The EMTs climbed out and took Amanda from Jared, strapping her onto a gurney. As they loaded her into the back, Jared climbed in.

"There's only room for one," the EMT said as Emily attempted to climb in too. "Besides, the cops want a statement." He pointed to the police car pulling up.

"Go. I'll stay with her, and when you're done, we can switch," Emily said.

Jared nodded and mouthed a silent thank you to Emily as the doors closed. He grabbed one of Amanda's hands and sent a prayer heavenward. *Please God let her be okay, please God.* He had no other words, and hoped God was hearing his heart, which felt like it was beating out of his chest. Though he'd only known her a few months, Amanda was a friend, and if he were honest, he hoped she would become a lot more.

When the ambulance braked, Jared fell forward a little. Chilly air rushed in as the back doors opened and doctors took over the gurney Amanda was on. Jared jumped down from the ambulance and hurried to keep up with them.

"Amanda? I'm Dr. Patrick, can you tell me what happened?"

"She can't," Jared spoke up. "I'm pretty sure she was drugged."

The dark-haired doctor turned to him. "And you are?"

"I'm Jared. I'm a friend, and I found her. Her eyes were open and seemed responsive, but she couldn't even shake her head."

"Okay, we'll take it from here. You can wait over there." He pointed to the waiting area. Jared wanted to protest, but he could tell from the look in the doctor's eyes that his protest would fall on deaf ears, so he nodded and stumbled over to a gray, vinyl chair. As he sank down, the weight of the night descended on his shoulders, and he dropped his head onto his hands.

He hadn't been able to stop it. Was this what Nikki had gone through? Was this why she left without a word? Would Amanda do the same thing?

"Hey, are you okay?"

Jared jumped at the touch to his shoulder ready to lash out at the intrusion, but relaxed when the eyes he saw belonged to Emily. "Yeah, I guess I'm alright. How are you?"

Emily sighed as she sat next to him and pulled her knees to her chest. "I've been better. They asked me a lot of questions. I couldn't answer most of them, so they'll be looking to talk to you too. But I told them what little I could. How is she doing?"

"I don't know," Jared sighed. "They whisked her away pretty quickly and haven't been back out yet. I'm worried, Emily."

"I am too," she said with a nod, "but the best thing we can do right now is pray." She took his hand, and they closed their eyes. "Father, our friend Amanda needs your help right now. Please be with her and give the doctors the knowledge to treat her. Lord also help us know how to help her in the future."

As they said amen, Jared added a silent plea for Amanda to be okay. If she wasn't, he wasn't sure he'd ever be able to forgive himself.

CHAPTER 2

*T*wo Months Previously

*A*manda Adams stared at the tiny gray room and sighed. This was going to be her new home away from home at least for the next year, and it was rather depressing.

"Well, it's got a lot of potential," her mother said with a false brightness as she looked around. Amanda raised her eyebrows. Potential? Maybe for a horror movie. Boring white walls dotted with myriad holes boxed the room in. Two small brown dressers with two drawers each separated two bare mattresses on metal frames.

Rolling her suitcase into the room, Amanda hoisted it onto the left bed and shivered at the groaning cacophony of creaks that answered back. She crossed to the right bed and pushed on it, hoping for a better outcome, but a similar noise resounded. "Right. Potential."

Crossing her arms, she emitted another sigh and surveyed the rest of the room. Two small closets framed either side of the doorway. One wall held a small sink and a vanity with a cloudy mirror. Two study desks took up the remaining space.

"Come on now. I know you can't paint the walls, but you can hang pictures, right?"

Amanda nodded. "We just aren't supposed to put holes in the walls, but I guess that's not a hard followed rule," she said as she glanced at the holes that contradicted her statement. "I don't think I brought enough with me though to cheer this up."

"So, we'll go shopping and get some more pictures. With your bed made up and some bright colored towels, it can at least look a little more 'homey.' And we're only a six-hour drive away, so you can come home on long weekends or we'll drive up."

"Yeah, I guess you're right." Amanda crossed to her suitcase, unzipped it, and began removing the clothes while her mother grabbed a towel and began cleaning the cloudy mirror. Suddenly, the door slammed open. Amanda dropped the shirt she had been holding in surprise and spun around.

A girl with long black hair shaved short on one side and a nose ring entered and narrowed her eyes at Amanda. "Who are you?"

Amanda swallowed and stepped forward, extending her hand. "I'm Amanda. I guess I'm your roommate."

The girl rolled her eyes and pushed past Amanda, ignoring the hand. "Crap. I told them I wanted a single."

"Oh, um, well maybe they ran out," Amanda stammered as she dropped her hand. The hair on her arms bristled at the girl's brusque demeanor. She looked to her mother for help, but she just shrugged.

The girl flung her backpack on the right bed and glared at Amanda. A chill ran through Amanda at the girl's icy blue stare. "Well, I'll be asking them to look again. I don't do roommates." She rifled in her backpack for a minute, turned and glared one more time, and then abruptly left the room, slamming the wooden door for a second time.

Amanda stared at the closed door and blinked. "Well, this should be fun."

"Maybe they'll change her room after all." Though the words were positive, her mother's voice was filled with doubt, mirroring Amanda's own.

"I can only hope." Amanda returned to the job of unpacking and when she had finished, she locked the door and followed her mother to her mother's car. They had driven up in two cars, so Amanda would have a vehicle to drive home in if necessary.

As they walked around the local Wal-Mart filling the cart with fun pictures and colorful towels, Amanda couldn't help thinking that it still wasn't going to be like home. She wasn't going to have many of her own things. There would be no brother and sister busting in while she was trying to study or Kate rattling on about the latest trends as they quizzed each other. And if that girl remained her roommate, it was going to be an uncomfortable year regardless of what she hung on the walls.

When they returned to the dorm, Amanda opened the door cautiously in case the mysterious, angry roommate was there, but the room was empty and looked exactly as she had left it. Taking the pictures out of the bag, along with the poster putty, she began hanging them over the bed she had chosen. Her mother cut the tags off the towels and hung one by the sink and placed the others in one of the drawers beneath it.

Amanda finished hanging the posters, stepped off the bed, and surveyed the room again. While it still didn't feel exactly like home, it did feel warmer than when she had first arrived.

"Are you sure you're going to be okay?" her mother asked, pulling her in for a hug.

Amanda rolled her eyes goodnaturedly as she hugged her mother back. "I'll be fine. You have to let me grow up sometime, Mother."

"I know, but I didn't think it would happen so soon." She wiped a tear from her eye and then pulled Amanda in for another hug. "Come home as often as you need to, okay?"

"Okay, Mom." After another few awkward hugs, Amanda finally ushered her mother out of the dorm room. As the door shut and the silence crept in, she turned back to the bed and sighed. She had hoped that she might meet another girl like Kate, someone she could relate to, but this roommate, whatever her name was, didn't seem like she wanted to be friends at all.

Rifling through her backpack–the only thing she hadn't completely unpacked–Amanda pulled out her Bible and prayer journal and sat on the squeaky mattress. Though her prayer journal was just a spiral notebook and not a nice leather bound one like Sandra's, it accomplished the same goal, and she'd had it since joining Sandra's prayer team three years ago. It was nearly full now, and she was excited about the prospect of having to get a new one soon.

Amanda flipped to the last entry and dug a pen out of her bag. On the next available line, she added 'patience to deal with my roommate, and the words to say to reach her.' She tapped the pen against her teeth as she thought about what else to add. 'Wisdom in how to further God's plan here.' Having no idea what God had planned for her at the university, she figured she should leave the request broad and just listen for his wisdom.

After closing the cover, she set the journal beside her on the purple bedspread. Then she picked up the Bible and flipped it open to John where she had last been reading.

As her fingers touched the page, she smiled. No matter how many times she opened it, the Bible always transmitted a feeling of peace and happiness. It had ever since she was a small child. Her mind drifted back to the day her father had led her in accepting Jesus as her savior.

"If you are ready for God to come in your heart, you just repeat after me," he said.

Amanda nodded at him. She wanted nothing more than to know this heavenly father he spoke so highly of.

"Father, I know I have sinned," he said.

"Father, I know I have sinned," she repeated.

"But I also know that you died to save me from my sin, and I want you to rule my life."

She repeated the statement and immediately felt a warmth wash over her. With wide eyes, she looked up at her father who smiled.

"You felt it, didn't you?" he asked.

She nodded.

"Good, now the next step is to know all there is about God. You can never learn enough. In fact, how about we start reading the Bible together and when you get old enough, you can read it on your own and we can discuss it?"

She nodded, eager to read with him. He pulled her onto his lap and opened the important black book to the beginning.

"Genesis Chapter 1," he said. "In the beginning, God created the heavens and the earth."

And that's what they had done. Amanda had been a precocious child and an avid reader at the tender age of five, but the Bible's vocabulary had been a little challenging until she was older. Even when she could read the words herself, she still didn't always understand the concepts, so he had set up a chart of the books with a point system, and she had earned points for every book she read and could discuss with him.

In this way, he helped her understand the parts she missed as they discussed it. Then she could trade the points in for treats. She had never told her father, but she would have read the books for free, partly because she loved learning about God and partly because she always looked forward to those discussions with her dad. He was often busy with work, but he always made time for her in the evenings when she wanted to discuss God.

At ten, he had baptized her, even though he wasn't the pastor. He had been a deacon of the church at the time though, and they had agreed he could. Amanda had only grown from there, telling everyone she met about Jesus and his love for them. It hadn't always been easy, especially in a public school where Christianity was frowned upon, but God had helped her stay strong, lead several friends to Christ, and helped her form a Fellowship of Christian Athletes at her high school last year that she hoped was going to continue just as strong this year.

Propping the pillow up, Amanda leaned back against the wall and drew her knees up to serve as a stand for the Bible. As she scanned the page for where she had stopped, the door flew open again and "the roommate" entered, stopping short at the sight of Amanda's open book.

"Oh gaud, you're one of those?" Disdain dripped from her voice.

"I'm sorry, one of what?" Amanda placed her finger on the spot she had just found and looked up at her.

"One of those Bible beaters." The girl's nose wrinkled in distaste as an ugly sneer crested her face.

WHEN HEARTS COLLIDE | 383

Amanda chuckled and smiled. "I am a Christ follower, if that's what you mean."

The girl rolled her eyes, mumbled something under her breath, and pulled out a pair of headphones. She plugged them into her phone and then turned up her music.

Flinching at the loud beat that escaped the headphones and filled the room, Amanda turned back to her Bible, trying to block out the noise. The words jumped on the page as she tried to focus, and after reading the same sentence four times, she decided to finish her devotional later. As she closed the book, her stomach rumbled. Food sounded like a much-needed distraction.

Though Amanda hoped the girl would decline, she figured it would be rude not to at least invite the roommate, since they were going to be spending a lot of time together. She waved her hand to get the girl's attention. The girl rolled her eyes, but pulled one headphone back. "I'm going for some food. Would you like to come?" 'The roommate' flicked her hand in dismissal, and relief flooded Amanda's body. Grabbing her key and ID card, she hurried out of the room before the girl changed her mind.

A dingy brown carpet ran the length of the hallway. Though Amanda had known the dorm hall was old, she had hoped maybe the university would have spruced it up some. Identical brown doors lined the hall and a set of stairs sat at either end. Amanda headed to the right and down the flight of stairs, which opened to another hall on the first floor. Though nearly identical to the second floor, an information desk filled some real estate directly across from the front entrance.

A mousy girl in glasses sat behind the desk, her nose buried in a book. Rows of mailboxes sat open behind her.

"Hi, can you point me in the direction of the cafeteria?" Amanda asked as she approached the counter.

The girl's eyes flicked up briefly. "We don't have one here. You'll have to go to Bledsoe-Gordon Hall." Her eyes dropped back to the book.

Amanda took a deep breath and clenched her teeth against the snippy reply trying to escape her mouth. Was everyone at college going to be this rude? "Okay, it's my first day, though, and I seem to have misplaced my map. Do you have another one?"

The girl turned and grabbed a piece of paper off a counter behind her. She held it out, never looking up from her book. It must have been riveting.

"Thank you." Amanda took the paper and sat down in one of the chairs near the counter to peruse it. Her eyes scanned the rectangles for the words 'you are here.' When she found them, she placed her finger there and read the names of the closest buildings to find Bledsoe-Gordon Hall. Sneed Hall, Doak, West, ah there it was Bledsoe-Gordon Hall. It certainly wasn't one of the closest buildings, but it didn't seem that far away.

Folding the map, Amanda placed it in her pocket, exited the doors, and turned left. Though Lubbock was, for the most part, flat and brown, the campus stayed relatively green, probably due to the sprinklers that ran incessantly. A few trees even popped up on the landscape though they were barren of leaves currently in the heat of late summer. Wishing she had remembered her sunglasses, she squinted and held up her hand as a shield until her sensitive eyes adjusted to the light.

Beads of sweat trickled down her back as she trekked across the grass. A few other people were out, most carrying boxes into other dorms, but some lounged at picnic tables reading or chatting with friends. Oh how she wished Kate had come to Texas Tech with her, but she couldn't begrudge Kate's choice to go to the same college her brother was attending. After nearly losing him to a drug addiction, Kate had wanted to be closer to him. Still, it would have been nice to have her best friend here with her.

Bledsoe-Gordon came into view, and Amanda turned up the cement steps. As her hand reached the silver handle, the heavy door flew open, knocking her down the steps and onto the jarringly hard ground. Her head flew back and her teeth snapped together, sending a pain across her jaws and down her neck.

"Oh, sorry are you okay?" a male voice asked.

Amanda shook her head to clear the stars and struggled to stand. Gritting her teeth, she blinked back the tears threatening to spill out from the throbbing of her rear end and head. Gingerly, she rose to her feet, dusted off her backside, and focused on the man on the steps.

Close cropped blond hair framed a ruggedly handsome face. His eyes were the color of the ocean, and his nose had a chiseled-from-stone appearance. A grey t-shirt covered his broad shoulders, showing off his muscular arms and chest. His waist narrowed, and under his shirt, he wore tan cargo shorts. Brown flip flops finished off the look, giving him a casual air.

"Sorry," he repeated. "I didn't see you there."

"Yeah, I got that," Amanda said. Though the stinging was subsiding, she knew she would be sore for a few days.

"Um, well hey, can I buy you lunch?"

"No, I'm fine, really." As she stepped past him, he grabbed her arm. Shaking off his hand, Amanda whirled, turning angry eyes on him. He stepped back, holding his hands up in defense. "Sorry," Amanda said, "but I don't even know you."

"I'm Caleb," he said sticking out his hand, "and I'm really not a jerk. Please let me buy your dinner."

Amanda cocked her head and regarded him. He appeared sincere, and surely there would be more people inside. "Okay," she agreed, smiling hesitantly and shaking his proffered hand. "Lead the way. I'm Amanda, by the way."

He flashed a charming smile and held the door open.

"Haven't you already eaten?" Amanda asked as they stepped in the hall.

"No, I live here. I was getting something out of my car for my friend."

"Won't he be wondering where you are?" The hallway in this dorm looked exactly like hers. Had none of these dorms been renovated recently?

"Nah, he'll be okay." Caleb led the way down the hall which opened into a large cafeteria at the end. Round tables full of students filled most of the room. The other side housed an assembly line where students could pick up food and then check out at the end.

After grabbing a sandwich, salad, and some fruit, Caleb and Amanda sat down at an empty table.

"So where are you from?" Caleb asked.

Amanda finished chewing the grape she had just popped in her mouth before answering. "I'm from Mesquite; how about you?"

"Houston. I can't say there's much to do here, but at least it isn't as muggy."

She nodded, remembering her trip to Houston in High school. Kate's aunt had lived there and one summer Kate had asked Amanda to go with her. The heat had hit as soon as she de-boarded the plane, flattening her red hair to her forehead in a sticky mess. To cool off, Kate's aunt had driven them to the neighborhood pool, but even the pool water had been so warm that they had been forced to sit in the hot tub first before jumping in the pool to at least make it feel colder.

"So, what are you studying?" Caleb asked before taking a bite of his sandwich.

Amanda narrowed her eyes at him, unsure how much information she should give out to a perfect stranger, even if he was a ruggedly handsome perfect stranger. "Counseling." She decided to keep it vague until she knew more about him. "What about you?"

"Business right now, but I'm not sure that's where my passion lies."

"What do you think you'd rather do?" she asked. Her counseling instinct had kicked in, sensing that there was a story behind the slight sadness of his statement.

"I think I'd rather be an architect." His blue eyes sparkled as he spoke, and her heart flipped and began beating faster. "I always loved building things, even as a kid."

"So why aren't you going into architecture?"

His face fell, and his shoulders sank. "My dad," he sighed, "He really wants me to go into business with him, but he owns a furniture store, and I just can't see myself really happy running it."

She nodded, knowing that feeling all too well. Though her own family had always been very supportive of what she'd wanted to do, she had known a girl in high school who had wanted to pursue acting, but her parents' desire was for her to become a lawyer. The girl grew so stressed every time "the future" was brought up in class that she had given herself ulcers. "It's not my place, but your career is the rest of your life. I think it would be hard to do something you're not passionate about."

"You don't know my dad," he said, shaking his head.

She shrugged. "I know, that's why I said it probably wasn't my place, but I do think sometimes as much as you want to please your parents, you have to do what's right for you. If it helps, I'll pray for you." Amanda stuck a grape in her mouth and watched for his reaction, hoping he wouldn't be offended by the offer to pray for him. He was intriguing, and she wanted to know more about him, but only if he were open to God.

"Thanks, I'd like that," he said.

Amanda smiled, and they finished the rest of dinner in a companionable silence. "Well, it was very nice meeting you," she said, standing and placing her trash on the tray. Caleb stood as well.

"Can we meet up again?" he asked.

Amanda bit her lip even as her heart fluttered. Should she give him her number? Though she didn't know him, he appeared genuine, and she could always use new friends in this unknown territory. Plus, it was just a number. It wasn't like she was going to jump into a relationship with him. Even if he was handsome, that wasn't her style. Curiosity tamped the small amount of trepidation, and she agreed. They exchanged cell numbers before saying goodbye, and then Amanda headed back to her dorm.

The dark cloud wasn't in the room when Amanda returned, but her essence remained. This was going to be a long semester.

CHAPTER 3

*J*ared Masterson unlocked the Students for Life office door and checked the answering machine. No calls yet, but it was only the first day of the new school year. When the parties started and people began hooking up, there would be many messages on the machine. While he loved being able to help people make a choice once they were in a bad situation, he wished there was something more proactive they could be doing to keep students from getting in those situations to begin with.

After he finished getting the brochures in order in case anyone visited, he pulled out a chair and sat down at the small conference table. From his backpack, he withdrew his Bible and placed it on the table. He tried to start each day praying that God would send them the people they needed to reach.

"Lord, use me today to do your work. Help me to see the people that need help and to have the words to say to them. And Lord, please send us new members to help spread your word this year. Amen."

As he ended the prayer and opened his eyes, he flipped to the back of his Bible and removed the photo he kept there. Though a little faded, the girl's green eyes and bright smile still touched his heart. His finger traced her face, and he wondered again if she were okay.

Nikki had been his girlfriend last year for half of the year until she met Caleb. Then, all of a sudden, she had decided she and Jared were no longer compatible and had broken up with him. Jared was crushed but had accepted her decision. Near the end of the school year, she had disappeared. Dropped all her classes and left without a word to anyone. Jared wished she had come to see him before she left or contacted him after. He just wanted to know she was alright.

"Still haven't heard from her?"

Jared glanced up to see Emily Peters throwing her gym bag in a chair across from him. Her blond hair was tied back in its usual ponytail.

"No," Jared said with a shake of his head. "Has she contacted you?"

"Sorry," Emily said as she sat down, "but we weren't that close, so I'm not surprised."

"Do you think he's still here?" Jared asked.

"Caleb?" Emily snorted. "Probably. He's a big man on campus here. Why would he go elsewhere and risk not being number one?"

"I hope we can stop them this year," Jared said, frustration boiling up inside him.

"We don't even know they did anything, Jared," Emily said, placing her hand on his arm. "Nikki could have left for a lot of reasons."

"You didn't know her like I did," Jared said. "Something happened to her, and I guarantee you Caleb West or one of his friends was involved."

❀

The blaring alarm elicited a sigh as it went off. Rubbing her eyes, Amanda glanced at the clock on her cell phone. Ugh, 6:30 was way too early. What had she been thinking taking the eight am classes? She loved learning, but it sure had been nice getting to sleep in all summer. With a final yawn and stretch, Amanda pushed herself to a sitting position.

Sunlight was barely filtering in the window, and across the room, "the roommate" was still asleep. Amanda still didn't know her name. As quietly as she could, Amanda pushed back the covers, crawled out of bed, and crossed to her closet, which sat on the right side of the door. After pulling on a pair of jeans and a light blue top, she brushed her teeth in the small sink and ran a brush through her hair, laced up her sneakers, and stuffed her backpack with the books she would need for the day. Grunting, she hoisted the heavy bag on her shoulder and quietly closed the door behind her.

The hallway was still dark as the lights in the hallway didn't give much light and there were only the windows at each end to let outside light in. Amanda took the stairs down, careful to hold the railing as the stairwell was even darker.

The bottom floor was lighter as it housed the front door and the administrative desk. Sitting down in a chair near a light, she pulled out her map. Her first class was in the math building all the way across campus. Second was History in Holden Hall and then Psychology back down by the dorm. At least all the classes were close together; even if they were on the other side of campus from her dorm.

Refolding the map, she pocketed it and pushed open the front doors. The cool morning air dispelled the last edge of sleep and invigorated Amanda's spirit. Though it would get hot later—one hundred was forecasted today—right now the temperature was seventy-one and perfect. The sun wasn't out just yet, but she patted the pocket of her backpack to make sure she had her sunglasses. She would need them later. The familiar bulge eased her worries as she began the trek to Bledsoe hall.

Very few people were out yet, and the quiet was almost unnerving. The birds chirping was the only sound. Even the sprinklers were silent this early in the morning.

Amanda couldn't help wondering if she would see Caleb at breakfast. They had exchanged numbers, but it was too early for him to call, and she wasn't going to call him first. Still, he was a face she knew, and it would be nice if he were there.

The cafeteria was sparse as Amanda entered. Only ten or twelve students dotted the tables and Caleb was not one of them. She chose some eggs and pancakes from the buffet and scanned the room. The choices were to sit alone or join someone at a table. Most students were immersed in their cell phones, but one blond girl in an oversized shirt sat alone, picking at a waffle. Amanda decided to try to be friendly.

"Hi, can I join you?" Amanda asked, setting her tray down.

The girl looked up, sadness emanating from her eyes. She shrugged, and then her eyes dropped back to her plate.

"Um, I'm Amanda. First year." Amanda hoped the girl would at least respond; she had no idea what the girl was going through, but her counseling instinct wanted to help. If only she'd had more experience. What she'd been able to do at JD's clinic hadn't been much, mainly filing paperwork and discussing vague scenarios with the actual counselor.

"I'm Jordan," came the mumbled reply, "Sophomore."

"Nice to meet you," Amanda pressed, but silence met her back. Jordan continued to push her waffle bits around on her plate. Her pale and splotchy face made Amanda wonder if she'd gotten any sleep the night before. "Are you nervous?"

The fork stopped, and Jordan looked up. Icy blue anger replaced the sadness, and Amanda shivered as the eyes bore into her own. "No, I just don't want to be here, but I couldn't afford to give up my scholarship." With that she grabbed her plate, stood up, and walked away.

With a sigh, Amanda loaded some eggs on her fork. Her first day was off to a stellar start.

❀

*A*s the last class ended, Amanda gathered her books and returned them to her backpack. It was time to head back to the dorm and tackle some of the massive pile of homework she had been assigned today. Funny, she didn't remember anyone warning her about homework on the first day or how much there would be. She was going to have her work cut out for her.

The bright sun blinded her as she pushed open the door of the building. Squinting, she reached into the pocket of her backpack and pulled out her sunglasses. While she loved the color of her green eyes, she often wished they weren't so sensitive to the sun, but that was an inherited trait from her father. At least she didn't need them for vision like he did. She could still hear him complaining about how the tint of the prescription glasses never got quite dark enough for him.

As the dorm came into view, Amanda whispered a silent prayer that "the roommate" wouldn't be there. She knew that wasn't very Christian of her, but the girl was such a downer, and Amanda just wanted to decompress after the first day.

The same mousy brunette was manning the front desk as Amanda stopped to check for mail; her face was still buried in the book.

"It must be good," Amanda said teasing her.

The girl glanced up, annoyance in her eyes. "Did you need something?"

"Um, just the mail for room 216, if there is any."

The girl turned, scanned the rows of slots, and shook her head before sticking her nose back in the book. Amanda nodded and started up the stairs, the mantra "please be gone" repeating in her head.

The door to the dorm room was shut, but that meant nothing. Holding her breath, Amanda turned the knob. Locked. Well, that was probably good. Fishing her key out of her pocket, Amanda unlocked the door and pushed it open. The room was dark, quiet, and blissfully empty. Sighing, she shut the door and dropped the heavy bag on the creaky bed. Then she pulled out the mountain of homework and spread it out at the desk.

It wasn't taxing work, really, but the quiet settled on her shoulders creating an unnerving sensation. At home, her little brother and sister would have been constantly interrupting her. As Amanda thought about them racing around the kitchen, loneliness set in.

On the first day of school last year, she and Kate had gone out for pizza and then walked around the mall. They had met up with a few other friends and the group had spent most of the year together. Though a small group, they had been close knit, and Amanda had always been surrounded by a great group of friends. Now, she had no one really.

Sighing, she stood up from the desk and crossed to the bed to retrieve her Bible. As she opened it, she searched for the source of comfort that usually accompanied it, but today nothing hit her. Her mind was not focused. With a sigh, Amanda returned it to the nightstand and decided to take a walk.

Amanda grabbed her sunglasses, locked the door behind her, and trudged back down the stairs. One thing was for sure, she was going to be in great shape after this year. As she stepped into the warm sunshine, her phone buzzed in her front pocket. Kate's number flashed across the screen, and she eagerly swiped the screen.

"Kate, how are you?"

"I'm good," she laughed. "How are you?"

"I'm okay, I guess. I miss you." Amanda crossed the grassy lawn to a nearby tree and sat down against the trunk. The rough bark bit into her back, but she didn't mind. Her best friend was on the phone.

"Uh oh, what's wrong?"

"I'm just a little lonely is all. My roommate is a nightmare, and I tried to make a friend this morning, but I don't think it went over well. I feel a little out of my element." Amanda hadn't meant to unload on Kate, but the words just fell out of her mouth.

"I get it. I have my brother, but we don't have any classes together. We got together for dinner last night, but he seems so much better I'm not sure I made the right decision coming here."

"Sounds like we both had unrealistic expectations," Amanda sighed. "I did meet a guy though."

"Ooh, do tell."

Amanda smiled at Kate's teasing tone and filled her in on the meeting of Caleb.

"He sounds hot," she sighed, "when are you going to see him again?"

"I don't know; we exchanged numbers, but I think I should wait for him to call, right? I don't even know the rules of dating." Amanda had been on a few dates in high school but none of them had panned out, and she'd been too focused on her grades to pursue any further.

"Yes, you should wait for him to call. You don't want to seem too eager. Oh crud, my roommate just returned and wants to get an early dinner. Can we talk again later?"

A hint of jealousy flared in Amanda's heart. How come Kate was given a roommate she could befriend while Amanda had the still-unnamed epitome of anger as her roommate? With a shake of her head, Amanda pushed the un-Christian thought away and hung up the phone, not sure if she felt better or worse. She pocketed the phone and pushed herself up from the grass. Might as well finish the walk.

After the walk and a dinner by herself—Amanda didn't feel like trying another awkward conversation—she returned to the dorm room. The roommate was sprawled on her black bedspread leafing through a magazine. She looked up long enough to roll her eyes and then returned her focus to the magazine.

Amanda stared at the contrast in the room. Her side of the room was bright and cheery while the girl's side was dark and monochromatic. Resolved to try to befriend the girl again anyway, she pulled back her shoulders and took a deep breath before asking, "How was your first day?"

The girl snorted in response, and a flicker of annoyance sparked in Amanda, but she swallowed it down. God obviously had a reason for pairing them together. Had she prayed for patience lately? She couldn't remember, but this situation would definitely be a way to practice it. "Can you at least tell me your name? I'd like to call you something other than 'the roommate' or dark haired girl."

The blue eyes rolled again. "It's Jade, but don't get attached. One of us will be leaving soon."

"Or we could become friends," Amanda tried.

"Doubtful," Jade replied and jammed the headphones that had been lying around her neck into her ears.

Amanda shook her head and grabbed her prayer journal. She had told Sandra she wanted to stay a part of the prayer team, but she hadn't been able to get the weekly requests before leaving Mesquite. Checking her watch to make sure it wasn't too late, she pulled out her phone and dialed Sandra's number. "Hey Sandra, it's Amanda Adams. Are there any new prayer requests?"

Sandra's voice on the other end was like a warm hug. After rattling off the prayer requests, Sandra filled Amanda in on the church service she had missed and asked how about her first day.

Amanda glanced at Jade. She didn't appear to be paying attention, but Amanda didn't want to chance it. "It was okay. Not as good as I'd hoped, but I know it will get better." She'd have to tell Sandra to add Jade to the prayer list the next time she called. "Be sure to say hello to Callie, JD, and little Hope for me," Amanda said as the conversation ended.

"Are you really going to pray for all that?"

Her eyes flicked to Jade who had obviously been listening and was now staring at her with one eyebrow raised. "Of course I am. These people need God's help."

"Why don't they just ask for it then?"

"They do," Amanda said with a smile, "but there is power in prayer, so more people praying can only help. Besides it keeps me connected to God."

"And what if God doesn't answer your prayers, what then? Won't you just have wasted all that time?"

Though the questions were snarky, Amanda wondered if they were laced with curiosity as well. Although people claimed to be agnostic, she had never met one who truly was. Most people either didn't know God or had been wronged and therefore hated God.

"It's never a waste to pray, and God answers our prayers every single time. We just don't always like or understand the answer."

Jade removed her headphones and sat up. "What do you mean?"

"I mean people always expect God to give them things, so they pray for money or cars, things like that. God does give us those things occasionally, but sometimes what we ask for isn't good for us. God always has three answers to prayers: Yes, no, or not yet. See, he has a plan for all of us, and while we don't know exactly what it is, he does. He answers in ways that will glorify that plan. We won't always understand his answers, but we can know he's always listening and watching out for us."

"That sounds stupid." Jade rolled her eyes and replaced her headphones. She laid back and rolled over to face the wall.

Amanda sighed as she reached for her Bible. Jade must hold the Guinness World Record for eye rolling, but something told her that the girl fit into the "had been wronged and was blaming God" group. Amanda clearly had her work cut for her and would need God's divine intervention.

CHAPTER 4

*a*s the first week ended, Amanda's loneliness settled ever deeper. She had spent every breakfast, lunch, and dinner eating alone after the disastrous breakfast on the first day. Classes hadn't been much better, as she hadn't met anyone she could connect with, and then there was Jade who seemed determined to try her patience every chance she got. Amanda wasn't used to not having friends, and while she wanted to be strong, she was contemplating driving home for the weekend just to see some familiar faces.

Amanda glanced at Jade who was scowling at some book she was reading. She seemed even grumpier than usual though Amanda had no idea how that was possible. Still, they were both alone, and they both needed to eat at some point. Maybe Jade would come to dinner with her. Bad company at this point was more appealing than no company at all.

"Hey Jade, I'm going to go get some dinner. Do you want to come with?" Amanda asked, steeling herself for whatever Jade might hurl back at her. Jade didn't even reply, just continued to shoot daggers at her book. "Okay, well if you change your mind, I'll be at Bledsoe-Gordon, probably eating alone." Still nothing. Sighing, Amanda grabbed her phone and ID and headed out of the room.

As Amanda shut the door, her phone vibrated in her hand. She swiped the screen to see a message from Caleb. She had assumed he had either forgotten about her or just taken her number to be nice as she hadn't heard from him all week.

Want to grab some dinner?

Relief flowed through her at the thought of having someone to eat with, and she quickly texted back a yes.

True to his word, Caleb stood outside the door of Bledsoe hall. His blond hair sparkled like spun gold in the sun, and he waved as Amanda neared. Her heart fluttered and a heat crawled up her neck. She hadn't had a serious boyfriend in high school and wasn't used to the feelings flashing through her body.

"Hey, how was your first week?"

His smile blew away the darkness she had been feeling. "Everything was great, except my roommate. I'm pretty sure she hates me."

He laughed. "I think all roommates are like that at first. My first year, I had this guy, Owen, who played video games all night long. It kept me awake many nights, but it turned out he was lonely, so after we started talking, he stopped playing the video games and became a really great friend."

"Well, I hope things work out like that for us, but she appeared genuinely agitated that she had to share the room. I kind of doubt that we'll be bosom buddies anytime soon." Amanda's gaze dropped to the ground and she bit the inside of her lip. "I'm also feeling a little lonely if I'm honest."

Caleb placed a finger under her chin and pushed her face up until she was looking in his eyes. "I can't imagine you being lonely, but I remember my first year. It does get better. You just need to get connected. It's why I joined a fraternity my freshman year."

His eyes were so mesmerizing that Amanda almost missed the word fraternity as it issued from his mouth. Her brow knitted together. He was a frat boy? The first inkling of doubt sprouted within her. She had heard stories of frat boys, and they weren't usually flattering. "I don't really want to join a sorority unless maybe it's a Christian one. Do they have those here?"

"I'm sure they do," he said with a shrug. "The bulletin board would be a good place to look. They have one in most cafeterias and at the student union. They're not all bad, you know."

"What?" Amanda asked.

"Fraternities and Sororities," he laughed. "I saw your face and heard the tone in your voice. I know we sometimes get a bad reputation, but I joined to connect with people. My fraternity doesn't even have the regular frat house, just a small place where we meet up once a week to catch up."

Heat seared across her cheeks as she stammered out an apology, "I'm sorry. I didn't mean..."

He held his hand up, interrupting her and smiling. "I was teasing you. Come on, I'll give you a quick tour of the most important places on campus before dinner."

As they walked around the campus, Caleb pointed out buildings and filled Amanda in on other aspects of college life. She tried to stay focused on his words, but now and then her gaze would wander down to his mouth. He had perfectly shaped lips, and she couldn't help wondering what kissing them would be like.

She'd had only one kiss and it didn't really count. In eighth grade, there had been a game where you tried to pull the tabs off soda cans and keep them in perfect form. If you were able to, you could hand someone the tab and they had to kiss you. Rick, the pastor's son had handed her such a tab one day as they walked the church yard between services. Then he'd leaned over and kissed her lips. It had happened so quickly that Amanda wasn't even sure if it had been real or if she'd imagined it.

"Dinner?"

"Huh?" Amanda's face blazed at the realization that she hadn't been paying attention to anything but his lips.

He smiled. "I asked if you were hungry. Do you want to get dinner?"

"Oh, uh sure," she stammered, and then, as if on cue, her stomach rumbled, punctuating her words. *Could this get any more embarrassing?*

Chuckling, he led the way back to his dorm. The smell of marinara sauce wafted through the hallway as they entered.

It was Italian night, and Amanda piled her plate with spaghetti, garlic bread, and salad. Caleb grabbed a small lasagna and a salad, but no pasta.

As he led the way to a table, Amanda's brow furrowed. Did he know something she didn't? "Okay, seriously, is the food poisonous?" she asked as they sat down.

A melodious laugh flowed out of his mouth. "No, it's actually pretty good, but it's not often good for you. During my freshman year I packed on the dreaded Freshman fifteen and had to work extra hard to get it off. I've just learned since then that salad is usually safer, so I fill up on it and just take a small portion of the main dish."

Amanda was thoroughly embarrassed. *What must he think of me with my plate piled high?* "I'll keep that in mind," she said in a soft voice.

"No one told me either my first year," he said with a smile. "Hey, what's your schedule next week? I'd like to meet you after your classes if it fits with my schedule."

"You don't have to do that," Amanda said, but even as the words left her mouth, her hand was fumbling in her pocket for the schedule as it wasn't memorized yet. Her heart raced at the thought of him meeting her after class though she tried to appear nonchalant.

"I know I don't have to. I want to."

The smile he flashed was pure gold and she reciprocated, feeling happy for the first time this week. She passed her schedule across the table to him, and he perused it silently.

"You have History near my last class, so I'll meet you outside your History class."

"Sounds like a plan."

After dinner, Caleb insisted on walking Amanda to her dorm. As the sun was setting, she agreed. The warnings of walking the campus alone at night had been drilled into her head before she graduated and then again at orientation.

The air was still warm as they crossed the luscious green campus, and the sprinklers were working late. Amanda's heart constricted when her dorm hall came into view as she didn't want the night to end.

Though the dorm had no strict visitor policy, Amanda wasn't ready to invite him in. She bit her lip, unsure of how to tell him that. Thankfully, Caleb seemed to read her mind and stopped outside the entrance.

He jammed his hands in his pockets, drawing her attention to his trim waist and the abs she was sure were chiseled underneath his shirt. Amanda forced her eyes to the side to avoid the heat she could feel crawling up her neck.

"Okay, have a good night, and I'll see you tomorrow," he said.

There was a moment of silence, and Amanda wondered if he were going to kiss her. Did she even want him to? No, it was too soon for a kiss. Again, as if seeing her thoughts, he leaned in and opted for a quick hug instead before turning back the way they had come.

Amanda watched him walk away, her nerves tingling at his touch. When he turned the corner and was out of sight, she entered the dorm and walked up the stairs. A dreamy smile played across her face. Even Jade wouldn't be able to spoil her good feelings tonight.

*Jared slapped the alarm off and rolled out of bed. Though he wasn't much of a morning person, he had found this was the best time to have his quiet time with the Lord. Grabbing his Bible from the nightstand, he sat at the small desk in the room and opened it up to Matthew 5, the last passage he had been reading.

"Lord, please help me be the light you speak of here. Use me to help reach others and share your word," he prayed as he finished the chapter. Then he shut the Bible and grabbed his shower caddy. Working at the Student Union wasn't his dream job, but it did put him in front of a lot people and allow him to be a witness to them.

*J*ared had just finished bussing a table and was headed to the kitchen with a tub of dishes in his arms when he spotted the beautiful redhead. She had stopped inside the entrance and was scanning the area as if looking for something.

"Can I help you?" he asked approaching her.

When she turned to face him, his breath caught in his throat. Her green eyes were a bright emerald color, and her skin was a flawless porcelain. Jared hadn't been captivated by someone so instantly since Nikki a year ago.

"Um, maybe," she said with a shy smile. "I'm looking for the bulletin board where they post groups you can join."

He nodded and pointed to his right, "They are posted on that column over there. Are you looking to get involved in something particular?" *Please say a Christian organization.*

"I don't even know what they offer." Her smile stretched further showing off perfectly white teeth, "but I'd love to get involved in some sort of Christian club and a pro-life group if they have one. I know a lot of clinics closed with HB2, but now that it's been overturned, I just have this feeling they will be coming back."

Jared's eyes widened and his mouth dropped open. He had been hoping those very words would come out of her mouth.

"What?" she asked.

"Nothing," he said with a shake of his head. "It's just that I'm a part of Students for Life, the pro-life group here on campus. We're having our first meeting Friday night at Holden Hall."

This time her eyes widened. "Really? That is amazing. What are the odds?"

"Astronomical I'm pretty sure, if God weren't in control. This is a huge campus, and we aren't that big of a group. A lot graduated and even more stopped coming once the Planned Parenthood closed in town two years ago, but a core group of about fifty of us have continued, and we are always looking for new members. I'm Jared, by the way." He transferred the tub to his left hip and stuck out his right hand. "I don't always look like this, but I'm working today."

"I'm Amanda," she said taking his hand. A tingle shot up his arm at her touch, but he tried to keep his face from showing his excitement. He would have to get to know this girl better.

"I don't have a flyer on me," he said, "but I bet there's one on the column."

He led the way to the column covered with flyers for all the different organizations, and after a minute of scanning, he plucked a bright orange piece of paper off and handed it to her. "Here you go; all the information about us is on here."

"Thank you and count me in," she said flashing another bright smile. "I'll be there."

As she walked away, Jared turned his face heavenward and sent up a "thank you" prayer to God. He knew He'd had a hand in his meeting Amanda, and he hoped God had more in store for them.

❀

*A*manda practically skipped out of the Student Union. Not only had she found information about the two organizations she was most interested in, but she had a feeling Jared would become a friend. There was something in his hazel green eyes and comfortable smile that made her want to get to know him more.

The buzzing of her phone halted any further thoughts of Jared. Her heartbeat quickened as she swiped the screen to see a message from Caleb asking if she wanted to meet up. Her fingers flew across the on-screen keyboard as she typed out her reply and headed his direction.

"How are you holding up today?" Caleb asked when Amanda was within earshot.

"Better," she smiled up at him and then dropped her eyes. "It's nice to have a friend."

"I'm glad," he said, grabbing her hand and lacing his fingers with hers. "What would you say to a movie tomorrow night?"

He pulled her hand tight against his chest, sending Amanda's heart into overdrive. She could feel his heartbeat against her hand. She opened her mouth to agree, but then remembered the meeting at the pro-life group. "I'd love to, but I have a meeting I promised I'd attend tomorrow. Can we do it the next night?"

A hardness flashed in Caleb's eyes for a split second, but then he grinned, and Amanda told herself she had just imagined it. "Sure. What meeting are you going to?"

"It's a pro-life group here on campus. I want to check them out to see if they're worth joining." Amanda could barely keep the excitement from her voice. Then a new thought popped into her head. "Oh, hey, do you know of a good church around here? I need to get connected soon."

Caleb's brow furrowed and he glanced away, sending alarms bells sounding in Amanda's head. "Oh, um, I've heard of this place called Experience Life."

"You mean you don't go anywhere?" He had never explicitly told her he was a Christian, but Amanda had assumed from his actions and his letting her pray for him that he was.

"Well, I've wanted to,"–he stroked her hand and stared deep into her eyes– "but I get so busy studying, and I've never had anyone to go with me."

The bells grew silent as a fog descended on Amanda's brain, and a shiver ran down her spine. Of course, that made sense. She didn't like going new places alone either. "Well, will you go with me this weekend?"

"Ooh, I can't this week, but next week?"

Amanda nodded, disappointed, but next week was better than not at all, and she had asked him last minute. She shouldn't be surprised he had plans already.

"I have some items to attend to, but dinner tonight?" Caleb asked. "I'll text you when I'm done."

Amanda nodded and floated back to the dorm on cloud nine. Images of Caleb flashed in her mind–his blue eyes, his perfect smile. She couldn't wait to see him again, and after grabbing the mail, she took the stairs two at a time.

As she neared the room, she stopped and looked again, her forehead wrinkling. A sock was tied to the doorknob. Was this some sort of weird ritual that Jade had? Was it a prank? She had heard there were often pranks in college.

Amanda glanced up and down the hallway, half expecting someone to jump out of a doorway, but no one else was there. It didn't appear to be a prank. Shaking her head, she opened the door. Immediately Jade's head and the dark-haired head of some stranger popped up from under the covers on Jade's bed.

Her hands flew to cover her eyes, and her ears burned up. "Oh, my gosh, what are you doing?"

"Don't you know what the sock means?" Jade demanded.

"No, well I guess I do now. This is not appropriate. I live here too." Amanda hurried to her bed and grabbed her Bible off the nightstand. "I'm going to go do my devotion, and I'd appreciate it if you weren't here when I return, whoever you are." Keeping her hands as a shield over her eyes, Amanda tucked the book under her arm and left the room.

She shook her head as she shut the door behind her. It was barely the end of the second week and Jade was hooking up with someone. How could people do that? She had always been taught that intimacy was special and something you reserved for your husband. While television portrayed it as okay to jump in bed with everyone you dated, Amanda had been sheltered growing up and never been around someone who did it. Oh, how she missed Kate.

Leaning against the wall, Amanda pondered where to go. She couldn't very well sit in the hallway because eventually the man would be leaving, and she had no desire to see him again. She tucked her ginger hair behind her ear and took a deep breath, trying to slow the adrenaline coursing through her veins. She closed her eyes and racked her mind. Study carrels. There were a few downstairs. Maybe they would be quiet enough that she could do her devotion and get her mind off Jade.

The study room was near the right end of the first floor. It was like a living room, quaint with a few mismatched couches and chairs, a television, and a bookshelf loaded with books. Thankfully, no one else was in the room, so Amanda curled up in a cushy brown chair to finish her devotion.

She couldn't focus on the words though. Her mind kept wandering back to Jade. What must the girl be missing in her life to be so willing to jump into bed with someone so quickly? No advice jumped out of the book, but someone who might have some sprung into her mind.

Taking out her phone, she dialed Callie's number. Though Callie was probably busy with little Hope, Amanda could think of no one else who could answer the question better. Callie had once lived with a boyfriend until she ended up pregnant. After deciding to keep the baby, she had then began speaking to local teens about the importance of loving yourself and your body.

"Hello?" Callie's breathless voice came over the phone, and Amanda hoped she hadn't interrupted something important.

"Hi Callie, It's Amanda, do you have a minute to talk? I have a problem I'm hoping you can help with."

"Sure, I just got Hope down for a nap, so I'm all yours for at least half an hour."

"I just walked in on my roommate and some guy, and it's only the second week of school. Could she be using sex to fulfill some need that's lacking?"

"It does sound like she's compensating for something. Sometimes when people have sex that soon, it's because they've had it with so many people that they've lost themselves. They now have a piece of all those other people with them which makes finding themselves and being happy with themselves so much harder. Are you close enough with her to ask about her past?"

Amanda bit her lip, wishing she could say yes. "Not really. I'm pretty sure she doesn't like me, though she did ask me about praying the other night."

"That's a start. The best thing you can do for her is to try to be a friend and pray for her. I'll pray over here as well, and I'll tell Sandra to add her to the list. Oh, and one last thing. I'd pray for some wisdom. Anyone who uses sex as a coping mechanism is bound to end up pregnant before they're ready. She may have either had an abortion in the past, will have one in the future, or both," Callie cautioned. "Just be aware and ask God to give you the right words when you speak with her."

Amanda thanked Callie and hung up the phone. As she put the phone back in her pocket, her stomach rumbled, but she didn't want to carry her Bible all the way to the cafeteria if she could help it. She wasn't concerned about being seen with it but about spilling food or drink on it.

A glance at her watch revealed more than an hour had passed. Amanda had no personal knowledge of sex, but surely that was enough time to finish. Deciding to chance it, she headed for the stairs.

The sock was gone from the handle when the door came into view, but worry still resonated through her at the thought of opening the door and them still being engaged. Closing her eyes, she sent a silent prayer, turned the handle, and pushed the door open.

"He's gone; you can open your eyes."

Jade's sarcastic voice snapped Amanda's eyes open. She stepped inside, still unable to look Jade in the eyes. Her eyes kept returning to the floor as if pulled by a tractor beam or a giant magnet.

"Have you seriously never heard about the sock before?" Jade asked as she pulled on a pair of black combat boots.

Amanda shook her head as she sat down on the bed. "No, I don't believe in sex before marriage, so I don't know all the code signs or lingo."

Jade stopped lacing her boot and stared at her. "You mean you've never had sex?"

"No, I'm waiting to do that with my husband. I've seen too many girls get pregnant or their hearts broken for one thing, and I want to follow God's command on the subject."

"Wow, you're really into this God thing, aren't you?" Jade finished lacing her boot and sat back.

Nodding, Amanda returned her Bible to its prominent place on the nightstand. "Yep, I've been a follower for thirteen years. He's always been there for me, even when people failed me." Something flickered across Jade's face. For just a split second, Amanda thought maybe her words had stirred some emotion, but then Jade's face hardened again.

"That's exactly why I stay away from God. I've known too many Christians who sure didn't act the part."

"I'm sorry you had bad experiences," Amanda said softly, "but people aren't perfect, and they will often fail us. Only God is perfect. I try my hardest to follow his plan, but I still mess up. The difference is I apologize when I do, repent, and try to do better next time."

Jade's eyes locked with Amanda's. Could they be about to have a conversation?

"And you think that's all it takes? Just apologize and it's all good?"

Her words were filled with so much hate that Amanda could only blink for a moment. What had hurt her so badly in the past? "No, I... I mean yes, you apologize, but I guess it doesn't always make it better."

"It is people like you who turn people like me off. You live in your rainbow and unicorn world, where probably nothing bad has ever happened to you, spouting off trite words about repentance and forgiveness, but you don't know what it's really like. You've probably never had to hide in a closet hoping your stepfather won't find you and will give you one night off from being his punching bag or his play thing. I doubt your mom has ever forgotten you in her drug-induced stupor, leaving you to walk home five miles in the dark."

Amanda stared at her roommate. Was this her past? "Jade, I'm so sorry," she said.

"Save it," Jade said, pushing herself off the bed and storming out of the room.

Sighing, Amanda sent up yet another prayer for patience. "God, I'm way out of my league here, and I could really use some help." Her cell phone vibrated in her hand, and for just a moment she wondered if God was answering.

Opening her eyes, she read the message from Caleb. He was ready for dinner, and thoughts of Jade flew from Amanda's mind like leaves in a windstorm. A smile crawled across her face as she locked the door and jogged down the stairs to meet him.

❀

"So, do you want to come up and watch a movie with me tonight?" Caleb suggested as they finished dinner and returned their plates and silverware to the kitchen.

The image of Jade and the unknown man in bed flashed before her eyes. "I don't think that would be a good idea," Amanda said, "but we can watch one down in the lounge."

Caleb's smile froze for just a moment. "Sure, I just thought maybe you'd want to be able to talk too."

"Well, are we talking or watching a movie?" Amanda asked with a laugh.

Caleb flashed another smile and led the way down the hall to the lounge. A big screen TV sat on the far side of the room. Next to it a shelf was teeming with movies. A few couches and chairs were set up around the room, very much like the study room at Amanda's dorm.

The room was empty, and Amanda paused. Would it be safe to be in here alone with him? She no longer trusted herself completely because new sensations coursed through her body every time they met up. There was no door on the room though, so she decided it would be safe enough.

Caleb picked out a romantic comedy and sat down on one of the couches. Amanda had hoped he would opt for two chairs, but swallowing her trepidation, she sat beside him.

Caleb opened his arm, clearly wanting Amanda to snuggle into it. She pursed her lips, trying to weigh the options. Deciding the pros outweighed the cons, she curled into the inviting open space. It was warm, comfortable, and the smell of his cologne reminded her somehow of home.

He placed his hand on her right shoulder and circled a slow pattern with his finger. A tingling sensation like nothing she'd ever felt before began bubbling in her stomach and crawling up her body, followed by a creeping warmth. Amanda snuggled deeper into Caleb's side, enjoying the masculine smell radiating from his body.

Her hand, seemingly with a mind of its own, found its way to Caleb's chest. The muscles tensed beneath her fingers, and the tingling sensation blossomed. Shifting slightly, Caleb cupped her chin and brought his soft lips down on hers. Amanda's breath caught in her throat as the tingling shot through her body, lighting up areas she hadn't even known existed. Her lips parted and Caleb's tongue touched her own. His hand edged under her arm, touching her side. An alarm began to blare in Amanda's head, and she pushed back on Caleb's chest.

"We should stop," she said, her breath labored.

Caleb turned his face away and ran his left hand across his face. "Of course, you're right. We should slow down."

Amanda nodded, but she hadn't been thinking of slowing down. She had been thinking of slamming the brakes and putting the car in reverse. Red flashes of light had shot through her head, telling her clearly they needed to stop. "I should go." Caleb's face fell, pulling on her heartstrings, so she quickly added, "I'll see you tomorrow if you're free before my meeting, but I think we need some space tonight."

Before he could convince her to stay, Amanda rose from the plush couch and hurried from the room. Her body still pulsed with desire, and she didn't trust herself to stay strong.

As she hurried back down the main hall toward the front entrance, she hoped the air outside would be cool enough to tame the fire raging inside her, but it was still warm. Sighing, she forced her thoughts to something else, anything else, hoping to tame the flame that way.

Amanda's face still felt flushed as she opened the door to the room. Jade looked up and grinned a malicious smile. "Uh oh, did the goody girl get some? Not so high and mighty now, huh?"

"What? No, I didn't," Amanda stammered, "but I can see how people lose control now. And I am not high and mighty."

"It's not a big deal," Jade said, "It's a normal part of life and yes, you are. You act like you are better than everyone with your Bible and your virginity."

Shaking her head, Amanda sat on the bed and grabbed her Bible for comfort. The textured black cover radiated calming waves as she held it to her chest, and her heart slowed. "I'm not trying to act like I'm better. I'm just trying to follow God's word. I know intimacy is a natural part of life, but it is supposed to be reserved for marriage.

Otherwise, it becomes natural with everyone you date, and it loses its special meaning."

Jade shook her head. "There's nothing wrong with that, and *it is special* every time, believe me."

"Do you really believe that?" Amanda asked. She didn't want to sound preachy, but if sex was as special as Jade claimed, why was she always so moody? "Don't you think it would be more special if you really loved the person, and they loved you back? If you were in a committed relationship?"

"You don't know anything about me."

Her hard exterior was returning, and Amanda knew she was losing her. "Not for lack of trying. I've been trying to get to know you the last two weeks, but you keep throwing up walls."

"Whatever. We have nothing in common."

"We might. If you'd talk to me, we might find lots in common. At the very least we wouldn't feel so alone."

"I don't feel alone," Jade said. "I have Gavin." And she turned back to her book.

Amanda stifled a small sigh, clasped the Bible tighter to her chest, and leaned back against her pillow. Jade was going to be a tough one, but she would keep trying.

CHAPTER 5

*A*manda swallowed the rather large lump in her throat as she dressed for the Students for Life meeting. Her nerves were jittering out of control. Jared had said it was casual, but the need to make a good impression weighed heavily on her heart. Her hope was that many of the people she met tonight would become friends. The Lord knew she could sure use some.

Deciding on a green shirt that complemented her hair, she pulled it and a pair of jeans on. After a final glance in the mirror and a quick fluffing of her long red locks, she left the room.

Even though the sun was setting, the air was still warm as Amanda crossed the green campus to Holden Hall. As one of the oldest buildings on campus, it had a regal air, though the architecture of it wasn't as striking as several of the other buildings.

She pulled open the large wooden door and stepped inside. The smooth white floor contrasted the exposed bricks lining the inside wall. Research had informed Amanda that this hall had once been a museum, and she wondered how it must have looked then. A small white sign that read Students for Life pointed to the right, and she turned that direction, her footsteps echoing through the large hallway.

As she stopped in front of room 101, she took a deep breath

before opening the door. Though large, the room was not as big as some of the lecture halls. There were round-tables and chairs set up about the room, and a small stage with a podium sat at the far front of the room.

Amanda wasn't extremely shy, but this scenario sent her heart racing. A sea of unknown faces stared back at her. What had she been thinking? A hand waved near the front, and she focused on it. It belonged to Jared and it felt like a life jacket in the unfamiliar water. While she didn't know him well, he was the only one she knew even a little. Squaring her shoulders and willing her nerves to relax, she pushed her feet forward.

"I'm so glad you could make it," Jared said as Amanda reached the table. One other guy and three girls were also at the table. "Guys, I'd like to introduce you to Amanda.... Sorry, I realize I didn't get your last name when we met."

Amanda's face flamed. "Oh, my gosh, I'm so sorry. It's Adams. Amanda Adams."

His green eyes twinkled as he smiled at her, and a calm flowed over her. What was it about him that made her feel so comfortable? "Okay Amanda. Well this is Chase, Sarah, Becca, and Emily," he said, pointing to each one in turn.

Chase reached out a hand first. He had dirty blond hair and friendly hazel eyes. His sharp features stood out on his clean-shaven face. Sarah's handshake was softer, though Amanda hadn't expected it with her steely eyes and hawkish nose capped off with spiky blond hair. Becca was a soft-spoken brunette with green eyes and a dusting of freckles across her nose. Emily came across as the sporty one in the group. Her blond hair was pulled back in a ponytail and the glistening of her face led Amanda to believe she'd either worked out just before or on her way here.

Though glad to meet new people she hoped would become friends, Amanda had no idea if she would remember all their names. She mentally went over them again as she sat down in the empty seat next to Jared.

The room quickly filled as others straggled in. A few came over to say hello to Jared and the others at the table. Jared was always gracious and introduced Amanda as well, and while she smiled and shook each person's hand, she knew she would never remember all of their names.

The sound of a hand tapping a microphone grabbed Amanda' attention, and she glanced up as a dark-haired woman stepped up to the podium. "Welcome everyone. I'm Tracy Martin, the president of Students for Life. I'll introduce the other officers in a minute, but I wanted to tell you all a little about what we do for the new people and a reminder for the returners.

"Last year we were mainly an educational group. We went to the fairs, and we distributed pamphlets about choices other than abortion. We will continue that this year. In fact, our first fair is next Monday. There are details by the door as you leave. I hope you'll sign up at the clipboard by the door, so we can contact you with future details of other fairs.

"As most of you know HB2, or House Bill 2, was repealed this year. This was the provision that made abortion clinics have to meet certain standards, and since most couldn't meet those standards, it forced many to close. We don't know what the repealing of this bill will mean yet, but I have an ominous feeling that it means more abortion clinics will be coming back. So, we are going to double our efforts this year. We may never get Roe v Wade repealed, but we can reach individuals and change their minds about abortion. We can show them the dangers of abortion and the humanity of the unborn."

Clapping erupted in the room. "Now, if I can ask the officers to join me up here, I'd like to introduce them."

"I'll be right back," Jared whispered and walked to the front. Amanda's eyes widened in surprise. She'd had no idea he was this involved. Sarah and Emily also stood and joined the group up front.

"This is Jared Masterson, our vice-president. Jared is a junior and has been involved with us since his freshman year. He's had a heart for the unborn ever since his mother told him she'd aborted a sibling before him."

Empathy tugged at Amanda's heart and tears pricked her eyes as she thought about her own siblings. She couldn't imagine knowing you should have a brother or sister, but that your mother had gotten rid of him or her.

"This is Emily Peters." Tracy continued, pointing to the petite blond. "She's a Sophomore and our Secretary. She'll keep notes of the meetings and send out emails if you miss them so you can stay up to date. Emily was adopted, so the sanctity of the unborn hits close to home. And finally,"–she pointed to the taller girl with the short blond hair– "we have Sarah Stewart. Sarah is a Senior and a communication major. She was conceived in rape, but thankfully her mother chose life. She'll oversee organizing events and putting the flyers together. We are all open to communication, so if you leave your email address on the sheet at the refreshment table, we'll be sending out our email and phone numbers to everyone."

Jared and the two girls rejoined the table, and Amanda's heart went out to him, to all the officers really. "I'm sorry about your sibling. I can't imagine what that must have been like. When did she tell you?"

"When I was fifteen, can you believe that?" he whispered, leaning forward, "She sat us down during a family powwow–I have a younger sister who was twelve at the time–and told us she'd gotten pregnant in college, but didn't want to give up her career, so she'd had an abortion. I asked her if she knew what the baby was, boy or girl, you know because I always wanted a brother, but she said she'd had the abortion too early to know. I don't know why, but it made me question if she really loved us. She tried to impress how important choice was, and that all children should be wanted. She made the baby sound like an inconvenience, and I told her that there were thousands of families waiting to adopt. I thought then, and I still do now, that she was being selfish. Our relationship has suffered since."

"Oh Jared, I'm so sorry. That has to be hard." Amanda had seen a few similar cases when she'd worked at JD's center. She still couldn't believe mothers would tell their children they had aborted a sibling, but the counselor on staff had said it was often the mother's way of processing their own guilt over the procedure. However, the news never sat well with the remaining kids as, like Jared, they almost always questioned why they were saved and not their brother or sister.

He shrugged. "It is what it is. It helped me find God. After that discussion, I was confused. I couldn't understand her, and it made me question everything. I found myself at church, and it was there I found healing. I pray for my mom every day to realize what she's done and repent, and I pray my sister doesn't follow in her footsteps. She'll be a freshman at college next year, and I know too well the temptations here."

"I'll add them to my prayer list too," Amanda said, laying a hand on his arm. "I have a friend who runs the prayer group at my old church. I'll have her add them to the list. We have at least fifty people praying every week."

Jared put his hand on hers and gazed into Amanda's eyes. A heat, starting at the point of contact, spread like wildfire up her arm, causing her heart to flip flop. "Thank you, I'd like that," he said. "Now, what's your story?"

"My story?" Amanda stammered trying to make her brain focus. She was having a hard time concentrating with his hand on her arm as it was sending her heart jumping. Why was his touch affecting her?

"This is my third year," he said. "Everyone has a story; some reason why they are pro-life and willing to fight for it."

"Oh," Amanda nodded, "Yeah, I have a story. My grandmother had a lot of physical issues growing up. When she married, the doctors told her she should never get pregnant, but she did. They recommended an abortion, but she chose to have the baby and my uncle was born. A few years later, my grandmother got pregnant again, this time with my mother. The doctors told her if she didn't abort my mother that she would die. If she had listened to those doctors I wouldn't be here, so choosing life is personal to me too."

"Did she die in child birth?" he asked.

"No." Amanda smiled. "She lived until I was ten."

"That's a good story. It's amazing how our stories can be so different, yet we are affected the same." He squeezed her arm before removing his hand. "Here, come with me; I want to introduce you to some of the others." He held out his hand and pulled Amanda to her feet.

She followed him around the room meeting other members of the club. Before she knew it, the room had thinned. Amanda glanced at her watch and realized she should be going too. She stopped at the table by the door to sign the email sheet before leaving. No way was she going to miss the chance of getting involved with this group; it was a perfect fit for her.

Amanda glanced around for Jared who had wandered off a moment before. She wanted to say goodbye, but he appeared deep in conversation with Sarah, so she decided she would just catch him later.

As she pushed open the outside door, the chill of the night air shook her. The sun had fully set as the meeting had gone on and now shadows loomed across the open campus. Amanda shivered, wishing she had come with someone so she wouldn't have to leave alone. Goosebumps broke out on her arms, and she rubbed her hands up them to quiet the attack.

❀

When the conversation with Sarah ended, Jared looked around for Amanda, but she was nowhere to be seen. He had been hoping to walk her home. Taking a chance that he had just missed her, Jared headed to the exit.

She wasn't in the hallway, but as he reached the main entrance, he saw a figure standing on the top of the stairs. Her red hair shimmered in the moonlight.

"Can I walk you home?" he asked as he pushed open the front door.

She turned to him, a look of relief in her eyes. "Thank you, that would be nice. I didn't realize it had gotten so late, and I didn't want to walk across the campus alone."

"I completely agree." Jared shoved his hands in the pockets of his brown leather jacket to keep from grabbing her hand. He had felt such a tingling sensation when they had touched earlier that he wanted to repeat it, but he didn't know if she had a boyfriend and he didn't want to overstep any bounds.

"I'm so glad I came tonight," she said as they walked down the steps. "This really seems like something I'll love."

418 | LORANA HOOPES

"I'm glad you did too. Tracy forgot to mention it, but we have a small office in Holden Hall that we run on a volunteer basis. Mainly we do a lot of planning there, but occasionally the phone rings. We have women who call us first if they aren't familiar with the clinics in the city, and we help get them set up. It's pretty boring most days and doesn't pay anything, but do you think you'd like to volunteer?" He held his breath as he waited for her answer. If she said yes, it would be a great way for him to get to know her better.

Her green eyes sparkled. "I'd love to. I'm not looking for a job, just a way to help, and that sounds perfect. Besides, doing God's work is never boring."

Her words brought a smile to his face. He had prayed so long to find a godly woman, and while he had met many, Amanda was the first one who had sent his heart racing.

"Oh," she said with a sigh. "This is me."

Jared swallowed his disappointment at the large dorm building. He didn't want to say goodnight to Amanda yet. "Thank you for allowing me to walk you home. I hope you can make it to the fair next week." He stopped just to the side of the front entrance and rocked back and forth on his heels.

"I wouldn't miss it," she said.

An awkward silence fell between them as Jared debated whether to ask her out or not. He opened his mouth to ask, but in the end, he decided to wait. Closing his mouth, he lifted his hand in a small wave and walked away.

"Lord, please give me wisdom about Amanda," he prayed silently as he returned to his dorm. "I feel a connection to her, but I want to follow your will."

❀

*A*manda returned the wave and watched Jared walk away. For a second, she'd thought Jared was going to ask her out. The thought had excited and terrified her at the same time because she was also seeing Caleb, but then he'd just walked away, leaving her even more confused.

Had she misread his affections? Did it matter? She was dating Caleb, wasn't she? Of course she had no idea what Caleb's idea of dating was. Her idea of dating was seeing only one person at a time, but she'd known many people in high school who went out with a different person each weekend.

With a sigh, she mounted the steps and pulled open the large front door of the dorm. A part of her longed for the simpler times of high school.

Jade looked up as Amanda entered the room. "What happened to you?"

While Jade was not the first person Amanda would choose to confide in, she had no one else at the moment. "Do you think it's possible to like two guys at the same time?" Amanda asked slowly as she removed her jacket.

Jade snorted. "Seriously? Of course, it's possible. I didn't think it would be for you, you know being such a prude and all, but for the rest of us, it's pretty normal."

Amanda let the rude comment slide. Her desire for knowledge outweighed a bruised ego tonight. "So, how do you choose?"

"Choose?" Jade wrinkled her forehead and looked at Amanda as if she were an alien. "You don't choose; you just date them both until you decide which you like more."

"I can't do that," Amanda said, sitting on her bed. "Dating is about finding your perfect match. I couldn't date both at the same time, but I'm no longer sure which one I want to date more."

Jade shook her head. "I don't think I'll ever understand you. If you date them both, you would be booked every Friday and Saturday night. Maybe they'll even compete and buy you things trying to win your affection. This could be very lucrative for you."

Amanda's mouth dropped open. Was she serious? "I could never do that. Stringing a guy along just to get presents would just be wrong. Besides, I'm not even sure Jared likes me. He had the chance, and he didn't ask me out tonight. Maybe I just misread the signs."

"Well then, problem solved," Jade said turning back to her book. "Date the other one, whatever his name is."

"It's Caleb," Amanda interjected.

"Fine," Jade said, waving her hand in a dismissive gesture. "He was first, and this new guy sounds like a prude, *if* he even likes you." She paused and looked back up at Amanda. "Of course, so are you, so maybe you should dump the first guy and date the second one. You'd probably be perfect together."

Though Amanda knew it was a dig, Jade's words were exactly what she feared. Jared did seem perfect for her. If she continued seeing Caleb, would she miss out on the guy she was supposed to be with?

CHAPTER 6

*A*manda smoothed her skirt and applied a layer of lip gloss in front of the mirror. Tonight would be her first real date out with Caleb, and her stomach had been in knots all day.

"So, you going to get some tonight?" Jade smirked from her bed.

Biting back the first reply that popped in her mind, Amanda took a deep, calming breath and faced her. "You know I'm not; I've already told you that, and you don't have to be intimate with everyone you meet."

Jade wrinkled her brow and tilted her head. "Who said I am?"

As Amanda sat on her bed, she prayed for wisdom. She wanted to reach Jade, but she knew she needed just the right words. "You did when you had your tryst here the other day. It was only the second week. There's no way you knew that guy very well."

"You don't know what I feel for him," Jade said bristling.

"Well, it's not from lack of trying," Amanda replied, "I've been trying to get to know you." Amanda bit her lip as she tried to soften her next statement. "Look, all I'm saying is that whatever you're looking for, a man probably can't supply. But Jesus? He can heal any pain you're feeling."

Jade snorted and rolled her eyes. "Yeah, Jesus has never been there for me. I've always had to look out for myself."

"Have you ever asked him?" Jade opened her mouth to reply but then shut it again. A knock sounded at the door, and both girls looked that direction. Amanda's heart sank a bit; she had thought there had been a moment when Jade was going to let her in. "That will be Caleb, but I hope we can talk again soon." Jade gave no answer, and Amanda sighed softly as she pushed herself off the bed and crossed to the door.

Caleb stood on the other side of the door, looking dapper in a blue shirt that perfectly matched his eyes. Amanda's heartbeat sped up as her eyes were drawn to the shirt stretched across his muscular chest. She turned back to Jade to avoid blushing. "Caleb, this is my roommate Jade. Jade, Caleb."

Jade harrumphed a half-hearted reply, and Caleb raised his brows. Amanda rolled her eyes and shook her head slightly to indicate she'd explain later.

"She seems pleasant," Caleb said as Amanda pulled the door shut behind them.

"I think she is underneath. It seems like there's some hurt in her past."

Caleb nodded and grabbed Amanda's hand. She smiled up at him as a tingle ran up her arm. For the moment, Jade was forgotten.

🍩

*A*manda's jaw dropped as Caleb pulled into the parking lot of the theater. The building was painted a bright purple with a marquis advertising the shows in bright lights. "Wow, it's so..."

"Hideous?" he asked with a laugh. "I know. They painted it last year, and I have no idea why they chose purple."

Amanda shook her head as she climbed out of the truck and walked around to meet Caleb, who grabbed her hand and led the way to the ticket agent.

"Two for Child's Play," he said, pulling out his wallet with his free hand.

The color drained from Amanda's face, and her throat constricted. "Is that a horror movie?" she asked softly.

Amanda had sworn off scary movies at the age of twelve after a scary slumber party. They had been watching some crazy show about a possessed doll that grew until it was big enough to kill everyone in the house. Though she had known it wasn't real, she couldn't shake the fear as she climbed into her sleeping bag. Her active imagination had run wild, and long after everyone else was asleep, her eyes were still wide open.

The house had grown eerily quiet, unusual with twenty girls filling the living room. Then a noise that she could only describe as the sound of something growing began radiating from a cabinet. Her eyes had stayed glued to that cabinet until morning.

Amanda shivered as the memory of the weird sound and the terror that had coursed through her body filled her mind again. The fear had carried over into her own house for another week. Some nights she even had to watch a silly cartoon before falling asleep, so the image of the terrifying doll wasn't the last thing in her mind.

"Yeah, I heard it's great. Don't you like scary movies?" He raised his eyebrow in insinuation.

Amanda felt like he wanted her to say yes, but she wasn't sure she could. Did she tell him the truth or hope her fear had been tamed with age? "Actually, I don't."

Caleb let out a deep breath. "Okay," he said slowly and turned back to the movie board listing. "Well, the only other thing playing close to now is a cartoon."

"I don't mind cartoons." Amanda squeezed his hand, hoping he would understand.

The movie attendant, probably a high school student by his baby face, shook his head but exchanged the tickets.

Caleb appeared to hold no ill will and held the door open for Amanda. After buying popcorn and drinks, they made their way down the purple carpeted hallway to the theater. Where did one even find purple carpet?

The lights inside the theater were already dimmed, but as

Amanda scanned the room, she could see they were the only people in the theater.

"Well, I guess there's an upside to cartoons late at night after all," Caleb grinned and headed to the very top of the theater.

Warnings fired again in Amanda's head. Though she'd never done it, she had heard many stories of couples making out in the top row of theaters where the movie attendant couldn't see them. In fact, she was almost sure that's how one of the many girls who had gotten pregnant at her high school had found herself in that unfortunate situation, but Amanda pushed the warnings aside as she climbed the stairs after him. Caleb didn't seem the type to force himself on her. He hadn't pushed her to be intimate, and after all, he had agreed to see a cartoon for her.

He sat down in the one of the middle chairs, and Amanda took the plush seat to his left. Even the velvet on the chairs was purple. She wondered who the decorator had been and if the manager who had approved the color scheme had been color blind.

The lights dimmed and the previews started. Though not a romantic movie, Amanda felt her face flush every time her fingers touched Caleb's in the popcorn bowl.

When the popcorn was gone, Caleb held her hand, and though he traced slow circles on it that caused her heartbeat to amplify in her ears, he never made a move to go further.

"You ready?" he asked as the movie ended.

"Can we stay till all the credits run?" Amanda asked.

"I guess," Caleb said, wrinkling his brow, "but why? The movie's over."

"I did a play once in High School. The actors got all the credit, but no one mentioned our light, sound, and tech crew who did all the backstage work. Without them, our play would have been a disaster. Ever since, I've wanted to stay through the credits as a thank you to the behind-the-scenes people. I know, it's silly," Amanda said as the expression on his face changed from curiosity to disbelief.

The corner of his lip pulled up into a smile. "No, I think it's sweet. I've just never known anyone quite like you."

When the last credit rolled and the lights came back up, Amanda rose and followed Caleb out of the theater.

As Caleb pushed open the door to the outside, Amanda shivered. Though still summer, the night air held a slight chill that bit through her short sleeve shirt. Not missing a beat, Caleb placed his arm around her shoulder and pulled her to his side. The masculine scent of his cologne wafted to her nose, and a spark of desire flared within her. Amanda wrapped her arm about his waist and smiled up at him.

As she climbed into his car, Amanda couldn't decide if she wanted to be closer to him or farther away so as not to inflame the desire. "So, are we still on for church on Sunday?" she asked. Perhaps if she reminded herself that the Holy Spirit was watching, her racing heart would calm down.

"What? Oh, yeah, church, sure." He turned his head away. "Did you want to try the Experience Life place?"

"That sounds fine. Do you know what time the service starts?"

"No, can you check?"

Amanda pulled out her cell phone and tapped the Safari app to open the search engine, but her email popped up instead. At the top of the Inbox list was an email from the Students for Life. Her heart skipped a beat. Could it be from Jared? She hadn't thought of him all evening, but his face filled her mind now.

Sneaking a glance at Caleb, she surreptitiously tapped it to read, and disappointment mingled with relief flooded her body. It wasn't from Jared, but it was a reminder of the information fair happening on Monday, which she was sure he would be attending. Promising herself she would read it more thoroughly later, she clicked out of it and to the web browser to search for the church time.

"Looks like 10:45," she said.

"Sounds good," Caleb replied, "I'll pick you up at 10:15 then." He pulled into the dorm parking lot and turned off the engine. He turned to Amanda and grabbed her hands. "I had a really nice time. Thanks for coming with me."

Amanda's breath caught in her throat at the intensity of his gaze, and her voice came out barely louder than a whisper, "Me too." All thoughts of Jared flew out of her mind as her heart pounded in her chest. Could he hear that?

Caleb placed a hand on the back of her neck and pulled her face toward his. Fireworks exploded in Amanda's head, and a tingling ran down her entire spine as his lips touched hers. This was so much better than her first kiss had been. *This* was what a first kiss should be like.

"I'll see you Sunday," he whispered as he pulled back.

Amanda could only nod.

❦

"*I*f you're that attracted to her, why didn't you ask her out?" Emily asked as she filled her mug with tea and returned to the table.

Jared sighed. "I don't know. I guess my nerves got the better of me. What if she turns out to be another Nikki?"

"What if she doesn't?" Becca spoke up. "Jared, we know you were hurt by what Nikki did, but you can't close yourself off to new possibilities."

Jared ran a hand through his hair. "I know you guys are right, but it's hard to open yourself up again."

"Open yourself up to what?" Chase asked, entering the lounge with his Bible under his arm.

"Love," Becca teased. "Jared's crushing on the new girl."

"The redhead?" Chase asked. "Good choice. She seemed nice and down to earth."

"You barely talked to her," Sarah said, looking up from her Bible. "How can you be so sure?"

"I'm a good judge of character," Chase smiled. "It's how I knew you had a soft side under that sharp, hawkish exterior you like to put on."

"Alright, you two love birds," Emily said, teasing the couple. "We should get started if we want to finish in time to get a good rest before tomorrow."

The others grumbled good naturedly but nodded. Though she

was the youngest, Emily had organized the weekly Bible study last year, and the rest had eagerly agreed. College was full of stressors and temptations, and the weekly meetings had helped them all stay on track and accountable to each other.

"I thought we'd start with prayer requests," Emily continued. "I could really use some prayers for my new roommate. She's…" Emily paused and took a deep breath, "tough to say the least."

"I could use prayer for my Chemistry test next week," Becca said. "Science is not my strength."

As the others continued to share their requests, Jared's mind wandered to Amanda. He could have invited her here. Then it wouldn't have been so much like a date as inviting her into their friendship circle, and she had said she could use more friends. Yes, that's what he would do. The next time he saw her, he would invite her to Bible study and maybe church.

"Earth to Jared."

Emily's voice broke through Jared's daydream, and he dropped his eyes. "Sorry," he mumbled. "I guess prayers for wisdom."

"And courage," Emily added. "Write that down, Becca. We gotta pray for this man to have the courage to ask Amanda out."

"I could use it," Jared said with a smile. He was so glad God had brought these people into his life last year. It had certainly made dealing with Nikki's rejection and disappearance easier, and now he had a great group of friends to rely on.

CHAPTER 7

*a*s Sunday morning dawned, Amanda woke excited for the day. She hoped she would love this church and be able to call it her home away from home church.

Jade snoozed across the room, and Amanda wondered what time she usually got up. She seemed to always be sleeping till at least nine or ten in the morning. Slipping out of bed as quietly as she could, Amanda gathered her toiletries and Sunday wear and headed to the showers.

After her shower, Amanda returned to the room to drop off her toiletries and grab her Bible. Jade hadn't changed position, and Amanda smiled at the deepness of her sleep. She had often wished she could sleep like that, through anything, but once the alarm went off, she was awake for good. Even on days she didn't set the alarm, Amanda could rarely sleep past eight. It probably had to do with growing up with younger siblings who were often up at the crack of dawn and rarely quiet.

Amanda glanced at her watch, and though she had a few minutes before Caleb was due to meet her downstairs she decided to wait in the lobby for him so she wouldn't wake Jade. Tucking the Bible under her arm, she grabbed a light jacket and headed downstairs.

"You look beautiful," Caleb said as she descended the steps. He was early. A blush spread across her face at the unexpected compliment.

"Thank you," Amanda managed. "Are you ready?"

He held out his hand, and after Amanda took it, led the way outside.

The drive to the church was short, but Amanda was very glad Caleb was driving as the church was in the newly renovated downtown area of the city where all the loops and overpasses converged. She didn't like driving in traffic anyway, but driving in congested areas when she didn't know where she was going was a huge fear.

As Caleb pulled into the crowded parking lot, sweat broke out on Amanda's palms. The church was huge, and the parking lot, which appeared to hold close to two hundred parking spaces was nearly full. How many people attended this church? Amanda's church back home had been on the smaller side, only about one hundred people in each service, and she rather liked it that way. It allowed her to get to know people in the church.

After circling the lot three times, Caleb finally managed to snag a spot as another car vacated it. It was at the very back of the lot, so they had a large piece of real estate to cross to get to the front doors. Amanda was glad she had chosen comfortable shoes.

A slew of people stood at the front entrance handing out brochures as Amanda and Caleb approached. Amanda took one, tucking it in her Bible to peruse when they sat down. The foyer was expansive, but the doors in front of them opened into a huge auditorium. Amanda held tighter to Caleb's hand as they joined the stream of people filtering into the auditorium.

Not generally a claustrophobic person, the sheer number of people in this building unnerved Amanda. Was this a church or a sporting event?

As Caleb led the way to two empty seats in the middle section, Amanda's eyes scanned the room. The auditorium which looked like it could hold a thousand people, was already filling up. "It's so huge," she said as they sat down. "So much bigger than my old church."

"It will be fine," Caleb assured her.

Out of the corner of her eye, Amanda saw Caleb glance at his watch and wondered if he had somewhere more important to be. Deciding she could ask him later, she pulled the brochure out of her Bible, expecting a small bulletin like her church back home had. Instead, it was almost like a college catalog. Every page was filled with a block of information and colorful pictures.

Amanda turned the pages, trying to find their belief statement, but none of the pages seemed to have it. What they did have was a choir, theatre, puppet shows, bible studies, pizza nights, game nights, work out classes, and much more. This church had a lot going on, and something for everyone, but it was so much Amanda wasn't even sure what to focus on.

When the music started, she looked up. She hadn't even noticed the entire band on the raised stage. As the music grew louder, it echoed throughout the room. The main lights dimmed and spots lit up the stage. Though upbeat and fun, Amanda found the music hard to worship to as it felt more like a concert than a worship service. The music continued for half an hour before a man started speaking.

He was ten minutes into his sermon before Amanda realized he was even the pastor as he was wearing shorts and a t-shirt. While she believed God didn't care what people wore, she had always attended a church where the pastor wore a suit or at least dress slacks. The image of the pastor looking more like he belonged at a beach than in a church created an odd dichotomy in Amanda's head.

Amanda snuck another glance at Caleb to see if he was having the same issues she was. His gaze was focused on something to the left. Discreetly, Amanda craned her head to see what had grabbed his attention, but all she could see was a group of college-aged people. Perhaps he was just scanning the crowd to see if he knew anyone.

Returning her attention to the pastor at the front, Amanda opened her Bible and forced her eyes to focus on the words of the page. As long as she didn't look up, she could follow the message without being distracted. It turned out to be a good one, all about keeping the focus on God. As the pastor ended, the band took the stage again and played for another ten minutes. Then the service was over.

"What did you think?" Caleb asked on the walk back to his truck.

Amanda pursed her lips as she thought. "The message was good, but I think the church is a little too big for me. I felt a little lost." She had, in fact, felt like a tiny fish in a gigantic pond, and while everyone had seemed very nice, she couldn't imagine calling the place her home.

"Right? Me too," he agreed as he opened the passenger door for her. "I even had a hard time concentrating because it felt more like a concert than a church service at some points."

Amanda smiled up at him as she climbed in her seat and he walked around to the driver's side door. She hadn't been sure Caleb had even been paying attention, but it seemed that he was on the same wavelength she was. "We can try a different one next week," she said as she strapped her seatbelt. "I'll do a little research online for a smaller one. I also want to find one that lists their statement of faith, because not all churches believe the same things, unfortunately, and I couldn't find one at that church."

"Oh yeah, that's definitely important." He started the engine and backed out of the parking space. "What uh is your statement of faith? I'm just curious if mine matches yours."

"Well, I believe that Jesus is the son of God, sent to Earth to die for our sins. I believe he is the only path to salvation, and that we must have a relationship with him. I also believe in the trinity and the pre-tribulation rapture."

"I'm sorry, I agree with everything else you said, but what's the pre-tribulation rapture?" Caleb glanced at her before returning his attention to the road.

"Well the rapture is when Christ will return and call all the believers back to Heaven. My family and I believe that will happen before the tribulation, but some people believe it will happen midway through the tribulation. That is called mid-tribulation. Then there's post tribulation, the belief that we won't be taken until the end of the tribulation. I just can't imagine that God would leave us to suffer through all seven years. I prefer to believe he will take us up to Heaven before the worst hits."

"I definitely like your stance better," he agreed. "I uh have some things to do this afternoon, but I'd love to hear more about the rapture tomorrow. I'm not sure my old church ever taught on it."

"Of course, I'd be happy to discuss it with you whenever." Amanda smiled at the interest Caleb was showing. There had been a few signs that made her wonder if he were a believer, but it appeared maybe he was and just hadn't attended a church that taught as much as hers did.

They pulled into the dorm parking lot and Caleb placed a quick kiss on her lips before Amanda waved goodbye and headed into the dorm.

"How was it?" Jade asked as she entered the room. She was awake, but she hadn't dressed; she was still laying in the bed sporting a cut off shirt and a pair of shorts.

"It was okay." Amanda returned her Bible to the nightstand and sat on the bed, folding her legs beneath her. "The message was nice, but the church was too big for my liking."

"How did Caleb like it?" Jade asked.

Amanda tilted her head at the question. Why did Jade care if Caleb liked church? "I think he felt the same, but he agreed to try another church with me next week." Amanda stood and crossed to the closet to change out of her dress and into more comfortable clothes.

"Hmm, he didn't seem the church-going type," she said.

"What do you mean?" Amanda asked turning on Jade. "You barely even met him."

"It was just a feeling." Jade held her hands up in defense. "You know him better, so I'm sure I'm wrong."

Amanda bit her lip as she returned to the bed. She wanted to tell Jade she was wrong, but she wondered as she replayed the morning in her mind. Caleb had seemed less engaged and his lack of knowledge about the rapture was interesting. Maybe he had never gone to church, but if that was the case, why would he say that he had?

CHAPTER 8

he fair was already busy when Amanda arrived the next morning. Dozens of colorful booths filled the street, and a crowd of people milled back and forth. Students for Life blazoned boldly in black on a white banner above a small booth. Jared and a group of others stood either in front of or behind the white folding informational table littered with pamphlets.

"Hey, glad you could make it," Sarah said, "have you ever done this before?"

Amanda shook her head, a little in shock at the sheer size of this fair. She had spoken with people when they had come in JD's center, but she had never been on the front lines, reaching out to those who may not want to hear what she had to say.

Sarah's eyes widened and her eyebrow shot up. "Well, I hope you have thick skin. It isn't always pretty."

A feeling of fear mounted in Amanda's stomach, and she swallowed. *Lord, give me the strength and the words.* Sarah handed her a stack of pamphlets with pictures of dismembered babies from abortions. Amanda's stomach flipped and the contents of breakfast threatened to make a second appearance. With great effort, she swallowed the disgust that erupted in her throat.

"Yeah, it hits all of us like that the first few times." Sarah touched her arm and then took up a position to Amanda's left. Jared came out from behind the booth, and after flashing an encouraging smile, he flanked Amanda's right side. As they were both taller than Amanda, a feeling of protection settled on her from their flanking.

"Help support life," Jared said, holding out a pamphlet to a blond girl passing by.

"Get lost."

Jared shook his head and turned to the next passerby. Amanda held out the pamphlet, trying to catch people's attention, but fear had constricted her voice to a whisper.

"What makes you think you have a right to tell me what to do with my body?"

"What you do with your body is your own business," —Jared's serious tone caught Amanda's attention, and she turned to see a blond girl who looked vaguely familiar, although she couldn't place her face, staring off with him— "but an abortion dismembers someone else's body."

"It's not alive," the girl shot back.

A courage descended on Amanda, and she jumped into the conversation. "Actually, he or she is. At just six weeks that baby has a distinguishable heartbeat. He or she has distinct chromosomes and DNA that is only half yours. The other half belong to the father which is why men should have a say too."

"Every child should be a wanted child," the girl replied, venom dripping from her voice.

"Every child is wanted." Amanda returned the girl's even stare, and the boldness cycling through her blood grew. "You may not want the baby at the time, but there are millions of couples waiting to adopt. They want that baby."

Amanda gestured to the surrounding crowd. "Americans will have garage sales to try to make money off unwanted junk, but instead of giving the most precious gift of a baby to a loving couple who desperately wants one, we choose to cut the living baby to pieces and throw it out with the trash."

The girl stared. Her mouth opened, but no sound came out.

Amanda stared back, not knowing exactly what was happening, but feeling power flow through her body. The surrounding noises stopped, and for a moment so did everyone around them. They seemed to fade into a hazy fog until it was just the girl and Amanda.

"Open your eyes and see." The voice that came out of Amanda's mouth didn't even sound like her own. An unseen electric current flickered between their eyes. Slowly, the girl's hand rose in the air and took the pamphlet. At the touch, the noise resumed, and the girl walked away.

With wide eyes, Jared turned to Amanda. "What was that?" he whispered.

"I have no idea." Amanda shook her head, her eyes mirroring the confusion in his. The power, whatever it had been, was gone.

❀

*J*ared watched Amanda closely the rest of the fair. She had seemed so unsure of herself at the beginning, but after her confrontation with the blond, a new boldness shone from her face. He wondered what she had felt in that moment. Though he had heard nothing, the air had appeared to grow cold when the two girls locked eyes, and then slowly the blond had accepted the pamphlet and walked away.

"So, how was it?" Jared asked Amanda as they packed up.

She bit her lip as she thought about her answer. "It was harder than I thought it would be. Some of them are so angry. I feel like I need to add all of them to a weekly prayer list, but I don't even know their names."

Jared nodded. "That part never gets easier, and I know exactly what you mean. Thankfully, God seems to know who we are talking about if we just pray for them in general. We have to remember that his plan is bigger than our plan."

"Thank goodness for that," Amanda said with a smile.

Jared inhaled deeply as he pondered his next words. "Would you uh like to go get coffee with me?"

Indecision flickered in Amanda's green eyes. "Uh, I would like to, but I feel the need to tell you that I'm dating someone or at least I think we're dating. It's pretty new."

Disappointment filled Jared's heart. He should have known she would be dating someone. "Oh, I understand. Well, are you still planning to come to the office on Tuesday to help out?"

"Of course," she said. "I wouldn't miss it."

❀

*A*manda's heart was troubled as she watched Jared's face fall. He had been so nice and he was attractive, so why hadn't she just said yes? The truth was she found Caleb more exciting. Jared was predictable and reliable while Caleb was... well, she wasn't sure what Caleb was yet other than unexpected. She had never thought she would fall for the fraternity type, but the way he looked at her sent her heart pounding in her chest, and she didn't get that feeling from Jared. Still, she didn't like hurting him, and there was some connection she felt with him.

After saying her goodbyes to the rest of the group, Amanda headed back to her dorm and thought back on the experience with the blond. Though the power hadn't returned after the experience with the girl, the feeling had lingered. That had been God speaking, Amanda was sure of it. But why that girl and no one else? Who was she and why had it been so important?

An intense pressure mounted in Amanda's heart, and the need to get on her knees and pray overcame her. She fell to the ground near a large oak tree, and the words tumbled softly out of her mouth. She prayed for Jade and for the unknown girl. She prayed for a revival. She prayed for herself, her family, and for Jared and Caleb. Names and faces jumped into her mind one after the other and Amanda prayed for them all. When she had finished, she was tired, but she managed to make it the rest of the way to her dorm room before exhaustion overtook her completely. Amanda crawled onto the bed and closed her eyes.

CHAPTER 9

*W*hen Tuesday morning arrived, Amanda rose from bed with an extra spring in her step. Today was the day she would be doing her first volunteer shift at Students for Life. Jared had warned her it might be boring, but Amanda was just glad to be getting connected.

She glanced over at Jade who was still sleeping, her dark hair splayed across her pillow case like spilled ink. Though still guarded, Jade had asked her about the Bible yesterday and they'd had a semblance of a conversation until she clammed up again. Amanda knew more questions resided there, but reaching Jade was like chipping away at a brick wall with a toothpick.

Inviting her to church would have been the perfect option back in Mesquite, but Amanda hadn't found a church home in Lubbock yet. She didn't want to take Jade to a place she wasn't comfortable at because for some reason, Amanda had the feeling she might only have one shot with Jade. She mouthed another silent prayer for the sleeping girl before she left for class.

Time seemed to drag as Amanda sat through each class. She continually checked her watch, tapping the face to make sure it was still working. Each class felt like three hours instead of one, and by the time the last class ended, she felt like she had been sitting for twelve hours instead of only four.

As she gathered her books, she stretched her sore back and checked the watch one more time. It was nearly one and she had told Jared she'd be there at one-thirty, so she had just enough time to grab a quick snack on her way.

Amanda stopped to zip up her light jacket as she stepped outside. Though still warm, the wind was fiercer today and carried a slight chill. The red, orange, and yellow leaves flew off the trees and danced in the air before lazily floating down to the ground. Her auburn hair lifted off her neck and followed a similar pattern.

A touch football game caught her eye as she crossed the quad. The guys were covered in dirt, but the sound of their voices belayed their enjoyment. The roar of a lawn mower started nearby, creating a cacophonous noise, and she was glad when Holden Hall loomed before her.

The heavy doors blocked most of the outside noise as they closed behind her, and the air inside the building was still and quiet. Quickening her pace, Amanda hurried to room 145.

Jared looked up as she entered, a welcoming smile on his face. "Hey, good to see you, Amanda."

Relief flooded Amanda that Jared didn't appear uncomfortable around her. She had worried it might be awkward after she turned down his coffee date request, but Jared appeared to have either forgotten it or gotten over it. "Thanks. I'm glad to be here, but I'm a little nervous."

"Don't be," he said. "First of all, I'll stay with you today, but you seem a natural. Also, we don't get a lot of calls, so it might be really boring."

"Doing God's work is never boring," she said with a smile. Amanda glanced around the small room, wondering where she should place her things. A small well-worn tan couch and coffee table sat against the back wall. A battered shelf filled with pamphlets butted against one wall and a few folding chairs leaned against the opposite one.

"Just drop your bag back there and pull up a chair," Jared said, seeming to read her mind. She followed his finger to the back of the small room and set her bag on the squat brown coffee table before grabbing a chair and returning to join him at the front desk.

"So, when a call comes in," he explained, "first we assess where they are. If they are agitated or seem adamant about an abortion, we take their number and transfer them to the crisis center. We take their number in case they hang up before the transfer goes through. In that case, we call the crisis center and have them call the girls. If they are simply looking at their options, as most are, then we discuss the available alternatives and get them set up with one. We can't actually counsel them, but we have numbers we can transfer them to. Do you have any questions?" he asked.

"Not about that," Amanda said, "It seems straight forward, but do you know a good church around here? Caleb suggested this place called Experience Life, but it was a little big for me."

Jared stiffened slightly and cocked his head. "Who's Caleb?"

A blush spread across Amanda's face, and her eyes dropped to study her hands. "Um, he's the guy I just started seeing, the one I told you about. I guess we're kind of dating. We haven't really labeled it, I mean." As the words tumbled out of her mouth, she realized she had no idea what Caleb and she were. Was he her boyfriend? Were they just dating? She would have to get some clarity on that subject.

"Oh, right" Jared said slowly. He leaned back in his chair and looked at his lap for a minute before raising his eyes again. "Well, I go to Indiana Avenue Baptist. It's big, but not too big. I haven't been to Experience Life, but I've heard you sometimes get lost in the shuffle."

"That's exactly what happened," Amanda said tentatively. Why was talking about Caleb in front of Jared so uncomfortable? And was it just her or was he feeling it too? "I'll check out yours then if that's okay. My church back in Mesquite was probably about one hundred each service. I don't want much bigger than that."

He smiled. "I can understand that."

For a minute, they sat in companionable silence then an uncomfortable silence. The phone stayed silent, the office empty, and Amanda hated that the talk of Caleb had stalled their normally friendly banter. She pursed her lips and tapped the desk lightly with her index finger, trying to think of something else to say.

"I'm glad you joined us," he began before being interrupted by the musical announcement of a text message on Amanda's phone. Blushing, she hit the silent button and looked up for him to continue. Just as he opened his mouth, the phone vibrated. "You better see what that is. Someone is persistent," he sighed.

"Sorry," she said, swiping the screen to see two texts from Caleb.

Where are you?

Want to meet up?

Amanda stared at the phone, at a loss for a minute. Though she did want to meet up with Caleb, she was also enjoying chatting with Jared.

"Is that him?"

"Huh?" Her eyes popped up, and a feeling of guilt coated her.

"On the phone, is that the guy?" He nodded his head, using his raised eyebrow as an indicator.

Heat flared across her face, and she knew it must now be the color of her hair. She nodded.

"Well, tell him to come by. I'd love to meet him."

"Really?" Her voice squeaked as it escaped her lips.

"Sure. We'll be spending a lot of time together. He ought to get to know me and the others when they're here," he hastily added. "Maybe he'll even want to join us." Though Jared's face held a smile, it didn't quite reach his eyes, but Amanda took him at his word and texted Caleb back.

Jared resumed his conversation and told Amanda about his life in California growing up. "I just wish–Jared visibly stiffened and Amanda turned to see what had caused the change. Caleb stood in the doorway, also stiff and cold.

"Jared." Caleb's voice was hard and flat.

"Caleb," Jared said, standing, "It's been a while."

Amanda glanced from one man to the next. "You two know each other?"

"You could say that," Jared said. Something in his voice was off. His friendly eyes had lost their sparkle, and they now appeared

WHEN HEARTS COLLIDE | 441

hardened. She shivered at the sudden change in his demeanor. They obviously didn't like each other though she had no idea why.

"Amanda, are you ready?" Caleb addressed Amanda, but his eyes remained focused on Jared. "I'm hungry, and I'd like to get something to eat before the snack bar closes."

Neither man had moved; it was like watching a standoff. A really strange, uncomfortable standoff. Amanda looked to Jared, unsure of what to say to diffuse the situation. "Um, okay. Jared, I'll see you Thursday, alright?"

She darted to the back table to grab her bag, hoping they hadn't started throwing punches while her back was turned. They remained in the same position, statues starting each other down. Amanda touched Caleb's arm, breaking the stare and followed him out of the room.

"What was that about?" she asked as soon as they were out of earshot of the room.

Caleb waved a hand. "Ah, nothing. We liked the same girl last year, but she chose me, and I don't think Jared ever forgave me."

Amanda's instincts told her there was more to the story, but she decided not to press the issue. "What happened to the girl?" Pictures of some beautiful blond swooping in and stealing Caleb back paraded through her mind.

He shrugged. "She moved. Back home, I guess. I'm not sure. We just... drifted apart."

The blond vanished in a cloud of smoke, and Amanda smiled. "Okay, as long as she won't be coming back to steal you away."

Caleb's blue eyes flashed, "Not much chance of that."

⊛

*A*s soon as Caleb and Amanda left, Jared's body began to shake. He sank into the chair and dropped his head into his hands. "Not again, Lord please don't let this be happening again." A seed of fury sprouted deep inside his chest and slowly clawed up his chest. He had to talk to Sarah; she'd know what to do. He texted her as he locked up the room and headed to her dorm.

The warm air did nothing to dispel his anger, and he was sweating when he finally reached her door.

"What's going on?" Concern colored Sarah's voice and face as she opened the door. He and Sarah had dated for a brief time before Jared met Nikki, but had quickly learned they were better friends. Still, Sarah had been his closest confidante when Nikki left.

Jared stepped in and sat down at the edge of her blue bedspread. He rocked back and forth, rubbing his palms down his pants. "It's him."

"Who's him? I'm afraid you're going to have to give me more to go on here."

"Caleb West, that's who."

Sarah nodded, "Okay, so you ran into Caleb. I still fail to see the connection."

"Amanda. The guy she's dating... it's Caleb. Maybe I should tell her what happened. Maybe I should fight for her."

"Whoa, whoa, easy fella,"—she laid a hand on his arm as she sat next to him— "Have you even told Amanda you like her?"

Jared ran his hand through his sandy brown hair. "No, I asked her out for coffee after the fair, but she told me she was seeing someone. I was disappointed, but kind of expected it. She's beautiful, you know? But then the "guy" texted her today and I told her to have come over, and Caleb walked in. It was all I could do to keep from punching him. What can she possibly see in him?"

"I don't know," Sarah said, "but that's not the point now. Nikki made her own choice,"—she held up her hand as Jared opened his mouth to jump in— "and we don't know what happened afterwards. Right now, it's important to keep a cool head. Since we don't know if the rumors are true, you want to be sure and stay friends with her in case things go awry. Getting all riled up will make that impossible, at least until you have proof."

Jared sighed, "You're right, but I don't want Amanda to get hurt. Is there any way to warn her without coming across, I don't know... pushy?"

Sarah shook her head. "Not really, but here's what you can do. First, and most importantly, you can pray. Second, you become a listening ear. Maybe then she will open up to you. She had to sense the tension between you two and will probably want your side of the story. If she asks, then you tell her what happened with Nikki, but stick to the facts, Jared."

Though he nodded, Jared was still unsure. He didn't know Amanda well, but there was something about her, and he didn't want a repeat of Nikki. "I guess you're right. Do me a favor though. Reach out to her too. I get the feeling she could use some good girl friends too."

"You got it, and I'll be praying too."

Jared knew she was right, but he couldn't shake the feeling of dread that encompassed him. Though no one really knew exactly what had happened to Nikki as she hadn't stayed on campus after the incident, the rumors had flown from person to person. If Caleb wasn't involved, his fraternity certainly had been. Jared knew Caleb well enough to know that he would get Amanda at that fraternity house one way or another, and he could only hope and pray that history would not repeat itself.

CHAPTER 10

$\mathcal{A}$s Amanda entered the Students for Life office on Thursday, she was surprised to see Emily sitting next to Jared on the couch. They were deep in conversation, not having noticed her yet.

"Hi, Did I get the date wrong?" she asked as she knocked on the doorjamb.

They both jumped and turned guilty faces her direction. *What had they been talking about? Had it been about me?*

Jared smiled, rising from the couch. "No, I just thought since we had been so slow on Tuesday that we could brainstorm ways to keep the group going and growing. I hope that's okay."

"It's more than okay, but how come I get the special planning meeting? I'm brand new." Amanda's gaze wandered from Jared to Emily and back. She appeared calm, but he kept balling and un-balling his fists, as if he were nervous about something.

"I uh thought that you might have ideas from your clinic time in Mesquite. Plus, you're new, so maybe you have ideas of how to reach new people that we've forgotten about."

Amanda narrowed her eyes. Emily was only a Sophomore and Jared a Junior. It wasn't like either of them were exactly "out of touch." Amanda didn't know what they were hiding, but she had been thinking the last few days about ways to help, and she was happy to share them. "Actually, I do have some ideas." She grabbed a folding chair and joined them at the back of the room.

As Amanda shared her ideas, Jared's and Emily's faces lit up. Wheels were turning in their heads as well, and the three hammered out some concrete ideas to present to Tracy. When the discussion began to simmer, Amanda chanced a glance at her watch and was surprised to see her shift time was almost over. She had hoped to get Jared alone for a minute to ask for his version of the rift between him and Caleb, but that didn't appear to be an option today. She would just have to try to get him alone another time.

Surely, it was nothing important. Men fought over women all the time. Amanda could remember fights breaking out in the High School cafeteria at least once a month and usually over a girl.

As she gathered her bag and waved goodbye, her phone rang. "I'll see you guys later," she said, hitting the call button as she exited the room. "Hi Caleb. Yeah, I'm on my way." All thoughts of talking to Jared exited her mind as visions of Caleb filled it.

The leaves crunched under her feet as she crossed the campus, and she breathed in the fresh air. Fall was her favorite time of the year with the bright orange and yellow colors of the leaves and the crisp chill that whispered in the air. Today was especially quiet outside, allowing her thoughts to roam as she crossed the campus. Everyone must still be in class or partaking of some other indoor activity.

Caleb was waiting when she arrived at his dorm, and after a kiss hello that set her entire body aflame, they walked together to his car.

Amanda turned to him as he pulled out of the parking lot, "Hey one of the people I met at Students for Life attends this church on Indiana Ave. Do you want to try it with me on Sunday?" While it wasn't a total lie, she felt just a tiny bit guilty not telling him the person was Jared, but she didn't want Caleb to say no just because of their history.

Caleb's eyes fell to the floor. "Oh, I would, but I promised my friend I'd help him move into an apartment on Sunday. I forgot we were planning to find a church."

Disappointment surged through Amanda, and she frowned. How did one forget about finding a church? "Oh, okay."

"Listen, why don't you check it out this week and next week I promise I'll go with you." He patted her thigh with his right hand before returning it to the steering wheel.

Amanda nodded, but her previous elation faltered a little. Tiny nuggets of doubt crawled into her head again. What if Caleb wasn't who she was supposed to be with? Shouldn't he want to be at church as much as she did?

Caleb must have sensed the change in Amanda's mood because he turned the car off, but made no move to unlock the doors when they arrived at the movie theater. Instead he turned to her and pushed a lock of hair behind her ear. His feather touch sent her nerves tingling and ground the nuggets of doubt to dust. He tilted her face up so Amanda's eyes were locked on his.

"I'm sorry I forgot about our plans, but I promise I'll make it up to you."

His voice flowed like silk over her bruised emotions and her doubt. She nodded, trancelike, as the familiar tingling sensation took over at Caleb's touch. Her lips parted and he leaned down to kiss her. Caleb's hands pushed at the back of her neck, urging her to respond in kind. As the tingling sensation pulsed and her breath grew labored, she pushed back on Caleb's chest, breaking the connection that was threatening her self-control.

"We'll miss the movie." She smiled up at him, hoping he would understand.

A fire of desire flared in his eyes, and for a second he looked like he wasn't going to stop, but then he took a deep breath, nodded, and unlocked the doors. Amanda's breath gushed out in relief as she climbed out of the truck.

After buying the tickets, they entered the brightly lit foyer of the theater. The hum of conversation filled the air along with the salty, buttery smell of fresh popcorn. As they surged forward into a line, a man yelled out and waved to Caleb.

"Oh hey, come meet my good friend, Trevor." Lacing his fingers through hers, Caleb pulled Amanda over to the dark-haired man standing in the next line over. He had chiseled features though his nose was a little too big for his face. A blonde with long legs and short shorts stood next to him, running a hand idly through her hair and twirling the ends, while her pouty pink lips smacked some gum. "Trevor, I want you to meet Amanda. Amanda, Trevor."

Amanda smiled and put forth her hand, but before he took it, Trevor's eyes roamed up her body. His eyebrows raised slightly, and a smile spread across his face. When he touched her hand, a feeling of nausea bubbled in Amanda's stomach, and she quickly retracted her hand and excused herself, citing a need to use the bathroom.

As she entered the black and white bathroom, she rushed to a sink. Turning on the water, Amanda splashed some on her face and then scrubbed her hands. Trevor's gaze and touch had left a dirty film, and she couldn't seem to get it off even with all the scrubbing. How could he be friends with Caleb? Was there a side to Caleb she didn't know?

Jared's reaction to Caleb returned to her mind. Caleb had said it was over a girl, but what if there was more to it? The questions that had plagued her earlier returned with force, pounding like a raucous parade in her mind.

A stinging sensation in her hands shifted her attention, and Amanda realized they were red and smarting from the scrubbing. She turned off the water, and after drying them gingerly with the paper towel, she headed back to Caleb, hoping he was no longer talking to Trevor.

He was, in fact, waiting right outside in the hallway. "Everything okay?" he asked, handing her a drink.

"Yeah, I guess so." Amanda bit her lip as they sauntered down the carpeted hallway to the theater, trying to find the words to ask what was weighing on her mind. "How good of a friend is Trevor?"

He turned to her, his eyebrows cocked. "Why do you ask?"

Amanda shrugged and ran her free hand over her opposite arm, which had broken out in goosebumps. "Just the way he looked at me; it kind of bothered me."

Caleb smiled. "Oh, he's harmless. He just knows a pretty girl when he sees one. In fact, he'll probably tell me later how jealous he is that he didn't meet you first."

"I guess." The explanation didn't soothe Amanda's nerves; instead it opened even more questions about Caleb in her mind.

CHAPTER 11

"Hey, how's your friend Sandra?" Jade asked from the other side of the room. Though still not close friends, Jade had begun talking more to Amanda the last few weeks. She had even asked a few questions about the Bible and Amanda's faith.

"Huh?" Amanda finished composing the text to Caleb and glanced up at Jade.

"Sandra, I haven't heard you call her lately. Are you no longer doing the prayer list thing?"

Her voice held just the hint of a challenge, and Amanda was about to retort back when she realized she hadn't called Sandra lately or Kate or Callie. Snatching the prayer journal off the nightstand, she flipped to the last page. Her eyes widened at the date. Was that right? It had been nearly three weeks?

Amanda glanced up at Jade who had an eyebrow raised awaiting a response, and her face flamed. "No, I still am. I guess I've just been a little busy with class." *Or Caleb.* "I'll call her tomorrow, I promise," she said, defending herself against Jade's knowing look.

"Why not now?" Jade challenged.

"I promised Caleb I'd help him study for a big test." The vibration of Amanda's phone punctuated her sentence. "There he is now."

"Uh huh," Jade said with a shrug. "Well, have fun."

A tiny kernel of guilt erupted inside Amanda as she exited the room. Amanda shouldn't have to justify her actions to the girl, but something in Jade's face sent her subconscious spinning. Was she spending too much time with Caleb?

Caleb was her first boyfriend; it was only natural that she'd want to spend a lot of time with him, right? Jade was probably just jealous because she had stopped seeing her "friend," or at least Amanda assumed she had as the man hadn't appeared in the room again and Jade hadn't mentioned him recently.

Caleb was waiting for her at the bottom of the stairs, and at the sight of him, the guilt flew from her mind. He pulled Amanda into his arms and touched his lips gently to hers. Warmth radiated through her body, and her head grew light.

"Jade is in our room," Amanda said. "We'll have to find another place to study."

"Let's go back to my dorm," Caleb suggested.

Somewhere at the back of her mind, alarm bells sounded, but they were distant and timid. Ignoring them, Amanda agreed and took his hand.

When they reached his room, Amanda made sure he left the door cracked. Though she was nearly certain she was falling in love with Caleb, there was no reason to open the opportunity to play with fire.

He took the desk chair, leaving her to sit on the bed. After rummaging in his bag, he pulled out a large textbook and passed it to Amanda. Flipping to the marked page, she drilled him on business terms and procedures.

An hour later, she closed the book, feeling as mentally worn out as he looked. He took the book from her hands and then joined her on the bed. As he brushed a hair behind Amanda's ears, a tingle traveled down her spine.

"My fraternity is having a party to celebrate Halloween. Will you come with me?"

His blue eyes bore into hers, scattering her thoughts. Amanda tried to focus; she did want to go, but she'd heard stories about frat parties.

"I don't know," she said in a hesitant voice. "Don't people just get drunk and... you know." Amanda's face flushed and she looked down at her hands at the innuendo she was alluding to.

"Some do, but ours aren't like that. Please." He placed a finger under her chin and tilted her face upward, turning his puppy dog eyes on Amanda. It was like he knew she was a sucker for those eyes.

"Okay," she whispered.

His eyes danced, and he dropped his head, placing his lips on hers. Nerves in Amanda's body ignited, and she leaned into him. Her hands slid up the hard muscles of his chest and around his neck. His hands dropped to her low back, pulling her closer.

As the kiss deepened, Caleb leaned Amanda back. When her head touched his pillow and she felt his hands breach the safety of her shirt, the alarm bells finally blared loud enough to grab Amanda's attention. She pushed against his chest until the kiss broke. He stared down at her with wild and hungry eyes.

"Stop. We need to take a breath," she said, panting.

Ice flickered in Caleb's eyes. Amanda flinched at the hardness that radiated from them. Had she gotten him all wrong? Another moment passed, and then his eyes softened, and he sighed.

"You're right. I just can't help it when I'm with you." He leaned down to kiss her again, but Amanda pushed harder.

"I'm serious."

"Fine," Caleb dropped his hands and rolled off her.

"I should go," Amanda said, sitting up and smoothing her shirt. Her emotions were running wild, and she needed time to think.

"No, don't." He reached out to her but made no move to get off the bed.

Amanda shook her head. Neither of them would get any more studying done tonight, and the promises she had made to herself earlier flared in her mind. "No, I promised Jade I'd do something with her tonight anyway. I'll see you tomorrow."

Without giving him time to respond, Amanda grabbed her bag and left the room. As the door closed behind her, she sighed. Dating was much harder than Amanda had expected. Her mother's admonishment to wait suddenly made sense.

Her mind knew saying no had been the right thing, but her body sure didn't understand, and it was becoming increasingly harder to say no. Should she break things off with Caleb? Though he had always stopped when she asked him, he never seemed pleased at the prospect. What if one day he didn't stop? Would she be okay with that? The thoughts circled in her head as she returned to the dorm. Surely, she could resist. She'd done it for years, and she did care about Caleb.

Jade looked up as Amanda entered the room. "You make that phone call yet?"

Annoyance flickered in Amanda briefly at Jade's persistence and insinuation, but she pushed it away. Jade's advice was needed. "No, I just left Caleb's. It got a little heated, and I'm having a hard time staying strong when I'm with him. I'm wondering if I should break it off."

Jade smiled, "Men are physical creatures. Once you let them down a path, it's hard to get them to stop."

"No kidding," Amanda returned. "All we've done is kiss, but I can tell he wants more."

"What would you say to a girl in your position?" Jade asked.

"What do you mean?" Amanda sat on her bed, curling her legs beneath her.

"I mean, what if Sandra asked you for advice?"

Amanda couldn't stop the laugh that escaped her lips. "Sandra is a sixty something year old widow; I doubt seriously she would be asking me for dating advice."

Jade rolled her eyes. "Fine, think of someone younger. Who's someone younger you might talk to?"

Well, there was Kate, but Kate was her best friend. They shared so much, it was hard to think about her representing someone she didn't know as well. Then Callie's face popped into Amanda's head. Callie had spoken at their high school last year. "There is this woman named Callie," Amanda began slowly.

"Okay Callie. What would she have told you?"

As the image of Callie solidified in her mind, Amanda could almost hear Callie's voice in her head. Amanda sighed. "She would say that if Caleb were pushing me to have sex, then he wasn't a good influence, and that as a Christian he should want me not to sin."

A stray thread in her comforter caught her attention as the guilt set in once again. It wasn't that she didn't believe Callie; it just was so much harder when it was happening.

Jade shrugged. "I'm no expert in Christian matters as you know, but that seems pretty reasonable.

Confusion tumbled around in Amanda's head. Somewhere deep inside, she knew Caleb was giving off signs that he wasn't good for her, but he was so handsome and he liked her. Nobody had liked Amanda in that way in a long time, maybe ever, and she didn't want to lose the feeling. And he had always stopped when she said no, so maybe he was just fighting his desire like she was.

"What's wrong?" Jade asked.

The thread garnered Amanda's attention again as she avoided Jade's eyes. "Um, he invited me to a frat party on Halloween, but I'm not sure I should go."

Jade cocked her head, and her right eyebrow shot up. "A frat party? I don't think that's a good idea. You do know what usually goes on at frat parties right?"

Amanda pulled harder at the thread, determined not to look up. "Yes, but I already said I'd go." Amanda glanced up from lowered lids. There was a little part of Amanda that was curious as to what actually went on in a frat party.

"I think you're playing with fire," Jade shook her head, "but it's up to you."

As Amanda turned out the light that night before bed, she realized she still hadn't called Sandra, and she hadn't read her devotional for the day. *I'll do it tomorrow*, she thought before falling asleep.

❧

"*D*o you know anyone in Beta Zeta Psi?" Jared asked Emily at their weekly Bible study. They were generally the first to arrive and Jared decided to use the time tonight to pick Emily's brain. He had heard some troubling information today.

"I don't know," she said with a shake of her head. Her forehead furrowed in confusion. "Why do you ask?"

Jared sighed. "I heard through the grapevine that they have a Halloween party planned. If I can't keep Amanda from Caleb, I want to at least be there to keep an eye on her. I know we don't know exactly what happened to Nikki, but we do know she left right after one of these parties."

"Amanda never asked for your side of the story?" Emily asked. Jared had filled her in on the encounter after his conversation with Sarah.

"No, and I really thought she would, but it's like he puts them under some kind of spell," Jared said. "I just need a way in, and then I can at least watch out for her."

"Okay, I'll ask my other guy friends," Emily said with a nod. "One of them must know someone, and I agree that Amanda shouldn't go in there alone. I only saw Caleb that once, but something about him just rubbed me the wrong way."

"Thank you," Jared said, as the rest of the group filed in.

CHAPTER 12

"*I*'m going on the record that I still think this is a bad idea." Jade said, flashing Amanda a reproachful look.

"Duly noted," Amanda said, checking her reflection in the mirror again. The last few days had been a litany of Jade telling her horror stories about fraternity parties. Then Kate had joined in when Amanda had finally remembered to call her and fill her in, but neither Kate nor Jade had spent time with Caleb. Once they did, Amanda was sure their concerns would fade away just as she was sure that nothing would happen tonight.

Caleb was waiting in the dorm lobby when Amanda arrived there. He stood and smiled at her. "You look great. Are you ready?"

"Absolutely," Amanda said with a smile and took his hand. Her smile faltered when they stepped outside the warm, lighted building though. An uncharacteristic fog had settled on the grounds and combined with the dusk and full moon, it created an eerie setting.

Caleb led the way off campus, stating the meeting house was just across University. As they walked the few short blocks to the house, Amanda found herself jumping at shadows and battling a foreboding feeling. What if Jade had been right? What if someone spiked her drink? That happened occasionally, right?

She wished she had thought to bring her own water bottle. No, that was silly. Why would anyone want to spike her drink? She was just being paranoid. A tiny voice insisted it wasn't too late to turn back, but Amanda tightened her grip on Caleb's hand and ignored it.

The meeting house was a single-story brick house with the Beta Zeta Psi banner across the front. Other than the banner and the music pouring out of it, it didn't look much different from the surrounding houses. As the door opened though, Amanda was surprised by how much room there was.

"We had it remodeled, so we'd have a bigger dance floor," Caleb said, answering her unasked question. "So now there's just a small kitchen and the open space here, and then the bedrooms and the bathroom are back that way."

The room already pulsed with people and the music was even louder inside. Flinching, Amanda resisted the urge to cover her ears. The electronic beat seemed to reverberate down her spine, causing her teeth to throb in their sockets.

Caleb pulled Amanda to the middle of the floor, and they joined in the dancing or tried to anyway. There were so many bodies that they were basically just jostled from one squished position to another on the laminate wood floor. Sweat poured down Amanda's neck and spine, and she glanced around for a way to cool off as she wiped a bead cascading down her forehead.

The front door seemed an ocean away, and they weren't near any windows, but the refreshment table stood out like an oasis just a few feet away. Surely a drink could wet her parched throat and then maybe she could convince Caleb to leave. While it had been fun seeing what a frat party was like, Amanda wasn't enjoying herself nearly as much as she had thought she would.

Amanda tugged on Caleb's arm and pointed at the table, motioning that she'd like a drink. Smiling, he pulled her close and pushed through the crowd.

"Sorry we don't have water, but would you like some punch?" he asked when they reached the table. Amanda nodded, assuming beer - which she wasn't drinking - was the only other choice. As Caleb picked up a paper cup and filled it with red liquid from the smaller keg, Amanda turned to scan the crowd. She blinked as she caught sight of a familiar face or at least she thought it was a familiar face. What would Jared be doing here? She was about to move that direction when Caleb tapped her arm and handed over the cup.

Amanda took the cup before turning her attention back to the crowd, but the familiar face was gone. With a sigh, she returned her attention to Caleb who held a bottle of beer in his hand.

"Aren't you going to have the punch?" Amanda asked.

He shook his head, "No, the sugar always gets me. Don't worry, I'll just have one." Caleb knew Amanda was not a fan of drinking.

Nodding, she took a large sip of the red liquid and nearly coughed it back up. There was indeed a lot of sugar in the punch. "Wow, you weren't kidding." Caleb smiled and nodded. Another small sip made the drink bearable, and she finished most of it that way.

"Let's go back there where we can talk a little easier," Caleb shouted, pointing toward the back. The foreboding feeling triggered again in her mind, but Amanda rationalized it away once more. Surely, they could go talk for a minute and be fine. There were too many people for him to try anything here. Nodding, she followed Caleb toward the back. Away from the music, it did get a little quieter. The pounding in her ears lessened to a dull ache.

"Whew, is the music always so loud?" she asked. As the words left her mouth, the room began tilting and going fuzzy around the edges. Swaying, she reached for the wall to steady her feet.

"Are you okay?" Caleb asked, holding out a hand.

"I don't know. I feel kind of weird." The room lurched again, and she fell forward into Caleb.

"Here, let's find a room and we'll lay you down for a bit." Caleb pulled her close to his chest. Alarm bells clanged like a five-alarm fire in Amanda's head and she tried to protest, but her mouth felt dry and heavy. She could only weakly shake her head back and forth. He wrapped an arm around her and began walking toward one of the rooms.

Amanda's feet refused to move, feeling like they were encased in cement. What was wrong with her? Her arms too hung limply at her side. Hoisting her a little higher on his hip, Caleb drug her the rest of the way to a room. He opened the door, pulled her inside, and closed the door. Amanda's mind tried to grapple with what was happening. The lock of the door clicked, and fear flashed through her.

Picking her up, Caleb carried Amanda to the king bed covered in a blue bedspread and hoisted her on it. He adjusted the pillow beneath her head and then sprawled beside her.

"There, that's better, right?" he said and caressed her hair, but his voice was off. It was cold, soulless. Amanda's eyes—the only body part still working—flicked to his. Nothing else was responding to her commands, though her brain seemed to be working perfectly, and she could feel the touch of his hand and the cotton beneath her. She should have listened to Jade. She should have listened to her gut. Fear crawled in as the realization sank in that she couldn't escape.

Caleb's hand trailed down the side of Amanda's face and he leaned in. His blue eyes were ice, chilling her to the core. His mouth touched her ear and his words stopped her heart. "Don't worry, you won't remember this tomorrow, and what you do remember, you'll think was a hallucination. You know you want this; I just gave you a little something to help you relax."

His lips then moved from her ear to her mouth as if this were a normal make out session. The urge to bite his lip and knee him in the groin flared inside Amanda, but no matter how hard she tried, nothing moved.

She flicked her eyes back and forth, trying to convey that this was not okay; this was not what she wanted, but his lips just curled in a sinister smile. Lowering his face again, his lips meandered down her neck. The word no flashed in her head, but it didn't escape her lips. Her finger twitched as she tried to push him away, but a twitch was all Amanda could manage.

"Let's see what you've been keeping from me, shall we?" He took one side of her shirt in his mouth and deftly flicked the button open with his tongue. "Nope, I need a little more." Another button opened and a chill hit Amanda's chest. "That's more like it," he said tracing the white lace of her bra. He finished separating the buttons and flung her shirt open. A solitary tear escaped her eyes. His hands roamed her chest, followed quickly by his mouth first on one side and then the other. Then his tongue traced a pattern down the middle of her stomach. "Now, isn't this more fun?"

He looked up at Amanda with those ice blue eyes and smiled before undoing the button on her jeans. Smiled! As if this was a game to him that she had agreed to play. He pulled the zipper down and she squeezed her eyes shut against the attack that was about to happen. Then the glorious pounding started.

"Amanda? Are you in there?" Jared's voice ignited a small kernel of hope inside Amanda, and her eyes popped open.

Caleb glanced at the door and cursed, but continued his crusade. Perhaps he believed the door would hold even against Jared's pounding. A large boom shook the door, but it held firm. Then another smaller series of poundings. The noise hit a nerve in Caleb. "I knew I should have had your friend taken care of."

Cursing again, he pushed off Amanda and began tearing around the room. Was he looking for something? The door rattled again. He ran his hands through his blond hair, uttered a final string of curse words, and opened the window. A glorious thud let her know he had landed on the ground.

Fear and joy intermingled in her brain, and another tear worked its way down her cheek. The door splintered open and Jared rushed in. Emily was close behind him. What were they doing here? Emily covered Amanda with the comforter, and gratitude flowed through her body. Then Jared picked her up, and Amanda let the encroaching darkness take over.

❁

*A*manda opened her eyes and looked around the hospital room. For just a second, she didn't remember why she was there, and then the memories came flooding back. Her fingers gripped the white sheet as the images overwhelmed her, pressing down like a ten-pound brick. The unusual taste of the drink and the dizziness that had come soon after. Leaning on Caleb for support as he took her into a room. The door opening and the large bed filling her vision.

Amanda shut her eyes against the invading memory, willing it to disappear, but it did no good. The image lit up, a movie screen in her mind. Caleb laying her down on the bed. His lips on her chest, where no man's lips had been before, the feelings of fear and despair as she realized what he was doing.

A sob escaped Amanda's lips and she curled into a ball. How could she have been so dumb? How had she let her guard down so much? She felt dirty and violated, and she wondered if she'd ever be okay again.

CHAPTER 13

Dr. Patrick entered the waiting area and Jared shot out of his seat like a rocket to accost him. "Is she okay? Tell me she's going to be okay."

The doctor held up his hands. "Physically, she's okay. She had some Ketamine in her blood, but it's working its way out. Thankfully, it looks like her dose was low, as she seems to remember the incident. We think you got there in time to save her from any intimate attack, but emotionally and mentally she is scarred. She can speak now, but she may not want to. You're going to have to give her time."

Jared's jaw tensed and his hands balled into fists. "Can we see her?" he asked.

The doctor nodded, and Jared and Emily followed the man down the hall to Amanda's room. She looked so fragile and pale in the white bed.

"How are you?" Jared asked as he reached the side of her bed. Amanda was listless and there was a distance in her eyes

"I'm okay, I guess, thanks to you guys." Though a half smile played on her lips, it did not reach her eyes, and the sparkle was gone.

"The police are going to be looking for Caleb," Jared said, "but they're probably going to want a statement from you."

She nodded. "Yeah, I figured."

Jared's heart went out to her. He wanted to tell her that everything was going to be okay, but he knew it wasn't. He had spoken with enough victims to know she had a long path to recovery in front of her.

"Okay, Amanda needs her rest," a short, stocky nurse said as she entered the room. "You can come back again tomorrow."

Jared nodded, though he did not want to leave.

"I wish I knew what else to do for her," he sighed as he sank into a chair in the waiting room.

"You be her friend, and you pray for her." Emily sat beside him and placed a hand on his arm.

"I know; it's just that it doesn't feel like enough, you know? I know God is so much bigger than you or I, but..." his voice trailed off.

"Sometimes, it's not about being perfect and having the right words," Emily said softly. "It's about being human and having empathy."

"Yeah, I just feel helpless. I feel like I should have done more to dissuade her from dating Caleb."

"You really care for her, don't you?" Emily asked.

Jared's lip curled in a half smile. "I have since the moment I met her. Is that terrible?"

"No, I think it's sweet, and I think you'd make a great couple, but I'm afraid it may be a while before she dates again."

"Excuse me, sir." Two cops stood before them. "Are you Jared Masterson?" Jared nodded. "We have a few questions for you if you don't mind."

Jared stood, following the officers to a small office. The room was barely more than a closet, and while he had nothing to hide and wasn't generally claustrophobic, the tight space sped up Jared's heart rate.

"I'm Detective Scott and this is Detective Delaney," the taller man said. "Can you tell us how you know the victim?"

Jared nodded and swallowed to ease the dryness in his throat. "I met Amanda this year, and we worked together at Students for Life."

"What is that?" Detective Scott asked, scribbling on a notepad.

"It's a pro-life college organization. We work together to inform women of options other than abortion."

"And how about Caleb West?"

Jared's muscles tensed as he clenched his fists tighter. "Caleb I met last year when the girl I was dating chose him instead."

Detective Scott stopped scribbling and looked up at Jared with a raised eyebrow. "So, would you say you held a grudge?"

Jared bristled at the implication in the detective's words. "I wasn't upset when Nikki began dating Caleb. I was, however, concerned when she disappeared without a word to anyone after a similar frat party she attended with Caleb. That is why I went to the party. I wanted to make sure nothing happened to Amanda." He stared pointedly at the officers. "I guess it's a good thing I did or she might be in worse shape than she is."

The two officers shared a look before Detective Scott asked, "Is there anything else you haven't told us? Anything at all?"

Jared shook his head. "I've told you everything I know."

***

*A*manda was released early the next morning. An orderly brought her out in a wheelchair and Jared cringed at the drastic change that had happened in just twenty-four hours. Amanda's eyes were sunken and surrounded by dark circles, and her ivory skin was paler than normal. Emily, who had come with him to pick Amanda up, gasped and placed her hand on Jared's arm. He nodded his agreement.

"Are you ready to go back home?" Emily asked, her bright and chipper voice sounding forced.

Amanda shrugged and looked down at her hands. Jared and Emily exchanged another glance as they walked out to his car.

The ride back to the dorms was quiet and uncomfortable.

"Is there anything I can do for you?" Jared asked as he opened the door for Amanda and helped her out.

"No, thank you. I think I just need some time." She walked into the dorm, leaving the two friends staring at each other.

"I'm worried about her," Jared said.

Emily nodded as she stated, "I am too. I'll try to talk to her roommate tomorrow and see if she knows of anyone we could contact for Amanda. Family or friends or someone."

"That's a great idea," Jared said. "Let me know what you find out and how I can help."

CHAPTER 14

$\mathcal{A}$manda walked into the dorm feeling much older than she had when she had left the previous night. She hoped Jade would be gone, so she could simply curl up in her bed and avoid questions. Amanda knew she would want to know what happened and why Amanda had been out all night.

Her hand trembled as she reached for the door handle. If she couldn't bear to face her roommate, how was she going to face the rest of the students in her classes? For that matter, how was she going to face Jared and Emily again who knew everything? With a heavy sigh, Amanda pushed the door open and entered the room, her head down.

The room was blissfully dark and empty. Without even removing her clothes, Amanda climbed into the bed, faced the wall, and pulled the blanket up by her ear. Though all she wanted to do was disappear, she couldn't get the image of Caleb's malicious grin out of her mind.

Except to use the bathroom, Amanda didn't get out of bed the rest of the day or for her class the next morning. At some point, she heard Jade enter, but the girl was eerily quiet. She didn't ask Amanda how she was feeling which led Amanda to believe Jared or Emily had spoken with her.

Whenever Amanda would get up to shuffle down the hallway to

the bathroom, she would see food sitting on top of her study desk, but she had no appetite.

※

*a*fter Jade left for the day, Amanda pushed back the covers. She had no plans to attend class, but the ripe smell coming off her body was starting to affect her, and she decided she could at least shower before returning to bed. Gathering her bath items, she walked, head down, to the bathrooms a few doors down.

Though the hot water didn't erase the violated feeling, it did soothe her raw nerves minutely. After drying off and dressing, albeit in baggy sweats and an oversized shirt, she headed back to the dorm room, ready to crawl back under the covers. Her sheets would need a wash soon too, but that was a problem for another day.

Amanda stopped in the hallway at the sight of the blond girl standing outside her room. The girl faced the closed door, clenching and releasing her fists, as if unsure whether to knock or not. Something about her seemed familiar, but Amanda's mind was unable to place from where.

"Can I help you?"

The girl's wide eyes met Amanda's. "Um, I was hoping maybe we could talk." The words were so quiet that Amanda wasn't even sure she'd heard her right. "You may not remember me, but I'm Jordan. We met at the fair. I felt... I don't know, some connection when we talked."

The memory surged through Amanda's mind again. Of course, the feeling of that other voice. "I remember," she said slowly, still not sure why Jordan was here. Why had she sought Amanda out? She waited for Jordan to explain, but when the girl stayed silent, Amanda figured whatever she had to say was important and not something she wanted to share in the hallway. "Come on inside," Amanda finally offered, opening the door.

When the door shut behind them, Jordan turned to Amanda. She rubbed her hands together and averted her eyes to the floor. "I know you're probably wondering how I found you and why I'm here."

Amanda nodded, dropping her bath items on the bed and sitting down. She motioned for Jordan to do the same.

Jordan hesitated, but sat down on Jade's bed across the room. She ran her palms down her pant legs. "So, I remembered your group Students for Life, and I went to their office. Your friend Jared told me where I could find you after he heard my story." A pause ensued as if she were gathering the courage to continue. "I... uh... heard you were attacked the other night at Beta Zeta Psi's house." She dared a glance from under lowered lids.

"I was." Amanda couldn't believe Jared would tell this girl where she lived, no matter what Jordan's story was, but since the girl was here, she decided to listen anyway.

"I was too. Not the other night, but at the end of last year." The girl's hands twisted in her lap.

A cold vice squeezed on Amanda's heart. "Was it... was it Caleb West?"

The girl shook her head, "No, a guy named Trevor. Trevor Jones, but I heard he was friends with Caleb."

Amanda's eyes widened, and she shivered. "I met Trevor. He gave me the creeps. So, this wasn't the first time..."

Jordan shook her head. "I've heard rumors that there have been others too. I don't think the whole fraternity is involved, just a close group of Caleb and Trevor's friends."

A hatred boiled in Amanda's stomach and overshadowed her fear and sadness. "I think we need to speak out about this. We have to stop them, no matter how many there are."

The girl curled inward. "I don't know if I can do that. I wasn't as lucky as you. No one was there to save me. Can I tell you my story?"

Amanda nodded, suddenly curious to hear Jordan's experience.

Jordan took a deep breath. "I was a freshman last year, new to campus and from a really small town. I hadn't dated much in high school, so when Trevor paid attention to me, I fell hard. I couldn't believe he would be interested in someone like me."

The words pierced Amanda's heart; they were so close to her own story.

"Anyway, near the end of last year, he invited me to a party at the

frat house. I was elated. I would get to walk in on Trevor Jones's arm.
I just didn't know I'd be walking out alone." She paused before
continuing. "I have little memory of that night. I remember it was
loud and there were a lot of people there. I remember being really
tired, and then it's all kind of blank. I woke the next morning, sore
and confused. Trevor was gone. In fact, everyone was gone. The
house was completely empty. I couldn't believe he had just left
me there.

"A few weeks later, I began vomiting several times a day. My
clothes felt tight and I was sore everywhere. After a trip to the clinic, I
found out I was pregnant. That's when I began to piece together what
had happened. I was a virgin before that night, and Trevor drugging
me and taking advantage was the only thing that made sense."

Amanda's hand covered her open mouth. That could have been
her fate if it hadn't been for Emily and Jared.

"I thought my mom at least would be supportive, but she told me
that I needed to have an abortion. I kept putting it off though I wasn't
even sure why. I didn't have any moral opposition to abortion. Finally,
I decided I couldn't put it off any longer and I looked up the closest
clinic, which was in Dallas. I was supposed to be going the day I met
you at the fair, but something wasn't sitting right, and I decided to go
for a walk. I don't know how I even ended up at the fair or at your
booth, but then you spoke to me, and something changed. I got this
feeling that I was having a son and that I couldn't abort him. I ended
up calling a health clinic here, and I decided to put him up for
adoption."

Amanda's heart went out to the blond. No one should have to deal
with what she was going through.

"It's not going to be easy carrying this child, especially after the
way he was conceived, but I realized it wasn't his fault either. And the
center gave me a job, so I'm answering phones there now and helping
other girls like me. I just wanted to say thank you. I was so depressed
this year, but having a purpose for this baby now, I feel like the cloud is
starting to lift. I hope you can find some of that too."

As Jordan spoke, Amanda realized they had met even before the
fair. Maybe she hadn't recognized her because she had been so

depressed the first time, but Amanda was nearly certain this was the girl she had met her first day of class in the breakfast hall.

Tears spilled down Amanda's face, partly from Jordan's story and partly from her own fresh pain. "I'm so sorry you are having to go through this. Can I pray for you, for both of us?"

"I'm not really into prayer," Jordan answered, "but I think I'd like that."

As Amanda bowed her head, she realized she hadn't prayed since the attack. She paused for a moment, asking for peace and forgiveness before letting the Holy Spirit give her the right words to say for Jordan. "I haven't really felt like going out lately," Amanda said after the prayer, "but when I do, would you like to go to church with my friends and me?"

Jordan nodded and the girls exchanged numbers.

"Thank you for coming today," Amanda said. "You have no idea how much I needed this."

When the door shut behind Jordan, Amanda fell to her knees in front of her bed. "Help me Lord. I don't know how to get over this attack. I'm so grateful that I was able to help Jordan, but now I need help. Please give me a sign and help me heal." No more words formed on her lips, but her heart continued to bleed out prayers. When nothing remained, she climbed into bed, mentally exhausted, and closed her eyes.

CHAPTER 15

"Should we have asked her first?" Emily asked Jared as they stood outside Amanda's door.

"She would have just said no," Jared returned, "and whether she knows it or not, she needs this."

"Okay, but if she gets mad, I'm telling her it was your idea," Emily said with a smile.

"Fair enough." Jared knocked on the door, knowing Jade was inside because they had planned the encounter with her. Jade had told Emily about Amanda's friend Sandra and sneaked into Amanda's prayer journal to get the number for them. Then Jared had called Sandra, who immediately asked them to bring Amanda back to Mesquite.

The door opened and Jade stepped back, allowing them entry. Amanda was in bed, dressed though, which meant perhaps she had at least attempted to go to class. That was a step in the right direction, but Jared knew they needed more help.

"What are you doing here?" Amanda asked when Jared and Emily entered the room.

"We're here for you," Emily said, "and you're coming with us."

"I don't want to go anywhere," Amanda shot back.

"I'm not giving you a choice," Jade said. "You've been living in your bed and the same three pairs of clothes all week. It's time to get out."

Amanda shot daggers Jade's direction. "Why? So people can stare at me and whisper behind my back?"

"Look I get it," Jade said. "I've been there, and it stinks, but you can't keep hiding in this room. That doesn't make anything better. Now pack a bag and try to grab something you haven't been wearing for forty- eight hours straight."

Amanda rolled her eyes, but she pushed herself up from her bed and lumbered over to her closet where she began flicking her hangers aimlessly back and forth, as if she couldn't decide what to wear.

Emily and Jared stood against the wall out of the way, unsure of what to say.

"Oh, good grief." Jade sighed in frustration and stomped over to the closet. "Take this"—she yanked a green shirt off a hanger— "and this." She held out a pair of jeans.

Amanda took the clothes and began packing them in a small bag. Jade grabbed her toothbrush and hairbrush and brought them to her.

"Why do I need all that?" Suspicion laced Amanda's voice.

"Because we'll be gone a few days," Jared spoke up.

Amanda raised her eyebrow, but grabbed the bag Jade had finished packing for her. "Gone a few days? What about church?"

"You didn't go last week, but we'll go to church where we end up," Emily said.

"Have fun," Jade said, practically pushing Amanda out the door and shutting it behind her.

"Shall we?" Jared asked. "Our chariot awaits."

Amanda didn't smile at his joke, but she followed them down the stairs and out to the parking lot.

"Can I help you?" Jared asked as he opened the passenger and back doors. Amanda held her bag out, and he placed it in the back of the jeep with his and Emily's bag.

Without a word, Amanda climbed in the back seat. Shrugging at

Jared, Emily climbed in the front seat, and Jared took his place in the driver's side. A GPS sat on the dashboard, and he programmed in their destination. Just over six hours of driving time. *Well, this should be fun.*

Jared started the car and pulled out of the parking lot.

❀

"Why are we here?" Amanda asked a few hours later as they passed the city limit sign of Mesquite. A slight tremor of fear laced her voice.

"We're getting you help," Emily said from the front seat.

A few minutes later, Jared pulled into the parking lot of Mesquite View Church. A few other cars dotted the empty parking lot.

"Come on," Emily said opening Amanda's door.

Amanda shook her head, the fear paralyzing her. "I don't want to."

"Please Amanda. We just want to help you," Jared said.

Jared's sincere eyes pleaded with Amanda. She didn't know what they had in store, but they had driven all this way. Swallowing her trepidation, Amanda unbuckled her belt and followed them into the church. Waiting just inside were Sandra, Callie, JD, and little Hope, who was crawling around on the carpeted floor oblivious to the tension in the room. Relief flooded Amanda when she realized her parents weren't here. She just couldn't tell them how stupid she had been yet.

"Hi Amanda," Callie said stepping forward to hug her. As Callie's arms wrapped around her, all the emotion Amanda had locked away burst forth, and she sobbed. One after another, the sobs wracked her body. Sandra rolled over and placed a hand on Amanda's arm and began praying aloud. Amanda vaguely felt the rest of the group circle around her, but she could do nothing except continue to sob into Callie's shoulder.

When the tears finally subsided, Callie pulled back, confusion filling her bright green eyes. "I'm so sorry this happened to you, sweetheart, but it wasn't your fault."

"It was though," Amanda whispered, finally accepting the shame. "I should have known better. There were signs, but I was too stupid to see them."

"We've all been there," Callie said. "Do you remember when I talked about my fiancé before I met JD?"

Amanda nodded. Callie had shared her story with the church and inspired Amanda to be a bolder example at her high school.

"Well, I'd been living with him for years and never noticed how selfish he was, though my assistant at work knew it. I was blinded from seeing the real him by my affection and by Satan. He preys on our weakness, you know."

Amanda's eyes dropped to stare down at her feet. "He was the first guy who showed interest in me that I liked back."

"But he wasn't the only one," Jared spoke up softly.

Amanda looked up at Jared. She had forgotten about that coffee date request. It seemed so long ago now, but she had thought he liked her at one time, hadn't she? "You liked me as more than a friend?"

"Girl, are you blind?" Emily said with a smile. "He has liked you since he first met you."

Jared's face flamed, and he dropped his eyes. "She's right. I have liked you from the first moment I met you, but I was too scared to tell you. Then you told me you were seeing someone, so I kept it to myself, but what happened is my fault." His eyes brimmed with sadness when he raised them. "I had a suspicion that Caleb was bad news, but I couldn't prove it. Still, I should have told you."

Emotions swirled through Amanda as she tried to understand. Jared liked her, but he hadn't warned her? What was she supposed to make of that?

"Look, the only one to blame here is Caleb. You didn't know"— Emily pointed at Jared— "anything for sure. And you"—she turned to Amanda— "were misled. He pretended to be a Christian and a good person, but he was the one who assaulted you. It was his choice, and he is the only one responsible for it."

"She's right," Sandra said. "You can't control the actions of others, but you can choose how to react to them. If you disappear inside yourself, Caleb wins, and I know you are stronger than that."

"You'd better come home with us," JD said finally. "It sounds like we have a lot we need to talk about."

CHAPTER 16

The sun filtering in the windows woke Amanda. Blinking, she covered her eyes and turned her head. The sun was brighter than it should be. The colors weren't right either, and the bed was too soft. Where was she? Pushing herself up, she glanced around the room, taking in the soft rose walls and the landscape pictures. Emily was sleeping across the room on a pull-out couch. Reality crashed back in on Amanda, and she fell back down. She was home, back in Mesquite, with a giant secret she was keeping from her parents.

Sighing, Amanda pushed back the covers and plodded out of the bed. Being careful to close the door quietly, she shuffled down the hall and into the kitchen. Callie sat at the kitchen table with a mug of coffee and an open Bible in front of her.

"Good morning, Amanda," she said, looking up as Amanda entered.

"Morning." There was more tumbling around in her head, but she was unsure of what else to say.

"There's coffee in the pot," Callie pointed and then returned her eyes to the page.

Amanda grabbed a mug off the bar and filled it with the steaming black liquid. After adding some creamer, she returned to the table.

Cupping her hands around the mug, she let the warmth flood her body.

"Do you think I should tell my folks?" The question tumbled out of Amanda's mouth before she could stop it. She glanced at Callie through lowered lids.

Callie met her gaze and took a deep breath. "I think they deserve to know. I think they could help you and not hiding it might help you heal."

Amanda's eyes dropped to the murky liquid. The white lines of the creamer swirled back and forth. "Do you think they'll hate me for being so stupid?"

Callie's hand touched her arm. "They could never hate you, Amanda. You made a mistake in judgment that's all. They won't be mad at you because what happened was not your fault."

"Do you think you could go with me? When I tell them, I mean?"

"Of course, I'd be happy to."

JD entered then, and after pouring his own cup of coffee, sat down at the table, and the conversation moved in a different direction. Jared came in shortly after that. He smiled hesitantly at Amanda as he sat across the table.

Amanda looked away, unsure of how she felt about him. The part of her that had liked him initially wanted to reach out and grab his hands, but the hurt part of her was still stinging over his knowledge and not telling her. He could have spared her the pain of the attack if he had just been honest with her.

The anger boiled up and her jaw clenched. How could she even consider dating a man who didn't care about her enough to warn her? But then the rational side of her mind spoke up. Would she have even listened to him? Her hands shook around the mug as the emotions battled in her head.

Emily entered the room as everyone else finished breakfast.

"Sorry I'm so late," she said sitting at the table. "I never sleep in like this."

"Then you must have needed it," Callie said. "Help yourself to whatever you find. JD is with Hope, but holler at him if you need anything. I'm going to take Amanda to her parent's house, but we'll be back soon."

"Thanks." Emily flashed Amanda an encouraging smile before she turned to the cupboards in search of a mug.

"You ready?" Callie asked.

"Not really," Amanda said with a sigh, "but we might as well get it over with."

Callie wrapped an arm about her shoulders and led the way out the car. Amanda sank down in the passenger seat, trying to make herself as small as possible. She would rather be going to the dentist than to her parent's house to tell them this.

Throughout the short drive, she tried to plan what she would say, but when her parent's single level rambler came into view, she still had nothing concrete.

"Just tell them the truth," Callie said as she parked the car. It was as if she knew what was on Amanda's mind.

Amanda nodded and opened the passenger door. The invisible weight still sat snugly on her shoulders as she trudged up to the front door, but having Callie by her side gave her a small dose of courage.

The front door swung open, and her mother's face appeared. "Amanda?" she asked in surprise. "Is everything alright?"

"Not really, Mom. Is Dad home?"

With concern etched on her face, she stepped back and opened the door. "He's in his office. Shall we talk in there?"

Amanda nodded, trying to bite back the tears that were threatening to overflow already. How would she make it through her story this way?

Her father looked up from his large oak desk when they entered. In a matter of seconds, his face went from surprised to excited to concerned.

"Sit," her mother said, pointing to one of the chairs. "Tell us what's going on."

Amanda sat in the grey office chair and stared down at her lap for a moment, trying to gather her courage. Callie and her parents remained quiet, waiting for her to begin. With a deep breath and a faltering voice, Amanda began at the beginning.

"I'm so sorry," she said as she ended the story, "and I'll understand if you hate me."

"Hate you?" her father asked. "Why would we hate you?"

"Because I lost my way. I ignored the signs that he maybe wasn't a Christian." Amanda wiped her wet cheek with the back of her hand.

"Amanda Lynne Adams, you were a victim. This was not your fault; do you hear me?" Her mother stood and wrapped an arm around her. "Did he..." She covered her mouth, seemingly unable to say the words.

"No, mom, I got lucky. Jared and Emily saved me before he could."

"Praise God for them." A sob escaped her mouth. "I'm sorry," she said sniffling, "this just isn't what I wanted your college experience to be like."

"We should all pray for God's grace in giving you amazing friends, for healing, and for this young man," her father said.

"And for the other victims," Amanda added softly.

"There are more?"

"At least one, Jordan, she came up to me a few days ago, but she wasn't so lucky. She's pregnant."

Her mother and father shared a silent stare. "We will have to find a way to help them too."

Callie had been silent throughout the discussion, but she spoke up after Amanda's father ended his prayer. "Please come back with us and meet Emily and Jared. They drove Amanda here, and they really are both amazing."

Amanda's parents agreed, grabbing their keys to follow in their own car.

"*Y*ou'll all be back for Thanksgiving, right?" Callie asked as she hugged Amanda goodbye the next day. After attending church with Callie, JD, and Amanda's family, the trio was ready to head home and back to college life.

The three shared a look and nodded. Amanda couldn't imagine any place she'd rather be for Thanksgiving. Jared shook JD's hand, and Emily hugged Callie and little Hope before climbing in the car.

Jared took Amanda's bag, and she smiled at him before opening the back door. Though she was still sorting through her feelings with him, she was trying not to jump to any rash decisions. Their conversation on the porch last night was still fresh in her mind.

After dinner, Amanda pulled Jared outside. Anger still swirled in her stomach, but the knowledge of all he had done battled it, and she owed him at least an explanation for her earlier behavior. Amanda motioned to the porch swing, and they sat in silence for a minute as she gathered her thoughts.

"I wanted to tell you that I liked you the first time I met you too. I had already met Caleb by then, but there was something about you that I was drawn to. It must have been your genuine love of God. I wanted to tell you"—she looked down at her hands— *"so many times, but I'd never really dated. I didn't know if seeing two men would be right. I didn't know how I felt about Caleb, and then I got blinded."*

His voice was soft as he spoke, like a comfortable blanket. "It's not important now. We both have regrets, but they don't have to keep us from enjoying the future."

"About that. I'm still processing, and I'm not sure how I feel about you not sharing your concerns with me." Amanda bit the inside of her lip. "I'm going to work on forgiving you and myself, but I might need some space while I work through all of this."

He nodded, and though she could tell the words hurt him, he didn't respond in anger. "I'll be here when you're ready," he said.

The image faded, and Amanda climbed in the jeep, buckling her seat belt. As the metal clicked, her phone rang. The number was not familiar, and a small thread of fear snaked down her throat, but she punched the button to answer the call anyway.

"Hello?"

"Hello, is Amanda Adams there?"

The voice was deep and unfamiliar. "This is Amanda."

"Amanda, this is Captain Griffith. I'm working your assault case. I wanted to let you know that we haven't found Caleb, but we did pick up Trevor, and we found a book."

"A book?" Amanda asked, her eyebrows knitting together in confusion. What did a book have to do with her case?

"Yes, a large black book filled with names. Did you know anything about this?"

"No, I'm sorry. Is... is my name in it?" She didn't know why, but the thought of her name being written down like it was all planned out filled her with fear. Had Caleb sought her out for a reason then?

"No, but the last entry was the end of last year."

Relief flooded Amanda's veins, but only momentarily. If the last entry had been last year that meant... she didn't want to, but she had to know. "Was there a Jordan?"

"There was," he paused, "how did you know that."

A vice squeezed on Amanda's heart. "I met her. She was assaulted by Trevor at the end of last year. I think you may have a list of assaulted women."

There was an intake of breath and then the pause on the other end stretched on. The man let out a low whistle. "I hope you're wrong. There are a lot of names here, but I fear you might be right."

"Are you going to contact them all?"

"We're going to try." His voice came out in a sigh, and Amanda didn't envy his position.

"Let me know if I can help in any way."

As she ended the call, a feeling of dread mixed with relief crept in. How many times had they gotten away with this? How many women were now out there and hurting?

Emily and Jared were watching Amanda from the front seat. It was obvious they had been listening and were waiting to hear the rest of the story. "Drive," she said, "I'll fill you in."

CHAPTER 17

*A*manda's heart raced as she faced the audience that was quickly gathering. A brown podium that held a microphone stood in front of her, and the media was setting up their own cameras and microphones in front of the stage.

After the police had picked up Trevor and the few other boys who had made entries in the book, they had called Amanda, along with all the other women involved. The women had all met at the station. Amanda had been the luckiest. Some had no memory of the night. Some had gotten pregnant like Jordan. A few of those had had babies and put them up for adoption. Many others had had abortions. At the sight of so many haunted faces, Amanda had decided to speak up about the incident, to tell men that what had happened to them was not okay and to tell women that there was help.

"Are you ready?" Captain Griffith asked.

Amanda glanced over at Jared and the rest of her friends from Students for Life, who had come to support her, and took a deep breath before nodding.

"Okay, let's get started." He stood next to Amanda at the podium and addressed the crowd. He began by informing the crowd about the incident, then finding the black book and picking up the boys from the fraternity who had been involved. "I'd like to introduce Amanda Adams. She was one of the latest victims, and she wanted to tell her story." He stepped back, letting her have the mic.

Swallowing the lump in her throat, she stepped forward. "Um, hello. This isn't easy for me to say, but I felt the need to step forward for all the other women I met. I was lucky that my friends"—she smiled at Emily and Jared— "saved me before the worst could happen. I know not all the other women were so lucky, and I wish I could go back in time to save them all. I want to warn other women to follow their gut. I had misgivings about the man who ended up attacking me, but I shrugged them off because I felt like I was finally getting noticed. Your instinct is your best defense, ladies; trust it.

"Also, you should avoid drinking anything if you go to parties. I was drugged by a punch they were serving. The drug compromised my ability to move, but I was awake, watching everything that was happening. To the men watching, this is not okay to do to women. Many of these women conceived children due to their incidents. All of us feel violated. This must stop. Intimacy should never be forced and should certainly not be performed while women can't fight back. If you have been a victim of an incident like this, I urge you to report it. We must unite and fight back against these attacks and the police need to take them seriously, so we can change the culture surrounding this. Thank you."

Amanda stepped back as Captain Griffith took over again. He reiterated the police department's desire to help women and to investigate these cases. Then he took a few questions from the crowd. When it was all over and the bright lights had been turned off, he turned and shook Amanda's hand.

"That took a lot of guts, and I thank you," he said, pumping her hand up and down. Captain Griffiths was the quintessential Texas stereotype. He had a deep southern drawl and always seemed to be sporting a cowboy hat on top of his salt and pepper hair. Amanda smiled at him before stepping down and walking over to Emily and Jared.

"You did great," Jared said and Emily nodded her agreement before reaching in her pocket and pulling out her phone. It must have been on silent as it hadn't even rung. Her eyebrows knitted together as she read the message and a frown stretched across her mouth.

"What is it?" Amanda asked.

"Nothing," she said and placed the phone back in her pocket. "I'm going to go... do something."

As she hurried off, Amanda turned to Jared. "What was that about?"

He shook his head as he watched her hurry away. "I think it's about her roommate. She filled me in a little on the situation when we were in Mesquite, but I think she could definitely use prayer."

"Whatever I can do," Amanda agreed. "You guys have been so great to me."

"We're glad we met you," he said with a small smile, and Amanda knew he mainly meant he was glad to have met her. She knew he still wanted to date her and she was pretty sure she wanted that to, but fear was holding her back.

"Can I walk you home?" he asked, breaking up her internal dialogue. Amanda nodded and fell into step beside him. When they reached the dorm, he bowed and waved a farewell gesture before turning back toward his own dorm. Amanda appreciated the space and she planned to use it to think on the situation and decide what she wanted to do.

"Oh, I'm glad I caught you," a voice said on her right as Amanda stepped up to the counter to grab her mail. Sarah rose from one of the foyer chairs and walked toward her. "Can we talk for a minute?"

Surprised, Amanda nodded and led her upstairs to her room. Once inside, Sarah sat on the bed, folding her long legs beneath her.

"You are probably wondering why I'm here," she said.

"I'm happy to see you, but the thought had crossed my mind," Amanda smiled. Sarah had been the hardest to get to know of the Students for Life group, so Amanda was very curious as to the reason for the visit.

She took a deep breath and bit her lip. Whatever was on her mind must be important. "It's about Jared."

Amanda's forehead wrinkled in confusion. She had just left Jared. "Jared? What about Jared?"

"I know he told you he knew about Caleb, and I know you're probably wondering why he didn't tell you. Well, that was my fault."

"What do you mean?" Amanda asked, narrowing her eyes.

"Do you remember the first day Caleb came to the office?" Sarah asked. Amanda nodded and she continued, "Well, Jared came to me afterwards. He was shaking, angry, and afraid. I don't know if he ever told you, but we dated for a time, and while it didn't work out between us, we remained great friends. Last year, he met this girl Nikki and he really liked her, but one day he saw Caleb and Nikki together. She told him they were just studying, but the next day she broke up with him over a text."

"That's awful," Amanda said, "but Jared already told me this..."

"Just wait," she interrupted, "Anyway, he never spoke with Nikki again, but a few months later, we heard rumors that she had been attacked at a party. Of course, we also heard rumors that she was pregnant, that she ran away, and that some family member died and that's why she left. My point is that Jared didn't know for sure what had happened to Nikki until they found her name in that book.

"He wanted to tell you that day, but I told him not to because we didn't know for sure. I didn't know you well enough to know if you would believe him or just think he was trying to break you guys up, so I told him just to be there for you and to pray." She sucked in her breath and her voice trembled, "So, it's not Jared's fault for not telling you; it's mine." She covered her face with her hands and her shoulders shook.

For a moment, Amanda just watched her, unsure of what to say or do. She and Sarah weren't close friends, but Amanda liked her. Her counseling instincts kicked in, and she moved to sit beside her. "Sarah, it's okay. You didn't know either. How could you? He fooled us all." As the words left Amanda's mouth, she finally believed them, and a weight lifted from her shoulders.

"But I've ruined it for you and Jared now. He cares for you so much." Her words came out in a muffled stream amid hitching sobs.

"I don't hate Jared," Amanda said. "I was confused about how to feel, and I've been working on it, but you just sped up the process. It may still take me a while to recover fully, but I don't have any reason to be mad at him, or at you," Amanda added quickly.

"Really?" she asked and lifted her head. Her hawkish nose was wet with tears, and her grey eyes glistened, ready to release another flood.

"Really," Amanda said. "I was already healing after the press conference today. What you told me clears up my remaining questions."

"Will you give him a chance?" she asked. The intensity that radiated from her eyes only convinced Amanda more that Jared was one of the good ones.

"I'd be crazy not to."

*A*manda woke, covered in sweat and shaking. Her eyes tore about the room, but she hadn't woken Jade. She still slumbered in her bed, back to Amanda.

Her heart slowly returned to its normal pace. The nightmare of Caleb's attack receded from her mind, but that didn't ease the fear. This was the third nightmare she'd had this week. She needed closure.

Amanda had hoped after the press conference that she would have it, but it hadn't stopped the nightmares. As if on cue, her phone began to ring. The number was unfamiliar, and she wondered if it was Caleb calling from somewhere. That had become a common fear with every unknown number, but then reality would kick in and she would ask herself why he would do that?

She tapped the button and whispered a soft "hello?" Her surroundings froze as the words from the other end filled her ear, and her knuckles whitened from the grip on the phone. "I understand. Thank you for calling me."

After ending the call, Amanda stared at the phone for a minute. Should she go? The idea filled her with fear, but the thought of closure held an appeal as well. Taking a deep breath, she closed her eyes and prayed for guidance. Then she tapped out a quick message to

Jared. She not only valued his opinion but had other things to discuss with him as well.

Half an hour later, a knock rapped at the door. Amanda opened it and stepped outside as Jade was still sleeping inside. Concern clouded Jared's green eyes. "Is everything okay?"

She nodded, trying to decide which subject she wanted to broach first. "Let's go downstairs."

Amanda led the way to one of the study carrels downstairs and grabbed two chairs. "Sarah came to visit me yesterday."

He looked up in surprise, but waited for her to continue.

"She told me how you wanted to tell me about Caleb, but she convinced you not to."

"I know I should have..." he began, but Amanda held up her hand to stop him.

"When you first told me you knew he was dangerous, I couldn't understand how you wouldn't have told me your suspicions, but Sarah told me the whole story. I understand why she asked you to wait. It makes sense."

Amanda's cheeks heated, and she glanced down at her hands before continuing. "I wish I had met you before I met Caleb, and I think in my heart I knew he wasn't the one I was supposed to be with, but... anyway, I'm sure I'll still need some time to heal, but I was wondering if you still were interested in me?" The last part came out as barely more than a whisper, and Amanda forced her eyes to his face.

A small grin played across his lips. "Of course I am," he said, grabbing her hands. "Watching you be so strong through all of this has just made me realize how much I admire you even more."

Elation filled Amanda's heart. "Good, then I need your help." She filled him on both the nightmare and the phone call.

When she had finished, he leaned back and ran a hand through his hair. "Wow, well I'm glad they caught him. I'm sure that will help with your healing and your nightmares, but seeing him? Do you think it will be a good idea?"

"I have no idea," Amanda said with a shake of her head, "that's why I wanted your perspective."

"Let's pray about it. God will tell us the right thing to do."

As he held her hands and began speaking, a feeling of peace and the knowledge of what to do flowed throughout her. When he finished, he squeezed her hands.

"Did that help?"

Amanda nodded; she knew what to do now.

❀

"Are you sure you want to do this?" Jared asked as they stood outside the jail. From the outside, it looked just like all the other brick buildings in this part of town—brown and nondescript, but he knew inside it would be very different, and he wasn't sure if Amanda was truly prepared for it.

"I'm not," she said with a slight chuckle, "but we are here; turning away now makes no sense." She took a deep breath and squared her shoulders, and Jared smiled at her strength.

He opened the door and led the way inside, hoping this would indeed give her the relief she was seeking. The initial room was a small, white area with a few chairs and a manned counter area shielded behind heavy glass.

"Can I help you?" The woman, a hardened tough looking blond with linebacker shoulders asked.

"We're here to see Caleb West," Amanda said softly.

"IDs please," the woman said "and sign here." She pushed a log book under the glass and waited for their IDS.

As Amanda signed the log book, the woman perused their IDs, looking from them to her computer screen and then back to Amanda and Jared. Her narrowed eyes stared intently as if she were trying to decipher if they were hiding anything. After inputting the information into her system, she pressed a buzzer that opened the door to another room.

Jared's unease grew as they entered this second room. It was another small colorless room where a male and female guard stood waiting to search visitors. After a quick pat down, they were led into yet another room with several tables.

"You can sit here," the male guard said, pointing to some tables. "I'll bring Caleb in."

"I'll stand back there," Jared pointed to the wall, "so you can say whatever you need to." He wanted to give her enough space to feel comfortable but not so much that she felt he had abandoned her.

Amanda smiled gratefully up at him before sitting down at one of the cold, metal tables. Her hands splayed then folded then splayed again across the top of the table in an obvious nervous gesture.

A few minutes later, Caleb appeared, clad in an orange jumpsuit. A sneer graced his face as he sat down across from her. "Did you finally decide you wanted it?" Jared bit his tongue and his desire to close the gap between them and strangle the man himself.

Amanda shook her head, and though she might have been scared, her gaze remained fixed on his face. "No, I wanted to ask you why. Why did you attack me? I was falling for you. I thought you were a good man."

"But you weren't giving me what I wanted," he said with a sneer and a shrug. "Besides, it's all about the conquest for me. I chose you because you were so innocent. I like them innocent; it's more satisfying when you get what they refuse to give you." His cold eyes gleamed with malice, and Jared saw Amanda's body tense. Even Jared hadn't known how awful Caleb really was. How had he hidden this evil running rampant through him now?

"But you could probably have any girl you wanted, why do you feel the need to take it?"

"Because I can. It's about power. I had it, and you didn't."

At his words, a smile broke out on Amanda's face. For a moment she said nothing, and Jared watched Caleb shift in his seat. "Well, now I have it and you don't. I feel sorry for you Caleb, but I'm not going to let you destroy my life. I'm going to pray for you and hope that one day you see how wrong you have been."

Caleb's mouth dropped open, but Amanda didn't give him the chance to say anymore. She stood, motioned for Jared to follow, and walked out of the room, never looking back.

"Do you feel better?" Jared asked as they left the jail. He knew the fresh air definitely felt better on his skin.

"I do," Amanda smiled up at him. "I was afraid it would bring back the fear, but I just felt sorry for him. He's obviously troubled. I am glad that he's going to go away for a while, but I'm not looking forward to the trial." She shuddered. "I know it's necessary, but I just want to be done with it, you know?"

Jared squeezed her hand in agreement. "How about some lunch to take your mind off it?"

"Sounds wonderful." Amanda flashed a smile and reached for his hand.

CHAPTER 18

By the time Thanksgiving break arrived, Amanda and Jared were officially a couple. As Jared's family lived much further away, he decided to go with Amanda to Mesquite for the break.

Amanda's family had agreed to host Thanksgiving at their house as they had more room and a larger family to move. Jared and Amanda arrived just an hour before lunch was to be served. Amanda made a beeline for the kitchen, offering to help, but her mother, claiming she had it all under control, ushered her to the living room.

Amanda sat on the couch next to Callie, who reached out and squeezed her arm while offering a smile. Returning it, Amanda glanced over at Jared who was conversing with JD. She still fervently wished that she had chosen Jared first, but God was healing her wounds and deepening their relationship. A part of her wondered if they would be as close if she hadn't gone through the harrowing experience.

An hour later, everyone gathered around the large wooden table. The table was fuller this year than it had been in previous years, and the faces surrounding it, though not all blood relation, were now all a part of Amanda's family. "I know there are more of us this year and it might take more time, but can we share what we are thankful for?" she asked, referring to a family tradition they had practiced for years.

"I think that's a wonderful idea," her mother agreed. She looked at her husband before saying, "I'm thankful that we've all met such wonderful friends."

"Agreed," he said. "I'm thankful that my family can all be here together." He turned to JD, who spoke next, followed by Callie, and then Amanda's brother and sister. Sandra's eyes misted as she declared her thankfulness for God's blessings.

Jared smiled at Amanda when his turn came up. "I'm thankful for meeting Amanda and for having a place to go this Thanksgiving."

"I'm thankful that God is allowing me to heal," Amanda said finishing the circle.

The silence hung suspended in the air for a moment as the words lingered on everyone's hearts. Then Hope banged her plate and shouted "eat." Smiles and laughter issued forth and the food began its rotation around the table.

After dinner, Jared pulled Amanda aside. "Would you like to go for a walk?"

"I'd love that," Amanda said. She was still full from the turkey and hoped it would relieve the pressure against her jeans. They threw on coats and headed out into the chilly air.

The sun was just setting, sending out rays of brilliant oranges, reds, and pinks as they walked. Jared grasped her hand, lacing his fingers in hers, and Amanda's lips pulled into a warm smile.

A little park sat a block away, and Amanda led them in that direction. No one was there when they arrived. The swings swayed slightly in the wind, but otherwise the park was still.

They stopped by a green park bench, but before sitting, Jared took her hands, staring into Amanda's eyes. "I'm so glad that you gave me a chance," he said.

"I'm so glad you have been so amazing through all of this."

Jared brushed a chunk of hair back from her face and cupped her chin in his hands. The electricity crackled between their eyes. Amanda's breath caught in her throat as she realized he was about to kiss her for the first time.

She closed her eyes, wanting to savor the feeling of his lips as they touched hers. A spark ignited from the very first touch, ricocheting down her body. Though she had felt passion with Caleb, it couldn't match this feeling with Jared. This was passion combined with love and a feeling of safety.

❀

*A*fter Thanksgiving, Amanda and Jared fell back into the routine of college until just before winter break. Caleb's trial was planned for the week after finals, and as it neared, Amanda grew more nervous.

Though she felt she was healing well, and the flashbacks had lessened to occasional night stirrings, she knew she wasn't completely healed. There were still times when she shied away from Jared's touch even though she knew he would never hurt her as Caleb had. Testifying at the trial was the right move, but Amanda wondered if reliving the moment would set her healing back.

"Are you ready?" Jade asked from across the room.

Amanda flashed a small smile as she smoothed her skirt. She and Jade had gotten closer after the attack, and Jade had even gone to church a few times.

"I think so," Amanda said with a smile.

Jared and Emily were waiting downstairs, dressed in their Sunday best as well. Though Amanda was the only one testifying today, the group wanted to put on a unified front. Jared stood as Amanda approached and without a word, he squeezed her hand, sending a shock wave of security down her arm.

Amanda used the quiet drive to the courthouse to collect her thoughts, going over the statement again and again in her head. Each time she repeated it, her heart pounded a little faster in her chest. When it got so bad, she thought her heart was going to bust out of her body, she closed her eyes and took a deep breath, forcing herself to calm down.

The courthouse appeared—a large two-story building that stood out with its alabaster color in comparison to the surrounding brown.

The vice grip Amanda had just managed to loosen re-tightened on her heart. Jared touched her arm and shot a comforting glance.

When the car parked, Amanda opened the door and stood, but had trouble making her feet move. They felt like they were made of lead and too heavy to lift. Emily, sensing trouble, came to one side and Jared to the other. Together they helped Amanda stumble in the direction of the front door.

Once inside, the group had to stand in line to pass through a metal detector before they could traverse to the correct courtroom. With each echoing step down the marble-floored hallway, Amanda's nerves wound tighter and tighter, coiling like a tight spring ready to burst.

The attorney, Paul Brooks, met them outside the room. His dark hair was perfectly combed, and he had trimmed his beard. His black suit coat and blue tie matched Amanda's dress. With a wave of his hand, he sent Jared, Emily, and Jade in to have a seat while he ran through some final items with Amanda. Although she nodded at all his statements, she barely registered them. When he was finished, he pointed to the bench she would have to wait at until it was time to testify.

Amanda sat down and smiled nervously at the security guard standing nearby. Was he to keep her from running or from talking to someone else? He needn't have bothered; the only thing she could even think to do right now was to pray.

Dropping her head, she opened her heart and began praying for a sense of peace, for the words to say, for the love of Jesus to be seen. She stayed that way—head bowed, lips moving silently—until a tap on her shoulder broke the connection and grabbed her attention.

"We're ready for you."

Amanda nodded, feeling a peaceful presence descend. As she entered the crowded courtroom, she barely noticed the people. Just like at the fair with Jordan, she felt more as if she were watching herself than that she was involved.

At the stand, she raised her right hand, placed her left on the Bible and solemnly swore to tell only the truth. The jury sat to her left, a mixture of old and young, men and women, professional and blue collar workers. The thirteen faces staring back at her stirred no fear, however.

Caleb sat to her right. Though physically still handsome, now that she knew his heart, she wondered how she had ever been attracted to him. He looked the part of the typical boy next door today in a nice pair of dress slacks and a blue button down shirt that brought out his eyes. No sense of remorse showed on his face. A female attorney with flowing blond hair in a smart black suit sat next to him. The irony of the choice of a female attorney was not lost on Amanda.

Paul began asking questions, setting up the night in question and walking Amanda through the attack. She answered each one calmly though her heart was pounding a double rhythm in her chest.

When he finished, the female attorney stepped up.

"Hello, Ms. Adams, how are you today?"

"I'm doing alright, thank you," Amanda replied, but her hands began to twist in her lap.

She also began firing off questions about Amanda's relationship with Caleb. At first, they were innocuous, about where they met, etc., but then she began asking very personal questions. Paul had warned Amanda this would happen, but the subject matter still colored a blush across her cheeks.

"If you didn't want to have sex with him, why did you go with him into a bedroom?"

"He drugged me," Amanda responded, struggling to keep her voice calm. "There was ketamine in my blood."

"I see," the attorney said, pursing her lips and walking from the stand to the juror box. "And how did he drug you?"

"He put something in my drink," Amanda responded.

The woman stopped her pacing and looked up at Amanda. "Did you see him put anything in your drink?"

"No," Amanda said, "but I turned my back when he was filling my drink, so he must have done it then."

"I see." The woman looked down at her notepad. "Didn't he pour you a drink from a keg though?"

"He did."

"So how could he have drugged you? Wouldn't the drug have been in the keg and affected other girls?"

Amanda had wondered this herself, but Paul had assured her it didn't matter. She only needed to tell the truth. "I assume it was in the keg and maybe they made sure other girls didn't drink from that keg. I honestly don't know, but he knew what was in the keg. He refused to drink it for one, and he immediately took me to the back of the house for another."

"But didn't my client say that it was just to talk since the music was so loud?"

"He did, but that wasn't his real motivation. As soon as the drug started kicking in, he took me to a bedroom and locked the door."

"Isn't it possible that the Ketamine just heightened your senses and you gave him the signal that you wanted sex, but then changed your mind afterwards and that's why you filed this complaint?"

Amanda clenched her fists in her lap and shook her head, sending her red hair rippling against her face. "I could barely move before he took me to the bedroom, and once he laid me down, my entire body went numb. I couldn't speak; all I could do was move my eyes. I tried to move them back and forth to let him know I didn't want his advances, but he ignored them and assaulted me anyway."

The defense attorney fired a few more questions at Amanda, trying to discredit her integrity, but the peace continued to flow around her, and she answered each one in turn.

When the judge dismissed her from the stand, she glanced over at Caleb as she took a seat next to Jared in the audience. Caleb didn't meet her eye, but whether that was from contriteness or something else, Amanda did not know.

At the end of the day, her energy waned from having to hear all the sordid details replayed in the courtroom. Amanda still couldn't believe how many other girls had fared much worse than she had. Though she had met most of them, seeing the actual black book admitted into evidence still hit her hard. Her Christian upbringing made it difficult for her to believe that men like this existed, men who would take advantage of women for the sheer sport of it.

"You did great," Jared said as they left the courtroom. "Do you want to get something to eat?"

Amanda was hungry, but more than that, she felt filthy. The reminding of the traumatic night had re-ignited the feelings of violation, and she wanted a hot shower to wash them off. She declined the dinner invitation with the excuse of being tired, and she and Jade headed back to the dorm room after being dropped off.

"You aren't really tired, are you?" Jade asked as they entered the room.

"I am, but more than that, I just feel dirty. I want to take a long hot shower and try to forget everything I heard today." Amanda shivered as another wave of disgust shot down her back.

Jade nodded in understanding.

Amanda gathered her toiletries and headed down the hall to the bathroom. Though a hot bath where she could soak the filth away would have been preferable, the hot water of the shower at least eased some of the loathing. The water droplets felt like tiny pellets stinging her back like a whip, but the image of the soap running down the drain made her think of sins being washed away.

After drying off, she redressed and returned to the room. Her pale skin was now a light pink from the heat of the water.

"Feel better?" Jade asked from her bed.

"A little," Amanda shrugged. "How did people do it? How did they get over it?"

Jade sighed. "I don't think anyone really gets over it, but from what I've seen, it gets easier. You start to think about it less. Some women change a lot though, taking self-defense or martial arts to protect themselves. Some hide away inside, but you've got God on your side, and I know with prayer and time, he will heal you."

Amanda smiled and chuckled as she asked, "How did you get so knowledgeable about God?"

"I had a persistent roommate who was a very good teacher," Jade said, returning the smile.

*T*he trial lasted another week. Both Jordan and Emily had to testify, and it was hard to sit through the story again and again, but the evidence was convincing, and the jury convicted Caleb of rape, attempted sexual assault, and drug possession. He, Trevor, and the other boys who were named in the book were all convicted to a minimum of ten years. It wasn't perfect, but knowing that they would be put away for a decade brought some relief.

"I'm glad that's over," Jared said as they exited the courtroom for the last time.

"Me too," Amanda said, snuggling into his side and enjoying the security of his arm around her. "This was not how I pictured my Freshman year, but I have to say, I think it will be much better from here on out."

"I wholeheartedly concur," Jared said with a smile as he pulled her even closer. Emily, Jade, Jordan, and several other friends joined them, and together the group walked out of the court house and into the crisp winter air, ready to tackle whatever else life threw at them.

*T*HE END!!

*I*f you enjoyed this book, please leave a review at your retailer. It really does help and only takes a minute. http://books2read.com/Whenheartscollide

DISCUSSION QUESTIONS

1. Lorana Hoopes used her alma mater, Texas Tech, in this story. What do you remember from college or if you didn't go, what do you think you would have liked the most?

2. What did you think of the book starting with something that just happened and then going back to the past? Did it make it more enjoyable or less?

3. Who was your favorite character in the book and why?

4. Amanda lost herself after the attack. While you may not have experienced anything that horrific, what are some things that distract you or cause you to lose yourself?

. . .

5. How can we ensure our daughters don't go through the same struggles Amanda did?

6. What did you learn about God from reading this book?

7. How can you use that knowledge in your life from now on?

8. Is there something you could do at your church to help inform or love on women in this position?

9. Have you ever had an experience like Amanda and Jordan did? What was it?

WOULD YOU LEAVE A REVIEW?

As an author, I highly appreciate the feedback I get from my readers. It helps others make an informed decision before buying my book. If you enjoyed this book, please review at your retailer.

Do you like free books? I'm offering a free sample of my next book Free Sample!

A PAST FORGIVEN

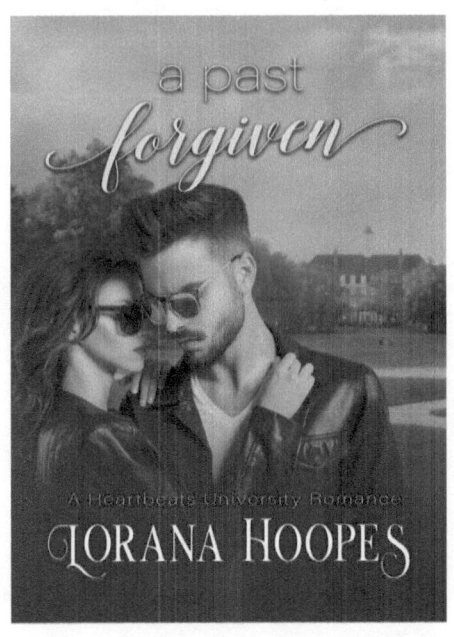

DEDICATION

Dedication Page:

To my family who allows me to sacrifice time with them to write these stories.

To my friends who inspire me even when you don't know it.

To women everywhere who have been forced to do things against your will, your Heavenly Father loves you.

CHAPTER 1

*J*ess Peterson stepped off the bus onto the campus of Texas Tech and took a deep breath. Though not her first choice of colleges - she'd wanted to get farther away - at least it removed her from the clutches of her "handsy" stepfather. In fact, if she never saw Paducah, Texas and it's one stoplight again, she would be fine with that.

She slung her black backpack over her shoulder and crossed the quad to Knapp Hall. A folded map resided in the back pocket of her cutoff denim shorts. However, Jess possessed a photographic memory and had memorized most of the buildings, on the east side of campus at least. Knapp Hall was a large, though non-descript, brick building of three floors built in 1948.

Jess registered the cracks in the cement steps as she pulled open the front door. They weren't surprising as old as the building was, but she hoped the interior had been updated more recently.

It was not to be. The dorm had been improved since 1948, but it still looked to be about ten years behind the times in terms of decorating. Variations of browns and greens were the main colors, interspersed with a few streaks of gray.

After stopping at the information desk on the first floor just long enough to get the keys, Jess took the stairs at the end of the hall two at a time to the third floor. 316. The closed door elicited a glimmer of hope that they'd gotten her the single she'd requested. She did not want a roommate.

As the door swung open, Jess swore softly under her breath. A blonde girl stood beside the left bed unpacking the suitcase in front of her. She looked up when Jess entered and smiled. Jess did not return the smile as she asked, "Who are you?"

The girl dropped the item of clothing she had been holding and stepped forward, extending her hand. "I'm Emily. I guess you're my new roommate."

Rolling her eyes, Jess pushed past the girl, ignoring the hand. "Crap. I told them I needed a single."

"Well, they ran out," Emily stated, appearing unperturbed by the rude behavior. "See, I'm a sophomore, but I offered to room with an incoming freshman if it was necessary. Since you're here," she shrugged, "I guess it was necessary."

Jess tossed her backpack on the right bed and glared at the blonde. "Well, I'll be telling them to look again. I don't do roommates." Her hand plunged into the backpack, rifling through the contents until she found the item she was looking for - the paperwork with the RA's name on it. Ah, there it was. Clasping it in her hand, she glared at Emily again, and then abruptly left the room, slamming the wooden door behind her. "Nope, nu uh," she muttered as she stomped down the hallway to the RA's room.

Room 350 was at the far end of the hall, and Jess rapped loudly on the wooden door when she arrived. A tall, leggy blonde with sparkly pink lips opened the door. "Hi, can I help you?"

Oh, great. My RA was probably the prom queen - every year, Jess thought as she shoved the paper clenched in her fist in front of the preppy blonde's face. "I'm Jess Peterson, and I'm supposed to have a single, but there's some goody-two-shoes who has already unpacked her things in my room."

The RA's perfectly arched eyebrows shot to the top of her forehead as she leaned back slightly and took the paper, lowering it to a level she could read it from. "Okay, well, first off, let's try not to call our roommate names." She unfolded the paper and glanced over it.

With crossed arms, Jess tapped her foot against the carpeted floor as she waited for the RA to explain they had made a mistake.

The RA looked up from the paper and sighed. "This says we'd try to get you a single, but that we couldn't guarantee it. Apparently, more upperclassmen returned than expected, and they get their choice of a single first. So, I can add you to the waiting list, but I'm afraid you're stuck for now."

Heat erupted in Jess's body and her hands clenched into fists at her side. "That's it? That's all you can do?"

The blonde shrugged and held the paper out to her, "Maybe try to get to know your roommate. I bet she's not as bad as you think."

"Aargh, you are worthless." Jess snatched the paper back from the RA's glittery pink nails and marched down the stairs. This could NOT be happening. She slammed the outside door open as she reached the final step. It banged against the wall before slamming shut, satisfying a small destructive desire burning within.

Leaning against the brick wall, she pulled a cigarette and a lighter out of the pocket of her shorts and flicked the lighter on. As she puffed on the cigarette, the nicotine went to work on her nerves, soothing some of the manic feeling. How was she going to make it through a semester with a roommate?

It wasn't that she'd never lived with anyone. She'd crashed with a few friends the last few months after moving out of her mom's house, but that had been a necessary evil and she'd been hoping to finally have a place of her own when she arrived at college.

As she inhaled, plans formulated in her mind. Maybe if living with her was awful enough, she could get the girl to leave. What would it take? Loud music? Being a slob? A parade of men? She would have to try them all until one worked.

The cigarette burned to a nub, and Jess dropped it to the ground, squishing it into the dirt with the toe of her boot before deciding to take a walk to calm her anger and solidify a plan.

When she returned to the room later, the girl was still there and had decorated. Red and black towels, displaying Tech pride, hung from the handle by the sink. Pictures of the Eiffel tower covered the wall above a soft grey bedspread etched with a black Flëur De Leis. The girl sat on the bed with a book open on her lap. Ice flooded Jess's veins as she realized what the girl was reading. She hadn't thought this roommate situation could get worse, but she'd been wrong.

"Oh heck no, you're one of those?"

"I'm sorry, one of what?" The girl's brow wrinkled as she looked at Jess.

"One of those Bible beaters." Jess had known enough "religious" people in her lifetime to know she wanted nothing to do with them. They always talked a big talk, but they never lived what they preached. Even her mother attended a church for a time, but dropped it when she met Jim.

The girl smiled. "I am a Christ follower, if that's what you mean."

With another eye roll, Jess mumbled under her breath, "Great, they paired me with a religious nut job." She grabbed her headphones from her bag, plugged them into her phone, and turned up the music. Though the girl said nothing, Jess could tell the music was bugging her, and she smiled a little inside. Maybe this wouldn't be too hard after all.

A few minutes later, the girl motioned for Jess to remove the headphones. She pushed one back just enough to hear the girl ask something about food. *Yeah, as if I'd want to eat with you.* Jess flicked a hand at her in dismissal and sighed in relief when the door closed behind the girl.

Turning off the music, she began to unpack her own things. There wasn't much, only what would fit in her large backpack. When she'd left home a few months back, she had taken only a few clothes and items, just enough to get by. She'd stayed with a few acquaintances through the summer before having to spend the last week in a shelter. It hadn't been that bad, and it allowed her to keep the small wad of money she managed to save up and keep hidden from her mother.

Thankfully, a scholarship arrived her senior year that covered college room and board. No fan of high school, Jess had done as little to get by as possible. But her Junior year, the guidance counselor, who understood a little of her unfortunate home situation, convinced Jess she was a good student and could get a scholarship if she worked hard. The counselor had been right, and the scholarship had been Jess's ticket out of the abuse she'd lived with for the last several years.

Jess pulled out her favorite black blanket, unrolled it, and covered the bed. As she looked at the bare walls, she wished she could have brought some posters from home, but there'd been no room. Her small wardrobe filled most of the space in the backpack along with necessary items. The contrast between her blank, monochromatic side of the room and the other girl's pride-filled side was nauseating and slightly comical.

An audible rumbling in her stomach sounded, and Jess realized she was hungry after all, but she had no idea which dorm the blonde saint had gone to. Knapp Hall didn't have a full cafeteria, but many of the nearby dorms did. As she didn't want to risk running into her, Jess decided it was time to see what the town offered.

University Avenue lay to the east, and she trekked that direction having seen a few restaurants from the bus when she arrived earlier. The sun still shone, though it was nearing dusk, and beads of sweat trickled down one side of her neck. She had shaved the other side hoping to deter her stepfather's advances, but it hadn't worked. However, it seemed to fit well with her "don't mess with me" attitude, so she'd kept it.

She crossed University at a crosswalk and debated. A pizza place, a burger joint, and a pancake house dotted the row of buildings. Not feeling much like breakfast or a greasy pizza, Jess opted for the burger joint, Ollie's.

The red and black building oozed Tech pride, and a picture of Ollie, a white dog with a black patch over one eye and a red bandana, completed the sign. Jess sighed at the gimmicky exterior, but figured the food couldn't be too bad. It was rather hard to mess up a burger and fries.

As she opened the door, second thoughts flooded her mind. She might as well have walked into an updated version of Cheers. Huge television screens adorned the walls. Booths covered in red vinyl hugged the large windows, and a few tables and chairs crowded a large bar. A lively group filled the room, including a group of jocks at the nearest table cheering at the big screens. Pretty, blonde girls in designer clothes sat at another table tapping away on their expensive cell phones. If there were two things Jess couldn't stand, it was jocks and Barbies.

She paused, hand on the door, and debated her options. Though not her scene, she was hungry, and there were a few empty booths. The renewed rumbling of her stomach finalized the decision, and with a clenched jaw, she crossed to a nearby empty booth. Why couldn't she be old enough to sit at the bar and order a stiff tequila drink?

She'd been drinking since the age of fourteen when she'd found the liquor in her mother's stash. The first swig had been awful, but she'd found after that the lightheaded sensation helped her forget the leers and touches of her stepfather. Jess wouldn't say she had acquired a taste for the liquor, but she had developed an appreciation to the mindless bliss it offered.

A college-aged waiter, clad in a white t-shirt, shorts, and bored expression arrived shortly and handed her a menu. New fears of the quality of the food deepened as the sticky menu ripped open with a squelching sound. Swallowing her disgust, Jess ordered a burger, fries, and a diet coke.

As the waiter turned away and headed to the kitchen, a large male slid in the booth across from her. With his short brown hair and broad shoulders, he looked very much like all the other jocks at the nearby table. A quick glance that direction confirmed her suspicion as the whole table had their eyes glued Jess's direction. The guy wasn't bad looking, but Jess held no love for jocks. Perhaps if she could give him a cold enough stare he would leave, but alas he opened his mouth, and at the sound of his thick southern drawl, Jess felt IQ points trickle out of her head.

"I haven't seen you 'round here before," the behemoth said. "I'm Randy. I'm a linebacker."

Though Jess watched football - she was, in fact, a closet Dallas Cowboys fan - she had no intention of letting this dolt know it.

"That's nice," she said sweetly, plastering a fake smile on her face, "now get out of my booth." The last words dripped with venom as her smile dropped and she glared daggers at him.

Randy held up his hands in defense. "Whoa, no need to be rude now. I just thought I'd say hi."

"Hi, now please leave."

"Whatever." He unfolded himself from the booth and lumbered back to his friends who cheered and clapped.

Jess rolled her eyes and sighed. Maybe she should have ordered in. She turned her attention out the window, and as she watched the cars pass, she wished for a different life. Thankfully, the table of jocks decided she wasn't worth any more trouble and left her alone.

A few moments later, her plate of greasy food arrived. Jess hadn't thought a restaurant could mess up a burger and fries, but she had been wrong. There was so much sauce on the burger that the bun had begun to disintegrate, and she was forced to eat the patty with a fork. The fries had evidently sat in the fryer a little too long as they were no longer a golden yellow, but an odd rusty brownish color. She could make a scene—demand a refund—but she wanted no more attention tonight. Better to just let it be and mark this as a place to never revisit. She shoveled down what little she could to satisfy the rumbling, paid the tab, and left. It was still better than home, she reminded herself as she stepped out into the humid night.

"Hey, you got a light?"

The voice came from the right where a guy with dark hair and a black leather jacket stood. Stubble covered his chin, making his blue eyes shine like a beacon in a dark storm, and the hint of a tattoo peeked over his collar. Jess's breath caught as her heart hammered in her chest. He reminded her of Adrian Paul's Highlander, a show that had originally aired before her time but that she had fallen in love with when re-runs began.

She nodded, forcing her voice to stay cool as she reached for her lighter. A slight tremor gripped her hand as she held it out, but he didn't seem to notice. He lit his cigarette and then handed the lighter back. Jess shook out her own cigarette and lit up next to him.

"What's your name?" he asked, nodding at her and taking a deep breath of smoke. It curled out of his thin lips in little wisps. Jess had never wanted to be a cigarette so badly.

"Jess. You?" She breathed in a deep lungful, careful not to overdo it. A coughing fit in front of this Adonis would be mortifying.

"Chad. You go to Tech?"

"Yeah, I just got here."

He nodded again and continued puffing. Jess watched as his hand rose to his mouth and lowered to his side in a rhythmic motion, and she wondered what the stubble on his face would feel like against her cheek. Would it be rough like sandpaper or was it softer? A heat seared across her face, and she turned away.

"Well, I guess I'll see you around." He finished his cigarette, flicked it on the ground, and then mounted a black Harley Davidson parked at the curb. His bad boy quotient rose even higher, and her heart pounded faster as she envisioned herself climbing on the back and wrapping her arms around his waist, the smell of his leather jacket tickling her nose.

As the engine roared to life, the image vanished, and the pounding in her heart slowed. He flicked a mock salute and rode away. Sighing, Jess finished her cigarette and began the trek back to the dorm room.

When the building came into view, her good mood faded away. If only she didn't have the perky roommate to put up with.

With a sigh, she pushed open the door to the shared room. Emily looked up from her book, but said nothing. Crossing to the little sink, Jess brushed her teeth, changed into her sleeping attire of a long t-shirt, and then flicked off the overhead light.

"Excuse me, but I was reading." Emily's voice held a note of annoyance, and Jess smiled to herself in the darkness.

"And now you're not," she retorted.

A sigh carried across the room, followed by the sound of rummaging around in a drawer. There was a click, and a little book light came on. Jess should have known Emily would be a prepared little Girl Scout. She rolled her eyes and turned to face the wall. Score one for the annoying blonde, but there was always tomorrow. She would just have to be more creative.

*a*s Chad turned off the motorcycle and dismounted, his mind revisited the raven-haired girl. With one side or her hair shaved and a nose ring, she was definitely trying to portray a tough exterior, but though he hadn't spoken with her long, he had sensed a sadness in her eyes. It was the same sadness he often saw reflected in his mirror, and he wondered what hurt resided in her past.

He hadn't always been into analyzing people. When he'd first come to Texas Tech, it had been to major in Mechanical Engineering, but two years ago his younger brother had been killed in a school shooting and everything had changed. Chad had turned from mechanical engineering to psychology, desperate for answers as to why people acted the way they did. He still wasn't sure what he planned to do with the degree, but if he could save even one person from going through the fate Kyle had or dealing with the aftermath as he was having to, it would be worth it.

He flicked on the light of his small apartment-like dorm room and sighed. The benefit of being a Junior was that he could live in West Village, but as he'd opted for a single apartment this year, the downfall was that loneliness often crept in.

Chad thought about calling one of his "hook-ups," but it would be his first day teaching tomorrow. His time would be better spent making sure he was prepared as he needed to keep this job to afford his housing. Besides, he was rather tired of last year's offerings. Hopefully, this year would wield some new and exciting flavors.

Again the girl from earlier flashed into his mind. She had been attracted to him. He had seen it in her face before she turned away, and she might be interesting. At least interesting enough for some good times. It was too bad he hadn't gotten her number. Tech was a big campus and the chances he would see her again were small.

He pushed the thoughts of her from his mind and focused on arranging his papers and rehearsing his lecture. Tomorrow would be soon enough to focus on finding new women to add to his list.

CHAPTER 2

*J*ess woke to the sun streaming in the window. Yawning, she stretched and sneaked a glance at the other side of the room. Emily's bed was made, but she was nowhere to be seen. A smile played across Jess's face as she realized she had the room to herself, for a bit at least. Who knew when the blonde would be back.

Ugh, she hated school, not because she was bad at it, but because it bored her. The only good thing about college was the ability to take afternoon classes. Not being a morning person, Jess rarely functioned well before her first cup of coffee.

What did she have today? Closing her eyes, she pictured her schedule - just Psychology and Math. Neither were her favorite subject, but she had taken Psychology hoping she'd learn to analyze people. Math, on the other hand, was just one of those stupid required classes in college. She knew basic math, enough to balance a checkbook and pay bills. Since math didn't change, anything beyond that seemed useless.

Rolling out of bed, Jess padded to the little cloudy mirror. The non-shaved side of her hair looked like it had been in a windstorm. She yanked a brush through it, hoping to tame it a little, but the result wasn't much better. With a shrug, she picked up her toothbrush, and after brushing her teeth, she pulled on a pair of black shorts and a matching tank top. Then she grabbed her books and a granola bar and headed downstairs.

Though the dorm didn't have a full cafeteria, a coffee pot sat on the table by the main desk, so she stopped to fill up a Styrofoam cup. It was strong, but not awful, and it would do until she could get a better cup.

As she pushed open the main doors, Jess's skin prickled at the change in temperature. The dorm stayed at a constant temperature of seventy-two, cool but not cold. However, the blazing sun outside made Jess glad she opted for shorts. She took a left towards the Psychology building.

One of the blander buildings on campus, the Psychology building was a giant brick rectangle with a myriad of windows. Jess pushed open the door and turned left to find room 110. The wooden door opened to a large lecture hall filled with rows of seats—almost like a movie theater except each seat contained a pull-out desk top on the side and was made of hard plastic instead of the comfy foam you found in the theater.

Jess took a seat at the back. She hated having people behind her, analyzing her, criticizing her. A handful of other people sat in the back row, and a few heads dotted the closer rows, but the room was mostly empty. Turning her wrist, she checked her watch to see ten minutes still remained until the class started. For once, she was early.

The door continued to open and more people filed in, filling the room, but none of them looked like someone Jess wanted to talk to. Slouching down in the chair, she pulled out her phone and aimlessly flicked through social media posts. She wasn't sure why she still bothered as she had no one she kept in touch with, having burned all her old bridges when she left Paducah.

A few minutes later, the door down front opened, and a dark-haired man entered. He laid a satchel on the table, and when he looked up, Jess's breath caught in her throat. Chad, the handsome biker from the night before, stood down front. She sat up straighter in her seat and wished for once she'd sat in the front row. This had just gotten interesting.

"I'm Chad Michaels, and I'm your TA for this class. Dr. Warren will rarely be here, though you can catch him in his office during office hours. I'm passing around your syllabus. Read it, live it, love it. Hopefully you already purchased the required reading because you need to read the first five chapters before our next meeting."

Chad continued speaking as he handed a stack of papers to the first row, but all Jess focused on was the sweet melody of his voice. She'd been attracted to him before, but now that he was basically the instructor, her desire for him increased.

As class ended, she realized she couldn't recall a single thing he had said after his name. She would have to hope everything he'd said was in the syllabus. Pretending to gather her books, Jess waited until most of the students left before ambling down front.

"Well, I didn't know I'd be seeing you again so soon," she said, turning on her most seductive voice and tucking a strand of dark hair behind her ear.

He looked up and narrowed his eyes, obviously trying to place her face. Then they widened as recognition flashed in them and he nodded, "Ah, Lighter Girl. You have time to get a smoke now?"

Jess shrugged, feigning indifference. No need to let him know how attracted she was to him. Though she had math in twenty minutes, getting to know Chad seemed a little more important at the moment. She flashed what she hoped was a sexy smile, lowered her lids, and said, "Sure. Why not."

He packed up his bag, and they headed out the side door. A shadow covered this side of the building, but it wasn't much cooler. They each pulled out a cigarette, and Jess produced her lighter.

"How long have you been a TA?" she asked him, trying to start up a conversation.

"It's my first year. You can't be a TA until your Junior year." He took a deep puff, and Jess forced her eyes away from his lips.

"Oh." *Stupid,* Jess thought, *stop asking stupid questions.*

"Where are you from?" he asked.

"A little Podunk town, Paducah. How about you?"

A tiny smile tugged at the corners of his mouth. "California originally, but when we moved out here, we lived in Seminole. It's a small town too." He finished his cigarette and then glanced at his watch. "I have to get to an appointment, but give me your phone."

The request took her off guard, but Jess pulled out her phone and handed it over. Chad's finger moved deftly over the screen. Then he flashed a sexy smile and handed the phone back. "I put my cell number in there. Text me so I have your number too."

Jess grasped the phone and bit the inside of her lip to keep from smiling like an idiot. "I'll do that."

He flicked a wave and sauntered off, and she strolled to math class on cloud nine. She'd only be a little late, and she doubted anyone would even notice.

When Jess returned to the dorm room that afternoon, Emily was gone. Jess sat on her bed, pulled out her phone, and flicked to Chad's number. She was looking forward to using it in the next few days. Not right away, but soon. Had to play at least a little hard to get. She laid the phone down and glanced over at Emily's side of the room. The Bible Emily had been reading the night before lay on her nightstand. Jess didn't know why, but the desire to look inside it suddenly burned within her.

After glancing at the door, she crossed to Emily's bed, sat down, and grabbed the book. It was heavier than she'd expected. The black, textured cover held Emily's name embossed in gold in the bottom right corner. Emily Peters. As Jess opened the cover, the words "To Emily, Love Mom and Dad" mocked her. Had she ever had a mom and dad who truly loved her? She held no memory of her biological father, but she had once believed her mother loved her, until the latest step-father entered the picture.

Jess flipped a few pages in and read the headings: Reward for Obedience, Punishment for Disobedience... Well, that didn't sound inspiring. A few more flips: The Lord Calls Samuel, The Philistines Capture the Ark. Who were the Philistines? She didn't remember them from History class. Another flip landed her in Psalms 106. "Praise the Lord. Give thanks to the Lord, for he is good; his love endures forever." Jess snorted. She had never felt any love from God if he was even real.

An exasperated sigh tumbled out of her lips. Nothing amazing resided in there, just a bunch of history and nonsense. Exactly what she thought. She slammed the book shut, tossing it back on Emily's nightstand before heading out to grab food.

⁂

"Well, how was the first day," Dr. Warren asked as Chad entered the small office. Dr. Warren was nearing seventy with a full head of white hair and matching bushy eyebrows.

"It went pretty well," Chad said. "It's a large class." He didn't mention the fact he was attracted to one of the students. Even though a TA and not the actual professor, he was pretty sure a relationship would be frowned upon.

"I have no doubt in your ability," Dr. Warren said. "If I had, I wouldn't have asked you to TA for me." Dr. Warren's tenured status allowed him the option to have a TA teach one or two of his classes so he could focus on the students seeking a doctorate. He had asked Chad to take over the Intro to Psychology class at the end of the previous school year.

"Thank you, sir. I won't let you down," Chad said, "but I better be getting back to my room. I have a lot of work from business class this morning. I'll see you on Wednesday." Chad had put most of his classes on Tuesday and Thursday when he didn't have to teach, but his business classes were only offered on Mondays and Wednesdays so he'd had to schedule them before his teaching.

Dr. Warren absentmindedly waved a hand at Chad as he returned to whatever he had been working on when Chad walked in.

As he crossed the campus back to his dorm, Chad's eyes took in the beautiful women in their crop tops and short shirts. Lubbock's warm weather and long summers often meant shorter shorts and tighter tops as women tried to escape the heat. Not that Chad minded the view, but today his mind kept returning to Jess. Maybe it was the look in her eyes, but something about her made him want to get to know her better.

🏵

*E*mily was in the room when Jess returned that evening. She glanced up from the book she was reading and asked, "How was your first day?"

Jess glared at her. Did the girl honestly think they were going to be friends? "Why do you care?" she mumbled in response before pulling out headphones and jamming them in her ears. In reality, she wished someone did care. Other than the meeting with Chad this morning, Jess had barely spoken with anyone. The truth was, she was lonely, but there was no way she would tell Emily that. She didn't need her making any more of a false effort to be friends when they had nothing in common.

"Hey."

The blonde's voice cut through her music, but Jess tried to ignore her, hoping she would leave her alone to wallow in her loneliness and dream of Chad, but she was persistent.

"Hey," she said again, tapping Jess's shoulder.

With a sigh, Jess pulled out one earphone and looked up at her. "What?" Her voice was flat and emotionless.

"I'm about to do my prayer time. I wanted to know if you'd like to join me or if I could pray for you in some way."

Her brown eyes appeared sincere as she waited for an answer, but Jess was unable to do more than blink at her. No one had ever offered to pray for her. Of course, since Jess didn't believe prayer worked, it had never mattered.

"No, I'm fine," she finally managed and shoved her earphone back in, but as the blonde shrugged and returned to her bed, Jess turned the volume down on her music. She wanted to hear what her prayer sounded like. Even though her mother had gone to church and claimed to be a Christian, Jess had never heard her pray.

The girl knelt in front of her bed and bowed her head. Her voice was soft as if speaking more to herself, and Jess had to strain to make out the words. "Dear Lord, I thank you for the blessings you have provided me. Thank you for the opportunity to make new friends. You alone know the desires of our hearts, and I pray that you will touch Jess's heart and grant the desires of her heart. Lord also be with Jared. Give him peace and protect Nikki wherever she is. I pray for a hedge of protection on all of us this year so we may be examples for you and show love and grace as you do. Amen."

When she finished, the girl pushed herself up and sat down at the desk where she opened a large textbook probably to do homework. Slowly, Jess turned the music back up, but the girl's words ricocheted around in her head. She'd prayed for Jess even though she hadn't asked her to and yet not for herself. Wasn't that what Christians used prayer for? To ask God to give them things? Yet Emily had prayed for others and only asked for to be a good example to others. A grey cloud of doubt filled Jess's head. Could it be possible she had the wrong idea about Emily?

*E*mily was gone when Jess woke the next morning, so she figured it was time to put the tactics she had brainstormed into place. After listening to Emily pray the previous night and wrestling with feelings she didn't want most of the night, Jess decided there was no way she was as good as she seemed.

After dressing and brushing her teeth, Jess scattered piles of clothes around the room. Then, she opened a few of her granola bars and tossed the wrappers on Emily's bed. It wasn't much, but Jess had more planned for the afternoon when she returned. Grabbing her bag and chomping on a granola bar, she headed off to Biology, hoping it would be less boring than math had been the day before. Maybe, if she were lucky, she'd have another hot teacher, like Chad, to stare at.

*D*isgust flooded Jess's veins when she opened the door to the room that afternoon. Emily had picked up all the mess and folded the clothes, placing them neatly on Jess's bed. She now sat calmly at her desk working on something.

"Don't touch my stuff again," Jess spat at her, slamming the door and crossing to the bed to knock the perfectly piled clothes over. She pushed them with such intensity that some flew off the bed and landed on the floor.

"Don't leave such a mess, and I won't have to." Her voice was matter-of-fact, and her eyes never lifted from her book.

"Don't tell me what to do; you're not my mother," Jess snapped. How could she be so calm? It was infuriating. She picked up a few articles still on the bed, walked to the middle of the room, and purposefully dropped them.

Emily looked up and said with a sigh, "No, but I'm trying to be your friend. Look, I talked to the RA, but all the rooms are full. Even if I wanted to go, there's no place, so we are stuck with each other for the semester at least. We don't have to like each other, but we could try to get along."

"Or you could find a place off campus to live." Time for the next step. Jess opened the window and pulled out her pack of cigarettes. Clicking the lighter, she lit up and puffed. Though most of the smoke was going outside, she knew at least a little was seeping back into the room.

Emily coughed. "Excuse me, but there's no smoking in here. You need to take that outside."

"It's a free country," Jess said. "If you don't like it, you can leave."

Emily took a deep breath and forced a smile on her face. "I already told you I can't. I can't afford an apartment. My scholarship is paying for my dorm room." She stared at Jess a moment, then closed her eyes. Her lips moved though the words she was saying were too quiet for Jess to make out.

"What are you doing?" Jess asked. *Is she putting a curse on me?* Jess saw no voodoo doll, but she would put nothing past religious nut jobs.

Her eyelids opened, and her brown eyes met Jess's in a piercing gaze. "I'm praying for you. For us, really. We will have to live together at least this semester, and I can't make peace alone, so I'm praying for patience and for guidance."

A loud snort escaped Jess's lips. "Yeah, well good luck with that." She finished the cigarette and flicked the butt out the window. Music and messes hadn't worked, smoking hadn't worked, that left men. She would see Chad tomorrow when she had Psychology again. She would just have to work her magic on him.

CHAPTER 3

*J*ess's eyes snapped open. Something wasn't right. It was too bright. Glancing down at her watch, she uttered a quick curse before bounding out of bed. She had overslept and would be late. Any other day, it wouldn't have mattered, but today was Psychology again, and she didn't want to miss a minute of staring at beautiful Chad.

A quick look in the mirror revealed an acceptable package. So, after a quick finger-comb of her hair, she hastily brushed her teeth, grabbed her books, and ran out the door. Though she didn't want to be out of breath when she arrived, she needed to walk at a quick pace or she would miss the first few minutes. As Jess trekked across the campus to the Psychology building, she wondered if it had been long enough that she could use Chad's number now. The loneliness was settling in, and some male company seemed liked the perfect remedy.

A glance at her wrist showed two minutes till class started. Jess quickened her pace and slid into a seat just seconds before Chad walked into the room. Taking a deep breath to calm her thudding heart, she smiled at him. She had chosen a seat closer to the front this time to see him better and so he would be sure to see her.

As he lectured, Jess tried to take notes, but her pen found its way to her mouth and her mind kept removing Chad's button-down shirt and revealing a six-pack of abs she longed to run her fingers over. Dropping her eyes, she tried to think of something else, anything else, to keep her obvious attraction from blazing like a marquee across her face.

The minutes seemed to both fly by and crawl at the same time. After her fourteenth glance at the clock, she began to fidget in her seat. Why couldn't the minute hand move faster? Jess wanted to catch up with Chad after class like she had on Monday.

When the class finally ended, Jess took her time gathering her things, hoping not to look too obvious. The door closed behind the last student, and she bounded down the front two rows and smiled at him. "Care for a smoke today?"

He looked up at her, his eyes traveling her body and taking in her tight shorts and black crop top. Jess was glad she had the figure to get away with them. "Actually, I've got the afternoon off," he smiled, "how would you like a private study session?"

She licked her lips, knowing exactly what he meant with his innuendo. His mind was certainly on the same track as hers. "I could definitely use one. I keep getting distracted because the teacher is so hot."

"Is that right?" he asked, matching her seductive tone. "Well then, your place or mine?"

Jess paused for a moment because she didn't know Emily's schedule yet. While she wanted to annoy Emily, she also wanted to make sure this happened. If Emily were already in the room, it might not. "Let's do your place. I have the roommate from Hades, and I don't know if she'll be there or not."

He chuckled. "Yeah, I remember those days. So glad to have a single now."

"Yeah, they were supposed to get me one, but some idiot in their office screwed up."

"All right, come on." He locked the door, and Jess walked with him out into the sunshine. Math would have to take a back seat today, but she figured that was okay as she would be practicing a little addition anyway.

Chad didn't speak on the trek to his building, but Jess didn't care. Visions of what was coming filled her head and sent her pulse racing. As they entered the building, Chad grabbed his mail and headed up the stairs. Jess hurried behind him. He stopped outside room 212 and pulled out his keys. Jess swallowed the emotion in her throat; this was really going to happen! After opening the door, he held out his arm in a gesture for her to go first.

His room was like a small apartment. A private bathroom was on the left and a small kitchenette on the right. The main hallway opened to a living room with a door off to the left. A big screen TV hung on the wall of the living room, and a battered brown couch sat across from it. A small table was to the left of the couch.

"Just drop your bag there," he said pointing at the couch, before turning to another small table in the kitchenette.

Jess tossed her bag on the couch and turned around to come face to face with Chad's chest. He had dropped his mail and then closed the distance between them when she had been facing the other way. His arms wrapped around her waist and his eyes bore into her soul. Jess could get lost in those blue depths.

He dropped his head, and his lips crushed hers. Jess eagerly responded, following his lead as he walked her toward the door she had noticed earlier. Pushing it open with his back, Chad pulled Jess into the room and closed the door.

❀

"*W*ell, you certainly know how to make a girl's first week enjoyable," Jess said, smiling up at Chad from the crook of his arm.

He returned her smile, but conflicting emotions battled in his head. He had thought a romp with Jess would be just like every other fling he'd had for the last two years, but when he'd looked into her eyes, he'd felt something. Something like he used to feel when he dated before Kyle's death. And it scared him.

"Yeah, well, always happy to lend my services," he said. His hand traced a slow pattern on her shoulder as he thought about what to do.

He needed to process and find a way to shut those feelings off again. "I should tell you though, I don't do relationships."

"I wasn't asking you to," she said, but he saw the flicker of hurt cross her face. A small part of him wanted to take his words back, but he was not a relationship guy. At least not since the death of his brother. Instead, he did what felt safest. He pushed her further away.

"Good," he said, "because while I'd love to do this again sometime, right now I need to get some work done." Chad stared at her, forcing his face to remain impassive.

A flush of embarrassment crawled across Jess's face. "Oh, right, okay, sure." She rolled out of the bed and grabbed her clothes from the floor, pulling them on as fast as she could. "I'll uh just get out of your hair I guess."

"Thanks for understanding." Chad rolled out of bed and pulled on a pair of shorts. "If you want to get together again, call me, and if I don't hear from you before then, I'll see you next week in class."

"Sure, sounds good," Jess said, but Chad could tell she was forcing the brightness. Still, it was better this way. He needed to be upfront with her and let her know he was only looking for fun. He walked her to the front door, planted a quick kiss goodbye on her lips, and ushered her into the hallway.

As the door closed behind her, he leaned against it. What was going on with him? He never had feelings for the women he let come over, so why was he feeling something for Jess?

Across the room, his cell phone rang, dispelling thoughts of Jess for the moment, but as he picked up the phone and looked at the screen, he sighed. It was his mother. Though he didn't feel like talking to her, he couldn't ignore her call. She was hurting too and lonely with his father working all day, Kyle gone, and Kendra in school all day.

"Hi, Mom," he said as he clicked the answer call button.

"Hello, Son. How was your first week of teaching?" Her voice held the same false brightness he had detected in Jess's voice a few minutes ago.

"It was all right, I guess. It's a big class, so it should keep me busy."

"Have you made any new friends?"

Chad rolled his eyes. "Mom, it's college, not grade school."

"Sorry, I mean have you met anyone interesting?"

Just Jess he thought, but he wasn't telling his mother that. Though she probably suspected his philandering ways, she had never asked and he had never offered the information.

"It's the first week, Mom. I've been a little busy with instructing and keeping up with my own classes."

"Oh, well," she paused, "have you found a church?"

Chad sighed. They had this same discussion every time she called. "I'm not going to church, Mom. I told you that."

"It wasn't God's fault, Chad."

"Mom, we've been through this. Maybe you can still worship a God who lets your son get killed, but I can't. Look, I'm glad you called, but I need to get ready for a test on Monday." It wasn't the truth, but Chad couldn't handle any more guilt about not attending church.

"Okay, Son. I'll be praying for you."

"Sure, Mom." As Chad hung up the phone, he wondered if he'd ever get past his hurt and anger.

❧

The door closed behind Jess, and a seed of disgust sprouted in her stomach. Why did she do this to herself? She knew nothing about Chad other than he was good looking, and yet she'd jumped right into bed with him.

A wave of anger boiled within her veins as she thought back to her most recent stepfather. He was the reason she did this. She hadn't been able to stop him from taking advantage of her, but once she'd found she could use sex to gain control in other relationships, the destructive pattern she'd been in the last few years had begun.

Unbidden, her thoughts wandered to Stephanie and Jess wondered if she were okay. Stephanie was technically Jess's cousin, but when Stephanie's parents died in a car crash, Jess's mother had gained custody. While Jess had no love for the girl, she hadn't wanted Jim to turn his attention on her. He was certainly sick enough to do just that. She'd tried to warn Stephanie, but like Jess's mother, the girl hadn't believed her.

"You're wrong, you know? Jim would never do that," Stephanie said, barging into Jess's room. *"He's been such a great father to us."*

"I know you don't want to believe it," Jess said, *"but he does. That miscarriage I had? The baby was Jim's."*

Stephanie narrowed her eyes into slits and shook her head. "I don't believe you. You're obviously sleeping around to make yourself feel pretty. It's not our fault you couldn't narrow the father down."

Jess flinched at the hateful words. While she had begun sleeping around, it was only to erase the memory of carrying her stepfather's baby, even if only for a few weeks. "You don't know what you're talking about," Jess shot back, *"but I'll be leaving for college soon and he'll have no one else. Do you think this was easy for me to tell you? I didn't ask for this. If you won't believe me, at least keep your guard up. Don't be alone with him and try to keep mom sober."*

"You're disgusting. I'll be glad when you're gone," Stephanie said and stomped out of the room.

With a sigh, Jess pushed the memory away and headed down the hallway. Jim was no longer her problem. She'd closed that chapter of her life and had no intention of ever going back.

Emily looked up from her Bible as Jess entered the dorm room. Her mouth opened as if to speak, but then she closed it and dropped her eyes back to her Bible.

Thank God for small miracles. Jess grabbed her headphones from the bed and turned up the music. The pounding beats made it impossible to think, which was exactly what she needed.

CHAPTER 4

riday was uneventful. As class ended, a part of Jess wanted to dial Chad's number to see if he was available. The other part of her still remembered the used feeling that enveloped her as he practically chased her from his room Wednesday. No, she might not have much dignity left, but she had enough not to call him this soon.

Jess didn't even stop at the front desk to check her mailbox as she entered the dorm. No one wrote to her, and her cell phone bill wasn't due yet. Though she didn't regret leaving home, she missed having someone to talk to. It wasn't like her mother had really listened in the last few years, but she had still been a warm body to throw words at. Some days, when Jim worked late and Stephanie wasn't around, they had watched movies together or baked cookies like old times.

She supposed she could have talked to Emily, but they had nothing in common besides being here on scholarship. No way could Jess tell her about Chad. Anyone who read their Bible and prayed as much as Emily did had no knowledge of lusty desires.

With a sigh, Jess stuck her key in the door and turned the knob, waiting for a barrage of questions about her day, but the room lay silent. Emily's bed was made but empty. Everything on her side of the room sat neatly in its place, as she always left it, but something was off.

Jess closed her eyes and pictured Emily's side of the room the way she had last seen it. The picture in her head scanned from left to right and when it reached Emily's nightstand, Jess's eyes popped open. Yes, there where her Bible usually sat, was an empty space. Since Jess doubted someone snuck into their room just to steal a Bible, she decided Emily must be off at some religious get-together.

As she dropped her bag on the bed, the desire to call Chad flared again. They would have the room to themselves, and if lucky, Emily might return while Chad was here, get offended, and leave for good.

Jess pulled her phone out of her pocket and swiped the screen, but as she clicked on the green phone icon, she paused. Calling today would make her appear desperate and nothing turned a guy off faster than desperation. In fact, the only thing worse than the used/discarded feeling was the feeling of rejection. No, she could wait a few more days to dial his number. Play a little hard to get. She shoved the phone back in her pocket, plopped down on the bed, and punched the power button for the TV remote.

The TV hung on the wall, an older model that worked only because the dorm supplied free cable. Jess flicked past the news and the evening game shows, but on a Friday night not much else was on, unless she wanted to watch reruns of Full House or The Golden Girls, which she didn't.

She flicked the TV off. There was always YouTube on her laptop, but Jess didn't feel like watching silly videos either. That left homework. There had been little assigned - being the first week of school - but she needed to catch up in the math class she had skipped. Jess pulled out the book and the syllabus, and after scanning for the missed assignment, she opened the book and tried to focus on the problems.

After reading the same problem three times, she closed the book and tapped her fingers on the cover. Entertainment! That's what she needed. This was a college town; surely a club existed near the campus.

Pushing the book aside, Jess stood up and grabbed her keys. After shoving her license, a credit card, and a twenty in the pocket of her shorts, she headed out the door, locking it behind her.

A mousy brunette with her face shoved in a book manned the information desk on the first floor. Though she looked like she could use it, Jess doubted she had ever stepped foot in a club, but her job was to know crap, so hopefully she had received good training.

"Hey," Jess said, tapping the desk to get her attention. The girl's eyes flicked up, but the book remained open, her index finger marking her stopping point. "Are there any local clubs around here that allow under twenty-ones?"

Her eyebrow inched up her forehead. "You have a phone?" she asked.

"Yeah."

"Then Google it." Her attention returned to her book.

"Thanks a lot," Jess said, though the words dripped with sarcasm. How that girl still had a job was beyond her. They must be desperate for help. Jess dug her cell phone from her pocket and pulled up a browser.

There were three clubs listed, but only one allowed underage entrance on Friday nights. The Hangout it was then. After plugging the address into her phone, Jess headed that direction.

The Hangout was a large brick building that looked like it had been a warehouse at some point. A large, muscled man with tattoos on his biceps, up his neck, and on his bald head stood at the door. Whether he was or not, he exuded a tough exterior and with his beefy arms crossed, he looked like a solid wall.

"ID please," he said as she approached.

Jess dug in her back pocket and pulled out her license. She no longer had her car, having sold it to have money for college expenses until she could get a job, but her license was still valid though rarely used now.

He perused it, flipped it over, and then handed it back. "It's a ten-dollar cover."

Jess nodded and pulled open the solid metal door. Another man, much smaller and wearing Buddy Holly type glasses stood behind a counter. She handed a twenty to him and he slid a ten-dollar bill back which she shoved in her pocket before scanning the room.

The room was large and open with a bar on the left and a dance floor in the middle, encased by a railing that separated it from the tables around the outside. Few people were on the dance floor yet as it was relatively early, but the music was blaring and lights lit up the floor.

Jess walked over to the bar and ordered a Diet Coke. She lounged on a barstool while she waited. A few minutes later, a glass slid in front of her and she sipped it as she watched the few people on the dance floor.

A girl with long brown dreads appeared lost in her own world, swaying slightly to the music while a chunky boy tried to gain the attention of the two blonde girls on the floor. They were adept at ignoring him, turning their back to him whenever he approached while making it appear they simply danced to the beat.

"You a people watcher?"

Jess turned to the bartender who leaned against the counter watching her watch the dance floor.

"Sometimes," she said with a shrug. "They're all basically the same though."

His brows knit together, "What do you mean?"

"I mean we all put on a show to get people to like us, but then our real colors come out and we just end up hurting each other."

He let out a low whistle. "Well, that's a very pessimistic view of the world. You seem a little young to be so jaded."

"It is what it is." She finished the drink and pushed it back to him. He had no idea what was in her past nor the right to judge her. "Have a good night." Suddenly, she didn't want to stay here with the intuitive bartender and the sparse crowd.

"Anytime," he hollered as she walked away. "I'm here every weekend."

*C*had looked at Jess's number in his phone. After the long week, he could use another release, but he wasn't sure he wanted to call her. Though he'd definitely enjoyed his time with her, he hadn't enjoyed the feelings she brought up in him. He wasn't looking for long-term. Long-term could lead to love and people you loved died. It was easier not to go near it.

No, he didn't need Jess. He needed a ride. Shoving his phone back in his pocket, he grabbed his helmet and headed downstairs.

The evening was perfect for a ride, clear and warm. He mounted the Harley and let the engine hum for a minute, enjoying the aggressive vibration of the engine. Then he pulled on his helmet, swung his leg over the bike, and released the brake.

The speed limit on campus was slow, but University Avenue loomed ahead and shortly beyond that - the interstate where he could ramp up past the speed limit. As he idled at the stoplight, a woman across the street caught his eye. He couldn't see her face, but her short shorts showed off long lean legs, and her shirt hugged her figure in all the right places. She looked like she enjoyed a good time.

When the light turned green, he turned her direction and pulled the bike up to the shoulder just behind her. He flipped up his visor. "Care for a ride?"

She turned and his smile froze on his face. It was Jess. What were the odds?

A sexy smile lit up her face. "Sure," she said. "I'm always up for a ride."

Who was Chad to deny fate? It obviously wanted them together tonight. He reached behind him and grabbed the spare helmet he kept attached to the back of the bike for just such occasions.

She took it from him, smoothing her raven locks back as she pulled it on.

"I don't have a spare coat," he said. Though the night was warm, the breeze would get chilly as they rode.

"That's all right, you can warm me up later." As she swung up behind him and laced her arms around his waist, the scent of some exotic perfume wafted over his shoulder. When he was sure she was secure, he throttled the bike, and they roared off into the setting sun.

CHAPTER 5

*J*ess's eyes snapped open at the presence of someone beside her in the bed. Chad's stubbled chin filled her view and she smiled. Then the memory of their last encounter crashed back in. He had let her stay the night, but without a doubt he would ask her to leave as soon as he woke and she wanted to avoid being dismissed again.

As quietly as possible, Jess slid out of the bed and dressed. With a final glance Chad's direction, she slipped out of the room. At least this way, she kept the power.

"Early breakfast?" Emily asked as Jess entered the room.

"Good night," Jess answered with a smile, deciding to make Emily as uncomfortable as possible. "I guess you did too since you were out late yourself. At least you weren't back by the time I left."

"I did," Emily said with a sweet smile, ignoring the innuendo. "Friday nights I have a Bible study with some friends. You could join us some week if you'd like."

"I'd rather get teeth pulled," Jess returned, crossing to the sink to grab her shower items. Of course Emily was off doing something religious. Did the girl do nothing else with her life?

After a quick shower, Jess returned to the room and dressed. It was

Saturday, and she had nothing to do. Perhaps it was time to find a job. Not that she wanted to work, but the money from her savings and the sale of her car would only last so long.

Jess smoothed her hair down and headed out the door. Plenty of businesses lined the campus. Surely one of them would be hiring.

The first shop she entered was a bookstore that also sold Tech merchandise. Jess made her way to the back counter where a girl about her age worked the counter. Unfortunately, she was clearly a preppy cheerleader type. Biting the inside of her lip, Jess forced a smile on her face.

"Hi, is there an application I could fill out?" Jess asked when she reached the counter.

The blonde cocked her head and flashed a smile that oozed pity. "Oh, I'm sorry. We aren't hiring right now. If you have a resume, I'd be happy to leave it with the manager."

Resume. Of course, why hadn't she thought to bring a resume? Maybe because she didn't have much work experience. She'd worked her Junior and Senior year at the one and only gas station in Paducah, but that was the extent of her job history and it wasn't impressive.

"Um, I forgot to bring one with me, but can I drop it by later?" Jess asked.

"Sure," the girl said.

Jess received the same story at the next five places she tried and two hours later, she returned to the dorm tired and worried. If she couldn't find a job soon, she didn't know what she would do.

"Hey," Jess cleared her throat - She couldn't believe she was about to ask Emily for help - "Do you know of any place that is hiring? I need to get a job."

Emily looked up from the book she was reading and studied Jess. "My friend Jared works at the Student Union. I think he said they were hiring. Do you want me to check with him?"

"Yeah, I guess that'd be cool," Jess said with a shrug. What was with this girl? She had been nothing but rude to Emily and she was still willing to help.

"Okay, hang on."

As Emily tapped out a message on her phone, the question that had been burning in Jess's brain burst forth. "Why are you willing to help me?"

She flashed a small smile. "Look, I won't say you've been super easy to live with, but I try to find the good in everyone. I don't know what pain you've dealt with in your past, but I know that God can heal it if you ask him."

"I appreciate your help in finding a job, but I don't need your sales pitch on God," Jess said.

"Fair enough," Emily said with a shrug, dropping the subject. A moment later her phone chimed. "Okay, he's there now and said he can get you a face to face with the director."

"Uh, sure," Jess said. "That would be great." She followed Emily out of the room, surprised that she had been willing to drop the topic of God so quickly. Emily seemed different from the other Christians Jess had met. They had tried to push God on her at every turn and one had even told her she was signing her ticket to Hell if she didn't convert. What made Emily so different?

The campus was bustling with activity as they made their way to the Student Union building. Games of Frisbee and flag football filled the open spaces and individuals lounged against tree trunks reading in the shade.

Emily pulled open the doors of the student union, and the quiet engulfed Jess. Due to the nice weather, most people were outside and not sitting in buildings. With a purposeful stride, Emily led the way to the cafe where evidently Jared worked.

The cafe too was quiet with only a few people seated at tables around the room, but as they entered, an average-looking male with brown hair approached.

"Hey, Emily," he said before turning to face Jess. "Jess?" he asked, holding out his hand.

She nodded and shook his hand. "Yeah."

He glanced at Emily with a raised brow.

"What she means to say," Emily said, shooting a pointed look Jess's direction, "is thank you for helping her out."

"Right," Jess mumbled. "Thank you for helping me out." Few

people in her life had offered such kindness, and she still wasn't sure how to process the feelings battling within her.

"Anything for a friend of Emily's," he said.

Jess opened her mouth to correct him, but thought better of it and smiled instead. Emily had probably already told him about her and therefore he was either being sarcastic or trying to be nice, and she didn't want to know if it was the former.

"Okay, well I leave you in good hands," Emily said. "I'll be praying you get the job."

Before Jess could say anything, Emily walked away, leaving her standing awkwardly with Jared.

"All right, well Darla is probably in her office. Follow me and I'll take you there."

Darla was a short, curvy woman with dark hair and red lips. She looked up from her desk as Jared knocked on the door.

"Hey, Darla," he said. "This is my friend Jess. She's looking for a job. Do we have anything open?"

"I don't know," she said with a smile, "but if Jared vouches for you, I'll take a look. Come on in."

Jess followed Jared inside, feeling like a charlatan as she sat beside him. They weren't friends; she had just met him. Why was he putting his name on the line for her?

"Let's see," Darla said, clicking the buttons on her mouse. "Well, I have an opening in food service in the cafe."

"Um." Jess needed a job, but she wasn't sure she could work in food service.

Darla laughed. "Yeah, it's not for everyone. Hmm, let's see. Well, the only other thing I have is a mail clerk position. You'd pick up the mail, sort it by departments, and then deliver it. There might be light filing as well. It's only ten hours a week though."

It was not her dream job, but Jess had no desire to return home to beg for money nor did she feel like losing her cell phone for non-payment or starving. Plus, the job sounded solitary, her specialty. "Thank you, I think it would be fine. Is there an application?"

Darla smiled and slid a piece of paper across the desk. "The application is merely a formality. I do have to run a background check, but I'm willing to take a chance on you."

Jess squirmed in her seat, feeling a smidgen of guilt for the false image Darla had of her, but she needed this job, and though she had plenty of other faults, she was reliable. Quickly, Jess scribbled down her information and passed the sheet back to Darla.

After taking a copy of her license, Darla shook Jess's hand. "I should have the background check back by Monday afternoon, so how about we plan to start on Tuesday? If something comes up on your report that would affect your employment, I'll call you Monday evening."

"That sounds great," Jess agreed. There was plenty of bad in her past, but it had all been done *to* her, and though she had technically broken the law drinking and smoking before she was legally old enough, she had never been caught.

As Jess followed Jared out of the office, her curiosity got the better of her, and she grasped his arm. "Why did you do this for me? You don't even know me, and I haven't been very nice to Emily."

His kind eyes studied her face. "I know, Emily talked a little about you last night at Bible study, but she also said you needed help and that's what we are here to do."

"You're one too," Jess said as the realization dawned on her.

"If you mean a believer," he said with a chuckle, "yeah I am."

"Well, thanks," Jess said.

Jess spent the rest of Saturday trying to sort through her feelings of confusion. Emily was like no one she had ever met, and though she'd only met Jared the one time, he appeared to be just like Emily. The two of them were calling into question every judgement Jess had made about Christians.

By evening, she wanted a distraction. Her hand reached for her phone to call Chad, but she froze before dialing. She had just seen him last night. Would he consider this too soon? With a sigh, she put the phone down and opened her laptop, but after a few minutes of scrolling aimlessly, she closed the lid and grabbed her phone again. It might be too soon, but Jess needed to get her mind off Emily and Chad was the only way she knew out to do it.

"I only have a few hours," he said over the phone. "I have plans later."

His words cut like a knife, reminding her that she was nothing more than a release for him, but she was too confused to care.

"That's fine," she shot back. "I have plans too."

Fifteen minutes later, Chad was in her room and five minutes after that, they were in her bed. As soon as his lips touched hers, Jess's confusion flew out the window. For the moment, her thoughts were consumed with his chiseled body and luscious lips. That is until the door opened.

"What are you doing?" Emily gasped from the doorway. "This is my room too. You can't do this here!"

"Actually, she can," Chad spoke up.

"I don't need to hear from you," Emily said, turning angry eyes on him.

Jess had never seen Emily angry, and after her help earlier this afternoon, Jess suddenly felt awful.

"I'm going to get dinner," Emily said, focusing her angry eyes back on Jess. "I want him gone when I get back."

The door slammed behind Emily, and Jess turned to Chad. "Maybe you should go."

"Yeah, whatever, the mood is ruined anyway and you're right. Your roommate is a piece of work."

Jess shrugged, unwilling to agree with him but not wanting to explain her change of heart.

As they dressed, an enormous guilt descended on Jess's shoulders. She often felt used and disgusted with herself after intimacy, but this was the first time she felt guilty. Was it simply because Emily had been so nice to her or was there some other reason?

"Next time my place, okay, babe?" Chad asked as he pulled open the door.

Jess nodded distractedly as she returned the quick kiss he planted on her before sauntering off down the hall. After the door closed behind Chad, Jess returned to her bed and curled her knees to her chest. Slowly her guilt turned to anger. Emily had no right to embarrass her like that, and she had no right to tell Jess she couldn't entertain a man in the room. She paid just as much for the room as Emily did.

By the time Emily returned, Jess had worked herself into quite a tizzy. "What's your problem?" she demanded when Emily entered.

She sighed as she dropped her wallet on the desk. "My problem is that I live here too. If you want to engage in that behavior that's your deal but I don't want to be a witness to it."

"You can't tell me I can't have him here," Jess spat back.

"That's true," she said calmly, "but I can ask you to respect my position, and I can tell you that he can't fill the void you have."

"You know nothing about me." Jess's hands curled into fists at her side, but she found herself angrier that Emily was right. How many times had she used sex to fill the feeling of emptiness inside her only to feel even emptier afterwards?

"Not for lack of trying," Emily said as she sat on her bed. "I've been trying to get to know you all week, but you keep pushing me away."

Jess wanted to hurl more hateful words at her, but none came to mind. With an angry huff, she shoved her earphones in and turned up the music. Emily was stirring up all kinds of feelings she didn't want to deal with.

❧

*A*s Chad left Jess's room, he wondered again what he was doing with a Freshman. He could have his choice of upperclassmen who didn't have uptight roommates, so why was he wasting his time with Jess? Except it didn't feel like a waste.

Every time he was with her, he felt.... different. Not so angry or something. He ran a hand across his jaw and shook his head. What was he thinking? The last thing he needed was to be falling for some woman. No, what he actually needed was a stiff drink. Something to clear his head.

Chad had never been much of a drinker, at least not until Kyle was killed. After Kyle's death, he had turned from prayer to the bottle.

Tequila didn't solve everything, but it dulled the ache of missing his brother.

Instead of heading toward his dorm, Chad turned toward University Avenue. Bruno's was open early and often had happy hour specials.

"What can I get for you, hon?" The bartender wore a tight fitting shirt with the words 'Liquor is my passion' across her ample chest.

"Shot of Tequila," Chad answered as he slid onto the upholstered barstool.

"Little early to be drinking, isn't it?" she asked as she turned to grab a glass.

"Not if you need to do thinking," he replied.

"I'm a good listener if you need ears," she said with a wide smile as she placed the glass in front of him.

Chad gave her another once over. She was pretty though she wore a little too much make up for his taste. However, she could probably distract him from Jess if he needed the distraction. "Thanks, I'll keep that in mind," he said with a wink as he picked up the glass and downed the shot.

CHAPTER 6

*J*ess was still processing Emily's behavior the next morning when she woke up. Emily lay in her bed reading from the Bible. Though Jess had seen nothing useful when she had glanced through it, something must keep drawing Emily back.

She bit her lip as she watched Emily. Even after the hateful words Jess had spewed at her, Emily had stayed calm and resolute. She seemed to believe in something rather than trying to be perfect or pushy like other religious people Jess had met.

"Why do you read the Bible every day?" The words escaped Jess's lips before she could stop them.

Emily glanced up, a look of surprise on her face. "Well, partly because God told us to, and partly because it gives me peace. If something is ever bothering me, I can usually find peace in the Bible."

"What do you mean? What peace? The only time I ever looked in one, I found it confusing."

She chuckled and nodded. "Yes, some parts of it are confusing, but it's also one of God's ways of communicating with us."

Jess chewed on her bottom lip, trying to understand what Emily meant. "You mean like I ask it a question and let it fall open and I'll find the answer?"

Emily shook her head. "No, it rarely works like that. It's not a Magic 8 ball. What I mean is, the more you read it, the more things will become clear to you. Sometimes you might read something that answers a question you have, but sometimes you'll read something about trusting people and a friend will tell you what you need to hear or you'll read something that makes you pray for something or someone."

She paused and pursed her lips. Then her face lit up. "Here, I've got an example. My parents wanted a baby, but for some reason, they couldn't conceive. One day, after praying with their pastor at church, they passed a woman heading into an abortion clinic. My mother blurted out to the woman that she wanted her baby, and the woman paused and turned to them. She told my parents she had been wrestling with the decision to have an abortion and had asked God for a sign not to do it. You see, my mother calling out to her was that sign, and my mother is a very shy person. Calling out like that wasn't in her normal nature at all. That's a pretty big coincidence, don't you think?" Emily's eyes danced as she finished the story.

Jess didn't know what to think, but she found herself wanting to believe it, to grasp onto something that might make sense in her messed-up life. "Were you that baby?"

"I was," Emily said.

"Didn't you ever hate your mother? I mean doesn't it bother you that she didn't want you?"

Emily shook her head. "No, don't you see? My mother thought she was trapped. She couldn't afford to have a baby, and the man had left tread marks in his departure from her life when she told him she was pregnant, so she felt all alone. I'm one of the lucky ones. My mother wrestled with the decision and prayed about it rather than rushing into it, and God saw fit to send my parents into her path. If they hadn't crossed paths that day, I wouldn't be here today."

"Does your faith really give you peace?" Jess asked. Though peace seemed foreign with her stained past, the thought was appealing.

"Yes, but just reading the Bible won't give you peace if you don't know Jesus. The peace comes from Him. Would you like me to tell you some about Him?"

Something deep inside Jess screamed 'yes,' but her pragmatic mind still wouldn't accept it. She felt the wall going back up. "No, I don't have time for stuff like that. I just wondered why you spent so much time reading."

Emily stared a moment longer, then she shrugged and turned back to her book.

"Hey, it's Sunday, shouldn't you be at church or something?"

Emily glanced down at her watch and frowned. "Yeah, I should be. Jared should be picking me up soon, but I guess he's running late."

"So that's your kryptonite?"

"Huh?" she asked.

"Your weakness. Going places alone? I wondered what it was. You seemed so perfect, but I knew there had to be something."

Emily smiled. "Well, first off, I am not perfect. I've never claimed to be. I'm just trying to do God's will, but yeah, walking alone into crowded places is pretty much my worst nightmare."

Jess regarded her for a second, feeling a little bad. "Well, I hope he shows up."

"You know, you could come with me," she said.

"I don't do church." Jess reached for her headphones. It was time to end this discussion.

"Have you tried?" she asked. "Look, all I'm saying is that whatever you're looking for, men probably can't supply. But Jesus? He can heal any pain you're feeling."

Jess snorted and rolled her eyes. "Yeah, Jesus has never been there for me. I've always had to look out for myself."

"Have you ever asked Him?"

She opened her mouth to reply but shut it again. A knock sounded at the door.

"That will be Jared," Emily said with a small sigh, "but I hope we can talk again soon." Her voice held a hint of sadness, as if she were almost considering staying to finish the conversation, but after a final glance Jess's direction, she grabbed her Bible and left.

Jess glared ice at the closed door. Emily didn't know her. But even as the words formed in her mind, she realized at least a bit of it was true. Jess didn't have any close friends, and whenever loneliness struck, she did turn to men for comfort, though the comfort only stayed while the men were there. Still, that didn't mean she was easy or whatever Emily had been implying.

Jess flopped back on the bed, but the silence inched in on her. She tapped her fingers against the mattress and tried to think of something to take her mind off the loneliness. She had some homework; maybe she could do that.

Pulling out her Psychology book, she opened it up to the chapter they were supposed to read, but the only thing popping up was Chad's face. With a sigh, Jess slammed the book shut, rolled over, and fished Chad's number out of the nightstand drawer.

Want to meet up? She tapped the message in the phone but then paused, trying to decide if she really wanted to send it. Desperation never looked good on anyone and they had gotten together Friday and Saturday. Her finger hovered over the send button, and ever so stealthily it tapped send. No taking it back now.

The seconds dragged on as Jess waited for the return bubble, and the screen timed out and darkened. With an agitated swipe, she turned it on again. How long did it take to reply? The phone beeped. *Sorry, can't right now* popped up on the screen. Disgust boiled in Jess's stomach, and she tossed the phone down. What good was a friend with benefits if he wasn't available when she needed to him? As the nervous energy built inside her, she paced back and forth in the room and decided she needed a smoke.

❀

C had pushed the guilt away as he sent the text dismissing Jess. She was lonely and he knew it, but seeing her three days in a row felt like starting a relationship and he couldn't do it. Besides, he needed to prepare for classes the next day.

The Psychology class had a quiz coming up that he needed to write, but as he sat down at his desk, Jess's face kept popping into his head. The sadness in her blue eyes and the feel of her skin against his plagued his mind. She reminded him of himself and he wondered what pain was in her past.

He reached for his cell phone and paused. If he texted Jess, he would be sending her all the wrong signals. No, it could wait. He could wait, but he couldn't deny he enjoyed being around her - more than he had any woman in the past two years.

Placing the cell phone to the side, he turned back to the Psychology book, but his mind and his eyes wandered to the phone every few minutes. He wondered what Jess was doing. Ugh, he would never get his work done this way.

Slamming the book closed, Chad grabbed his keys and headed out the door, deliberately leaving his phone on the desk. If he didn't have it, he couldn't be tempted to call Jess, but maybe a ride would clear his head enough to focus.

CHAPTER 7

"hat is the matter with you?" Chad asked, propping himself up on his elbow and causing his biceps to bulge. Though he hadn't been available yesterday when Jess had texted, he had responded this morning, and offered to come over after class. Since she knew Emily would be in class, she agreed.

His blue eyes stared down at her, expecting an answer she didn't have. She should be into this. He was built like a god, and the light sheen of sweat glistening on his body made his muscles appear to ripple, but as Jess lay beneath him, all she could think about were Emily's words - that men couldn't fill the hole in her heart, but Jesus could.

Jess shook her head as she looked back at Chad. He was handsome, but she knew nothing about him, other than he was a TA, rode a motorcycle, and stirred lustful emotions in her body. And while the immediate pleasure was nice, the void always remained when he left, and with it came the fear. Fear of pregnancy, fear of STDs, fear of labeling. Jess had been used for so long that her self-respect now depended on a man's attention. The worst part was it rarely even mattered which man.

"I'm sorry," she said, trying to clear the thoughts. "It's just something my roommate said."

"The prude who walked in on us the other day?" He knitted his dark brows together. "Who cares what she thinks?" He leaned in to kiss Jess again, but her hand pushed him back. Her traitorous hand. What was it doing? She should let him kiss her and allow the pleasurable sensation to overwhelm her, but she couldn't. Her mouth followed her hand's actions, speaking without permission.

"I know, it's just... what's your favorite food?"

"My favorite what? Never mind." He pushed himself up, and his blue eyes bored into hers. His mouth opened as if he to say something, then closed. With a shake of his head, he stood "This just got too real. I'm not looking for a relationship, just an easy hook-up. Call me again when you're ready for that, otherwise, don't call me." He lumbered off the bed and pulled his clothes back on. After flashing one last incredulous look, he left the room.

The emptiness crowded in worse than before as Jess retrieved her own clothes. *Stupid, stupid, stupid. Why did you do that?* As she yanked on her shorts, hatred simmered in her stomach for Emily. She had been at peace with her life before Emily's words dug in and took hold. Sure, it hadn't been great, but she had learned how to cope with it. Why hadn't she gotten the single she had asked for? If she had, this never would have happened. This was all that goody-two-shoes's fault, and Jess wanted to make Emily pay.

After pulling on her shirt, she glanced over at Emily's side of the room. What could she do to her that would send Emily into a tailspin like she was in? She could tear down her pictures or deface them, but Emily would just get more. No, that was too easy; it needed to be something bigger, something that would hurt her more. Jess's eyes landed on the Bible. If she tore it to pieces that would hit Emily; she was always reading the bloody thing.

Stomping to the nightstand, Jess reached for the book, but a heat blazed against her hand. Jerking it back, she stared at the book, and her heart thudded in her chest. What was that? She had touched it before and felt nothing. Jess stepped away from the book and returned to her bed. Pulling her knees up to her chest, she stared at the black book that now held an unexplainable power and tried not to panic.

❦

I have to end this, Chad thought as he left Jess's room. *She's getting attached.* He knew the signs. He'd seen it in many of the girls over the last two years. Normally, this would be the time he would stop calling the girl, pretend to lose her number, and find another one. It's what he should do with Jess, but he couldn't. He couldn't keep her piercing blue eyes and soft lips from re-entering his brain. He needed time away from her. Away from the feelings she was stirring in his heart.

The best way he knew to do that was to find another woman. Someone he didn't have feelings for. Maybe the bartender from Bruno's he had met the other night. Though not his usual type, she was pretty and had seemed attracted to him.

He was heading that direction when his phone rang. Pulling it out, he looked at the number. The area code was the same as his hometown's but he didn't recognize the number.

"Hello?" he said, punching the button.

"Hi, Chad, it's Amy. Can you talk?"

His heart dropped to his stomach. Amy had been Kyle's girlfriend and a staple at their house before Kyle's death, but Chad hadn't spoken with her since the funeral. However, he knew she was still attending church with his parents and kept in touch with his mother.

"I have studying and planning to do," he said with a sigh, forgetting the blonde bartender. "What do you need?"

"Actually, I think it might be something you need. Can you come home this weekend?"

Chad avoided going home except for major holidays, summers, and when his mother begged him. Mostly it was to avoid memories of Kyle, but also it was because his parents always insisted on dragging him to church. Chad had given up God when Kyle's casket was lowered into the ground.

"Please. I think you need to see this," Amy said when Chad hesitated.

His curiosity got the better of him. "Fine. I'll be there on Saturday."

⊗

"*W*hoa, you look like you've seen a ghost." Emily said when she returned that afternoon.

Jess looked at her and then glanced over at the Bible. "What's in that book?" Though her voice sounded calm, her heart still beat erratically in her chest.

Emily's brow wrinkled, "What book?"

"Your Bible." Jess pointed, feeling eerily like the ghost of Christmas Future. Her hand trembled slightly.

Emily crossed to the Bible and picked it up. "I've already told you. God's instructions to help us live. Why?"

"I wanted to destroy it," Jess began mechanically.

Emily's eyes widened. "Why?"

"You got in my head with your words and I may have ruined things with Chad because of it. I wanted to hurt you, but when I went to touch it, heat flared against my hand. What sort of voodoo magic is that?"

"It's not voodoo," Emily sighed, shaking her head. "It was God. He's trying to get your attention. He loves you, and he wants you to come home."

The words pierced Jess's heart. "No one has ever loved me, and I don't have a home any longer." Tears pricked her eyes as images of the day she left home flooded into her mind:

"*Where do you think you're going?*" her mother asked, hands akimbo, brown hair wild and frizzy. The smell of alcohol radiated from her pores and her eyes couldn't seem to focus.

"*I'm leaving,*" Jess replied, shoving clothes into her large duffle. "*I have to get away from him. I can't stay here and watch him do to his own daughter what he did to me.*"

"What are you talking about? He's been a great father to you since we married, and he's taking care of us."

Jess's knuckles whitened as she clutched the shirt she was packing even tighter. "No father should do to a daughter what he does, and the only thing he's taking care of is your drug habit."

Her mother's eyes narrowed as she stumbled across the room and slapped Jess's face. "How dare you! Why would he even want anything from you? Look at yourself; you're so ugly. And you're always whoring around. Why would he want that?"

Tears stung Jess's eyes, both from the physical slap and from the emotional pain of the cutting words from the one person she thought loved her. "I can't believe you would side with him over me. I only started sleeping around after my miscarriage. That baby was your husband's by the way. But why should you believe me? I'm just your daughter."

"I don't have a daughter," her mother spat and faltered from the room, grabbing the walls to steady her gait.

Jess let the tears flow as she finished shoving what she could in the big black bag. With a final glance around the room, she slung the bag on her shoulder and left the house she had called home for eighteen years.

Emily pulled the desk chair around and sat in it facing Jess. "First off, I'm sure someone has loved you, even if it doesn't often feel like it. Second, God has loved you forever. He knit you together in your mother's womb, and he knew every hair on your head then and now. He sent his only son, Jesus, to die for your sins so you could spend eternity in Heaven with Him. So, you do have a home, a heavenly home, and even though you can't go there now, one day you will get to see it in all its glory. Our life here on earth is so fleeting. It's important to remember that even though life here will not always be what we expected, what's coming next makes it worth it."

"Do you really believe that?" Jess asked. She wanted to believe—there had to be more to life than what she'd seen so far—but there had been so many hurts, so much pain.

"With all my heart." Her serious tone matched the intensity blazing out of her eyes.

"I'll think about it." Jess rolled over and stared at the wall, but her mind replayed Emily's words over and over again.

CHAPTER 8

*J*ess sighed as she stared at the empty room. Emily was out, probably with Jared and the rest of her group again. She had told Jess about the others over the last few days, and while she'd invited Jess along, Jess wasn't sure she was ready to be immersed in Emily's crowd yet.

On top of that, Jess had been avoiding Chad all week, and he hadn't called either. Her old habit would have been to go out to a club, pick up a handsome man, and bring him back home, but every time she dressed for that occasion, her stomach would clench up and Emily's words would parade back through her head. Was God trying to get her attention?

From across the room, the black book called out like a beacon in a storm. Would it shock her again? Running her palms down denim clad thighs, she pushed herself up from the bed and crossed to Emily's nightstand. Jess's hand hovered over the book, but no heat licked at it this time. Had she imagined it last time? Tentatively, she dropped a finger to the cover. Nothing. Gathering the last of her courage, she placed her palm flat on the cover and closed her eyes.

A spark of light and the image of a cross filled her vision. Startled, Jess pulled her hand back and stared at the book. There was no pain, but why was she seeing visions? She had never seen visions before. Were they permanent? She held her breath and touched the book again. Nothing. No light, no cross, just the textured cover. Jess sat on Emily's bed, pulled her knees to her chest, and opened the book, deciding to look towards the end this time.

The red text jumped out at her. "I am the way, the truth, and the life. No man comes to the father except through me." She turned back a few pages. "For God so loved the world that he sent his one and only son that whoever believes in him shall not perish but have eternal life." Eternal life? Was this for real? Jess raised her brows but kept reading. "For God did not send his son into the world to condemn the world but to save the world through him. Whoever believes in him is not condemned, but whoever does not believe stands condemned already because he has not believed in the name of God's one and only son." Was she condemned? More importantly, if she was, could she change her fate? A desire to learn all she could filled her soul, and Jess eagerly turned back to the book.

The sound of the door opening interrupted Jess's reading, and she slammed the book shut and replaced it on Emily's nightstand. As she pushed herself up from the bed, she smoothed the comforter. Only a few wrinkles hinted at her intrusion on Emily's side, but Emily looked too preoccupied to notice.

"Whoa, what happened to you?" The normal smile that framed her heart-shaped face was missing and her flawless, olive skin appeared paler than usual.

Emily shuddered. "I just feel dirty. Some guy came up to me as we were leaving the restaurant and he practically undressed me with his eyes. I think I need a dozen showers." She shivered and rubbed her arms as she sat on the bed.

"Welcome to my world," Jess muttered.

"What do you mean?" Emily looked up, and her eyes were so sincere that a chunk of the wall Jess had built around her heart crumbled, and she found herself telling Emily about her stepfather. "Oh my gosh, Jess, I'm so sorry." Emily rose from her bed. She crossed the room and sat beside Jess.

Jess shrugged. "I'm kind of used to it. He wasn't the first, just the worst. The first time my mom fell to drugs, she hooked up with a real winner. He had a temper, so I never knew whether he was going to hit me or"—she stared down at her hands, embarrassed and let the sentence trail off.

"That is not okay. It should never have happened to you. Is that why you're so... guarded?"

"Maybe," Jess said, tracing a line on her left palm with the thumb of her right hand. "You're less likely to get hurt if you keep walls up, you know?"

Emily's brown eyes stared into Jess's with a blazing intensity. "I know you aren't a believer, but can I pray for you?"

It was the second time Emily had asked her, and while Jess still wasn't sure she believed in prayer, Emily seemed to, and her voice held a sense of urgency. What could it hurt? Jess nodded, and Emily bowed her head and closed her eyes.

"Lord, my friend Jess is hurting because of her past. Please heal her and show her your love."

As Emily continued praying, Jess felt another chunk of the wall she had so carefully created crumble. Tears welled up inside and threatened to overflow. She sniffed and ran a hand over her eyes, willing them to stay dry. The effort was futile. They spilled out, creating wet, shiny tracks down her cheeks. Her shoulders heaved as six years of hurt slammed against the dam, crumbling it to bits. When Emily finished praying, she grabbed Jess's hand

"Can he take it away?" Jess sobbed. "Can he make me forget my past?"

"Your past is always with you," Emily said. "But he can give you a brighter future. You don't have to be a slave to your past."

Suddenly Jess wanted that more than anything. She didn't know if Emily was telling the truth, but if there was even a possibility, she wanted it. "Tell me what to do. I want the peace you seem to have."

"Just ask God to save you. Tell him you know you're a sinner and you want him to guide your life."

Jess said the words through tears, and when she finished, Emily hugged her. Though she was not generally a "huggy" person, she found her arms returning the embrace as a weird need to laugh bubbled inside.

A tiny chuckle escaped along with the words. "What do I do now?"

"Now you read. You learn everything you can, and you try to live it. I won't lie; it isn't always easy, but it's always worth it."

"What about the emptiness? I still feel it."

"You have to give that to God. It won't go away instantaneously, but he will begin to fill it, if you let him."

Jess nodded, smiling at Emily and enjoying the lighter feeling. Though the emptiness remained, it felt like a heavy blanket had been lifted from her shoulders.

"Hey, will you come to church with me Sunday?" Emily asked. "There's a really great college crowd at my church."

Jess nodded, almost mechanically, but her mind wondered if she would be accepted with her shaved hair and nose ring?

❦

Chad's throat grew dryer the closer he got to Amarillo. He had been home a few times in the summer, but as his dorm allowed him to stay on campus during the summer, he had claimed his summer work of clerking at a counselor's office kept him stuck in Lubbock and had avoided spending much time at home.

Though he was coming into town to see Amy, he knew he would have to make at least a quick stop at his parent's house, but he decided to do it on the way out of town.

He was surprised to see a moving van in front of Amy's house when he pulled up. Intrigued, he locked the car and walked up the steps. Before his hand even hit the doorbell, the door swung open.

"Oh, hello, Chad," Amy's mother said from the other side. While he hadn't spent much time here, Amy's parents had often joined them for dinner and festivities when Kyle was living. The last two years had added a few streaks of grey to her chestnut hair and a few new wrinkles around her green eyes, but otherwise she looked exactly the same.

"Hello Mrs. Bledsoe. Is Amy here?"

"Of course dear. She's in her room finishing packing. It's the second door on the left down that hallway." She pointed behind her to the hallway now devoid of family photos and knickknacks.

"Thank you." Chad stepped over the threshold into the nearly empty living room. Blank bookshelves and a couch were all that remained. He wondered where they were moving to and if the move had anything to do with Amy's cryptic call.

The second door on the left was only partially closed, but Chad still knocked before pushing it the rest of the way open. Amy's head popped out of the closet at the slight squeak of the hinges.

"Oh good, you came. Give me a second," she said and a moment later she re-emerged, a stack of clothes slung over one arm. She laid them on the bed and looked up at him. "I guess you can tell we're moving, huh?"

"Yeah, where to?" Chad asked. He didn't really care, but it seemed impolite not to ask.

"California. My dad got a job out there, so off we go. Not the way I wanted to spend my Senior year, but I guess those are the breaks sometimes, right?" A sad smile crossed her face for an instant before she wiped it away.

At least she would have a Senior year, Chad thought. Kyle never got that chance. "Yeah, life isn't always fair," he said aloud.

She caught the tone in his voice and opened her mouth as if she were going to say something, then thought better of it. Instead, she crossed to the roll top desk, which was devoid of anything except a notebook. Picking it up, she turned back to him and held it out.

"What's this?" he asked, taking the spiral notebook from her.

"It was Kyle's. Our English teacher made us keep a journal. At first Kyle hated it, but then he got into writing out his feelings and he wrote in it all the time. I guess he left it here one day when we were studying. I found it under my bed." She tucked a strand of dark hair behind her ears and dropped her eyes to the floor. "You need to read it because he wrote about you." Her eyes lifted to Chad's, and in them burned an intensity. "He really looked up to you," she said. "You meant the world to him."

Chad returned her gaze for a moment before opening the notebook. The first few pages held short, choppy paragraphs, and after scanning them, Chad could see this was when Kyle was writing just to fulfill the assignment. But as he turned the pages, the paragraphs grew longer and more detailed. Near the end, the entries were full pages, sometimes more. The last entry in the book was dated only a few days before Kyle's death.

I'm worried about my brother, Chad. He used to be so strong in the faith, but college has changed him. He no longer talks about God much and I haven't seen him pray in ages. Now, all he talks about is girls and I'm afraid he is caving into the pressures of the world. I hope God sends an angel to protect him.

Chad looked up from the page. Kyle had hoped God would send an angel for him? He should have been praying for Kyle's protection, but as he thought back to his Freshman year, he realized Kyle had been right. Chad had started slipping away from God even then. Not like he had after Kyle's death, but with little things - not reading his Bible daily, forgetting to pray, rationalizing physicality in relationships.

"Can I keep this?" he asked Amy. He wanted to read it more in depth and it was a link to Kyle, a side of him he hadn't seen.

Amy nodded. "I can't think of anyone Kyle would want to have it more."

"Thank you," Chad said, clutching the notebook in his hands. He turned to leave, but then paused and faced Amy again. "Kyle cared for you too. I hope you know that."

Tears glistened in her eyes as she nodded. Before her tears could fall and encourage his own, Chad exited her room and the Bledsoe house.

He placed the notebook on the passenger seat beside him before backing the car up and heading toward his parent's house.

CHAPTER 9

*J*ess stared into the sea of black that was her closet as Emily dressed the next morning.

"What's the matter?" Emily's voice carried over from her side of the room.

"I have nothing to wear. Everything I own is black or holey or"—Jess shrugged—"Not what you wear to church." She didn't know much, but she didn't think miniskirts and crop tops seemed appropriate for church. Tears pricked at the back of her eyes, and she blinked furiously to keep them at bay.

A small, knowing smile spread on Emily's face, and her eyes lit up. She held up a finger, then turned to her closet. After flicking hangers back and forth, she pulled out a blue dress and held it out to Jess. "God doesn't care what you wear, but it is important to feel comfortable. It's not your usual style, but the blue would look great with your eyes, and I think we're close enough in size."

The tears forced their way to the front and blurred Jess's vision. She couldn't remember the last time someone had told her she looked nice when they weren't trying to get her into bed. "Thanks."

As she grabbed the dress, Jess turned her head to wipe the tears away before Emily saw. On one hand, it was just a solid blue piece of fabric, but on the other it was a symbol for so much more.

After slipping on the soft cotton dress, Jess looked in the mirror, stunned at the transformation. The blue did bring out her ocean eyes. Her skin looked pale but smooth, and even her hair appeared less severe.

"See?" Emily asked, coming up behind her. "Beautiful."

Jess nodded, still stunned at how different she looked.

"Oh, they're here," Emily said as her cell phone beeped.

"They?"

"Yeah, Chase and Sarah. Jared needed to go in early today, so Chase and Sarah offered to go with us. Don't worry, they're nice. They're both members of the Students for Life group I'm in." Her eyes dropped back to her phone as she typed back a message.

Jess's nerves crumpled in on each other, and a small voice whispered in her head. Sure, Emily accepted her, but would her friends? She wasn't even sure about this church thing and now she had the added pressure of meeting new people at the same time? Was she doing the right thing? "Maybe I should stay home," Jess said, and the voice agreed. "I don't even have a Bible."

"Don't worry," Emily said, holding out hers. "You can borrow mine. I have it on my phone too."

The small voice rebutted: It wasn't hers; people would know; she could never really fit in. Jess shook her head to stop the negative thoughts and grabbed the Bible. Though it didn't ease all her worries, it seemed to silence the voice. For now, at least. She ran her free hand down the borrowed dress, though no wrinkle was in sight, nodded, and followed Emily out of the room.

A tall guy with sandy blonde hair and an almost equally tall girl with short spiky blonde hair were waiting for them at the bottom of the stairs.

"Chase, Sarah, I'd like you to meet my roommate Jess," Emily said.

"What's up, Jess?" Chase said with an easy grin.

"So nice to meet you, Jess," Sarah said. Her grey eyes sparkled as she shook Jess's hand. They were the most interesting color she'd ever seen, like the color of fog in the evening. Though her features were sharp, her voice was soft and friendly, and she emitted a calming presence.

"Nice to meet you too," Jess said but her voice lacked its usual confidence. Fears kept popping into her mind. What if the others weren't like Emily and Jared? What if they mocked her for coming? Did she really want to give up a Sunday for this? What if she hated it?

Even as they walked to the parking lot, the questions cycled in Jess's head. Sarah claimed the front seat next to Chase, easing some of her nervousness. Sarah seemed nice, but not knowing her, Jess didn't want to answer a lot of questions or attempt small talk. She swallowed to ease the knots as she climbed in the back seat next to Emily, but they remained resolute.

A few minutes later, they pulled into the church parking lot, and Jess's eyes widened. A large white building loomed in front of them, and the parking lot teemed with cars. "There's so many."

She thought she had only spoken in her head until Emily touched her arm. "It'll be all right. We're all right here with you, and it probably won't seem like so many inside."

Nodding, Jess opened the car door. Other college-aged students meandered in the parking lot. "Is this a University only church?"

"No," Chase laughed, "but they have a great program for high school and college aged students, so a lot come here."

Several young adults stood at the entrance to the church handing out brochures of some kind. Curious, Jess took one, and the group entered the large, open room. Rows of chairs filled it, and a large raised platform occupied most of the front. A piano, drum set, and several guitars sat atop the platform. Three large white screens hung at the front of the room as well, one in the middle and one on each side.

Chase chose a row in the middle aisle and they filed in. Sarah took Jared's left side, Emily his right, and Jess sat on Emily's right, closest to the aisle. As the others chatted quietly, she opened the thin brochure. A listing of activities filled the left side. Groups for men, for women, for teens. It carried into the middle partition.

She couldn't believe how many options were offered. Jess had thought church was just a Sunday thing, but there was something happening nearly every day of the week. A men's and women's ministry on Monday, choir on Tuesday, drama ministry on Wednesday, Teen/college ministry on Thursday, and movie night on Friday. The only day where nothing was listed was Saturday. On the far-right panel, a section for prayer requests filled the top and the bottom held a "Staying Connected" card that you could fill out to give them your information.

As people filled in around them, the hum of conversation grew louder. Jess looked up from the brochure, expecting to see a sea of dresses and suits, but men and women alike sported pants, some even jeans. Maybe Emily had been right about God not caring what people wore.

A few minutes later, several people took the stage. A woman sat down at the piano, a man at the drum set, two men grabbed guitars, and four other men and women picked up microphones Jess hadn't noticed before. The music filled the auditorium, and while the music was not what Jess usually listened to, she enjoyed the sound. She knew none of the words, but her foot tapped along to the rhythm.

When the music ended, the pastor took the stage. As he spoke about Satan using insecurities to pull people away from God, his words hit Jess's heart, and she remembered the voice from earlier trying to convince her not to come. Had that been Satan? She glanced around to see if others were affected. *Is he speaking just to me?* The more he spoke, the more it felt like his words were for her alone, and emotion began bubbling up inside. She wiped her eyes, pretending an eyelash or something was in them and hoping no one else would notice.

When the service ended, people began filing out. Jess followed, but the pastor's words tumbled around in her head. Could it be that she sought male companionship because she was so insecure? Was that Satan attacking her? Even as the group went to lunch, Jess continued to process the words of the preacher.

*A*s Chad sat between his parents and his younger sister in church, a feeling of unease crept in. He felt like a fraud, not having been inside a church in over a year, but his sister had begged him to stay the night when he'd showed up at the house yesterday.

When he'd agreed—only due to his guilt over not seeing her as often as he should—his mother had suggested he attend church with them the next morning. Chad had initially declined, stating his lack of attire as a reason. He hadn't planned on spending the night and therefore hadn't brought a change of clothes with him, but his mother had insisted.

Now as he listened to the pastor's words, he thought back to Kyle's journal. He had read it cover to cover the previous night after dinner. Kyle had been so strong in his faith, and Chad wondered if he had ever been as strong or if he had been merely putting on a show. He certainly couldn't remember thinking the way Kyle had - putting others above himself. Chad had always thought about himself first. Why would God take Kyle who would have been a much better example for others to follow?

"You can always come back to God," the pastor said, his words breaking through Chad's sidetracked thoughts. "He is always waiting for you with open arms. No matter what you've done, God will forgive you if you just ask. Let us pray."

Chad watched as heads around him bowed, but he couldn't follow suit. Not yet. Though he felt something, he wasn't ready to give up his anger yet. God had taken his brother and he needed to know why.

CHAPTER 10

For the first time, Jess dreaded going to class on Monday. It had been over a week since she had spoken with Chad, and after attending church Sunday, she felt more than a little guilty about jumping into bed with him. How was she going to make it through the rest of the semester in his class?

Jess stared at her reflection in the mirror. Though she didn't look that different physically, she felt different. No longer wanting to attract men at every turn, she now opted for longer shirts and shorts that weren't quite as revealing. She wasn't sure if she wanted to keep the shaved part of her hair, but if she parted it down the middle, it was barely noticeable.

Though still new to praying, Jess turned her fears over to God. He would know how to soften this situation with Chad. "Lord, I'm so new I'm not sure if you deal with stuff like this, but I think I messed up. I am not even sure how I feel about Chad now, but I have to see him twice a week, and I'm asking for strength not to fall into temptation again and for peace. Help me get through this semester. Amen."

Jess was glad Emily wasn't in the room as the prayer felt awkward. Did it get easier with time? She'd never been a big fan of public speaking and praying aloud seemed similar, but as stilted as her prayer might have been, a measure of peace blanketed her when her eyes opened.

Chad wasn't in the lecture hall when Jess arrived, and she sighed a breath of relief as she slid into a chair at the back. It was short lived though, as when he walked into the room, her heart thudded in her chest. Why was she still so attracted to him? Was it because they had been intimate or was there something more?

Dropping her gaze to her paper, Jess found she could concentrate on the lecture a little more if she didn't watch him. Still, every once in a while, he would say a word that would trigger a memory in her head and send heat across her cheeks. Would she ever be able to get him out of her head?

"Hey, I saw you at Indiana Avenue Baptist yesterday, right?"

The voice startled her, and Jess looked up in surprise at the guy in front of her. With her focus on avoiding Chad's gaze as she gathered her books together, she hadn't noticed this stranger approach as the rest of the students filed out.

"Uh, yeah," she responded as she stood and slung the backpack over her shoulder. "It was my first week."

"I wondered," he said with a smile. "I didn't think I had seen you there before. I'm Randall, by the way."

As Jess took his hand, her gaze wandered down front to find Chad staring at them. Their eyes locked for a moment before he shoved the rest of his papers in his satchel and exited the side door. A part of her wanted to run after him, but the more rational part realized it was better this way. Perhaps Randall was her answer to prayer as a way to avoid temptation.

"Uh, Jess," she said, focusing her attention back on the dude in front of her. "I'm Jess."

"So, did you like it?" he asked as they walked out of the row towards the door.

"Yeah, I did," Jess said. "I'm new to church but it was nice there, and my roommate Emily Peters attends there."

His eyes lit up. "Oh yeah, I know Emily. She played on the church softball team last spring."

"The church has a softball team?" Jess asked as the two stepped into the sunshine.

"Yep, and a volleyball team during the winter. Can you serve?"

"I don't know," she said with a laugh. The truth was, she'd never given sports a chance in high school. She had wanted to avoid the camaraderie that generally went along with team sports as she had wanted no one finding out about her home life. Plus, she had never known when her mother would be sober and allow her to attend games or be drunk and forbid it.

He raised his eyebrow at the response and Jess shook her head. "It's a long story," she said. "Suffice to say, I didn't play any sports in high school, so I have no idea if I'm good at any of them."

"Well, you should definitely try out this year then," he said. "We have a lot of fun."

"I'll think about it," she agreed. "I'm this way." Jess pointed to the right where the math building lay.

Disappointment filled his brown eyes. "Oh, I'm this way." He pointed to the left. "Well, it was nice to see you again, Jess, and I guess I'll see you Wednesday, right?"

"I'll be there," she said and returned his wave before he walked away. As she continued to the math building, she found herself wondering if Randall's interest had been purely platonic or if he were interested in her. Having never had a "normal" relationship, Jess found she had no idea how it was supposed to work. Her history had always been find a man, hook up, repeat. She would have to ask Emily how to navigate these new, unfamiliar waters.

❦

A feeling of jealousy welled up in Chad's stomach as he watched the boy interact with Jess. He shouldn't be jealous as he hadn't called her in a week. Plus, if she were willing to jump into bed with him, she had probably already found someone to take his place, but the feeling remained.

Maybe he should have answered her question. What did he care if she knew his favorite food was Chicken Alfredo? The truth was - he didn't. He had been scared. Scared that she wanted a relationship that he wasn't ready for. Was he? Frustrated, he shoved his papers in the satchel and stormed out the side door. A cigarette, that's what he needed.

As the door closed behind him with a soft click, he dropped his satchel and leaned against the brick wall. He snaked a cigarette and his lighter out of his pocket and flicked the flame on. The calming effect was nearly immediate.

What was wrong with him? He didn't need to be developing feelings for some girl. But Jess wasn't just some girl. She intrigued him in a way no woman had in years, and he didn't even know why. What he did know was that she occupied his thoughts a lot, more than he wanted, but falling for her meant opening up a side of himself he had closed off with Kyle's death.

Ever since Amy's call, Chad's life had been in a tailspin and going home had only made it worse. The journal from Kyle, seeing his sister, and attending church had all stirred up feelings and emotions he thought he had long ago buried.

The cigarette burned to a nub, stinging his fingers. With a curse, he dropped it to the ground and smashed it into the dirt with his toe. He needed answers before he could really process his feelings.

CHAPTER 11

*A*voiding Chad grew a little easier after that. Though he often popped into Jess's head, she found ways to fill her time to avoid focusing on him. Her job kept her busy for one, and on Friday nights, she attended the Bible Study with Emily. The roommates had also started a Saturday movie night to keep them both out of trouble. Plus, Randall started sitting next to her in class and walking her out each day.

"I ought to like him, right?" Jess asked Emily as she pulled the popcorn bag from the microwave and opened it. The sweet buttery smell of the popcorn filled the air as a cloud of steam billowed from the bag. Careful not to burn her fingers, Jess tilted the bag until the oily, yellow kernels filled the metallic bowl. Though she loved microwaved popcorn, she had never liked eating it directly out of the bag due to the residue it left on her hand. Plus, it was harder to share that way.

"You want my honest opinion?"

"Of course."

"Well, just because he's nice and a Christian doesn't mean you'll be attracted to him," Emily said as she popped the DVD in the player. Jess had rented When Love Returns, the small town love story from the Redbox at the Student Union before leaving work for the day. "If we were attracted to every Christian man, that would be a mess. I mean if that were the case, I'd be attracted to Jared and Chase and…"

"You mean you aren't?" Jess teased her. "I've seen the way you look at Jared."

"No way," she said with an adamant shake of her head. "Jared and I are just friends. We tried dating last year, but it didn't work out. Besides, he likes this new girl, Amanda. Anyway, it's not about liking Randall exactly; it's about finding a guy with those qualities. Someone of faith who loves the Lord."

Jess joined Emily on the bed and placed the bowl between them. "I guess you're right. I just feel bad. Like I should be attracted to him, but honestly… I can't get Chad out of my head."

"Is that the guy I walked in on?" Emily asked with a raised eyebrow.

"Yes," Jess said slowly and then continued in a hurry before Emily could interrupt, "I know it's wrong - that he's wrong for me, but thoughts of him just keep flying in, even when I don't want them there."

"Have you tried praying about it?" Emily asked.

"All the time," Jess said with a sigh. "It's probably selfish, but I was really hoping God would make me magically forget how attracted to him I was. It hasn't happened yet."

Emily popped a kernel in her mouth and chewed slowly. "Well, have you tried praying for him?"

"What?"

"Pray for him," she said. "He is in your life for a reason. He's may not be healthy for you right now, but maybe God's plan was to have you be a seed in his journey to redemption. I also think you should avoid relationships for a bit anyway. Get to know yourself and what you really want before trying to blend your life with someone else's."

As the movie began, Jess leaned back against the wall and pondered Emily's words. She was right that Jess needed to find herself, but she didn't understand how she could be a seed for anyone's redemption. There was still so much in her past she was ashamed of.

※

"Thank you for meeting me," Chad said as he sat across from the chaplain. Not being a church goer, Chad was unfamiliar with the pastors in the area, but he knew the campus had a chaplain on staff.

"Of course," the man said. He was older, with salt and pepper hair and laugh lines around his eyes. "What can I do for you?"

"I have some questions," Chad said. "About God."

"Well, that is my specialty," the man said with a smile, "but I don't claim to know everything. Only God does that. Still, I'll be happy to answer what I can."

"Why does God allow suffering?" Chad asked.

"Ah," the chaplain said, "that is a common question. The truth is that we don't know the answer. God allows free will and because there is sin in the world, often that free will leads to suffering for others."

"But why would he take someone good? See, my brother had a heart for God unlike me. He was a true believer. So why would God take him instead of me?"

"Oh, son, I'm sorry you lost your brother, but God doesn't work like that. Your brother was affected by someone else's free will, and sometimes that means bad things happen to good people. But, it sounds like your brother was prepared to meet God."

"But couldn't God have stopped it? Couldn't he just have kept my brother from getting killed?" Chad pushed.

The chaplain sat back in his brown leather chair. "I suppose he could have, but let me ask you this - if your brother were still alive, would you be here in my office?"

"What do you mean?" Chad asked.

"You said your brother was a true believer. I take that to mean you weren't, that you acted as if you were, but you weren't really, am I right?"

Chad shrugged, not liking where this was going all of a sudden. "I guess. I mean I attended church, but I wasn't dedicated like Kyle was."

"So, am I safe in assuming if your brother was still alive that you would still be on that path? Talking the talk but not walking the walk?"

"Are you saying my actions got my brother killed?"

"Not at all, but I am saying that we don't know God's plan. We only see the lower story, what's happening down here. But God sees a much larger plan from his viewpoint."

Chad sat back and thought about the chaplain's words. Could it be that his anger had been misplaced?

As if reading his mind, the chaplain leaned forward again and said, "You know God understands when we are angry with him. It doesn't make him love us any less, and He is still waiting to accept us with open arms when we are ready to come home."

Chad nodded as he thanked the chaplain and headed out of the office. Kyle's last few journal entries had been about wishing Chad would renew his relationship with Jesus. Could he do that? Could he get over his anger at God and be the man that his brother had hoped he would become? And what about his lifestyle, would that have to change too? And where did Jess fit into all of this? Chad had come to the chaplain for answers, but he was leaving with a lot of questions too.

CHAPTER 12

The next morning, Jess awoke with a start. Something was wrong, but she couldn't put a finger on it. It was dark for one thing. As she didn't have classes until the afternoon, she rarely woke before the sun, but that wasn't the main issue. Today was Sunday and there were no classes anyway.

As Jess tried to focus on what had woken her up, her stomach seized, and she suddenly knew. Throwing back the covers, she vaulted out of bed and rushed to the sink. She would never make it to the bathroom down the hall in time. This would have to do. With a final clench, her stomach heaved its contents into the sink.

When the sickness subsided, Jess rinsed the sink and her mouth out and then splashed cool water on her face.

"Jess, are you okay?" Emily mumbled from her side of the room. "What time is it?"

"Early," Jess answered. "Go back to sleep. It must have been something I ate. I'll be fine." But as she walked back to her bed, she wondered if that were true. With a cast iron stomach, Jess couldn't remember the last time any food had made her sick.

The sunlight peeked in the next time Jess opened her eyes. Emily still slept on the opposite side of the room. Saturdays and Sundays were the only days Emily could sleep in though to her that meant eight am and not Jess's idea of nearly noon. The room lay quiet aside from her rhythmic breathing. Jess paused for a moment, testing her stomach, but it appeared to have settled.

She pushed back the covers before sitting up slowly and planting her feet on the floor. So far so good, but as she stood, her stomach clenched again, and she hurried to the sink a second time. What was wrong with her? She hadn't thrown up this much since...

Her eyes widened, and she raced back to her bed, grabbing the backpack from the floor and pawing through it for her birth control pills. Her mother had put her on them at sixteen when she found out about the miscarriage. Jess suffered through her mother's lecture on safe sex, but couldn't find the courage at the time to tell her the baby was Jim's. After all, she hadn't believed Jess when she'd told her mother he touched her, why would she have believed that? And the pill opened the door to other men after that, ones Jess could choose to help her forget her stepfather, if only for a time.

Jess's fingers grasped the package, and she pulled it out, flipping over the cover. All the pills had been taken, no gap existed in the line. A sigh of relief escaped her lips. What would she have done if she were pregnant? So as not to forget, she popped out the pill for today and froze. Today's pill was labeled Saturday, but it was Sunday morning. Had she skipped it yesterday? No, she remembered taking the pill shortly after waking up yesterday. Friday, then?

With a sinking feeling, Jess plopped down onto the bed as she realized she had no idea when she'd missed a pill. This pack or last? In fact, she couldn't even remember if she'd had her period with the last pack. Typically regular like clockwork and light enough that she barely noticed it, she had stopped charting her period and just known it would hit when the pills changed color. Unfortunately, now she couldn't place having one in the last month which meant there was a very real chance her "sickness" was morning sickness.

Across the room, Emily stirred and stretched in her bed. "You feeling better?" she asked, her voice still fuzzy sleep.

Jess couldn't tell her. She wanted to, but she couldn't. The need to process the situation seemed more important. "Um, not so much,"

Jess said. "I think I'll have to skip church today. I don't want to get anyone else sick."

"That bad, huh?" She tugged a hand through the tangled blonde mess on her head.

"Yeah, I think I'm going to try to sleep this off, whatever it is." She hated lying. The first thing she planned to do when Emily left was head to the campus drugstore for a pregnancy test. Hopefully they would be open on Sundays.

"Do you want me to get anything for you while I'm out?" she asked as she gathered up her shower items.

"No, I'm sure it will go away on its own." Or with some help, she thought.

❦

C had looked at his reflection in the mirror and wondered again what he was doing. Attending church two weeks in a row was a foreign concept to him, but he couldn't shake the sensation he needed to be there. He had no idea where *there* was though. Lubbock was one of the most churched cities in Texas. You could barely go three blocks without running into one.

After asking around, he found Indiana Avenue promoted a strong college program and that many students from the University attended there, so he had picked that as his first choice to try. If he didn't find what he needed there, he would try another church the next week. The only problem was Chad didn't know what he needed or what he was looking for, but he felt sure he would know when he found it.

The parking lot teemed with college aged students when he arrived. He maneuvered the Harley into a spot and turned off the key.

Chad joined the throng of people funneling into the entrance and found himself in a large foyer. Ahead he could see the open doors of the sanctuary and he continued that direction, finding an empty seat near the back. He stowed his helmet under the chair and then perused the brochure he had been handed at the door.

When the music started, he glanced up and realized the room had filled up around him. Empty seats remained though not many. Most of the surrounding people stood as they sang. Self-consciously, he rose though he didn't know the words to a few of the songs.

Relief flooded Chad when the pastor took the stage and the congregation sat. However, that relief was short-lived as the pastor began to speak on being different from the world.

"You see, Jesus called us to be in the world but separate from it. However, that has gotten much harder with technology. TV and movies tell us that smoking, drinking, cursing, cheating, and intimacy outside of marriage are not only okay but the norm. And the media assaults us with the mantra that if it feels good, we should do it, that God would want us to be happy. But the truth is, God wants us to be holy.

"Now some of you may ask yourselves, 'But doesn't God forgive our sins if we ask?' The answer is He does, but mercy and grace were never meant to be an excuse to sin. It was to save us with the expectation we would then turn away from our sin. Remember he told the woman at the well to 'go and sin no more.' He expects the same from us, and it's hard, but if we love Christ, we should want to be different.

He paused and scanned the crowd. "Some of you may be wondering what to do now because you have already started down a path created by the world and not by God. The answer is to repent, to turn away from your sin, and to follow Jesus."

As the preacher ended the sermon with prayer, Chad felt the weight of his sins bearing down on him. He had been doing nearly everything the preacher spoke on. Chad knew what he needed to do, but he wasn't ready yet. Something held him back from fully re-committing his life to Jesus, and as he walked outside the building and mounted his motorcycle again, the pastor's words began to fade and with them the sense of urgency.

❦

*J*ess stared at the small plastic stick. Though she had been nearly positive she was pregnant, seeing the two blue lines confirming it still elicited a shock. What was she going to do now? She hadn't even spoken to Chad in weeks; she had little money and no way to raise a baby. As much as she didn't want to think about it, abortion seemed like the best option. It would allow her to have the fresh start she was looking for and she wouldn't have to tell Emily...

No. Correction. She could never tell Emily. Emily would not understand, but Emily was not in her shoes.

The sound of a key in the door snapped Jess back to reality, and she shoved the stick under some clothes on her bed mere seconds before Emily entered the room.

"Hey, Jess, are you feeling any better?"

"A little," Jess said which wasn't a total lie. She had been able to keep down food the last hour. Still, guilt crept in for not telling Emily the whole truth. "How was church?"

"Really good. The pastor spoke on not following what the world says and standing strong in faith."

"It sounds like a good one," Jess said. "I'm sorry I missed it." Inside though Jess was glad she'd missed it. She felt guilty enough about her plan to have an abortion. Listening to the pastor would have probably made it worse. She just needed to take care of it this week and then she could repent and really focus on doing God's will.

CHAPTER 13

*J*ess slipped out of bed as quietly as possible. She would have to come up with some excuse to explain to Emily where she'd gone when she returned, but she had to get this taken care of before she lost her nerve.

Last night, she'd researched abortion clinics on her phone and found the closest one lay in Fort Worth - six hours away. Unfortunately, Jess didn't have a car, so she also looked into buses. The earliest one left at six am, so she'd set the alarm for five and turned it to the quietest setting she dared. She wasn't sure if the alarm had woken her, or if she'd never gone to sleep the night before.

Jess grabbed her toothbrush, toothpaste, wallet, jacket, and shoes and slipped out of the room. Having slept in the clothes she planned to wear today to cut down on the chances of waking Emily, she now padded silently to the bathroom to brush her teeth and pull on her shoes.

Five minutes later, Jess pushed open the dorm doors and trekked across the dark campus to the bus stop. The street lamps cast an eerie glow across the grass as the sun was not yet out, and a sense of relief filled Jess when the small bus shelter came into view. She huddled in the corner, pulling her knees to her chest to combat the cold and waited for the bus to arrive.

*C*had thought about what he would say to Jess as he crossed the campus. He'd spent the previous evening thinking about Kyle and his own life. Though not sure he was ready to commit - either to Jesus or to a relationship - he needed to apologize to Jess for his behavior. Plus, he wanted to see if she still wanted to hang out, so they could get to know each other this time.

As he neared the Psychology building, a female figure near the side door caught his eye. Could it be Jess waiting for him? Was she having second thoughts as well? But when the girl turned, he realized it was not Jess.

His heart sank as the distance closed and he realized the girl was Jess's uptight roommate.

"Have you seen her?" the girl asked when he was within ear shot.

"Not yet, but class is about to start. She should be here soon."

"Can I come in and wait for her?" Worry lines creased the girl's pretty face.

"Why? What's wrong?" Chad asked as a sinking sensation filled his stomach.

"I don't know." The girl tucked a strand of hair behind her ears. "Maybe nothing, but she was gone this morning when I got up. She's never gone. She sleeps until noon. And yesterday she was sick, throwing up and she skipped church. I'm just worried about her."

"Maybe she was still sick this morning and she left early so she wouldn't wake you," Chad offered, but in his heart, he didn't think that was the case, and now a seed of worry joined the sinking sensation, creating a churning nauseous feeling.

"Can I just check?" she continued. "I'll leave if she's not there, but will you tell her to call me if she shows up after I'm gone?"

"Sure, yeah. Come on," Chad said, opening the door for her. The two scanned the crowd, but Jess was nowhere to be seen. Chad dug a paper and pen out of his satchel, scrawled his number on the paper, and handed it to the girl. "Text me, so I have your number, and I'll text back whether or not she shows up."

"Thank you." The girl took the paper from him, scanned the crowd with worried eyes one last time, and then turned and exited the room.

Chad took out his supplies for class, but his mind was elsewhere. Where was Jess? And was she okay? It would be a long hour.

※

*J*ess looked at Emily's number flashing across her caller ID and sighed. Emily had been calling every hour since seven am. She should have known Emily would worry about her. Maybe she should have left a note or maybe she could text and at least let Emily know she was ok. But what would she say?

"Boy troubles?"

Jess looked up at the woman next to her who had spoken. Kind brown eyes stared back at her from a weathered and wrinkled face. The woman had to be in her seventies.

"No, my roommate," Jess said. "I left without telling her this morning and she's worried about me."

"Ah," the woman said with a knowing nod. "Why don't you just tell her where you're at?"

"I…" Jess didn't know. Emily couldn't stop her now even if she told her, but the truth was Jess never wanted Emily to know what she was doing, and she had no lie concocted yet.

"It's the secrets that hurt us the most," the woman said, and sadness clouded her eyes. "I remember my Maggie used to be so carefree until her secrets festered inside her. Then she grew distant and she stopped coming around."

"What happened to her?" The words slipped out of Jess's mouth. She didn't want to engage this woman in conversation, but she wanted to know.

"She took her own life a year ago. In her suicide note, she wrote about she couldn't handle the guilt of what she'd done, and she hoped God would forgive her for taking another's life."

Jess's hand flew to her mouth. "She killed someone?"

"A teenage girl," the woman said. "She was driving drunk and ran a red light. She served over a year in prison, but she sobered up while she was inside. I wish she had told me when she got out how she was feeling. I know what she did was wrong, but every life is precious to God."

A new wave of guilt washed over Jess and she wished she had never conversed with the elderly woman. As her phone buzzed again, Jess reached for the power button, but her eyes landed on the caller ID screen and she paused. The number flashing this time was not Emily's but Chad's. Why was he calling her?

Jess let the call go to voicemail and then listened to the message. "Jess? It's Chad. Your roommate came looking for you. She's worried about you and frankly so am I. Where are you? At least let us know you're okay, please?"

The tone in his voice was the last straw. Tears spilled out of Jess's eyes and coursed down her cheek. What was she doing? She couldn't have an abortion; she hadn't even told Chad she was pregnant.

"Are you all right, dear?" the woman asked.

Jess shook her head. "I'm not, but as soon as I can get off this bus I will be. Thank you for sharing your story with me. I…. I'm pregnant and I was headed to Fort Worth to have an abortion, but your story and that call…. That was the baby's father. He doesn't even know…"

"Are you a believer, my dear?" the woman asked with tears in her eyes.

"I'm almost ashamed to say I am after what I was considering," Jess said, "but I'm very new to this."

"My daughter was a believer too when she had her accident," the woman said. "I think it's what made her guilt even worse. I prayed often for her to come back to me and when she didn't, I was angry for a time at God. But then He showed me that good things can come out of tragedies and so I began to pray that Maggie's story would help others. He answered my prayers today."

At that, more tears escaped Jess's eyes and the two women hugged and prayed together before the bus stopped and Jess deboarded to switch busses for one headed back to Lubbock. As she waited for the bus that would take her back, she sent a text to Emily letting her know she was okay and one to Chad asking him to come by her dorm that evening. She knew she would have to tell them what she had almost done, but it needed to be in person and not over the phone.

❀

*R*elief flooded Chad at Jess's message. She was okay. That was the main thing, but where had she been and what did she have to tell him? Had she found someone else? Would he be okay if she had? The more he thought about it, the clearer the answer became. No, he would not be okay. His worry over her today solidified the feelings he had been denying. He cared for her, and regardless of what she told him tonight, he would tell her how he felt.

CHAPTER 14

*J*ess gathered her courage in the hallway before opening the door. As soon as Jess crossed the doorjamb, Emily bounded across the room and engulfed her in a hug.

"Where were you? Why didn't you leave me a note? Or text me you were okay? I was so worried." The words streamed out of Emily's mouth with a rapid-fire intensity.

"I'm sorry," Jess said. Was she really going to tell Emily? What if Emily hated her afterwards? What if she no longer wanted to be friends? Jess shook her head to clear the thoughts. Emily wouldn't do that. "I need to talk to you, but you should sit down."

Emily followed Jess's lead and sat down on her bed, her hands clasped in her lap.

Jess opened her mouth to speak, but then decided evidence would be more powerful. She crossed to her dresser and retrieved the white stick from under the clothes where she had stashed it at her first opportunity.

Emily's eyes widened as she realized what lay in Jess's hand, and her mouth dropped open in a perfect "o" shape. "Oh, Jess, I'm so sorry, but we'll figure something out. We have several places you can contact for information on adoption or financial assistance if you decide you want to raise the baby." Horror dawned on Emily's face. "Or did you…."

Tears flooded Jess's eyes, blurring the room around her. She sank onto the bed next to Emily. "I didn't, but I was on my way, Emily. I knew it was wrong, which is why I didn't tell you, but I have nothing. I thought it would be easier if…"

"Don't even consider it," Emily said. "That could be me. That was going to be my fate until God stepped in. He has a plan for you too, and it does not include getting rid of this child."

"I was so worried you would hate me," Jess said. "I've messed up so much."

"Jess, I could never hate you. You're my sister in Christ, and no matter how much you mess up, I will be there, and Jesus will be there for you." Her eyes widened. "Does Chad know?"

Jess shook her head. "I asked him to meet me here at seven, so I could tell him."

"Jess, it's six forty-five," Emily said.

"Oh, crap," Jess said, jumping up from the bed. "What do I say to him?" She paced back and forth in the room. It was a good thing the floor was already old because Jess felt like she would have worn a crevice in a new carpet.

"The truth," Emily replied. "Whether he wants to be a part of it or not, he deserves to know he has a son or daughter coming. I'll step out to give you privacy, but I'll be right downstairs if you need me."

Jess nodded, but her heart continued to pound a beat in her head. She'd practiced what she would tell him on the bus ride home, but now that the time was nearly here, her stomach twisted in knots. Taking a deep breath, Jess smoothed her shirt and sat on the bed, tapping her fingers on the mattress. Her leg jiggled back and forth of its own accord.

"It will be okay," Emily said from across the room.

Jess envied her calm demeanor. Of course, she wasn't the one carrying the baby, but she somehow thought even if Emily was that she would be calm.

A knock sounded at the door, and Jess's heart jumped. Emily flashed a thumb-up as she walked to the door. Chad, dark and sexy, stood on the other side in a black leather jacket and jeans. At the sight of him, Jess's heart sped up. He still affected her, and though she saw him twice a week in class, seeing him out of class and in her doorway felt different.

"I'll just let you two have some time," Emily said, squeezing past Chad.

As Chad stepped into the room and closed the door behind him, Jess felt her old nature start to kick in. The words could wait. She could pull him onto the bed and lose herself in his arms. After all, she was already pregnant, so there was no fear of that. No, that was no longer her life. She would stand up to temptation.

"Jess," he said, closing the distance between them.

She placed her fingers on his lips, trying to ignore the tremor of emotion that shot through her. "Wait, let me go first before I lose my nerve."

Chad nodded and reached for her hand, but the smell of his cologne was intoxicating. Jess had to distance herself. She crossed to the window, gathering her thoughts, before turning to face him. "Um, so okay you remember when we..."—she looked down at her hands and then at her bed, unable to verbalize the act, but he understood and nodded, prodding her to continue. "Well, I'm pregnant."

His eyes widened. His mouth opened and closed; then opened again. He ran his hand across his stubbled chin. "Are you sure? I mean it's been so long. We were together the last time over a month ago."

Jess's face flamed. "I know, but I hadn't realized I was late until I started getting sick. I took a test this weekend, and I've only been with you."

"Wow, okay um." His hands trailed down his denim-clad thighs before he turned his blue eyes on her—oh, those eyes. "What do you want to do?"

"I'm going to have the baby," she said. "I thought I wanted an abortion which is where I was today - on the way to the nearest clinic, but your call, an old woman, and God changed my mind." She chuckled at his puzzled expression. "It's a long story, but I'm not asking anything from you. I'll put the baby up for adoption."

He nodded, blinking a few times. Then his hand again grazed his chin. The simple nervous gesture sent her heart racing. What was wrong with her?

"No."

"No?" she asked.

"Well, I'm not sure. Look, Jess, I don't know if I'm ready to be a father. I didn't even think I wanted a relationship, but I can't stop thinking about you. I've been making some changes in my life too, and I'm sorry for the way I treated you the last time we were together. It was selfish and wrong, but I was pushing you away because of fear. That's a story for another day. However, after Emily came looking for you today and I didn't know what had happened to you, I couldn't deny I had feelings any longer. I want us to be together, the right way this time. Let's get to know each other and then we can decide about the baby."

Jess's head dropped forward, and her eyes widened. Was he for real? She had thought he would push her to have an abortion or run screaming at the very least, but here he was telling her he had feelings for her. "I don't know, Chad," she managed to stutter. "I mean I'm not the same person. Jesus is a part of my life now, and I'm trying to live the way he wants me. And you," she stepped back as he approached her, but there was nowhere else to go - she was backed up against the window. "You are like playing with fire. I'm not sure I could date you and behave."

The last words came out little more than a whisper as his hand circled her neck and tangled in her hair.

"I'd like to try," he said in a husky voice before claiming her lips with his own.

🐚

*A*s Chad left Jess's room later, fear and elation cycled through his veins. Kissing her had been amazing - he had definitely missed it - but his desire for her hadn't changed, and it had been hard to stop himself this time. So hard! The bed was right there, and her scent had driven him crazy. But he had refrained. However, he knew more time spent together would mean more temptation to face. He would have to give that to God.

It was funny how the thought of losing someone made everything so clear. Not only had he decided he wanted a relationship with Jess when he'd heard she was missing, but he had wanted to talk to God then too. As he crossed campus, he wished Kyle was still here to talk to. He might have been younger, but from his journal he appeared to have his life more together than Chad did.

When he got back to his room, Chad pulled Kyle's journal out of his desk drawer and sat down to read it again. His brother's words had been so full of wisdom, and as he read over Kyle's entries of dealing with his own temptation around Stephanie, Chad knew what he had to do.

"Jesus? I know I wandered and thought I could do things my own way, but I realized I need you. Forgive me for sinning and help me to follow your ways now. Give me the strength to resist the physical temptation and show me how to be a man of God."

As he finished the prayer, Chad looked back down at the journal. At the bottom of the entry, Kyle had penned: Pray Unceasingly. *Okay, God,* Chad thought. *I'll pray and trust that you'll show me the way.*

CHAPTER 15

*J*ess stood outside the brick building trying to calm her heart. A gentle touch at her elbow caused her to turn to Emily who flashed an encouraging smile. "Thanks for coming with me."

"Of course," Emily said and gestured to the door.

Jess knew she had to go in, but her feet felt encased in cement, and her arm stuck like Velcro to her side. Taking this step would change her life forever, and she wasn't sure she was ready.

Emily held out her hand, and Jess managed to move her arm enough to grasp it. Emily pulled open the door with one hand and Jess forward with the other. Though slow, Jess's feet stumbled forward, and she stepped onto the smooth floor.

The foyer broke into several halls, and a large curved desk sat in the middle manned by two women. An ocean of beige carpet separated the girls from the desk, but Emily plowed forward, dragging Jess along.

"Can I help you?" the woman to the left asked at their approach.

Jess cleared her throat, hoping her voice would work better than her feet had so far. "Yes, I'm pregnant, and I wanted to speak to someone about help."

"Absolutely, you can have a seat over there"—she pointed to the waiting area just to the side—"and we'll call you back as soon as we can. Also, I need you to fill out this paperwork." She handed over a metal clipboard with several sheets of white paper attached, which Jess grasped tightly as she turned to the chairs.

The chairs, upholstered in a blue fabric, formed two rows of ten chairs each. She plopped down in one of the empty ones on the first row, and Emily sat next to her. Clicking the back of the pen, Jess began to fill in the paperwork. Name, address, date of last period. It seemed to be a standard medical history form, and the monotonous scratching of the pen eased her nerves. After finishing the first side, she flipped it over. Questions of a different sort filled this side.

Has anyone been adopted in your family? What kind of adoption would you like to have? *Kind? There are different kinds?* The questions continued, and Jess answered them the best she could. Yes, she would need help with medical care. No, she didn't have family close by. Yes, the father knew. No, he wouldn't fight the adoption. Or, at least she thought he wouldn't. They hadn't really discussed it much after the kiss.

"Tara, it's so good to see you," Emily said. Jess looked up from the paperwork as Emily rose to greet a blonde girl about their age. The girl wore a loose fitting blue shirt and black pants. "I didn't realize this was where you worked."

"Yep, ever since the day we spoke at the Students for Life office. I started answering phones, but I recently got a promotion, so now I get to start the process."

"That's so amazing."

"Are you here with Jess Peterson?" Tara asked Emily, before glancing Jess's direction.

"Yes, she's my roommate," Emily said, then turned and made introductions.

"Nice to meet you Jess. If you'll follow me, we can talk in a more private room."

Jess stood, still grasping the clipboard like a flotation device in choppy water and followed Tara and Emily down a long grey hallway and into a tiny grey room. A small desk crowded one corner of the office. Two blue chairs, like the ones in the waiting area, sat across from the desk. Books filled a small bookshelf in the other corner, and pictures of parents holding a baby lined the wall behind the desk. Though packed full, the room felt cozy.

"Did you unite all those families?" Emily asked, pointing to the wall as they sat down.

Tara smiled, "No, I inherited this office and the pictures, but these three are mine. Or at least partially mine. I answered the phones on the day they called and got them to come in." She pointed to the bottom three pictures.

"So, how does this work?" Jess asked, interrupting. She hadn't meant for the words to sound rude, but her nerves were on edge. She was here to give her baby away and that was tough to deal with.

Tara recovered nicely and even flashed a smile. "Well, we'll fill out a list of what you'd like in adoptive parents. We'll get the paperwork started for the financial aspect, and you can look through the binder today if you'd like."

"Binder?" Emily asked.

Tara pulled a large black binder to the center of the desk. "This is a listing of all the couples waiting to adopt in the near area. You can read all about them, see pictures, and decide if you like any of them. I suggest you pick five to six couples you like and then narrow it down from there. Of course, you can meet any of the couples you'd like as well." With a swipe of the mouse, Tara brought the computer screen to life. "Okay, let's get the basic questions out of the way. Do you care if the couple has other children?"

Jess's eyes were glued to the binder. Were the people who would adopt her baby in there?

"Jess," Emily poked her, and Jess's head jerked up.

"I'm sorry, what was the question?"

"Do you care if the couple has other children?" Tara repeated patiently.

"No, I don't think it would matter."

"Okay, religion? Do you want them to be religious and do you have any specific religion?"

"Just Christian is fine, but yes, that's high on my list." Though still learning about God herself, Jess wanted the baby to be in a loving, Christian home like Emily had grown up in.

Tara clicked a few keys and continued to rattle off questions. There was so much involved in the process, and Jess wanted to finish so she could look through the binder. Finally, the questions were complete.

"Do you have any questions for me?" Tara asked.

"Does the binder contain pictures of the couples?" Jess's fingers itched to open the cover and devour the pages.

"Of course." Tara turned the binder around. "This was my favorite part when I decided on adoption. Just a few more months to go." She patted her belly, and Jess did a double-take. The idea that she was like Jess, young and unmarried, gave Jess hope that things would work out for her.

"How is it going?" Emily asked.

As Tara answered, Jess's attention returned to the book. She touched the cover, suddenly unsure. What if none of the people called out to her? Swallowing her apprehension, she flipped open the cover.

A nice-looking man and woman stared up at her. Beneath the picture, a bio of the couple and what they were looking for filled the page. Jess skimmed it before turning the page. Another couple, blonde. Another, brunette. The couples seemed so similar, and there were so many of them. How would she ever decide?

As Jess continued to flip through the pages, she found it easier to eliminate couples than to pick couples. She didn't want the parents to smoke; she wanted a two parent household; some education was a must, but by the time she reached the end of the binder, Jess still wasn't sure.

"Did you find a few you liked?" Tara asked.

Jess bit her lip and shook her head. "I don't know. Do I have to decide right now?"

"Of course not," Tara said with an encouraging smile. "You can think about it and come back and look through the binder whenever you'd like or if you have a list of items you know are necessities or deal breakers, I can run it through the system and send you potential candidates."

"Okay," Jess said. "What about the father? Does he have a say? Should I be asking him?"

Tara's forehead furrowed, and she looked from Emily to Jess. "Is he in the picture? I only ask because usually they aren't, so I just assumed."

"Um, he's not, I guess. I mean we're together, I think, but he said he wasn't ready to raise a baby. I simply wondered if he had a legal say in any of this."

"Only if he decides to fight the adoption," Tara said. "Otherwise, it's pretty much your decision as long as he signs the papers. Of course, if you are together, you're welcome to bring him in and have him look with you. Maybe his perspective will help you decide."

Jess nodded, trying to process all the information. Suddenly, she was no longer sure of anything. "Can I take time to think about it?"

"Absolutely," Tara said. "We have the process started which is the important thing. You can come make changes whenever you'd like. We are here to help you."

"It was good to see you again," Emily said to Tara as the girls stood to leave. "I'm so glad things seem to be working out for you."

As the two walked out of the office, Jess couldn't help but wonder if things would work out for her.

☙

*C*had stared at the bouquet of red roses in his hands and smiled. He had no idea if Jess even liked flowers, but what woman didn't like roses? And if she hated them, then perhaps she would at least appreciate the gesture.

He rapped gently on her door and waited for it to swing open.

"Oh, Chad, they're beautiful," Jess said as the door opened, and her eyes landed on the flowers. "But, I have no place to put them." Her brow furrowed as she turned to survey the room.

"Don't worry, I'll see what I can find," Jess's roommate said as she rose from her bed and took the flowers from Jess. Chad would have to find out her name again.

"So, where are we going?" Jess asked as she took his arm.

"You'll see." Chad led the way to his motorcycle parked downstairs and handed her the spare helmet. When he was sure Jess was secure behind him, he fired up the bike and headed toward his favorite park.

As the air was cooling the closer it got to winter, Chad had packed a few blankets along with the food in his saddlebags and told Jess to wear a coat. Her jacket looked old and worn though, and he made a mental note to purchase her a nice leather one soon, especially if she would be riding with him more often.

"So, you once asked me what my favorite food was," he said after turning off the engine and removing his helmet. "I thought instead of just telling you, I would share it with you." He swung off the bike and helped her down before grabbing the supplies from the saddlebags.

"I can't believe you remember that," she said with a soft smile. "I thought as fast as you got out of there that you wouldn't remember my silly question."

He returned her smile. "I may have behaved badly, but it didn't mean I wasn't listening. Now, I am not a great cook, so I have to admit that I got this to go. I hope it's still warm enough."

"I'm sure it will be fine."

Chad led the way to a large tree that still had some of its leaves and spread the blanket out underneath. Then he opened the boxes he had picked up from Carino's and handed one to Jess. "Chicken Alfredo. That's my favorite food. Along with French Bread and pretty much anything Italian."

"I love Italian too," Jess said with a smile.

Chad liked seeing that smile on her face and he decided he would do his best to keep it there.

CHAPTER 16

The next Psychology class was hard to sit through. Chad's eyes kept wandering to Jess's, and she felt like everyone in the class could tell they shared a secret. As the class ended, Chad kept glancing her direction as he packed up and Jess felt sure he would call her down or come up to her, but before he could, a body blocked her line of sight.

She knew before her eyes even reached his face that it was Randall. His plaid shirts were his trademark, and today he wore a blue and green plaid button down.

"Can I walk you to math?" he asked.

Discreetly, Jess leaned to the left as she grabbed her bag and glanced down to the front of the room, but Chad was gone.

Disappointment washed over her, but she knew she'd be seeing him later. "Sure, that would be fine," she said and followed Randall out the door.

It was mid-October. A chill had descended this week, making the air outside cooler than normal. Jess shivered as the cold seeped through her jacket. Pulling up the collar, she stepped a little faster. Randall matched her pace.

"So, I know you usually do a Bible study on Friday nights," he said, "but I was wondering if you'd like to go to a movie with me this weekend."

"I'd like to, Randall, but I'm kind of seeing someone."

Though his face fell slightly, he nodded. "Oh, yeah, of course you are. I should have known that."

Jess's heart went out to him. He was nice, and he deserved someone. But even if she had been single, she felt no emotions that way toward Randall.

⁂

"*W*hat was with the guy cornering you after class?" Chad asked Jess that evening as they sat together in the cafe of his dorm.

"Randall?" she asked after she finished chewing the French fry she had just stuck in her mouth. "He wanted to ask me out."

"What did you say?" Chad asked, trying to keep the jealousy he was feeling from showing in his voice.

"I told him I was seeing someone," she said, picking up another fry. A feeling of relief doused his jealousy, but it was short lived as Jess continued, "That brings up a good question though. Should I stay in your class now that we're dating? I mean what if someone finds out and claims special treatment or something?"

Chad hadn't thought about that aspect of it. There was probably some policy against dating students. "Yeah, you might have to change classes, though it will be so much harder teaching without seeing you there every day."

"You'll still see me every day," she said with a smile.

"I know, but it isn't quite the same."

"Ooh, hey, do you want to come to the Bible study Friday night? You can meet the rest of Emily's friends."

"I'd love that," Chad said. Three weeks ago, going to a Bible study would have made him cringe or run the other direction. However, after re-dedicating his life to God, he found he wanted to do anything and everything he could to learn more.

"Good." Jess popped another fry in her mouth and smiled.

CHAPTER 17

As the days went on, Jess threw herself into studying the Bible and praying. Even though she was dating Chad, the need to discover herself echoed continually at the back of her mind. She'd gone from being abused to using and being used and was just now figuring out how to be useful to God. Of course, the child growing inside her complicated that, but still she felt... free.

She no longer slept until noon. Her mornings began at nine with a healthy breakfast and silent time with the Lord. After that, she would head to class - Psychology was a lot less interesting now that she'd switched out of Chad's class, but at least she still saw him most evenings.

After classes, her job at the Student Union filled the remaining afternoon hours. It had been a godsend, giving her money for food and her phone, which was getting a lot more use now that she had friends. Plus, the monotonous work gave her time to reflect and pray.

As she finished for the evening, she shrugged on her coat. Fall in Texas was unpredictable and the last few days had felt more like the early tinges of winter than late November.

Her stomach growled as she stepped into the cool, crisp air. Instinctively, she placed her hand on her belly. There had been no discernible movement yet, only strange fluttering sensations that often caused her to pause.

"Are you all right?"

Jess would have known his voice anywhere. Her eyes lifted from her abdomen to Chad, clad in jeans and his trademark black leather jacket, and she smiled. He held a wrapped box in his hands.

"Is it the baby?" he asked, his eyes dropping to Jess's midsection, but not with his usual smolder. This time concern colored his gaze.

"Yeah, but you can't feel the movements from the outside yet. It's just a weird fluttery sensation in my stomach. It's hard to explain, but it's a little like butterflies flying around in there."

He looked at her, a strange expression on his face. "Do you" - he shoved his hands in his pockets and glanced down at the ground before meeting her eyes again - "Do you ever think about keeping it? The baby, I mean."

"All the time, but we're so young, Chad. I don't know if it would be best for the baby."

"Oh. Yeah, you're probably right. Have you picked parents yet?"

Jess shook her head. She hadn't even gone back to the adoption center since the first visit. She knew she needed to, but something kept her from being able to finish the adoption process. "What's in the box?" she asked, switching the path of the conversation. She needed more time to think about the adoption before she could really discuss it. Even with him.

His eyes lit up. "Oh, it's for you," he said, holding it out to her. "It's a one-month present, and my way of apologizing that I have to work over most of break and can't take you home to meet my family."

Jess smiled as she took the box. She'd been disappointed when Chad told her he had to work over Thanksgiving break and would only be going home for Thanksgiving Day. Jess stated she wouldn't mind being alone the other days, but Chad insisted he wouldn't be able to work knowing she was all alone. Thankfully, Emily offered to take Jess to her home. That was a nice second choice though she hoped she would get to meet Chad's family soon.

She tore into the paper and opened the box to find a smart, black leather jacket similar to Chad's.

"It's for when we go riding," he said. "You seemed cold the last time. Plus, this will offer much more protection."

"Thank you," she said as her eyes filled with tears. Was this what it was like to have a real relationship? To have someone who truly cared about her?

"Hey, it's not supposed to make you cry," he said, pulling her close and wiping a tear from her cheek.

"Don't worry; they're happy tears," she said as she leaned up to kiss him. The feel of his lips on hers sent tingles down her spine.

"Oh, good. I was worried there for a second," he said as they parted. "Here, let's try it on." Chad helped her pull the coat out of the box, shrug out of her old one, and put on the new one.

The feel of the leather was cold on her arms at first, but it warmed quickly. However, when Jess tugged on the zipper, she realized quickly the coat wouldn't fit much longer. Not when her belly got much larger.

"Well, I guess we'll have to get another one in a few months," he said. "Now, let's get you inside. It's getting cold out here."

As his arm wrapped around her shoulders, Jess snuggled against his chest, enjoying the warmth and security he provided.

❀

*C*had smiled as they walked back to Jess's dorm. He was pleased she liked the jacket and it looked good on her, but they would have to continue this discussion of the adoption. Ever since he had heard the first heartbeat with Jess, his desire to keep the baby had grown. She might not be ready, but he was beginning to think he was.

He would have to tread lightly with Jess though. She hadn't revealed everything to him, but he had a feeling her fear of raising the baby had a lot to do with her home life. Jess never talked about it, and the one time he had asked her, she had clammed up and changed the subject which only solidified his hunch.

Her dorm came into view too quickly. Chad had been hoping to take Jess home to meet his family, but Dr. Warren had gotten sick and tasked him with covering another class for the rest of the semester. He needed to spend the majority of the break working, and while he planned to return home for Thanksgiving dinner itself, he didn't want Jess having to be alone in her dorm room the rest of the break.

"Have a good trip," he said, giving her another kiss - a longer one this time as it had to last him four days. It did not disappoint and as he watched her walk into her dorm, he wondered how he was going to make it the next few days without her.

CHAPTER 18

"**Y**ou ready?" Emily asked as she zipped up her suitcase.

"Are you sure they'll be okay with me tagging along?" Jess asked as she rolled up the last shirt. Because she had nowhere to go and Chad had to work, Emily had invited Jess to her family's house for Thanksgiving.

"Of course they'll be okay. My house was the hangout during high school anyway."

"But, do you think they'll care, you know, about the baby?" Jess was now in the second trimester and starting to show and though Emily and her friends accepted her, Jess still worried what others thought. With no ring on her finger, did they condemn her or pity her?

"I'm adopted, remember?" Emily asked with a smile. She crossed the short distance between them and flung her arm about Jess's shoulders. "Stop stressing about what others think about you. You made a mistake, you repented, and now you are making the best out of a difficult situation. A lot of women wouldn't make the choice you did. I'm proud of you and any true Christian would be too."

Her words soothed a few of Jess's insecurities and she pulled the drawstring of her duffel bag closed. As she passed the mirror on the way out of the room, Jess glanced at her reflection. The tough exterior might be fading away, but the insecure girl underneath still resided there. *God, grant me confidence*, she thought as she shut the door behind her.

*E*mily's house was a two-story brick home on the outskirts of Dallas. After the six-hour drive, it felt good to stretch. Jess's belly wasn't big yet, but it was larger than she was used to and so getting comfortable in the car had been harder than usual.

The girls grabbed their bags from the trunk and approached the front door. "You ready?" Emily asked as she opened the door. Jess offered a small smile in response.

Emily's house was warm and inviting and smelled of chocolate chip cookies. Emily led the way to the kitchen where a blonde woman who, surprisingly, resembled Emily greeted them. How could they look so similar while not being blood related? "Emily," she said with a wide smile.

"Hi, Mom," Emily said, returning the hug her mother had engulfed her in. "This is my roommate, Jess."

The woman turned her friendly green eyes on Jess. "Hello, Jess, and welcome to our home."

"Thank you for having me," Jess said.

"Oh, Emily's friends are always welcome here. Emily probably told you our house was the unofficial hangout when she was in high school."

Jess smiled at Emily. "Yeah, she did."

"Okay, let's go drop off these bags," Emily said leading the way to her old room. Trophies and medals lined shelves hanging on the walls.

"Wow, you really are an athlete," Jess said. She had never won a trophy or a medal unless you counted the ribbons in elementary school they gave out on field days.

"Yeah, I played a lot, but you want to know a secret?" she asked as she hefted her suitcase on the bed.

"Sure." Jess glanced around the small room looking for a place to drop her stuff. A brown, roll-top desk took up most of one wall and while there was a window seat under the two windows, it didn't look large or comfortable enough to sleep on.

"Oh, it's a trundle," Emily said, evidently noticing Jess's questioning gaze. She lifted the flowered bed skirt and pulled out a second twin mattress on a rolling platform. When it was free from the bed, she motioned Jess over. "Here, help me out. There's a bar we have to press to get it to raise."

Jess reached under where Emily was holding and felt a cold metallic bar. As the girls pressed it up, the mattress raised as if on a lift until it was even with Emily's bed.

"We'll get you some sheets and a blanket later, but for now you can put your stuff there," she said, pointing to the mattress.

As Jess placed her bag on the mattress, she returned to the previous conversation, "So, what's the secret you were going to share?"

Emily smiled a sentimental smile. "I kind of feel like I missed childhood. If I could go back, I might take time off, not play so many games, and just be a kid, you know?"

Jess knew. Not that she would go back to High school, but she would love to go back to early childhood, when her mom was sober, and it was just her mother and her. Her mom had worked a lot then, but at least she was present every evening. She'd read Jess stories and tucked her in and on weekends she would make smiley face pancakes.

"Ready to meet the rest of the family?" Emily asked, breaking into Jess's reminiscing.

Jess nodded, but as she followed Emily back into the kitchen, she couldn't help wondering if she could be a mother like that - the good kind. Like before her mother had found solace for her loneliness in a bottle. Or would she end up as her mother eventually had, broken and overwhelmed? Her mother had been a teen mom and Jess knew there was sometimes a cycle to these things, but could she break it and keep her child?

*T*he smell of turkey and sweet potatoes greeted Chad as he walked into the house.

"You're home," his sister, Kendra, yelled as she accosted him in the hallway.

"I told you I would be," he said with a laugh, returning her hug. When he'd recommitted his life to Christ, he had also recommitted to his family, calling them at least once a week to keep them informed.

He'd told them about Jess, but he hadn't mentioned the baby yet. It wasn't that he was hiding it, but he felt that Jess needed to be there when he had that conversation. Plus, he wanted to be firm in his decision of either keeping the baby or putting him or her up for adoption before telling them.

"Come on," she said, tugging on his arm. "Lunch is almost ready, and the football game is on."

Chad smiled as he followed her. It felt good to be home, and while he missed Kyle, he was glad to have his family back in his life.

"Hello, Son," his mother said as he entered the kitchen. She dropped the spoon she was stirring a pot with and walked over to envelop him in a hug. "When are we going to meet this mysterious girlfriend of yours?"

"Soon," Chad said. "I would have brought her with me, but I have to work when I get back and I didn't want her stuck alone in her dorm room."

"Well, that was very chivalrous of you," his sister spoke up, "but I'm starting to wonder if she's even real."

"All right, that's enough," his mother said as Chad lunged playfully at his sister. "It's dinnertime, so why don't the two of you go join your father at the table?"

The table was overflowing with platters of food, from turkey and stuffing to sweet potatoes and green bean casserole. Once again, his mother had cooked enough for an army - a trait she'd had for as long as Chad could remember.

A pang of sadness washed over him as he glanced at Kyle's empty chair. This would mark the third Thanksgiving without him and Chad wondered if it would ever get easier. But he didn't have time to focus on his sadness long as his father greeted him with a hug and his mother and sister took their places around the table.

"Frank, would you pray for us?" his mother asked.

"Actually, Mom, can I do it?" Chad spoke up.

She flashed him a smile and though she said nothing, Chad could tell she was glad to finally have her prodigal son back home again.

※

"So, Emily tells me you're planning on putting the baby up for adoption," Emily's mother said as Jess helped wash the dishes that evening. Jess had offered to help clean up as a thank you for allowing her to come and crash at their house.

"I honestly don't know anymore," Jess said with a sigh. "I know adoption is the smart move because I'm young and single and know nothing about raising a baby. However, as my belly grows and I feel the strange movements, I think about what he or she might look like. Then I wonder if I'll be strong enough to give the baby away. And the baby's father is back in the picture which makes it even harder."

With a nod, her mother turned wise eyes on her. "I'm sure you're not alone in that feeling. I can't imagine how hard it must be for you to feel the baby growing and know you won't get to see him or her grow up. Have you tried praying about it?"

"Every day," Jess said with a sad smile. "Maybe I'm doing something wrong though. I thought I would hear an answer or see something like I did when I tried to destroy Emily's Bible." Her mother raised an eyebrow. "It's a long story," Jess continued with a laugh, "but I haven't felt or heard or seen anything. Is that normal?"

"You know, a lot of people think they can ask God a question and hear an answer like we're talking right now, but He doesn't really work like that usually. Sometimes, the answer will come in feelings like you'll feel conflicted if it's not the right decision."

Jess shook her head. "I feel conflicted with both decisions, so I'm not sure that helps."

Emily's mother smiled as she continued, "Sometimes the answer will come through actions of others. Someone you know will do or say something that makes the answer clear." No, Jess wasn't having that either. "And sometimes, you'll actually hear God speak to you, but he speaks in a still, small voice, so you have to be very focused on listening for it. I know it seems confusing now, but I'm willing to bet that God will reveal himself when he's ready."

Jess took that nugget of wisdom to bed with her that night and chewed on it over and over in her head as she lay in the foreign room. Was she trying to rush God's timing? The pastor had often spoken about God's upper plan being different from what we could see down here, and maybe even though time felt short for her, it surely wasn't for God.

CHAPTER 19

*J*ess's phone rang as they were driving back to Lubbock. She smiled as she recognized Chad's number. Though they had spoken a few times over the break, the conversations had been short, so he could work. She was looking forward to seeing him again tonight. "Hello, Chad."

"Hey Jess, will you be home by seven?"

Jess looked at her watch. It was barely one. They had headed back right after church ended. "Yeah, we should be home by six barring traffic."

"Great. Will you meet me at the Starbucks on University at seven?"

"Sure, but what's up?" She had expected to hang out in his dorm, not at a coffee shop. What did that mean?

"I don't want to tell you over the phone. Please? It's important."

"Okay. I'll see you at seven." As Jess hung up the phone, she couldn't help but wonder what the secrecy was about. Her old insecurities seeped in. Had Chad found someone else while she was gone? Had their whole relationship been a sham?

"What was that about?" Emily asked.

"I have no idea," Jess responded with a slow shake of her head. "I guess I'll see at seven."

❦

Chad sat a table in the coffee shop and tapped his finger against the table top. The last few hours had crawled by as he waited for seven to hit. His visit home had solidified his feelings, and he knew now he wanted to raise his child. He hoped Jess would feel the same, but he could no longer sign adoption papers.

A chill breeze swept through the room and Chad glanced up. Jess stood in the entrance scanning the room. His face lit up at the sight of her and he crossed quickly to embrace her.

Her arms wound around his neck as she returned his kiss, and a heat spread through his body. "I've missed you," he said as they parted.

"I missed you too," she said with a smile.

"Come, sit down," he said, taking her hand and leading her to the table he had been sitting at. "Would you like a coffee or something to eat?"

"No, I'm okay. What's going on, Chad?"

His eyes held her gaze a moment and then dropped to the tabletop where his finger tapped again. After a deep breath, he raised his eyes again. "I know I said I wasn't ready to raise a child, but after going home on Thursday and seeing my parents, I've found myself daydreaming about you and the baby and us as a family."

He paused, waiting for Jess to say something, but she only blinked at him.

"I guess what I'm saying is I don't want you to give the baby up for adoption. I want us to raise the baby together. I want what my parents have."

"Chad, I'm so young. I'm only nineteen," Jess began.

"I know we're young," he said interrupting her, "but younger people than us have done it. I'm almost out of school, and I can support you while you finish." His eyes pleaded with hers.

"But why? Why do you want this baby so badly?"

His gaze was frank and unwavering as he stared into her eyes.

"Because I love you, and I see my future with you. I honestly think we'll regret the decision if we give this kid away. Our family will never feel complete, you know?"

Jess looked as though she was going to object again, but Chad jumped in before she could.

"Let's at least try," he pleaded.

"Okay, let's try," she said with a laugh.

He reached across the table and grabbed her hands, sending a tingling sensation down his arm. "I know you think I'm crazy, and maybe I am, but I'm also serious about this."

"Okay, let's raise a baby."

"I'll show you, Jess. I'll show you I can be father material. I still have some prep work for tomorrow, so I have to run, but let's do dinner tomorrow."

❧

*J*ess nodded at him, still unable to find the right words. He squeezed her hands and then stood and walked away, leaving her in a happy but dazed stupor as she watched him leave.

In her pocket, her phone rang. Still reeling from the last few minutes, Jess tapped the answer button without looking at the caller ID. "Hello?"

"Jess?"

Her mother's voice caused the hair on Jess's arms to stand up. What did she want? And did Jess even care what she had to say? The broken part of her wanted to ignore the call, to pretend it had never occurred and just hit the end call button now, but the other part of her—the part that God was healing—decided she should at least see what her mother wanted.

"Yes, it's me. What's... what's going on?" What was with today? First Chad and now her mother? Could it get any stranger?

"I wanted to see if I could come see you. I kicked Jim to the curb. You were right about him. I'm sorry I didn't listen to you."

Jess held the phone away from her ear and stared at it. As much as she wanted to believe her mother, so much hurt existed between them. If she gave her mother another chance, would she just end up hurt again? A tiny voice inside her head whispered "forgiveness," but there was so much pain in the past.

A sudden bolt of inspiration hit her, and she responded, "Yeah, I guess you can come, but only if you come to church with me." Jess knew this would dissuade her mother if she weren't serious.

Silence descended.

"I didn't know you were attending church." Her mother's voice was hesitant, soft.

"I am now. I am trying to repair the damage you did to my life, so take it or leave it. You want to see me, then you come to church. Otherwise, don't bother."

"Fine, I'll drive up Saturday morning. We can spend the day together and attend church the next morning."

Jess agreed and hung up the phone. Shock rolled off her in waves. What had she just agreed to? Her hands began to shake, and the urge for a cigarette gripped hard even though she hadn't smoked in a month. Trying to focus on anything else, Jess stared out the window.

"Jess?"

She turned around to see Chase staring down at her, wearing the traditional green apron of Starbucks' employees. How had she missed seeing him when she walked in? "Yes, hi, how are you?"

"I'm good, are you okay? Can I get you something?"

"Um,"—she was about to tell her usual—coffee, black with one sugar, but she caught herself, "Sure, I'd love a green tea." She could have ordered a decaf, but it wouldn't be the same, so she might as well have tea instead.

"Not a coffee fan?" he asked smiling.

"Something like that."

He returned a moment later, and she cupped her hands around the mug, enjoying the warmth that traveled up her arms. She sipped the steaming liquid as she tried to make sense of the last ten minutes.

When her drink was finished, she began the walk back to the dorm. The last half hour felt like a dream, but perhaps telling Emily would help it feel more real.

CHAPTER 20

*J*ess stood in front of the closet, surveying the dark contents. Even though she was no longer wearing mostly black, she still preferred darker colors, but nothing was jumping out at her today. What did you wear when you hadn't seen your mother in months and the last time you did was shrouded with anger and disbelief?

Deciding on a simple long-sleeved blue shirt, Jess pulled it and some jeans on. She was only a few months along, but already her jeans were starting to fit snugly. She would have to buy some new ones soon.

A look in the mirror revealed the fear and insecurity in her blue eyes, but there was no turning back now. As much as she wasn't sure she wanted to see her mother, she didn't feel okay leaving her sitting in a restaurant waiting either.

"You look good," Emily said from her side of the room. "Are you sure you don't want me to go with you?"

Jess shot her a grateful look and shook her head. This, she had to do alone. Taking a deep breath and sending words heavenward for wisdom, Jess headed out of the room and to the coffee shop she had agreed to meet her mother at. It was the same coffee shop she had met Chad at just a week before.

As she pushed open the dorm door, a gust of cool wind blew against her, causing goosebumps to rise on her arms. She should have worn a heavier coat, but the walk wasn't far.

By the time Jess reached the coffee shop, her cheeks were numb and probably pink from the cold. She pulled open the door and scanned the shop. Her mother was not one of the patrons, and Jess sighed in relief.

Chase was working the counter again, and his smile calmed the jitters running through her. After ordering a tea, she took the cup to an empty table and sat down to wait. The liquid warmed her insides, dispelling the last lingering tendrils of cold.

Her mother walked in a few minutes later, and Jess almost didn't recognize her. Her dark hair was combed and had regained some of its sheen. Her blue eyes appeared unclouded and focused. Had she gotten off drugs? Her lips curled in a small smile as she stepped in Jess's direction.

Jess had forgotten how much she looked like her mother. The resemblance was unnoticeable when she was on drugs. But now her mother looked clean, and Jess could see what she might look like in another fifteen years.

"Hi Jess." Her mother stood awkwardly. Jess stared at her, unsure if she were expecting a hug or just awaiting an invitation to sit. She pointed to the chair, not ready to embrace her mother yet.

"You look good," her mother said, pulling out the chair and sitting down. "Different."

"Yeah, I am different," Jess said. "You look good too."

Her mother's eyes dropped to the grey tabletop. "Thanks," she said softly, "it's because of you. When you left, I... uh I didn't know what to do. I got worse for a while, I think, but then Stephanie told me Jim was touching her too. I remembered your words, and I stopped taking drugs and started paying attention. You were right about Jim, and I'm so sorry I didn't believe you. When I realized I couldn't ignore Stephanie too, I knew I had to take her, leave, and get completely clean. I just hit my ninety-day's clean milestone."

"That's great, Mom, I'm happy for you." The words sounded insincere because while happy for her mother, Jess was also guarded and still angry. Her mother had given up drugs a few times before, but it had never lasted.

"I know it will take time, but I want to see if I can be a part of your life again."

Jess was tempted to tell her no, that she had been hurt too often. However, she had learned that God was about forgiveness, and that if she were forgiven, she should forgive her mother as well. It wasn't easy as the words lodged in her throat, but eventually she managed. "I'd like that."

"I'd like to hear how your year is going.... If you don't mind telling me about it," she said.

Jess dropped her eyes to her cup and twirled it around. Did she tell her mother about the baby? It was a pretty important piece of her life, but did she want to share that information yet?

"My year has been interesting to say the least," Jess began slowly, deciding that if her mother were making an effort to be in her life that she could make an effort to trust her. "But I guess the most important thing to tell you is that I'm pregnant."

Her eyes widened, and her hand flew to her open mouth. "You are?"

"I'm having the baby," Jess said. "We didn't do it right the first time, but we are committed to following God's way now."

"We?" Her mother asked. "So, the father is in the picture?"

"He is," Jess said. "You can meet him at church tomorrow."

Jess waited for her mother to balk or come up with an excuse not to go, but she smiled and said, "I can't wait. You obviously found a part of religion I never knew and I'm looking forward to finding out what it is."

"It's not about religion, Mom. It's about Jesus." Jess smiled as she continued to share the story with her mother of how she came to know Christ.

*C*had swallowed his feeling of trepidation. He knew this was the right move, but it didn't make it any easier. This had been a part of his life for the last few years and he wasn't sure who he would be without it.

"Can I help you?" The salesman was an older man with a pot belly and a bald spot.

"Yeah, I need a car," Chad said. "A nice, safe, economical, family car."

"Yeah? We got lots of those. Follow me."

The man led Chad through the parking lot to the used car section. After test driving a few and haggling over the price, Chad followed the man into the sales office and spent the next half hour filling out forms.

CHAPTER 21

When Sunday rolled around, Jess couldn't tame the butterflies in her stomach. Would her mother really go to church with them?

"You ready?" Emily asked with an encouraging smile.

Jess swallowed and nodded.

At the base of the stairs, Chad waited, looking more handsome than Jess had ever seen him. His black leather jacket still graced his shoulders, but underneath he wore a blue button-down shirt that enhanced the color of his eyes, and a pair of black slacks that accentuated his other assets. This was not his first time attending church, but it was the first time he had dressed so nicely.

"Wow," Jess breathed. "You clean up nice."

"Thank you," he said. His normal bravado was missing from his voice, but the remaining tone was rich and silky. He closed the distance between them and met Jess at the stairs as her feet were still not cooperating. Taking her hand, he locked eyes with her. "I told you I would prove I was father material to you. This is just step one."

As he led the way out to the parking lot, Jess wondered what he had in mind for the other steps.

"Uh, my car is this way," Emily said, pointing to the right.

"I thought we'd take my mine," Chad said with a smile as he led them to a silver Chevy Traverse.

"When did you get a car?" Jess asked. The only vehicle he had ever talked about was his Harley.

"Yesterday, when I sold my Harley."

Jess's jaw dropped. "You sold your motorcycle? But I loved riding it with you."

"Do you have a car?" Chad asked in a teasing tone.

"Well, no, I sold mine to help pay bills when I moved out of my mom's house," she said.

He squeezed her arm and smiled. "Then one of us needed a car to put a car seat in. We can always get another motorcycle later when we can afford it."

Jess blinked at him. The baby wasn't even due until late summer and he was already thinking about car seats?

"Besides, in a few months, you'll be too big to ride behind me," he said with a glint in his eye.

Jess playfully slapped his arm, but he was right. In another few months, holding on to him would have become a problem.

"All right you love birds," Emily said. "Let's get going. We still need to get your mom, right, Jess?"

"Yes, we do," Jess agreed. "You don't mind, do you?"

⚘

Chad didn't mind. In fact, he was super curious to meet anyone from Jess's family. She had only ever mentioned her mother, but even those mentions had been few and far between.

He pulled into the hotel parking lot Jess directed him to and parked the car. "Do you want me to go with you?"

She shook her head. "No, I'll run in and grab her and be right back." Jess jumped out of the car before he could say anything else and hurried into the hotel.

"Have you met her yet?" Chad asked, turning to Emily.

"No, but I hope for Jess's sake she really has changed."

Chad wondered what that meant and made a mental note to ask

Jess later. If they were going to do this right, he needed to know all of her, even the stuff she wanted to keep hidden.

A few minutes later, Jess and an older woman emerged. Other than the few grey streaks sprinkled throughout her hair and the few extra wrinkles on her face that hinted at her older age, the woman could have passed for Jess's older sister.

"Mom, this is my roommate Emily," Jess said as she opened the door and ushered her mother inside. "And this is my boyfriend, Chad."

"Nice to meet you both," the woman said. "You can call me Diane."

Chad hoped he would have the chance to ask Diane questions later. He had a lot for her, but for now, church awaited them, so after everyone was buckled in, Chad pointed the car that direction.

❀

"What did you want to talk to me about?" Jess asked her mother as they walked around the campus. After church, the group had gone to lunch and then Chad had dropped them off at the dorm, so he could finish up work for the next day. Her mother had asked for a tour and Jess obliged, feeling the need to stretch her legs.

"I uh need to ask you for a favor," her mother said, dropping her eyes.

"I don't have any money, Mom," Jess said with disgust. She should have known it was too good to be true. Her mother was obviously about to ask for money for drugs.

"What?" her mother asked. "Oh no, Jess, I don't need money. I told you I'm clean. I need you to testify against Jim."

"No way!" Jess shook her head. "I've finally gotten past those memories and you've left him. Why on earth would I testify?"

"Because Stephanie needs you to. She will testify too, but the case would be much stronger with your added testimony. There's a chance he'll get away with it if it's just Stephanie's word. You know how persuasive he can be."

Jess shuddered at the memory. She knew firsthand how persuasive he could be. It was how he got so close to her before she realized what was happening. "I don't know, Mom. I'll think about it, but I'm trying to put that behind me. There's a baby to think about now."

"I know, and I'm sorry to have to ask. I'll understand if you can't, but I truly think it might help with your healing as well," her mother said.

Jess bit her lip and shook her head. How was she going to heal if she kept having to revisit the nightmares of her past?

CHAPTER 22

The crisp autumn air cooled as December hit. Jess had picked up a heavier jacket from a local thrift store as the weather forecast often threatened snow now, and her stomach had grown just enough that her leather jacket didn't zip. The new jacket kept her warm even though the wind had turned the air a little colder on the walk to and from class.

It was one of these especially chilly days when the semester ended. Jess zipped up her coat as far as it could go, and after throwing her backpack on, she jammed her hands into her pockets to warm them up as best as she could. Though the rooms were warmer than outside, her hands were like ice today.

As Jess pushed open the door and a wintry chill ambushed her, she wished she had bought a scarf at the thrift store too. Dropping her head, she braved the short walk back to the dorm, wishing there was a fireplace to warm up in front of. She'd have to throw on a heavier sweater and crawl under her covers to warm up. Jess was considering the quickest option when she heard her name being called.

Chad was hurrying after her, a smile lighting up his whole face. "I'm glad I caught you." His breath came out in labored gasps. How long had he been running after her? "My mother said there's a storm coming tomorrow, so are you okay if we head out tonight?"

Jess and Chad had planned to drive to Amarillo to spend Christmas with his family. Her nerves were in a bundle since it would be her first time meeting them.

"Sure, I'm mostly packed. Just have to give Emily her gift."

"Great, I'll swing by to get you in an hour after I finish packing." He leaned in and kissed the corner of her mouth before hurrying off toward his dorm.

Though it had been short, just the touch of his lips on hers had sent a warm sensation flowing through her body. Jess didn't think she'd ever tire of kissing him. She hurried the last of the way to the dorm, relishing the disappearing warmth from his lips and looking forward to the heat that the building would offer from the pervading cold outside.

"Hey," Emily said looking up from the suitcase she was packing as Jess entered. "I will miss you." She was going home to Mesquite for the break.

"Me too, but it's only a few weeks," Jess said, putting down her backpack and pulling out her own bag to finish filling it. "Be sure to say hi to everyone in your family for me though. Oh, hey, before you go, I got you this." Behind her pillow, Jess had hidden a colorfully wrapped gift. She grabbed it and turned around, holding it out to Emily.

"I've got one for you too," Emily said, holding out her own box. Laughing, the girls exchanged boxes and ripped into the paper.

"Emily, it's beautiful," Jess sighed as she pulled out a delicate silver cross necklace. A small silver ribbon marked by tiny footprints wrapped around it. Ever since she had heard the Footprints in the Sand poem, she had loved the idea of it, and a cross that represented that was a perfect gift. Jess fastened it around her neck and touched the spot where it lay.

"I'm so glad you like it. I know mine always gives me peace, and I wanted the same for you." She finished unwrapping her gift and smiled. "Jess, thank you, my old one was getting so full."

Jess had found the perfect leather journal for Emily to write her prayer requests in. She held it to her nose sniffing the leather and smiled over the top.

"Oh, good. I didn't smell it, but I thought it was perfect," Jess said with a laugh. Emily crossed the room to throw her arms around Jess in a giant hug which Jess reciprocated until a knock at the door grabbed the girls' attention. "I'll get it," Jess said, crossing to the door.

Chad stood on the other side, his blue shirt making his eyes appear like the ocean after a storm. "Hey beautiful, are you ready?" He pulled her in, placing his lips on hers longer this time. Sparks ignited in her body. "Hi Emily," he said when he finally separated from Jess.

"Hi Chad," she waved from the bed, smiling at the show and the blush that spread across Jess's face.

"Come on in, I'm almost ready," Jess said, recovering. She grabbed his hand and pulled him inside.

"Okay, I have to go," Emily said, finishing packing her bag. "Have a great break you two." She hugged them both before flying out the door.

Jess smiled at Chad as she shoved the last few things in her bag. This would be their first test at being completely alone since they had decided to no longer have sex. Chad had told her his family was religious, so she wasn't worried about anything happening at their house. However, it was a nearly two-hour drive there down stretches of road that were not always heavily populated. She and Chad were both growing in their relationship with God daily, but they were still both human and physically attracted to each other.

"All done," Jess said and zipped the bag closed. One final glance assured her nothing was plugged in or forgotten. Picking up her bag, Jess followed Chad out the door.

As soon as the door shut, Jess's nerves kicked in. Chad had told his family about her when he'd first told them of his decision to follow Christ again, but he hadn't told them about the baby, and they planned to today.

Jess's stomach wasn't that large, but they wouldn't be able to ignore it much longer. Chad had assured her his family would be sympathetic and understanding, but past experiences still filled her mind. Sensing her discomfort, Chad squeezed her hand and flashed an encouraging smile.

The ride to his family's house was quiet and comfortable with no stops along the less populated roads, but the nerves still tangled in Jess's stomach. Her throat grew drier the closer they got, and her head pounded as they pulled into his family's driveway. The SUV crunched over a light dusting of snow. Though it had missed Lubbock, Amarillo had gotten the tail end of the first storm that had passed through a few days ago.

Jess accepted Chad's help in climbing out of the truck and self-consciously ran her hands across her stomach as he crossed to the back of the truck to get the luggage. The blue coat she had picked up hid most of the protruding bump, but it would be seen as soon as the coat was removed.

"You look beautiful," Chad said, rounding the truck with the suitcases and noticing her nervous gesture. Jess shot him a grateful smile as they ascended the steps. Though still the handsome and intriguing guy she had first met, Chad had accepted the role of encourager easily, which had only deepened her love for him.

"Chad," his sister shouted as the two entered. His sister was a freshman with long brown hair, big brown eyes, and wire-framed glasses. She threw her arms around Chad's neck, squeezing until he cried Uncle. "I knew I could get you one day," she said triumphantly before turning inquisitive eyes on Jess.

"Hey, Kendra, this is my girlfriend Jess."

Kendra stuck out her hand and smiled at Jess. "It's nice to meet you. After he came home for Thanksgiving alone, I wondered if you were even real."

Jess laughed and returned the handshake. "Well, here I am."

"Come on, Mom's making cookies," Kendra said before spinning around and dashing ahead of them down the hallway.

Chad and Jess continued into the kitchen where his mother was indeed rolling dough into little round balls. She had the same dark hair as Chad and his sister, and a warm smile.

"You must be Jess. I'm Tanya."

Jess nodded, expecting a handshake, but instead Chad's mother pulled her in for a hug. Jess's eyes widened as she realized his mother would feel the baby bump. The surprise registered on his mother's face as she pulled back, and Jess shot Chad a glance. They would have to spill the news even earlier than planned.

Chad took the hint and jumped in, grabbing his mother's attention. "Hey, Mom, is Dad around?"

His mother nodded, calling for her husband, Frank, to join them. She put the tray into the oven, set a timer, and wiped her hands on a nearby towel. His father, an older version of Chad, only with a full beard and salt and pepper hair, stepped into the kitchen and hugged Chad before turning to shake Jess's hand.

"Can we go in your office for a second?" Chad asked.

His mother and father exchanged a glance but nodded and led the way. Jess's heart thudded in her chest as they followed.

Frank's office was small, but inviting, decorated in earth tones. Family pictures lined the walls, giving it a homey feel as well.

The door shut, and Chad grabbed Jess's hand and gave it a squeeze. They had decided on the way here that she would start the conversation, but her throat was now dry and scratchy. A long swallow returned a semblance of peace, and she opened her mouth.

"Um, so I wanted to thank you both for inviting me to come and spend the holidays with you. My relationship with my mom is still a little rocky, but I wanted to be honest with you. I"—she glanced over at Chad—"We made mistakes before finding God this year, and, um, I'm pregnant."

Frank's eyes enlarged to the size of saucers. Tanya had probably already suspected this information, but her mouth pulled into a tight line.

"Jess was going to put the baby up for adoption," Chad said, stepping in, "but I convinced her to keep it. We're going to raise the child together."

"You're going to what?" His father's words exploded from his mouth causing his head to shake with the ferocity.

Tanya laid her hand on Frank's arm. "Is this what brought you back to God, Chad?" Her stoic face held no emotion, but her soft voice was full of love.

Chad nodded. "It started with Kyle's journal as I told you, but I really committed when Jess told me she was pregnant. I know we're young, but I couldn't get her out of my head, so we started dating, but I kept thinking about the baby. When I came home for Thanksgiving and remembered how great it was to be a family, well, then this feeling covered me, and I knew we had to keep the baby and be a family."

He squeezed Jess's hand again, and though the words were meant for his parents, he said them with his gaze locked on Jess. "I promised Jess I would clean up my act, and I have. We know we messed up, but we're trying to make it right."

Frank's face was still a few shades darker than his normal color, but his mouth had closed and his anger was starting to fade.

"That is admirable," Tanya said. "It's not the way I hoped to become a grandmother, but if this event has brought you home, then I can't say I wish it hadn't happened." Frank nodded beside her though he appeared to be deciding if he should say more. "There will be no sharing of rooms while you are here under our roof though."

"No, ma'am. We haven't anyway since we got back together." A blush colored Jess's cheek as she offered up the intimate information.

"Good," his mother said. "Well, let's not let this news ruin our evening. We will pray for this baby and the path you now face, which will be harder, but not impossible. We're glad you have changed your paths though, and we hope the two of you will remember this as your relationship deepens."

"We will, Mom," Chad said, squeezing Jess's hand again and shooting her a soft smile. Relief flooded over her. She couldn't believe how amazing his family was being.

Chad's mom nodded. "Now, I need to finish baking cookies. How about you come and help me?" She grabbed Jess and pulled her back to the kitchen to finish helping with the cookies. Jess donned an apron, happily chipping in.

❦

*a*fter dinner, Jess helped Tanya clear the dishes, and then Chad whisked her away for a walk.

"Don't go too far," his mother called after them. "The snow is supposed to hit any time now."

Jess and Chad shared a secret smile as they bundled up. The December air was crisp, and their breath rose in smoky wisps from their lips. A light dusting of white made the yard seem almost magical. Chad thought back to the many winters he and Kyle had built snowmen or had snowball fights.

"Your parents took the news better than I thought they would," Jess said as they walked up his driveway.

Chad chuckled and clasped her hand. "They're still angry or maybe disappointed is a better word, but too polite to show it while you're here."

"Is it hard?" she asked. "Being home where memories of your brother are stronger?"

"It's always hard," Chad said. "Some memories never go away." He saw a flicker of something cross her face and was just about to ask her what was wrong when a drop of coldness touched his cheek. He glanced up to see snow falling slowly from the sky.

"Come on, we better get back in before your mother freaks on us," Jess said, tugging on his hand.

Chad raised his face and stuck out his tongue, attempting to catch a snowflake. "Juth a thecond," he said. Laughing, Jess grabbed his arm and pulled him back to the house. They were still laughing as they tumbled through the front door.

"There you are. I was just about to send your sister after you. There's hot chocolate in the kitchen. Why don't you go warm up?"

After hanging up their coats, they wandered into the kitchen and poured two mugs of hot chocolate. The rest of the family was gathered in the living room, and Chad and Jess joined them, mugs in hand.

*J*ess took a seat next to Kendra on the tan leather couch. Chad sat beside her. With a small smile, Kendra passed Jess a Bible, which she opened and followed along as Chad's father led a Bible Study. It felt a lot like the small group back home with Jared, Emily, Chase, and Sarah. More than that, though, it felt like home.

The Bible study had just concluded when Jess felt her phone buzzing in her pocket. She knew, without even pulling it out, who it was. Her mother had been calling all week and Jess had been avoiding her calls because she still didn't know what she wanted to do. However, since she didn't want her mother bugging her all break, she decided to take the call and tell her mother she needed more time.

"I should take this," Jess whispered to Chad. "I'll be right back."

His brow furrowed together in confusion, but he nodded and Jess slipped out of the room, punching the call button as she went.

"Hi, Mom," she said quietly as she walked down the hall to the room she'd be sleeping in.

"Jess? Oh, I'm so glad I finally got ahold of you. Why are you whispering?"

"Because I'm at Chad's house and I don't really want anyone to hear this conversation," Jess hissed.

"You haven't told him yet?" her mother asked.

"No, I haven't told him yet. If I tell him, I'll lose him. No man wants a woman with a past like mine. So, please stop calling me before you ruin everything."

"Jess, I need to know your answer. They moved Jim's hearings up. They are happening next month."

"I'll think about it, Mom. I promise, but I have to go now." With that, Jess ended the call before her mother could say anything else.

"What's going on, Jess?" Chad said from the doorway.

She hadn't heard the door open and she cursed herself for not paying closer attention. "Nothing," she lied, letting the old habit sneak back in. She had once been a master at lying. "Just a professor who needed to speak with me about one of my finals."

Jess had no idea how much Chad had heard, but as his face dropped, she knew he had heard enough to not believe her story.

"That wasn't a professor, Jess," he said, and she cringed at the emotionless tone of his voice. "What's really going on? Is there someone else?"

"Is that what you think?" Jess asked. Anger boiled inside her. He was just like all the other men she'd known after all.

"I don't know what to think," he said. "You won't talk to me. You've been withdrawn ever since your mother came to visit. I thought maybe you were just worried about your finals, but they're over now, so what is it? What's going on with you?"

She knew she hadn't been acting completely normal, but she couldn't believe he would immediately think there was someone else. "You know what? If you think I could just jump to another guy, then maybe I should. It's all you'll ever see me as, right? The unfaithful tramp."

"Jess, stop," he said, shaking her shoulders. "I'm sorry. I shouldn't have said that, but I'm worried about you and I'm worried about this secret you're keeping from me."

The anger fizzled, and tears flooded Jess's eyes. "I can't tell you. It will change everything." She crumpled to the floor and dropped her face in her hands.

"Jess," he said, sitting beside her. "I don't care what's in your past. Whatever it is, we can make it through, but we won't make it if you keep secrets from me. That's no way to start a marriage."

"Marriage?" she asked, splaying her fingers enough to look at him.

"Yeah, marriage," Chad said with a lopsided grin. "This isn't quite how I planned it, but I was going to ask you to marry me, Jess Peterson." He reached into his pocket and pulled out a small black, velvet box.

Her breath caught in her throat, sending out a hitching sob as he opened the box. Inside was a small gold band with a single tiny diamond in the middle.

"I know it's not much," he said. "You deserve way more and one day I promise I'll get you a better ring, but I want us to be married before the baby comes."

"It's beautiful, Chad," Jess said as she dropped her hands, "but I can't say yes until I tell you everything. I should have told you before, but I'm so ashamed." With a final shaky inhale, Jess gathered her breath and began the story of her sordid past.

❦

*A*s Chad listened to her speak, an intense sadness filled his soul. No one should ever have to go through the unspeakable acts Jess had endured. That sadness was quickly replaced with anger when she reached the part about testifying.

"That monster's still alive?" Chad hissed.

"He is," Jess said, "and I have the chance to speak at his hearing. My testimony could put him away, but I'm not sure I can do it."

Chad took her chin in his hands. "Jess, you are the strongest woman I know. You can do this, and I will be right there by your side."

"You mean you still want me?" Jess asked, her voice incredulous.

"Of course, I still want you," Chad said. "None of what happened was your fault. You were a victim. It doesn't change my opinion of you one bit, except maybe to make me love you even more. So, will you accept my proposal now and agree to be my wife?"

"Your proposal could use some work," Jess said with a laugh.

"I'll keep that in mind," he said, pulling out the ring. "Though in my defense, this was not the proposal I had planned."

"I'm sorry I ruined it," Jess said.

"You didn't ruin anything," Chad said. "I don't care about the proposal as long as the answer is yes. So, is it?"

"Yes," Jess said as he slid the ring on her finger. "It's a yes."

CHAPTER 23

"Okay, so we have the church booked and the pastor taken care of," Tanya said as she tapped the pen against the paper. "What am I missing?"

"Invitations," Jess said. "I know we're calling people since it's such short notice, but I'd still like to send out traditional invitations to your friends and family since we have a few weeks, and I'd like to have one as a keepsake."

"What about your friends and family?" Tanya asked.

"We can send one to my mom," Jess answered, "but all my friends are the people I've met this year, and I don't know their dorm addresses, except Emily's and that's only because it's my address too. Besides, most are probably home on break, and I don't even know where all of them call home."

"Okay then," Tanya said, scratching the pen across the paper. "We'll have fifty made to send out to our side of the family. That leaves...."

"Cake," Kendra answered entering the room. She had a bag of carrots in her hand. Jess bit back a smile because over the last few days, she had learned Kendra was obsessed with food. Jess rarely saw her without something in her hand though it was usually healthy. And on the few occasions she wasn't eating, she was chomping on gum.

"Right, cake," Tanya said, adding it to the list. "We can visit some shops today and taste some. I'm not sure if they'll be backed up, so we better do it as soon as possible. Also flowers. I'm not sure what you had in mind, but we should look into those quickly too."

Jess had no idea what she had in mind. She had honestly never thought about marriage after her mother's failed attempts, so there had been no girly daydreams growing up. And she had only been engaged for five days, so she'd had little time to think of what she wanted, but she understood the need to rush the planning.

She and Chad had agreed they wanted to have the wedding before the baby's birth and that pretty much left weekends, Spring Break, or the rest of winter break. Doing it on a weekend had just seemed too hectic, and Jess had opted for winter break over Spring Break so that she wouldn't be huge walking down the aisle. Though most of her friends already knew about the baby, she still fought the emotions of feeling like people were judging her and getting married while she was still only slightly showing would help with that. Plus, since college breaks were longer, it gave them nearly a month to plan the wedding before classes started again.

"Can we look at a dress too?" Jess asked quietly. "I don't have much money, but hopefully there's a rental store or something around here that I can afford."

Tanya put down the pen and crossed to Jess. "Actually, my dear, Frank and I would like to buy your dress as a wedding gift to you."

"Oh, I couldn't let you do that," Jess said.

"No, we want to. It was always our plan to pay for the honeymoon, but since it seems you two won't be having one right away, we would like to do this instead."

Jess shook her head. "I don't know what to say."

"Say thank you," Kendra said and then chomped down on her carrot stick.

"Thank you," Jess said, blinking back the tears that had suddenly filled her eyes.

❀

*C*had walked in as Jess ran a hand across her eyes. "Hey, what's this? I thought this was going to be a happy day."

"It is," Jess said. "Your mom offered to buy my dress."

A feeling of deep gratitude filled Chad, and he mouthed a silent thank you at his mother. He knew Jess had little money and her mother was still getting on her feet. "Sweet. When do we go?"

"You can't go with her to pick the dress," Kendra said. "You can't see the bride before the wedding, remember?"

"So, I'm stuck here all day while you all have the fun?" he asked.

"No, you can come with us to pick the cake, flowers, and invitations," his mother said. "Then you can do something else while we pick the dress."

"Sounds good," Chad said. Ever since their big conversation and the proposal five days ago, Chad hadn't wanted to let Jess out of his sight. Though he knew it was unfounded, a tiny piece of him worried she would change her mind and run away. He had been glad when she opted for the quick wedding.

"Great. Are we ready now?" Kendra asked. "I could use some cake."

Chad and Jess shared a glance and snickered.

"What?" Kendra asked. "What's so funny?"

"Nothing," Chad said. Telling her would ruin the fun of teasing her.

"Let's go," his mother said, glancing at her watch. "It's after ten already and we have a lot to do."

❀

*I*t was after four by the time the group made it to the dress shop. Chad had excused himself to get a cup of coffee from the nearby cafe while the girls picked out a dress.

An older woman with a kind face approached them as they entered. "Hello, my name is Angela. What can I do for you today?" she asked.

"We are in need of a dress," Tanya said.

"Of course," the woman said, looking at Kendra. "Congratulations. What are you, about a six?"

"Oh, it's not for me," Kendra said with a laugh. "It's for my soon-to-be-sister-in-law, Jess, here."

The woman turned her attention to Jess.

While her eyes held no condemnation, Jess felt as if the woman was examining her.

"You're with child, are you not?"

"I am," Jess said softly, wanting to sink into the floor. Was this woman about to chide her for sex outside of marriage?

Angela smiled and reached for Jess's hand. "Congratulations, my dear. Now, you seem young. Am I right that money might be limited?"

"I'll be covering the cost of the dress," Tanya said.

"Wonderful. I believe I have just the thing. Come with me."

Jess followed her to the right side of the store where rows of wedding dresses hung from metal bars.

"Let's see," Angela said, flipping through dresses. "I bet you're a six, right?"

"Well, maybe before the pregnancy," Jess said.

"We can adjust for that," Angela said. "Ah, here it is. I designed this custom wedding dress for a client, but she cancelled the wedding. I couldn't give her a refund as it was a custom order, but I can give you a discount on it." She pulled out a long white satin gown and handed it to Jess. "There's a dressing room right there," Angela said, pointing to a pink door. "Why don't you go try it on and see how it looks?"

Jess took the dress into the room, slipped off her clothes, and pulled the dress over her head. It was a simple dress that hung in a clean silhouette from her shoulders to her toes. The sleeves were a sheer fabric and a small line of pearls lined the neck of the dress. At her feet, the dress pooled in a white billow of fabric.

A look in the mirror elicited a small gasp from Jess. Though her baby bump was visible in the dress, the overall effect was stunning and drew the eye away from her midsection. Jess had never felt more beautiful. With tentative fingers, she opened the door and stepped out for the others to see.

"Oh, Jess," Tanya said with a sigh. "You are indeed a vision."

"It's perfect," Kendra agreed.

"I knew it," Angela said. Her hands were clasped together under her chin and a wide smile lit up her face.

"We'll take it," Tanya said.

CHAPTER 24

"Are you nervous?" Chad asked as they finished their Bible study. They had been doing one nightly since they arrived at his parent's house nearly a month before but opted for an extra one this morning before the wedding. Chad was glad because Jess seemed preoccupied. "Everything for the wedding is ready and in just a few short hours we will husband and wife."

"It's not that," she said with a shake of her head. Her sapphire eyes met his. "I'm excited to be marrying you, but I'm worried about the hearing. I know I said I could do it, but now I'm not so sure."

Chad sighed. Of course, the hearing against her stepfather was scheduled for just a few weeks after the wedding. She'd agreed to testify, but Chad knew it was only for Stephanie's sake. Jess held no desire to relive the abuse that had been inflicted on her.

"You know what we haven't done?" he asked. "We haven't prayed for him."

"Pray for him," Jess said with surprise. "What good will that do?"

Chad smiled and took her hand. "God has changed far harder hearts than your stepfather's, but it might also give you peace. Remember, God said to pray for our enemies? Perhaps praying for him will take away some of your nervousness."

"I'll try anything," Jess said. "I don't want this cloud to ruin our wedding."

Chad led the two of them in prayer for Jim and for Stephanie and Jess when they would have to testify. As he said 'Amen,' the feeling that he should continue praying for Jim settled on his shoulders and Chad determined it would be his priority until the trial.

*J*ess, you look so beautiful," Emily said as Jess surveyed herself in the mirror.

Jess could hardly believe the transformation herself. Kendra and Emily had curled her hair and pinned it up in such a way that the shaved part was barely visible. Dark ringlets hung down and framed her face and the touch of make-up Emily had applied completed the picture.

"You do too," Jess said, turning to her friend. "I'm so glad you were able to come for this."

"I wouldn't have missed this for the world."

A knock sounded and then the door cracked open. Kendra's face appeared in the space. "You ready? It's time."

"As I'll ever be," Jess said. She thought she would be nervous, marrying Chad, but she had woken this morning with a sense of peace. And everything had come together. The cake had arrived, the church was decorated, and everyone that was supposed to show up - had.

Jess grabbed her bouquet of red roses and sniffed them. She knew it was cliché, but red roses were the first flowers Chad had given her and they seemed like a perfect fit for her wedding.

Emily grabbed the two similar bouquets of white flowers and handed one to Kendra. The contrast was beautiful. The two girls in their red dresses with white roses and Jess in her white dress with red roses. It had been Tanya's suggestion and Jess was more than pleased with the outcome.

Kendra led the way to the sanctuary doors where Chad's groomsmen waited. Jess knew it was unorthodox that she had no one to walk her down the aisle, but she'd never had a father figure growing up. However, God was her Father and she wanted the place beside her to belong to him, even if he couldn't be physically seen.

As the music started, Kendra and Emily gave her a quick hug before taking the arm of their groomsman. Jess closed her eyes and sent up a prayer. "Lord, thank you for the many blessings you have given me. Thank you for taking our mistake and turning it into a gift. Lord, bless our marriage and help us be the husband and wife you want us to be."

A feeling of warmth surrounded her like the warmth from a soft fire. Jess flashed one last smile heavenward and then, when the music changed, she opened the door to the sanctuary. The crowd rose to their feet and Jess blinked at the number of people. She had only invited a handful. Were all the rest of these Chad's family and friends?

Her feet froze to the floor for a moment in fear, but then her eyes found Chad's and a small voice whispered in her head, "Fear not, daughter, for I am with you."

That was all Jess needed. She began the walk down the aisle toward the man she loved.

"Dearly Beloved," the pastor began as she reached the front, "we are gathered here today to join this man and this woman in holy matrimony."

The pastor continued, but Jess didn't hear the words as her focus was on Chad. She couldn't believe how much both of them had changed.

"I do," Chad said and placed the ring on her hand.

Jess blinked, startled. Were they already at 'I do?' She had missed more than she thought.

"Do you Jess Peterson take Chad Michaels as your lawfully wedded husband, to have and to hold, in sickness and in health, in good times and bad, for as long as you both shall live?"

"I do," Jess said, sliding Chad's ring on his finger.

"Then by the power vested to me by the great state of Texas, I now declare you husband and wife. You may kiss the bride."

As Chad's lips touched her own, the baby kicked in her stomach and Jess smiled. Everything was going to be okay.

CHAPTER 25

Chad and Jess were unpacking the last box when Jess's phone rang. He looked up as she answered.

"Hello?" she said and then paused as the person on the other end spoke. "What's that, Mom?" Another pause and then her mouth dropped open. "What?... Are you sure?... Okay, thanks Mom."

Jess hung up the phone and looked at Chad with wide eyes.

"What is it?" he asked with concern. "Is it the baby?" He rushed to her side, but Jess waved her hand in dismissal.

"It's Jim," she said slowly. "He confessed, so there's no hearing."

Elation flooded Chad, and he picked her up and swung her around. "That's wonderful news. I've been praying that God would resolve this and he did."

"Yes, I guess he did," Jess said with a smile. "I love you, Chad."

"I love you too, Mrs. Michaels," he said, setting her down before lowering his face to plant his lips on hers.

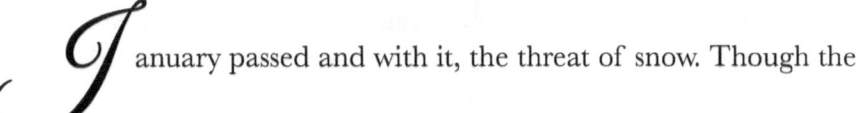

January passed and with it, the threat of snow. Though the

air was still chilly, the biting wind had calmed to a nibbling breeze. February arrived, and for the first time in a long time, Jess was looking forward to Valentine's Day. Plus, this month, her ultrasound was scheduled. Though Jess was nearly certain she was carrying a daughter, she wanted the surety of the ultrasound.

On the morning of the appointment, butterflies zoomed in her stomach. She placed her hands on her stomach, hoping to feel the baby move again. The feeling was an unexplainable sensation, but one she wouldn't trade for the world, and today she'd get a grainy picture of the baby. Pulling out her newly acquired stretchy pants from the dresser she now shared with Chad. she pulled them on over her enlarging belly and headed out to meet him.

"You ready?" he asked as he set down his coffee mug and stood.

"Yeah, I think so. I'm nervous though," she said.

"Me too." He grabbed their coats, "But it'll be fine, and we'll finally be able to start thinking about names."

Though Chad had been tossing names out - Jackson if it was a boy, Kayleigh if it was a girl - Jess had been unable to decide on a name until she knew for sure what they were having, but today she would finally know. She pulled on her coat and followed Chad out the door.

The parking lot was mostly empty as they pulled in. Jess hoped this meant they would get in and out quickly. After checking in at the small desk, they found two empty seats in the waiting room. Another pregnant woman and an older man sat in two other chairs.

A few minutes later, a blonde technician called Jess's name and led the way back, down a short hallway carpeted in gray to a small room. There was an exam table, a computer, and two chairs in the small room.

The technician took a seat at the computer and patted the bed. "Hop up and let's take a look."

Jess climbed on the exam table and laid back. Chad positioned himself on the other side of the bed from the technician who folded Jess's shirt up and poured a glob of blue liquid on her stomach.

"Sorry, it's a little cold," she said as Jess shivered. She picked up the wand attached to the computer.

As she touched the wand to Jess's stomach, the black screen lit up. The heartbeat was audible almost immediately and Chad's mouth dropped as he watched the screen.

"Okay, I'm going to take some measurements first, and then I can look for gender if you want." She moved the wand back and forth, stopping to click some things on her computer. Jess strained her eyes to see what the shapes were, but the screen was so grainy that she wasn't sure if she was seeing an arm or a leg. The wand continued to move back and forth. "Okay, I'm all set, do you want me to see if I can tell the gender?"

"I want to know," Jess said and then looked at Chad, "Do you still want to see or wait?"

"See," he said. His answer was decisive and made her smile. They hadn't discussed whether they hoped for a boy or girl, but it was obvious he had been thinking about it.

A smile broke out on the technician's face. "Okay, let's see what we have." The wand moved again. "So, here's the head and the spine."

Jess looked close at what the technician was pointing out, but she couldn't tell one white part from another. She had never thought much about an ultrasound technician's job, but now it was obvious why they received so much training.

"Here are the legs, so let's see, well it looks like a little girl. Now, girls aren't as accurate as boys because the baby could just be hiding that part, but I'm pretty confident that you are having a girl."

Tears welled up in Jess's eyes. Somewhere deep inside, she had known she was having a daughter, but hearing the words triggered an emotion she hadn't even known was residing there.

The technician printed off a few ultrasound pictures and handed them to Jess. "Okay, I'm going to show some of the scans to the doctor just to make sure everything looks good and then you'll be free to go. Here's a towel you can use to clean your stomach."

She handed Jess a towel and left the room, leaving Jess and Chad staring at each other, in awe of God's creation and the perfectness they could see in the tiny grainy images.

The technician returned a few minutes later with a smile on her face and a disc in her hand. "Okay, you're good to go and here's a video for you." She held out a disc.

"A video of what?" Jess asked.

"The ultrasound. Everything we did today. It's on video now."

Jess grabbed the CD, an unexplainable feeling surging through her body. "I didn't know they did this. Thank you."

CHAPTER 26

The rest of February, March, and April flew by. Jess and Chad had moved into a two-bedroom apartment in his building, and Chad spent the mornings teaching and the afternoons setting up the nursery or studying. Jess still worked at the student union, so he tried to have dinner ready for her when she returned home each night as well.

As May began, and the uncomfortable stage of pregnancy hit for her. Jess's belly had now grown out far enough she could no longer see her feet, and she definitely couldn't lean over to tie shoes. She had asked Chad to tie her shoes for a few days, but finally had resorted to a pair of slip-ons.

A nasty case of heartburn had also started in the last month, and after burning through an entire bottle of Rolaids in one week, she had asked the doctor about it. The doctor had prescribed Ranitidine, which at least tamed the fiery beast enough that she could sleep. Unfortunately, as she could no longer sleep in her favorite position, she would often toss and turn keeping Chad awake.

It was after one such sleepless night that he had done some online research and found the perfect gift for Jess (and himself).

"Come on," Chad said, grabbing her arm and pulling her to the

Traverse. He had surprised her after her last class with a bouquet of flowers and a chocolate milkshake, her current weakness.

"I have work, Chad," she said, handing the flowers back to him. He noticed she kept the milkshake tight to her chest.

"Not today you don't. I talked to Darla and got you the afternoon off. Now, come on."

"Where are we going?" she asked before taking a large sip of the milkshake.

"It's a surprise." He grinned like a kid at Christmas waiting to open his first gift.

Smiling and shaking her head, Jess allowed herself to be pulled to the SUV and for him to open the door and help her climb in.

Ten minutes later, Chad pulled into the parking lot of a mattress store. Sleep City blazoned across the roof and two sheep decorated the front windows.

"Uh, Chad, I don't understand," she said, turning a raised eyebrow on him.

"Just wait," he said with a smile that sent his eyes sparkling in delight.

He jumped out of the SUV, nearly skipping to Jess's side to help her out. She followed him into the store, but confusion was still clearly written all over her face. Chad scanned the store for a salesman, and after gaining one's attention, he whispered a request to the man.

The man, a middle-aged, bearded man with glasses, nodded; his lips pursed, and then his eyes lit up. A smile etched across his face, and he motioned for Chad to follow him.

They followed him around several mattresses, bedroom furniture, and finally to the back of the store where pillows and linens lay. The salesman picked up a giant pillow, almost as tall as he was, and held it out to Jess.

"You want to buy me a pillow?" she asked in a hesitant voice. It was clear she had missed the gesture.

"Not just any pillow," Chad said. "This is a contouring body pillow. It's supposed to help pregnant women sleep better. My mom swore by one when she was pregnant with my little sister."

Jess smiled as the thoughtfulness of his gift sank in. "Thank you," she said with sincerity. "I can't wait to try it out."

❀

"How are you feeling?" Emily asked from the living room as Jess dressed for the day. They had finished finals yesterday and had agreed to have a final hurrah to celebrate today.

"Like a giant melon," Jess said, entering from the bedroom. "I miss my feet. Do I have on matching shoes?" It was a running joke between the two girls. Ever since Jess had switched to slip on shoes, she would ask Emily this, even though she only had one pair.

"You do," Emily laughed, "You're good."

"You know, I'll miss some things," Jess said, "like feeling her move around. That really is a unique sensation, but I can't wait to see my feet again."

"Do you ever worry?" Emily asked.

Her serious tone chilled Jess's playful mood as she knew exactly what Emily was asking. Even though she prayed, the thought plagued her nightly, sometimes just a passing thought, but sometimes an agonizing hour-long focus. Could she and Chad really give this girl a good life?

"I do," Jess nodded, "but Chad has been amazing. I know it won't be easy, but we will be okay. After all, we have God with us, and I know for sure we're going to love this girl."

The front door swung open, and Chad's dark head popped in. "Hey, you two ready yet? I'm starving. I've been thinking about brunch since I woke up."

"We're ready," Jess said as she waddled toward the door. "I just move slower these days."

"I know," he said, planting a kiss on Jess when she reached the doorway, "but you're still beautiful."

"Ah, come on, you two," Emily teased. "It's a good thing I haven't eaten yet."

"Your day will come," Jess said as she locked the door. "I hear Randall's been coming around to see you."

A rosy blush colored Emily's cheek before she could turn her head. Jess laughed. She was glad Emily had found someone and Jess knew Randall was a good guy.

Though the IHOP wasn't far, the trio loaded up in the SUV as the distance was too much for Jess to walk in her current condition. Just going up and down the stairs left her winded, and by the end of the day, she would have to prop her feet up to let them rest after walking all over campus.

"I'm so glad it's summer break," Jess said as she stretched the seatbelt across her belly. "I'm going to spend all day tomorrow just sitting on the couch."

"You can have one day," Chad said, "but remember the doctor said you should keep moving."

"Yeah, yeah," Jess said in a good-natured tone. "Just drive. I've been craving pancakes with blueberry syrup for a week now."

Chad smiled and pulled out of the parking lot.

❀

"To a wonderful year," Chad said holding up his glass of orange juice as the trio finished their food.

"Cheers," the girls agreed and clinked glasses. Jess lifted the glass to her mouth for a sip and then froze. Her eyes widened.

"What is it?" Chad asked, his eyes wide with concern.

"It's time."

There was a moment of silence and then everyone spurred into action, speaking at the same time. "I'll get the check, I'll start the car, Are you okay?" Emily grabbed the keys from Chad and darted out the door.

Chad waved the waitress over and asked her for the bill. When the waitress returned, he didn't even look at the bill, just pulled two twenties out of his pocket and threw them in the black folder. Then he hurried to Jess's side of the table and held out his hand to help her up.

Emily had the SUV running as they reached the parking lot and Chad helped Jess into the front seat before climbing in the back. After buckling in, he pulled out his cell phone to text his family.

"What are you doing?" Chad asked as he noticed Jess retrieving her phone as well. "Aren't you in pain?"

She paused for a minute as if thinking. "Actually, no." Her eyes widened. "Is that a bad thing?"

"How would I know?" He threw his hands up in the air in a gesture of exasperation and then tugged one through his hair, creating an uneven part. "I've never had a baby."

A small smile tugged at Jess's lips. "Neither have I," she reminded him. "It's my first time too, so I have no idea what to expect."

"Don't look at me," Emily said from the driver's seat. "I'm still a virgin."

As Chad laughed, his nerves calmed a little. They were in this together, and everything would be okay.

✿

*A*s the whooshing hospital doors parted at the trio's entrance, the nurse at the front desk looked up at them.

"Can I help you?" she asked.

"Yes, ma'am," Jess said. "I'm pretty sure my water broke."

"You're pretty sure?" The woman asked. "You mean you don't know?"

"Well, it's my first time in labor, so I'm not sure what to expect, but there was a lot of liquid."

"Alright, we'll have the doctor confirm," the nurse said. She turned to her computer and clicked several times on her mouse. "Let's get you checked in."

When the check-in was complete, an orderly appeared with a wheelchair and whisked Jess down the hallway to room 105. He helped her out of the chair and onto the hospital bed before exiting the room and leaving her alone, momentarily.

The door opened a minute later, and a dark-haired nurse entered the room holding a blue hospital gown. "Hi, I'm Nancy," she said. "We need you to get changed into this. Dr. Stevens will come check you. If your water has broken, we'll get you moved to a delivery room and your husband and friend can join you."

"Thank you," Jess said as she took the gown. As soon as Nancy exited the small room, Jess climbed down from the bed, removed her street clothes, and put the gown on. It was a cloth one at least with little white flowers, but it was still completely open in the back. Jess couldn't tie it herself, so the cool air sent shivers down her spine.

A knock sounded and a short woman with graying hair entered the room. "Hello, I'm Dr. Stevens," she said as she crossed to the antibacterial dispenser and rubbed some on her hands. "I hear you think your water broke."

"I'm fairly certain," Jess said, "but it is my first birth."

"Congratulations," Dr. Stevens said. "Okay, lay back and put your feet here in the stirrups."

Jess did, trying to ignore the cold that was creeping in through her socks. The doctor poked and prodded a bit, and Jess tried not to grimace. She hated this part, always had.

"Well, your water definitely broke," the doctor said. "You aren't feeling any contractions though?"

"I don't think so," Jess said. "I'm not feeling any pain."

"Alright, we'll give it another few hours to see if labor kicks in. If not, we'll put you on a Pitocin drip. I don't want to let it go too long with your water broken."

Jess nodded though she had no idea what that meant. No one had ever mentioned Pitocin in the few birthing classes she had attended and all the movies she had watched had the women screaming in labor shortly after their water broke.

The doctor exited, and Nancy returned to help Jess down the hall to the delivery room. Chad and Emily were already inside. Chad jumped up from the chair he had been sitting in as Jess entered.

"Calm down," Jess said. "No active labor yet."

Nancy helped her into the bed and then attached a belt-like device around her stomach. "This will monitor your contractions," Nancy said, "so don't take it off. It's on a long cord so you can stretch it into the bathroom. I'll leave my number on the board for you." She pointed to a small whiteboard on the wall. "Call if you need anything."

As Nancy exited, Chad crossed to the bedside and took Jess's hand. His hand was sweaty and warm. "You sure you're ready for this?" she asked.

"Not at all," he said, shaking his head, but a smile remained on his lips. "We'll figure it out though."

The next few hours flew by in a whirlwind. Chad's family arrived, bringing balloons and flowers. Jess's mother showed up moments later and introductions flowed around the room. Emily and Randall entered after that, having returned with clothes for Jess and the packed diaper bag that had been sitting by the front door of Chad and Jess's apartment in preparation for this day.

Then the doctor entered to check on Jess's progress again. Her eyes widened a little at the number of people in the room, but she politely asked them to stand back as she grabbed the white readout paper from the machine to the left of the bed. Her forehead wrinkled as she surveyed.

"Are you feeling any contractions yet?" Dr. Stevens asked, turning her dark eyes on Jess.

"I don't think so," Jess said. "I have some discomfort, but no pain. Would it be pain?"

The doctor nodded, almost absently, and then checked the belt around Jess's stomach again. "It looks like we'll have to give you Pitocin to speed up the labor," she said, and her fingers clicked across the keyboard of the computer.

Jess's pulse quickened at the words. "Can it wait? I'd like to have as natural a labor as possible."

"I can give you two more hours, but no longer. We don't want to risk infection."

Jess nodded. Two hours wasn't that long, but hopefully it would be long enough.

The doctor shuffled out of the room, and the tense silence descended again. Eyes shifted back and forth. No one seemed to know what to say. Jess readjusted her position in the bed, trying to get more comfortable, and the small move seemed to break the stillness.

Chad's father offered to pray for the delivery, for Jess, and for the future of the baby. Everyone circled around the bed and clasped hands.

*N*ancy entered a few hours later and put her hands on her hips. "I don't know how you all got in here, but we have a three-guest limit in the room during delivery. Some of you will need to go wait in the main waiting room until after the baby comes."

Everyone looked to the person nearest them. No one wanted to volunteer to leave, which left the decision up to Jess. She knew she wanted Emily in the room, and even though she felt closer to Chad's mother than to her own, the look in her mother's eyes said she would be disappointed if she couldn't stay. "Okay, Chad, Emily, and Mom can stay until the baby is born. Then the others can come back, right?"

Nancy nodded, and the others shuffled from the room.

"So, Chad, where are you from?" Jess's mother asked. Though they had met twice before, Jess's mother had been more focused on Jess those times and hadn't asked Chad many questions at all.

"California originally, but we moved to Texas when I was in High School because my dad got a job here."

"And what do you do?" It was odd to see her mother taking such an interest in a man in her life, but nice at the same time.

"Right now, I'm a TA for a psychology class, but eventually I hope to have my own counseling practice."

"Really?" Jess asked from the bed. He had never mentioned wanting to be a counselor.

"What else would I do with a psychology degree?" he asked, a smile stretching across his face. "You pretty much either have to teach or be a counselor."

The nurse re-entered with a clear bag and hooked up the IV. "You should start feeling this soon; it might be a little cold. If you start feeling contractions and want the epidural, just hit the button, and I'll send the anesthesiologist in."

As the cold liquid entered her arm, Jess cringed. It wasn't exactly painful, but the feeling of ice mingling with blood wasn't comfortable either. An uncontrollable shiver ran over her body.

"Would you like an extra blanket?" the nurse asked.

Jess nodded as her teeth began to chatter slightly. The nurse ducked out of the room, returning a minute later with a warm blanket. Slowly the chills subsided, and Jess began to warm up again. With the heat came an intense pain in her abdomen. Her eyes widened, and she held her breath until the pain ceased. Had that been a contraction? The paper readout of the monitor next to her displayed a spike in the graph, confirming the hypothesis.

"Was that a contraction?" Emily asked.

Jess nodded, her jaw slowly unclenching. The pain had been bad, but not unbearable. As the afternoon wore on though, it became harder to tolerate. When she could stand it no longer, Jess punched the button on the call pad. The nurse popped in a few moments later, took one look at Jess's face, and left the room again promising to be right back.

When she re-entered, she had another new face with her. "This is Michael. He'll administer the epidural."

Relief flooded Jess at the words. She had wanted to be strong, but the pain had quickly become unbearable. Michael and Nancy helped her sit up and lean forward – not an easy task with a large belly.

Michael cautioned her to be still, but the contractions were even stronger when she leaned forward. Tears flooded Jess's eyes at the intensity of the pain. Chad hurried over, offering support and distraction until the needle was inserted in her back.

The pain dulled as they helped Jess lay back. A glorious numbness took over. The nurse checked the read out again before exiting the room with Michael.

"Better?" Chad asked.

Jess nodded. There was now just a dull throb, but none of the intense pain. The time seemed to pass ever more slowly. The nurse returned, checking the monitor read out again.

"Are you feeling any contractions?" she asked.

Jess shook her head. The pain was completely gone.

The nurse's brow furrowed, and she left the room, returning a moment later with the doctor.

"Feeling no pain, Jess?" she asked.

"Nothing. Should I be?" A tiny inkling of fear stirred in her belly.

"I'm sure it's all fine. Let's take a look, shall we?" She motioned for the others to stand at the far end of the room, so she could perform the physical examination again. "Oh, there's the top of the head, so it looks like we're ready. I need you to push the next time you feel a contraction."

"But I'm not feeling any contractions," Jess said, fear mounting in her heart. "I don't feel anything."

"No worries," Dr. Stevens smiled, "I'll tell you when to push."

As Nancy took her place beside the doctor, Chad hurried to the head of the bed and grabbed Jess's hand.

"Okay push," the doctor said.

Jess pushed like the nurse had told her, hoping she was doing it correctly.

"Okay, relax. And push again."

The process continued a few more minutes, and then the baby cried. Jess's heart seized with emotion. The nurse placed the baby on her chest for a minute as the doctor finished checking Jess. When the doctor was finished, Nancy took the baby to be weighed, measured, and checked. A few minutes later, Nancy returned with the baby bundled in a receiving blanket.

"Are you ready to hold her?"

Jess nodded and held out her arms. The tiny baby was perfect. Just a dusting of black fuzz covered her head. Jess's heart filled with love. She would move heaven and earth for this child, and as Chad leaned in to look at the baby, Jess saw the same emotion in his eyes.

"She's so beautiful," he said, touching her head hesitantly.

"Yes, she is." Jess kissed her tiny angel on the forehead, then motioned her mother and Emily over. A smile broke out on her mother's face as she approached. Regret and love fought for prominent placement on her face.

When the doctor and nurse were finished with all the checks on the baby and Jess, they left the room, allowing the rest of the brood in the waiting room to join the group. Baby Kayleigh was passed back and forth, oohed and aahed over, rocked, and cuddled by everyone in the room.

At the end of visiting hours, the new nurse on shift came and asked everyone to leave. Chad and Jess were left alone in the room, which now seemed unnaturally quiet without the noise from everyone else.

Jess held the sleeping angel, stroking her hair while she slept, and poured her heart out to the little girl. "Darling daughter, we didn't do this right, but we promise to love you and do all that we can to give you the best life possible." Jess kissed the little button nose and looked up at Chad who smiled before kissing her forehead lightly.

Jess spent the night with Kayleigh curled in her arm. When the nurses would come in to check the vitals, they would always point out the bassinet. "You could get better sleep," they would say, but Jess shook her head. Sleep was not necessary tonight, but bonding with her daughter was.

Jess's eyes wandered to Chad's sleeping form on the couch. The love he had for his daughter had shone from his eyes every time he held her, and Jess knew that whatever might come, he would always do what was best for Kayleigh. He would never be like the abusive father figures that had been in Jess's past.

With a smile, Jess reflected on the past year and how different her life had turned out all because of a perky blonde and her God.

The End!

DISCUSSION QUESTIONS

1 . What did you like best about this book?

2 . What did you like least about this book?

3 . What other books does this remind you of?

4 . Share a favorite quote from the book. Why did this stand out to you?

5 . Would you read another book by this author? Why or why not?

. . .

6. What feelings did this book invoke in you?

7. If you got the chance to ask the author of this book one question, what would it be?

8. What do you think of the book's title? How does it relate to the book's contents? What other title might you choose?

9. What do you think of the book's cover? How well does it convey what the book is about? If the book has been published with different covers, which one did you like the best?

WOULD YOU LEAVE A REVIEW?

As an author, I highly appreciate the feedback I get from my readers. It helps others make an informed decision before buying my book. If you enjoyed this book, please review at your retailer.

Do you like free books? I'm offering a free sample of my next book Free Sample!

WHEN LOVE RETURNS PREVIEW

There it was. The one stoplight Brandon thought he'd never see again, still blinking its irregular red pattern that no one ever paid attention to. As most of the shops were centrally located, few people drove in town. Their cars were used for driving to neighboring cities when what they wanted wasn't available in town. There was no real need for the stop light, but the people had decided the town needed at least one stoplight to be called a proper town, and so it had been erected.

There had been a huge ceremony the day it was christened; the whole town had shown up. The mayor had been forced to stand on a ladder to cut the red ribbon as someone had placed it too high. Once he was up the ladder, another member of the city board handed him a giant pair of silver scissors. Then it became a balancing act as the mayor tried to open the giant scissors without losing his balance – that had been comical – and the town had watched in awe as the stoplight blinked, blinked, long pause, blinked, blinked.

The awe had faded quickly, and a squabble had broken out among the adults about the brand new broken light. The whole affair had been rather disappointing to a sixteen-year-old, who had been looking forward to getting his driver's license. That day was the nail in the coffin that solidified Brandon's idea of leaving the tiny backwards town and returning to normalcy.

Then he had met Presley, and his life changed.

"Are we there yet, Daddy?"

Brandon glanced in the rearview mirror at his daughter, Joy, strapped in her car seat. Her dark curls came from him, but her blue-grey eyes were her mother's. Joy was the one good thing that came out of this town.

"Almost, Bug."

She resumed her stare out the window as they continued down Main Street. The Diner still sat on the corner, probably still run by Max, the same uninspired owner who wore a ball cap and plaid flannel shirt to work every day. His choice of attire left a lot to be desired, but he was a good cook. To this day, Brandon was not sure he'd had a better burger.

Next to the diner was the small Post Office. Brandon had never spent much time there growing up, but he knew the man who worked there, Bert. An odd man to say the least – always trying out new ideas that never seemed to work. One year, he had tried raising chickens to supply eggs for the general store, but he had become attached to one of the chickens, naming her Stella and carrying her from place to place in a little bag like wealthy old women do with tiny dogs. The chicken had escaped the bag one day in the middle of The Diner and wreaked havoc, incensing Max. Stella disappeared after that, and Brandon was fairly certain she ended up on Max's menu, but he could never prove it.

The general store appeared next. It carried groceries and a small selection of clothing and household goods. Brandon had been shocked by the meager selection when he first arrived, but the town wore on him and had a way of making him forget the outside world moving on around it. By the time he graduated high school, Brandon had been accustomed to the small offerings until he arrived in Dallas and felt like a total hick, at least three years behind the times.

"Daddy, look, cupcakes. Can we get one?"

Twisting in the black leather seat, Brandon followed her finger pointing out the opposite window. There had been no cupcake shop four years ago, but there was indeed a shop there now, where the laundromat had been, sporting a colorful cupcake sign and logo on the window. Sweet Treats. Not a highly original name, but neither were most of the stores in town.

"We'll come back by later." Brandon was curious about the owner. Who would choose to put up a new shop in this sleepy little town?

Her bottom lip turned out in an adorable pout, but she didn't continue to fight him. For her, this trip was like a vacation to a new and unusual place. The two rarely ventured from Dallas, mainly because Brandon's work kept him too busy for vacations. For him, it was a return to a past he had hoped to forget. Too much pain and too much sadness resided in this little town.

Brandon made a right down Cooper Street, the road that led to his parent's house. Though it had been years since he had been back, he could drive the route blindfolded, partly because it was a simple route, and partly because he walked it so many times as a teenager.

The two-story yellow house looked exactly as he remembered it, though the paint was chipping in a few more places and faded in others. The gravel of the driveway crunched under the tires as he pulled in. Brandon parked the car and took a deep breath.

"Let me out Daddy," Joy called from the back seat.

Sighing, he opened his door and then reached in to unbuckle her. Though five, she was still too small to qualify for a booster seat, and Brandon felt safer having her in the bigger car seat anyway. No one ever told him that when he became a parent, he would have crazy nightmares about all the ways he could lose his daughter. The car accident was always the worst.

Joy scurried out of the car, her faded pink bunny clutched in one petite hand. On the day she was born, Brandon's mother had given her a soft pink cuddle bunny. Joy latched onto it, sleeping with it every night. When she began crawling, she would often pick up the bunny in her mouth, dragging it across the floors. Even after she began walking, the bunny would go outside with her to play in the dirt or be flung around the room. The bunny had seen better days, but she refused to part with it for any longer than an occasional trip in the washing machine, and of course, no one sold this bunny any longer.

Brandon had scoured the internet one day looking for a replacement, but come up empty. He dreaded the day it fell apart, and he couldn't replace it.

As Joy scrambled up the wooden porch, Brandon popped the trunk and grabbed the two suitcases he packed the night before. His hope was that they'd only be here a week, but he had no guarantee and therefore packed for at least two.

Joy was banging on the door when Brandon reached her side. She hadn't been around his parents much, as Brandon had moved to Dallas shortly after Joy's first birthday, but they had visited a few times. Joy always clung to them when they did as if she knew the time wouldn't be for very long. Now, she had created this idea in her head of what they would be like while she was here and regaled Brandon with it the last few days. He hoped she wouldn't be disappointed, but was afraid she might. His mother probably wouldn't be able to spend much time with her as she would be taking care of his father, at least when he got released from the hospital.

Brandon's mother opened the door and broke into a smile. She looked older than he remembered. More lines crossed her face and more grey streaks colored her hair, but her eyes still twinkled the way they always had.

"Joy." She bent down with her arms out.

"Nana." Joy ran into her arms, squeezing the woman tightly about the neck. "You smell like cookies."

A smile played across Brandon's lips. His mother always smelled of vanilla and sugar, and while she had often had a plate of cookies waiting for him when he arrived home from school, she hadn't every day, and he wondered how she still smelled of cookies on those days.

"That's because I have some in the kitchen." She tapped the end of Joy's nose, earning a giggle. "Now, come in, and let's get you settled."

"Then can we have cookies?" Joy bounced up and down, sending the lights in her pink sneakers into overdrive. His mother nodded, smiling at her enthusiasm.

Brandon pulled the two suitcases into the homey entrance and shut the door behind him.

The house hadn't changed a bit. A wooden coatrack still sat just to the right of the front door, holding his father's derby cap and a few coats, and the sign, announcing "As for me and my house, we will serve the Lord," still hung prominently on the wall. Brandon shed his coat, adding it to the rack and then removed Joy's as well.

"Let me show you to your room." His mother grabbed Joy's free hand and led her down the beige carpeted hallway. Pictures of Brandon and his sister, Anna, lined the walls. His mother never let an opportunity to take a picture go by, and Brandon was almost certain she bought every school picture they ever had so she could display them all on the walls. He had tried to remove one once and replace it with something else, but she noticed right away and forced him to rehang the picture.

His mother opened the door to the guest room. She had obviously added some decorations for a younger child to enjoy. The daybed had been covered with a flowery pink and purple bedspread, and a blond doll sat propped on top. An old dollhouse was near the dresser along with a faded toy box filled with toys.

"This is all for me?" Joy's eyes were wide as she looked up at Brandon's mother.

The lines around his mother's eyes grew more visible as she smiled. "Yep, all for you. A girl needs proper toys."

"Especially in this town," he said under his breath. Not quietly enough though as his mother shot a look full of daggers his direction. How quickly she could change from sugar to fire. Brandon held his hand up in silent apology.

"Where is Daddy staying?"

"Right across the hall." His mother opened the door to Brandon's old room which looked very much like it had in high school. His football awards still lined the shelf, though a fine layer of dust coated them now, and the tattered posters of his favorite bands covered the walls.

"Didn't feel like updating this one?" he asked.

His mother shrugged. "Maybe I would have if you came around more often."

Brandon wanted to reply, but he didn't want to start a fight, so he bit his tongue and carried the suitcase inside. After dropping off Joy's suitcase as well, they followed his mother back towards the open living room and into the country-themed kitchen. Brandon hated the flowered wallpaper trim that circled the kitchen, but his mother hung it herself and had always loved it.

A plate of chocolate chip cookies sat in the middle of the scratched kitchen table. The usual wild flower display had been pushed to the side. Joy turned eager eyes on Brandon, the unasked question evident.

"You may have one." He held up a finger. "I don't want you to spoil your dinner."

She climbed up in a chair and snatched a cookie off the top of the pile, shoving most of it in her mouth.

Brandon shook his head. "You could chew more slowly."

Her ravenous munching changed to a thoughtful chewing, and he joined her at the table, plucking a cookie for himself off the pile.

"How is Dad?" Brandon asked before taking a bite. His father was the whole reason he was here. He was in the hospital after falling off a ladder and fracturing his skull. Though Brandon's mother claimed he hadn't needed to come, he couldn't very well stay in Dallas if there was a chance this was life threatening, and brain bleeds often were.

Plus, he figured his mother might need some help with his father when he got released. He would probably not be as active as he was before the accident. However, Brandon was in the middle of a big presentation, one that could set him up for life with an even bigger company, so he had left strict instructions with his assistant to keep him in the loop.

A flicker of doubt erased his mother's twinkling eyes for a moment before she recovered. "He is doing better today. The nurses say he only had a few instances of confusion yesterday, but they want to run another CT tomorrow."

"Any idea on when he'll be released?" Brandon took a bite of the cookie, enjoying the warm chocolate goodness. He had missed his mom's cooking.

"Probably another few days, but it depends on what the scan shows. He has a pretty big brain bleed."

"Your brain can bleed?" Joy's head popped up, her eyes as wide as saucers.

His mother shot an apologetic look and without saying it, the two agreed to finish the discussion later when little ears were not present.

"Don't worry." Brandon patted her arm. "The brain is amazing and can heal itself. When does Anna get in?" Anna, his younger sister, was away at college studying to become a nurse.

"She has finals this week, so she's coming as soon as she finishes the last one. Oh, and guess who else is back in town?"

Brandon raised an eyebrow at her; he had never been a fan of the guessing game.

"Presley Hays."

Presley Hays. The name knocked the wind out of him like a sucker punch. He hadn't thought of her in years. In high school, Presley had been his best friend – the one person who had made this town bearable – but for some reason they had grown apart when Morgan entered the picture, and then one day Presley had come over to tell him she was going to France to attend Le Cordon Bleu.

"The cupcake shop?" Brandon said the words for himself, but his mother smiled and nodded.

"Who's Presley?" Joy looked from Brandon to his mother.

"Just an old friend," Brandon said. *Just an old friend.*

Click to continue reading When Love Returns at your favorite retailer.

ABOUT THE AUTHOR

Lorana Hoopes is an inspirational author originally from Texas but now living in the PNW with her husband and three children. When not writing, she can be seen kickboxing at the gym, singing, or acting on stage. One day, she hopes to retire from teaching and write full time.

ALSO BY AUTHOR

If you enjoyed this story, be sure to check out Lorana's other books.

When Love Returns
> **Once Upon a Star**
> **Love Conquers All**
> **Where It All Began**
> **The Power of Prayer**
> **When Hearts Collide**
> **A Past Forgiven**
> **The Billionaire's Secret**
> **Brush with a Billionaire**
> **The Billionaire's Christmas Miracle**
> **The Billionaire's Cowboy Groom**
> **Lawfully Matched**
> **Lawfully Justified**
> **The Scarlet Wedding**
> **Lawfully Redeemed**
> **Lawfully Pursued**
> **The Still Small Voice**
> **Love Renewed**
> **When Love Returns**
> **Once Upon a Star**
> **Love Conquers All**
> **The Cowboy's Reality Bride**
> **The Reality Bride's Baby**
> Her children's early reader chapter book series:
> The Wishing Stone #1: Dangerous Dinosaur

The Wishing Stone #2: Dragon Dilemma
The Wishing Stone #3: Mesmerizing Mermaids
The Wishing Stone #4: Pyramid Puzzles
The Wishing Stone Inspirations #1: Mary's Miracle
To see a list of all her books

authorloranahoopes.com
loranahoopes@gmail.com

www.ingramcontent.com/pod-product-compliance
Lightning Source LLC
Chambersburg PA
CBHW030919020726
47498CB00001B/33